A DISTANT TRUMPET

BY PAUL HORGAN

PAUL HORGAN

A
DISTANT
TRUMPET

A NONPAREIL BOOK
David R. Godine, Publisher
BOSTON

This is a NONPAREIL BOOK first published in 1991 by
DAVID R. GODINE, PUBLISHER, INC.
Post Office Box 450
Jaffrey, New Hampshire 03452

Reprinted by arrangement with Farrar, Straus and Giroux
Originally published in 1960 by Farrar, Straus and Cudahy
Copyright © 1951, 1952, 1953, 1954, 1960 by Paul Horgan
Preface copyright © 1991 by Paul Horgan
Introduction copyright © 1991 by C. P. Snow

Library of Congress Cataloguing-in-Publication Data
Horgan, Paul, 1903–
A distant trumpet / Paul Horgan
p. cm.—(Nonpareil books ; 65)
Reprint. Originally published : New York :
Farrar, Straus and Giroux, 1960
ISBN 0-87923-863-1 (pbk. : alk. paper)
I. Title II. Series: Nonpareil book ; 65.
PS3515.06583D57 1991 90-55278
813´.54—DC20 CIP

Second Printing, January 2000
PRINTED IN CANADA

Dedicated
with affectionate thanks
to
Colonel and Mrs. Livingston Watrous
of the Army
who told me at dinner in Washington
on the eve of my separation from the
service in 1946 the family anecdote
from which this whole story took form.

CONTENTS

PREFACE

to the Thirtieth Anniversary Edition

i

Anyone who tells a story wants it to sound real. When I set out to tell the following large story that would contain many inner stories I foraged through various fields of my experience to support the persons, places, and events I was working with.

First of all, the army. Military life is a sort of separate world within the broad national character. From early youth I had a taste of it as a military school cadet. Later, returning to the school as a faculty officer, I had nearly two decades of contact with a succession of regular army officers and their families who were stationed there. They were in the cavalry. Ever so many airs, virtues, prejudices, and strengths of that service made the social and professional character of their lives. I could observe all that through my friendship with those officers and wives and children. My experience of the military life was enriched through reading—histories, biographies, novels. Above all, my own active life as an army officer during four years of service in World War II brought me my own further authority in the ways of those who wore the uniform. They thought of everything in terms of rank, privilege, style, duty, and, vaguely but seriously, the possible necessity, in some ultimate way and time, of sacrifice.

When I came to write A DISTANT TRUMPET throughout a span of ten years or so I saw what my book was to be. It had to be told, of course, through the lives of men and women, and these had to be real enough to me and to the reader to convince both of us that what they did during their lives on my pages was real for as long as the book was open. Their lives would lead me in my attempt to recreate the world of the United States Army in the nineteenth century. This was a richly peopled society, peculiar unto itself, yet acting in representation of the nation; and the two great themes that gave it dignity and purpose were the historical effects of the Civil War and the opening up of the western frontier. The scene of the drama was the whole continent, with life in the sophisticated eastern nation figuring as vitally in the narrative as the primitive endurances and heroisms of the huge empty West.

ii

An engulfing fire starts with a spark. I have hinted in my dedication how a single anecdote told to me by an army family set off this whole chronicle. It was told with so much charm, humor, and love for an ancestral reality that it summoned up for me acute impressions of what a certain young officer and his young bride must have been like—the two about whom the little anecdote was told—and there was a third person in the action, an Apache Indian of the Southwest desert. These three became so real to me in the next few days that as I saw them in my mind they began to create for me their immediate surroundings in a remote army post of the 1880s near the Mexican border of Arizona. I already knew that landscape. They now inhabited it. Then, I began to know not only what they looked like, but what their parents had been like; what conditions of family, local, and national history had molded their lives; how their lives had interlocked with other lives which came clear—and by this time I was making notes so compelling that they threw out tendrils in every direction. They wove a fabric so rich that I knew I had a very long story to tell. It had to be told through people who must be believed if the events of their lives were to interest me—or anyone else.

As any novelist will tell you, characters for his scheme are almost always composites. These are drawn from people he has known, or from individuals he has invented, or, in large part, from himself—or from all three. Discounting those parts of myself that helped to impersonate my characters in this book, I will identify other models for a few of my people.

Matthew Hazard became visible as a boy through my memory of a schoolmate named Jack Shuttleworth, aged seven or eight, at the Nardin Academy in Buffalo. He was sturdily built, with dark hair, level black eyebrows, a slightly challenging posture that came more from curiosity and interest than from aggressiveness. He spoke little, but then to the point. He was generous with his lunch box. He rarely fought, but then with calm fury. He loved railroad trains and swords. Rivals in class, we were not close friends, but his positive character kept him alive in my memory for half a century as I began to write this book. I never knew him grown-up, but his style and looks merged with ease into Matthew Hazard's manhood, which I modeled on a distinguished friend. He was a lawyer who became chief judge of a circuit court of appeals on the East Coast, and was within rumor distance of Franklin Roosevelt's Supreme Court. He gave me much of Matthew's mature person—brilliant black-and-white gaze, a warning zone of personal dignity, serious high spirits, and an almost militant sense of honor. I put him into the army instead of the law—the challenges transferred nicely.

Matthew's mother-in-law Drusilla Greenleaf was easy to catch. She was a family friend of my parents in early life. I saw her only in my impressionable late childhood, but her ruling traits of mon-eyed arrogance and whaleboned certainty of her perfect rightness were there to be made fun of out of sight—and to remember; and so was her habit of not listening to anyone else as she continued her grand monologues of self-satisfaction. Her husband Colonel Greenleaf, engulfed by her serenely fixed power, was molded from an officer I knew who was content to be perfectly tailored and socially well-connected. He knew his army regulations to the last section, article, and sub-paragraph. He never saw a battle. He had lost the important one of his life at home.

Captain, later Brevet Lieutenant Colonel Prescott, a man born for greater things than ever came his way, had his springs in another officer I knew who, having reached colonel, was well-deserving of a brigadier's star. He was never granted it, but continued to pursue duty with baffled good sense and a private belief that anyhow, he had come to a natural limit in his life. This made him an endearing companion, a splendid husband, and an outwardly tough, secretly tender, commander. I drew as accurately as I could his stocky figure, bald head, considering stare, and his flares of temper that subsided in rueful humor.

His wife Jessica came together from several models. One was an army wife whose slightly ironic air was the mask for a sense of realism that came close to a tragic view of life. Another was a woman of upstate New York who had a dynastic sense of herself which was borne out as an acute, but non-interfering, responsibility for others. And another—I hope she will forgive me—was the entrancing actress Helen Hayes. When I took Jessica Prescott through her big scenes, I saw Helen Hayes doing them in every shade of powerful feeling. (When she finished the book Miss Hayes sent me the warmest letter I ever received about it. "What am I going to do," she wrote, "without Matthew and Laura, Jessica and Hiram, and the General, and Isabel Mercer, and Trumpeter Rainey, and all of them?")

The cast of dozens would go on for pages, but I will trace the origins of only one more. That would be Major General Alexander Upton Quait. He had several ancestors, private and public, in my notebooks. The first was my geometry teacher in school—Major J. Ross Thomas, at New Mexico Military Institute, seventy years ago. He was as tall and thin, as tough and resilient as cattails in winter. His temperament reflected the ordeal and triumph of a recovered tubercular. He had a comically pedantic vocabulary which he used to educate us in precision of statement. His wits were ghoulish at times. He spared none of us real hardship in work, having survived it himself. Barking his words, he drew deep breaths with difficulty, and he snapped heads off for mendacity as readily as he took the truth for granted. He gave the wretches in his classroom a sense that if doom lurked grinning around the corner, the only thing to do was to spit—no, expectorate—in its face. He was joined by another figure whom I knew—Major Elkin Franklin, U.S. Cavalry, from whom I took two traits: his headlong manner of conducting formal troop inspection, and his whirlwind style of ballroom dancing, dangerously booted and spurred. From three more figures whom I knew through public knowledge I transposed some edges of reality for General Quait. One was General George Crook, USA, not for his nature, but for the achievement of his conclusive campaign against the last belligerent Apaches. Another was George Bernard Shaw, with his inexhaustible eruptions of opinion, sage or absurd; his extensive but too easily displayed learning; and the deep-seated unease that obliged him to show off. The final attitude for my General was lifted from what I'd read about Field Marshal the Earl Montgomery, who, if anyone lighted tobacco in his presence, stiffened into outraged silence until the offender either extinguished or fled—the social tyranny of the highly-placed prig.

iii

Such examples—treating only a few out of the dozens of characters who carried my story forward—reflected my effort to make things real so far as human nature was concerned. Other aspects of the fictional world also had to be translated by the imagination after the model of the real world: places, memories of history, styles of speech, ideas in their time.

I was lucky in having known all the important actual backgrounds of my story—the Middle West, New York City, upstate New York, Buffalo, Washington D.C., the vast Southwest, north Mexico. They came to mind like lighted pictures as I needed them in my intention to make the past of such places seem immediate. To the same purpose, I remembered that people long ago said some things differently in their speech and writing, often with charm amounting to more than quaintness. My modern ear listened for such expressions as I read memoirs and records from the American past; and where needed, I made up styles of expression to help bring the American nineteenth-century to mind.

When I wanted a ballad for Hiram Hyde Prescott to sing with his guitar twenty years after the Civil War, I wrote one that included references to Lincoln: "Johnny, did you say goodbye? Oh, yes, Father." I used it to tide over an intimate moment of feeling between the middle-aged Prescotts and the young Hazards in the commanding officer's primitive quarters at the little one-troop cavalry post in the trackless desert. The ballad seemed to give an air of reality to the scene and its historical time. I was both amazed and delighted when after my novel appeared the ballad was given musical settings by different folk performing groups of the 1960s who sang it in their concerts as a genuine folksong. One such group planned to record it and consulted me about the plan. I was obliged to deny them the use of it, since I had granted the copyright to a musician friend who had already composed a melody for it. So it was that the novelist's use of impersonation extended not only to character but to period idiom of sentiment and style.

A larger and to me an even more gratifying stylistic masquerade was General Quait's autobiography from which I "quoted" extended "passages." In his final Indian campaign the General has extraordinary adventures to describe, including tactics inspired by a ghostly visit to the desert past and episodes of an immense and perilous mission which he entrusts to Lieutenant Matthew Hazard. If I were to narrate these in the general tone of the rest of the book, I feared that I might not capture their epic and almost nightmarish extremes of endurance. It then occurred to me that if Matthew's extraordinary ordeals were to come to us through the General's later account of them, I could take advantage of his love of classical eloquence. Surely he was a devoted reader of Gibbon and Macaulay—I immersed myself in their histories to find the General's idiom, and I came out to write the luxuriant pages I needed from his book which I titled "Honor and Arms, The Autobiography of Alexander Upton Quait, Major General USA." To support the imposture I gave him a fraudulent footnote citing the title, author, publisher, place and date of publication. The footnote did wonders for plausibility in the matter; and I think it fair to say that General Quait's elevated and heroic style did the rest.

For I soon had evidence that my literary imposture succeeded in unexpected ways. In 1959 I was in Rome to work in the Vatican archives on research for my biography of Archbishop Lamy of Santa Fe when I received a cable from Macmillan, my London publishers. It said they were delighted with the manuscript of A DISTANT TRUMPET, they looked forward with enthusiasm to publishing it, and the rest. But several in the House raised a serious question. Was it proper in a work of fiction to include so many pages from an actual autobiography? Might I please reconsider? . . . You can imagine the pleasure I had in replying that I had composed every word in question. Again—the joys of the successful swindler were mine when I had many requests from readers for information about how to find complete copies of the General's book; they had consulted public and academic libraries, and even the Library of Congress, but could find no record of it. My hours with Gibbon and Macaulay—and General Quait—were not wasted.

iv

Abraham Lincoln fathered so much of empowering good for the nation that the spirit of it endures, perhaps not always visibly in daily lives, but it is there, like the hum of history in our background. True to his legend, he is alive to people in these pages on various occasions and is referred to for his charm and compassion. In Matthew's childhood, President Lincoln, in a purely fortuitous meeting, bestows Matthew's vocation upon him and gives him the talisman of it—an army officer's cap—to hold in secret while the powers of character and dedication grow into fulfillment. Hiram's ballad takes on the voice of Lincoln. Jessica remembers a family anecdote about him that exactly catches his waggish gaiety. He is actually seen by the Prescotts on their honeymoon in Washington when an armed escort comes clattering through the streets—and there is the President, in his seedy old wartime carriage: he feels something radiant and special in the just-married young captain and his bride as they salute him from the sidewalk, and he takes off his hat to them as he goes by. They will never forget it.

Again, at the very end of this story, Matthew's talisman, with its memory of his high hope and its promise of a man's good future, is brought to light in one last echo of Lincoln's inexhaustible legacy to dedicate Matthew's little son to his father's vocation in the nation's army.

v

A work of fiction calls into play all that might evoke the reader's belief. As an historical novel A DISTANT TRUMPET has a double obligation: without scholarly postures, to be true to a given historical environment; and to seek truth in the human nature of its characters.

P.H.
Middletown, Connecticut
1991

INTRODUCTION

C. P. Snow

A DISTANT TRUMPET is an historical novel, and a very good one. It can be read for that, and nothing else—but, if so, a great deal will be missed. As with all Paul Horgan's best work, both in fiction and literary studies, there are messages lurking beneath the surface, modest, unobtrusive, not strident, but with deep significance, for those able to catch the tone. This aspect of Horgan's talent has still to be fully recognised. That is the reason why it is mentioned here at the beginning of this essay and why it will be stressed at the end. There are a fair number of good writers, but not many wise ones. When we are given a writer as wise as Paul Horgan, it is worthy of anyone's trouble to penetrate to what he is really saying.

The central story of A DISTANT TRUMPET is set in the 1880s. The geographical domain is the far Southwest of the United States, which was then called the Arizona Territory, and in today's terms is part of the states of Arizona and New Mexico. This is the region which for fictional and other creative purposes Horgan has made very much his own. Early in his career—this novel was first published in 1960—he became, in various kinds of medium, fiction, travelogues, biographies, the epic poet of the Southwest. That was long before the Southwest was fashionable, but Horgan was showing the insight, or foresight, or prophetic sense which sometimes possesses writers without their knowing it. Dickens wasn't conscientiously forecasting the spirit of the great nineteenth-century cities when, just out of boyhood, he made his first shots at becoming the epic poet of London. So far as one knows, Horgan hasn't told us whether, forty odd years ago, he was predicting the demographic shift of the American population towards the Southwest. It doesn't seem specially likely. Anyway, however it happened, it was a brilliant intuition and has brought distinguished creative rewards.

In the 1880s the last of the American frontier was not quite closed, but nearly so. The Indians in the Arizona Territory were putting up what, in the light of history, we now know as their final fight. The French and Americans called them Apaches which became an international word: in fact, it referred to a loose collectivity of tribes. These Indians, like all other American Indians, didn't show much capacity for military organization (or any other kind of organization, as far as that goes), but they were ferocious guerilla warriors.

They were operating in a terrain, harsh, mountainous, beautiful in a kind of lunar style, which Horgan evokes in his splendid verbal description, and also in his drawings.* He is one of the few modern writers who could have made a success as a visual artist.

This terrain was peculiarly well adapted for Apache purposes, and equally unadapted for the American soldiers who were trying to subdue them. The nearest experience in British experience would be the Northwest frontier of India, where for three generations British military fought against varieties of war-like Muslims. These were small but merciless wars, which Kipling wrote about with relentless honesty. "When you're lying for dead on Afghanistan plains/ And the women come out to cut up what remains,/ Jest roll to your rifle, and blow out your brains,/ And go to your Gawd like a soldier." In Horgan's novel, the army outpost at Fort Delivery, Arizona Territory, was in something similar to a Kipling situation. Horgan doesn't parade the horrors, but they were there. When one of the little garrison is caught by Apaches, he is duly eviscerated, castrated, killed, just as he might have been on the Afghan plains. That is enough to tell us what this kind of soldiering is like.

Horgan is very good at making us understand his soldiers. A young man just out of West Point arrives at Fort Delivery. He is intelligent, competent, courageous, made for the military life. He

*Unpublished illustrations.

is not rich enough, nor socially grand enough for the girl he is engaged to, who has an ambitious mother back in Washington: but he is a man, the girl loves him, and she duly joins him in the desert. It is everyone's prediction that he will go a long distance in the Service. Promotion, though, is slow in the tiny regular U.S. Army of the 1880s. Matthew Hazard will have years to wait before he can make Captain.

An excellent professional officer, with a splendid record in the Civil War and afterwards, comes to the outpost to take over command. In middle age, he is still only a major (none of this would have been surprising in the British army of the period). Deliberately, Horgan is using a device which he may have studied in Trollope: Major Prescott is a foreshadowing of young Hazard. He has similar military virtues and sense of honour. He was born to enjoy the military existence. Horgan has never been affected by contemporary Anglo-American intellectual modes, and he makes it clear that good men, intelligent men, can actually relish being soldiers. Some men, Horgan likes disclosing, are capable of diminishing their egos in the satisfactions of duty.

There is another resemblance between the middle aged man and the beginner. Prescott's own marriage, harmonious and beautifully depicted, started against the same opposition as Hazard's. There is a delicate interplay in the novel, as there often is in Trollope, between the contrasts and similarities of the two mentalities and the two fates.

Many of the soldiers, officers and enlisted men, are not so well adapted to war. Major General Quait is admirably adapted, though in a remarkably idiosyncratic manner, scholarly, thoughtful, original, with an inner core as tough as old boots. To an Englishman he is something of a surprise. He reminds one of an odd British general who in his spare time wrote academic treatises on obscure languages in the Punjab. Quait might have been an eccentric British product. Horgan is always accurate about his social details, and it is easy to accept that similar phenomena occurred in the nineteenth century U.S. Army. Characteristically, and this would have been as true in London as in Washington, Quait's oddities prevent him getting the highest jobs, though he stands out as much the best military mind in the whole of this record.

Horgan takes a Kiplingesque pleasure in showing men at work, which must have seemed strange, and vaguely reprehensible, in the literary climate of the 1950s and 60s. He likes techniques and expertnesses of all kinds. Some of the officers are sloppy and oughtn't to be in uniform at all. One or two of their wives, bored by the depot routine, look out for extra bedmates or serious love affairs. On the other hand, the outpost surgeon, English by birth, getting on towards retirement, is happy in his job, and even happier when he can take over command as a regimental officer, at which he is abnormally good.

Rank and file are as mixed a bag as anyone could collect in a volunteer army. There are as many scrimshankers as there would have been in a British detachment. Very few have seen action before, and the action of guerilla war is a test of nerve even for brave men. Experienced officers such as Prescott don't know which of their troops they can trust. In the 1880s, as now, no one had been able to devise an estimate of courage before the event. As usual, there was cowardice in unexpected quarters, and equally unexpected gallantry.

There was supreme gallantry evinced by one of the Apache scouts, whose name was White Horn, but who was known to the troops, with jocular contempt, as Joe Dummy. White Horn is a central figure in the novel, and he is, simply by his existence, responsible for the final dramatic climax and the moral crisis. It is about him that Horgan shows a complex of delicacies and powers. No one quite knows—the otherwise omniscient author isn't certain—why White Horn has committed himself to being a scout in the U.S. Army. There are practical reasons. He may believe that, after one of Quait's campaigns in which White Horn was fighting on the losing side, that the Apaches stand no chance, and the only course for his nation is to make what terms they can. But it is not so completely commonsensical as that. White Horn has become dedicated to the American Army and in particular to the officers he is serving. He is a marvellous scout (maybe just a shade too marvellous to a hypersceptical reader), and is as good a soldier as the officers are.

He is given honorary rank as Sergeant. He becomes linked with silent stoical loyalty to Matthew Hazard. Again there are parallels to this relation in Anglo-Indian literature. Together Hazard and White Horn bring off feats of endurance and cool-headed bravery. Some of these adventures are described with formal Victorian decorum by General Quait, in Horgan's pastiche autobiography which is one of the nicest touches in the novel.

In the end, Matthew is sent on a mission to Rainbow Son, the last significant Apache chief left resisting. The U.S. Government has decided on a final solution, which Quait has been sent to the Southwest to execute. Rainbow Son and his forces must be followed and persuaded to surrender. Otherwise all-out war. If they surrender, they will be treated charitably, and the entire Apache nation collected together in Florida.

So, in one of the adventure-travel narratives at which Horgan is a master, Hazard and his silent scout, just the two of them, track down Rainbow Son's movements through the Mexican wilds. They have to go through the mountains a long way south of the present U.S.-Mexican frontier. They are lucky to survive. At last there is the confrontation with Rainbow Son. The deal which Hazard has to offer is not attractive, but the young man knows that in the long run the Apache has no option. His nation will be looked after in Florida. The army scouts, White Horn in charge, will organize the journey across the continent. Hazard cannot give any guarantee, either for the nation or for Rainbow Son himself, whether and when they will be allowed to return to the old Apache lands in the Southwest. But it is an honourable settlement, and they will be treated with honour.

That is all very well and good, and might be the end of an excellent adventure novel, enhanced by some unusually perceptive revelations about people. But we haven't finished yet. As often with Horgan, there is something in reserve, so much in reserve that it might have escaped us. Horgan, like many reflective members of the Catholic church, is an expert in the ethics of situation.

The American officers on the Southwest frontier are portrayed as not pre-occupied with the ethics of their situation. They are doing their duty, according to instructions; and that duty is simple, even for thoughtful men like Quait and Hazard, carefully represented by Horgan as eager to understand the Apaches, and by nineteenth-century standards uncommonly free from racial prejudice. Yet the duty they are carrying out is harsh. It is also simple. American policy is to dispossess the Indians of the last of their ancestral lands, and in the process (though this is not explicit) it will be for the general good if the Indian population is reduced.

It is hard to see how the West would have been made to flourish without such a policy. But it is also true that nineteenth-century Europeans were singularly unsqueamish about genocide, when they came into contact with primitive societies. The British settlers in Tasmania met the most primitive of all human societies, and massacred its members as though they were so many rabbits, leaving not one Tasmanian aboriginal alive. Australia was too large for total extermination but the settlers did their best. The Spaniards in South America for centuries operated likewise on the Indians.

American Indians were, from the first contacts, a special problem to Europeans. They weren't tractable, as many Africans were. They wouldn't work. They couldn't be made into domestic servants. They died off easily. Some of them, like the Apaches, were homicidal warriors who committed atrocities with enthusiasm. Roger Williams, one of the loftiest spirits among the first New England colonists, called his local Indians wolves with the minds of men. One would have to go a long way in the early centuries of white America to find persons who didn't accept that Indians were better eliminated.

The most humane of Horgan's soldiers want the Apaches treated with consideration, so long as the West became safe. If that should mean transporting the residue of the Apache nation thousands of miles to Florida, that had better happen. Up to this point, there is no ethical dilemma for Horgan's characters.

It is here, though, that Horgan plays, very quietly, one of his characteristic cards. The Apache scouts, White Horn and the rest, are duly sent to herd their fellow Apaches into Florida. These scouts have been on the books of the U.S. Army for years. White Horn has shown gallantry equal to Hazard's own. He has saved American lives. He is a comrade in arms. Quait and Hazard feel for him absolute trust, and he returns the trust.

Then the highest army authorities in Washington make a decision. It breaks solemn pledges. It is ruthless. For security's sake, all Apaches without exception, including those attached to the army, including White Horn, are to be kept in the reservation in Florida. This is a final decision.

What are Quait and Hazard to do? Here is the kind of situation where the deepest layer of Horgan's talent reveals itself. Love of his country, a visual artist's happiness in the great vistas of the

West, pleasure in the comedy of manners—these are his gifts which allure us and lead us on. But he is a more unusual writer than that. He is a profound and decided moralist. How does a man behave, tormented by the ethics of such a case? How should he behave? How, living in the dilemmas of the real world, can one lead a decent life?

Quait, now getting old and near retirement, goes as far as a conscientious officer can go. He protests that this new decision is a shameful breach of honour. It is a stain on the army. He is listened to politely, but he doesn't carry enough weight. His record of eccentricity counts against him: he has been suspected of excessive partiality for Indians. Anyway, no protest from anyone would have prevailed. *Realpolitik* has conquered. He argues with himself that any gesture he makes will not help White Horn or any other comrade. That is true. The sane, unpicturesque course is to soldier on until he retires. He may still be able to do something, small things, but possibly useful, which can bring more civility into the official policy.

That is exactly what one of the wise, upright, experienced characters in Trollope would have done—and probably what most honourable men who have lived in affairs in our own time, would have done.

Hazard, however, is too passionate not to make a gesture. He is too sensible to believe that it will have any effect. He has enough self insight to realize that in a sense he is indulging his own pride. There is a fierce pleasure in sacrifice. He behaves with formidable dignity. With military propriety he returns the Congressional Medal of Honour which he has just been given, in recognition of the expedition in search of the Apache chief. Immediately afterwards he resigns his commission.

The army has lost a future general. The book ends on a dying fall, with Hazard and his wife planning to go West. There he will make money, everyone assumes. That is not what he was born for. The irony is not underlined, but virtue has not been triumphant.

The whole of this display of situation ethics takes up quite a small part, a couple of chapters, in a long book. Without realizing what he implies, though, one is skimming over the hard core of Horgan's art. He would be a fine writer without it, but it is that core which gives him the bone of his originality.

BOOK ONE

Scenes from Early Times

"If my father's child can get to be
the President, your father's child
can make his heart's desire."
—Abraham Lincoln

i

"Do you know?" Matthew Carlton Hazard used to say in happier times, "the earliest chief thing I knew in my life?"

"No, what?" they would ask.

"It was to know while I was still a little boy who I was and who I was going to be."

"Who were you?"

"I was my father's child," and then they would come to know how this was and what it meant.

ii

In those early times of our American grandfathers and great-grandfathers, two prevailing visions dwelled above their lives. One was the spiritual design of national union which in the Civil War took so much bravery and sacrifice to secure. The other was the continental destiny of the United States which in the conquest and settlement of the West took so much work and love to fulfill.

The Civil War was the universal event of the nation in the nineteenth century. It was the watershed of millions of destinies. It was the source of emotion and the crucible of character. It made histories and personal unions and generations. And after its time, it yielded the nostalgia into which children were born, and it gave to the future a fabric of common experience which made our national condition.

The opening and taking of the Far West began before the War, and continued after it, and made promises where the War made memories. It brought people from both sides of the War together in a new purpose, and to those who went west it presented danger, hope and a share in a heroic creation. Having saved the Union, our grandfathers with their bodies and their acts of work found for it new lands to grow in, to forgive in, and to die in, for the sake of that which though it lived in their spirits was yet greater than they.

The War and the West—together these held nostalgia and promise for the men and women who made their immediate, concrete acts of life in terms which reflected those two grand abstractions in their country not quite a hundred years ago.

iii

Independence, in this life, was required early of Matthew Carlton Hazard. He was too young to meet it in material affairs when the need arose. During certain of his early years he lived on borrowed protection, and in every wordless way, yet with all of an energetic boy's most passionate earnestness, he vowed to be free of dependence upon anybody else as soon as ever he could.

Matthew, the only child of Richard and Emma Hazard, was born in Fox Creek, Indiana, four years before the Civil War. His parents were both tall and dark-eyed and dark-haired. Physically they resembled each other to a startling degree, and people sometimes said they could have been brother and sister. They were handsome and much loved in the town where they had come after their marriage in Pennsylvania.

Richard Hazard had a little capital saved from hard work as clerk, later as manager, in a dry-goods emporium in Pittsburgh. He took his bride to Fox Creek, Indiana, for he thought emigration to the West was surely going to grow more lively, and the tracks of the Pittsburgh, Fort Wayne and Chicago railway line had already come to Fox Creek and beyond. He already knew a few people there through business connections in Pennsylvania. The little town of seventeen hundred people was sure to have a future. He liked the idea of growing up with it. His wife Emma, who had been employed with him as a clerk in the Pittsburgh dry-goods store, knew he was a man of good judgment, pleasant nature, lively imagination (which in business meant confidence) and much energy. She went with him in joy.

Opening their own dry-goods shop in Fox Creek, they earned a modest prosperity. They ran a close margin of overhead and profit, but with the two of them to do the work, and make friends, and give their lives to the little town, they walked comfortably ahead into the years which, they knew, must bring them substantial position in time. This they wanted less for themselves than for the children they hoped to be granted. But it was many years before their son Matthew was born, and he was never joined by a brother or sister.

The parents took their disappointment privately, and found much joy in their son, who grew up even more like the two of them than they were like each other. He had all their distinguishing marks—thick, black, glossy hair, black eyebrows sweeping in gallant strokes sidewise along his finely porched brow, which threw a band of shadow over his eyes. His eyes were deep and black, and made sparks of brilliant light under their brows. His nose was straight, short and a little thick. He had a wide and fully modeled mouth, and a stout chin like his father's. His color was the color of a ripening peach, gold as well as red, and with some blur of silvery down over it that blended the whole effect into a tawny glow. He was an appealing little boy, and, as could happen in a small town, a personage in his own right because of his arresting appearance of health, good looks and intelligence.

His parents worked hard not to spoil him. They affected an offhand air with him, required him to do his share of chores about the house, and made him behave in a mannerly fashion at all times.

"Please be polite without groveling," they said to him, and "if you are ever afraid of anything, do not *deny* it, but *behave* as if you feared nothing," and—his father speaking—"Learn the value of a dollar."

They smiled to hear him repeat to his dog—a loose-skinned mongrel predominantly hound—their earliest precepts of good manners. The hound, whose name was Major, listened with abashed attentiveness; his eyes watered as though in regret at his own shortcomings; he tried to kiss Matthew during the lecture, and he ended by shaking paws as though his conduct however reprehensible had been forgiven.

iv

Fox Creek had its dusty, shady streets, many of them cut in two by the creek that wandered from north to south through sloping meadows and stone-walled orchards. Several of the streets had wooden bridges across Fox Creek. The tracks of the Pittsburgh, Fort Wayne and Chicago line came from the east between deep-grassed fields, went by the gray wooden station and its narrow gables edged with wooden cut-outs, and on across the creek and out of sight into low wooded hills. The highest point in town was called School Knob. It stood on the northern outskirts, and commanded a view in all directions. On its gentle summit sat what was called Old School. There went the children in elementary grades. Farms lay all about, and—again to the north, but under the western slope of School Knob—stood a grain mill which used the water power of Fox Creek controlled by a dam.

The mill was the town's great business, for it was the only mill in many miles. Here farmers brought their grain and sold it to the mill's owner. Like every town, Fox Creek had its rich family whose wealth and position dominated the community life. In this case it was the family of Major Robert Pennypacker, who owned the mill and much else. Matthew's dog was named after the great man's title of "Major." The citizens had wry jokes about the name Pennypacker. It seemed to describe the habits by which had been amassed the fortune it controlled. The Pennypackers lived in a large house called The Fortress on the western slope of the hill. It was a pseudo-Gothic mansion of wood with turrets, crenelations, and a round tower in which the Major kept his library. Matthew, like other children of Fox Creek, thought it was a real fort, and equipped it with soldiers and artillery, and imagined it as the scene of sieges and battles which he read about. He wished it was all his.

Matthew's best friend in town was Mr. Clarny, the station agent. It was a one-sided friendship, for to Mr. Clarny, Matthew was just another small boy who came to watch the trains go through. But Mr. Clarny, as custodian of glorious engines with their stovelike iron pots emitting thick smoke, was almost heroic to Matthew. Mr. Clarny was short, pear-shaped and deliberate. He wore an eyeshade and spectacles and never lifted his eyelids all the way up. He carried a moist, dead cigar butt cuddled against his sloping front. When he put it into his teeth the effect was calmly tremendous. In spite of Mr. Clarny's sandy irritability, Matthew wanted to be exactly like him, and could imitate him for other boys, and often did so.

v

When Matthew was four years old his father went to the Army in the first months of the Civil War.

Emma Hazard kept the store open and Matthew was much with her, "helping out." Times were hard. Emma, who worked faithfully, was unable to push the family business forward in the manner of her husband. Her best qualities as a woman were not those which would bring ingenuity and shrewdness to the ideas and acts of trade. Moreover, people had less money to spend. Everyone knew certain privations. To her privation of heart at the absence of Richard in conditions of risk and danger, Emma had to add worry over the store. She concealed as much of her feeling as possible from Matthew, and made sacrifices for him so that he would have good and plentiful food, and gave him as much untroubled companionship as she could. In his own way he felt the worries of his mother, and even of the town, and without knowing just how or to what degree, he did as much as a small boy could do to sustain her, and to make her smile, and to make her show him her love in spite of her efforts not to spoil him.

Mr. Clarny received the telegram at the station when news came from the Adjutant General of the Army that Richard Hazard had been killed at the battle of Chickamauga.

He walked in person to the store bringing the apricot-colored telegram form on which he had written the message as it came from his telegraph clicker.

"Good morning, Mrs. Hazard?" he said with inquiry in his voice, for he saw Matthew playing near her before the counter.

"Yes, Mr. Clarny," she said, and her voice dropped deep into her breast, until it sounded from her very heart. She saw what the visitor held in his hands—in the left, his luxurious squashed cigar, in in his right the telegram. She knew what the little paper must say.

"Matthew," she said, turning down to the child in the luminous shadow where he made his willful world of play, "just run out to the well and fetch Mother a ladle of water, we must give Mr. Clarny a drink after a walk on such a warm day."

Matthew turned his head without looking at his hero, or at his mother, and went down the store and out the back door. His breath felt dry and his insides felt squeezed. He did not know why.

Mr. Clarny put his cigar to his mouth and seemed to take speech from it. Huskily and with halved gaze, he said:

"I am obliged to hand you this message, Mrs. Hazard, from the Army at Washington."

Doing so, he raised his eyeshade and replaced it as if it were a hat, used in a gesture of respect.

"Yes," she said, "thank you," taking the telegram and not reading it, but folding it, and reaching to the counter for her black purse into which she placed the paper.

"My deepest condolences, madam," said Mr. Clarny, in an echo of many telegrams of similar occasion. He left the store by the front door which Emma shut and locked after him. She then pulled down the faded blue shade on which appeared in scrolled letters the word "Closed" carried on a ribbon supported by doves, all drawn in gold paint. She went out the back door, locked it after her, and met Matthew with his ladle of pure cold water. He walked carefully to spill as little as possible. Looking up at her with a hearty breath of accomplishment, he lifted the ladle to her. She bent over him in the wan sweet sunlight which made summery shadows of their presence in that place and that moment of hidden feeling, and took the ladle saying:

"Mr. Clarny has left, and so I will drink it, for you brought it to me."

She drank. He watched her with love making a lump in his throat, and with pleasure at being able to do for someone else something which was accepted. So she fostered his confidence in life.

"Come," she said, "we are going home."

She took his hand and led him to the well where they replaced the ladle, and then started walking homeward. To do this at such a time of day, leaving the store empty and shut, was puzzling to Matthew.

Their house was a small cottage of clapboard painted gray. The lines of the boards gave it from a little distance an engraved look. There were sycamore trees and lilac bushes about it. It had three rooms and a lean-to kitchen.

They walked home in silence, and Matthew felt his mother's hand cold and thin in his hot strenuous grasp. Her wonderful dark beauty was drained out of her. Though frightened, he skipped and whistled along by her side pretending that all was well. When, at home, in the front room darkened for cool in the heat of the day, she had to tell him that all was not well, and why, she tried to preserve her principle of dealing with him without frank emotion. But her voice at last betrayed her, and he saw her eyes fill, and he began to cry at the contagion of her anguish, and at that she gave up, took him in her hungry arms and crushed him to her heart and wept, ashamed and helpless, and without hope.

Matthew stopped crying then, and tried to pat her tears to stop in their turn. She saw his father in him, and thanked God for this, and at the same time could hardly bear to look at him, for the reminders.

She came back to herself presently, and just in time, for neighbors and friends, having heard from Mr. Clarny of the War Department telegram, began to come, to take up some of the burden of sorrow that had come to the Hazards. The War was coming home everywhere, changing lives suddenly and remorselessly.

vi

Emma despite her best efforts could not maintain the store. She lost everything they put into it. She sold what she could and closed out the business, and was thinking of returning to Pittsburgh with her boy when a way was found for them to stay in Fox Creek.

Major Robert Pennypacker came one day to see her at home. His namesake, Major, the hound, greeted him with shambling suspicion and a long, wet growl, for which Matthew reproved him, but without conviction, for he did not like Major Pennypacker himself. The major was a plump man with a pale face on which an apologetic expression lingered, as though to excuse himself for the superior station he occupied in the life of the modest town of Fox Creek. His hair was sandy, and his eyes were light blue and he often blinked them both together when he smiled, to ingratiate himself. He tried too hard to seem what actually he was—a kindly man of middle age. But because of a suspicious nature he knew little happiness.

He condoled with Emma, and blinked at Matthew, and then came to his business.

"As you know, Mrs. Hazard, my wife is an invalid and is now unable to manage or even direct the affairs of my house."

Emma murmured an appropriate regret.

Yes, continued the major, it was a sad cross to bear, not only for his wife, but for him, as there was no one else to conduct a proper household. He came here today to inquire into the possibility that Mrs. Hazard might consent to become his housekeeper. He could offer her comfortable quarters for herself and boy, at a generous wage of six dollars a week, in addition to lodging, full found and keep. He was pleased to repeat to her what all agreed upon to be true—that she was known to be capable, gently mannered, honest, and diligent. There would be a cook and an upstairs maid to obey her directions, and a coachman-gardener to do heavy chores at her behest.

"And for the little fellow, here," he added, turning his doleful good will upon Matthew, "think of the ample grounds to play in, and the fine books and albums in the library to look at, and the horses to ride."

Matthew's face burned dark red. His eyes shone like coals of fire. His breath went hot over his lips. He wanted none of what was offered.

But it was for his sake entirely that Emma agreed to think the matter over, and that she decided after a few days to accept the position of housekeeper at The Fortress. She knew that nowhere else might she find for her boy such comfortable living. They went to live at The Fortress on West Hill. It was then that Matthew, as a little boy, having lost his independence along with his mother's, began to fight to recover it in any way he could imagine. The struggle remained in his imagination alone for a long time. But to be in a rich man's house, and yet not of it; to live like a rich boy and yet own nothing; to see his mother subject to other people's wishes and orders—he knew what all this meant soon enough, and he hated it all.

He was glad when he was old enough to go to school every day up on School Knob, for then he was out of The Fortress, which once he had so coveted from a distance.

vii

In the late summer of '64, when school was barely begun, and bees were still above the clover in the meadows, and boys ran barefoot, and women went every day to read the Army lists on the post-office door, the town of Fox Creek, Indiana, heard some rousing news. Though he was not compaigning for re-election, it appeared that President Abraham Lincoln was obliged to make a trip by the steam cars in the second week of that September, and on a certain morning would pass through Fox Creek, westbound. Mr. Clarny had the news, and for the next few days was the most important man in town. A committee called on him to telegraph asking the President to stop in Fox Creek and say a few words from the rear car of his train. There was self-doubting anxiety until a message came back over the telegraph that said, "I will. A. Lincoln," and then followed great pride and delight.

On that September morning everything in town shook and shone in the golden sunlight. From Matt's school window up on the Knob the extra flags in town looked brand-new. Nobody worked. The firehouse band was standing loosely about the station much too early. Now and then a brass horn of the band would squeeze down the sunlight into a single blaze and send it back with a blinding glory. Nobody studied or did lessons. It was for everyone, ever since early morning, a matter of holding the breath.

The school children knew who was coming—it was Father Abraham. *Voom!* they said, firing with their mouths the cannons of the War of their fathers and older brothers and young uncles. Of all those who had never seen the War, the children were oddly nearer to knowing what it was like than their elders. But for all, the War was personified in the President. To the children he was like a grand figure in a storybook. Seven-year-old Matthew Hazard thought of him often, the Commander in Chief.

He thought of him in a great blue uniform with golden shoulder fringes and buttons, and a long cavalry saber with a gold knot, and a white horse. He saw whole meadows full of men exactly like one another following him with bayonets at the port, knees bent in arrested running, dots of light along the ranks of their black patent-leather visors. He saw the shining Army right there, crossing Fox Creek after their Commander in Chief who held out his saber to order "Forward!" It was a creek to run out of woods and through a whole lifetime. It was a heroic creek for Matthew even before he entered the first grade of school, for one frosty afternoon in early winter he saw a red fox among rusty weeds at the edge of the water; and for years he believed that the name of the creek, and of his home town, came from the very fox, that individual animal, whom he had seen: Mr. Fox of Fox Creek, Indiana, himself. And now that the Commander in Chief, President Abraham Lincoln himself, was coming here, the little creek became one of the great rivers of the world. Matthew Hazard was so excited that what meager breakfast he ate would not stay down. His mother worried until she saw him run up School Knob right afterward as muscularly wild and inventive as a large kitten.

Matthew's seat in the schoolroom was by a window that over-looked town, and the tunnels of trees on the streets that led down to the tracks, and the station, and the tracks coming to town and going. A great result of his position was that before anybody else he saw smoke at the horizon where the eastbound tracks must be. Without thinking to get permission he ran out in the school hall. From the cupola of Old School a good stout rope hung down inside the building. He seized it and swung. High above him the school bell rang out. He sang with it—"*Blanngg, mrrongg.*" He danced and the rope took him up and he came down with it. He would crack the bell if he could. He told the town with his bell that the President's train was almost there. Children streamed out of their classrooms and out the main door.

He left his bell to die like the old cat, and ran with them. He came to lead them. By acting his most naturally, he had imposed himself, his will, and his effect upon others—all the children, the whole town. He was already a power in life, without knowing it. Sweetness, inno-cence and energy made his power. Its expressions might change in long later days, but never its source. The children following him tumbled and spilled all the way down the hill. Part of the way went over a boardwalk. The weeds in the cracks blurred green with the speed of Matt running, who believed he flew.

He was the first boy to reach the station platform. There he saw Mr. Clarny inspecting the last loops of red, white and blue bunting that were being tacked up by a firemen's committee. For the past several days Matthew had seen himself as Mr. Clarny and had acted like him. Who else was in charge of the President's visit? He rushed up to him now and asked,

"She's right on time, isn't she?"

Mr. Clarny did not even glance at him but replied with terrible civility,

"This will be a *special* train. It's not on a schedule. It'll only stay a minute."

The mid-morning breeze lifted the bunting. People hurried down the road to the station. They could all see the smoke in the eastern sky. It seemed to come and go. Now it was dense and again pale and silvery like a wave of heat. When no steam engine took form in the distance, someone said that the smoke must be a hay fire at about the old Carruthers place. Murmurs of agreement went around. Someone else asked when was the train due in, then? And Matthew answered:

"This will be a *special* train. It's not on a schedule. It'll only stay a minute."

And then it was asked why everyone had broken their necks to get down here if the train wasn't even *due in,* and if it could only stay a minute, at which Mr. Clarny scratched his brow under his green eyeshade with the thumb of his cigar hand and said inside his fat cheeks,

"Somebody rang the bell at Old School," and with that all the children, the teachers, finally everyone, turned upon Matthew and all their voices spoke over him saying, "He did it!"

It was a hard moment, full of responsibility. There was the band from the firehouse. There, the mayor's committee. Mr. Clarny and his sober preparations. Every man, woman and child. Matthew saw his mother in the crowd on the platform. She lifted her head and smiled at him as if to tell him she was proud of what he'd done, regardless. It was enough. He too felt proud, then, and his confidence became his truth, and he cried out,

"He's coming, all right!" and then threw himself down on the tracks to put his ear on a rail and listen for the faraway train. He shut his eyes and listened hard. His heart banged away on a sharp edge of a wooden sleeper. He hungered to listen to the whole United

States of America, and slowly something cleared in his hearing. It was a faint thin humming, and it grew stronger, and he opened his eyes to be sure in another sense, and he shut them again, and he heard. There was a clear jarring ring of the track now. He jumped up waving his arms, vindicated.

"It's coming!" he called out, "I heard it!"

On top of his words there came on the wind like the song of a long cloud the cry of the oncoming engine's whistle out of the east. The crowd quickened, leaning out over the track to see. Other small boys fell to the tracks to listen to the rails like Matthew, and were angrily pulled to safety.

viii

Then they saw it. It let out smoke and it stood far away there up the track. They could tell by the smoke that it was moving, but it seemed to be both furious and slow. Those waiting in the little town in the late summer fields felt something must crack if they had to wait much longer for the world to come down the tracks to Fox Creek. But of course the engine grew and grew, and soon the high wheels clanked by with their shining drivers, and with a golden blast of sunny steam and a ringing scream of her iron brakes the engine ground to a halt. The name of the locomotive was "Flying Dutchman," for it said so in a yellow and green sign under the engineer's window.

The rear car was four cars back, quite a way beyond the end of the station shed. The crowd broke and flowed to the rear, followed by the band. The train conductor with telegrams in his hand hurried to the office of Mr. Clarny. Matthew ran down the cindery path beside the cars. Up ahead the engine grunted and sweated and leaked. Back to the rear the crowd fanned out facing the rear platform of the train. Running low, Matthew managed to come in around the crowd by its front knees and at once began to climb up on the last car. Someone plucked him off and made him stand down properly. He was hardly where he should have been, staring upward at the canopy of the car, and the long wood-ribbed door, and the festoons of guard chains on the rear platform, before the door opened slowly, and then let itself shut again, as though someone inside had changed his mind, which made anguish for those waiting; and then again the door opened, slowly, and stooping to get out free under its top came a very tall man in a stovepipe hat and a long black rumpled coat.

The crowd let go and the band blared and drummed in general tumult. There were cries of "Old Abe!"

Matthew's mouth dropped open. There was some mistake. He had not come to see an old brown man with a scarecrow frame. He was looking for the blue and gold Commander in Chief. He wanted President Lincoln. He stared about. The grown-up faces were raised and lighted. He looked up again to the rear car.

Gazing down at him with a frown that was at the same time a smile, the man pulled off his rubbed tall hat from the back frontward across his face, and then broke at the knees like a grasshopper and gravely set the hat down on the floor and then came up again.

The crowd laughed and clapped and Matthew wildly did not know why.

The man held up one hand for silence. It fell. Fox Creek, the fields, the United States held their breath and waited. There was going to be a speech. In the stretched quiet Matthew tugged at the citizen nearest to him and asked out loud,

"Where is President Lincoln?"

"Right up there, that's him, now you hush!" was the answer, accompanied by a hard clout.

"Is *that* him?" asked Matthew and stared up at the platform, while images fell shattered for him.

The tall brown man heard him and looked down and nodded solemnly at Matthew, as if to say, yes, this was him, such as it was, and nothing could be done about it. Then the President squared his shoulders and slowly raised his right hand over the crowd again, and then scratched his neck and opened his mouth to speak.

Exactly then the engine up front let go a leak of steam with a pounding screech, and the President closed his lips and clasped his hands over his hollow middle and waited, looking blank-faced and patient. The band took the opportunity to blare and thump for a few seconds. Suddenly the engine quit screeching, and the President made several little nods, and then began again, saying,

"My—"

Blast went the engine again, and cut him off, deafening him and everyone else. He looked down at Matthew and frowned, sharing with him, now that Matthew knew who he was, an opinion about that pesky engine. He looked like a farmer making a joke, trying to be serious and scary, while all the time he really felt peart. Somebody poked Matthew and gestured, to say that the President was making up to him.

Matthew put his head down and turned hot in shame that he had not known who Mr. Lincoln was, at first. He now had to act more indifferent than ever. He scraped his foot and he knew that everybody was trying to see the boy whom the President of the United States was making up to in the midst of all the racket. The President made his thumb over his shoulder at the engine where the noise came from that shut him up, and he raised his eyebrows, and waggled his jaw making his beard go, and put apart his hands to ask what could be done about the whole scrape. He smiled. His face was so tired and marked with lines that when he smiled it was enough to turn over the hearts of those who watched.

The next thing anybody knew, the conductor was swinging up on the side of one of the cars up ahead, and the steam cut off, and the engine began to hoot out smoke, and the wheels started to turn. They went spinning, then took hold on the rails, and the President's train was moving out. Heavy soot came down over the crowd and they yelled and waved. The President bent down and took up his hat and waved it back. As the train slowly pulled out it gave several blasts with its saluting whistle.

The whistle seemed to wake Matthew up. He gazed after the last car where the President still stood looking at everyone, and Matthew thought he looked sadly at him, because— Matthew suddenly jumped with a fearful thought. The President was almost gone away, believing that Matthew Hazard did not know who he was and didn't care!

"No, there!" cried Matthew, but there was too much noise and nobody heard him.

He hit the air in a leap and began to run up the tracks after the special train under the smoky sun. He was determined to catch the train and make things right with the President. He knew he must win a race to do so, for not far to the west of the station, the tracks crossed Fox Creek on a wooden trestle with open air between the ties. If he tried to run across them he would surely put his leg through and break it. He had to catch the train on this side of the trestle. He put up his head and tried harder. He thought he was gaining, but the clackety-clack of the wheels ahead of him went faster.

Then he saw Mr. Lincoln lean out from under his rear-platform canopy into the sunlight to help him.

"Come on, come on!" said the President, though nobody could hear him.

The President clapped his hands and Matthew flew.

The President stomped his big right foot in time with running, and Matthew puffed and romped.

The engine blew and Matthew was ready to burst. The space widened between him and the last car. He was going to lose. He faltered.

"No, no!" shook the President with his head up there, and waved, "Come on, come on!"

The trestle was just ahead. Mr. Lincoln could hardly have known it was there as a trap for Matthew, but just as if he did know, he suddenly put up his long arm and took the signal cord under the roof, and yanked it hard many times. The train at once began to slow down, it rolled on to the trestle, and stopped with only the last half of the rear car on solid ground this side of Fox Creek.

ix

When Matthew saw that, he knew it had stopped for him. He came up to the rear car. The door opened and some other men came out to see what had happened to jerk the train to a halt. One of them was a young officer in blue uniform. The President turned to them and nodded that things were all right, he had taken charge. They just stood there then.

The President gazed down at Matthew and said,

"Well, now."

Matthew went hollow, now that he was where he meant to be, and said nothing. The President leaned down, took Matthew by the arm, raised it, got his hand, then his other hand, and hauled him up over the guard chains and set him on the platform.

"You came to see me?" he asked seriously.

Matthew nodded.

Mr. Lincoln scraped up behind himself an unfolded chair made of fancy green and brown carpeting, and sat down. On his knees he placed Matthew.

"What about?" he asked

Matthew knew well enough what about, but he could not speak. He hung his head. The President said,

"Just had to see the old hound dog anyhow, is that it?"

One of the men produced a watch and with barely respectful impatience, said,

"After all, Mr. President, we haven't got all day."

"Maybe you haven't, but I have, if somebody is about to break wide open unless somebody else will sit down and pay him a little mind."

"Yes, sir," said the man furiously.

The President winked at Matthew over what got grown men all het up, and asked,

"You live back there in Fox Creek?"

Matthew nodded.

"Say yes, my boy."

"Yes," said Matthew.

"That's done her. Now we can talk. What's your name?"

Matthew told him.

"All right, Matthew Carlton Hazard. What does your pappy do?"

"He was a soldier."

"He was, was he?" A long, sweet smile went over the tired old man's face. "In this war?" he asked.

"Yes, sir."

"Did you lose him?"

"Yes."

"When? Where?"

"At Chicka—"

"—mauga?" finished the President on the difficult name. "Chickamauga. Last year." He put his hands on Matthew's shoulders and gripped him hard. "God bless him," he said. "Is your mother all right?"

"Yes, sir."

"And are you?"

"Yes, sir."

"And so are we all, my boy, for we are trying to do what is right." He drew a deep, staggering breath. "Now let me tell you something, Matthew. Whatever you want to be, and do, if it is a good thing to be, and do, you can be, and do, in this land. Do you know that?"

"Yes, sir."

"If my father's child can get to be the President, your father's child can make his heart's desire. Do you hear?"

"Yes, sir."

Mr. Lincoln put his long finger like a bayonet on Matthew's breast. "Who is your father's child, then?"

Matthew thought for a moment, and then he knew.

"Me."

"That's who he is, all right! Now then. What do you want to be?"

"Like my father."

"You mean, a soldier?"

"Yes."

The President turned to the young officer beside him and said, "Captain, if you please."

The captain leaned down to inquire what his Commander in Chief wanted, and Mr. Lincoln reached up and took from his head his little blue cap with the squashed-in front on which were crossed rifles of brass.

"I'll make it up to you, Captain," he said, and put the cap on Matthew's head. It was somewhat too large, but it was real, and it was put there without any idea that it was funny or make-believe. "It does not fit you now," said the President, "but it will fit you some day, Matthew. And when it does, maybe you will remember kindly who put it there. Will you?"

"Yes, sir."

"When the time comes, you find your congressman and tell him you have to go to West Point. You tell him we want to get to where we won't need wars and killing, but you tell him if the Republic needs soldiers, you're aiming to be one. He'll pay attention to you, if you stick out your wishbone and dog him enough. One thing though—" The President put on a joking look. "One thing, don't tell anybody I sent you. It might do you no favor ten years from now. Who knows? Who knows?" he added with sad politeness. "Anyhow," he said, brightening, "far's I'm concerned, you're a soldier right now! It's just a case of the Army waiting a while for you!"

With that he stood Matthew off his knees, and got up and lifted him over the chains down to the ground. For the first time, he noticed that people were coming along the tracks from the station to see what had stopped the train. The President waved at them, turning away, ducking his head, as if to say that enough was enough. He nodded to a member of his party, the signal was sent to the engineer, and the train began to pull away. President Lincoln looked once more at Matthew down on the ground, waved good-by to him with an air of having finished up a good piece of business, and stooping, went inside the car through the rear door.

"What was that?" asked the nearest people, crowding about Matthew to see what he held. He pushed the officer's cap inside his shirt and ran off to the creekside. Major Pennypacker called after him, "Matt, Matt! Come right back here and tell us what the President—" but without effect. They gazed after the running figure which made a receding disturbance in the high-flowered meadow, like a small, straight wind that took its course there, bending aside the tall stalks of Queen Anne's lace and goldenrod and silver-burst long grasses, took its course as it had to do, heeding no power that sought to call it back or make it change.

He took the cap back to The Fortress and hid it with his treasures. The cap was now invested with magic, for it represented to Matthew a talisman for his whole future. It meant that one day he would be able to achieve his independence. The town had seen him receive it from the President, and thereafter, if anybody asked him about it, he lowered his head while keeping his black, brilliant gaze upon his questioner, and simply refrained from replying. It was what Emma called his "black look." It made him formidable, even as a boy, and more handsome than ever.

x

In his twelfth year Matthew had an idea which was all his own, and which he tested against grown-up obstacles.

One day he went to see Mr. Clarny at the station. Mr. Clarny was busy with his brass and copper insect, as Matt saw it, or, as others saw it, the telegraph key. Matthew waited until there was silence from the key, whose language only an adept like Mr. Clarny could understand. Then,

"Mr. Clarny," he said, "I want to work here, for pay."

Mr. Clarny performed actions which separately and together meant "No." He put his cigar butt into his pale mouth and took it out again. He inclined his portly figure forward to his leather-topped table and with a careless, superbly expert throw of his shiny stout fingers, he re-engaged the key and made it resume its chatter, which filled the wood-ribbed room and made any other concern but the obscure messages of the key seem like an impertinence. Matthew stood waiting for almost half an hour, but Mr. Clarny never again glanced at him, and finally he left, pondering about possible mistakes in his manner of approach to the station agent. He could discover none.

He waited a week, and came back with the same request, and again he was ignored. He came twice more, with the same results. The fifth time he came just after sunup, bringing a broom. He swept the station platform, and pulled weeds that rose above the planks and between them, and he dusted off the window sills of the bay window through which Mr. Clarny, when seated within at his key, could look uptrack and down. Mr. Clarny arrived for the day to find him as he finished his task.

"Here, there!" cried Mr. Clarny, waving his short thick arms wildly at Matthew. "Get away from there! You. What do you think you're—"

"I swept off, and I took up the weeds, and cleaned the window ledges," said Matthew.

Mr. Clarny, looking deeply offended, unlocked the waiting-room door and disappeared within. Matthew sat down on the edge of the platform, feeling too foolish and sad to go away immediately and thus reveal his disappointment. He heard the telegraph key start up, and he supposed Mr. Clarny would now be lost to him once again.

But in a few minutes, while the key continued to talk, a bulky shadow flowed across Matthew, starting him up from his daydream of puzzled sorrow, and Mr. Clarny said through his cigar shred,

"Well then, come on inshide, and we'll shee."

By his simple persistence which arose out of the planned desire in his mind, Matthew had prevailed. He was hired at fifty cents a week to come every day before school and sweep out the station office and waiting room, and to keep "the grounds," as Mr. Clarny called the area about the station, in a condition of neatness. Further, when occasionally there should be time for it, Mr. Clarny would undertake to teach Matthew how to understand the telegraph and to operate the key, with the strict understanding that he was never to touch it in the absence of the proper authorities, by which awesome plural Mr. Clarny meant himself.

xi

Matthew, in trying even so young to govern the conditions of his life, had his purposes. Earning money of his own, he imagined that soon he would be able to take his mother away from The Fortress and support her himself. He saved his salary. Emma was proud of him, for his frank nature was unable for long to conceal its motives, and as she saw him grow up faster within than he did visibly in his body, she knew an ache of pride for him, and a prayerful concern that life would use him kindly. She tried not to show him her dwelling love to its full extent, but he knew of it anyway.

To the rest of the boys in Fox Creek he was an acknowledged leader. Who else among them was a railroad man? Who made his own money at other than chores about the house, and was paid in more than mere pennies? But not only his position as an employee of the railroad gave him primacy. Who knew so well *how things were,* and could tell others of his age, and yes, even older?

In late winter of 1876, Matthew discussed his plans with Mr. Clarny.

"Mr. Clarny, I am considered an employee of the Pittsburgh, Fort Wayne and Chicago, ain't I?"

Mr. Clarny regarded him in silence with a halved gaze. He had grown fatter with the years. His cheeks had pouches like those of a chipmunk, and the impression existed that instead of keeping nuts inside his cheek pouches he kept words which he produced slowly and importantly as needed. He finally said,

"For the first year I paid your wages myself. But when I made certain you were t'be trusted, I added you to my office worksheet. The company never questioned it. So I sh'd say you are an employee of the Line."

"Good. I can ask you this, then. As an employee, am I eligible for a pass?"

"A pass," said Mr. Clarny, to be sure he understood.

"Yes."

"Where to?"

"Fort Wayne."

"What for?"

"I want to go see the new congressman there."

"What about?"

"About an appointment to West Point."

"Fixing to leave us?"

"Well, sir, you know how it is."

Mr. Clarny looked aside like one betrayed.

"I'll consider it and let you know," he said.

It took him a whole day to think it over, but in the end Mr. Clarny agreed that Matthew was eligible for a pass, and he wrote one out for him, "good for thirty days."

Within the week Matthew rode over to Fort Wayne on the morning train with his head buzzing. It was a wet snowy day. The fields were white. The creeks were black in thawing ice. Russet woods marked the distant hilltops. The gray sky seemed to hang low. Blackbirds now and then circled upon it. Earth's scents were sharp and penetrated deeply into the mind and heart. It was a day to make sorrow heavier and happiness sweeter. Matthew was happy. In his vision he animated the scene that must soon take place when he should confront the congressman. He took with him a brown-paper parcel. It contained the officer's cap which President Lincoln had put on the head of that small boy so many years ago. He would show it to the congressman, and by the power of this token he would force the congressman to grant him what he asked. It was a luxurious daydream, and Matthew refined it in its every clear detail.

But when he sat down in the congressman's dingy law office—a room in every shade of brown silvered by dust—Matthew put dreams away and presented only himself in his own daylit mind and strength. The officer's cap he left in its neat parcel. He never mentioned President Lincoln. Something drove him to ask for his lifetime's favor on terms that were his alone—what he could show and give to a stranger. This did not mean that the magic had all gone from the Lincoln cap or the scene of its presentation. Quite the contrary. It had simply accomplished its magic through the years of Matthew's growing faith that he must be of the Army and that nothing could prevent his acceptance. "Your father's child can make his heart's desire." There lay the power of President Lincoln's tender kindness to an unfathered boy during the War. There lay the long-submerged source of Matthew's conviction now as he laid his appeal before the congressman.

The congressman was of an appearance which could signify any age from thirty-five to sixty. He was whiskered at random like an old mongrel dog, wearing a collar and a suit too big for him, within which he inched around as if to find his mental attitudes in physical trials at various positions. He wore his tin-rimmed spectacles up on his ridged brow and he gazed at his caller out of filmy blue eyes, while he chewed tobacco which made him clear his throat every few seconds.

He listened without asking questions while Matthew talked himself out. In effect:

"I was born in 1857, at Fox Creek, Indiana," said Matthew. "I attended the early grades and high school there. Here is a record of my marks. I have always been in the upper ten of my room. My teachers and my principal wrote me these letters of recommendation. Here is another one from my employer, Mr. Cyrus E. Clarny, agent of the Pittsburgh, Fort Wayne and Chicago line. I am in tiptop health. I am convinced that I will be able to serve my country as an efficient officer of the Army. My father was a soldier in the late War. He was killed in the battle of Chickamauga. Ever since then I have never wanted to be anything else but a soldier. I have worked in my spare time to contribute to the support of my mother. I believe a standing army commanded by trained leaders is a matter of great importance to the United States. I think it will be many years before the Far West is pacified. I believe there is going to be much work for our Army on the Indian frontier. Property rights and the safety of settlers must be protected. A nation without a well-trained and well-kept armed force is a second-class nation. My purpose in life is to help this to be a first-class nation. That is why I have come over here on a railroad pass as an employee of the Line to ask you to appoint me as a cadet in the United States Military Academy, sir."

The congressman scratched himself against the spine of his creaking high-backed swivel chair and said,

"I have already assigned my last appointment, but I would be prepared to consider Mr.—" He pawed and tapped at Matthew's papers on his desk—"Mr. Hazard two years from now."

Matthew said nothing, but simply let his will stand between them. His abundance of health, determination and confidence spoke for him. The member of Congress, with a shift of his comforting cud, swiveled about to look through his cobwebbed window at a prospect of the street outside, where figures moved along in the snow on errands which happily had nothing to do with demands upon him. His eyes watered, his whiskers thrust and fell in the movements of his chewing jaws, and his hands, like dried tobacco leaf, seemed brittle and aimless as he sought to resist the invading force of vitality, youth, and comeliness that faced him across his littered table. He risked a few suspicious, sidelong glances at Matthew, but each one cost him a grain of his official resolve, and he took refuge in an elaborate act of dignity that occupied several minutes. He produced and opened his penknife, and took up his plug of tobacco, and made himself a new mouthful of shavings from it, while his lips reached out for the stinging pleasure of the first taste of the new chaw. All this delay was intended to seem deliberative and statesman-like. When it could no longer be extended in the face of Matthew's calm refusal to be denied, the congressman leaned forward, spat at his cuspidor and stated that, as it happened,

"I have not yet notified the candidate whom I had in mind, though I had reached a tentative—purely tentative, mind you—understanding with the candidate's sponsors, and I might just not, I just *might not,* notify him, if—"

He broke off his thought, weighing the uneasy political consequences of changing his mind. But it was plain he was obliged by the power that was working in Matthew to view the matter simply on the basis of what, in this case, would be good for the Army. If he had ever seen any young man who promised to make a good officer, he was looking at him right now in his law office upstairs over the Citizens' Union State Bank of Fort Wayne, Indiana.

In a sudden gesture of quixotic determination, the congressman sat forward to his table and rattled through Matthew's papers.

"I reckon it's all here," he said. "I'll do her; you can count on me."

The affair was settled. They shook hands on it. Matthew's tawny face turned a deeper color in a sudden blush. The congressman wheezed out a laugh of gratification at having brought such strong pleasure to such a strong young man in such a strong cause. Matthew went home with the promise that he would soon receive an official letter of appointment.

xii

Entering the military academy in the summer of 1876, he succeeded in realizing the terms of his life. He was independent. He was a soldier. Major Pennypacker was no longer his private enemy because the major now had no further power to do him favors. Keeping the secret of it now, as always, he took the Lincoln cap with him among his few private possessions.

In the following year when the invalid Mrs. Pennypacker died, Emma Hazard married the widower. This, by now, had no pain for Matthew. His mother would now be mistress where she had long been servant. That the major had made this possible proved how respectfully and gratefully he must have taken the services of Emma Hazard through the years. He must long since have ceased to regard Emma as a hireling and have come to need her as a wife. Ready as he had been to provide for his mother when he could, Matthew was happy that she would have all her remaining life in comfort and protection, even if these should not come from him.

On his first leave he went home to Fox Creek to visit his mother and her husband. The Fortress was now not only a familiar but also a happy place to him. Major Pennypacker was proud of him in his tight, short-jacketed gray uniform. Since the major's own military title owed more to courtesy than to martial experience, he was fiercely gratified that a real officer was now enfolded within his family. Matthew allowed him his sentimental pride, but did not feel obliged to encounter it with any regularity. He spent his second leave in Washington as the guest of his classmate, Cadet Harvey Greenleaf, whose father was a colonel stationed in the office of the Secretary of War.

Harvey's mother kept an establishment of some grandeur which held little interest for Matthew beyond the fact that it was the residence also of Harvey's sister Laura. Holding himself throughout his visit in a convention of impersonal civility, for he was still between the years of boy and man, Matthew had no event of striking significance to record or remember of that holiday.

But he was sure he had never seen anyone prettier than Laura Greenleaf. He had never heard a voice which so pleased him simply to listen to, irrespective of what it said, as hers. He suddenly became aware of clothes, women's clothes, the things she wore. It must have been because it was she who wore them. When they went to a ball together, along with Harvey and another girl, Matthew decided that at last he knew what the dancing instructor at West Point meant by all his insistence on the value of the lancers, the waltz and the schottische to the well-rounded young officer. She was full of energy and high spirits, and she gave these equally, so far as he could judge, to all young men—and there were many—who put themselves forward for her notice. He had the advantage of staying in the same house with her, and thus saw her not only on arranged occasions, but also incidentally.

When his leave was up, he asked her,

"May I write to you? Would you answer my letters?"

Lightly she replied,

"*Of course* you may write to me. You *must* write to me, if only to give me news of Harvey, who never, the wretch, absolutely never writes home. He is the most unsatisfactory brother imaginable. I don't know why I adore him, but I do, like everyone else."

xiii

Before marrying Huntleigh Greenleaf, Laura's mother, Drusilla Godwin, was a Camden girl, a member of a famous South Carolina family which had two branches. One lived in Charleston, and this was the socially dominant branch. The Camden branch had more money, more slaves, but—it was a family mystery—less prestige. Drusilla Godwin was aware of the distinction between her own people and her cousins in Charleston. In consequence much of her energy and ingenuity was spent in trying to erase it through all her life. In fact, with the passage of time, she forgot the immediate envy which had provoked her forces and formed her character, but simply continued to exercise these with all the vitality of her self-will and her charm.

When she married Lieutenant Huntleigh Greenleaf, who came of a socially impressive Philadelphia—a Northern!—family, her governing motive was to show her Charleston cousins that she could marry someone even more distinguished and just as aristocratically poor as any of them. Her husband's mother was descended from a Signer. A young uncle, prematurely dead of the varioloid, had accompanied the mission of Washington Irving to Spain. During a youthful visit to London, her husband himself had dined in company with Lord Melbourne, who liked to stare at Americans. Through an odd foreign connection, a great-uncle in the Greenleaf family had been a cardinal in Rome. Not herself a Catholic, Mrs. Huntleigh Greenleaf liked to make her remark about how odd was the position of the Church in modern society—it seemed that Catholics were either cooks or corporals on the one hand, or kings and queens on the other

—nothing, really, in between. In marrying her, the young Northern lieutenant married an heiress. He also married into bondage.

When their children were to be born, Mrs. Greenleaf said,

"I cannot imagine having my babies anywhere but in my ancestral home in Camden."

She journeyed south with many servants and a personal physician when her son Harvey was due to appear in 1857, and two years later she repeated the journey to her ancestral shrine for Laura's delivery. She did this in spite of her resentment against her own family for not having belonged in Charleston. Her husband was granted army leave to go with her, though he went merely as another member of the maternal entourage. The great mansion in the sandy flats on the outskirts of Camden was opened and restaffed for a period of four weeks and there Laura made her first cry in the world. When she and her mother were strong enough to travel, the whole household returned to Fort Jay, on Governor's Island, New York, where Lieutenant Greenleaf was stationed. They never returned to Camden, for two years later the Civil War made that temporarily impossible, and loss of slaves and deterioration of the great empty house made any later return both painful and extravagant.

Mrs. Greenleaf was cut off from her cousins by the War. Privately she almost enjoyed the troubles that befell them. Publicly she presented the image of a heroic woman who suffered with grace the tragedy of those whose loyalties must in the circumstances be divided —a Southerner born who was wedded to a Northern soldier. When tactful sympathy was proffered her by her friends in the Army she permitted her fine blue eyes to be clouded with tears, even as she raised her head and her bosom and demonstrated that she was a dutiful wife and mother whose first loyalty lay to her husband and his children.

To give himself any sort of character, Huntleigh Greenleaf adopted the slightly detached, severe air of a critic of fine living. Style became more important to him than substance, as would be natural to one who had made his particular compromise with life. He was punctilious, almost a martinet, as an officer. His uniforms had to cling to his figure without wrinkles, especially at his waist and over his buttocks, of whose trim outline he was vain. In speech, manner, judgment, he became fastidious and attentive to fashion. He sometimes had the illusion that he could, and did, set fashions. He started his "collections"—engraved flintlock pistols, Georgian silver snuffboxes, and royal autographs, including what he called a rarity, a signature of Louis XVI, who, said the colonel, wrote so little. These had to accompany him wherever he went in his army stations.

For the most part, his stations were assigned or accepted according to Mrs. Greenleaf's wishes. It suited her to be the center of an active social life. Remote frontier posts or battlefields could give her little of what she wanted. Her husband's career, in consequence, was molded to her needs, not his. Even during the Civil War she contrived to have him contrive to be retained in Washington on staff duty.

"This war," she would remark with dashing charm which barely concealed her will, and in an accent which prettily confessed her important Southern origin, "this war will be won by brains, and we have all too few in Washington, as I was saying just now to General Meigs. Huntleigh has agreed to sacrifice a field command in order—" and so on. Dreamily she looked forward to the day when he should be promoted general, without considering that her policy might be the one sure way to deny him the rank she regarded as her due.

xiv

Their children saw through the Greenleaf parents at an early age. Harvey and his sister Laura were drawn together in an alliance of opinion about the purposeful grandeurs of their mother and the weak, gallant airs of their father. Sometimes the two youngsters would burst out laughing as they looked at each other in the midst of family occasions. So self-centered was their mother and so self-deceiving their father that the healthy mockery of their children never appeared to them for what it really was. The ostensible solidarity of the family was preserved for years in precarious balance. But this was a doubtful substitute for confidence and love based on unselfish devotion.

Harvey naturally enough grew up to be indifferent to the over-fastidious standards set by his parents. As a boy he was always being hauled home from adventures in the poorer quarters of whatever town was the family station. He preferred disreputable friends. He learned much about the seedy excitements of the pool room while still a boy. In spite of his mother's "fainting" fits over his behavior, he failed to reform.

Harvey was much like his mother physically. He had her delicate coloring, her hazy sweetness of expression, and her small-boned, animated and energetic body. But in him these qualities were charged with a grinning masculinity which made him essentially as unlike her as possible.

"I simply cannot understand him," she would say. "How any son of mine can like the things he likes, and prefer the people he prefers—gambling, and racing, and common women, and actors, why, even as a boy in his teens, he—" and she would toss her hands to her shoulders and let her glance flutter to the ceiling. Unable to control Harvey, she told her husband to handle him. But Huntleigh Greenleaf thought it rather dashing to have a buck and a beau for a son, and murmured about wild oats, and wistfully hoped Harvey would confide his adventures to him for vicarious enjoyment. The son never did this.

But the brother did.

Harvey would fascinate Laura by the hour with descriptions of his low-life companions and their world. He never told her all. He loved her adoration, and he feared to shock her love away from him if he told her fully about his life. Deleting those parts which had to do with his own cheerful sins—mostly to do with affairs purchased from working-class girls or prostitutes or musical-hall chorines—he gave her lurid stories about the edges of their worlds that made her shudder and thrill. They began a delicate comedy in which she would try to save him from his worser self. But, in spite of her prayers for him, she did it half-heartedly, and his promises of reform were just as tacitly insincere. After each of his falls he would come to describe it and be forgiven. It was one way to cement their bond of inner resistance to the family masquerade in which they had lost faith.

Harvey's subsurface life in no way altered his affable and effective position as a member of polite society. Seeing him at dances and parties Laura would marvel at his charming and innocent appearance, and feel superior to the pretty girls and fresh-faced boys who knew nothing of the other world to which she was made privy by her brother's reports. When he entered the military academy on a presidential appointment she was glad he would now be rescued from his indulgences, for she was devout and she suffered for the state of his soul; but she was also a little regretful at losing her contact with a life larger than her own.

XV

As she grew up Laura was outwardly her mother's doll, to be beautifully dressed, to be put through social paces, to be moved about according to Drusilla Greenleaf's proprieties. In childhood, Laura was able to retain her composure in this role. She liked clothes and enjoyed making an effect. She heard grownups often exclaim over her as such a beautiful and mannerly little girl. She learned to hear such tributes without seeming to notice them, and if on occasion they were not forthcoming, she knew how to elicit them by redoubling her grace of behavior. In time she took for granted her position as the most admired and sought-after young lady of her time and place.

But she was, too, as she grew into late girlhood, increasingly aware of missing something. What was it? She found it hard to say, but nothing, really, gave her any warmth of feeling. It was this which people meant but could not identify when they were afraid she was somewhat spoiled. Laura took the wages of her charms simply— preferments and gifts and condonings—not realizing that she made of them substitutions for the thing she had always most wanted and had never had. This was a sense of love, ease and hidden strength given to each other by her parents in their life together. Laura dearly wanted to care about something or someone, but there seemed to be little chance to discover what or whom in the course of her active days directed by her mother.

Mrs. Greenleaf's precepts were steadily laid before her daughter. A lady should always have her way, and any man who was a gentleman would agree without argument. A lady must learn the art of dissembling her real opinions, revealing only those which brought advantage if she hoped to be socially successful. A lady must never permit herself to grant to any man any degree of favor which would make it difficult for her to withdraw her interest from him at any time. Though she must perfect the art of seeming to trust and love everyone, a lady must never make the mistake of trusting any other lady. A lady must never, never in any circumstances show disappointment in anyone, but should privately note the occasion of it, and bide her time until an opportunity for indirect reprisal should come to her, when she must use it with swift and deadly accuracy.

Laura could not help being affected by such scraps of a remorseless philosophy. But though they gave her an armory of weapons with which to wage social life according to her mother's tested code, they did not satisfy her.

She had inherited from her grandmother Godwin a set of jewels consisting of half a dozen crescent brooches set with diamonds, earrings of pearls and diamonds, and a necklace of pearls. When on the grandest occasions she would wear these, she would find herself wondering whether they were admired for their beauty or their worth in dollars; and from that thought she would proceed to wondering whether anybody really looked at her to find the heart and spirit within, or merely saw the beauty and animation of her presence enhanced by her mother's arts and known fortune.

For many years there was only one person who seemed to take her for what she herself thought she was, or, if she presented herself falsely, who loved her enough to take this, too, and await her early return to her own truth.

xvi

This was her Uncle Alex—Major General Alexander Upton Quait, who had been married to Huntleigh Greenleaf's only sister. Widowed for many years, he recognized that his connection with the Greenleafs was now tenuous, at best. Yet he spoke of them as his "family." There was nobody else in the world to whom he might so allude. The sighing, bored hostility of Mrs. Greenleaf, and the offhand civility of Colonel Greenleaf, were not enough to turn the lonely old brother-in-law away. Whenever he was in Washington, General Quait made his *devoir,* put his calling cards in the silver dish on the hall table, and in his own strange way, in his latter years, began to achieve something of a success with the Greenleaf circle of guests. Drusilla Greenleaf explained it by shrugging reference to what two stars seemed able to do for almost anyone. But major generals were not so rare in the capital that his autumnal triumphs could be explained by his rank alone. His reputation did much for him—it was unlike any other in the Army; and so did his conscientious efforts to enter into the occasion, whatever it might be. Moreover—in the Greenleaf house, anyhow—he had a real reason to return. Many grownups would never have understood it if they'd known of it.

This was the affection that existed between Laura Greenleaf and her Uncle Alex.

She met him first when she was five or six years old, and at first he frightened her, because he loomed so tall, and had such a rapid, whistly way of speaking, and threw his arms about so alarmingly. In fact, his appearance was considered irregular enough, which was not to be wondered at when it was recalled that armies prefer uniformity to all other qualities.

He was well over six feet tall, and bone-thin. He wore his white hair trimmed close to his skull, and yet his mustache and beard were allowed to grow as long as those of a Chinese sage. His beard was brushed apart into two long forks that came halfway to his gold bullion lace belt with its starred buckle. His eyes were black and piercing. From years of squinting in the sun and at the pages of books, he had developed deep sets of wrinkles that ran from his eyes down the hollows of his cheeks until engulfed by his whiskers. His mouth could not be seen under his mustaches. The skin of his face and hands was tanned to a walnut brown. If his thinness suggested a skeleton, his movements even further underlined the impression. He almost clattered when he walked or sat down or gestured. His gestures were free-flung. He often hung his right hand by its bony claw in his beard while he talked or speculated—and he was often lost in speculation even while gazing at someone with whom he was supposed to be conversing. He had a wet, thin cough which wracked his angular frame frequently. When this happened, he would fix his interrupted remarks in the air with a lifted finger, and smile brilliantly through his cough to excuse the nuisance.

If his thinness and his cough gave the impression of ill health, there was truth in it only to the extent that the illness was an out-lived one: he had been bedridden for two years in his youth with tuberculosis. It was an astonishment that he had recovered. It struck observers that his recovery had been an act of will, mind over matter, spirit over flesh. This was true. The illness had left him with his cadaverous frame, his thin, slightly husky voice, and a little habit of taking many short breaths which could be heard a little distance away.

In his youth Alexander Quait had never seemed young. This was generously accounted for by those who had raised him from infancy with the explanation that as an orphan, he had missed softening early influences.

But they misjudged him. He was not particularly aware of missing anything. He had no self-pity. His early hungers were easily satisfied, and in fact his appetites never required much in all his life. He wanted to know how the world was, and he liked to see a clear cause produce an appropriate result, and he looked for the design of logic in everything.

Because books contained most of the sorts of answers he hoped to find in life, he became attached to them in their every aspect while very young. He loved their look, their feel, their type, their presence singly or in great quantities, as in libraries. His origins were lost in mystery, so nobody could explain where his traits and tastes came from.

xvii

As soon as Laura Greenleaf in her childhood became used to her Uncle Alexander Quait's appearance, she thought him funny, and without malice would laugh out loud and clap her hands even when he was simply his most usual self.

Her parents, being too sophisticated to get the point, thought she was being impolite and tried to bring her to manners. But Uncle Alex, seeing how she regarded him, patiently acknowledged that he must indeed seem absurd to a child, and made himself consciously so, to save her from reproof by her parents. He never came without bringing Laura a little present, and he loved to have her sit with him and listen to stories.

"Do you want to hear a real one," he would ask, "or a made-up one?"

"A made-up one."

"So you want me to stretch my feeble old wits. Very well."

And he would launch into a fantasy of such brightness and such surprise that she would be lost, watching his eyes as if to anticipate in their quivering search the next turns in the story he invented behind his sight.

It was her innocent policy to charm everybody older than herself, and she tried two or three times to turn her full battery of blandishments upon Uncle Alex. He was never fooled. He would regard her gravely, and without a rebuke or shake of the head he would simply let her spend her charms until even to her they became insincere and foolish. He rejected that part of her mother which would now and then show. Laura would blush, and subside, and wait for him to resume his connection with her in his animated recitals.

"What on earth Laura sees in the old fool I cannot for the life of me imagine," declared Mrs. Greenleaf.

General Quait was absent from Washington for long periods of time and Mrs. Greenleaf hoped that Laura would "outgrow" him.

But her brother-in-law, without trying to be, was more clever than she. Whenever he returned, he continued to interest Laura simply by being who and what he was, and even in her most affected phases of girlhood, he gave her the happy relief of letting her come back to him in a completely honest relationship.

Harvey Greenleaf was strangely bothered by his uncle. Alexander Upton Quait was the only living being who made Harvey feel the smallest sense of shame for his own sins of self-indulgence. Not that the General knew anything of these—he did not. But by his mere presence, the uncle seemed to visit a silent judgment upon the nephew, and the nephew was uncomfortable in the face of it.

In consequence, Harvey, though always polite in a worldly way, made himself scarce when Uncle Alex was in the house, and afterward, alone with his sister, he would ask rather too casually,

"What did Uncle Alex have to say? I suppose you two had a good gossip about me?"

"Why, no, of course not," she would answer in some puzzlement, "we had a thousand other things to talk of. Besides, don't you suppose I am *loyal*? I would never dream of speaking to Uncle Alex about my darling brother and all his wicked ways."

xviii

Laura was particularly lonely in her busy and trivial life after her brother Harvey went to West Point. When he came home for Christmas, 1877, in his second year as a cadet and brought with him a dark, simple, tall young man from out West somewhere—Illinois, was it, or Indiana?—or some such outlandish place—she made judgment upon him offhand with her mother's standards, according to which he was without interest.

But she showed him no hint of this judgment. Her arts were by now so practiced that she could be as clever, as lively, as pretty for him, Cadet Matthew Carlton Hazard, as for any of the attentive young gentlemen who flocked about her in Washington. She went to dances with him and other young people in a group, and she endured his dancing, which was formal to the point of awkwardness. He was given to long, rather speculative silences, which sometimes made her uneasy, as though he were searching out something in her, and she wondered, whatever it might be, whether he would fail to find it in her. He had a kind of dark, brooding look which, because she could not fathom it, seemed almost rude to her, when his steady black eyes gazed at her with shocking directness, even as he held his head lowered so that his gaze came through a band of shadow cast by his brows. Then she would pointedly ignore him for a few minutes, waiting for him to reclaim her with some audacious move.

He did not make it.

She smiled. He was not worth troubling about. She had always known that her brother Harvey took up with strange creatures. She remained lightly civil; the vacation would soon be over, the two cadets would leave the house, and she would not always be finding Mr. Hazard underfoot.

It was a nuisance to wonder what sort of impression she had really made upon him—not that she cared, he was nothing to her—but she had to put up with not knowing. He was cheerful, polite and acquiescent in her presence. That was all she knew about him.

When, at the point of leaving to return to the military academy, he asked if he might write to her, and if she would answer his letters, she was perversely cross with him for waiting so long to show that she interested him. She turned him off with some light snub or other —wasn't it something about obtaining news of Harvey through him? She really could not be bothered to recall just what—and with a sigh of relief saw him depart. It was enough that he had admitted her attraction for him. With this reassurance safely in her collection, she could forget him.

After he was gone, Mrs. Greenleaf, who never shirked an instructive duty, made a few laughingly dismissive remarks about him.

"The poor young man," she said, "he did seem a fish out of water here. Oh! Whatever shall we do about Harvey and his choice of hangers-on. Still, poor, earnest, fumbling Mr. Hazard must not be entirely blamed. It was clear that he had had few advantages. Still, as I say, there is no use, is there, ever expecting him to change?

I've no doubt he will be a good, solid junior officer who will probably never rise much above the mentality or manner of a platoon sergeant. What *do* you suppose Harvey was thinking of to risk embarrassing the poor creature by bringing him *here?* I do think I see signs that democracy is taking root at the military academy to an alarming degree. Huntleigh should use his influence to do something about it."

Mrs. Greenleaf beamed at Laura with brimming eyes of conspiratorial fun, and continued,

"I am pleased and I am proud for the way you tried, my dear, tried to put our visitor at his ease. By your manner nobody could ever have guessed that you must have found him shrieking dull."

In a cloudy movement of ribands, ruchings and laces, Drusilla Greenleaf impulsively embraced her daughter for being such a dear and accomplished pupil.

Laura smiled. Her mother really need not have gone to all that trouble to warn her away from further interest in Mr. Hazard.

Within a week Mrs. Greenleaf—slightly to her disappointment as she had counted on nothing but ignorance of amenity from him—received a letter from Mr. Hazard thanking her like a proper guest. The letter was skimmed, a check mark meaning "bread-and-butter" was put against his name in Mrs. Greenleaf's social ledger, and the letter was torn up with more energy than necessary.

Laura had a letter too.

It was almost impersonal. It paid her no compliments, reached out for nothing about herself, but only gave an account of a remarkable experience he had had going up the Hudson River by train:

The train stopped at Haverstraw station while the engine was watered. I got out to walk about a bit. At once I heard a very strange noise in the air—I could not at first account for it. Then I looked out over the river and I saw that it was full of ice floes going downstream.

They rubbed together and as they rubbed, they caused a squealing, ghostly sound to arise. This made me think of something else. The only time I stopped over in New York I went down to the Battery to see the bay and the ships, and there I saw and heard sea gulls for the first time. Well, the sound of those ice floes was like the sound of thousands of sea gulls as I should imagine it if heard from far away.

It was almost evening. The air was bitter cold. All the trees were bare and the only lights to be seen for all around were the smoky yellow lights of the oil lamps in the railroad cars, and the goldlike, yet sooty, glow of the station windows (like the station windows back home where I worked for the railroad as a boy). All this added to the strangeness and fascination of the ice action on the darkening river, though for my life I cannot tell you exactly how.

With all respects, I am

Yours faithfully,

Matthew C. Hazard, Cadet U.S.A.

His handwriting was large, quite firm and consistent, and extremely legible.

Laura tore the letter slowly into four pieces.

What complacency on his part, to think that a description of ice going down a river was of any interest to her. He had put it down just because it happened to him. What did she care what happened to him? And in any case, why had he waited nearly a week to write to her about it?

Then she recognized that the thing he had described had remained vividly in his mind for all those days, and this gave her a sudden entry into his mind, and she felt a little leap of pleasure at being there, and she remembered him clearly.

Not knowing what she thought, she went to the pantry and made a little dish of paste out of flour and water, and with strips of paper mended his letter until it was again whole. After all, it would be only polite to answer it (allowing a suitable lapse of time to indicate indifference) and before doing so she really should read it again.

xix

All the rest of that winter, and into the spring and summer, Laura Greenleaf worked to maintain her position of indifference toward Matthew Hazard; yet hardly a day passed in which she did not discover that she was frowning over some reminder of him.

Once when her father had lounged affably through tedious reminiscences of staff crises in the War Department, Matthew leaned forward, his hands clasped between his knees, and listened to the colonel with every sign of honest fascination.

Once, bringing her a plate of supper at a cotillion, he had walked

so carefully that he spilled the glass of claret cup which he held in
his left hand and stained his white glove pink.

Another time at the family table at home, when Mrs. Greenleaf
spoke of someone's bump of adhesiveness, he had had no idea of
what she meant, and said so.

He once said to Laura that in his opinion money was more of a
bore than a pleasure.

On all such occasions, she had had a right, she said to herself, a
right to feel superior to him in every way. If she recalled these later,
surely it was but for the comfort of remembering what she had
thought at the time. Nothing else.

He continued to write to her, and she—"common politeness," she
said privately, and she, for one, would never give *him* an opportunity to find a flaw in *her* good breeding—would answer his letters.

Her mother was not deceived but knew how to play out her line,
trusting to her long-range powers to see that the strange attraction
which her daughter felt would come to nothing in the end. The
only comment Drusilla Greenleaf permitted herself was to say one
time, when at the breakfast table she was sorting her way through
the family mail to keep her information up to date about what letters
each received,

"That young man"—tossing Matthew's latest envelope to Laura—
"won't stay written to, will he?"

Laura saw him again in late summer, and again the following
Christmas. On the surface, matters remained much as they had been.
It was displeasing to her that Matthew seemed to feel no uneasiness,
no impatience, at this. But he knew he had another year at the
academy before he could be in a position to ask her to marry him,
which was what he intended to do. He seemed exasperatingly confident, and she was not at all complimented by his attitude.

It was a sharp blow to her when after planning to come to Washington with Harvey in the vacation period of his last summer Matthew
suddenly changed his plans and went instead to Fox Creek. The
occasion was imperative and sad—his mother was ill, and it seemed
that she would die. He must go to her when he could. Laura wrote
to him.

My dear Matthew Hazard,

It is of course your duty and your desire to go to your home to
attend your mother in her illness, which I trust will soon and hap-

pily be succeeded by swift recovery, despite the fear which you express as to the outcome. Harvey is surely much disappointed that you were unable to accompany him home for the vacation. My parents join me in wishing all good news for you at home.

Remember, Hope is a source of Strength. Be of Good Heart.

With cordial greetings,

Yours sincerely,

Laura Greenleaf.

If she had meant simply to do him a pretty kindness with a formal note of encouragement and hope, she was shaken to discover that she meant it. To think of his having to endure a saddening experience made her heart contract with sympathy. She seemed to feel what he would feel. Her throat thickened. Her eyes filled with tears which she winked away before they could fall. She saw him, tall and hardy, brave with health and so mysteriously composed no matter what he might be thinking; and to think of that strong creature visited by a sorrow that must fill him through and through, as a child would be filled, though unable to show it—this gave her a wild little sorrow of her own. It was an experience new to her; she found herself caring about what someone else felt. It was the first sign of being in love which she admitted to herself. Since he had never made her an avowal, she could admit her discovery to no one else.

XX

Another of Matthew's classmates was occasionally in Washington— Cadet Adrian Brinker. He knew Matthew and Harvey, and he was aware of the tradition, fostered chiefly by Harvey, which coupled Laura and Matthew romantically. But he thought there was "less to it than met the eye," as he cleverly put it, and he set out to pay court to Laura.

He was a tall, blond, self-confident young man with world-weary manners and a developed capacity for being ingeniously disagreeable. Ambitious, he knew how to make himself attractive to older people. Mrs. Greenleaf thought him an ideal "possibility" for Laura. His father was General Brinker. The Brinker family, like the Greenleafs, had "money on the outside," as army cant said. They had traveled much abroad. The names of titled acquaintances fell from their lips with false deprecation. Cadet Brinker preferred everything foreign, however outworn, to anything of his own country, however original and promising. In company he gave a continuing performance of how he felt a distinguished European would behave. Languid and precious, he smiled kindly upon the young men of his generation, and devoted himself to stunning the ladies with his gossip about people in high places. His hero was the German chancellor Bismarck, whose military and political policies he endorsed, lamenting that there was no one to lead the United States with Prussian wisdom and firmness. His classmates nicknamed him "Bismarck" because of his obsession. In Matthew's absence he laid siege to Laura, beginning with elaborate frontal maneuvers before Mrs. Greenleaf.

Laura was amused by him and saw him whenever he called. It was not long before he felt that he was doing very well for himself. It must surely be only a matter of a little time until he would make her confess that she could not live without him. At such time, he would decide what to do about it. He enjoyed talking about Matthew.

"There's no doubt that Hazard is a wholesome fellow," he would say. "Everybody at the Academy feels that about him. Why does it happen so rarely that wholesomeness is accompanied by intelligence?"

Under the rules of coquetry, Laura was obliged to defend Matthew in order to pique Bismarck.

"I consider him not *only* wholesome but *also* intelligent," she said coolly. "It may be that your interests do not call forth his most lively response of mind."

"I should dashed well hope not. I'd hate to find myself excelling at anything a bumpkin could comprehend."

"Bumpkin! He has beautiful manners."

"So beautiful they creak, like a new pair of shoes."

"Oh! You're hateful! How can you speak of *any* classmate so!"

"Oh, what rot, to carry local patriotism and institutional loyalty that far. I'll tell you something else; when I mentioned Adelina Patti in his hearing on one occasion, he asked *who she was!*"

"Well? Is that such a crime, not to know?"

"And when I told him, and said he mustn't miss hearing her if he ever had a chance, even if he had to pay fifteen dollars for a ticket, which people do pay to hear her, he said he had other uses for fifteen dollars, thank you. Worse than a bumpkin. An insensitive clod."

"Oh, you are dreadful. Cannot you see that he was telling the simple truth? And if he was, is not that simple dignity? Matthew is not wealthy. Fifteen dollars *does* mean more to him than it would to you, or—or me. Why should he pretend to be other than what he is?"

"I give up."

Bismarck all unknowingly by these remarks did Matthew a great favor, for by leading Laura to defend him, he led her into saying what she found herself believing. If Matthew—now that she knew it, for she herself had said it—did not pretend to be other than what he was, then what he was made her heart go faster, and her eyes grow deeper in color as she gazed off into her memory of him: his stride, and his thin smooth hard cheek, and how he sat, both correctly and comfortably with his back straight, and the grain of his voice, and the dark shade cast by his brows over his sparkling black and white glances.

"What?" said Bismarck, for she seemed to have left him while remaining right there.

"Nothing," she replied with a smile that cast a bright light over her beauty. "Everything."

Emma Pennypacker died while Matthew was at home. He wrote to Laura about her last days. His letter was like an elegy for his whole boyhood and youth, though he did not mean it to be. But through it Laura received strong impressions of his little town, and the father who had been lost to it so long ago, and the mother who without complaint had worked for her son so long as she had had to, and the peace that had come to her, the mother, and him, the son, when he had made his own independent way in the world, and the pity of her illness, the sweetness of her resignation, and the benediction of her death, for she had smiled at him and touched his hand with hers at the end, and in her face and under her fading touch he knew that her love for him was made principally of her faith in him and her modest pride.

Laura wept as she read his letter. She longed to be with him to give him comfort. Her heart filled with untellable gratitude to him for the new power that came to her—the power to care about someone or something beyond herself.

Matthew had to return direct from Fox Creek to West Point.

xxi

Laura did not see him until the following Christmas, when once again in the old habit, Harvey brought him to Washington.

Their meeting was curiously formal.

"How nice that you could come."

"I was delighted to have the chance."

"There are many parties arranged. I hope you will be free to attend them."

"It must depend on what you do."

"Oh! I have been engaged for all the holidays for weeks."

"I see. Well. Whatever my luck, then."

Mrs. Greenleaf was witness to these exchanges, which perhaps, in her presence, could not have been more ardent. But matters were no easier at later moments when the young people were briefly alone. How long must they avoid the admission they ached to make to each other?

Bismarck was also on hand, and Laura played up to him recklessly, which brought forth Matthew's "black look" with some regularity. One evening there was a party at the British Legation to which all the young people were invited. Matthew declined.

"But why?" she asked.

"I believe you know well enough."

"How absurd. Of course I don't."

She was plainly dishonest, and Matthew disdained to discuss further what affected his feelings to the point of not going to the party: she was going with Bismarck. Her throat dried up. She was afraid. She had handled the whole thing badly. She should have admitted that she knew how she had hurt him. But she had never openly given him the right to be hurt by anything she might choose to do. What if he were as indifferent henceforth as he now seemed to be? Was he going to control her by fear? How could she endure that? Bismarck arrived, and she went off with him in a great whistle of silks and circumstance.

When she returned late at night she had Bismarck and Harvey with her. In her mind lived a shadowy picture of what she had hoped for all during the party. She saw the scene just as she wished it might be. She sent Bismarck home at once in his carriage, for it was very late; and for the same reason, Harvey went right upstairs to his room. Now she sought her picture.

She went into the front drawing room to turn out a lamp that cast its pale glow into the crimson-carpeted, dark-paneled hallway.

Matthew was there. As soon as he heard the carriage come and go, and heard Harvey's steps retreat up the stairs, he knew that she was now alone, and his heart began to beat and swell.

He rose out of the shadows and faced her silently. Her picture was coming true. He wore a baleful look, but it was not enough to conceal the marks of real suffering in his eyes. It made her breath go shallow to see a man so strong as he and certain now show the marks of miserable uncertainty. That this change in him came about because of her was sweet and wonderful, she thought. She went closer to him.

"But you are still up!" she exclaimed lightly, while a pulse went rippling in the pit of her throat. "It is so late."

"Have you had a happy evening?" he asked in a muffled tone. His words sounded absurd to him, but he knew he must say anything at all in order to establish communication with her.

She raised her arms in a gesture of remembered delight.

"I have never had a better time," she said, seeing how it hurt him to hear this.

When he said that he was glad to hear it, his voice was almost a croak, for the emotion that filled him. He rubbed his brow as if to clear away a blinding pain.

"You are not feeling well, Matthew?" she asked, and at playing a game with him who was so deadly in earnest she felt a flicker of guilt try itself like a little flame in her breast.

"Laura," he said, near to her, rapidly and softly, "you are just about killing me, you must know that, you must see it."

Their hearts began to choke them, for all was about to come plain between them, and they both knew it.

Bowing her head she tried to distract herself by taking off one of her long white gloves, but he caught one of her hands away from the other, and leaned down and kissed her fingers. In another moment they were in each other's arms, delivered of their hunger and their long-protracted game of evasion by their first kiss.

They loved each other for what they were, each of them. All obstacles and traditions, all disparities of position and advantage, disappeared. They confessed themselves to each other, now in their embrace, later in words. They sat late together in the dim drawing room, pledging all.

Laura was the first to return to practical considerations.

"Now that we are engaged, we must keep our engagement secret from everyone, even my parents, until your graduation in June. Then we can make formal plans."

"I will not even tell Harvey."

She smiled. In this resolve there was a portrait of her brother, who must speak whatever he knew, especially a secret.

"And you must not go *looking black* if I continue to be ravishing when I am around Bismarck and the others. It will help to keep our secret."

"I won't care for that."

"It is best."

"But I know best."

"About most things. About everything else. Not this."

He lost hearing her in looking at her.

xxii

In June, 1880, he received his commission as second lieutenant of cavalry and his first assignment to duty. He was to proceed to Arizona, on the Indian frontier, and report to Fort Delivery.

The lovers were not prepared for an assignment of such rigor and remoteness, but they said it did not matter; they would go anywhere together. Laura and her family were present at the graduation on Harvey's account, and when a suitable moment came, Matthew went to make his request for Laura in marriage. Colonel Greenleaf listened to him. They were privately together on a grassy edge of the palisade overlooking the Hudson. The colonel was amenable. He liked and admired Matthew, though his code of raised eyebrow and privileged behavior made it impossible for him to show this frankly.

"Yes," he said, "Mr. Hazard, your request is not amazing to me. I am not blind, you know, nor have I been for some time, in this matter. I'd be inclined to give you my blessing. I believe you will make a career. I am glad Laura chooses to stay in the Army. It is my life, as you know." He became visibly proud in his superbly molded tunic. He glared briefly like a war horse. So great was the power of the externals of his vocation upon him that he really saw himself as a fighting man. Becoming mild again, he added, "However, I shall of course have to discuss your proposal with my wife."

Matthew's heart sank, even though he had expected to hear this, for he knew where his real obstacle lay.

He was right, though he was spared having to witness how Mrs. Greenleaf took the news. She was opposed. The terms of her opposition were the more dangerous because she did not faint or have a heart attack or burst into hysterical tears; she lifted her chin and put her hands on her cheeks and broke into a little rill of laughter which contained everything but amusement. The proposition was too absurd for any other reaction. She murmured about the susceptibility of two pretty things thrown together incautiously for years, who, now beguiled by the emotions of graduation, thought they were in love and, being in love, must marry forthwith. Such things could only pass off harmlessly.

Colonel Greenleaf was not fooled by this, nor was Laura. They knew that under her frills Drusilla Greenleaf was deadly serious about the matter. But if Mrs. Greenleaf hoped to be rid of it by treating it lightly she misjudged, for once, the quality of her opposition. Laura, Harvey and even her husband were solidly in favor of an immediate marriage, so the new lieutenant could take his bride to the frontier with him.

When she saw these forces arrayed against her Mrs. Greenleaf withdrew into a wounded calm. She refused to speak to anyone in her family, but punished them by being absent in their very presence, as it were. She denied Matthew an audience at West Point. She swept her people back to Washington, and never let Laura out of her sight.

Matthew followed with Harvey, both on graduation leave. Harvey became an emissary between the exiled lover, who took a room at a boarding house, and the fortress he would penetrate. After days of negotiation, Matthew was sent for. There was a conference in the state drawing room of the Greenleaf residence. There he heard the ultimatum. Mrs. Greenleaf gave it.

She was wan and charming, like one who has survived a trial. Her voice, which could be shrill, was dovelike. She gave a falling inflection to her phrases—the mortal reasonableness of an invalid who tried to lighten all burdens for those dear to her, among whom she now, in pity for his absurd dilemma between ardent passion and poor judgment, included Matthew.

"Matthew: my dear boy: sit down beside me here on my little sofa. We have much to work out together and you must help me with your understanding and your good heart."

It was an ominously new tone for her to take with him. He begged Laura with his eyes for some hint of what might be coming, but she, pale and calm over an inner trembling, pressed her lips together and shook her head almost imperceptibly.

"I will try, Mrs. Greenleaf," he said in a chastened voice.

"Of course you will: you are a reasonable boy, and you have done wonders with your own life. All my friends quite dote on you, and I feel it is wonderfully to your credit that in your circumstances you have somewhat distinguished yourself. I know something of your early years and the struggles that came to your family, and believe me, my heart knows something of youthful trials." She paused briefly as though to invite her hearers to look back with her at all humble origins and rejoice at any triumph over them. Matthew was beginning to look black at her condescension, but he felt Laura pleading with him in silence and he gripped his hands between his knees, leaning forward in his familiar attitude.

"I should think your present circumstances, while honorable," resumed Mrs. Greenleaf, "were not entirely those to justify an offer of marriage to a young lady accustomed to certain comforts and a real stability in life. There is, of course, a future in the Army for anyone who shows devotion to duty. But how slow we are in our stodgy old army, and how often even real merit is somewhat lost in the shuffle!" She put her hand on his arm to indicate her sympathy for him in the future she had just foreseen for him. "Oh," she said, swept into another vein of her role by the effect upon herself of her gesture of fatalistic sympathy toward Matthew, "I know, I know too well, what it is to be young, and ardent, and impetuous. But"—her smile was a wistful shadow over her lovely mouth—"I know too the duties of a mother."

His answer lay there. He had only now to hear the terms of her refusal. When they came, he was amazed to find a ray of hope in them, and it was this he peaceably reached for, exactly as Mrs. Greenleaf, in her skill, had meant him to do.

She said she would agree, provided the lovers would wait one year, to consider the proposal again. If at the end of that time they still persisted in their desires, Matthew was free to return, and the marriage could take place. In the meantime, though all announcements would be of course withheld, they might if they liked consider themselves betrothed.

In the silence that followed, Matthew saw that Laura had been made to agree to this in advance. Colonel Greenleaf nodded sagely—he considered it an endurable compromise. Most marriages, he seemed to say, occurred only after long engagements, anyway. Mrs. Greenleaf was so happy in her reasonable mood that she hardly bothered to conceal her conviction that a long separation would bring her child to her senses—meaning her mother's will. Harvey, whose nature made him cheerful under any circumstances, broke the family silence.

"Yes," he said, "it might be fairer to Laura if Matt went ahead to the West, to see what conditions prevail at the little frontier post where he wants to take her. You see, in this way, when the time actually comes, Matt, you'll be more able to prepare Laura for the kind of life the Army lives out there. It is pretty hardy, you know. Most of what we hear about it is true, you know."

"Et tu, Brute," said Matthew to his classmate, who laughed with delight at the classical learning of his friend. But he could see that there was something to recommend the proposal, for Laura's sake. He bowed to it.

As a reward, he was permitted to see her alone a few times before he had to leave on his long journey westward.

They vowed that nothing would make any difference to their love. They were destined to be together. Delay would only seal their devotion. Their plight was a familiar one in the circles of junior rank. They were lost in a combination of rapture and grief. It was a good mixture for the nourishment of their ruling emotion. When they parted they were more in love than ever. Laura said that so long as she had him to live for, and think of, and pray for (her love made her pious), she could endure anything. Her heart seemed to take flight from her breast, like a spirit freed. Gone was all her earlier obsession with herself. She had learned to love beyond herself, and her happiness was great, even as she wept to say good-by.

Matthew was strong enough to think more of her than of himself. Their parting had a kind of peace in it. It was the peace of perfect trust in one another.

xxiii

A few weeks after Matthew's departure, the Greenleafs were transferred to Fort Porter, at Buffalo, on Lake Erie, where Colonel Greenleaf was to take command.

Mrs. Greenleaf's first concern was to know whether the post would
bring a star to her husband's epaulet. The possibility, she had to
admit, was remote. No general officer had commanded Fort Porter
for years. Still, she had connections, and before she left with her
mountains of furniture and luggage, she had a conversation with
her brother-in-law, General Quait, who had lately come to town for
conferences at the War Department before returning to his command
on the far Indian frontier. She despised everything about General
Quait but his rank, and that she resented, but the pressure of her
urgent concern was enough to blind her to his maddening oddnesses.
Hearing her prettified statements of her otherwise naked ambition,
General Quait was full of animated evasions, but promised to make
the proper inquiries. It was the best she could get.

"Inquiries," she stormed to herself, knowing that nothing could
possibly come merely of "inquiries." Colonel Greenleaf left for Fort
Porter without a promotion.

"Politics," said his wife, and managed to include him in her scorn.

Laura, too, saw her Uncle Alex.

"Did you get my letter?" she asked.

"Letter?"

"I sent it to you out West."

"Ah. No. I must have been traveling and so missed it. What did
your letter say?"

"I told you of my engagement to Lieutenant Hazard."

"Should I know him?"

"I don't think so, not now, but I hope you will, Uncle Alex. He
has been assigned to your department. He was sent to Fort Delivery,
Arizona, when he graduated last month."

"Yes. I know of the place. I have yet to see it. I shall see it. My
area of observation is larger than France, Germany and Spain together. I am constantly moving about and my movements must bring
me to Fort Delivery in due course. —Let me bless you, Laura my
dear child."

He kissed her cheek. She set out to beguile him.

"Will you watch out for him, please, Uncle dear? He is a wonderful soldier and a beautiful man. I love him so. I have to wait a year for him. I shall die. Keep him for me."

This was the other Laura whom he always allowed to disappear leaving the real one. He smiled on her in silence, and in a moment she laughed softly and said without elevated style,

"Yes, I know, Uncle. But you do know what I mean. I want him to be all right."

He could answer this.

"You want special consideration for him?"

"Yes."

"Tra-la-lá. Now we are honest. Well: Laura: I intend to compliment your maturity by what I will now say." He took her hand. "If I should encounter your lieutenant, I shall deal with him, in all matters of *duty,* precisely as I should deal with any other officer of my command."

"How bleak."

He pressed her hand to indicate that he was not finished, and said,

"But I honor your *love* for your future husband, and I will state freely that I shall pray for his safety in his service, which is hazardous, and I will pray for your fortitude, until events may bless you with the marriage which you so impatiently await. Love and duty, my dear child. Let them never be separated, but equally kept."

For years he had amused her. For this she loved him.

Now he taught her. Wearily she saw the value of what he taught, which would accompany her while she waited for the next summer.

She began to gather her trousseau. Her mother permitted this, even though she saw it as an act of faith which would be expensively wasteful, when the engagement should come to nothing.

What was it like where Matthew was going? asked Laura of herself in many a lonely, precious moment. She had heard and read much of the Army's work and the Indian's fury at the white man's settlement upon his lands. She could not imagine anything beyond the popular romance of the subject as it came to print, and the private grief that attended its realities when some army family in her friendship lost a man in the West. Matthew was ordered to the Apache country of Arizona. She shut her eyes and saw herself there with him in a year's time. All she saw was herself with him. She could have no way of knowing the kind of man, and the power of a whole people's dream, which the Army had not yet found a way to conquer.

xxiv

A certain Apache Indian of the Chiricahua nation was born during the 1830's at an encampment site in southern Arizona. Years later he alone remembered the exact place of his birth and his early years, when he had long since left it, but on several occasions his travels had taken him past it again, and upon each such occasion he paid it reverence in the way known to him as proper. He rolled himself on the ground first to the east, then to the south, the west and the north, in obedience and gratitude doing homage to the world whose forces of life had granted him body and breath.

His birthplace was a long narrow shelf of flat grassy land by the side of a meager creek that ran out of a mountain several miles away to the north. At the creek grew willow trees and cottonwoods to give shade and shelter, and the land bounded south toward grand plains of a desert character. Away off far in that direction other mountains were manifest by day when blowing dust did not hide them. These were in Mexico, where his people came from.

There was a time when nobody else ever came there but Indians of the Chiricahua family. There was then no war at home. Game animals were found in the mountains in certain seasons. If game was sparse, then the people went garnering seeds and berries to live on. When these were scarce, the most able men and youths went raiding eastward to the ranches of New Mexico, often reaching as far as the Rio Grande, to steal cows, sheep and horses, and to kill white men and women and capture white children, returning home then with riches for the belly and merit for the spirit, since to live at all the people must eat, and to live virtuously, must destroy their enemies.

This particular Apache child was given no name for several years, for by a circumstance of his birth, he seemed to his parents destined to be a remarkable man: when he appeared from his mother's womb, he was silent, and when cold water was thrown upon him to make him breathe, he remained silent. He took his first breaths without crying. As everyone knew what this meant, it was plain, then, that he would be a strong man. They decided to wait to name him until some event of his own life should suggest a suitable name. He was called This Boy for the time being.

Earlier than most babies he was able to hold up his head, and so was the sooner able to be put into his specially made cradle board, which had its sun canopy of red-barked dogwood edged in buckskin. Like most of the people his parents loved children, prayed for them, worked over them, and hoped to deliver to them wisdom inherited through the ages.

They called their doctor to bless the cradle board. He blessed it with pinches of *hoddentin,* or pollen, and he fastened to it protective amulets such as loops of turquoise beads, pieces of lightning-riven wood, and buckskin sacks of *hoddentin.* This Boy's mother added her own prayer objects to the doctor's. To guard her son from fright, she put the right front paw of a badger; to protect against sickness, a scrap of cholla wood; to propitiate nature in general, the claws of a hummingbird and a tuft of wildcat skin. The child's bedding was of wild mustard well-packed, and his pillow was filled with aromatic pine needles. He was securely strapped in the cradle and its board was bound to his mother's shoulders when she walked or to her thighs when she rode. When he could stand, his father, one night of a new moon, took him in his hands and lifted him four times toward the moon in order to make him grow tall.

xxv

This Boy seemed to grasp the idea of life—of the fact that all things contained life—early in his childhood. One thing seemed to lead to another, he noticed. For example, the mountain had a power in it, because everybody spoke of it, and this made him think of something else but connected, which was that the sun was the size of a mountain, and this in turn made him realize how he could feel the sun's heat in himself, and how it was cooler in the shade of trees, and so—directly consequent and quite wonderful and delightful—in order to keep cool in the sun, he should wear on his head, as so many of the people did, a wreath cut from a young willow and wound together to provide shade that could go about with him. This Boy's mother showed him how to make willow wreaths and after that he could make his own.

He went around dressed in nothing else as a boy. He would be proud when the time should come for him to wear a fringed buck-skin shirt like his father's, and a buckskin sling high between his legs with a knee-length flap in front and another that almost reached the heels behind. Though he lived in the hive-shaped one-room dwelling of his parents with his younger sister, he never saw the adults naked, or observed their intimacies. He was required to be polite to them and never to question the rightness of their way or their orders or their opinions.

When he asked where someone was who had not been seen in the encampment for many days, they said simply that the person was gone. This Boy could not be sure of how he found out that this meant the person had died. But he heard of death somehow, and one day, though told not to do so, he watched a burial procession as it left the village for some dunelike hills to the east. He followed it and saw the corpse put in the ground and covered up.

He was distressed, and asked his mother later,

"Won't the dirt get in the man's eyes?"

She hushed him sharply, for it was dangerous to speak of death and dead things, and she said,

"They have a way of not letting the dirt get into the man's eyes. Now go away and play."

His play thereupon consisted of killing grasshoppers and holding miniature burial ceremonies with them. He was not yet afraid of death.

But when he was seven years old, he became afraid of it because of a dream.

xxvi

He had a dream of ghosts one night. The ghosts were like nothing he had ever seen or thought of, except that they had coarse dust running out of their eyes in dry streams. This seemed to him so dreadfully against the natural stuff of eyes that he was terrified. The dust-weeping ghosts were trying to catch him. He tried to run, but though he ran, he seemed not to move, and the ghosts came all about him.

It was a pitiful and fearsome dream. He was sure he might have died of it but for something else that came next in the dream and saved him.

Above and beyond the ghosts he saw a large, beautiful, pale deer with white antlers. The deer had brilliant eyes. They shone with water-like purity, completely different from the ghost-eyes with their weeping dust. The deer lifted his head at This Boy, beckoning him to come and follow. The deer did this four times, and it was as clear as being spoken to. This Boy said to himself in his dream,

"Why, I am the boy who can do anything he has to do!"

With that, he was able to walk right through the ghosts and follow the deer to safety. When they reached safety the deer bowed to him and one of the tips of his noble white antlers fell off and This Boy knew it was a gift. He picked it up, saying,

"My name is White Horn."

He then awoke from his dream. He knew he was the same person as This Boy, but he knew too that he was someone else entirely new.

What he saw when he woke up was strange and splendid. The fact was, his dream had come to him in a deep illness which had brought him nearly to die. When he thought he was simply asleep as usual for a night, he was actually in furious fever for many days. His parents, and in fact the whole village, were in terror and grief for him, and a number of doctors were brought to pray, to treat, and to dance for his recovery.

When This Boy awoke he saw the masked fire dance in progress, and spoke, and all knew then that he would recover, though his father was not yet done with the curing ceremony in which he took part. This Boy was proud of his father for what he was doing, though it also made him fearful, for his father took great risks in the way he addressed his power to make it free the son from illness and danger. The father was among the doctors with their great tall wide masks which had wooden branches tipped with feathers and terrible faces painted on. He chanted and spoke to his power saying,

"My little son is ill and we fear he may die. Do not let him die, I plead with you. What has he done to offend you? Why should you make him suffer? If you must make someone suffer, make me suffer. I have done bad things in my life. But he has not. How could he? He is but a child. You are unjust if you punish him instead of me."

The father's voice grew angry and he became rough in his way and he scolded his power savagely.

"Have you no eyes to see the truth? You are behaving miserably. I am ashamed of you as my power. Stop being so cruel and so stupid. Free my boy. Let him live. I want him to live a long time on this ground."

His voice changed and again became prayerful.

"I bend myself down to the ground and I beg for this little life from you. I humble myself before you. Be good to him. Be good to us. You are brave and gentle and you will help us."

The father was weeping.

"Listen to me, power."

The smoke ranged upward from a great bonfire, and the sparks behaved like wild stars. The masked doctors looked huge in the wavering light. People were all about. The night was all gathered inward over this one place of prayer, fire, dance and will. This Boy was shaken out of his fever by the wonder and the force of all of it.

The next day he told of his dream. It was then perfectly clear that he had found his real name. He was named White Horn by his father and mother.

They talked to him of other dreams, and of meanings.

"If you ever dream of fire," they said, "you must try to wake up at once, and then immediately build a real fire, to wipe out the fire of the dream, as fire, though it can be useful and good, can also be ruinous and cruel. You will learn that this is true of many things in life, too."

There were good dreams as well as bad.

"Perhaps one day you will dream of summertime, with everything in the dream growing sweetly, and green grass and green leaves everywhere, green, green, and rain clouds over the mountains, and waters running white and cool in their courses, wet, wet. If you dream this way, you will know on awakening that it means that all things you may plan to do, all conditions of your life, are good and proper, and must come to pass as you intend them to. —Everything means something," they concluded.

White Horn (as it was now proper to call him) learned the facts of the world from his elders.

Nobody knew how the earth was created, exactly, but it seemed that the power named Life Giver made it. It was enough to know this, without asking how and when. The sun and moon were as big as mountains and were fixed in their places. The heavens moved about them. The earth was a woman. Lightning and thunder were persons. Lightning shot arrows which flashed and cracked through the sky and often hit the earth. Thunder spoke with his special, particularly loud voice. Long ago, lightning and thunder acted as huntsmen for all the people, killing all the game they needed, but the people were not polite and grateful, so the hunters of the sky stopped helping them.

Since then it was necessary to keep out of the way of lightning and thunder. The people did so during thunderstorms by imitating the call—"piš, piš"—of the speckled nighthawk which swooped and darted so fast and so cleverly that lightning could not strike it, and thus, presumably, lightning could not harm anyone who even sounded like the hawk. Animals, birds, reptiles, were long ago just like people, and what one of these creatures in particular did had consequences forever for real people.

This was Coyote.

It was Coyote who by one of his most reckless and wicked acts made it necessary for people to die. Thus: one time he threw a stone in the water saying that if it sank, then all living things must eventually die. If only he had not said that. Sad to tell, the stone sank, since it was in the stone's nature to sink when thrown into water. People died thereafter. What danger there was in words, and the thoughts behind them.

Coyote created all the wickedness that people found in themselves to do. Before anyone, he lied, he cheated, he stole, he raped, he ate himself insensible, and the rest. When they did wrong, people were "following Coyote's trail."

Fortunately there was also someone else long ago whom it was nobler to follow. He was called Child of the Water, who was the son of White Painted Woman and of Water himself. He was a glorious hunter, conquered giants, the fierce bull buffalo, and other dangerous creatures. Those whom he conquered he forced to become useful servants of mankind. He and his mother and father retreated beyond the sky long ago after they had done their good work for people.

In common with all other boys, White Horn knew all these things. It was good to know them, but he did not give them as much attention as he did the things near about him which could be seen, and other things which needed to be done. To feel and touch and do were more natural ways to know things. He was busy doing what his father made him do—the same things other fathers made their sons do.

xxvii

He had to spend hours practicing how to run. His father showed him the vast reach of the plains and deserts and said all boys had to learn to cross them in speed and safety when necessary. White Horn was sent out to run. He worked on his legs. He fed them fat with his fingers at meals, rubbing grease into his growing thews. He learned to run upright, and bent over; fast for short distances, slowly for long; straight in the open, and dodging in shadow and bush for concealment. Running made his chest grow, too, and his heart tough. He sometimes listened with pride to the pounding pulse in his head and felt it in his breast when he threw himself down to rest.

When men went to hunt he was taken along with other boys. The boys were not permitted to kill, but only to watch and learn on their first trips. They spent much time at practice with bow and arrow. They had a game which helped them to perfect their skill. One boy would shoot at a target, and the others would then shoot at the arrow of the first, trying to hit or cross it at the target. The boys worked at riding, too, without saddle or bridle, and then with halter. They learned every kind of movement with the horse.

They were ordered to do many things just because they were difficult things to do, or painful, or so foolish that obedience required strength over self-ful opinion.

"Go and fight that tree," White Horn was told by his father.

He went and attacked the tree with his fists, his nails, his teeth, his gripping knees, until he was scraped raw in places.

In winter, before dawn, he was ordered to rise and run to the mountain and back for no reason but to train his legs and his will. When a thin film of ice came on the creek, he was sent to throw himself into the water, cracking the ice with his body as he did so. When he was completely wet, he could return, but he was not permitted to come to the fire to dry and warm himself.

All this time he was required by the custom of all boys at his stage of life to reserve himself from the company of girls, and even from thoughts about them. Despite this prohibition, however, he talked with other boys about the female nature and kind, and together they knew what they knew.

Sometimes Coyote took hold of a boy or a youth, who went to lie with some older woman, maybe a really old woman, who had no husband and who longed for a man's power in her secret body; and if he did this, all knew that he would fall ill and perhaps die, as a consequence of mingling his flesh with that of an old woman. Sometimes a young woman or a girl took a boy, and gave him a boy's knowledge to share with his friends. It was wrong to do what he'd done, they all agreed; but everyone was interested. White Horn's father, like any other father in the village, tried to frighten his son away from women during this time of life.

"Be careful," he said solemnly, expecting his son to believe him, "if you put your branch into a woman, you may lose it, for they have teeth in there, and the teeth will bite it off, and then what sort of man will you be!"

White Horn believed this until he found enough courage to discuss it with other boys, who reassured him with jokes and laughter based on experience they had had or knew for certain otherwise to be true. They loved to talk about the subject. There was much of Coyote in everyone. There was a Coyote story for every situation which had to do with the impulse and emotion and assuagement of desire. Coyote had done everything wicked that a man might at one time or another desire to do. To tell about it by way of Coyote stories was a satisfaction. Perhaps it disposed of the matter for a little while.

But it was dangerous to dwell upon anything by itself for a long time. Witches had their opportunity at such times. If Coyote was not a witch, he was probably a very close confederate of witches. To call anybody a witch's son was to give the gravest insult. Most people tried to be good—good according to what everybody else regarded as proper. Becoming proper was difficult and arduous. White Horn like other boys endured the process and grew by it.

xxviii

When he was sixteen he knew by the bulk and power of his body that it was now proper for him to present himself as a novice for war training.

This was expected of him, though nobody prompted him. He was accepted. Not tall, he was built like a cat, with sliding muscles and power beyond his size. His face was wide at the cheeks, and his forehead was shallow. His long black hair was brushed apart and fell beside his cheeks and was held in place by a band of cloth. His winter shirt was of buckskin, fringed at the seams and edges. His breechclout was knee-long in front and fell to his Achilles tendon behind. He wore it day and night except when he practiced running, when he liked to go bare. His eyes were bright black coals within little triangular openings under his almost hairless brows. He had no beard or body hair. Long ago, like all the men, he had fastidiously begun to pluck out every hair but those of his scalp, eyebrows and lashes. His mouth was a thin wide line and his jaws were bony. He gave a slightly hunchbacked effect, not from any misshape in his spine, but from his habit of hunching up his shoulders to peer farther at whatever he was after, either visible before him, or invisible in his thoughts. He always seemed concentrated and focused and ready to spring. He spoke little and listened much. He laughed more than most of his friends. People liked to be with him because he had a jolly nature, even if he said less than they. It was said of him that though he was a small young man, he did not feel small, and therefore was, in effect, a large young man.

Like all novices in training, White Horn was regarded and spoken of as though his name for the time were Child of the Water. This was a powerful way of bringing him into kinship with that godlike being of long ago.

White Horn had to wear a special sort of little hat as a novice, made by the novices' doctor, who also made and blessed with pollen other accessories of the new duties—a drinking tube (for the novices had to drink in a special way until they were graduated), and a skin-scratcher to toughen them, and the like. The novices did all the heavy work of the training journeys on which they were taken along as observers.

They were not allowed to raid for horses and cattle like the men, or to fight if they encountered enemies. For four raids the novices could only travel and watch and work as servants. They had to speak a special language. "Home" was called "the place where I abide," and "my blood" was "the red river within me," and such. They had to move in a special way, never looking up for fear of causing storm, never looking to the rear without first glancing from an eye corner over the shoulder. They must be chaste in act and word. They must eat only cold food. They must not laugh. They must be alert and prompt and uncritical of all that happened to them in training. They

must study hard and keep every lesson of the elders and of the land
and of the sky and of the distance, for one day the novices would
use their knowledge for themselves and for their people.

Lessons were born of the land.

When traveling alone it was best to set out at sundown and travel
all night, resting and hiding during the day, except in mountains,
when because of available concealment travel by day was permissible.
A man should carry a week's supply of dried and pounded meat and
fat. If he must find water, let him go to a high place and look for
green places. There would be water. But he must not go for it in
daytime, for if he had enemies they would look for him there. He
must thirst until nightfall, then go to drink his fill and fill his water-
skin. If he was drowsy and must rest in the daytime, where should
he rest? Well: where would an enemy first look for him asleep? In
the deep shade of trees if there were trees. So he must content himself with taking his ease in the meager but sufficient shade of a little
bush in the open, from which he could spring into action more
readily if need be, or make for cover elsewhere. Should he be moving
or still in deep grass, and should he hear a strange sound, he must
make no sudden move; rather he must take a clutch of the long grass
and rise slowly holding it before him and gaze through it to see what
he could see. Thus nobody could see him from a distance. So too in
trees he could carefully move a leafy branch across himself and be
invisible while observing the world.

If he saw someone in the distance but did not know whether friend
or enemy, what should he do? He should find an open place from
which he could escape to nearby cover. In the open place he should
make a little fire, putting evergreen on it to make heavy smoke. Let
it rise for just a moment or two, then put it out. Then what? Well:
then: the person seeing the fire would come to investigate, and the
novice would see who he was, friend or enemy, and could come forth
from cover either to greet or to kill. Smoke had every other possible
use, too, for messages and news. Even ashes told things, and the
novice must learn to read the age of dead fires, and the size of them,
and thus the time and number of travelers whose trail he came upon.
Much else could be told from the ground—horse droppings, their
quantity and degree of freshness, human ordure, depression of grass
and plants, efforts to obliterate trail, and such signs: a language to
be learned.

Meanwhile, on the raid, the party moved in force toward their goal, whether it was to steal horses or sheep or to fall upon cows and butcher them and run away with the meat.

Sometimes the owners of such animals gave fight.

The raiders killed when they could. There was honor in killing enemies. After the raiders killed, they mutilated, which was a way of really killing someone absolutely dead, killing him twice, killing with mockery of his honor and manhood, forever, and by such many killings they proved their living excellence; for did they, the killers, not survive, and was he, the enemy, not dead and naked and cut apart and emasculated, with his man's members cut off and stuffed into his own dead mouth and disgraced? There was power to gain from such acts.

The novices were never permitted to engage in conflict on their training raids, but were ordered to remain far in the rear, out of danger; for they were for the time being under sacred protection, the blessing of Child of the Water and all the doctors who spoke for him. For a novice to be hurt or killed at such time would be disgraceful to the expedition and its leaders. But the novices watched and knew, and White Horn learned what the warrior did when he raided and killed, and how all approved the ways which had been the ways of life ever since the time long ago when Life Giver first made everything—though nobody could say how he had done it, or just when.

Returning from a raid, the novice was cautioned especially to govern himself, for this period, just after a raid, was one of delicate importance. What he did in those first few days would by virtue of his state of blessed power become his nature for all his life.

Therefore he must avoid gluttony now if he was to be spared its appetites throughout his years. He must be truthful if he was not to turn into a liar. He must be continent lest he become that pitiable object, a man who slavered after women like a dog after a bitch in season.

He would be watched and his conduct discussed. Nobody spoke to him directly about it, but his novitiate was weighed and judged. Going out on his second, third and fourth raids—four was the sacred number for everything—he made great strides toward manhood. His endurance of hardship and his bravery and ingenuity in danger must pass test after test. Sometimes in a battle the men would have to leave the novices far away to protect them, and the novices might be cut off from their life party, and then would have to manage for themselves. Youths were known to have been lost forever to the vast earth at such times. White Horn thought as much as anyone about what to do then. He never had to do it, but in his state of dedication and awe, what might happen was almost as real to him as what did happen. He vowed himself to be a great and true man, if the elders should accept him at the end of his fourth raid.

He was accepted. He was officially a man. Everything now told him so. He was by training a master of the land and all its life. He could now smoke. He could marry. He could admit to himself that figures in the masked dances were men, not gods—something he had always known, but had never dared think about until now. He could imagine a long future for himself full of honors as a raider and full of wealth as owner of a great band of horses.

Events ordered otherwise for White Horn.

xxix

He married soon and was a father within a year.

It was against the propriety of his people that a man should hold congress with his wife until after her child was weaned. This often meant two or three years of continence for him. Many men ignored the delicate law and either took their wives again or went after other women. But there was in White Horn a strain of probity, some vein of loyalty, which held him true to beliefs and promises and persons when once he had given them his allegiance. He prided himself on his endurances, and he believed that the more virtue he could hold in himself, the more he would have to give into his sons with his very seed when he begot them on their mother.

He worked hard, went on many raids, killed and mutilated men in the accepted style, outwitted many a desert or mountain passage with all its hazards of weather and distance, animal hunger and human craft. He was being thought of as a possible chief for the village. The great chiefs of the Chiricahua—Rainbow Son, who lived in the mountains of northern Sonora, and Sebastian, who commanded a large and roving town which ranged with the seasons in eastern Arizona, would age in time, and one day there must be new chiefs to keep the people. White Horn—who knew?—might well be one.

But change came in three ways to his life. The first was a change in the life of his family. The second was a change in the life of his

Apache nation. The third was a change in his own condition of mind, and consequently of his daily circumstance.

His little son died at the age of two and a half, in spite of every effort to save him—fire dances, doctors, sacrifices. A few weeks later the child's mother died, and White Horn was left alone.

He was urged to marry again, and this time to take not one but several wives, for he could afford it, and it was a mistake to become too attached to any one woman as he seemed to have done in the marriage so sadly disrupted by evil and death, from what source none could say.

He refused to marry again.

He thought much on death—too much, his friends said. If you think of one thing, that very thing often took charge of you. Many cases were known of how men had thought themselves to death. This was immoral, against every view and desire of the people. They loved life, and put death for themselves away as far as possible. Even their dear dead ones must be dismissed, and never referred to or their possessions retained. Even the dwelling they had occupied must be destroyed and a new shelter built for survivors.

Yes, but he had been struck twice by death, said White Horn, twice within a few weeks. What had he done to deserve this? How could anything mitigate his loss, which was so great that it sat upon him almost like shame? He bitterly recalled how long ago as a child he used to play death, and in all observed solemnity to hold mock burials for grasshoppers. Perhaps all his life he was meant to think about death, and play with it—or else it meant nothing; and if it meant nothing, then perhaps nothing else meant much, either. He made an ugly gesture that scorned all that was sacred. Perhaps that wretch Coyote, he declared, Coyote who obtained all his ends by every trickery and meanness and obscenity, perhaps Coyote had the right way of life. If you could believe all you heard, Coyote got along very well indeed.

White Horn in his grieving petulance made his elders shake their heads. They even smiled over him. It was the end of youth speaking, not the clear, warm noon of manhood. He would get over it. He would come around again. The best thing for him would be a succession of many raids.

XXX

They came, and with them, the change in the Chiricahua life which affected him more, perhaps, than most of his fellows.

For many years, white men in growing numbers had been coming across the lands of the Chiricahuas, and in consequence there had been much warfare and many raids, and in the end the Chiricahua people had been forced to flee into Mexico to remain for a time. But settlement in the grand deserts and mountains of the territory had not come so heavily as expected, and outside of a few towns there had been only widely scattered ranch homes where good horses and cattle were to be found, from time to time, with little danger of full-scale punishment against raiding parties.

Now suddenly all this seemed to change.

What made the change was the building of long heavy iron lines laid on squared timbers tamped into the ground across the whole country. On these lines rode heavy wagons pulled by an even heavier thing full of fire and noise. It brought many people, first to work on its way, later to ride in its wagons. It brought also every kind of thing for people to buy, sell, work with, use in any task or need or pleasure. Where these lines ran, towns grew; and where towns grew, farms appeared roundabout; and where farms spread, food could be had, but the farmers meant to keep it for themselves. With all the people at hand in the white man's towns, and with all the soldiers stationed to protect the railroad and the farms and horses and cattle of the white men who came now in thousands, the Chiricahua people had to think about things, and to realize that the world no longer belonged to them.

They were being pushed away from their very deserts. They were being told to contain themselves or another force than their own would contain them against their will. Their freedom was gone and they raged to lose it. For longer in time than anyone could fix, the Chiricahua people, given their world by Life Giver, and consecrated to their ways by Water's Child, and served by sun and moon (both as big as mountains), had made their own life reach as far as need be for good, for glory, and for knowledge. It was not to be thought that they would agree to lose easily what was theirs in all justice and right of possession: so the elders believed and told.

The whole nation of Apache people would have to work on their plans together, if they were to make any great effect upon the white men who kept coming to stay. Until that grand design could be managed, the best any individual, or group of individuals, or village, could do was to go out raiding continually, to do as much hurt as possible to the invaders, and if accomplishing nothing else, to remind them again and again, like wasps stinging though they must eventually retreat to the hive or die, that for what they did, the white people deserved to be robbed and killed, just like any other enemy, such as Comanche Indians or Navajos or Lipans, who had also dared through the centuries to come upon Apache lands as though to stay.

White Horn became a chief of raiders, then, and led the raids north and east against ranches and farms.

He suddenly looked older than his years. Deep-furrowed wrinkles were tooled into his wide leathery face by the sun. His mouth was grimly set, showing no lip. Everyone noticed how, since the deaths that had changed him, he spoke hardly at all. He gave commands by signal, and he answered yes or no with a nod or a shake of his head. He had little else to communicate.

He was in his early forties when he led his last raid.

It was his last because in the course of it, his entire party was defeated by a troop of soldiery. Many Indians were killed in the battle and the remainder were captured. They too expected to die, for it was well known that the white warriors never kept a prisoner, but shot him to be left for carrion.

But White Horn's party, to their amazement, found themselves guarded, and fed, and with their hands tied behind their backs given horses to ride, until they arrived at Fort Bayard, New Mexico.

There they were well enough treated, but for weeks nobody except the guards and the mess orderlies saw or spoke to them. They were confined in adobe cells with small barred windows too high up in the walls to show anything but vacant sky. If punishment had been designed to break the spirit of prisoners who ever before had known only the open world, the Army could not have done better. One of the Apache captives went insane in confinement. Others could not eat.

White Horn was numbed in mind and body. He fought all night with terrible dreams, and all day he rehearsed the events of his last battle to discover where things had gone wrong. He could never put his finger on the single error, the main mischance, which had brought him down with his followers. The fact simply was that the Army was there, and there were too many of them, and they knew too well what they were about, and they simply succeeded. White Horn remembered how the soldiers had appeared out of nowhere, from behind meager bushes, out of little declivities of the earth where they must have been hiding flat on their bellies, their shapes broken by the broken shadows of leaf and branch, just like Apaches.

There was the key!

White Horn spat in misery and disgust. The soldiers had fought not like white men in ranks and columns—they had used the earth, the cover, the shadow, the dazzle of light, to come over their enemies. Who had told them so much? Who had made Indians of them in order to kill Indians? Whoever it was, he had a power which Apaches had not tasted before.

xxxi

It was a power which came to its maturity in the life of Alexander Upton Quait. As a very small child he was brought through the Delaware Water Gap from the East in a household wagon covered with Osnabrück linen in 1827 by his parents who were emigrating to the West.

They came to Germantown, Pennsylvania, one night and parked their wagon by the wall of an inn and took a room upstairs. The inn caught fire during the night and burned to the ground. The wagon standing beside it was destroyed. Several people lost their lives, including the parents of the infant Alexander. Wrapped in a blanket, he was thrown from the low second story by his father, and he was caught on the ground below by a volunteer fireman, who stood as close to the house as the flaming heat would permit.

In the morning the inn register, charred and soaked, was found, and the names of the family and their child were just barely discernible. Where they had registered from was illegible under the brittle black along the last column of the scorched ledger. The covered wagon of the family and all its contents were now ashes. The volunteer fireman took the baby home where his wife cared for him. He grew up in their family. They were orderly, frugal and undemonstrative people of the Pennsylvania "Dutch" community. All the baby had left of his father's possessions were his name and the team of mules which had drawn the wagon. Alexander's foster father, whose name was Odenbaugh, took charge of the animals in trust for the child. Shrewdly he sold them before they were too old to be useful to a buyer. The revenue—eighty dollars—he saved for the time when the boy should need cash.

The time did not come for many years. Alexander Upton Quait went to a Quaker school in Germantown, and the Odenbaugh family clothed, fed and housed him in strictness along with their own children. In return he worked for Mr. Odenbaugh at the paper mill on the edge of town.

He went to Philadelphia one time with Mr. Odenbaugh and saw many arresting sights.

One was a printer's shop where Mr. Odenbaugh delivered a consignment of fine-laid paper made with a special watermark. The print shop put a spell on young Alexander. He loved immediately the smell of ink, the ranks of type in their wooden cases, the stages of bookmaking all about, the grand press with its great lever, and even the wood-engraved portrait of Dr. Franklin which hung in the office. He had read Benjamin Franklin's aphorisms and he knew about his scientific mind. Franklin was one of his heroes. He knew the story of young Benjamin's entry into Philadelphia. He wanted to make his own entry to stay, as soon as possible. Mr. Odenbaugh gave him up to a job in the printer's shop, when Alexander was thirteen. He was, clearly, to be trusted. He received his eighty dollars in silver and the affectionate good-bys of all the Odenbaugh family. Alexander Upton Quait went to live at Philadelphia in confidence and ceaseless curiosity.

xxxii

His new employer, Arthur Waddell, found him a small room in a boardinghouse near the print shop for a dollar a week. In due time Mr. and Mrs. Waddell made a habit of inviting him to Sunday dinner. They lent him books. Mrs. Waddell tried to fatten him up, but without success. She had three plump children, two girls and a very small boy, and her standards were set by their fat and hearty flesh, which echoed that of her husband and herself, and so seemed excellent.

Alexander's conversation astonished them. For a boy it was disturbingly knowledgeable. His delivery—nobody knew where he had picked it up—was like that of a lecturer in a lyceum. He would underline his point with his finger, and he enjoyed making a little mystery of whatever story he might tell.

"And then, what on earth do you suppose happened next in the order of things?"

And when he reached his climax, he sometimes rose off his chair a trifle and his voice grew higher in pitch and softer in volume, and they all strained to hear, fascinated by his thin, animated face, and if they did not actually come up from their chairs themselves, they seemed to, until he dropped them all back with his conclusion. Mr. and Mrs. Waddell often shook their heads over him, wondering what would ever become of him. They were glad to have him around, but they were even more glad that none of their children was anything like him.

In the shop Alexander Quait was an eager apprentice. He did all the usual boy's chores, but beyond these he also learned to set type, operate the press, bind books and act as salesman in the display room at the front of the shop. There came many of Philadelphia's best people, to buy books newly imported by Mr. Waddell, and to pick up copies of the weekly news broadside which the shop printed for its editor, and to have invitations printed.

Mr. Quait, as his employers called him when in the presence of customers, had a rather courtly and attentive way with him. He knew the stock well and soon was an authority on the tastes of buyers. Though always ready with his own suggestions of what a customer should buy, he was patient if the customer preferred to make the decision. One lady, Mrs. Sylvester Greenleaf, who came from a great family in an old shabby house behind Independence Hall, could never make up her mind, but would return several times to examine paper samples, styles of type, and suggested phrasings, before ordering her invitations. Mr. Quait was always just as delighted to see her the third time as the first. His bony young smile never left his face, and he followed her musings with every mark of respectful attention.

But the fact was, he could divide his concentration, and while everyone thought he was paying them strict attention, he was actually far off in the liveliest part of his mind, thinking about something which had occurred to him early in the day—something which all day he would develop and test in his thought. He made a discipline of selecting a topic for the day's consideration:

Possible Applications of Energy Arising from Heat in *Gaseous Form;*

What Might Have Been the Effect of the *Absence* of Lord Byron from the Greek Struggle for Independence;

In Bacon's Essays, What *Uses of Statecraft* Were Suggested; et cetera, in the style of one who enjoyed nothing more than the giving and taking of examinations. Mr. Quait rarely deluded himself that he came to great conclusions. He knew he was young—though he never remembered having felt young—and he must believe that his conclusions could not be worth much.

He went to a good school for half of each day, and there, with diffidence related to politeness, mastered in two or three gulps what it took other students days or weeks to understand. He did not despise the elementary learning in the conventional subjects taught in his school. All of it was interesting and useful, if too simple. He made his own way faster by reading in his room than listening in school, and he was satisfied.

In the schoolyard he did not often join in the games of other boys, but would watch them with an eagerly critical light playing over his lonely face. The systems of their play interested him more than their thoughtless joy in physical expression. If on rare occasions he was induced to play, to complete a team, or a "side," in the absence of another boy, he entered violently into the game, but usually without winning effect. His tall, thin frame had strength in plenty, but he could not govern it with the instinctive economy and style which gave to movement that completeness and form upon which all athletic prowess rested. When he missed a ball, or ran the wrong way, he was always able immediately to explain in detail just how he had made his mistake, which was a matter of technical interest to him, though not to his companions.

Boys sometimes walked part way home with girls.

Mr. Quait did so, for he was always amenable to convention, on the basis that what the majority of people found suitable might—though not necessarily—by the very fact of its continued practice have reason behind it.

His occasional female companion after school hours was a girl his own age whom he had seen in the printing shop with her mother. She was Miss Jane Elizabeth Greenleaf. If anything, she was more prim than he. She had little to say, but listened to him as he gangled along with his head in the air and with his arms swinging wide to shape the outline of his discourse, and she thought it was a pity that his humble circumstances made it inconvenient to see him at her house. He always left her at the corner of Independence Square to go to work.

He worked late into each evening, and Mr. Waddell trusted him to lock up the shop. Frequently he stayed until after midnight reading the new books when they arrived from Boston, New York and London. Since he could not own the books, he wore cotton gloves to keep the pages clean.

xxxiii

When he was sixteen his ardor of spirit and his overgrown physique combined to bring him down with a fever which persisted in spite of Mrs. Waddell's best efforts to nurse him.

She took him into her house and there he stayed for nearly two years, a victim of consumption.

Even in his weakness he was almost aggressively cheerful. Mrs. Waddell at first tried to keep his books away from him, but the family doctor presently decided that the patient did better with than without them, and ordered them restored with the condition that he must sleep two hours every afternoon and stop reading when darkness fell. Late at night Mrs. Waddell would hear him coughing in the dark, and she would bite her lip in concern for his wakefulness. What really troubled her was the idea that there he was, lying awake, and *thinking*.

For a long time he seemed to grow no better and no worse. With his laughing intuitiveness he said to her one day,

"Now, Mrs. Waddell, you must not worry."

"I do not worry. —What about?" she asked, folding her full lips with her stout, restless fingers.

"About me. I am not going into a decline and die."

She was touched to the point of fury by his exposure of what in fact did trouble her day and night, and she railed at him,

"Well, how can you be so sure, if you keep on refusing to eat

properly, and put some flesh on your poor bones, and keep your poor
mind racing like that!"

"Oh, yes, I can be sure. I am not going to die simply because I
do not intend to."

She thought at first that this must be just another of his unsettling
bits of cleverness, but she saw that he meant it, and, moved by powers
far beyond her comfortably limited knowledge, she told Mr. Waddell
that she guessed they'd all been too het up about Mr. Quait, and that
perhaps he had just grown too fast, and when he caught up with
himself, he would probably come well.

There was a certain matronly wisdom in this, and in time she was
proved right.

When Alexander did actually recover he was better in every way.
He had learned patience in his long inactivity. His pace was slowed
down and his mind was tempered by his invalid's habit of thinking
long, instead of rapid, thoughts. He had come to a number of conclusions, the most important of which was about himself. It was the
sort of conclusion which a father would ordinarily make for his son.
Having no father, Alexander was obliged to offer himself fatherly
advice.

He considered that his mental development far outstripped his
physical abilities. It was time to turn his attention systematically to
these. Reviewing the various vocations open to a young man of
eighteen, in order to isolate that one which most demanded physical
stamina, and application of physical forces under control, for a purpose susceptible of direction, he concluded that the profession of
arms met his inquiry better than any other.

He resolved, then, to apply for entrance into West Point, and to
make the Army his career. He felt he could be trusted during all his
life to preserve and enhance his intellectual powers by himself, no
matter what his calling: the Army would never succeed in imposing
its disciplines upon his mind. Cheerfully he would submit his physical
and social capacities to the Army, therefore, in the belief that he
would thus become a more balanced and well-rounded man.

Mr. Waddell, while privately certain that Mr. Quait would never
make a soldier, and kindly regretful for the disappointment which
must come to him, helped him to take his first steps toward his
ambition. Mr. Quait took his examination and scored the highest
mark of all who were examined with him.

As in the case of his earlier schooling, the curriculum of the military academy served Cadet Quait mainly as a point of departure for his real exercises of mind. As though saying "Yes, of course," he swallowed up and demonstrated with ease the class assignments, moving ahead, when called upon for discussions, to what lay beyond the Greek or Latin texts, the fixed problems of mathematics, the irregularity of French verbs, or the neuter gender in German. While other cadets rubbed their skulls over syntax and theorems and reflexives and abstract concepts, Cadet Quait wanted to inquire aloud whether Strabo actually discussed the political structures of the city-states, and if so, precisely in what book, chapter and paragraph, or to discuss the systems of military tactics cited *passim* by Herodotus and Caesar, or the value of triangulation in ballistics, or national character as revealed by linguistic idiom. He was not often given free rein in his recitations, as by military regulation a certain number of pages had to be covered every day in each subject, and time would run out for this if Cadet Quait were indulged. His powers, being recognized, served to render him less than popular.

For the rest, he learned to become a superb rider of horses. His thinness made him light on a horse, and his gristly strength and length of leg gave him a sensitive instrument for controlling his animal. If he began equitation with a personal theory of coordination between the movements of man and horse, he soon ceased to apply it consciously. He was baffled if another cadet might seem afraid of horses. Much as he tried to understand such a feeling, he could only revert to the rational query, Was not the least of men superior in brain power to the best of horses? How, then, could fear become a factor between man and horse?

xxxiv

He was graduated first in his class in 1846. The Mexican War was already under way, Taylor had already taken the lower Rio Grande, and the whole immense Mexican borderland was awaiting the United States Army.

Second Lieutenant Alexander Upton Quait, U.S. Dragoons, was posted to join Colonel Stephen Watts Kearny's expedition against New Mexico. When he reached Fort Leavenworth, Kearny had already marched west on the Santa Fe Trail. Lieutenant Quait, traveling with a courier party and escort, overtook him on the plains.

He was from the very beginning of the experience fascinated and uplifted by the West. In his time this was not an unusual emotion—the whole nation was obsessed by the West. But he met it with powers of observation, intuitive grasp of its nature and its problems, and love for its landscape in all its components (geologic, botanical, zoological) of uncommon breadth and acuteness. By the time he entered Santa Fe with Kearny's forces he felt like a veteran of the plains.

In Santa Fe he learned the great lesson of his military life from Kearny, who had been promoted. General Kearny conquered New Mexico without firing a shot. Once he had conquered, he governed the population with courtesy, fairness and sympathy. The lesson lay in this: that the best way to gain political ends by military means was to possess great force of arms, but to use them sparingly, or if possible, not at all, and to remember that an enemy was also a man deserving of human respect. These large, simple premises might at first knowledge seem obvious to the point of banality; but the behavior of many of his associates and the histories of wars (and Lieutenant Quait had read most of them) all too sadly underlined the value of reminding men of the truths he saw so ably demonstrated by General Kearny.

When Kearny moved on to California in September, 1846, Lieutenant Quait was assigned to accompany Colonel Doniphan and the Missouri Volunteers on their march south along the Rio Grande to Chihuahua, Mexico. As a regular officer on liaison duty, he was out of place amidst the rough crew of free spirits from Missouri, and was made to feel so. But he did his share of fighting in the battle of Brazito forty miles north of El Paso, and he saw how untrained volunteers, when the time came, could act in concert like the best of trained troops. Mankind, he concluded not for the first or last time, was a remarkable species. In the Army such an observation was irrelevant, and would therefore cause uneasiness.

In Mexico he was shifted to General Wool's command nearabouts Saltillo and Monterrey. There he saw much that sickened him in the behavior of the volunteer regiments and the Texas Rangers—depredations, sportive crimes of lust and torture and murder—and he wondered at times whether he had after all chosen the right career. Something about great throngs of men turned to the purposes of war seemed to invite and almost justify their worst, most deeply buried impulses. The Mexicans were no better in this aspect of the conflict. Lieutenant Quait began to search for examples of the opposite tendencies of man—those which made him commit mercy instead of murder, charity instead of rape.

He found plenty of examples and gratefully noted them in his pocket journal, in which he carefully entered his observations of each day. He thought of it as his Good Book.

"Leave the worst to others," he said to himself, "and let me record the nobility of mankind under suffering."

This softness of heart, induced in him by the hardness of duty, he carefully concealed from his associates. They began to say that nobody ever knew what Quait was thinking. His eyes were black and bright and active, and they could see that his mind was working away lickety-split, but until he chose to give it, his opinion, his inner attitude, was a mystery. He didn't give it often. Mostly they thought of him as buried in some book or other.

He returned from Mexico with his mustache and beard well-started, and reddish-brown in color. He brushed his beard with a part down the center. He was only twenty-four, but seemed ten years older. His scholarly reputation had drifted as far as the bureaus of the War Department, and someone there considered that he would be an excellent one to serve in the Adjutant General's Office, since he could read and write, and seemed to like all that.

The quality of his reading and writing had nothing to do with such an assignment, and he knew it would be drudgery, but cheerfully he took it on, in order to widen his experience of the Army. In three years in Washington he learned enough about the endless strife between headquarters and the field to last all his life. He vowed that if ever he became the commander of the whole Army, he would order that everyone who served in Washington war offices must first have served in the field, preferably at the most unpalatable duty, including battle.

XXXV

In these three years of clerical duty he conducted a program of further systematic self-improvement.

He now felt confident not only of his mental powers but also of his physical quality. If he had a lack in his total effect it was, he believed, in the social arts. If he should one day attain to high rank, he must be able to behave in a high-toned style. He began to tour the drawing rooms of Washington society on their hostesses' days at home.

One place he particularly enjoyed going to was the house of former Secretary of War James Hamilton Mercer and Mrs. Mercer, where the conversation always amused him, and was often *about something,* besides.

By this he meant that the talk dealt with ideas, public issues, and international intelligence, rather than merely with local gossip, food, clothes and fashion. Honora Mercer had a particularly pleasant way for him, for she always singled him out.

He never suspected that in this there was response not so much to his gifts as to the awkwardness which made him seem eccentric among her other guests, and which for his sake she must ease.

There was always a little square bulge inside his military tunic.

"What is that curious protuberance below your beard?" Mrs. Mercer asked him one day.

He inhaled sharply and colored deeply as he unbuttoned his tunic and took out a small but thick little volume.

"It is volume three of my Gibbon," he said and then held his mouth fixed as though to whistle: in this way he controlled his desire to laugh with pleasure at her interest.

"And do you always carry a book?"

"Always. Who knows when he may have a few stray moments in an otherwise busy day?"

"How heavenly," said Mrs. Mercer. "I shall start to keep a book with me wherever I go."

He called on her a week or so later on an off day when she was not receiving generally. A parlormaid asked him to wait. He sat in a sofa and began to read, and when Honora Mercer came in he was so absorbed that he did not even see her. She let him read on, until turning a page he looked up and beyond his book saw the compassionate smile on her face. He blushed above his beard and waved his book.

"I am reading Horace's Odes."

She leaned to see.

"In the *original Latin?*" she asked.

"In the original."

"How perfectly heavenly."

"Oh, one needs a special interest to—"

He did not mean to sound superior, but managed to do so. Try as she might, Honora Mercer was never able to make him adopt easy airs in society. Something—was it his early life in the families of hard-working tradesmen with their blunt simple ways and their creature silences that had fixed him forever in his idea of social intercourse?—something made him feel and act like a fish out of water when he came among well-born and cultivated people, with their casual give and take, and their airs of comfort in any situation. He held himself stiffly in body and mind, and took refuge in a tendency to do all the talking. His monologues were in themselves excellent expositions, but in their subjects and manner of delivery they were not often of interest to anyone else. All people could do was admit that he was brilliant, and shy away from exposure to him. He felt this, and it did not help him in his campaign of social experience.

He was rescued in due course by assignment to the field. Two companies of his regiment of dragoons were assigned to duty in the mountain west, where Indian raids were endangering white settlements from Colorado to the Texas border. There he had his first encounters with Indians. Obliged to fight them on occasion, he became a student of their tactics. In 1855 he was with a detachment that defeated a large band of Sioux in southern Nebraska. Many Indian women and children were captured, and nearly a hundred Indian warriors were killed—some of them after capture. Captain Quait did all he could to prevent what he regarded as outrage and stupidity. He said to his commanding officer,

"Let me have the captive men."

"What for, in God's name?" asked the commander. "I have given orders to shoot them. After the things they have done to our people, it is better than they deserve."

"Yes, yes, sir, I know. I agree, so far as this particular group of Indians is concerned. But this is not the only group we will have to deal with. We will be fighting people like them for decades. If you give me the captives, they will, I believe, help me to defeat their kind sooner in the end."

"Captain Quait, you are a very high-toned and advanced kind of thinker, but, sir, I'll be slam-damned if I know what you are trying to say, and I misdoubt if you know yourself."

"No, sir, I know. I believe if we have a chance to study these people, to examine and know what they know, which can only be managed over quite a period of time, we may use this knowledge of them to teach us how we may more fully and more quickly bring the Indian troubles to an end, and the Indians themselves into our citizenry."

"Our citizenry?"

The commander was infuriated by Captain Quait's theory of Indian conquest.

"It will be the only guarantee of lasting peace," said the captain.

"Captain Quait, you will take command of the execution squads," said the commanding officer, "and you will execute the male Indian prisoners immediately. You will personally give the command to fire in each detachment of executions. You will report to me giving a full description of the executions when they are done."

Captain Quait saluted and went to do his duty.

In his tent that night he made an entry in his pocket journal, describing the events of that day, then adding:

There is much to be said for the practicality of the orders which I carried out today. I will not enlarge on the problems of logistics and management which retention of the now-dead prisoners would have entailed. Still, I believe there are overriding principles which I would defend in any further discussion of my proposal. The first of these is the principle which I indicated: we will the sooner and the better defeat the Indian enemy if we know him well. The second principle is of another dimension and quality. It is this: Indian savagery and cruelty, ingenious and remorseless as they are, are but fragments of *humanity's general capacity* for savagery and cruelty. Indians do not have a monopoly on these traits; nor do we white people have exclusive claim to virtue and enlightenment. Not condoning savagery and cruelty in any degree, we must see these as expressions of evil common to all mankind. We must broaden our view of our mission, tragic as it is, and bring compassion and even humility to our fulfillment of it. Evil must be overcome, but without righteousness or any feeling of personal exemption from liability to its power within ourselves. Let us know more of all humanity in whatever guise, and bring love and trust to this awareness, and we shall one day long hence perhaps come truly to be men worthy of the name.

Whenever he could, in the next years of duty against the Indians, he learned as much as possible about Indian principles of belief and behavior. Though he never succeeded in persuading anyone to adopt his ideas, which were genially described as "hare-brained" by his colleagues, he slowly won a sort of reputation as an expert in Indian affairs.

"Yes, sir," they said, "listen to Quait, and then do just the opposite. It takes an expert to be as reliable as that every time."

Nobody denied that when it came to fighting, Alexander Upton Quait was as effective and ingenious as many another man. Recommendations of his promotion were accordingly almost always approved.

xxxvi

On a visit to Washington in 1857 he called at the house of Major Huntleigh Greenleaf and found an old friend.

It was Miss Jane Elizabeth Greenleaf, his schooltime companion of long ago, who was visiting her brother. She was a confirmed spinster, but her old admiration for Lieutenant Colonel Quait was quickly rediscovered, and as his program had always included the plan that he would some day marry, he began, in his own fashion, to lay siege to her.

He was thoughtful of her comfort, he talked to her as if she too had a lively intelligence (which was true, though few others gave her credit for it), and brought into her life a largeness of view which she had never expected to know. She accepted him. The engagement astonished everyone, and made his prospective sister-in-law groan. But Mrs. Huntleigh Greenleaf had no direct authority to block the match, and it came off.

The marriage was a success but for one respect. The Quaits had no children, though they hoped for a family, in spite of their mature years. With marriage, some of Colonel Quait's oddness seemed to be eased. As a husband he felt more nearly accounted for and explained among other men. To share his life seemed—as he noted in his book —to bring him more of life in return.

Early in the Civil War he was given a regiment and assigned to the western campaign. He took a box of books and went off, leaving Jane Elizabeth in Philadelphia in her family home. She died there of pneumonia a year later without seeing him again.

The news of his loss reached Colonel Quait on the very eve of a battle. It came by letter. For long nobody else knew about it, for he felt that in the first place his suffering belonged to him alone and he was almost jealous of protecting what it stood for from those about him. In the second place, he thought that some quality of his leadership might be lost if his officers knew that he had a double burden to carry at a moment so critical in military operations, with the lives of so many men dependent upon his highest effectiveness.

The battle was not a decisive one but Colonel Quait's regiment performed well, and was commended by the commanding general.

Some time later with the arrival of newspapers in camp, Colonel Quait's bereavement became known to Pennsylvanians in his command. The news filtered through the regiment. Not knowing the reasons for his reticence, the soldiers thought him really a cold fish not to have told anyone, but to have gone about his job showing no more concern than a billygoat. He felt their attitudes, and he suspected what lay behind them, but he knew that men through the whole course of human time were inclined to make hasty judgments on insufficient evidence, and he hoped he might be spared from committing the same error, and he forgave them in his obscure heart.

His fortitude had a curiously effective influence on his subsequent promotion. His superiors, hearing that he had conducted himself and his command so well at exactly the time of his greatest private concern, considered that he was really to be trusted with more responsibility. Preparations for Grant's operations along the Mississippi were quickening, and Lieutenant Colonel Quait was promoted colonel and assigned assistant brigade commander. A year later he was raised to brigadier general, and six months after that brevetted major general, a rank he held until the close of the war, when he reverted to permanent brigadier general.

Within the frame of his opportunities, General Quait's performance in the war was superior from first to last. It earned him the abstract respect of his superiors and the puzzled devotion of his subordinates.

If he was not loved by his troops, it was because he lacked the ability to come close to men in the mass with warmth of feeling. His attentions and decisions and championings on behalf of his men were all more cerebral than emotional in their character, and the result was that many a less gifted commander received the hero worship which soldiers were so willing to give to anyone fulfilling an enlarged idea of themselves. If General Quait had had one great opportunity to fight a battle of the largest consequence, he would much sooner have become a famous man and a legend, in spite of his lively austerity.

After the Civil War he was sent to command troops on the Sioux frontier in the Dakotas.

It was work he liked, and he did it well. Once again his love of the open life in the West, and his eagerness to treat with the Indians through a grasp of their culture and their nature, satisfied him, and brought the nation good returns. His mission was interrupted by a new assignment in 1870—one which only he in the Army could properly fill, as they said generally in the War Department.

He was promoted major general not only as a mark of prestige for himself but for his country, and sent to Europe as a military observer of the operations fought by both sides in the Franco-Prussian War.

He made a great impression on the German generals with whom he dealt, for his mind, so quick with theory and so rich with historical precedents, seemed to them extraordinary, "for an American." With the French he made a somewhat lesser success, for though he applauded their lucidity and their logic, the French generals appeared at times to act upon their emotions rather than upon their military philosophy, and his judgment could not be hidden from them, however politely he put his views.

He watched the debacle which overcame France. He saw the Emperor Napoleon III at Metz during his disastrous retreat. He could have foretold these mournful inevitabilities even before the battle of Sedan. During the siege of Paris he established himself at the Hôtel de France et de Guise in Versailles, and kept a journal of events as reported from the capital, where pet cats were eaten by beleaguered citizens. He became fluent in written and spoken French, though his accent was a marvel of the age to all who heard it. When Paris capitulated he entered the city to watch the Prussians take possession, and recorded his opinions of their lack of grace as victors.

Before returning home he visited England, and was pleased with her monuments to the history, law and literature whose great residues had illumined his mind since boyhood. One evening in London he was taken as a high-ranking guest by the American minister to a reception where he met Benjamin Disraeli, who was for the moment out of office. There was immediate intellectual sympathy between the two, many flashes of wit were exchanged, and in return for a character sketch of President Grant by General Quait, Mr. Disraeli gave one of Queen Victoria. When they parted, Mr. Disraeli expressed the hope of one day visiting the United States, especially since he could now expect to see the savannahs of that remarkable nation peopled not only by red savages but also by major generals who evidently commanded in addition to troops every flight of classical learning.

General Quait brought home and delivered to the Secretary of War a voluminous and highly readable report of his military observations. His main professional conclusion was that employment of troops in close field formations must henceforth be wasteful and ineffective, and that emphasis should be placed instead on massed artillery, with troops deployed as thinly as possible, yet in groupings capable of ready mobility.

Almost at once he was assigned to new duties in which this lesson which dealt with similarly armed and organized opponents had no application.

He was sent to the Southwest to put down depredations practiced on a wide and barren terrain by nomadic Indians, chiefly Apaches. The work took him several years, and called for many improvisations of military method. He ranged from western Texas, across southern New Mexico and into Arizona and even into Mexico. His Mexican foray was diplomatically risky until in the Treaty of 1875 Mexico authorized American armed pursuit of Apaches on her soil. Thereafter he was seen in the mountains of northern Sonora, which he inspected with an eye to the future.

"It may well be that here we will play the final scene," he remarked to his staff.

In the course of these operations he became almost as great a master of the deserts, the mountains, the skies, the tempers of the great land, as his enemies.

The campaign was formally ended when he captured the Apache leader, in a skirmish above the Salt River Canyon. The captive, with many others taken at the time, was granted life by General Quait. The Indians were removed to recently established reservations. General Quait was recalled.

He promptly told officials in Washington that the campaign should be continued for many more years, until the actual spread and strength of civilized settlement in the Southwest would of itself render the Indian power ineffectual through peaceful means.

But the War Department, influenced by a strong faction in Congress, disagreed with him, and cut off appropriations for massive reconnaissance and maintenance of troops on the frontier. A few scattered companies of cavalry and infantry had to be responsible for order in the extended Southwest. In the government's policy, it seemed to those who lived out there, the Indians were favored over white settlers.

Philosophically defeated once again, General Quait took up duty in the War Department. But he kept abreast of all discussion and modulation of policy in Western Indian affairs, and he never lost from his mind the bright images he had gained of the Southwest, and the realities they stood for, in his years of service there as a youth and as a seasoned campaigner.

xxxvii

If he was a lonely man in those later years, he was too obliging to confess it in behavior.

Nobody really knew much about how he lived, and many would have been amazed to learn of one of his activities. He made an organized effort to seek out people in distress of poverty, and after examining their needs and estimating their capacity to receive help sensibly, he undertook to contribute to the support of a number of families out of his salary, which constituted his only worldly means. The one condition he imposed was secrecy. His charities were conducted through a confidential agent. He did not want his benefactions to be known even to the recipients.

"I find the gratitude of others," he said to his pocket journal, "a heavy burden to bear."

In this there may have been the diffidence of a man who counted himself for so little that he could not imagine receiving the gifts of love and thanks from another; fearing he would never have them, he must repudiate them in advance. All the repayment he asked was to hear of good results from his charity.

In his sixties he was an elderly ascetic such as might turn up in any profession now and then. He had seen enough of society, and continued to see enough, to know the signals of gallantry, and in company he made them himself; but the result was often grotesque. He could throw a gleam of approval at young people in their romances, as if to endorse a generally accepted principle of life in the world, though he left it to others to illustrate it through their instinctive pleasures.

Late in life he granted himself an indulgence. It was joy in gastronomy. He could eat rapidly and tremendously, though without gaining a pound. People could not help wondering where he put all his food, and also how, hardly pausing between bites, he could talk so steadily.

Married late, widowed early, and childless, he was drawn to children.

"I do always, it seems, prefer the potential," he noted, "to the fulfilled."

xxxviii

After some weeks White Horn discovered who had designed his downfall.

He was taken from his cell one afternoon and marched to an office in the headquarters building of Fort Bayard, and there he was faced to stand before a tall, thin, white-bearded old man with piercing black eyes and a strange, high, husky and beguiling voice. With a gesture he told White Horn to sit down, and with another he sent away the guards. For a long, an extremely long time, he sat in silence and gazed at White Horn. He did not move. His eyelids were severe across his gaze. He breathed audibly in long, slow, regular draughts. He seemed to be drinking in all knowledge of White Horn. White Horn tried to retain himself wholly, but he felt himself losing something of his own secrecy. He did not like the feeling, but he could not make it stop. All he could do was match the silence and calm of the man opposite to him and pretend that he himself were elsewhere.

Finally, taking inward a little series of noisy breaths—"h'h'h'h' "— the old man clapped his hands once as though to awaken himself from his thoughts, and spoke. He used Apache words and Spanish words as he needed to, and he made himself understood absolutely.

"I am General Quait of the United States Army. Your name is White Horn. How do you do. I have much to say to you. You will do well to hear me seriously. Now:

"I have had much experience in dealing with the Apache people in both peace and war. I was in your country many years ago and I have returned now to see what must be done.

"For myself, I prefer peace.

"But I am capable of war, if necessary, as you and your men now know. I, myself, commanded the action which brought you and others to captivity or death. I was victorious for various reasons, all of which I well know. The important ones to mention here are these: first, I had more men than you; second, I know how the Apache people use the earth as warriors, and I practiced your lessons."

He paused and nodded many times toward White Horn, to add thrust to the things he had said, and to drive them deeply into White Horn's being. The old man hung his right hand by its fingers fixed like claws in the thick of his white beard at the fork. He seemed to nibble something briefly, but it was only the working of a thought which made his hidden lips act with it. He soon spoke again.

"Now I want you to know that if the Apache people will not live in peace with the white Americans who have come here to stay, and to increase their numbers and their works in this land, then I, General Quait, with as many thousand soldiers as might be needed for the task, I will be obliged to destroy the Apache nation in war."

White Horn listened in silence. He listened to doom. He believed he knew the truth when he heard it and he was hearing it now.

General Quait moved to a wall and slapped a great map showing the Apache world.

"This is a design of your land." His hand moved over the design like a wind that knew the country. "Here is a railroad running all across. This is a village. This is a town. Here is a place where soldiers are kept until they go out to punish wrongdoing. Farms are put in places like this and this. Across, and across, and up and down, my people come to live. They will remain. They are put here for their own purposes. Their purposes are generally good. They prefer peace to everything else." His arm swept the whole space to show where the Americans lived and would live. "Here is much land, enough for everyone. But"—he cupped his hand on the map and showed where the Apache people would have to stay—"here is where your people are put, surrounded by soldiers who will keep you there—until we can make peace with you. If you will be peaceful, we hope you will be free one day to go where you will, to farm, and trade, and take your place and make your children's place with other Americans. This is good."

General Quait broke off, and said in a half-voice to himself in English,

"Yes, it is good, but it is not what he has always known, and being strange it is therefore undesirable. Still. We must do our best. H'h'h'h—" drawing his breaths inward. He continued in White Horn's language,

"There are some people in my government who want to have every Apache man, woman, child and dog put to death. Plenty of our men are tired of hearing what your Indian people do to my people. Even so, there are others, including myself, General Quait, who believe it is better to make peace, and exchange promises, and *keep promises,* and make life for people, better these than to settle something by killing, killing, everlasting killing. —What do you think?"

White Horn, if he thought, said nothing.

General Quait took a deep whistling breath through his white whiskers and resumed his remarks.

"Now I know you are a chief of raiders. You have shown your people an example of power and leadership. Yes, and good judgment under their laws. You now have another chance to show this example again to them. Do you want to hear how?"

White Horn half-blinked his eyelids—the merest intimate muscular response that might indicate a willingness to hear what General Quait wanted to tell him. General Quait laughed and slapped his high boot with his riding whip, and exclaimed, in English, "Capital!" and went on to speak in Apache words.

"Now I want to get my work done, and done quickly, and with good feeling and mercy. It might take months, or it might have to take years. If it will take years, well, then, it will take years—but there is one thing everybody must know already: no matter how long it may take, it can end in only one way, and that is, with the white people on top. Regardless of how you like it, is this true, or is it not?"

White Horn said nothing, but a little seep of liquid started along his eyeballs from the corners of his eyes and took a sliver of light laterally for a second, and if it had been a lens, it could not more clearly have shown to someone so observant as General Quait what White Horn thought, in grief.

"Well, then, since we are agreed," said the general, "I want to call upon all intelligent men, Apache men, especially Apache leaders, to bring peace to the land. Now listen. I want to find enough skillful Apache fighters, with enough dignity to keep an oath, to join the

United States Army as paid scouts. I know Apache ways; and where I am, these ways will succeed. But I cannot be everywhere. The scouts will help soldiers to know desert and mountain, and the fighting ways of the Indian people, and the signs of trail and movement."

The general put his hands under his beard and lifted its forks up and forward in a gesture strangely expressive of delight, and his eyes lighted with surprise at his own persuasive ideas.

"And what will a scout receive in return for such service? Well, first, he will be trusted. Wonderful. The greatest of rewards. He will go free from his prison cell. He will help to bring peace to his people. He will help to prevent years of wasteful and cruel warfare. Some people say the Indian people do not know right from wrong—that when they commit horrors upon our people they are innocent because they do not know good from bad. But I say, let a white man do these things to an Indian, and the Indian will know well enough what is good and what is bad. We can understand things alike if we work together. The scout will find friends among the soldiers. If he has a family they will be taken care of. His pay will be generous and if he wishes to, he may have it in silver, whenever the soldiers are paid. People say to me, 'But General, aren't you afraid to trust these Indians?' and I reply, 'In the first place, I am not afraid, generally, and in the second, if I give honor enough to a man he will keep it just because it is honor.' No, I am not afraid. I want you for a scout."

White Horn leaned stiffly back in his chair and gazed past the side of General Quait's head. The idea he had listened to was something that had to be considered in silence and perhaps for a long time. He did not reply.

"Did you understand me, White Horn? Do not nod or shake your head. Answer me aloud."

"*Si,*" replied White Horn.

"Very well, that will do for the time, then," said General Quait, and rose to fling open the door for the guards to enter and remove White Horn to his cell. "You will tell me what you will do when you know."

xxxix

How did he think, then, for many days and nights in his cell?

He, himself, was conquered; a prisoner. Might not all other men of his people be conquered also? Should they be killed or put into cells, or given freedom on their promise? He asked what he had to fight for if the fight was already lost. He knew from the swelling of his heart that if his wife and son were not dead, he would never surrender, but would fight in their name, their honor, until he too was dead, and splendidly.

But where were they?

With the grasshoppers, in their graves.

How had that white old man spoken to him?

Like a man explaining something to another man, and giving him time to know what he thought.

And then White Horn would think of his people, and the village with which he had traveled all his life; and at the idea of leaving them to serve their enemies, he would taste something hot and sick in his throat.

Then he would sleep, and then he would awaken, and remember that whatever he did, his people would be overcome, and if he could help them sooner to peace, and their children to peace, why should he not do it?

He was like Coyote, trapped and raging from one side of his cage to another. He was good man and bad man at the same time. He prayed for resolution.

It came in a dream.

For four nights running, he dreamed of his power—the deer with white tips to his antlers. The power appeared to him in his sleep each night, and nodding his horns, told him to *do something,* but without explaining what, but to have no fear, but to do it. On awakening, White Horn saw that the only thing he was to do was to accept the general's proposal.

And then for four more nights in a row, he dreamed the summer dream, with all things blooming and growing, and making life. On awakening he knew that he was being told that only good must follow upon his joining the Army. He was then at peace with himself. The decision had come from without. He must obey his power, and he must live according to whatever made things grow and turn green and prosper as in summer. If becoming a scout meant this, then he was prepared to become a scout, and take his oath, and keep it.

On the ninth day—how did the white old man know how long the dreams would have to take?—General Quait came to White Horn's cell, dismissed the guard, walked in leaving the cell gate open, sat down on the packed earthen floor facing White Horn, and asked him what he was going to do.

White Horn looked upon him for quite a long moment, and then, in his habit of not speaking when he could make his meaning plain otherwise, he dabbed the fingers of his right hand together, and put his hand forward in the air, and with it made a small circular movement, suggesting by it a wafting of opinion toward the general, an agreement by indicating the general repeatedly with those tapered fingers in their gesture of compliance.

"Do you mean that you will accept the appointment as a scout in the Army?" asked General Quait.

White Horn leaned backward a small way, an action which lifted his fixed gaze above the general, and after a last hesitation which concealed strong feeling, he replied,

"*Si.*"

The general put out his hand, and they shook hands, after which the general stood up and walked out of the cell, motioning to the returning guard not to close the cage. At a rapid gait which made him tall and then less tall with every pair of steps, he disappeared in the direction of the Fort Bayard headquarters.

White Horn sat still, reflecting upon the actions of the white old creature.

One thing seemed clear—he had gone off that way, leaving the jail door open, to prove to White Horn that he trusted him. But he had not said to him that he must arise and go free. Accordingly, and with a stubbornness related to suffering, White Horn resolved to sit there on his dirt floor facing the open door, and not move, until someone came to ask him to walk forth as a free man.

When mealtime came, a sergeant of cavalry went to see where White Horn was, and at last thought of looking for him in the least likely place, which was his open cell. He found him there, led him up to his feet, and took him to mess. White Horn stood in line with his graniteware plate and tin cup just like another soldier, and the soldiers stared at him, wondering, and he kept his eyes away from them, and slowly made a stout meal, sitting by himself.

Halfway through it, General Quait came strolling with his loose-flung gait out of the headquarters office and over to the shade where the men were taking their lunch. He put them at their ease before they could spring to their feet, and walking along the irregular line, he peered at their rations, exchanging a word or two without stopping to stand.

"Hearty appetite? Well and good. —Do as you will, but I must advise, advise only, mind you, to take coffee without sweetening. The taste is soon acceptable, the effect better on digestion. —Slumgullion. I have relished it all my life. —You have a boil, my man, on your neck. Report for poultices. The doctor will advise hot salt packs. —If you sit up rather than recline, your food will the better find its way," and so along the line.

Coming to White Horn where he sat apart, he did as much for him, neither more nor less.

"You now have a tin cup. Keep the tin cup. It will be your best friend on the march," he declared, and passed on to the next man. By this, the soldiers, and White Horn himself, understood that a new order had been established with naturalness and authority and kindness.

xl

Some of the other Chiricahua captives also agreed to become scouts. After a few weeks at Fort Bayard, they were assembled one day on the parade. In a few minutes the muslin door of headquarters was slapped open vigorously to give passage to General Quait and his staff of two officers. They strode rapidly to the formation of waiting scouts. The general was in full-dress blue uniform with gold epaulets, gold sash, dress sword and white gloves. A squad of soldiers fell in behind his advance. Coming to the Indian scouts, General Quait halted facing them. The duty sergeant called all present to attention.

He allowed a long silence to dwell over the scene while he stared at each Indian scout in turn. His invisible nibbling went on, making his beard quiver in the staring sunlight. Then having given the effect of gathering all the scouts in his knowledge and memory, he made them a speech in their language, ending by reciting his own translation of the army oath. When he had finished intoning it in a high, intense monotone, he asked if they understood it.

They replied in unison that they did.

Would they keep it?

They would.

"I believe you," he said. Then he turned to the sergeant, and said, "Sergeant, the rifle."

At this the sergeant ordered the squad of soldiers forward. From the first he took his rifle and handed it to the general, who moved to the line of scouts and presented the rifle to the first man in line, who was White Horn. In a symbolic presentation of arms, the same rifle was handed briefly to all the scouts.

"Here is your power and your honor," said General Quait, looking sharply into White Horn's eyes.

The only reply to this—but it seemed sufficient to General Quait—was a lowering in almost invisible degree of White Horn's eyelids. The general passed down the line to ordain the remainder of his new troops. When he was done he returned to headquarters to change from his dress uniform. The scouts saw him soon afterward in his fatigue tunic and knew that he had worn ceremonial dress in honor of their solemn induction.

xli

Within the year the scouts were sent away to their new posts. White Horn was assigned to Fort Delivery, Department of Arizona. He carried written orders and travel vouchers. Accordingly he went to the Rio Grande at El Paso, and there boarded a railroad train of the Atlantic and Pacific line and rode westward to Driscoll, Arizona.

On board the train he was addressed by a young man in army uniform who saw White Horn's regulation flannel shirt and its brass collar ornaments.

"Are you authorized to wear that uniform?" asked the young soldier, seeing his first Indian.

White Horn did not understand him precisely, but the glance

and gesture that went with the question made him bring out his official papers which he handed over to be read.

"Good enough," said the young man presently, handed the papers back to their owner, and clapped him on the shoulder. "We are going to the same place. My name is Second Lieutenant Hazard."

When they reached Driscoll and left the train they found an army ambulance waiting to leave for Fort Delivery—a journey of two and a half days' duration. Lieutenant Hazard was expected, but not White Horn.

"I ain't *about* to take no Indian in my wagon," said the sergeant in charge, after spitting on the ground. "No Indian is going to ride in it like any white man."

"What is your name, sergeant?" asked Lieutenant Hazard.

"Sergeant Blickner, sir."

"Take this man in your wagon, Sergeant Blickner."

The sergeant hesitated.

"Take him, sergeant," said Lieutenant Hazard.

The sergeant felt silent support for his position from the handful of enlisted men standing behind him. He remained irresolute. Lieutenant Hazard was not pleased with this behavior.

"What is the matter with this detachment?" he asked in a flat voice. "I have just given an order."

"I know, sir. I heard you. But I have been long enough where Indians belong to the other side. I don't hardly expect to—"

"I will take the responsibility, Sergeant Blickner," said Matthew. "I have seen this man's orders. He is in our army as much as you and I are." He turned to White Horn and with a jerk of his head toward the open leather curtain at the end of the wagon, said, "Get in."

White Horn entered the wagon. Matthew climbed in after him and sat down beside him on the side bench. He did not know it until long later, but Matthew, in those few moments made a friend and partisan for life in White Horn, who would never show his feeling.

In the course of the journey overland to Fort Delivery, there was time for the lieutenant to meditate about the state of discipline at his new post as demonstrated by the ambulance party. The drawling insolence of Sergeant Blickner and the silent confederacy of his small command gave Matthew an impression of the commanding officer at the fort.

"Who is in command at Fort Delivery?" he asked.

"First Lieutenant Mainwaring," said the sergeant. "He's acting in command. Our new C.O. is supposed to be here long ago, but he ain't come yet."

"How many men are at the fort?"

"One troop. F Troop, Sixth Cav'ry. Little biddy under strength, we've got fifty-eight men and four laundresses."

"How do you like your post?"

"Sir, I wouldn't shit you, it's just outdoors of hell."

Lieutenant Hazard withdrew into high, cold calm. His propriety as a newly graduated officer was offended. The strength and justice of his displeasure were felt by the men who traveled with him. It made them uneasy even as they despised it.

The sergeant had time to recover his manners as they traveled over the desert. He had intended in the first place by his treatment of the Indian to show the new lieutenant how people in Arizona felt about Indians. He had guessed wrong about this particular Indian, and this particular lieutenant. He now tried many times to fall into conversation with White Horn as they traveled.

"You make-um medicine, U.S. Army?"—whatever this was to mean.

White Horn with silence and calm made a large world of which he was the precise center, and to this he gave his fixed attention. The sergeant had no existence on the periphery of White Horn's defined gaze.

"Hot damn, you steal-um plenty cows, sheep?"

Silence.

After other trials at recovering his good standing by further baiting White Horn, Sergeant Blickner winked at his fellow soldiers, and said,

"I guess ol' Joe Dummy, here, don't have much to say. Mebbe ol' Joe Dummy can't reely say anythin', mebbe somebody cut out ol' Joe Dummy's tongue, somewhere back there, when ol' Joe got caught doin' what he hadn't ought to be caught doin'."

The sergeant had his partisans, and now they laughed with approval of his fun. They picked up the nickname, and when they all reached the post after three days of wagon travel, they used it in the most natural way in the world, and the new Apache scout became known by everyone, even the officers, even the lieutenant who had befriended him and given him dignity, as Joe Dummy—though Matthew Hazard usually said just "Joe."

Joe Dummy bore little resemblance to the youth White Horn or the child This Boy.

His age, judging by appearances, could be anything from forty to seventy. He was still somewhat hunched, still showing a keenness of apprehension, a reaching to know which his body reflected from his mind. His skin was walnut dark, and as wrinkled as a shelled walnut, and his teeth were damaged and some lost, so that his lips caved in a bit; and wearing clothes, scraps of uniform, he represented only the movement of a body instead of the visible free movement of a naked figure. His red headband—all scouts wore a red calico headband as part of their uniform—was already dark with sweat. His shirt, whether a trooper's flannel or a trading-post calico—hung outside his sacklike trousers and was secured at the hips by a rawhide belt. He was not accustomed to washing a shirt, but wore it until it gave way into rags. His trousers were treated in the same way. About his belt he kept various accessories and attributes—little pouches containing his private treasures, such as *hoddentin,* and his little twig of lightning-split wood, and other possessions which he treasured for their power or their association. He was indistinguishable from any of hundreds of Indians who might be gathered for a parley or a trading fair or a reservation roundup.

Who knew that he had been nobly named for the white horn tips of a princely deer who had come to him in his sleep and was his power? The pathetic splendors of his inherited vision of life were never known or suspected by any of his new associates in the United States Army. Nobody knew the story of his bereavements which had so changed him. He was a smallish, grimy, fast-moving, taciturn Apache of the Chiricahua people, once enemy of the Army, then captive, now soldier. Few enough read through to the man within his stale-smelling, alien person. Those who did saw at last a human being capable of loyalty, and a man of extraordinary intelligence when dealing with the natural materials of his inheritance and his world.

xlii

The ambulance party with its outriders crossed country that faded and swam in the heat of the day and cracked with cold at night. Matthew said to himself that it was like crossing a succession of great blazing platters whose rims were mountains. The color amazed him—some of the mountains were of reddish rock, and others took every shade of blue at odd times of day. There were whole passages of white earth, and others whose prevailing color was a pale yellow, from a short bush that grew in profusion over the flats. He saw many varieties of cactus, and much mesquite and greasewood, and he saw these change hue and even outline when dust rose on hot winds to scour the desert and all things in it. He longed to see water, and he passed many a place where water had long ago done its work—dry gullies whose carved walls reflected the slicing power of storm water. How could any people live on such land? And yet he knew that this was the very theater of the enemy he had come to oppose, and of the other American soldiers with whom he would oppose him.

Matthew had formed an image of the place where he was going. Before leaving Washington, and after having said good-by to Laura, he had gone to the Adjutant General's Office in the War Department to take up extra copies of his orders. There he had asked an assistant adjutant general who was handling his papers,

"What does anybody know about Fort Delivery, Arizona?"

The clerical officer turned to a bookcase behind his desk and removed a large thick volume which he handed to Matthew.

"Look it up in here," he said. "You will find a description."

Matthew took the book to a vacant table and sat down to read. The volume was a report of the Surgeon General to the Adjutant General on the hygiene of the Army. The subject required a description of the living conditions at all regularly maintained army posts. As he read, Matthew learned much about Fort Delivery, and with an hour to spare, he ended by asking for paper and pen and ink so he might make a copy of the pages which concerned him.

Now on his journey by ambulance from Driscoll on the railroad to the fort, he took out his copy and read it again.

xliii

FORT DELIVERY, ARIZONA TERRITORY
Information Furnished by Assistant
Surgeon William O. Sennis,
United States Army

This post is situated on the northern Sonoran deserts in latitude 32° 30' north and longitude 113° 39' west, at an elevation of 1650 feet above sea level. It is reached by the rail lines of the Atlantic and Pacific Railroad from east and west, via the junction point of Driscoll. From Driscoll a distance of ninety miles must be traversed to the fort by waggon or horseback. From the east, the railroad passes through the town of Tucson, which is the territorial capital, lying ninety-six miles from Driscoll. From the west, the railroad, stretching from the west coastal terminus of San Diego, passes through almost no settlements. Since its complete establishment in 1882 and subsequent operation on schedule, the rail line has received little threat from Indians. Overland travel by waggon, however, and movements of cattle herds, horses, and marching troops, as well as isolated settlements, are still in danger of Indian attack. Letters posted at Washington take from ten days to two weeks to reach the fort.

The terrain in the vicinity of the post presents monotony nearby and variety in the distance. Hardly perceptible undulation of the desert floor appears to have influenced the placement of the post. The post, which is roughly rectangular in occupied area, lies with its long sides at an angle to the north, and is consequently oriented north-east to south-west. The immediate vicinity is open desert country, with pasturage of gramma grass southeast of the habitations. North of the post lies a dry gully varying in width from ten to twenty feet, and in depth from five to fifteen feet in a distance of two miles in each direction from the fort. Five miles east is a range of low sandy hills whose drainage in storms has created the dry gully already described. To the north at about thirty miles' distance rises the rocky profile of the Phantom Mountains, so called, according to local tradition, because of their relative invisibility in dust which is swept up against their skirts by constant desert winds. To the west and south at a distance of four to five miles is a wide lowered basin whose western rim is broken by innumerable little gullies and canyons that look like the spaces between spread fingers. Sixteen miles further

west is the only live water source in the area other than the wells
at the fort. This is called Arrel Spring. It lies at the foot of a rocky
ledge and supports a single cottonwood tree. In times of quiet among
the Indians, soldiers from the post occasionally range as far as the
spring on grazing parties. Indians use it as a watering place on their
travel overland on foot or horse. To the south of Fort Delivery
nothing is visible but the desert, reaching to Mexico sixty miles
distant and, beyond the border, into Sonora.

Mesquite, ironwood, creosote bush, palo-verde, artemisia, various
species of *opuntia* and *cereus,* and *cactaceae* in abundance may be
seen in the area. Great sweeps of gramma and other grasses occur
as wilderness pasturage in various places. These grasses are used as
cover for their movements by Indians advancing to the attack of
camping grazers or overland travellers. Such lands, valuable as ranch
properties, are sought by prospectors and agents, often against Indian
claims which have no legal evidence for their validity.

In the Phantom Mountains ores are undoubtedly present in com-
mercial quantities. Scrub and live-oak and pine of large growth occur.
Building timber is almost all in inaccessible situations. Quail and
rabbits are abundant in the desert, and deer, bear and wild cats such
as the puma are present in the mountains, though less frequently
than in the northern parts of the territory. Coyotes, rattlesnakes,
scorpions, lizards (including the gila monster), centipedes and
tarantulas are generally wide-spread. The soil is dry and porous, and
with distance passed, shows varying colors, as yellow of ochre, white
of gypsum, pink and grey from sandstone, and pale brown of ordinary
sand.

Fort Delivery was founded as a one-company post in 1872 when
active operations were conducted against the Apache raiders of
northern Mexico and southern Arizona. It was abandoned with the
temporary pacification of these people in the campaign of the mid-
seventies. One year ago it was reactivated again as the base of a
garrison of a single troop of cavalry. It is the farthest west and south
of the Arizona armed establishments, and is employed usually as an
observation and listening post for the movements, activities and
temper of the Chiricahua Apaches who range indiscriminately between
the Arizona territory and northern Sonora, Mexico.

The climate is warm and dry. By day in summer the thermometer
may show a maximum heat of 120° F. and by night within the same
twenty-four hour period a minimum of 45° F. Thunderclouds frequently show above the Phantom Mountains, but their delivery of
rain as they pass to the southward and eastward rarely occurs more
than once every six weeks, when it may take the form of cloudburst,

with consequent flow of water in the gullies and other eroded passages. In winter the rains are lighter though of much longer duration. Snow falls on the mountains but not on the desert. For most of the year the winds are variable and light, except when immediately preceding a thunderstorm, when they are tempestuous; and during the spring and summer months, and even occasionally in winter, when they blow steadily from the southwest often carrying driving storms of heavy dust lifted from the desert surface. In such storms visibility is often reduced to zero.

The structures of Fort Delivery are built around a parade ground 380 feet long by 260 feet. The long sides lie east-west. The buildings are arranged along the sides of the parade-ground as follows: on the west is the main gate, which is wide enough for the entry of waggons and heavy caissons, though no major artillery is found at the post. The gate is continued on both sides with extensions of palisade made from saplings plastered with mud, standing eight feet high. On the north side, turning the corner from the palisade, there is open space for about ten yards. There follows at the west end of the north line the quarters of the commanding officer and post headquarters. Three sets of officers' quarters complete the north line. Again turning the square there is ten yards of open space. On the east line are a storage building and stables behind which is the horse corral. A fenced yard for beef cattle is attached to the south. Another stretch of open space as at other corners marks the southeast corner. The south line comprises a blacksmith shop attached to which is the guardhouse. The long barrack of company quarters and quarters for laundresses are situated in the south line. The parade is without turf. The surface is dusty. The flagpole stands before the headquarters building. A well providing clear, cold but strongly alkaline water is situated in front of the company quarters. Water is taken by bucket to all points of use. Cooking facilities are separate from residential quarters, and are built behind, and close to the back doors of, each building. The sinks for each set of quarters and the barracks are beyond the cook-houses, and consist of deep trenches enclosed by walls of brush and earth plaster. For ornament and shade a row of cottonwood saplings was planted to line the inner rectangle of the post, and was watered assiduously for two years, at the end of which time the trees, evidently reaching with their roots to a stratum of concentrated alkaline salts, died. They have not been replaced.

All structures are built of adobe, with earthen floors, mud roofs (with exception noted below) and open fireplaces. After heavy rains, leaks appear in the roofs, and repair is constant. The commanding officer's quarters is the only building with shingled roof. It is 42 feet wide and 36 feet from front to back. A hall 14 feet wide runs through the center of the house. The front door opens into this from a porch with a low wooden pediment supported by two posts. At the rear of the hall is a back door. From this hall on the left front opens the headquarters office 14 feet wide by 16 feet long. Beyond it is the sitting room, 14 feet wide by 20 feet long. Across the hall on the right are bedroom and dining room in matching dimensions. Ceilings are 10 feet high. The next two sets of officers quarters consist of three rooms each, while the last set, much smaller, contains one room and a recessed alcove large enough for a double bed.

The company quarters consist of an adobe building 150 by 20 feet, containing dormitory, company office, and a walled-off wing entered separately which is used as the hospital. The dormitory is lighted by twenty windows, is warmed by stoves and fireplaces, is well-ventilated, and is furnished with iron cots. It provides 900 cubic feet of air-space per man.

The post vegetable garden is located east and north of the commanding officer's quarters. Owing to scarcity of water, the crops cannot be large. The same privation makes bathing facilities less than satisfactory. The men are not permitted to bathe more often than once a week, but this is required. Drinking-water is cooled by means of porous *ollas,* or clay pots. These, when filled, are suspended in a current of air, and protected from the direct and indirect rays of the sun; evaporation occurs readily, and thus the temperature of the water is reduced.

The cemetery is distant about an eighth of a mile southeast of the buildings. It measures 50 by 40 feet, and contains the graves of 9 soldiers and 3 citizens.

The means of subduing fire are buckets and barrels, kept constantly filled.

Consolidated sick report for Fort Delivery cannot be submitted for the current year owing to incomplete data. Present figures indicate the following among *General Diseases,* A: typho-malarial fever, 2 cases; remittent fever, 1 case; intermittent fever, 31 cases; other cases of this group, 6 cases. Among *General Diseases,* B: rheumatism, 4 cases; syphilis, 11 cases; consumption, 2 cases, 1 death; other diseases of this group, 1. Among *Local Diseases:* catarrh and bronchities, 29 cases; pneumonia, 3 cases; pleurisy, 2 cases; diarrhoea and dysentery, 54 cases, 1 death; gonorrhea, 4 cases; other local diseases, 97 cases. *Alcoholism,* 2 cases. Among *Violent Diseases and Deaths:* gunshot wounds, 4 cases; arrow wounds, 1 case, 1 death; suicide, 1 death; other accidents and injuries, 18 cases.

Fort Delivery lies sufficiently distant from the existing Apache Indian reservations so that regular commerce with the Indians is not maintained. Occasional Indian parties which appear are invariably members of the untamed Apaches who maintain their bases in northern Mexico, and who now and then penetrate into the Territory either for raids or to obtain information on activities of white settlements and garrisons. When possible, they are apprehended and sent under escort to the reservation. More often, so great is their skill as travellers, hunters and raiders, they obtain their quarry and retreat swiftly to safety beyond the border 40 miles distant. A word as to the construction of these people may be appropriate.

The physique of these Indians, to a casual observer, does not appear to be at all a striking or unusual one, either in respect to size or development, but on closer inspection it will be observed that they are compactly built, and are generally well-muscled and sinewy. Their chests are generally deep and square, the sternum and clavicles standing forward prominently, and well up, indicating great chest capacity. Their hands and feet, of both men and women, are remarkably small and delicately formed, the ankles and wrists remarkably so. The women are more heavily muscled than the men, owing to the constant drudgery they undergo. They carry readily two hundred pounds or more upon their backs. The physiognomy of these people in repose is very mild, and as pleasant as their coarse, semi-mongoloid features will permit, but during excitement it lights up, and every feature, particularly the eye, betokens deviltry and bloodthirstiness. This ferocity of countenance in these people has even been observed by the writer during the excitement attendant on their witnessing a dance by masked figures. Their morality as regards truth and honesty is found to be high. A liar is contemned and tabooed among them, debts are scrupulously paid, both among themselves and when dealing with whites. Still, it must be said that many of them will steal when opportunity offers, and when at war, or engaged on missions sanctioned by their people as a whole, they are capable of the most unconscionable and indeed indescribable atrocities.

In summary it can be said that where other posts of the United States Army are located primarily for convenience and comfort within a given strategic area, Fort Delivery stands where it does, removed from almost every source of comfort and convenience, for reasons based on strategic considerations alone.

Respectfully submitted,
Wm. O. Sennis,
Ass't Surgeon, U.S.A.

As he finished reading this description, the image which passed in strong light through Matthew's mind was not that of the sunny, dust-swept post, but that of Laura.

"How will you like it, my darling?" he wondered, looking out through the rear opening of the canvas over him. His belly went hollow at the thought of so much reinforcement—the unpromising aspect of Fort Delivery—for the masterly campaign of Mrs. Greenleaf. And then he felt his face turn hot, and his mind, too, as he said in his thought, "They won't stop us. She will come because I will be there." He felt beloved, and therefore strong, and thus equal to creating anywhere in any condition the life Laura would ask of him.

xliv

A week after Matthew's arrival at Fort Delivery the wagon was to leave with mail for the railroad. He sent with it a letter to Laura, enclosing the official description of the post which he had copied in Washington, and giving her his first impressions, including these:

The officer who wrote the report on this place was accurate and thorough, but seeing it makes a difference. It is the difference between a map and the country it depicts. Things standing up on the ground and throwing shadows are different from flat outlines. But the physical aspect of things is fairly well caught, and you can trust his words.

The human aspects are another matter, for of course these change, and he didn't set out to describe them anyway. I don't know if I can. Anyway, I was received by the acting commanding officer, First Lieutenant Theodore Mainwaring. He has been in command for months, expecting the new C.O., a Major Prescott, every week. Evidently orders have been mixed up. It is a pity, for the quality of command at present leaves much to be desired. The state of the garrison is deplorable—lazy, insolent, complaining, and generally below par in health. In a place like this, where things at best are difficult, effort ten times over must be expended to render life worthwhile and rewarding. Mainwaring showed me around the day after I arrived—we got in after dark—and at every example of bad discipline and poor order he was too eager to explain and apologize before I had made any remarks at all. He looks at me out of the corner of his eye to see what I think. Well, I am the lowest ranking officer here, and my thinking remains private. But if the new C.O. don't come along soon, we must have trouble of some sort or another. When matters decline, if they are not reversed, a crisis must come.

Mainwaring is personally agreeable enough, and so is his wife, whom he calls Kitty. He is a big, rather soft, loose-skinned fellow, eight or ten years my senior (class of '70). Nice-looking and always grinning. You can't help liking him when he puts himself out for you. She is small, thin, pretty with pale eyes and dark lashes like a kitten, hence Kitty, I suppose. Very social. Loves to entertain, and gasps over the idea of entertaining *here*. She calls it 'Fort Deliver-Me.' Is madly in love with Teddy, as she calls him, and when she says anything to anybody else, she keeps watching him as if it is meant for him. They have no children, but keep a big greyhound, named Garibaldi, a fine animal whom she adores. She is kind and helpful, and swears she will make my quarters attractive, though I'd be glad to fix them up myself. I'll describe them below.

The other officer here is the surgeon, Captain Gray, and his wife. They live in quarters #2. (The Mainwarings of course occupy #1, the commanding officer's quarters.) The Grays are elderly, very nice, both English-born, and keep rather to themselves, though of course in so small a place, we all see each other constantly. He has said to me that as soon as he thinks I have digested my impressions of Fort Delivery, he intends to have a talk with me. I shall welcome this, though it may create certain difficulties, for already I feel that I am caught between two conditions. One, my proper loyalty and demeanor as a subordinate, and two, my professional conscience as an officer who must refuse to let near-disgraceful conditions continue to exist, if they can be improved. For now, I'll content myself with remarking that the men simply have not got enough to do, and are deteriorating of it. Not enough to do, and this in a place where the most active reconnaissance and patrol action should be maintained at all times! Well, don't get me started.

My quarters are at the end of the line. They offered me #3, also vacant at my arrival, but I decided to move now into #4, as I would only have to shift from 3 to 4 when the new C.O. does arrive. Adobe, flat roof, thick walls, one room, but with a kind of recess where a big bed could stand. Right now, I am still cleaning it out, and having some men paint the walls inside with whitewash, and put glass in the rear window, and fix the front door so it'll actually shut and stay shut. We are sprinkling down the earth floor every day and tamping it to harden it, so the dust won't continually blow up off it. I have an iron cot from the company barracks, and a table, and a canvas chair, and an oil lamp, and a mirror, and a basin, and a locker, and my own few things I brought along, dearest and best of which is the little French enamel box you gave me with you-know-what inside. I hold it in my hand when I am sitting and thinking, and when I go to sleep at night. At night when the moon comes in the brilliance is unbelievable, it makes a shining white page on my floor. I look at it and think that the same light shines upon where you are, and it puts me with you. Do you feel this too?

My room: all I can think of is what it will be like after you come here to do the right things to it. It really can be made very nice. Mrs. Mainwaring says she is going to make me some curtains, but I don't want them, and don't know how to tell her so. I will think of a way.

One thing may help the general situation. Now that I am here, Mainwaring says he may devote all his time to the office, and make me troop commander. I'd have much to do. I would start with the horses, who have a generally neglected and dejected air about them. Meanwhile, I'd come to know the men, and they me. I expect the horses will like me better.

You will worry until I tell you how I take my meals. The Grays and the Mainwarings both invited me to share theirs, and so I do, by turns, and will make up out of my ration allowance each month what is due each family. It is kind of them. They are all most kind, and seem glad to see me; but this is only because I am an event, as a newcomer in so remote and outlandish a spot.

He closed with endearments which gave him deep happiness which lasted, after a spell of hot, quick sadness which did not.

xlv

Matthew amused himself by thinking that Captain A. Cedric Gray, Surgeon, U.S. Army, seemed to carry his character around with him as an exhibit of which he was indignantly jealous and proud. It would have astonished Captain Gray to hear of this impression. He was entirely unself-conscious. If he impressed Matthew, and other Americans in this way, it was because he was in their eyes so different from themselves. The difference which to him was native and unremarkable lay in the fact that he was an Englishman by birth and tradition, though since his nineteenth year he had lived in the United States and considered himself as good an American as the next man.

But his accent remained English, his kind of mental process was crisply logical to an unusual degree, and his outspokenness was sometimes unflattering, which often disconcerted the libertarians among whom he had come to live. He was of medium stature, his hair was grizzled and short, his mustache and beard were trimmed close, and his light-blue eyes under a habitual scowl held a challenging vitality of gaze. If he seemed generally critical in his views, this did not mean that he liked nothing. In fact, he so much wanted the best in life for creatures who worked to deserve it, or who could not help themselves, like children and common soldiers and domestic animals, that anything short of it made him cross on their behalf.

One evening after supper, which they had shared with Matthew, the Grays asked him to linger for a special treat—a sip of Scotch liqueur. They were comfortable in the sitting room, where over the ragged easy chairs Mrs. Gray had thrown large paisley shawls. By lamplight, which drew moths in the hot evening, which they ignored, they talked about what most engaged their thoughts—those things which were nearest, and those farthest away.

"I expect you know what you think, by now," said the surgeon to Matthew, "about all this." He gestured to indicate the whole fort.

"I do, sir. If I may speak unofficially, I don't think we can wait much longer for the new commanding officer to clean things up."

"Nor do I. But short of insubordination, what could be done?"

"I don't know, sir."

"Oddly enough, I was a line officer in the war, and I commanded a battalion in action. I could manage here well enough. But my orders don't authorize me to take command here."

"You were a battalion commander?"

Mrs. Gray smiled at the diversity of her remarkable husband.

"He is a patchwork quilt," she said. "You never saw so many shapes and colors. All of them bonny."

"Aggh," said the surgeon, "when she becomes Scotch, look out. She's turning over in her mind a long story."

"It is natural," she replied, "so far away, in a place as strange as this, to think back to other days and places. —Let me show you," she said, putting aside her sewing basket. She went to a cabinet and brought out a portfolio and opened it, showing Matthew a thick sheaf of water-color drawings—landscapes, soldiers in groups, formal rows of brick houses in a city street, aspects of ships.

"He did them," she added. "Everywhere he goes, he makes a record of what he sees. Everywhere but here."

"I've had no time," said the doctor. "I have time for everything, and so I do nothing. It takes a busy man to do anything extra, like drawing."

"They are very pleasing pictures," said Matthew, who had never looked at pictures, and did not know quite what to say. These now interested him more as expressions of Doctor Gray's personality than as works of art. "I would like to look at them more carefully sometime."

"You shall." The portfolio was put away. They all knew he would never see them again.

"Sir," said Matthew, "Mr. Mainwaring said he might give me command of the troop. Has he said anything to you about it?"

"No. But I wish he would. I can see that even with all your inexperience you would do better than he." Mrs. Gray made an inward sigh at this frankness. "Well, Maud, I mean it, and so shall say it."

Matthew felt obliged not to pursue the matter since it contained the materials of shock. He said respectfully and with interest,

"Doctor, are you English?"

"I was. I was born near Lechlade, Gloucestershire, where my father was estate manager for the Earl of Faringdon." He looked in mind at the desert around him and then at the country of his birth. "First in life I knew deep forest and water meadow. Through them ran a little stream where I played. When I heard that it became the Thames, that ran to the sea, I was taken by the news. It was not unusual for a boy of my time and station to think of the sea as a career. And so did I. When I was twelve, my father turned me over to a shipmaster he knew. I was articled as a cabin boy."

"Cedric," said his wife, "Mr. Hazard doesn't want to hear all this."

"Don't you?" asked the doctor flatly of Matthew.

"I do, of course I do," said Matthew, leaning forward with his hands clasped between his knees.

"There," said the doctor to his wife. "I shall proceed, for it is my experience that in out-of-the-way places it is our past lives by which we make our new friends and command the future. —My father drove me down to Folkestone through Fairford and Winchester in a two-wheeled cart and said good-by to me with the fiercest look

I had ever seen on his face. I know now that his loving ferocity was an attempt to make his lad a man right there and then."

"To a surprising degree," said Mrs. Gray, "it worked."

"I had a handful of sovereigns tied in a handkerchief which Lord Faringdon had given me. Two years later on my first return home I still had them."

"He kept them, actually," said Mrs. Gray, "until he arrived in New York in 1844 on a sailing packet."

"That is so. There I stepped ashore, changed my money, and remained to become an American."

"He used to say he came ashore once too often."

His time aboard ship in all those years had been given to his duties and to reading. He loved best of all to read medical books, such as his first captain kept in his cabin in case of emergency among crew or passengers. On later voyages in greater ships he made friends with the surgeon if there was one aboard; and he knew he wanted to become a doctor in his turn. For his first year in America he worked in the New York office of an importing house. He saved much of his wages, and when he could, he went to Philadelphia to begin his training for medicine. Here too he had a job, but his energy seemed boundless. His sense of responsibility, acquired at sea, and his own lively intelligence assured him of steady employment. Between his job and his studies he worked fourteen hours a day and prospered on it.

He even found time to haunt the libraries and museums of Philadelphia. He particularly enjoyed the Peale Museum with its combination of exhibits in natural history and the fine arts. He became an amateur of drawing, and formed the habit of a lifetime in making sketches.

In 1849, when he was twenty-four years old, he returned to England for a visit with his family. He was anxious to marry. The girls he knew in America were all very well, but he wanted a wife who would know him not only as he was, but as a child of his old country. After a few days spent at home in permitting his parents, and old Lord Faringdon, to be proud of him in their uncommunicative fashion, he borrowed the two-wheeled cart and rode over to Cirencester for divine services in the ancient church there. The curate, an elderly man long since resigned to the remarkable persistence of life in his vicar, had a daughter eighteen years old.

"Her name was Maud Cantwell. I met her in the churchyard after vespers."

"He blustered a bit," she said.

It pleased Cedric Gray that even his most blustery opinions seemed acceptable to her, as they had not seemed to be to girls in Philadelphia, who were inclined to wrangle with him in a maidenly way.

"I took his manner for granted," said Maud Gray. "I had seen it before. Englishmen are born knowing—and all but saying—what is right and what ought to be done, and done promptly, whether at home or anywhere else in the world."

He asked her after several visits to her in Cirencester whether she might ever think of living in America.

"Do you remember what you answered?" he asked.

"I do. I thought it over, and then I said that it would not matter where I lived, if my place in life should take me away from home, for I had faith in God, and I believed people everywhere tried to do the best they could, and I thought I could do my share of duty in America as anywhere else."

Would she consider becoming the wife of a man of medicine, which might at first be a difficult life?

She considered the healing art to be a noble vocation, and would be honored to assist it in any way in her small power, if she should be called upon to do so.

It was then proper for him to ask her if she would marry him when he received his degree, which would take three more years.

She believed that she would be able to give him her answer if they would write to one another in the interim and know one another through a frank exchange of their inmost thoughts and hopes.

It was such a reply as must have been approved by the Queen in her exemplary family life. The curate approved the tentative engagement, and Cedric Gray returned to Philadelphia considering himself as good as married.

"In 1852," he said, "she came alone by sailing packet to Boston." He looked proudly at her now as he had then. "It took courage to cross the Atlantic alone in those ships. I had offered to go home to fetch her, but she told me that the expense was considerable, and we would need all our resources to weather the first years of marriage and the uncertainties of a new medical practice." He looked at her again and said as if admonishing history itself, "Maud Gray is one of the few women in the world who knows how to be a darling without sacrificing everyone else to the idea."

They were married in Boston's Trinity Church, with witnesses provided by the rector.

"I did love Boston," she said.

They expected to spend a week there. Through their new friend at Trinity Church they met a few people, and finally an old surgeon who might do with a young assistant. After various restrained interviews by the old doctor, Doctor Gray found himself as the assistant in a flourishing practice. Boston did not take eagerly to strangers, but Doctor Gray had the advantage of impeccable local sponsorship, and if a man *must* be a stranger in Boston, the best kind for him to be was an Englishman, and one so grainy in temperament and clear of mind as Doctor Gray.

"We were happy there," murmured Mrs. Gray.

In Boston were born their two children, a boy and a girl. There Doctor Gray found enough ferment of opinion and individuality in conversation to interest him. There Mrs. Gray became an American without having to endure contrasts in atmosphere too sharply different from life in England—such contrasts as she might have encountered farther west. Boston was the real center of the American conscience, and admitted it, especially in respect to the issue of slavery. Abolitionist sentiment, debate and action were constant and lively in Boston during the '50's, and Doctor Gray strongly expressed his views against slavery and any individual or institution which condoned it for any reason whatever.

When the War came in 1861, he arranged for his practice to be divided between several other doctors in Boston, and offered himself to the first volunteer mustering of Lincoln's army as a medical officer. He was accepted immediately. Maud Gray and the children remained in Boston throughout the War.

Doctor Gray passed much of his time in war in a state of controlled rage.

In the first place, it seemed to him abominable that the matter of slavery had to be fought over; any civilized man must admit offhand that slavery should be abolished by law and the law never again challenged. In the second place, the issue took too long to be decided. He resented every casualty which the War, and the philosophical and economic argument of its occasion, continued to cost month by month through the years. In the third place, he was nearly consumed by the anger which rose up in him at the incompetence of so much of the War's administration on both sides.

In his third year as a front-line surgeon he was attached to a unit commanded by an elderly major who, with every advantage on his side, yet withdrew his battalion in the face of far weaker but more gallant enemy forces.

"Stupendous imbecility!" roared Doctor Gray, and though he obeyed orders to retreat, he made his opinion plain far and wide.

Word of the action came to the ears of the general officer commanding in the vicinity. An investigation was ordered, and Doctor Gray volunteered to testify. The general himself presided, and heard Doctor Gray denounce the miserable old major in terms of "unparalleled pusillanimity," "cowardly disregard for the mission," "simian incompetence," and so on.

"What would you have done under the circumstances, doctor?" asked the general.

"I would have pulled out the center and sent it around the left flank, and closed the front-line gap by extension—" and proceeded with a fully developed plan of aggressive action which revealed, if he did say so, a full grasp of tactical and strategic principles. When he was done he was ordered to report in private to the general, who offered him a command as a line officer.

"If good surgeons are desperately needed, doctor," said the general, "good commanders are even more in short supply."

"I told him," said Doctor Gray, "that I could not abandon my medical duty on the grounds that casualties would continue to mount up, needing my help."

The general disposed of this by saying,

"Is it not better to prevent than cure?"

Doctor Gray reddened and agreed.

"Done!" said the general—it was Brevet Major General Alexander Upton Quait—and sent Doctor Gray to take command of his old battalion with the temporary rank of major.

So, having thought like a soldier, Major Gray became one, and finished the War in the line.

"So far as we knew," said Mrs. Gray to Matthew, "he was the only medical officer in the Civil War who also achieved the status of line officer."

The four years of the War were the greatest experience of Major Gray's life.

When the War ended he returned to Boston, intending to pick up again the threads and patterns of his civilian life. The attempt was a failure. He loved the Army too well to forget it. Maud Gray had no separate opinion of what the family should do. When he said to her that he would above all else like to be back in uniform as an army surgeon—for he still loved his medical work—she saw that he could have the substance of both his worlds if he returned to the Army. She encouraged him to go to Washington to see what could be done about obtaining a regular commission in the medical corps.

He arrived there just in time to see General Quait, who was preparing to leave for the Dakotas and the Sioux campaign. General Quait wrote a strong recommendation for him. Six months later Cedric Gray was again an officer, though with reduced rank. Gathering up his family he left Boston forever. His first station in his restored military status was with Quait in Dakota.

Among the things he loved about the United States was the extraordinary variety of experience which lay open to the men of his time and place there.

He did not feel unique in his history—almost everyone he knew on the frontier had a remarkable diversity in his background. If he had stayed in England he might never in his life have moved beyond London—perhaps Cheltenham and even Cirencester might have been his farthest horizon. His portfolios of sketches were a record of the changes, and contrasts, and degrees of learning which his hardy life brought to him, to which he was equal in his energy of action and opinion. His wife, saying little about her feelings, was equal to them too. Coming to the Indian West where hitherto their values had little relevance, they, and others like them, gave with their being the civilization which had made them.

They saw their children grow with satisfaction. Their son entered Harvard College. Their daughter married early, into the Army. Captain Gray and his wife proceeded on orders to Fort Delivery in 188–, unencumbered by anything, veterans of every possible discomfort in other army posts, and indifferent, he brusquely, she calmly, to whatever inconvenience and danger might await them.

"We have not, I suppose," said Mrs. Gray, "actually seen worse, but after years in the Army, it is all a same of a sameness."

They had made Matthew an occupant of their memories, and though there were many deep privacies which he could not know, and though the Grays themselves could not say forth all that they were and meant to each other, the three of them in their long evening together made, between them, a considerable awareness of each other.

Mrs. Gray was still small and delicate in appearance. Her hair was white. Her cheeks showed their fresh English color. She still spoke slowly and softly, but now in her years firmly. Her voice was appealing. There were marks of life in her face, and at moments she looked tired and drained, but then if she smiled, she seemed to lose years. Her husband loved to look at her. To him she was the most beautiful creature in the world. He sometimes wondered how she had endured all the storms that had come her way for living with him. Upon marrying she had resolved that her husband must always be right, in whatever situation. He did not realize, as they matured together, how often he decided what was right on the basis of what she would think. If he had his power, she had hers.

"Are you familiar, Mr. Hazard, with all our regulations?" asked the doctor in a brisk change of subject.

"Most, by now, I suppose."

"I'd only urge you to know best those dealing with safety."

"Oh: yes: those."

"Most important—never to go off post alone unless under orders. The women, of course, never, never without armed escort and then only for necessary travel in large parties."

"Yes, sir."

"All seems quiet. You would never believe such rules advisable. But then most of all is the time to be true to them."

"Yes, sir."

"The men get impatient. Who can blame them? They like to try their superiors. They like to risk a dare. Boys. Watching you with their tongues sticking out of the corners of their mouths, to see how far they can—" He shrugged and laughed. "They're not a bad lot, unless you think all humankind a bad lot, which I do not, being made, like the rest, of bone, gristle, fatty matter, guts, lungs, heart and hair —*and* the breath of God in all of it. If you know *where* you are, and *who* you are, you'll do, even here." He paused, looked down, and then again straight at Matthew. "That's the difficulty with Mr. Mainwaring. He may know where he is, but he doesn't know who he is."

"Cedric."

"Aagggh. I've done it again."

Matthew stood up and said good evening.

"We've been glad to have you. Some day you must get back at us by telling all about yourself."

"You had something to tell, sir. I have nothing. Yet."

When he was gone, Doctor Gray turned to his wife and said, "I love him for that 'yet,' don't you?"

xlvi

A few days later Matthew, on returning from the stables where he and Joe Dummy worked some young horses, found Mrs. Mainwaring in his quarters hanging new calico curtains at his rear window. The front window was already newly dressed.

"Oh!" she cried, blushing wildly pink, which made her blue eyes darker and her curly hair, moist with exertion, even more in disarray, "I meant to be finished and gone before you returned!"

His thoughts darkened. He did not want any woman but Laura to touch into his manner of living. He put his wide-brimmed hat and his sweated gloves on the packing-box table and lifted his hands to help her down from the stool on which she stood.

"But I am not finished!" she said.

"I will finish it. Thank you."

"Oh. I have intruded. I have made you cross. But I was only trying to—"

"No, no, Mrs. Mainwaring, thank you, it is ever so kind. They're very pretty curtains. They will keep me much cooler in here. But you mustn't go to any more trouble."

He took her hand and steadied her to the floor.

She stared up at him, stricken to think that again, again, once again, a gesture she had made to reach someone had somehow gone wrong; why, she could not say. How different it was to have been. . . . Busy work in secret, to surprise a nice, handsome young stranger who would add so much to the limited interest of life at the post; careful watching to see when he would be out so the surprise could be installed and ready for his return; his return, his delight, his instant visit to thank her, to admire her handicraft, to be touched by her ardent kindness, to realize what a splendid wife she made to a post commander; his admiration for her husband coming alight as a natural consequence of what he owed her for her generosity; a wonderful new friendship, and—and—other details of imagined pleasure. But what was the fact?—only a glum, dark young man, hot from work, and disarranged to find an unexpected female in his Spartan quarters, doing something for him which plainly he did not particularly welcome. Why? Oh why? She could not see that having invented a little drama which was to be played out according to her will only, for her gratification alone, it might not necessarily be gratifying to anyone else, and so must fail her rapturous fancy. She felt a chill of pride come over her. She lifted what of herself would lift—eyebrows, cheeks, shoulders, manner, and said, in her style of commanding officer's wife,

"So hope you will be more comfortable, Mr. Hazard. Do come to see us when you can. —Thank you—" the door. Holding a gather of her long skirts, she stepped her way in the sandy glare rapidly to her house at the head of the north line, a little distance away. Matthew watched after her, shaking his head at his clumsiness, and feeling her unspoken unhappiness, and taking blame—too much blame—for it upon himself.

That evening, when supper tasks were done, and the swift dark had fallen on a late twilight, the Grays could hear, and so could Matthew in his room, the ebb and flow of discord in Quarters 1.

Matthew did not know that he was the occasion for it. All that reached him was the alternation of stridencies with deeper-voiced grumbles. The two voices rose and fell, telling vaguely of misery and unpleasantness, want and denial. Matthew groaned at the vulgarity of it, and covered his ear with a pillow; but the night was not yet cool enough to permit that soft weight, and he uncovered, thinking crossly that when he should marry people would see what marriage could be like.

"I would not have told you, would I?" asked Kitty Mainwaring in the darkness of the bedroom where she lay with her husband, and whose open windows carried the tone if not the words of their continuing quarrel down the north line, "would I?—if there had been anything to concea? Would I be that much of a fool?"

"I don't like your bringing up that possibility at all. It never occurred to me."

"Then why do you heave and growl so, just because I made him a set of cheap little calico curtains from leftover material? Can't anybody do a simple kindness without being accused of—"

"I'm not accusing at all. I just don't think the wife of the command-ing officer—"

"Oh, the wife of the commanding officer. If you were anything of a commanding officer, you wouldn't even have to think about how to be one, much less use your wife to keep you full of—"

She desisted on a quick intake of breath. She had not meant to say this. She had even refused to think of the subject. She had no desire to kill anything in her husband's poor pride. Further, to scorn him as an officer was to throw away something of her own worth as his wife. She felt in the dark how she had wounded him. She bit her lips. Her heart surged toward him. He was so defenseless. He tried so hard. He was so generous to her. No man was perfect. Her heart felt a little stab of humility and pleasure: he had even been jealous because she made curtains for the handsome and lofty young lieu-tenant who had arrived at the fort. Poor Teddy, she said to herself, and, having hurt him as only she could hurt him, she was now faintly swollen with loving and protective feelings for him.

"Teddy, darling . . ." she whispered.

He refused to reply. Lying in the darkness, large, soft and mortally young in his vulnerable heart, he let tears of sorrow for his lot gather and sting along the edges of his eyelids. She was right. Her grasp of the truth was always horribly right. But why did she have to beat him with it? Other women became, or behaved like, what a man wanted them to be. Why not Kitty? But he knew why. It was because he could not make her conform to his will. How often he had vowed to show her: just as he vowed daily to show them, the others, the Grays, the soldiers, the War Department: show who was master around here, and who, however it might look for the moment, really had the long-term answer for—for everything.

The abiding concern of the Mainwarings was what others thought of them, and in every degree of dissembled anxiety, they searched for the reflections of themselves in their associates and superiors in the Army, who might have dismissed them as snobs except for the fact that they were both more or less miserable much of the time, making each other so, and even extending to others around them their bridling uneasiness; and for the further fact that with all their weak-ness and vanity, they possessed appealing traits which made claims upon friendship.

It was these traits which had drawn them to one another in their younger days, when what later came to seem like trying characteristics then seemed in the health and freshness of youth to be droll little vagaries which could be laughed or kissed away.

Kitty as a girl was proud, high-headed, inspired in her will, and determined to establish out of unpromising beginnings her own excellence. As a woman, years later, she bore the watered-down and matured reflections of those qualities, and now they seemed like anxiety, envy, willfulness and doubt.

Ted as a youth had been easygoing, cheerful, clumsy as a puppy and as playful; and as a man in middle life, he had become the victim of those traits until he seemed lazy, overeager to please, soft and troubled by the mystery of his failure to "go farther."

What had happened to them?

Teddy Mainwaring met Kitty Dodge in New York during a weekend in 1869. She was a working girl with whom he had an encounter one winter evening on a Fifth Avenue horsecar. The step at the rear of the car was icy. She slipped and fell in mounting it. He was waiting to enter the car behind her. He helped her up. She clung to him, shaken, and thanked him, and then bridling with virtue and ladyship, she detached herself and proceeded into the car under her own power. By the light of the oil lamp in the front of the cabin he watched her find a seat. She wore a little green velvet cap shaped like a canister. A voluminous cloak of black broadcloth trimmed with bars of green velvet swept from her shoulders down over the wide spread of her hoops. It was tied beneath her pointed little chin with a large bow of ribbed black silk. Ted Mainwaring had to smile because it made her look like a kitten. He was pleased with himself for noticing this, for he knew that ordinarily his imagination was not active.

On the bench where she sat there was room for him beside her, and he took it. She stared straight ahead to discourage familiarities from a West Point cadet in uniform, for she knew "all about" those young men of the Academy.

But he would talk to her, he was merry and at ease, and she lost her suspicion of him. She permitted him to see her home to her doorstep, confessing that she was still shaken by her small mishap, but he could not tell whether this was or was not a true statement.

She lived with her widowed mother whom she supported by work as a sempstress in a downtown dress factory. Her specialty was "finishing."

What was this? he asked.

"Oh, sewing braid, and cord, and bugles, galloons and fancy buttons, on the frocks which the other girls put together."

The work was hard and ill-paid, and she hated it, but what could she do? She was clever with her fingers and it was all she could find.

"After Papá died, and Mamá was so ill, and we realized we were so poor, *somebody* had to do something, and I was that somebody, and so . . ." she spread her hands in comic gallantry which touched him, as it was meant to do. Many of the other girls in the shop— she delicately made plain—were of a type no lady could enjoy knowing. She was pathetic and firm about being a gentlewoman in unlucky circumstances. Her eyes blazed with determination to free herself of that life somehow, but the terms were going to be her own, and proper, and "nice."

Ted asked if he could call again at her lodging house in West Twenty-third Street, and she replied that she would be pleased to have him meet her mother, who was a semi-invalid. It was not entirely a romantic opening, but it sufficed. He saw her whenever he could come to New York. He became her habit, and she his desire. He achieved it one night in his boardinghouse a few blocks from hers. The extent of her joy frightened him, but not so greatly as that of the horror which came in a storm afterward. Her self-hatred was surpassed only by her hatred of him; and the only way he could restore calm and perceive any future at all was to promise that they would be married. Immediately upon being graduated with his class, he found himself a married man with an ailing mother-in-law to keep, in addition to a bride.

He was a kind young man, mild in all his humors, and Kitty won dominion over him by her high-keyed prettiness and vivacity. If she fell into low spirits fairly regularly, he knew what lay at the root of these, and he would hold her little sharp chin in his big thumb and fingers, and shake it playfully, and tell her she was not to go on all her life brooding about that mistake of theirs in the boardinghouse before they were married. What was done was done, and they were man and wife, and what difference did it make?

But *she* knew—oh, *she* knew, and even if nobody else knew, that was enough: and sometimes she thought people looked at her as if *they* knew, too.

He would say, in various ways,

"You know something? I'm not sorry it happened. I'm glad. How do you like that?"

"Teddy!"

"Yes, because you know why? You might not have married me if I hadn't taken advantage of you"—this was her officially established version of the episode—"and then where would I be?"

She loved him for this. If he ambled through life in a loose, hound-like way, gentle and undemonstrative, taking things as they came, she was alive with inner pulsations of ambition which he could feel when he held her, and he was choked with love which he could not readily express when he felt the contrast between his big, heavy, slow self and her little, thin, troubled and determined person.

Mrs. Dodge lived with them wherever they went—Fortress Monroe, Fort Porter, Fort Leavenworth—until she died in 1879. More often than not Lieutenant Mainwaring was assigned to quartermaster duties, though his branch was cavalry. This was a source of pity and annoyance to Kitty. She was glad her husband was mostly safe from hazardous duty, for then she need not worry about his safety, or about (a buried thought) what would become of her if he should be incapacitated or killed on duty. But she was also cross and sorry that he was not given more dashing duties, with troops, such as all the really stylish officers seemed to have. Correspondingly, their wives seemed more stylish and dashing than she did.

"There is," she would sometimes blurt out in one of her tirades, "there really is a difference between being a storekeeper's wife and the wife of a fighting man!"

Ted would sigh and admit it, and beg her, if she must quarrel, at least to keep her voice down so the whole post—Monroe, Porter, Leavenworth—would not know that the Mainwarings were going at each other again. At such times he just held on, remembering that after each time she let herself go, she seemed for days or weeks to be her sweetest self, and his life was again easier under her ingenious and efficient attentions.

Everyone else was fond of Kitty in her "good times," too. At such times she could not do enough for others. She interested herself in the problems and needs of enlisted men's wives, and their children, and when there was anything of a party going on in the officers' circles, she was always to be counted on to perform small miracles of festivity. She cooked special dishes and made remarkable desserts. She had an eye and a hand for decorating tables, making place cards with her little water-color box, and arranging bouquets, and remodeling party gowns until they looked like new. When busy with such projects in such periods, she looked years younger, her eyes shone, her cheeks were hot and pink, her sharp little voice lost its edge and took on warmth and charm, and everyone would be moved to say that Kitty Mainwaring, all in all, was really a dear little thing, so capable, so useful to have around.

And then, and then—at some fancied slight, or some vagrant recollection of what she had meant her life to be instead of what it had come to be, or an innocent bit of obtuseness on Ted's part, she would change in a flash, and their little world was turned into a prison for both of them, where they were shackled to each other and barred from happier atmospheres.

Her mood would cast him down until he sank into sensations of failure. What did others think of him? He would peer anxiously to know. Was the C.O. planning to ask for his transfer elsewhere? The thought was enough to keep him awake at night, next to Kitty, who seemed often to sleep with angry dreams. But if the C.O. would casually happen to greet Ted with a smile or offer him a cigar or tell him a racy story, Ted would be raised by such mild acts of comradeship to a thudding happiness and restored faith in himself; and for the C.O., or anyone else who showed him civility even a trifle above the ordinary, he would carry vague but powerful feelings of loyalty, even—hazily he would muse—even to the point of dying in combat for him, if such a dramatic necessity should arise.

Everyone said there was no harm in him anywhere, but nobody thought of him first if there was a matter of responsibility or sharp judgment to be handled. In his lumbering, pleasant figure lived an eternal boy. It was this whom others addressed when they used his nickname, "Teddy."

When the Mainwarings acquired a dog, everyone was glad. Teddy had a creature to command, Kitty a pet to love, somewhat inordinately. When they were ordered to Fort Delivery they took the dog with them, for they *knew* he would pine away and die if they should leave him behind, or—better yet in terms of sentiment—they *knew* he would set out to find them, wherever they were, as dogs had been known to do when separated from masters they adored.

They always made a splendid first impression wherever they went, for they knew how to present themselves at their best until habitude and familiarity slowly wore away the exhilaration of the new, and its concealment of their troubling self-doubts.

"Teddy"—her whisper was slow and full of pity for the human

capacity of error. After their gusts of despisings and accusings they would humble themselves for their bad tempers, and come together again in a sort of mutual protective association, each finding in the other's weakness a consoling image of his own.

"Teddy . . ." she said, coming close to him, and sounding more than half asleep, "I made you cry, and I am sorry. I am a horrible woman. Scold me."

Her tones were seductive. She settled herself in the swells and hollows of his body. He sighed with creature comfort, and took comfort of heart from that of his flesh. His sigh was enough for her. She slept; and so at last did Fort Delivery.

xlvii

But the next morning forgiveness did not emanate from the commanding officer to all those around him. He sent for Lieutenant Hazard.

"Now at last he's going to give me the troop!" said Matthew to himself. But when he stood in the headquarters office he was not so sure. Lieutenant Mainwaring let him stand for a moment while he continued to lean over some papers on his roll-top desk which stood in a corner and thus gave the back of its user to the room. Presently, with an unconvincing start as of a man emerging from deep concentration, he turned to see Matthew, and then swung about in his high-backed swivel chair.

"Well, Hazard," he said. "Good morning. I won't keep you. I just wanted to let you know that on thinking it over, I believe it best for me to retain permanent command of the troop. I will also keep the first platoon, but will delegate Sergeant Fry to act as platoon commander. I have assigned the second platoon to you, as of today. Good luck with it, and don't hesitate to bring your problems to me."

He smiled widely, which made his eyes water slightly. He seemed to plead for forgiveness after giving an order which must displease Matthew. The commanding officer, making the gestures of command and decision, seemed unconvinced of their justice, and so convinced nobody else.

"Yes, sir," said Matthew.

Mainwaring gazed at him. What was there about Hazard which led happily married females to put themselves out making curtains for him? Whatever it was, Mainwaring did not like it, he feared it, and deviously he must express his feeling.

"Thanks, my lad," said Mainwaring, nodding genially in dismissal. He had proved how strong he was in his weakness.

The orders designating Matthew were read aloud by himself as acting adjutant at the evening parade on the same day, and in the following days he entered upon his duties with the second platoon. He had twenty-seven men. They ranged in age from nineteen to the mid-forties. Several were English-speaking foreigners from the British Isles or colonies. One was a German immigrant, two were Swedish, one was a Frenchman who had fought in the Franco-Prussian War. The remainder were native Americans. Joe Dummy was attached to the second platoon as scout. Matthew drilled his platoon separately whenever possible. He believed in daily drill. He explained why to the men, and if they did not believe him, they obeyed him with some hidden flicker of smartness and pride as he put them through their evolutions across the bare, dust-drifted parade ground.

He carried with him something of the flourish of the military academy. He was one used to walking beneath plumes. His figure was agent of an inner smartness of spirit; and that spirit was proud not only of itself but also of the purpose to which it had been called. At drill Matthew was impersonal, sharp, demanding; he saw every man at every second, or so the troopers believed. His eye was like an eagle's. His voice was direct. It rang out in his commands and in his corrections. Walking, his shoulders were so straight and his back so arched that if his men gave even a poor imitation of him, they began to look soldierly. If he made them sweat, they sweated no harder than he. Each man had but to drill himself. The lieutenant had to drill them all. He would walk in step close behind a man in ranks, and bark the cadence into his ear, and at a new command execute it in close step with him, giving advice between counts:

"Hup-two-hup-four, hup-keep-hup-straight, hup-two-piece-up, hup-don't-hup-slouch, hup-two-hup-four, ve-ry-good-four, front-rank-hold-down, hup-two-hup-four."

At the end of each drill period he would seat the men and discuss the day's exercises with them, giving a critique as to a class of officers. The military culture he brought to them was that of the parade. It might not in itself be useful against enemy Indians, but it made an atmosphere of command and obedience in which could grow the harder lessons which the troopers might be called upon to apply.

Repeatedly he obtained permission from Lieutenant Mainwaring to drill his platoon separately. The first platoon, under Sergeant Fry, performed its own drill at the opposite end of the parade ground. During drill period, Mainwaring came to look on, approve all, and return to his meager duties in the office.

At the corral, Matthew gave his men the school of the horse. He was a good rider, though not a spectacular one. He began with instructions on care of the horse, and the platoon spent hours grooming their animals, rehearsing treatments for various sicknesses and injuries, and feeling their way to identify with them. He made them repeat almost endlessly the acts of bridling, saddling, mounting, dismounting, unsaddling, unbridling, riding bareback with hackamore, riding (in the corral) bareback without hackamore, making the mount lie down and rise, lie down and rise.

Such exercises were performed too by the first platoon, as prescribed by regulations. But the style and energy with which Matthew pursued work made his subcommand, when compared to the other platoon, seem like an independent unit. Its tone and spirit improved daily, the incidence of sickness among its troopers fell sharply, and Doctor Gray found reason to worry.

"I hesitate to speak to the young man about it," he said to his wife, "for fear of depressing his impulses toward hard work. But while he improves his own platoon, he breaks the unity of the troop, and in the long run this may be more dangerous than letting both platoons drift along at the common level allowed by that incomparable ass in the headquarters office."

"Cedric. You must not shout."

"I am not shouting. I am being as murderously calm as a man can be who sees other men being mishandled."

"You are shouting inside. It is bad for you."

"I'm damned if I'll give Hazard even an oblique hint of advice. He just proves my case for me that troops under hard work are healthier than troops with time to think up ailments."

Inspections were occasions for further differences between the platoons. The second platoon, in barracks inspection and in troop inspection on the parade ground, had the benefit of their lieutenant's incessant attention to detail. One day Sergeant Fry—a mournful young West Virginian—came to him and asked his help in demonstrating to the men of the first platoon how to memorize the proper positions of articles in a locker opened for inspection.

"Has the troop commander authorized your coming to me?" asked
Matthew.

"No, sir."

"Why not?"

"Sir, I didn't ask him."

"Do you think you should have?"

Sergeant Fry looked soberly into the eyes of the young officer. They
both knew that if the conversation went further, the soldier and the
officer would come to agreement about certain matters which ought
not to come clear between them. Matthew wondered if he should not
refuse the sergeant's request; but if he did so, too much might later
be made of the difference between the platoons, which would em-
barrass Lieutenant Mainwaring. He agreed to help the sergeant. He
made his demonstrations as briefly and clearly as possible and returned to his own men. From that moment, all men in the post
regarded him virtually as troop commander. Discontent began to
appear among men of the first platoon at the quality of their own
platoon leader. "What is the second platoon doing?" they wondered
at every turn, when they should have been thinking of their own
work. Kitty Mainwaring knew more about the true state of feeling and
opinion in the troop than her husband.

She knew by watching from her piazza how matters went at drill
and inspection. She knew by the behavior of men off duty as they
pursued their vagrant recreations on the south line across the parade
ground. She heard the conversation of soldiers on duty cultivating
the post garden behind the north line. She knew by her contacts with
the laundresses.

These were four women who lived in their adobe rooms—"Soapsuds Row"—behind the company quarters, and who did their huge
weekly washes in lean-to sheds built against the south wall of their
house. The only women on the post aside from the two officers' wives,
they were amiably willing to discuss their concerns, however trivial,
with the commanding officer's wife when she came to see how their
work went, and whether she could do anything for them, and how
went things otherwise.

By "otherwise" they all meant the reach and repulse; the kindled
interest and the happiness of desire; loneliness and the hope of folly,
which in their turns came to pass between so many men and so
few women, isolated together under conditions of strict convention

so far from any other congress with their kind. One of the women was engaged to a trooper; but under a regulation prohibiting family life to any of the enlisted men stationed at Fort Delivery, she was not yet able to marry him. Her connection was well-known and respected. The other three laundresses—one a German immigrant woman of twenty-six, known as Dutchy, one a middle-aged Missourian named Wilma, one an Irish-American woman just twenty, called Annie—were the objects of incessant attentions and rivalries among the troopers. Like many other states of feeling at the fort, that which existed between the soldiers and the laundresses was held in a precarious balance. The soldiers kept the laundresses, an ever-present provocation to them, in an almost angry surveillance, to make certain that no man above others should gain joys wanted by all. Another attitude grew out of this challenging watchfulness. It was a rude code of chivalry. Woman, so precious and rare among them, must be kept inviolate. So through hunger itself, guarded by jealousy, the barracks and washhouse society found its morality.

Soldiers spoke to the women of all their concerns. They gave their views of Matthew. In turn, and with tact masquerading as absent-mindedness, the women reflected these to Kitty. What she heard made Kitty suffer two pangs. One was for her husband—Ted, who was her substance and dimension of life, and who infuriated her at times for his Teddishness, and who made her vulnerable by his need of her. The other pang was as unexpected to her as to anyone else. It drove to her heart. It struck her with so strong a sense of Matthew's quality, his effect on all those about him, the troopers, the laundry women, that, in her way of blushing violently and readily, she revealed even as she felt it a hot hope of him in his manhood.

Dutchy, Wilma and Annie exchanged a look at what they saw in her face.

In their position at the fort, they had become expert at observing and estimating desire. When Kitty left them they had a raucous laugh over their tubs and washboards at her state, and then, women who felt with all women, they sent a sigh after her.

xlviii

She resolved to let it make no difference. Nobody would ever know, least of all Mr. Hazard. She invited him to supper perhaps more often than before, just to prove that she could dominate the feeling that troubled her.

Matthew wondered what made her so excitable during those evenings. Her natural animation was noticeably increased. She began to dress up more than usual. She made Ted tell all his stories, and she laughed so at them that she had to touch away tears with her lacy handkerchief. In her ardor there was something winning; yet it was marred for Matthew by various flourishes of manner which seemed deliberate and therefore somewhat disheartening. Determined at all costs to make her supper table into a pool of gaiety and amusement to which he would always want to return, she made fun of herself and everyone else. Teddy would be proud; Matthew fascinated. Great ladies, she had heard, were given to outrageous remarks and gestures at times. She risked one now.

"Mr. Hazard," she said, half-closing her eyes to give humorous shrewdness to her prettiest expression, "everybody, simply everyone, is wondering why such an eligible young man as yourself is not married."

Some pulse sounded in her voice which betrayed to her own ear, if not to Ted's or Matthew's, a troubled want that underlay the idea of Matthew and marriage.

"Now, Kit," said her husband. "Nobody ever ought to ask a fellow that. Look at him. He don't like it, and I don't blame him."

Matthew had his head down, and his black look shone forth at her. The power of spirit behind it pierced her. Her heart hurried itself. What a fool she was to risk bringing up the subject. She was not a good actress, try as she would to dissemble. But with both men at her supper table leagued against her in her inquiry, she lifted her head higher and said,

"You must have been told all your life that you're handsome. You have a safe and solid career ahead of you. Plenty of girls would—"

"I am engaged," said Matthew flatly.

"Oh." She caught her breath with more than dramatic effect: the

news was full of chagrin for her. She hated the woman who had betrothed him. "When was it announced?"

She had asked him the one question which must rob his news of
some of its point.

"It is not exactly announced, yet," he replied. "We will be married
next year."

"But you are waiting? You are *both* waiting?" Her tone asked why.
By following rapidly upon her advantages, she made less experienced
people, like Matthew, say what she would hear, whether they wanted
to speak or not.

"Miss Greenleaf's family thought it wiser to let me serve a year out
here alone, at first. I agreed."

"Greenleaf!" she said. "The Colonel Greenleafs?" He nodded.
"Teddy, we met them once, you remember? They came to Monroe on
an inspection. —My oh my," she added, bridling on her chair with
mock elegance so that her hidden silks made a little shower of sound.
"You are marrying into society, I must say."

Her spirits were suddenly high, for if he had a year to wait, and
if he spent it, as he must, at this post, where she was, who knew
what might not come to pass, with a slightly older, still pretty, selfless
and devoted woman at hand to perform for him those small attentions which he would miss if he ever became accustomed to them?
She knew how to be a perfect darling. He would see. She savored
these reflections, which appeared in complete detail before her private
vision, with no sense of the infidelity to her marriage which they must
imply. She felt no loss of virtue. Her cheeks were rosy. Her eyes
danced. What she felt was reflected in her face. Ted stared at her.
Sometimes he did not know her at all, he thought. He looked at Mr.
Hazard, who saw nothing.

xlix

A new sound broke into their circle.

"Mainwaring!" cried a rough voice, while a knock sounded on
the front door. "I'm coming in."

It was Doctor Gray. Ted went to meet him, and was backed into
the room by the energy of the doctor, who was scowling with concern.

"I'm sorry to be unceremonious like this, and I hope Mrs. Mainwaring will forgive me, but the commanding officer ought to know what I just discovered on the south line."

"Yes, captain?" asked Ted.

"I was going over a couple of men in the infirmary, and all they could talk about was Sergeant Blickner and Annie, the laundress."

"Well?"

"They have disappeared, and two horses are missing. Evidently this has been the case since mid-afternoon. If they went for a pleasure ride—against regulations, of course—ordinarily they should've returned by dark." He looked at his thick silver watch. "It is now forty-three minutes past nine. That they got away without being noticed is extraordinary. That they have not come back is more than alarming. I felt certain, sir, that you should know, in order to act."

"My God in heaven," said Ted, sinking into his dinner chair. "What do the men think?"

"Think?"

"I mean, about why they went, and where?"

Doctor Gray glanced at Mrs. Mainwaring and would not say in her presence what the men thought: that a young and vivacious woman and a hungry soldier had gone off together in search of that which they were not permitted to find within the fort. Kitty understood him well enough. She drew her breath sharply, and asked,

"Doctor, what do you think could have happened to them?"

"They might have lost their way after dark, madam. However, this is not likely, when the lights of the post can be seen for thirty miles. One of their horses might have become lame, in which case they would return more slowly than they went. It is possible that they simply meant to go away and not return at all. And it is possible that if they do not return it is because physically they cannot."

"Doctor, then, you think . . ." said Ted, and his face paled.

"They may be dead, or captured, if Indians are about us. This we do not know, as no patrols have been ordered out for some time, as I recall."

Matthew lowered his eyes to avoid the look of pain that crossed Ted's face on hearing this openly critical remark. Doctor Gray was biting his jaws together with a grinding effort at self-control.

"Teddy," said Mrs. Mainwaring in a suddenly cool voice, "you will do whatever is wise and needful in this matter. I will leave you and your officers to decide upon it."

Turning her head in order not to see Captain Gray as she left the room, Kitty was a traveling monument to her own conception of a commander's wife, who must use the snub when necessary. Captain Gray smiled after her in pity.

"They went against standing orders!" exclaimed Ted, taking refuge in the one fact he knew.

"Indeed they did," said the doctor. "But that is past. What next?"

"I will order out a search and pursuit party immediately," said Ted, gathering himself as if to move.

"I might suggest, sir," said the older officer with a severe tone of official respect, "that this would compound risks to this garrison. A mounted party away from the fort at night would hardly be able to find anything, and might be open to ambush."

"Yes, I thought of that."

Matthew had a sudden certainty now of what awaited him in this matter. Mainwaring turned to him.

"Hazard," he said, "take the best squad from your platoon, and prepare to move out just before daybreak to look for the missing parties if they have not returned. I want them back without fail. And with their mounts, too."

"Yes, sir."

They heard the front door open and close. Kitty was crossing the parade to see the remaining laundresses, to learn what she could, and to give encouragement to them for the safe return of their companion.

"Thank you, captain," said Ted. "I appreciate your action in this matter."

"You are welcome, sir," said the doctor, and took his departure.

"Sir," said Matthew, "perhaps I'd better interview the men to see what they know. Blickner may have confided in someone. In any case, I will get ready at once. I will take my scout, Joe Dummy, with me in the morning."

"I was about to suggest it." The acting commanding officer nodded in dismissal. His great need was to be alone for a little while, without anyone to observe what he did or failed to do, or to tell him what he must do.

1

Moving between lanterns and stars they readied themselves before daylight.

The air was chilly and pure; and when the first streak of day came like a visible waft on the eastern darkness, the sense of purity grew. Matthew breathed something of it and it plumbed deeply his tense breast and belly. He was acutely aware of all details in this, his first mission with possible enemy contact; and as he worked, rapidly and precisely, he saw emerge under his touch the value of long and frequent practice. His squad was in proper condition. His men knew it, too. He was taking seven troopers, the post trumpeter and Joe Dummy. He inspected each man's supplies of food and water, even though he himself had supervised the issue and packing of these during the night. The squad carried enough rations for seven days. By lantern light the lieutenant examined arms and ammunition, the condition of hoofs, saddle girths and bits and bridles. Most of the troop awoke and came to watch the preparation and the departure. Since the recommissioning of the post, this was the first expedition to ride out on extraordinary orders.

Lieutenant Mainwaring came. With him was his wife. She wore a Spanish shawl over her head and shoulders. She kept herself in the background while her husband spoke to Matthew and the squad, who presented themselves in line, dismounted, at attention.

"You men," said the acting commanding officer, "are ordered out to do a duty which is important and may be dangerous. I hope you will find and return to us the two people from our small official family who are missing. They will be punished on their return, for they have deliberately disobeyed standing regulations. They have also removed without authority two valuable pieces of government property—the horses they took. We must recover these, too. So you see you have something worthwhile to do. As for the dangerous part, there is a possibility that Indians may be about, and may be responsible for the continued absence of Sergeant Blickner and his companion. In the event of an encounter, I know you men will give a good account of yourselves. Gook luck. We'll be waiting for you. —Lieutenant, the command is yours."

The officers saluted each other.

Kitty came to Ted and took his arm.

"May I say a word to Lieutenant Hazard?"

There was a certain military impropriety about her request, but Ted, taken by surprise, nodded. She went forward to Matthew, who saw her just as he was about to address a command to his squad. He hesitated. She reached him in another step or two. He could see her face now in the paling day. Her eyes were lighted by some odd energy.

"Just a word, Mr. Hazard," she said, "which may be useful to you. I talked to Dutchy and the other laundress. I asked if Sergeant Blickner had been paying any special attention to Annie. They didn't know of anything special, just about like everyone else who was a friend of Annie's. Then I asked if she had talked about him much, and they said, not much. But they said this didn't prove anything, as they weren't with Annie every minute."

She paused. He frowned. Was that all? She shrugged. With her mouth slightly open she made a wordless sound. It had a strange, desperate, dry quality. What on earth was the matter with her? he wondered. She acted as though she were seeing her husband off, instead of him.

"Thank you, Mrs. Mainwaring," he said. "I'll try to think over what you report. It may be helpful—" though he could not imagine how. He began to turn away, but she said in a low voice,

"You must not misunderstand my—my interest in you, I just wanted to say good luck, you know."

But she searched his face with her eyes to see if a sudden kindling in him of the desire she denied in herself would appear there.

"No, no," he said politely, "of course I don't; and thanks for the luck."

Now he did turn away to his men, and Kitty drew her shawl across her mouth. A shudder went through her in the day's first twilight; she thought of Sergeant Blickner and Annie—desires beyond their power to control had overtaken them. To what had it brought them? She stepped back.

Matthew's voice rang out in the command to mount. In another moment the squad was moving out at a walk following after their lieutenant. Beside him rode his Apache scout. They rode out between the corral and the forge to the open desert. In common impulse,

everyone held silence—those who went and those who watched behind. Only sounded the dim thud and shuffle of hoofs in dust, the
twist and creak of leather, bit chains shaken by a horse.

li

"Joe, this is your game."

Lieutenant Hazard swept his arm over the desert earth. Joe
Dummy nodded. He gestured for a halt behind the corral. While the
squad rested, he went slowly forward on foot. The first sunlight
threw long shadows and gave brilliant relief to the very grains of the
sand. He saw a wide spread of hoofprints—the marks of weeks made
by horses taken out and brought in for drill, exercise and forage.
Hundreds of crescent-shaped small low ridges threw their shadows.
Amidst them Joe sought fresh prints. Walking in a pose of meditation
over the hoofprints, he soon found what he wanted, and followed
for ten or twelve yards until he was sure. He then gestured to Matthew
to bring up the detachment. He knew where to go now.

They followed him—he was now remounted—as he pursued the
marks of two horses leading eastward. The sergeant and Annie had
gone at a walk, probably to avoid attracting attention with the dust
and sound of trot or gallop. After going half a mile eastward from
the corral, they had turned to their left, northward, until reaching
the near rim of the arroyo. At the bank, they had paused, and then,
probably with the sergeant leading, and even holding on to Annie's
bridle, they had taken their mounts at a scramble down the steep,
sloping, red-earthed wall, until they had found the protection of the
deep dry gully. In soft sand they had ridden the arroyo bed. Presently
they had taken up the trot, but not for long, perhaps because Annie
had not been used to riding. At a walk they had proceeded for the
next two miles or a little more, and then had taken their way out of
the arroyo over the north bank.

Three miles away were the low hills out of which, when rains
came, the gully had long ago been formed and was periodically re-
plenished. The hills contained miniature ravines, long slopes, and
winding hollows. Toward these Sergeant Blickner and his companion
had then taken a direct course. They had once again tried the trot,
and then had broken into a gallop, riding close beside each other,

with one horse slightly in the lead, as though the sergeant had held Annie's bridle for her protection at unaccustomed high speed. After about half a mile the gallop had come down to a walk, and then to a halt, while the riders had dismounted, and the horses had moved idly about, stamping. It had been a brief pause, yielding marks of no other action, and it had perhaps taken place to permit a catching of the breath, possibly a discussion of plans, and then a remounting.

Resuming their course eastward, they had come to the rise of the hills, where they had turned first to the right, or south, and then to the left, or north, entering a shallow trough between two low hills covered with short, sharp, dusty grass. Hoofprints now became dim, and soon vanished altogether, in a texture of the hard grass and loose but impervious white gravel.

"They certainly came this far, anyhow," said Matthew to Joe.

Joe did not reply in sound, but with the fingers of his right hand tipped together he made it clear that the riders had gone farther into the shallow valley in which the squad was halted. Up there, indicated Joe, on the ridges, they would have been visible. On the slopes, they would have ridden in discomfort. The marks at the entrance of the valley had gone in only one direction: they had not come out. Therefore, he said, the squad should continue the march up the defile.

Matthew gave the command accordingly.

Joe Dummy turned his mouth down in a sour expression. It concealed his satisfaction that his young commander reposed trust in his judgment.

In the care of their study of the trail, the column had taken almost three hours to come into the hills. It was now after eight o'clock in the morning, a late August day, and the light was turning from golden to white as the day advanced. The heat was already wavering off the desert crust in visible reflections, and dust was hanging forward on the drying wind out of Mexico many miles away. The defile was pale in color—dust lay on the rocks that jutted from the low slopes, until from some distance the rocks looked like rags of cloth or paper in the beating light, and the grass made a ragged shimmer. Grass crushed by hoofs gave up a wry, piercing odor. Ahead of them the hills time after time folded away any distant view; but revealed with every turn of a fold another stretch of the low valley that showed nothing new: dusty rocks in random attitudes, the only surfaces to catch the light and make pale interruptions of the dusty olive green of the sharp grassed slopes.

There, said Joe, riding beside Matthew, with a movement of his crabbed arm.

"Where?"

Joe showed the lieutenant a cluster of pale ragged surfaces that took the light like the outcropping rocks of the whole passage—and yet somehow did not look quite the same. Matthew leaned sharply forward and halted the column with a hand signal. Various pale objects about sixty-five yards ahead—nothing in his experience prepared him to know what they might be, even remembering all the possibilities which had brought him here.

But if Lieutenant Hazard had never seen dead naked and hacked bodies lying to catch the sunlight under a dusty white sky in a desert defile, Joe Dummy had, and often. He knew what he saw.

The lieutenant knew, too, soon enough. So did his men. The column approached at a walk the works left by murderers. No soldier said anything except a young Pennsylvanian; and he said with sudden vomit what his mouth could not frame in words. Matthew glanced at him, and said,

"Cranshaw, dismount here and wait for us."

The trooper, shaking in his pallor, nodded and came to a halt. They left him there, sitting on his own shadow, with his horse's bridle caught around his right ankle. It was most curious, thought Matthew even as he drew ahead with his attention fixed on what they had come to find, most curious how unsafe it was to predict what any given man might do in situations of unaccustomed difficulty. Cranshaw was robust, well-favored, seemingly confident. He was liked in the platoon, he had a stock of jokes and farces, and he gave freely of them to entertain his fellows. When offered alcohol he drank readily and was drunk sooner than anyone, and then, more droll than ever, he was much applauded for his blithe obscenities and music-hall turns. Matthew had already marked him for possible promotion, for he was quick and clever at his tasks, and men learned from his demonstrations at these. Now at the sight of mutilated death, he failed the rest, showing them an example of weakness. Matthew reserved his judgment: Cranshaw perhaps must simply get used to what now the other men saw in immediate clarity. The column halted ten feet from their discovery and dismounted. Matthew went forward alone with Joe Dummy.

Yes, this was how, all was proper, nothing had been neglected— so Joe Dummy seemed to say as he took in the scene. If he held views about the death of Sergeant Blickner, who had abused him, he did not reveal them.

Matthew was more slow in accumulating all the details. The victims were naked. Their limbs were severed from their bodies, and slightly scattered. The woman's body showed a mortal mercy. Powder burns close on her breast indicated that Sergeant Blickner had shot her before she could be taken prisoner. His own flesh showed bullet wounds of farther origin, and lance and knife cuts. Further specifications of unspeakable treatment suffered by the two corpses would be reserved for the official report to the commanding officer of Fort Delivery, Matthew decided. He was pale. His lips were white, and felt stretched.

He turned to his troopers and said,

"Trumpeter, hold the horses. The rest of you men come forward if you wish to see."

They came. Trumpeter Rainey, holding the squad's bridles, craned his neck. A sense of injustice possessed him. In due time it was relieved, for the lieutenant ordered the men back, and permitted him to come forward in his turn. He was the youngest man in the detachment. Matthew watched him study the recognizable pieces on the ground. The trumpeter closed his jaws and squeezed down his eyes almost shut in his hardened face. He looked twice his age for a moment. Then he glanced at the lieutenant, and nodded, and the effect was of his saying that it was the worst thing you ever could see, but if you had seen, and felt, anything of life before, this was something you just had to put along with all the rest of it, good and bad, to keep on going yourself.

"Rainey," said Matthew, "go back and bring Cranshaw up here. If he wants to see, before we decide what to do next, you stay by him. But don't *make* him look."

" 'S sir," said Rainey, saluting as he went. He was more of a stylist at soldiering than the rest.

Matthew moved aside with Joe Dummy.

"How were they, how many, and where have they gone?" he asked.

So: this and this: they were about four in number, and they were mounted. They now had two extra horses, along with whatever arms and ammunition the sergeant had carried, and all equipment including saddles and food and water. They had two places to go. One was there, north, to the Phantom Mountains, and one was there, south to Mexico.

When did they do this?

This: and this: and so: the blood on the ground was black and that on the stumps was black and also tarry, and these, and these, where some had been eaten by creatures, out of the sky, and from the open earth, vultures up there, and here, coyotes, a wolf, insects, these places were dry and hard; and what from far had looked like pale ragged rock catching the light, was now seen closely to be very pale blue in color; and all such information indicated that the thing had been done yesterday during the twilight.

Yes. And when did the others leave here?

So. And so. And so. Speaking from his own old customs, Joe Dummy was sure they had left very soon afterward. Once the proper things had been done, and the loot taken, there was every reason to go away from death and leave it behind.

"They were Apaches, do you think?"

Oh, yes, yes. Tshaa. Nobody else.

"Do you think we could ever catch them, Joe?"

Off there, that way, south, yes, they would go south for greater safety, for they had more places to hide once they were in the mountains in Sonora, they would arrive there long before anyone who went after them, but they could be found there, they could be found.

"How would I know them? I mean, the very ones who did it?"

One would have this, and one that—a U.S. Army carbine, or a Colt's revolver, and there would be the two horses, and all the equipment. And then the scalped hair—they could be identified by such things.

Matthew considered his duty. It embraced a dilemma in command. The bodily remains of Sergeant Blickner and Annie the laundress must be returned to the fort for burial. Should the whole squad take these back, or should one man be detailed to the task, while all the rest mounted a pursuit? What was his stated mission? The commanding officer had asked for the persons, and also for their horses, to be returned. Matthew believed he should recover the horses. Nothing had been said to him about capturing Apaches, if indications suggested that Apaches had been involved in the extended absence of the sergeant and his companion. But how could he capture stolen horses without taking Apache horse thieves?

Watching his thoughts as they made successive pictures of his alternatives for him, Matthew also saw Rainey bring Cranshaw near the slowly shrinking objects on the dusty short grass. Cranshaw looked his fill and then turned away. Rainey put his hand on Cranshaw's shoulder. It was like a father heartening a child. Wondering whether Cranshaw could ever take death as a soldier must, Matthew said, "He would not be the one to send back to the fort with a blanket full of remains," and in this thought, concerning the quality of one of his men, he discovered that he had made his decision.

He would detail someone to go to Fort Delivery, while with the rest of the squad he would take up the pursuit toward Mexico.

He then moved rapidly. The trooper whom he designated to return to the post was ordered to lay out his blanket and two others were directed to gather upon it the remaining components of the two bodies. These were then folded tightly into the blanket which was secured with rope. The heavy bundle was lashed to the trooper's saddle.

"Get back as soon as you can to the post," Matthew told him, "and report in detail what we found. Tell Lieutenant Mainwaring there is no doubt at all that Apaches have been, and may still be, in this vicinity, so he can alert the post. Tell him I am going in pursuit, and that I consider myself on a war mission. I will remain in the field until I can capture the murderers and recover our horses, or as long as my supplies hold out. My course lies southwest. Keep yourself a strict lookout on your way back. Don't halt to fight. Run for it if you are attacked. That is all."

lii

"The school of the desert," said Matthew to himself as they rode to the southwestward in the second day. By this he meant Joe Dummy's instructions to him, and so to the rest of the detachment. Joe had found signs of the raiding party on that morning. They pointed to a recent and brief encampment, and indicated that he was right in his assumption that the raiders were retreating southwesterly. He showed how he made his conclusions. Horse dung, its degree of moisture; hoof marks without other prints of heavy saddles thrown off; the site itself, open, without even the shelter of scattered bushes such as would be desirable overnight.

Moving once again, the detachment learned from Joe Dummy how to use the faculty of vision upon the distance. The ground gave great reflected glare. Hold the forearm over the face just below the eyes to place a shadow upward instead of the unimpeded glare, and you could see much farther. He halted the detachment when a stir of dust appeared far ahead. If it drifted steadily aside with the prevailing wind, it was caused by movement of bodies. If it rose and vanished after a short while, it was a desert gust whirling upward, and meant nothing. The present flare of dust soon disappeared. The column moved on.

At night they used no campfire. The guard was changed every two hours. The work of the day was exhausting. No man should lose more than two hours of sleep at night. The troopers slept like the dead, Matthew thought, once they were down. The guard called his relief quietly. The relief took his place with loaded carbine. He learned to see at night by using the corner of his eye instead of direct peering vision. He listened and he watched. The horses were picketed far enough way from the sleeping men so their night sounds would not disturb, and yet near enough so the guard could see them in the starlight at all times.

The rations of all the troopers were gathered every night in two large saddlebags. These were placed under the care of the guard who in the event of attack from ambush could save the supply, moving with it to the picket line to be ready for emergency saddling. Night was cold on the desert. Dreams came shafting through the contracted forms of the sleeping soldiers, and made them murmur and hold themselves against the cold and against the instrusions of images induced by cramped positions on hard ground. The last guard of night was to awaken the lieutenant. When Matthew arose, he always found Joe Dummy sitting awake near him.

"Don't you ever sleep?" he asked.

Joe slept like anyone else. He knew how to sleep deeply, like a rock, for there was value in it if hard work awaited in the day. But much was astir in the hour before dawn, and it was his lifelong habit to be watchful then. That was all.

"Joe, Joe," said Matthew, laughing.

The scout understood the warmth and the respect in how this was said. He understood the principle of command. He was now subject to it. He understood also the inarticulate truth of friendship. This too under the young officer's command he was coming to know.

liii

Under his duty as trumpeter, to whom the commander in the field would give commands to be relayed by bugle, Private Rainey rode at the head of the column with the lieutenant. There were long hours of riding when watching the distance the leaders of the column were able also to converse. Trumpeter Rainey was talkative. Matthew listened to him and regarded him now and then sidewise. Rainey was artless. Anything that had ever happened to him was fit matter to tell about. Matthew put down smiles now and then, and now and then he was moved by the vividness of a place or an event which Rainey evoked with unconscious style. A commander never knew, thought Matthew, what went into the making of his men. Every one of them was different in his way from the others, and yet in their official and natural similarities of body and endowment, they were to be counted as exactly alike, for military purposes. It was a rare man who gave himself up so openly out of his past as the trumpeter. He was young, only nineteen. He would no doubt discover reticence as he grew older.

This man; those men; the lieutenant was responsible for them; they were responsible to him, and to each other; community held them. If it made them strong together, it made Matthew stronger than all—or so he prayed in feeling beyond words. Private Rainey's summoning up of the days when he "was young," as he put it, gave Matthew a close sense of identity with his troopers.

The trumpeter was not tall, but he was stoutly made. He gave a generally blunt effect. He often wore a scowl which looked to Matthew like an effort to focus himself—to give detail to his blurred face, with its freckles, and sharpness to his mind, with its youthful vapors. Otherwise he seemed like a boy much younger, afraid, for the sake of manliness, to seem too good-natured. Matthew had never heard the bugle played so truly as Rainey played it. The same true feeling came free as Rainey talked to his commander.

Olin Rainey's mother, Cleora, said to him one Saturday afternoon when he was bothering her in the kitchen, back home in Galena, Illinois, where he was born,

"Olin Rainey, you'll have me taking a lank fit with all your askings for your doings. Sometimes I wish you'd do instead of ask. No I don't," she added at once. "All right, I'll see what your father says about it."

"Don't ask him!" said Olin. At fifteen he was coming into a blunt-nosed power that made him try everything to have his way. "Don't tell my dad," he insisted.

"Your dad is my husband. I've got to."

"No, you don't. You didn't tell him when you let Bethesda go to the magic-lantern show."

"He wasn't fit to tell, that's all why."

"Maybe he won't be fit to tell about me going to Cedar Rapids, then."

Cleora said, "You should be a lawyer."

"No, Mordell's more likely for lawyer."

"All right," she said, "I won't tell your father. Go along. Come here." She hugged him. "Now go along or I'll think of what you could do for me that'd keep you here, so go on."

She thought he didn't hear her, but he did, when she added under her breath, "And don't come back, ever, my honey, but go on to better people and places and chances for yourself."

He had the permission he needed. It was permission to take the first trip of his life—to go, tomorrow, Sunday, with some slightly older friends of his in a buggy to attend an outing in Cedar Rapids, Iowa. They would leave Galena, Illinois, early in the morning. It was a fine prospect. Olin knew of only one place where he could go to think about it in peace.

His haven was a little open room of willows facing the Mississippi River which ran by Galena. He spent all possible time there on the bank of the river under the bluff on which the town of Galena rested. He often went alone, though the river was the playground of most other boys he knew.

Galena was a river port where the old side-wheel steamer *Menominee* called. Olin would watch her, and imagine going away on her some day, perhaps next week, maybe next year, to steam downstream (never upstream—why was that?) to another world where nobody knew him. He did not know what he longed to find, but he knew well enough what he wanted to get away from.

His father, Ruben Rainey, worked hard in the lead mines at Galena for little pay to support his large family. They lived in a narrow red brick house on one of the streets high above the center of town. There was not room enough for everybody in comfort; the family had to double up in beds, share every corner, and (so it seemed) apologize for their individual existences to maintain any sort of order in their horizonless world. When he looked ahead, Olin could only see himself coming home at night in his turn from the lead mines, with his face gray and his hands dark with the rubbed-in grease of the velvety mineral which was taken out of the earth in such great quantities and yet earned so little in wages.

He would like to get away from pretending that his father was not a drunkard and a braggart who refought his days in the Civil War every other night, sitting around in Ferguson's store. If he couldn't help his dad, and he didn't know how he could, Olin was ready to get gone.

He would like to get away from sleeping with his brother Mordell, who was a year younger than he and skinnier, and more full of words. Like him, Mordell also wanted to be alone sometimes, but alone in a different way. If Mordell had a book—any old book, it seemed— he could be alone in the middle of everything. Mordell never minded to have the other children around—Jane Mary, next youngest; then Bethesda; then Martha Mary; and then Benjamin, the baby. Knowing all these people better than he did anyone else in the world, Olin still thought they were practically strangers.

He would like to get away from having to come home afternoons wondering "how things were," and then having to see that look on his mother's face sometimes, when she would go white and all but fall. He and Mordell would sometimes manage to catch her. Once she fainted *sitting down* and that was the worst of all. Doctor Jimson said he didn't know what caused it—she was just "subject" to it. Relieved to be left with only a familiar worry, they thanked him for not finding anything terrible. The doctor surely knew. He had a roomful of books and was always buying more.

Finally, Olin wanted to get away from being Olin Rainey as he knew him, so he could be Olin Rainey as he wanted to be. He could not say just yet what this was to be, but his dream did not seem entirely hopeless. Somebody else had once lived in Galena and had gone away, and Olin often dawdled past the house of this man which was two streets lower toward town than the Rainey house. The man was Ulysses Grant, who in Olin's boyhood was President of the United States. President Grant's house was not much different from Olin's. Years ago it was part of the town lore that Ulysses Grant, as a clerk in his brother's harness store in Galena, would never amount to much, and the fact that he'd proved everyone wrong didn't seem to make them any the less pleased with themselves. If they ever thought of saying the same thing about Olin Rainey, the miner's son, perhaps they'd be wrong there, too.

Everything about going away kept Olin interested. He liked to go to the levee to watch the old *Menominee* come in and tie up, and unload, and load, and then cast off. Cautiously she'd backwater with one big paddle wheel while the other went slow-speed ahead. He cocked his head to hear the bell signals somewhere deep inside her. The dark water by the steamer dock was churned up white. Red brick buildings in the reflection shattered and broke. Birds flipped up from treetops back of the shore.

The *Menominee* let go with her whistle and began to pick up speed, letting the water come back to black glassy stillness. Her twin stacks side by side rose high in the air and ended in iron crowns blackened by smoke. Her windows looked black except where the fancy curtains showed, looped apart. Her deck was only a little way above water. People on deck walked close to the water. If only he were on board, Olin would lean over all day long and watch the water go by under him as he went away. Sometimes he would go to his willow brake to watch the *Menominee* as she trundled herself downstream like a wide duck on the sailing current. He saw the steamer safely receding into the engulfing light until she vanished. He always went there to watch her away as she took some part of him along.

At other times he kept returning to his grove of river willows for another purpose which at first he did not rightly grasp. He went to listen. He liked to sort out the river sounds. There were all kinds, once he listened for them separately.

The difference between the sound of water close in to the bank, and water far out in the stream.

The kinds of wind, high or low, in branches or in grass.

What a steamer whistle did upwind and downwind.

Best of all, the songs of birds.

Olin would listen with his cheek turned toward a bird singing somewhere, and then he would try to imitate it, whistling. Then he would wait for an answer. It was some time and many visits to the river before he got his first answer, and when it came, he fell down on his little floor of damp river grass and hugged his ribs and rolled over and back, laughing fit to be tied. When he got his breath he stood up and tried again, and again the bird answered him. From that time on, so true and pure was his whistling, he could make birds answer him whenever he wanted to. He did not say so to himself, and nobody else knew, of course, but this was music. He was trying to make music, using the only instrument and the only teachers within his reach.

But there were other tunes, and he practiced these too, and on that Saturday afternoon when he had his permission to make the excursion tomorrow, he went down the river to his place, and after a few exchanges with whatever old birds happened to be around, he set to work practicing his best pieces. He began with "The Brown Eyes Polka," and worked his way through "Tenting Tonight" and "Darling Nellie Gray" to the "Boston Waltz." It seemed possible that tomorrow, on the way, or actually at Cedar Rapids, someone might want to hear him whistle. He meant to be good and ready.

liv

"On Sunday morning four buggy-loads left for Cedar Rapids," said Trumpeter Rainey to Lieutenant Hazard as they rode, "and I filled the last seat."

The young people were all going to attend the band festival which was staged every few years in springtime by members of the Cedar Rapids Bohemian colony. The understanding was that if Olin would help to care for the horses and make himself generally useful, he need not worry over expenses, for his friends would see that he got fed. The rest of them were paired off boy-and-girl. Olin had never been out with the young people before. They thought it was high time.

The trip over saw the birth of his social sense.

"Well, let's all do our part," they said to him. "Can you tell us a story? How about a riddle. Can you sing?"

No, but he could entertain with his whistling.

"Your *what?*"

He showed them. The buggy horse pricked up his ears and so did they. First he gave them birds. The sweetness and wit of this made them laugh with delight. Then he tried his real tunes, and on the inspiration of the moment, he mixed in a few bird sounds with these, and they all said the effect was way downtown. They applauded.

"Let me show you, lieutenant," he said to Matthew, and demonstrated how he mixed bird songs with real tunes. The horses in the column, and the troopers, lifted their heads to listen. Just so, on the ride over to Cedar Rapids, he had lifted the spirits of the young people. He also released their real reason for making the trip to Iowa. Much sparking and daring came out between the young men and women of the party. Olin caught his first glimpse of courtship. It made him wonder and then it made him more secret than ever with his feelings which, under suppression, were dear and bothersome.

One of the girls took a liking to him and pretended to prefer him to her fellow, just to bring advantageous jealousy into the air. Olin's head swam. Shucks. He grinned. His features felt as though they blurred together at what he felt. The others pointed to him and laughed, but not unkindly. He gripped his hands together between his thighs. He felt far from home.

But the band festival wiped out all his other new excitements. Several bands competed in the festival. He listened to them all. The greatest, and the winner, was a band of silver valve cornets—the John Huss Silver Cornet Choir. He had never imagined, much less heard, such beautiful sounds. He followed the players around when they were through, and finally got up enough nerve to ask one of the younger musicians to let him see his silver cornet.

"Here, you want to hold it?"

Olin took it and pressed the sparkling valves with their inviting action cushioned on little trapped columns of air. He held it to his face as if to play it, and then lowered it.

"Go on, try it once," said the young Bohemian.

"I don't know how."

The player showed him how to fix his lips, inflate his cheeks and make a tone. Olin tried it, making some cracked noises which embarrassed him. The owner nodded with encouragement and he tried and tried again, until he heard himself blow a long, pleasant, if somewhat breathy, tone.

"Good. Good," said the cornetist. "You'll catch on easy!"

The leader of the choir was nearby. He came over and smiled generously at Olin's first trial. Then, taken by what he saw in the boy's face, he asked him if he would like to learn to play the trumpet.

Olin blushed and nodded. He felt like a bump on a log.

"Here, there," said the leader, "you come over here, once," and led him to a grove of trees away from where the festival crowd were eating their picnic. Right then and there the professor gave him a lesson on the cornet, and when they were done, he said that Olin Rainey had a natural talent for music and for the cornet, and added,

"When you get home, you tell your pa and ma, you tell them to get you lessons."

"Thank you."

Olin knew the thing was hopeless. Why did *anybody* have to want what they couldn't have?

When he came back to Galena from Cedar Rapids he was somebody else. His mother recognized this at once, for she had known well who he was when he went, and now he could see her wondering what kind of somebody else he was who came home from the outing she had let him have, for which she had had to pay dearly over the weekend.

Olin didn't say anything, but on Tuesday afternoon his mother came into the kitchen and saw him with her china beehive in his hands.

"Olin Rainey! Drop that, no don't drop it, give it here to me, you—oh!"

In the china beehive was the money she had saved. It was the treasure she kept against calamity. He handed it to her and she boxed his ear.

"I was not stealing it," he said. "I was just counting it."

Now over her fright, she saw he told the truth.

"What for?" she asked.

"To see if there was enough for us to get me what I saw down in Mr. Ferguson's store window."

"And just what is that?"

"A secondhand valve cornet."

She folded her hands across the beehive against her bony breast and stared at him. So this was what had happened to him in Cedar Rapids. Music. And all the while she'd figured what else. She nodded and in a few words he told her what he had discovered on the outing. He knew he could speak to her without sounding like a fool, and all his longing became an open secret between them.

"How much is it?" she asked.

"Nine dollars and four bits."

She did not have that much money. It may as well have been

thirty-five dollars so far as the beehive was concerned. It angered her and she beat back at injustice.

"I'll certainly not give you any nine dollars and four bits. And what if one of us fell sick? Medicines cost money. And what if Bethesda or Benjamin or the others need clothes to keep warm? Or what if your father gets taken so he can't work for a while and then who buys what I must cook for my hungry mouths? Just so you can have a brass horn to make noises on! You may be the oldest, but that don't fit you to have everything and the rest nothing! Do you know who is always after me to buy him books? Mordell is, that's who. Did I, though I would if I rightly could? No!" She went to the closed shelves and put the beehive back where she always hid it. "I'm not going to hide it in a new place," she said, "for I trust you."

"Yes, you do, yes, and you can."

Her eyes suddenly held a sting. She winked it away.

"Maybe Ferguson don't have to ask that much for it."

"Yes. I asked him."

"He always was *near.*"

Like other discussions which skirted crisis in that family, this one ended only in a gradual settling back of silence, and of old familiar troubles.

lv

To Olin these seemed sharper and more hopeless as new discoveries came his way.

The next time a steamer arrived it was not the old *Menominee* which, they said, was laid up for repairs downriver. It was the United States mail and passenger packet *New St. Paul,* a younger, grander ship. When she came in, Olin was at the levee, for she tied up after school.

The channel was narrow and she lay athwart it at a long angle. Her bow touched the shore, and dockhands first unloaded her from the bow and then took new cargo up along inclined planks. From the side she looked like a two-story store front with wooden galleries. On top was a deckhouse and on this again was the pilot house, which resembled a miniature bandstand. Just behind it rose her twin stacks tall and black. Her side wheels were encased in great half-drums which carried her name. Somewhere down under breathed her engines, asleep and softly hissing out steam. Olin tilted his head. There was another sound.

He came closer. What would they do to him if he ran up the planks? Perhaps he could find a bundle of some sort to carry which would justify his going aboard. For a moment he hesitated to take the risk; but what he heard pulled at him, and then, scowling forcefully and striding like a man, he simply walked straight across the levee, fell in between two work parties, and marched right up to the foredeck of the *New St. Paul*. Once there he continued the march until he was inside the main saloon cabin where he found the source of the sound that called him.

It was the sound of a square pianoforte. Framed by yellow velvet draperies looped with gold ropes and tassels, the piano occupied the center of a shallow little stage at one end of the magnificent steamboat room. An old man who looked like Andrew Jackson in the history book was making long fancy glides on the keys. When he reached the top he would linger and tremble his fingers until Olin was dazzled by the brilliant blur of sound. Then he would swoop downward to the thunder of the other end, and scowl, and make rumbles, and grind his teeth, sinking his narrow, bony, loose-skinned chin inside his stand-up collar. Knowing someone was listening, he played all the grander and harder. Even if he knew it was only a boy, he had to show what he could do, and at one point he rose off his cut-velvet piano stool and flipped out his coattail as if it were part of the music and came down again on the stool and suddenly went limp. He rolled his eyes to heaven and then shut them and made a pursed smile and his fingers played like gentle rain on the keys, and he seemed to show that he could be a poet of all moods. Then suddenly he changed, stopped playing, woke up, and asked Olin,

"Well, what can *you* do, now?"

"No, I can't do anything. Except listen. It surely was mighty fine."

The artist shook his head and showed his long, yellow, horse teeth in a sad smile.

"Oh, it was, once upon a time. It was, for certain. These hands have played before crowned heads and they have won gold medals and scrolls at many an international exposition of science, art and industry. But what are they doing now? Playing storm effects and moonlight mush for passengers who hardly listen on a moth-eaten old Miz'sippi steamboat."

"I don't think she's moth-eaten. I wish I was on her."

"Could you earn your way?"

"I don't know doing what."

"I lost my orchestra at Natchez last month, by which I mean my horn player. Can you play a cornet?"

Olin's heart took a jump.

"No, but I surely wish I could learn."

"I can teach you, if you have a cornet."

Olin felt like crying for the first time in many years.

"I don't have one. I know where I can get one, but it costs too much."

"What makes you think you could play it, anyway?"

"The bandmaster at Cedar Rapids told me I could learn."

"Well, he probably knows. Can you do anything else with music?"

"Well, it isn't music, just like that, but I can whistle."

"Then whistle."

The pianist turned to his keys and began to make up music that called for birds in the trees. Olin, at first hesitantly, then more confidently, began to do his birds. In a very short while the two performers were one in creating a kind of music that went right along.

"Try this!" cried the pianist without pausing, but switching to a real tune which Olin knew—the "Boston Waltz." Olin whistled the melody, but he kept his birds in too, and the result moved the old man to stand up and clap his hands once or twice.

"You're an entertainer!" he sang out. "What's your name? I am Professor McKlarney. Whistling won't do forever, but if you can learn to do as much on the trumpet, you'll never starve!"

"Olin Moresby Rainey. I can learn it."

"Oh, my gracious, how I need a trumpeter! That's all they'll listen to when they get to really having a good time on board. —Do you drink?"

Olin was both complimented and shocked at this.

"No, sir."

"Well, that's a relief. I lost my last one through drink. But what'm I saying. I can't take you. Oh, you could come along and whistle, but that would do only till you learned the cornet. And you haven't a horn and neither have I, nor do you play."

Professor McKlarney knew too much of old disappointments to

spend much time on new ones. He shrugged his bony shoulders, swept his long gray hair out of his collar, and sat down as if to resume his study of music.

"If you ever get a horn, speak to me again," he said, and began to exercise his hands in octave scales.

There was a short, shaking blast from the steam whistle of the *New St. Paul.* The professor angled his head at Olin to tell him to get off—they were about to sail. Olin left him, taking along the remarkable knowledge that he was—according to a professional—an entertainer. With him, too, went the sorrowful certainty that nothing could be done about it.

lvi

That night at home they all held their breath.

It was past nine and the father had not yet come home. They all knew, even little Benjamin, that when he came, matters would be much worse even than this stretched feeling in the stomach, which everybody got by looking at the mother. Her face was white and when she smiled to ease their fears they could have sobbed drily.

Olin and Mordell stayed close to Cleora and moved still closer when they heard footsteps on the porch.

They were firm steps, slow, heavy and important. Ruben Rainey when at his worst acted deliberately. His rages built themselves up out of the depths of his wounded silence. For a long time he would not say a word, but only hang his head forward and stare at them all in turn. His silent accusations were borne along his hot, red-rimmed gaze which looked as if it must hurt him as it left his eyes. Though he was powerfully built, his menace was something beyond body.

He came in this night and spoke to nobody but went and sat at the kitchen table.

"Would you have your supper now?" asked Cleora.

He shagged his great head about to see her and made no reply. His head swayed forward and back slowly, like a heavy weight delicately balanced. Cleora motioned to her sons to go to bed. The younger children were already upstairs, but wide awake, listening for the fury which sooner or later must explode.

"Not him. Him," said Ruben, indicating that Mordell was to leave, but Olin was to stay.

Cleora nodded and Mordell departed, walking backward until he was in the dark of the narrow steep hall. His stomach tasted in his throat. If his father struck his mother tonight, just this once more, he would come flying down the stairs and do his best to kill his father. With this resolve it was possible for him to leave as ordered.

In the kitchen nothing moved but the brass pendulum of the walnut clock on the shelf above the sink.

Olin knew that his father had been aggrieved for days because he had gone to Cedar Rapids. He knew that his mother was still in danger for having let him go. His guilt was unbearable and it moved him to speak.

"It wasn't her fault," he said. "I begged her to let me go and not tell you because I thought you would say no if we asked you."

A look of weary sweetness came over Ruben's work-grimed face and lingered there briefly. At last the excuse had come to him to break the hard thick shell of his own trouble.

"Come here," he said to Olin, almost lightly.

Olin glanced apprehensively at his mother as if to ask whether to obey.

"Don't look at her," said Ruben thickly but in a gentle voice. "Just come here to your father."

Olin went to him. As he went, he watched his father's heavy arm draw back to gather the distance from which it would strike him when he was near enough.

When the arm was as far back as it wanted to be, Ruben's face went broken and wild. His body tensed stiff as iron, braced to destroy. His voice let go with a shout. He smashed Olin to the floor with one strike and picked him up to do it again. His lungs were bellows blasting out the sounds of his humiliation and his hatred before the whole world.

Olin bled. He put his young arms across his head, his face, but still he bled. The house shook the small hearts upstairs.

"Not good enough, are we," bellowed Ruben and struck again. "Get away whenever you can, hey," and struck. "Go crawling around asking the price of a valve cornet, will you," and slapped his son with an open hand like a hickory board, "when nobody here has enough to eat, hey?"

Olin on the floor assumed protectively the shape of an unborn child. His mother came to cover him.

"You," cried her husband, and sent her across the room with a crashing swing. The air was rank with the breath of the corn whisky which had brought him home as temporary master of his world.

In the door appeared Mordell. He saw Cleora pulling herself upward by holding to a chair.

"Did he strike you?" he yelled, "for if he did, I will kill him!"

Ruben Rainey heaved himself aback and stared at his second son. Anger went soft and melted into grief. He sank against the table, covered his face and wept aloud in a hooting voice for the son who would kill his father. Upstairs the little ones clutched each other and hugged with relief. Like Olin, they knew that the nature of the terror below had changed, and that presently peace would descend, after the father had been hauled to his bed as if never to awaken again.

lvii

When Ruben was safely lost in sleep, Cleora came to the boys' bed and, as she expected, found Olin awake. She took him quietly away, in the dark, to the kitchen, and lighting no lamp, she bathed his cuts and bruises with cool water, as if to bathe his beaten heart. As she worked, she held a whispered conversation with him.

"We've got to fix it for you to go," she breathed. "I shouldn't have waited for tonight to know it."

"Go where?"

"Anywhere. Can't you think of where to go? I know your father. He's got his mind set now about you. It'll only get worse the longer you stay."

"Why does he hate me."

"He don't hate you sober, son. He just can't stand to know he can't be what he would be to you if he could. He sees you're a man, just about, and it makes him feel less a man. I don't know. I don't know."

She spoke in mysteries, but never had she failed him in her good sense, and he tried to know what she meant.

"Where can you go, Olin?"

"I could have gone today, only I couldn't."

"Where!"

He told her about Professor McKlarney, the want of a valve cornet, and the United States mail and passenger packet *New St. Paul.*

"He said I would never starve if I could learn the horn."

"Do you figure he meant it, or was he just talking for talking?"

"I figure he meant it."

She gasped between a laugh and a catch of her breath and put her cheek to his brow for a moment of hidden leave-taking. Then she got them both to their feet and said,

"Go to bed and sleep, my honey. It may take a bit to fix everything, but whatever it'll have to happen afterward, it'll be worth it."

He was so drowsy with assuagement and love that he hardly heard her, and only remembered her words when the *New St. Paul* was reported to be scheduled for Galena again on the following Wednesday.

On that morning, Cleora said to Olin as he was about to leave for school with his lunch in a newspaper packet,

"Come home at noon."

He held up his sandwich and gave her his best look of comical puzzlement.

"I know," she said, "you've got your lunch. But you come on home. Alone."

When he came at noon the house had another of its particular stillnesses. This one was created by young children who were told to stay upstairs in the bedroom with the door shut no matter what.

As he came to the house, he heard her start to make busy noises, slamming this and shoving that, like a woman working so hard she don't know which way to turn. So it was that she managed to look cross when he stepped in, and the slapped-at tears on her face might have been beads of honest sweat. She hardly gave him a moment to turn around, but said straight off,

"Now Olin Moresby Rainey, you take this bundle." She reached it out from under the kitchen table. He took it. It was a bundle of a few of his clothes, tied with twine. It was heavy because of something inside it. She went on, "The *New St. Paul* is to be here this afternoon, for I asked and they told me down to the levee. Now you go and keep yourself somewheres out of sight till she comes in. Do you know a place to go?"

"Yes. I have a place by the river."

"Well, wait there till she's ready to go off again, and then you run lickety-split and you climb on, and go find your piano professor, and you just tell him yes: there you are: you have come to work for him. You know what's inside that bundle. First I went to the beehive and took some out. Don't look so, there's some left. Then I got Mr. Ferguson to give the cornet to me to pay the rest on it so much a week and when you're rich and famous you can send me some money to make it up. You stay out of sight, now, hear? And if the *New St. Paul* keeps coming back to Galena, you just lie low till she's gone again. Not that she will, once the *Menominee* is back on the run."

"Mother."

"I know. I know. Now don't you go to saying it. It's hard enough as 'tis." She opened a cupboard. "Now here's some extra sandwiches to tide you over. And here"—she reached in her apron—"is what can be spared out of the beehive to start you off in the world."

He reached for her fisted money and then broke against her in a wild hug. At the moment when she gave him the freedom he longed for, he would not go. She kissed him hard and set him away.

"Go on, my honey. Don't you let me see you till you can come back stronger than all of us."

She took him to the door and put him out. He went down the hill and turned to see if she was watching. She was not. He knew she could not have borne to watch him go. . . .

Trumpeter Rainey fell silent, thinking about something he heard a long time afterward from his family.

"After I left home that day," he said to Matthew, "she waited till she heard the whistle blow on the *New St. Paul* and she knew I was safely gone. Then she fetched out her china beehive again, and took out what was left. It was two dollars. Then she marched down to Doctor Jimson's office, and she said, no, she told him, it's not for me, I'm not sick, she said, but I want you take this two dollars here, she said, and next time you send for books, Doctor, send for a two-dollar book for my son Mordell Rainey, to read and keep, and help *him* on *his* way for the way *he* wants to be, she said, when the time comes. —*That's* the kind of woman she was, sir."

Matthew nodded seriously. It was enough of a tribute for Trumpeter Rainey, who knew that his lieutenant was moved to hear of a mother like that, and maybe, even, was thinking about his own.

"I told everyone I was twenty," said Rainey, "and nobody believed it, but I felt like it soon enough."

"How did you ever get into the U.S. cavalry from a Mississippi steamer?" asked Matthew.

The trumpeter sighed strenuously.

"Just the way life does you," he said, with every accent of a personally earned philosophy. "I made good money for several years, and then Professor McKlarney took sick and died, and I lost everything I had, waiting to get a new job. I was every kind of a danged fool, sir; I had too much freedom all of a sudden. Gambling and likker and women—one woman specially. Anyhow, I knew it was time for me to straighten up. I enlisted. They sent me to Fort Sheridan, someone heard me blow a cornet, and before I knew it, I was an army trumpeter. And here I am."

lviii

The rate of their progress toward Mexico was difficult for the troopers to measure or even observe. They proceeded mostly at a walk, mounted. So seen, the ground passed slowly by beneath them, and the distance showed no change even to the fixed gaze. The only sense of advance they could know came through spending the hours with no regard for accomplishment. Sighting mountains far to the southwest in the morning, the soldiers if they looked at them again in the late afternoon saw a slight alteration in the mountain outline. Matthew could imagine that he had remained stationary, and that sometime during the day some great hand had given a quarter-turn to the row of mountains without bringing it any nearer. But he recognized his progress, to which his patience was exactly equal, with none left over. Joe Dummy cautioned him against a pursuit too close. It would be as unfortunate as a pursuit too slow.

"Too slow," Joe had made plain, "would lose the quarry for good. Too fast would warn them. They would perceive dust far away. They would watch to see if it came for them, however, far and slowly. If it did, they would make a plan to meet, and then they would scatter and disappear, and nothing would come of this pursuit."

Matthew accepted the advice of superior experience; and, in his private impression of it, the pursuit crept forward halfway between everything ahead and behind.

His men were generally at ease, if not entirely comfortable. The heat was great. The dust made thirst, and water was rationed. Few of the troopers had ever ridden so far at a time. Some developed raw skin from the chafing of thigh and calf. Matthew inspected such damage during the hourly halts. The men wanted to put water on the hot sore areas, but he refused permission. Water was precious, and besides, the abrasion would heal sooner if kept dry. He ordered them to tie their yellow silk neck cloths around the sore limb to ease the sliding contact between skin and the thick wool of army trousers, manufactured of "sky-blue kersey." When the soldiers asked if they might remove their dark-blue flannel shirts for coolness under the sun, the lieutenant refused permission, telling them that thick cloth, even if it trapped heat, kept the body cooler under direct sunlight than air itself.

They grumbled at believing him, but believe him they did. They knew already that as he gave them care, he would give them safety, fairness and bravery when these too should be needed. He knew them well by now. He felt their tempers without working to do so.

Generally these remained good—though he wondered now and then about Cranshaw. Cranshaw was not yet his entertaining self. He seemed thoughtful since the discovery in the hills. When Matthew would catch his eye he would smarten in his saddle, and with a pleading look to let his moment of chicken-heartedness be forgotten, he seemed to make himself brave, worthy and personable for the eye of his commander. Matthew heartened him with a nod and a wink; but later, unobserved, he would notice that Cranshaw was again downcast. Perhaps he should have sent him back after all, to Fort Delivery, on the squad's mortal errand. He shrugged. There was nothing to be done about it now but adjust a balance between hardship and the available comforts.

Chief of these was "Rio" coffee, which the soldiers drank at every meal but supper, when Joe Dummy would allow no campfire for the smoke that would stand forth in the low rays of the setting sun and the cooling air which rose from the desert. The coffee was boiled until all its natural flavor was gone. They carried no tea, for this was famous as "the laundress' drink," and the troopers were self-consciously truculent about showing indulgence for the slightest effeminacy in their own habits. Baking powders and lime juice were included in the rations of the expedition—Doctor Gray had seen to that, with a word to Matthew about the value of both starches and antiscorbutics on a long march away from garden vegetables or canned fruits with acid content.

By evening of the second day the column was near enough to Mexico to be ready, if the command were given, to cross the border during the following morning. News of this came to Matthew from Joe, and Trumpeter Rainey heard it too. Presently the whole squad knew it.

In their various ways they made their acts of inner readiness.

lix

Darkness fell without a moon. The moon was waning and would rise late and lean its misshapen way over the heaven and persist into the next daylight. Between all the men of the detachment there was a sense of unspoken mystery. Matthew felt it on his own account, and also on theirs. They were thinking that tomorrow they might enter Mexico. What they would find there they could not imagine in any clear detail. But they felt that this would be a fateful step, and contemplation of it filled them with awe and wonder.

What came into their minds with power was the exact recollection of what had been done to two members of their community by the creatures they now pursued. No man among them was so indifferent that he did not in thought see his own flesh crawl as if those horrors had happened to him and might yet happen, if the Apaches were engaged and should win. But no man spoke of this or showed open concern.

They made camp under the lieutenant's direction and waited for his designation of the guards for the four watches of the night. The roster was taken in strict rotation as to which four men went on duty—all knew that on this night they would be the lieutenant himself, who took his turn in order to bear every burden of the common hardship, Joe Dummy, Trumpeter Rainey and Private Cranshaw. What was yet to be announced was the order of their watches.

During his supper of cold biscuit, cold bacon and canned apricots, Matthew considered his decision. The most important watches were the first and the last. The Indian enemy almost never attacked in full night, but in early night he might be making observations, and in the hour before dawn he might fall upon a sleeping camp. The hours between were relatively secure. Therefore, decided Matthew, and told his men so,

"Joe the scout will take from nine to eleven. I will take from eleven to one. Cranshaw will take from one to three. Rainey will take from three to five. We will march at five thirty. Get all the sleep you can. Wake up promptly to relieve the guard who wakes you. He wants his sleep as you do. Be especially careful to watch the picket line. Call me at any time if you observe anything the littlest bit suspicious. We're getting closer. We've got something to do. We'll do it, but only if every man does his share. I'll say this, I never saw a better squad."

They hungered after his words, and when he praised them, they held their faces still, forgetting that the young officer had never before had a squad. They lived in his serious regard for them, and accepted it as their due.

The night was well ordered.

Matthew's last reflections before sleeping were full of satisfaction. Joe Dummy was the right man to guard the first watch. He could see shadows on the desert even where no moon shone. Matthew himself would span the midnight when the moon would rise. For the following watch, when least responsibility would be required, Cranshaw was the right man to assign, since even if weak he must do his share, and be given a chance to heal his inner wounds of that fear which he had helplessly exposed. As for the dawn guard —Rainey's story had given Matthew a rooted confidence in him. The trumpeter had become a man, a survivor of ambition, sorrow and folly, early in life. He could deal with the world as he found it, even if it brought danger.

lx

Between three and four o'clock the lieutenant was awakened by a rough hand on his shoulder. He came awake and bolt upright instantly. Joe Dummy was by him.

"Joe! What is it!"

Joe was faintly visible in the waning moonlight. He gestured over the camp. There was no guard.

"No guard!" exclaimed Matthew. "Where is Rainey!"

Rainey was still asleep.

Nobody had awakened him.

"But I put Cranshaw on duty myself," said Matthew, rising. "He was to call Rainey." He called out, "Cranshaw!" over the sleeping figures. The men awoke. Nobody answered the name. Cranshaw was absent.

"What time is it?" asked Rainey thickly.

The air was still cold. The men shivered as they felt it in their waking. Matthew asked,

"Does anybody know where Cranshaw is?"

There was no reply.

"Very well. Trumpeter, it is your watch. It is about ten minutes to four. Take up your post."

"Yes, sir. Where are the rations?"

Matthew indicated the sentry post where he had established the collected saddlebags between the camp and the picket line and which he had himself guarded earlier. In a moment Rainey called out from his post,

"Sir, there's something wrong here."

Matthew joined him to see.

There was something to see, and more to think. Half of the rations of the detachment was missing. In a moment they discovered that one of the horses was also gone. Cranshaw had deserted during his watch.

"No wonder he didn't call me!" said Rainey.

"Which way did he go?" asked Matthew.

In the faint darkness Joe Dummy made a slow wide circle with his arm. It said that Cranshaw could have gone to the rim of the world along any line from this point at the center. In the darkness nobody could tell. They must wait for daylight to read the ground.

To be trapped by the night did not improve Matthew's temper. He was filled with rage almost to sickness by the corporate hurt done to his command by Cranshaw's breach of moral law. That a man for whatever ends of his own could steal from his comrades half of the stuff they needed to survive in the desert for a limited and fixed time—this was the personal, sickening part of the event. The other, official part was that a soldier doing duty in the field should desert on approaching the enemy. Cranshaw running away from something which no one could name was also running straight toward the hardest judgment of which the Army was capable in peacetime.

Matthew sent the remaining troopers back to sleep, if they could sleep, and Rainey continued his guard. Joe went to kneel at the outskirts of the camp watching for light in the east. Matthew sat on a blanket and came to new decisions.

His total rations on marching out were meant to last the squad seven days. This was now reduced by Cranshaw's theft to half that time. The pursuit into Mexico must be abandoned because of inadequate supplies. A new pursuit must be taken up—Cranshaw must be found and taken under arrest to Fort Delivery. The deserter had changed the mission of the detachment and its conditions of living, and even its internal relations, for some of the troopers with supreme bitterness wanted to get their hands on Cranshaw and kill him for his bad faith. One or two others felt more lenient. They talked in low voices. They said he was not himself. They said they didn't entirely blame him for feeling the way he did, though they would never have gone as far as Cranshaw in acting upon his feelings.

"You men:" said Matthew sharply after allowing the talk to continue for a few minutes, "settle down and get all the sleep you can. You'll need it."

The camp was quiet but wakeful. Matthew gazed at Joe, and saw him lift his shoulders and head toward the sky. In dim silhouette he looked like a wolf or a coyote making silent expression of doleful meaning. But he was sampling a new condition of the air which was making its way so gradually that no one else perceived it at first. Joe came to Matthew, and gestured toward the leaning moon. He wafted air toward his nostrils with his hand and sniffed audibly, like a dog intent.

"What is it?" asked Matthew.

He looked at the moon. It was beginning to dim. It was held in veils of air thickening toward the wide darkness. It looked like a great airy misshapen pearl in rings of nacreous dust. A vast dust storm was rising out of Mexico, and its first breath was the scent in the air of fine acrid particles of drifted earth. The scent alone was what Joe Dummy had first detected. Soon the dust itself could be seen. Joe showed with turbulent motions how the storm would grow and grow, until by full morning nothing could be seen.

"How long will it take to blow over?" asked the young officer.

Joe showed one, two, maybe three days, with fingers. Who could say? It would have to last until it was over.

"Well, we will look for Cranshaw anyway," stated Matthew. "Find me a trail if you can."

They found one with daylight. It showed tracks leading westward, toward the path of the setting moon. Cranshaw had a lead of three hours. Once beyond earshot of the camp he had taken up the gallop. His lead in distance would be even greater than his lead in time, for the detachment still proceeded at a walk. This was required by Joe Dummy, who pointed out that a march at high speed—sustained trot or long gallops—would cost the horses and men the loss of much perspiration. With reduced water rations, this could be dangerous.

"But he might get entirely away from us," protested the lieutenant.

No, said Joe, they would find him. You could always find what you were after in the desert if you kept after it long enough, and knew what to look for, in what places.

"We're going to be short of food in two days," said Matthew.

Joe looked at him with a flat face. His meaning, which came through, was that men could live much longer on nothing than they thought they could—even white soldiers without all the things they thought they must have.

By eight o'clock the full storm was upon them. The sky was filled from rim to rim with flying heavy dust. The wind was strong. It drove the dust into the skins of the troopers, stinging. It choked their nostrils and mouths. They made mud about their eyes with tears stung forth by the hot wind and the driving dust. The ground was swept steadily and the marks of the trail were obliterated. With their heads down, the soldiers marched westward. Once or twice during the morning the sun came to sight in rifts of the sandy cloud that covered all. The sun was like a disk of pale blue metal. The dust closed over it soon again.

"Is there any shelter anywhere about here?" cried Matthew into Joe's ear.

It seemed that there was a low mesa, called Bear Mesa, along their westerly course. If they could find it in the storm, they could come to its north side and be protected from the worst of the blow. If Cranshaw happened upon it, he would probably take shelter there too.

"Let us try to find it," ordered Matthew.

Though he showed it to no one, a bitter concern filled him. The one faculty which made search useful in the daytime desert—sight itself—was now useless. The dust blizzard benefited only the deserter who had nothing to lose by riding on, no matter what conditions descended from the sky. Matthew doubted the value of leading his men on a blind pursuit.

Further, he was filled with a sense of failure. On his first expedition against the enemy in the field he was obliged to abandon his mission because of a crime against the Army by one of his own men. He felt blame for the crime. Cranshaw had shown weakness in his presence. Why had he trusted him? He saw now that an experienced commander would have handled Cranshaw altogether differently. Matthew, by treating him like all the rest, had hoped that he would behave like all the rest. It was a grave miscalculation. Its consequences could be serious, even deathly, for other men in his charge. He would have a sorry report to make to his acting commanding officer when he returned to Fort Delivery.

The wind was like an oven breath. The dust thickened toward noon. They halted for a brief meal. The horses faced away from the driving wind, and the men crouched with their backs to it. When it was time to resume the march, Matthew asked his scout,

"Where is west?"

Joe indicated it.

"How do you know?" asked Matthew. There were no shadows, the sun was gone, the day was placeless and all pale-colored like the tawny fur of a mountain lion.

"Well, I know," replied Joe.

Matthew took his word for it. They mounted and moved out again.

"The mesa," said Matthew. "How much farther?"

Joe did not know, but he expected to see it by now. He was looking hard for it, because he felt certain that Cranshaw would have seen it and taken refuge there until sure of his freedom from pursuit. The mesa had many little depths in its cliffs where someone could hide. Joe Dummy had used it long ago. If it had rained here recently, there would be water in basins where animals and men could drink.

An hour later the air cleared a little. The distance was extended. As the light turned from sand color to white, lines of the earth a few miles away became visible. Joe Dummy swept the limited horizon, and then halted.

There. Behind them. Bear Mesa. They had passed it in the thick of the storm. It rose sharply at each end and showed a flat top about a third of a mile long and four hundred feet above the surrounding surface. Even in clear weather it could be hidden by the swell and hollow of the ground over distance. Now the storm was not yet over. If they were to use the mesa they should go to it now.

Matthew ordered the column about. They rode to Bear Mesa. Their spirits came lighter. Here at least was an event, a possible haven, in the threatening monotony of the overblown day. They came to the mesa's west end and rode around to its north side. It was mid-afternoon. Under the north cliffs there was an effect of hollowed calm, for the wind and dust drove over the edge and came scouring down to earth at some little distance from the base. Matthew dismounted the soldiers to rest for a little while. He let himself back upon a rocky slope and shut his eyes wearily. His weariness was more in his thoughts than his flesh. He did not sleep, but the feeling was one of sudden awakening when he smelled on the air a new clear scent. He sprang up. He smelled rain. He looked at Joe, who nodded. Rain was coming from the south behind the dust.

Let everybody come to work, Joe asked. The men joined him. He showed them where to place small rocks and how to pack these with loose earth, to make rims for catching rain water at the ends of runnels in the sloping sides of the mesa. They could fill their canteens after the shower. It was wise to be ready for the water.

The day turned dark. It was a blue darkness and it drove away the thick continuing squall of the dust which choked the eyes, the mouth, the very skin. The sky roared with the coming downpour. The drying heat of the air gave way to chill downdrafts off the mesa top. Matthew put his men in shelter under rocky flanks of the mesa clefts.

With sudden pounding energy the rain came down the north side of the mesa as the cloudburst moved across the flat top. A trooper gave out with a yell of excitement and thankfulness for the cooling rain. The others turned to see him. He was hauling off his shirt, and then his boots and breeches, and in a moment he was bare. He thrust his clothes into the rain shadow of a big rock and he ran out into the thick downpour. The soldiers glanced at Matthew to see what he thought of this unordered action. He grinned and began to take off his own shirt. The rest took this for a signal. All but Joe Dummy were in another minute standing forth under the cold pounding rain, bathing their stifled skins and breathing the wet rain and sweetened air. The scout remained in his shelter squatting with his arms about his knees. The transported men refreshing their hot, dirty, bare bodies in the sluicing rain looked to him like witless boys taking useless exercise. Lightning split the sky over the mesa and thunder shook the rocks. The soldiers cried back at the elements and capered with joy. Joe briefly prayed them free of danger in their folly of defying the powers of the sky.

lxi

The mesa was like a palace of rock. Here they should stay the night, said Joe Dummy.

"Why?"

So: the water now caught by the improvised basins was muddy with reddish earth. In a few hours much of the sediment would settle, and by morning the water would be pure and clear. Then all canteens could be refilled to last for two more days.

"But what if Cranshaw got too far ahead of us? We still have a few hours of daylight."

Yes. And so. And well. Before moving ahead from here it was only wise to search the great flanks of the mesa to see if anybody was in hiding there. That would take a long time, and must be done, for secrecy and surprise, by one man. Night would come before the search could be ended. It would proceed better after dark, even, than before. So. And this.

"Why?"

Because so. This way. If there is a man in the rocks, with a horse, there will be small sounds which are better heard at night. Not seeing, the searcher will listen the more acutely.

"But what if he gets away during the night while we are all asleep?"

That. So this. After the rain, the tracks of anybody moving out of the mesa in any direction would show for weeks. He could be followed almost at anybody's own time and pleasure and one day when he least expected it he would be overtaken.

It was then decided. The detachment would stay overnight on platforms of talus under the overhanging walls of Bear Mesa. The sol-

diers were glad to know this. They asked if they might have a fire to
make coffee and heat their beans.

No. And no. And no—this was Joe Dummy's opinion. Rosy light
off the rocks would be a warning, if anybody was watching after dark
for pursuers. There would be one pursuer. It would be Joe Dummy.
He would set out to find his way alone to the top of the mesa. From
the rim he would be able to see down into all the long folds of the
rock. He could put his ear over the edge to listen. When he heard,
and then saw, what he expected to find, he would bring Cranshaw
back.

lxii

He did so at half past five in the following morning. Leading Cranshaw's horse, and marching Cranshaw ahead of him at carbine point,
Joe Dummy appeared coming along the northern base of Bear Mesa
from the east.

Matthew saw him first and motioned to him to halt below.

"You men," ordered Matthew to the others about him, "remain
here. Private Cranshaw is a prisoner. He will be protected until I
deliver him to the guardhouse at the fort. None of you will speak
to him at any time for any purpose without my permission. You will
all stay away from him, except the man I designate to lead his horse."

Matthew went down the rocky slope until he was face to face
with Private Cranshaw and his captor. The young officer felt his
heart pounding, and wondered at it. His exertions coming down the
talus were not so violent that his heart must beat after them. What
troubled him almost uncontrollably was anger, now that he confronted the thieving deserter of his command. He, the lieutenant,
had been the victim of a betrayal like a betrayal in love. The excellence of someone had been granted and trusted; and it had turned
false. The healthy, happy and comely presence of a companion had
been shown to conceal corruption. A man for whom he was responsible, and thus a man for whose safety and well-being he would have
fought and died if necessity had asked, was now known to be unworthy of such guardianship. Matthew looked at him.

"Hello, sir," said Cranshaw, tentatively, with his head turned a
little away but with his clear, doubtful blue eyes on Matthew's. Cran-

shaw's smile was as charming as ever. His brow was wrinkled with appealing perplexity. His mouth was fixed in a half-smile of hope. He had pulled off his hat and his curly pale brown hair fell in a boyish lock over his forehead. Every expression and attitude that he had always found successfully likable now showed in him as he stood a prisoner before his young commander. He looked as if he had already exempted himself from all blame, and was only happy to be back again with the squad.

A chill settled about Matthew's heart and brought him calm. If Cranshaw was without remorse, then he was irredeemable, and Matthew need waste no feeling over him.

"Private Cranshaw, you will speak to me only when spoken to," said Matthew, in accents which recalled the impersonal severity of his cadet life. "Turn about and walk around the side of that big boulder. Joe, keep him covered."

In a moment the three of them were out of sight of the squad higher up. Joe tethered Cranshaw's mount.

"Stand there facing me, Private Cranshaw," said Matthew. To Joe he said, "Is that his carbine?"

"Yes," said Cranshaw cheerfully.

"You will address me as *sir* at all times."

"Yes, sir."

"Very well," said Matthew. "I now officially inform you, Private Cranshaw, that you are a prisoner of the United States Army, charged with abandonment of your post while on sentry duty, desertion while in the field, and theft of supplies, rations and other government property."

Cranshaw's face paled and then he blushed violently. His eyes shone with sudden light. His cheeks seemed to be dragged downward showing the shape of bone. He licked his lips. He looked like a young man who had never heard of any such charges as were now made against him. But his habit of charm persisted, and he smiled deprecatingly at the lieutenant.

"You have nothing to smile about, Mr. Cranshaw," said Matthew. "You will answer my questions. Your answers will go into my official report."

"Yes, sir." Cranshaw was now serious. He had never before seen this impersonal stranger in Lieutenant Hazard. Much must have happened to change him so from the strict but friendly young officer

of the second platoon. Matthew's black eyes were hardened and their
light seemed to come off steel points.

"Why did you run away, Mr. Cranshaw?"

"I heard something and went after it."

"*Sir.*"

"Sir."

"What did you hear?"

"Someone rustling around near the picket line, sir."

"What did you do then?"

"I went to investigate and then I thought I should follow, sir."

"Why didn't you call me, or wake someone else?"

"I wasn't sure, sir, yet, so I thought I would make sure."

"What did you do next?"

"I took my horse and saddle, sir."

"Then what."

"I went out where I thought I heard the disturbance and I walked
after it, sir."

"What else did you take with you?"

"Nothing else, sir."

Matthew pointed to Cranshaw's saddle on the tethered horse. Extra
saddlebag and canteen were lashed there.

"Oh, yes, sir," said Cranshaw with a self-forgiving smile at his
omission, "I did not know how long I would have to follow the
Indian, and I thought I should have some rations along." He risked
a comradely smile in reference to the common lot. "A man has to
eat, sir, after all."

"What Indian?"

"Oh, why, the Indian I thought I heard out by the picket line."

"How did you know it was an Indian?"

"Why, I didn't think it could be anything else, sir," said Cranshaw
in an aggrieved voice. Matthew pierced him with a look.

"Now let us see, Mr. Cranshaw," he said. "You went out to investigate a noise which you were sure was made by an Indian, and
before waking anyone you decided to be certain of what were after all
merely suspicions. In order to make certain of these you saddled a
horse and attached to it enough supplies to carry nine men three and
a half days, or one man for almost a month. You were prepared to
go quite a distance to make sure before waking me or someone else.
Having made sure, Mr. Cranshaw, say at the end of ten days, were
you prepared to turn around and inform me of what you found out?"

Private Cranshaw looked at the ground.

"You are lying to me, Mr. Cranshaw."

"I left half of the rations behind, sir," said Cranshaw, with an involuntary catch of breath that was like a dry sob. "I didn't take them all."

Matthew bit his jaws together at the desperate absurdity of this defensive statement. The confusion in Cranshaw's statements exasperated him, and the cowardice which, he was certain, lay behind these made him contemptuous. Yet if cowardice was alien to Matthew's nature, he was driven to dig for its motive in Cranshaw. He felt that he must try to understand it, for his own satisfaction if nobody else's, though what other good was now to be accomplished by such understanding he could not say.

"When did you make your plans, Mr. Cranshaw?"

"Plans sir?—I guess just at the time I thought I heard the Indian."

"When did you make your plans, Mr. Cranshaw, to steal our food, and crawl away during sentry duty, and walk softly until it was safe to mount and gallop? These matters were not spontaneous."

Cranshaw gave him a pleading look.

"But I told you, sir . . ."

Matthew remained silent and simply posed his own presence. It spoke out with righteousness and physical power under control. All that he was stood against Cranshaw like a world lost to Cranshaw forever. Could anyone despise Cranshaw so wholly as the young officer seemed to? Cranshaw could not believe this and yet he must. It cost him his imposture. The eager, thoughtless, impulsive youth vanished in Cranshaw, and his place was taken by a weak self for whom he sorrowed. Tears came up to his eyes. His mouth trembled. The charm he had tried to invoke now inadvertently came to his being, and in his misery he gave Matthew for the first time a qualm of sympathy for him as a fellow being in mortal trouble.

"The idea came to me," he said, "as we rode down toward Mexico after we found the—the sergeant and Annie."

Yes, Matthew remembered Cranshaw's obscurities of behavior. Bitterly he chided himself for not having taken them as grave warnings.

"As you worked out your scheme," asked Matthew, "didn't you give a thought to the men you were going to leave hungry and thirsty?"

"I did, yes, sir, I did, I did, but I couldn't help it. I couldn't forget what I had seen." Cranshaw was sobbing now in widely separated gasps. The sound hardened Matthew toward him further.

"We had all seen it, Mr. Cranshaw."

"Yes, sir, I know, I know. But I kept thinking of what it would be like if something like that happened to me."

What leaped out in this was Cranshaw's dearness to himself. It was so dear that Matthew had no reach of the imagination to grasp it.

"We had a good chance to fight for our own safety, Mr. Cranshaw."

"Yes, sir, I know, sir, but you don't understand how I— And then we got close to Mexico, and I thought of when we would go on into the Mexico mountains, and there they would be, and if one of us got killed, or taken, then it might be me, and I can't stand the idea of what they did to Sergeant Blickner, and if they did it to me, sir, I—" He choked to silence. Revealing with a gesture the memory that had driven him to his ruin, he cupped his big tawny hands over his groin. His shapely face was fixed in the ruefulness of a weeping child. He raised it forward toward his commander begging for comfort and reassurance. Matthew, unable to offer these, withdrew from the whole allusion of Cranshaw's unspeakable concern. He took refuge in a calm resumption of his interrogation.

"Where were you planning to go, Mr. Cranshaw, once you had escaped from the Army?"

Cranshaw shuddered himself away from thoughts and replied,

"I was going to get to the railroad, and pick up a train for California, and find me a job there, probably up North somewhere, and take a new name, and start all over. I know I could make a success out there."

"If you were going to change your name, you knew you had done something wrong, then, Mr. Cranshaw?"

"Oh, yes, sir, I knew it was officially wrong."

"Officially?"

"Yes, sir, but I bet the other men would feel just as I did about it, if they had the chance."

"Many of us might feel afraid, Mr. Cranshaw. But not all of us would admit it by running away."

"No, sir."

Matthew was exasperated to the point of silence. He had never confronted a personality so elusive. Cranshaw, ostensibly healthy, well enough spoken, and certainly popular in his time at Fort Delivery, seemed unable to grasp the realities of his present situation. Further, he angered Matthew by being the agent of so many changes of plan. It was now time for the lieutenant to make his next decision. He weighed the pertinent circumstances.

"Joe," he said, "we have recovered most of the rations stolen by this man. Do you think they would stretch far enough, if we took up the trail after the Indians again?"

"Oh, no, sir!" exclaimed Cranshaw. His fright was plain. Matthew ignored him.

And yes: some people could go on those rations for quite a while, and so: so, replied Joe. More important, he felt, was the fact that the Apaches now had gained an additional two days' lead over the pursuing squad. But even that might be overcome, with much luck and skill. So. But who could promise, now?

There was, then, doubt about the outcome of resuming the chase, and therefore the wisdom of it. Matthew's first decisions in the field were of great discomfort to him. They were all based on unresolved possibilities and lost opportunity. Yet—so he hotly asked himself— would new opportunity be created if he were more daring? Why had he to figure and weigh and compromise? He knew well enough why— he was regarding the welfare of his men. But a great commander always seemed to behave as though no one but himself need be considered—his own dash and brilliance could move whole armies, bestowing on them dash and brilliance until they moved as one man, in the likeness of the commander. All seemed simple and clear in Creasy, like the difference between day and night. But not so with Matthew. He found no clear mark between the black and the white of his condition now. Was this what command was—to wish he could be sure of being right, and to hope that others would think he was?

"We are returning to Fort Delivery, Mr. Cranshaw." Cranshaw's relief at this was sickly to see. Matthew continued, "Your horse will be led. You may ride with your hands unbound so long as you make no move to escape."

Cranshaw was dumfounded at this.

"You mean I will be treated as a prisoner, sir?"

"Yes, Mr. Cranshaw, for that is exactly what you are, and I told you so before."

"Oh, I didn't know it would be this way, I didn't know it, I didn't know it."

"Mr. Cranshaw, do you have any idea what the penalty for your offenses can be, even in peacetime?"

"I guess not, no, sir."

Matthew squinted earnestly at the soldier's still watery eyes, and read there only a bewildered desire to be liked as he used to be.

"Then I won't tell you, now," said Matthew. It was as near to mercy as he could bring himself. He turned to Joe Dummy. "Joe, we'll get to moving now."

To be given silence was Cranshaw's worst punishment so far. If he spoke to anyone in the detachment he was not answered. Matthew's eye was upon the men. They looked at him and kept still. During the afternoon of their second day's march to Fort Delivery, Cranshaw called out,

"Listen to this, you fellows," and began to sing:

> There are bonds of all sorts in this world of ours,
> Fetters of friendship and ties of flowers,
>   And true-lovers' knots, I ween.

His voice was light and true, and into it he put all his powers of beguilement and appeal, such as had made him so popular in barracks. Giving now of his talents, he rose up in his heart. He presented his excellence to his comrades. How could they not receive it and ask for more?

> The boy and the girl are bound by a kiss,
> But there's never a bond of old friends like this—
>   We have drunk from the same canteen,
>   The same canteen.

He held the last syllable, letting it fall away sweetly. Then he looked about for all the faces of his friends. They need not have heard him, for all the response they showed.

"Hey, what's the matter with you all?" he asked in a lightly chiding tone. "Don't you want to hear old Crannie sing for you any more?" When there was no answer to this, Cranshaw laughed shortly and shrugged. His face whitened. His mouth dried up. He was amazed, and then fearful, and justly so.

lxiii

First Lieutenant Mainwaring, listening in his headquarters office to the report of Second Lieutenant Hazard, maintained an air of noncommittal gravity. Matthew showed him on a wall map of Arizona Territory where the detachment had gone, and what, in each significant place, it had done.

When he was finished Matthew waited for comment. It was long in coming. Teddy gazed out the window and whistled a tune in a whisper.

Across the parade was the guardhouse, at one end of the forge. In it reposed Private Cranshaw. He was seen only by the guard and the soldier who thrust his food through his briefly opened cell door. Cranshaw in the guardhouse exerted a greater power of presence upon the post than he had ever done in freedom. Nobody could glance toward the blacksmithy without thinking of the man behind the bars. He was the first prisoner to be lodged there since the present garrison had arrived. One of their number was shut away from them. Every man to one or another degree was able to think of himself in Cranshaw's state. Many fought away the sympathy they felt, cursing the prisoner for his deeds. Others were more courageous, and spoke up for him, and risked censure for their charity.

The acting commanding officer was the man most affected by the astonishing circumstance of having a thief and a deserter behind the guardhouse walls. He hated Cranshaw for presenting him with a heavy problem in discipline; and yet in a secretly pleasurable way, he was glad to have an opportunity to show what he would be capable of as a post commander faced with stern necessity. They would see. He was equal to the hardest challenges. It would not matter if they all thought him wrong in his decisions. Kitty would believe him right. That was enough.

He turned his wide, rounded face to Matthew, and in a mellow voice which was meant to convey the gentleness of a strong man performing hard duty, he said,

"Mr. Hazard, please write down the substance of your report as you gave it to me verbally."

"Yes, sir."

"I feel obliged to make one or two remarks on your conduct of your command."

"Yes, sir."

"Had I been in command of the detachment, I would have issued orders other than yours at certain points. I would have returned here with the whole squad bringing the remains of Sergeant Blickner and the laundress."

"Sir, my orders were to recover the missing persons, and the horses they had taken. I did recover the remains, and then I set out to overtake and recapture the horses, and if possible, the murderers."

"Circumstances in the field alter decisions. I would have armed a much larger force here and then set out in pursuit. With a larger force, even if Cranshaw would still have defected, I would have been able to continue the direct pursuit toward Mexico while detailing a smaller force to apprehend the deserter. In this way the primary purpose of the expedition would not have ended, as it did, in accomplishing nothing."

Matthew stood silent. Perhaps Mainwaring was right. Teddy took his silence for criticism.

"You do not agree, sir?" asked Teddy.

"Sir, I may have been wrong, but I came to my conclusions after weighing all the circumstances."

"I do not indicate that you deliberately did wrong. I only question your judgment."

"Yes, sir."

Having presented his planned severity, Teddy grew more friendly.

"Well, well, what's done is done. We will do what we can, now, to take cognizance of enemy action in this neighborhood. There are going to be changes around here. I count on you to help to make them effective. Meantime, I'll be preparing my disposition of the case of Private Cranshaw. I imagine you'd be interested to know what that will be?"

"Yes, sir."

"In due time I shall forward a request to convene a general court-martial to try Cranshaw, and I shall press for the death penalty." Matthew was astounded, and showed his feeling. "Abandonment of sentry post, theft, and desertion in the field," continued Teddy, "all the charges you yourself have filed against him."

"But sir, we are not in a state of war. The death penalty, as I understand it, applies only in wartime."

"State of war may be subject to interpretation, lieutenant. We must make an example of the man."

"Yes, sir, I agree. The discipline here is—" he halted.

"You will see discipline, lieutenant. Give me a day or two. When word gets out of what I intend for Cranshaw, you'll see discipline, all right."

"Lieutenant, I beg your pardon if I presume, but I would hesitate to speak of a sentence—an execution by firing squad—before a trial is held, when the court-martial might not arrive at the penalty you recommend. If it did not do so, the effect would be to weaken the command for having failed in its announced purpose."

"Again we differ in a matter of judgment, Matthew," said Teddy with an effect of largeness of nature. "I believe we'll just leave this to the acting commanding officer."

"Yes, sir."

Teddy grew gently serious.

"It was most affecting," he said, and his voice took on a mealy richness, "when we held services for the sergeant and Annie. We buried them out there in the graveyard. Captain Gray read the prayers. The whole garrison sang my favorite hymn, 'Safe Across the Stormy Waters.' It was beautiful. —And then, at the very end, this was remarkable and no one could have predicted it, my greyhound— we had never noticed that he was anywhere near—my greyhound set up a long, doleful cry, and he kept it up till the graves were half-filled. My wife broke down, and I nearly did. The only thing we lacked was Trumpeter Rainey to sound taps. But of course he was on the march with you."

The acting commanding officer stood up to terminate the interview. The propriety of the funeral services in the post cemetery had restored his comfort of temperament. He shook Matthew by a shoulder and said,

"Don't feel too bad about the little expedition, my boy. It was good experience for you. You'll do better next time."

lxiv

"From a man," wrote Matthew to Laura a week later one evening—a mail bag was going out the next morning by wagon to Driscoll— "who has never, so far as I know, been more than fifty yards from this fort since he got here eight months ago, such a remark is fairly hard to take. The joke is, I have already had more real experience than he has so far as activity in the field against enemy raiders is concerned." He paused. Would Laura think he was whining? If she were here, he would be able to discuss the whole affair with her, and she would see in his eyes and hear in his speech how honestly objective he was trying to be. And yet his feelings smarted, and deep inside his thought flickered the idea put there by Mainwaring—the idea that perhaps he had not handled matters as well as possible in the five-day march. He resolved to confine himself to a simple report for Laura of the whole movement he had led, and of what had happened since his return. It was enough to make a full letter. Resuming his page after the chronicle of his expedition and Mr. Mainwaring's critical remarks, Matthew wrote:

My self-respect was somewhat restored by a call from Captain Gray at my quarters late the same day. He said the C.O. had given him an accounting of my report, and that he (the doctor) had stoutly commended my course of action. At this Mainwaring grew lofty and closed the discussion. I asked the doctor if he knew what M. is planning to do about Cranshaw. He said no. I told him. He could hardly believe his ears, and then he erupted into fury. He thought the plan to let the men know that the prisoner was facing general court-martial and prosecution under the death sentence was sure to be ruinous as far as the state of society here is concerned.

Well, my dearest, he was right; and because I thought the same way, so was I. Mr. Mainwaring sent for Sgt. Fry, acting commander of the first platoon, and told him to let it be known in the barrack that Pvt. Cranshaw would be held prisoner for general court-martial and that he, the acting cndg. offr., would press for death sentence. He told the sergeant that an example had to be made, and that no penalty was too severe for a man who was capable of defecting in his duty at such a time, etc., etc., and if it was the last thing he did, he

was going to see that the new C.O. when he arrived would find a
garrison smartened up in every respect.

Sgt. Fry was stunned, as he said later. He did go back to the
barrack, and he did tell what he had heard. He knew, and so did
Captain Gray, and so did I, what any group of soldiers would think
on receiving such news of one of their number. The first thing they
all said was that this was peacetime, and only in wartime would, or
should, the death penalty be considered for desertion etc. It was what
you could expect—but what did then occur was something none of
us imagined might come.

I was dining with the Grays when we heard odd noises coming
across the parade. The captain went to see, and then in a cold, flat
voice, called me. In the late twilight we could see a gathering of men
coming and talking loudly and heading for the headquarters. At the
foot of the hq. steps they halted, and one of their number went up
the steps and rapped on the door. It was Sergeant Fry, as I could tell
by the outline of his figure—he always stood with his upper body
slouched, and his legs sloped straight backward at a long angle.
Soon the door opened and let light out on the porch and the mob—
for this was a mob. "Mutiny, by George," said the captain beside me.
He nudged me forward and we went over to the side of hq. porch to
see and hear better. Mainwaring said, "Well, Sergeant Fry, you have
business with me?" The sergeant saluted and held out a paper. "What
is this?" said Ted, and his voice trembled a little, and the sergeant
said it was a petition, which he presented on behalf of almost the
whole troop, who had signed it, and he had been the first to sign.
"What does it petition for?" asked Teddy, and the sergeant said if
he would read it, he would see that it asked that Private Cranshaw
might be disciplined or reprimanded but that he ought not to be given
court-martial with recommended death sentence for what was a crime
in time of war but only a military offense in time of peace.

The doctor whispered to me that the devil of it was, the men were
right.

Teddy Mainwaring began to shake with outrage, and maybe a little
fear mixed in. "Sergeant Fry, this is mutiny, and you are the ringleader of it. I take it very ill to have action like this come to my
attention. You are relieved of your assignment." He turned around
to find help, and saw me and the doctor. He called me over. He
ordered me in front of the demonstrators to arrest Sergeant Fry and
lodge him in the guardhouse, and to march the men back to barracks
and to hold the troop at reveille formation the next morning until the
commanding officer appeared.

I stepped forward to the men and called them to attention. Nobody moved. It was a tight second or two, and then Sergeant Fry said, "All right, you men, you heard the lieutenant. Snap up to it," and because he had endorsed my command, they obeyed. I was in the strange position of being thankful to the soldier I was arresting that he had acted to support my authority. I marched them all across the parade, and there at the barracks, I halted them and faced them toward me and spoke to them briefly. I told them that evidently we had a problem which concerned the whole post, and that the only way to handle it was to keep order, do their duty, withhold their judgment, and give things a chance to be worked out. I said I would arrest and confine any man I knew of who made any further mutinous gestures. But I said I would be as fair and friendly as I had ever been with all men who conducted themselves in the right way. They began to say, yes sir, yes sir, but we can't let that happen to any one of our troopers, and added uncomplimentary remarks about the c.o., but I stopped them, and said that was all, and dismissed them, and then personally took Sergeant Fry to the guardhouse, and locked him up.

Cranshaw recognized my voice in the darkness, and came to ask me if it was true, the thing he had been told, that he was to be tried and sentenced to death. I couldn't see him, but he put his hand on my arm, and he felt like an old man, clutching and letting go over and over, and his voice was dry and cut in two. I told him he was not tried and convicted yet, and that he had a long way to go before he was. It was all I could say. I left feeling sorry for him for the first time. And if I felt sorry for him, how could I be amazed or censorious if the troopers felt so too?

I saw Doctor Gray later that same evening, and he laughed when he saw my face. He hit me on the chest and said, "Hazard, I'll bet the thing that bothers you the most about this is that you can't believe it can happen in the U.S. Army." I don't know how he knew. He went on and said that the sooner the better for me to learn that the army is like any other human institution—it contains all kinds and descriptions of men, capable of every error, just like men on the outside; and that I must not lose my ideal of the army because of this.

Well, to jump to reveille the following morning, Teddy appeared and said that he had acted with the proper speed and severity against the ringleader of last night's petition, but that he had not read the names signed to it, as he did not want to know who did and who did not sign it. But he said that the innocent unfortunately had to suffer with the guilty, and disciplinary penalties would have to be endured by the whole troop. There was to be a formation after breakfast under the command of Lt. Hazard, who would lead the garrison in troop formation out to the brush on the desert, where the men would cut enough brush for each man to make himself a stiff broom. On marching back to the post, the troop would take their new brooms, and beginning at the east end, they would sweep the entire parade ground, every inch of it, until all loose dust was gathered at the west end. They would then shovel this dust into bushel baskets from the warehouse and carry it and dump it in the arroyo back of the north line. This task would be performed daily until further notice. He then ordered the troop dismissed.

So for three days we carried out this senseless work. There is no bottom to the amount of dust we can raise by scraping long enough at the surface of this desert. I had many a private moment of wondering how long the men would continue to do it, or even why they consented in the first place. Gray says it is out of respect for me. I can hardly think they would care anything about my feelings or success or failure as a commander. But I suppose habit is strong, and isolated as we are, men here must prefer to cling together even under bitter and distasteful conditions rather than risk the anarchy that must follow wholesale disobedience.

Teddy asked me on the third day how the men were doing, and what I thought generally. I could not escape the impression that he might be asking me for some way out of the condition he had brought to the fort. I told him I thought the men had had enough of it—not of work, for it has been lack of work that prepared the way for bad feeling and judgment; but they had had enough of *useless* work. Indeed, he wanted to know, and what would I consider *useful* work? Luckily I had an answer, for I have long thought that the open corners of the post area represented real danger—gaps at each corner of the rectangle about thirty paces wide. There, I said, the men should be put to work building revetments out of earthen mounds, or of adobes—bricks made of water and straw and earth. It would work them harder than ever, and there would be something to show for it. He looked out the window and whistled a silent little tune, and said he would think it over, and nodded me out. But later he sent for me and gave orders to do just what I had proposed.

So, my dearest, for the last several days, and for as many ahead as I can see, we are improving our defenses with earthworks. Luckily I have my engineering books with me, and my copy of Hopkinson on Fortifications. Following drawings which I made in ink outline, and which Doctor Gray shaded with his water colors (he paints in water color) the troopers are erecting fine crescent-shaped revetments. We will have fire-steps, parapets, crenellations and extern trenches at each. It must be weeks before we can be done; but I wish you could see the interest with which these troopers come to their work every day—not that they do not grumble, for they do, and make worse of the heat, which is bad enough, for they do; but when you hear one man criticize another's work, or make a suggestion for improvement, or keep track of how much was done on a given day, you know there is at least some pride in what they're doing, for they can see that it is a useful thing to be doing.

Meantime what of the prisoners? Nobody moves faster than a man unsure of himself. Mainwaring has prepared a report of the case for higher authority and has sent it along with the prisoners under escort, to Department Hq. for a decision—just what to expect, nobody knows. Mainwaring has let it be known that he personally feels that mutiny is just as deserving of the death sentence as desertion, and that therefore Sgt. Fry is exactly in the same case as Pvt. Cranshaw.

Meanwhile, it is all the men can talk about. They are all uncertain, and uncertainty is the soldier's worst disease. The rest of us only wish the new C. O. were already here to take up the matter.

This, Laura my darling, is what life is momentarily like at Fort Delivery. I shall hope in my next to have happier things to report, and will close this, only thinking that anything that happens here, because it affects or concerns me, must be of interest to you. . . .

and from there, stirred by the sense of how he and Laura were locked together in heart and mind each for the other's sake, he gave himself up to words of love.

lxv

Beyond all this there was one matter about which Matthew did not write to Laura.

One evening in the last week he was sitting on the threshold of his lopsided adobe doorway watching the darkness draw over the world from the east. He was tired, thinking of nothing, and at peace. He had refused invitations to supper and had instead prepared his own meal, which he had devoured with relish after working in the sun all day building fortifications. His sentiments were hardly clear at the edge of his mind, but they dealt generally with Laura and the future, and they filled him with vague desire which was like a blissful dream. He was a lonely and hardy young man lost in a reverie of love. It was a state of being which brought to a higher degree of expression his natural attributes—his ruddy color, the intensity and depth of his eyes, a little ridge that shone in a moist line around the edges of his lips, the strong charge of his blood as it beat its slow, steady power through his pulse.

Suddenly from the direction of the arroyo behind the north line sounded the hornlike baying of a hound. It was the Mainwarings' greyhound. He barked in long, excited cadences. Something there disturbed the dog. Matthew went to investigate. He found Kitty Mainwaring standing at the edge of the arroyo, gazing below, wringing her hands above the deepening shadow of the bank.

"What is it?" asked Matthew, coming up beside her.

"Garibaldi has trapped something down there, I cannot make it out—some small creature near those clods of earth. I am terrified it might be something that would harm him!"

Matthew scrambled down the bank and came up to the dog, which was dancing about in clamorous fury. Matthew tried to pull him away from a little heap of fallen clods, and as he did so, he saw a large white scorpion with its shelled tail quivering over its back. It was like some miniature survival from a prehistoric sea. It might have been more imagined than real, but Matthew thought he smelled an odd, musty, yet acid essence in the air, released by the defensive insect. He knew that its sting could be gravely troublesome to a man, and that it might prove fatal to a dog. He glanced about for other clods, found a couple, and hurled them down on the scorpion. They broke, making a dome which concealed it for a moment. In that moment, he found a rock which took both his hands to lift. The scorpion tunneled its way out of the loose earth over it and began to streak for the bank of the arroyo to find a hole. Matthew stoned it and broke it. The rock rolled away. Exuding its thick fluids of life, while its flexible horny scales slowly unfolded into inertness, the poisonous small creature died.

Matthew kicked earth over it. The dog tried to scratch the earth away.

"Back, sir!" commanded Matthew, and then called up to Kitty on the bank above, "Call him, Mrs. Mainwaring!"

She called. The dog ignored her.

"Oh, bring him by his collar, Mr. Hazard," she cried. "I saw that creature. It might sting him even yet."

Matthew put his stone to make a grave over the scorpion, and then led Garibaldi up the steep wall until they were with Kitty.

"Oh! whatever would I have done without you!" she said, swaying a little toward Matthew, and laughing faintly at her weakness. "I was out for a little walk with my beautiful beastie here, and before I knew it, he was down the bank and attacking that thing! What eyes he has, to see it in the twilight. —Thank you, Matthew," she added, and her voice was close and shaken.

"You are most welcome, ma'am."

He glanced toward his house as if to take his way there, but Kitty made no move to walk homeward, and out of politeness he stayed. It was most curious: whenever he had seen her lately, she had seemed tense, about what he could not imagine. Some inner excitement made her voice shake a little, and sound a little higher and louder than usual. Everything, even the smallest thing that happened when he saw her seemed to mean more to her than to anyone else. A dog barking at a scorpion was hardly enough of an event to make her look so tragic and sound so significant.

"He'll be all right," said Matthew, patting the tall greyhound on its narrow head. Garibaldi licked his hand and sat down like a heraldic supporter.

"He likes you," said Kitty.

"He knows I like dogs."

"Oh, so do I. Do you like cats?"

"Oh, yes, cats are often very funny to watch."

"But you don't love them—I can see that. I always say I *like* cats, but I *love* dogs." Her voice was breathy. She looked at him and even in the falling evening he could see that her eyes shone with extra moisture. What in the world did she feel like weeping for, he wondered.

He could not know, she said to herself expertly, having rehearsed a hundred times the feelings that made a turmoil in her mind and heart, he could not know the burdens she had to bear. Her pride lay in ribbons, as she privately described its condition. Her husband the commanding officer had lately acted like a man either afraid or foolish. She had been forced to conceal from Teddy her opinion of his recent official actions. It was humiliating to lie beside him at night and be forced to reassure him a dozen times about his wisdom and strength of character. When he asked her to find out for him what people were saying about him at Fort Delivery, she wanted to scream at him and refuse. But she agreed. The laundresses would presently tell her, if she approached the matter delicately enough.

And to think that she was facing, soon, what must amount to an eviction, when the Prescotts would arrive to take over Quarters I— this was painful, and intruded between more pleasant thoughts at any time of day or night.

Worst of all was the trouble that beset her about Lieutenant Matthew Hazard. Her mind flooded hotly with different views in succession as she dwelled in thought upon him. He went his way, doing his work, thinking of his Laura Greenleaf, gaining the good respect of the men which her husband ought to hold and could not. So far as she knew, Matthew never gave her a thought. But at what he aroused in her she suffered hours of discontent and wonder. What kind of woman was she, after all? Was she no better than those common guttersnipes among whom she had worked years ago in New York? If being a lady and preserving virtue went together, then was she no lady? She had allowed herself to be betrayed before her marriage. Must this haunt her all her life? She could remember the feelings of that time. They were brought alive in her again, now, by this quiet and dedicated young man beside her in the dusk. It was cruel that he must bring "that" out in her all over again. Perhaps the only way she could quiet it and transcend it was to bring it out *in him,* too.

But when she showed him feeling which, coming from any pretty woman, any man would receive with interest, he simply did not recognize it. Her will was denied. It was—even she herself knew this— a fierce will, and when denied, it worked the harder to prevail. Laura Greenleaf! A fiery thread of feeling went through her. She could make him forget Laura Greenleaf!

But how could she live in the same row of officers' quarters with him if, should she declare herself, he would not respond with his love? He showed no sign of knowing what it was—the only thing— that she longed for, even as she told herself that she had no right to long for it. His love—but he seemed not even interested in her in any way.

She turned abruptly away from him and saw the first stars given light by the darkening east. She was flooded with a choking tenderness, a feeling which seemed to resolve all her troubled interlacings of willful thoughts. She felt lovely and calm when she heard herself say,

"Matthew, aren't you lonely?"

With a smile in his voice he answered,

"I certainly am, Mrs. Mainwaring."

She faced him in a swift attitude of yielding grace.

"Oh, why won't you call me Kitty! Lonely, lonely, I am dying of it, and yet here we are, the two of us. I think we are waiting for each other!"

Having said it at last, she was suddenly sick with fear. He was so amazed at what she meant, which at last he recognized, that he took a little step backward. His action was involuntary. It told her all—the worst—she had to know.

"Oh, no, Matthew," she said quickly, "I cannot imagine what made me say a thing like that! You must forget it. I am such a goose, I always have strong sympathies, and I suppose I felt too strongly how lonely you must be, thinking of your Miss Greenleaf so far away."

He was not deceived, but he was grateful for her desperate work of pride. He moved to help her in it.

"Well, Kitty," he said gently, "I did not know it showed so plainly in me. I am thankful for your concern. Under other circumstances, it might make me forget myself."

"You would think of me in that way, Matthew?"

"Who knows?"

She leaned to stroke the dog beside her. When she spoke her voice was sad and full of courage for those to whom she could give it.

"I think it is best to admit how you feel. I can help you to overcome it. We all live very close to each other here, and also very far away from wholesome distractions. We must all put forth a little extra effort in keeping our promises to those we love. —We really should be going back. Thank you for rescuing us—" she laughed and patted Garibaldi.

"I'll walk you home, Kitty," he said.

"But no gallantries," she said. "You must promise."

"I promise," he said, accepting the character she put upon him of the hotheaded lover who must be guarded against. They walked up the north line escorted by Garibaldi. Of the three, only the dog was not playing a part.

Conversation of any sort was desirable. Kitty said,

"I cannot help wondering what they will be like."

"Who?"

"The Prescotts. —Have you heard? Teddy has had notice that they will be arriving at Driscoll next week. We are to send an ambulance and an escort for them."

"No. I did not know. Doctor Gray has never met them, but he knows of them, and what he knows he likes."

"I shall see for myself," said Kitty. "I imagine *he* will be very commandery-officery, and *she* will be very ranking-lady. Poor old Fort Deliver-Me!"

Matthew had a qualm of pity for her restless fears which had to be prepared against long in advance.

They walked on to headquarters where new occupants would soon live.

lxvi

Hiram Hyde Prescott was born in Batavia, New York, in 1840, the third son, and fifth child, of Ezra Mulligan Prescott and Martha (Baynes) Prescott. He was much younger than his brothers and sisters. His mother survived his birth by only a few months. Until the age of twelve he was reared by his sisters.

His father, a farmer, was a God-fearing man of reluctant expression who hoped his sons would succeed him as proprietors of his farm. In this hope the father was disappointed, though no one knew the depths of his regret when his two older sons left him to work as boatmen on the Erie Canal. To help him with the farm he hired a middle-aged man who drifted into the farm one day asking for work. The stranger was a veteran of the Jackson campaign against the British on the lower Mississippi. One of his duties was to teach young Hiram Hyde what he could about farming, soldiering and hunting.

The boy was silent by disposition and lonely by habit. He had little active friendship with his father, who seemed too old to understand him and too pessimistic to stimulate his imagination. Hiram's sisters taught him to read, and read aloud to him in the evenings. Their family literature consisted of the Bible, the novels of Walter Scott, Fenimore Cooper, and Charles Dickens, and the tales and histories of Washington Irving. It was years before the boy realized that the books read to him were not historically and exactly true. When he learned this, he seemed to lose interest in books and reading and listening. Perhaps it was that his time of life was ready to bring him a livelier interest in the actual world; perhaps he felt dimly betrayed by the discovery that everything people told each other was not factual.

In any case, he fastened his interest increasingly on Luke, the hired man, who took him hunting in the low wooded hills near Batavia, and along the little creeks that came through meadows, misty in morning and evening, and pure and clear by noonlight and moonlight.

He developed a passion for hunting. Game—birds and small animals—abounded in the intimate and lovely landscape of western New York State, and all nature seemed to him full of open secrets, known to him alone. He became an excellent shot and he learned the craft of the trapper.

Like his father, he was taciturn; but this did not mean that he had no life in his thoughts. Always in terms of the actual, as he had experienced it, he came to many conclusions and convictions, which he shared with nobody. His sisters knew him for an intelligent boy, but they could not penetrate or alleviate his loneliness. They discovered that he had a smoldering temper, but almost never did he permit it to show itself in impulsive anger. It was years before he learned to blow up when he was angry or out of sorts.

Luke took him to Buffalo one time on a canal boat on which one of the older Prescott brothers worked. It was supposed to be a great adventure—to go to Buffalo, the city of twenty thousand people, and see the sights. Hiram was interested enough, but nothing could persuade him (so he told himself) to live in a big town.

The United States was a real place to him, a place he loved, but its image was not cities, with their broad, muddy streets, their noise and confusion and costly pleasures, their sense of hurry and strife. His nation was, in his mind, an enlargement of the land around Batavia—woods, meadows, little wild valleys, the blue drifts of autumn air in the distance, scarlet maples, the pure mounding snow on wintry hills with ranks of bare trees marching like armies with fixed bayonets over their crests, and the stirring hum of spring in the woods and fields, and the drenching drowsiness of full summer when his thoughts droned sweetly through him like bees heavy with honey.

In his youth he thought less about citizens, people, men and women, as those who shared his nation with him, and more about the adroit foxes, weasels, partridges, pheasants, doves and owls whom he knew so well. When he hunted and shot them, he did so with excitement stretched fine under control, and with love for his victims.

These elements were the basis of his patriotism until at the age of twelve he added another, which brought into his life the power of an ideal.

In 1852 his father and sisters decided that he was needful of more education than they could give him at the farm. Accordingly he was sent to live with his mother's brother in Albany, a schoolmaster called Joseph Baynes. One of Hiram's first lessons out of his new books dealt with the life of General George Washington. He learned what General Washington had fought for—the independence and internal order, the self-respecting freedom of the American states. It was a large subject, and the thing that brought it within Hiram's grasp with the power of an ideal was this—that in his youth, George Washington, like Hiram in his boyhood, had been a forest man, a hunter, a trapper, a walker of the wilderness. In the greater scale of Washington's years as a wilderness surveyor Hiram saw all the things he loved most in his own small, lost world of Batavia, which on going to Albany he had left never to return. Washington's life completed his concept of the United States, and confirmed his love for his country. He would never have been able to explain it, or write it all down.

He was a slow but thorough student, and he took pleasure in reading the newspapers with all their reports through the years of the trouble that was building up about slavery, the Western territories, and such large matters. In the mid-1850's there was already talk by extremists of possible war between the Northern and Southern states over the abolition of slavery, and the balance of power with respect to the matter in the Congress.

Hiram had no notion of war other than that absorbed from the maundering tales told by Luke back on the farm. These dated from 1815, which was almost like prehistoric time to Hiram. At six he had heard sweeping rumors and odd reports from the war with Mexico far away on the Rio Grande and beyond, but these meant less to him than the torchlight parades that celebrated various victories, and the impression he received one day when some neighbor women came with news to tell his sisters. While his sisters listened and consoled, the other women wept into their fringed shawls over the death in Mexico of a husband, a son—someone they loved who had been killed in battle or who had died of disease. If war ever happened, Hiram knew he would be a soldier, but not a leader.

He matured early physically, which induced other boys to turn to him for leadership. But he never felt he knew enough to tell others what to do. He preferred to be among them and for the most part did not see the need for anyone to tell anyone else what to do.

He was popular because he was strong, stocky and honest, and because he had such a fine hand and a good head for handling horses. He used to ride in the race meets down the Hudson as a youth, and in time his opinion was sought when a horse trade was in order. Horses and dogs invariably trusted him. He knew their natures for what they were, and while working to make them better through training, he never impatiently required of them more than they could perform. In time he came to apply this gift to dealing with people.

He learned to do it in a hard school.

lxvii

In 1861 the war between the states actually did break out in consequence of the Republican victory and the election of Abraham Lincoln, who ran on an anti-secession platform.

Hiram was one of the first young men in Albany to enlist in response to the President's call for troops. Commissions were being arranged for their young men by influential citizens, and Professor Baynes was in a position to obtain a lieutenancy for Hiram.

But Hiram refused.

He refused, too, the position as lieutenant of cavalry when his volunteer troop elected him to the rank. Again he felt that he did not deserve to take charge of others. His regiment was shipped by steam cars to a camp in Pennsylvania, where he spent months waiting for the Army to decide that he and his comrades were ready to march. Drill, firing, guard duty, training horses took up his days until his regiment was called south to the defense of Washington.

It was a life he slowly came to like in spite of its crowds, its lack of privacy, its uncertainties about the future. Hiram was a man who saw the world in concrete terms. In the Army he found man, vastly multiplied, and fixed in the least abstract of situations and circumstances. He found himself increasingly at home amidst his fellows; and the time came, even, when he thought he could do something for them better than they could do for themselves. It was the beginning of him as an officer.

His promotion came to him on the battlefield.

He was in the column moving south into Virginia under Sheridan when his platoon was separated from the command by traffic confusion in a supply train at a crossroads. Hiram's lieutenant led the way on a detour by a field. In the field the platoon was ambushed by Confederate infantrymen who lay in wait for the supply train. Hiram's officer was killed and several other men were killed or wounded. Out of sheer demoralization the whole platoon was ready to be captured until Hiram rallied them with violent exertions of body and language. He brought them back to the main road fairly intact and reported to his captain. Word of his performance was carried on up the line until he was summoned by General Sheridan, who confirmed his assumed lieutenancy with official promotion.

It was the best possible dedication to the Army for Hiram Prescott. Circumstances had forced him to put himself forward. In doing so he proved himself capable of command, and thus were quieted many self-doubts that would have plagued him if he'd been given command before events revealed him to himself. He now knew that he was capable of meeting challenges which lay within the frame of action. Other challenges, residing in powers of mind and imagination, he hoped he would never meet.

He served through the first Virginia campaign earning promotion until he was brevet captain in command of his troop. In bivouac he was strict, fair, and profane when angered. In battle he was oddly quiet. He then seemed wholly self-forgetful, and all his faculties were given over to seeing clearly what was happening in the fight, so he might better be able to move his men wisely and protect them as he sought to damage the enemy. In his rare opportunities for recreation and indulgence while quartered in towns, he found much the same kind of fugitive assuagement through women as the rest of his men, with no confusions of romance, but yet with a certain gentleness and gratitude which told as much about other men at war as it did about him.

For if with hundreds of thousands of men he was engaged in the business of willful killing of other men, he could not help bearing invisibly the marks of such action. More than many men, he felt the hurts and deaths of the soldiers of his daily association. That death and wounds came to men often through his orders he accepted without guilt; but not without fellow feeling. Some grand, delicate balance was somewhat restored when after performing the gestures of destruction he—and other soldiers—performed through assuagement of desire the gestures of creation.

lxviii

He was wounded one blue and gold morning in autumn on the edge of a creek in a Virginia woods. When the momentum of battle passed beyond him he was left to die.

But he did not die, and a day and half later he was found, brought to a field hospital, and then evacuated to Washington on a halting steam train that carried with it its own swarms of flies. Hiram Prescott was mostly unaware of the journey. He was lost in fever, dreams, alternating drifts of peacefulness and pain.

"Captain! Captain! Look out! Look out!" he heard someone cry over and over again, but when he looked to see who warned him, there was no one there, and he said to himself, passing his hand across his face, "I am confused," and then he saw again that vast and rapid dark bulk in the air above him, hurling its might across him, taking away the light of the blue sky, and he threw up his arm against it, but to no avail, for out of it, that dark riding fury like a cloud, came a strike like lightning, and he knew at the time that it was not lightning, but the blade of a cavalry saber, which flashed directly toward him, until he felt it enter his breast and leave him fallen upon the rusty oak leaves of that creekside in Virginia where his blood ran over little white pebbles to join the clear water rippling its way in the crisp sunshine of that early winter day.

"Captain! Captain!" cried the voice again, and he tried to rise toward it, though he could not see who called to him. But why should anyone call, now, at all, for was he not already wounded and lying there alone by that creek, which flowed into the Rappahannock? Would he die without being known about by anyone, ever again? "Captain!" he heard, once more, and threw himself upward, and met resistance, and awoke.

To awaken so was a great shock. Who would hold him like this? And that cry—he knew now that it was his own voice which called "Captain, captain."

"Hush, captain," said someone.

He looked wildly. His head bobbed like a puppet's. His breath was hot and strident. He was running with sweat. He had died, in dream, of his wound.

"Lie down, captain. You had a nightmare. It is all right now. I will bathe your face."

Weakened by pity, he went back to the pillow and licked his lips, which tasted to him like the rim of a tin army mess kit. The dream receded, but slowly. It spoke out from him once more, even though he was now fully conscious and remembering fact.

"I was wounded by a Rebel horseman," he said in a gasping whisper. "I had already been wounded by a bullet in my leg. I couldn't move. He rode right over me, and if his horse hadn't taken a jump over me, the horse would have killed me too."

Leaning over him to bathe his forehead, Jessica Dryden smiled and said softly,

"You were not killed by anybody, Captain Prescott. Do hush now and rest. We must not disturb any of the others. They are trying to sleep. I believe your fever has broken at last."

He stared at her. There was light on one side of her face only. It dwelled on her smile and it made a golden spark for a second deep in her eye. He glanced aside. He was in a long wide-high-ceilinged room with lofty windows. Heavy shadows draped all he could see. He believed that rows of beds reached all down the room from where he was. Here and there a tall screen stood about a cot and made shadows like up-ended boxes standing together. A few lamps were burning low. Far outside in the hall through a black doorway a candle made a pinpoint of distance that frightened him because it was so infinitely far away and so still. He turned to her.

"What is this?" he whispered.

"This is the Armory Square Hospital."

He was determined to sound intelligent, though it cost him a pain in his head.

"Where is it?" he asked.

"In Washington."

"Who are you?"

"Miss Dryden."

"But how did I get here?"

She was quietly withdrawing her attentions from his needs, hoping to bring him gradually to sleep.

"A hospital train brought you to Washington. You were assigned to my ward. You have been here a week."

"A week!" He shut his eyes in disgust. A week and nobody had told him about it! She watched him. His eyes remained shut. In a moment he slept. It was deep, easy sleep, and she gave her folded towel a little pat of satisfaction, as if to say, "There, now. The worst is over." She turned the coal-oil lamp a trifle so that its improvised mask, made of a brown manila government envelope, would cast its pale golden glow on the foot rather than the head of the cot, and leave the captain in quiet shade yet not in such total darkness that he would be fearful on awakening. She had seen enough in her months of service as a hospital volunteer to know how the strongest men when lost in dangerous illness could reveal if never confess the fears and even the hopes of childhood.

It was time for her to go home. The night orderly had come to his place at the duty desk in the hallway. She had had a full day, and she had stayed longer than usual because she had heard the surgeon say that he suspected that they would know, one way or the other, about Captain Prescott, before another day came around. She was glad to have stayed, for she had seen the captain in his suffering for that whole week, and when before her eyes a few minutes ago he had come from war to peace, awakening in safety from the fevered dreams which had held him in torture for that whole week, she could not repress a feeling of triumph in her breast. To see the look on his face change from blind anguish to ineffable relief— this was a moment she believed she could never forget, no matter how accustomed she might be to the woes of the hospital, where one day was like another, and one man seemed like another, and time itself had little momentary meaning.

Jessica sighed deeply and left the ward to go home. The atmosphere of the place went with her always, in her plans for the next day, and her feeling for the patients.

She was one of the volunteer helpers who came to work with the Army's professional nurses and doctors. The hospital was understaffed and crowded. The food was abominable. Proper sanitation was almost wholly missing. The place stank and the very air seemed hopeless of the restoration of health to the rows and rows of sick and wounded men in their canvas cots. In performing little services the volunteers—Jessica herself—became expert in meeting and even anticipating the wants of the patients. They would read them their mail and take letters by dictation to be sent home to families and sweethearts. They learned what little dishes of food might taste good to the men in their assigned sections, and these they would bring in late afternoon, when the patients were most likely to be feverish and disconsolate. They would bring if they could find them little articles which the sick and wounded asked for—caprices of their former interests. Most of the volunteer workers were women. Some of them were young, and of these a number came from what Washington regarded as its first families. Miss Jessica Dryden was one such young woman.

She thought much about the meager information on the card which hung at the foot of the captain's cot. She tried to make it tell her more than it could about him.

Prescott, Hiram Hyde, Capt. Cav. b. Batavia, New York, 14 Mar. 1840. Unm. Parents:dec'd; notify:sister, Miss Eliza P., Batavia, N.Y.

She translated these impersonal items. He was twenty-three—so young to be a captain; he must be a famous soldier. If she read correctly, he was unmarried. His parents were dead, and in case of necessity, his sister was to be informed. Batavia, New York, must be a small community. Prescott was a fine-sounding name. Did they live in a great square board house with tall shuttered windows, and a glass lookout, and a wide lawn, set in a grove of dark hickory and sycamore trees? To look at him, unshaven for so many days, and so ill, she thought he might be anything up to forty years old, and a poor farmer.

But why on earth did she think of all this? She laughed at herself, as her mother had taught her to do years ago in her willful childhood.

lxix

The oldest child and only daughter of United States Supreme Court Associate Justice Lycurgus Tewkes Dryden and Isabel (Mercer) Dryden, Jessica was born in Washington in 1843. Twin brothers followed her into the family three years later.

The Dryden residence stood in the row of plaster houses on the same side of Lafayette Square as the private house of President

Madison on the corner, where Mrs. Dolley Madison was still living when Jessica was born. The White House was within sight in its often muddy park at right angles to these houses.

One of Jessica's earliest memories was this: to an iron balcony fronting the street she would be carried by her mother for a look at the park in the square. Her mother was a tall, slender woman with much grace about her. She held her young daughter up to wave to friends who went past in varnished, open carriages when the days were fine. It was a pretty spectacle—the high-stepping horses, the coachmen and footmen on their boxes, the ladies with parasols in summer or muffs in winter, the gentlemen in glossy top hats of the best Western beaver, the twinkling of polished carriage spokes. The little girl happily took all this as a pleasant arrangement for her own pleasure, even when, as often happened, the President of the United States and Mrs. Polk drove by and waved to Mrs. Dryden, who waved back. So did Jessica, comfortable in her child's order of the world.

No matter what visited her later in life, Jessica seemed able to retain a sense of serene comfort which could sustain even deep personal suffering with a sort of spiritual good manners. This gift was composed of a number of elements. One was her religion, for which she had a feeling so true that it was almost without thought. Others were a sense of high position calmly recognized, and natural good health, and an innately aristocratic knack for assuming that matters of inconvenience should be dismissed. Finally, her sense of flowing harmony in life came from the presence, never spoken of but daily revealed, of a really rich happiness between the father and the mother, the Justice and his wife. It was an enfolding and reassuring atmosphere in which to grow up. The alliance of the parents was so all-pervading that the children took from it their own life-long sense of safety, contentment and justification.

Mr. Justice Dryden was at first glance a formidable man, tall, heavy, richly whiskered, big-voiced, and given to disconcerting fits of scowling when he was thinking most actively.

Jessica was much like him in a certain abruptness of manner and strike of thought, though these traits were transmuted by her modicum of her mother's charm and grace. Judge Dryden, like so many men of his vocation, was inclined to grant opinions in domestic matters rather in the manner of decisions handed down from the bench. As she grew old enough to know what a Supreme Court justice was, and the law, and to differentiate between the manners of people as they talked, Jessica dared to tease her father for his heavy ways. This might have been perilous but for his devotion to her, which was almost inordinate. He had married late in life, she was his first-born, she resembled her mother whom he adored with secretly abject gratitude that shook him in his most obscure fastnesses of spirit and heart, and in general Jessica could do nothing that he would not suffer, even when if she was in error he brought his grandest legal battery to train upon her in judgment.

Mrs. Dryden came of an interesting family. Her father had been Secretary of War—the Honorable James Hamilton Mercer. His name was a modification of the French name Mercier which took plant in the United States just after the nation's victory in the Revolutionary War.

In the command of Admiral Rochambeau with the French warships which fought for our independence was a young naval officer of the line, named Vicomte Étienne de Mercier. After the War he resolved to settle in the United States of America, went ashore, bought a farm in New Jersey, doffed his uniform and title, and became a philosophical agriculturist. In a world so new, a political atmosphere so without precedent, Citizen Mercier's views, innocent and passionate, seemed appropriate. Actually they were a naïve mixture of Rousseau, Locke and Pascal, but their inner contradictions did no harm when it came to building a manor house or planting a garden or even engaging local farmers to make things grow and to harvest them when ripe.

The ex-vicomte founded a family, died early, leaving a heritage of debts and social confusions, and a penchant for public affairs which drew his son into running for Congress. In the course of the campaign for his seat, the name Mercier, in deference to the speech habits of the American voter of the time, was modified to Mercer. This congressman served several terms and then received cabinet appointment as Secretary of War. His duties in this position took him to the West for personal observations, and while he was not one of the first or greatest of surveyors or pioneers, he was one of the most orderly, with a strong sense of posterity, and his name was commemorated by a number of geographical names beyond the Appalachians.

His wife Honora was equal socially to his official responsibilities, and the drawing room of Mrs. Secretary Mercer on the second and fourth Tuesdays was always attended by the most interesting people in the capital. Isabel Mercer, a daughter of the house, grew up amidst the glisten of candles and prisms, and later, gaslight, and the rich hum of talk muffled by velvet draperies and thick Turkey carpets, and a sense of government as embodied in people—the very people who carried it on. She married Mr. Justice Dryden right off a sofa in her mother's drawing room, as she herself once put it.

The justice had been coming to the Tuesdays for years. Nobody knew it but Isabel herself, even as a child; he came not to see famous men or listen to Mrs. Mercer's rattling talk but to see Isabel grow from child to woman—the woman he adored in secret and never hoped to win. Isabel helped him to make his secret plain to her almost against his will. He proposed and was accepted.

Though not without difficulties raised by her parents in duty, affection and perplexity. The Secretary was shocked at the wide difference in age between his daughter and her fiancé. It was Mrs. Mercer who decided the matter. Glancing in her mind's eye across the company she commanded—judges, diplomats, persons of unde-fined but weighty authority, clever clerks and of course people of rank in the Army and Navy—she saw no one with quite the dis-tinction of Mr. Justice Dryden, and she approved the match.

As a child, Jessica loved to hear from her mother, Isabel Mercer Dryden, the story of this marriage and the obstacles that had beset it, and as in any familiar and beloved story when the same tri-umphant outcome came true each time she heard it, she clapped her hands at the bravery of the lovers and the defeat of the wicked parents who would thwart them.

lxx

When she was about ten years old she ceased looking like a brother of her twin brothers and began to look like a miniature woman. Her garments were thick, bulky, overwarm reproductions of the clothes her mother wore, with tight uppers, overlapped sleeves, several layers of wide woolen skirts on taped hoops, and coarse black stockings and high leather shoes with buttons like the eyes of rabbits dotted each with a point of light. When she went out of doors to walk or to ride in the family carriage she wore a heavy shawl folded into a triangle, and a bonnet with a spray of pheasant feathers. So much clothing—in color dark, ranging with various costumes through brown, green, gray, violet, crimson and black—concealed the tender and troubling swellings of adolescence which came to her early. She began to take a longing and passionate interest in how she looked, begging in prayer that she might be exactly like her mother, who was the prettiest woman she knew, and also the most amusing, and also the most dependable.

The Drydens were Catholics. Mrs. Dryden came by her faith through its descent upon her from her ancestor, the emancipated Vicomte de Mercier, who for all his fashionable skepticisms, had never left the Church. The fact that Mr. Justice Dryden was also a Catholic had much to do with the success of his suit for young Isabel's hand. There were few Catholics in the membership of the Supreme Court, but Mr. Justice Dryden, like Mr. Chief Justice Taney, served both his faith and his judicial duty with impartial gravity. As a child Jessica Dryden knew God as someone to whom she could whisper secrets, certain that they would be heard and safely kept. As she grew older, her prayers remained impassive; private meditations in which she could come to the realization of life's varied experience, to meet which she would need strength. She could ask for this, quite aware that what she asked might not, out of a wisdom larger than her own, be granted. But the asking, and the certainty of being understood, gave her a power of belief in the general worthiness of mankind which grew in her with all the troubles she ever encountered—her own, or those of other people known to her. Her habit of faith was like the breath she drew. She could not imagine living without either. It would have to be a calamity or an aberration which would rob her of her cherished fragment of God's grace. Even as a schoolgirl she could shudder in genuine concern for those who for whatever reason had lost the shelter of God's arm and were alone and cold outside it.

In her twelfth year, Jessica was sent as a day student to a fashionable school for girls in Washington. She there discovered, through the solicitous remarks of her realistic schoolmates, that she was not pretty, and probably never would be—pretty in the conventional, and therefore desirable, style. It was a severe blow, for she had always felt—and been made to feel—that she was pretty. It was the spirit of the family which had given her this happiness in her condition of early life.

Her response to the discovery was characteristic. After a few days of secret misery, and many queries in prayer, she thought she would do well to discover if what those other girls said was true or not. If it was not, she need pay no attention then or thereafter to anything else they might say. If, on the other hand, it was true, then she must determine what could be done about it.

It did not take her long to agree that what they said was true. She was more plain than pretty, though her expression was attractive —surely it must be attractive, she urged in her prayers, since she felt so warmly toward everyone and all of life.

She began, then, consciously to make up for the deficiencies in herself which she thought apparent to the world. By this course she achieved what few people do—she deliberately created her own character. Her criteria were both simple and worthy. One of her precepts was to be busy.

In her school she became the most influential young lady, until the habit of command was well lodged in her. Her studies embraced a list of conventional subjects: English, history, French, penmanship, geography, music, cotillion dancing, embroidery, manners, watercolor painting, decoration of china, elocution, dramatics and the Bible. The students were expected to learn at home such crafts as cooking, housekeeping, sewing, simple remedial medicine, style in entertaining, elementary gardening, croquet, diabolo and, in prescribed apparel, the riding and driving of horses.

Jessica showed proficiency in all such formal and informal matters of learning. She brought something of her own to all this systematic preparation for life—something which those who lacked it tried anyway to imitate. It was a decisiveness, an ability to make up her mind, and to give reasons for doing so. In an age when it was considered becoming for a maiden to show diffidence and helplessness, Jessica's crispness of thought, her clarity of view, and her often lightly given but never lightly meant conclusions were noticeable.

Her mother once said to her,

"Sit down and listen to me, my pet."

Jessica sat down and folded her hands in her lap.

"Yes, Mamá."

"You are very good at the things you do, aren't you?" said Isabel Dryden.

"I mean to be, Mamá."

"Yes. And do you think other people always like to see you meaning to be, and actually being so?"

"I never thought of it, Mamá. Everybody else tries to do their best. Why mustn't I?"

Isabel put her hands on her daughter's and smiled with love into the clear young face, and answered,

"You should, my darling. But when you succeed so often in what you set out to do, it gives you—it would give anyone—a sense of being always right, and therefore somewhat better, than anyone else, not only in the thing done, but in all things. I speak of this only because I would hate to see you in spite of yourself become a wilful female."

It was said so fondly that Jessica instead of being hurt began to laugh.

"Mamá! Do you mean to call me a shrew?"

Isabel, with some relief and a surge of love for the good sense of her child, said,

"No, I mean something worse—I mean a woman who knows better than *anybody* what is good for *everybody*."

Jessica thought this over for a moment, and then she hugged her mother, and admitted that perhaps she had been in danger of taking charge of everyone.

Again with her clear-headedness she assessed her nature and worked to govern this aspect of it. Deliberately she withdrew from certain eminent positions which had fallen to her in school—she was to act and sing the leading role of Egeria in the opera of that name by Bowlton, and she was to provide the charades for a Saint Valentine's Day party, and she was the newly elected chairman of the Martineau Forensics Society (Miss Harriet Martineau had recently lectured before the student body with telling effect). All these, with other conspicuous honors, Jessica gave up, meeting protests with assurances that she was abandoning nothing and no one, but would take part to the fullest like everyone else; but she would just not direct everything. Her modesty and unabated enthusiasm combined to win her even greater success than before. As legends could, one came up about her out of the simplest ingredients, and in repetition acquired a solidity which gave substance to her in the grown-up society of the capital. Justice Dryden's daughter Jessica, even before she was presented to Washington society, was a personage.

lxxi

Following a supper party given by President Buchanan and his sister in the White House for the Drydens and their closest friends, Jessica made her debut at a reception across the square in her own house. It was a famous party. Jessica was, for the moment, spoken of as the catch of the season—of many seasons.

She had gone beyond needing to look pretty.

At eighteen she was handsome. Her color was high. She held herself beautifully. Her brow was wide and open, and her eyes were brilliant in their blue-gray color, under dark brows. Her cheekbones were rather prominent and when she smiled or held a hazy smile they seemed to rise a trifle more.

The night of her party she wore a complicated, many-layered and repeatedly draped gown of white satin. Her hair was dark gold, drawn back from her face in easy waves, and dressed low on her neck. Above her brow was a wreath of small pink rosebuds made of thin velvet, and more of these little flowers were set in garlands upon her immensely wide, shining skirts. Her bosom was daringly exposed. It was the first time she had worn a low-necked dress. She was conscious of it all evening, and to deny this to herself, she resisted strong impulses to hold her fan in concealment or lay her hand above her heart. She felt that she was dear to look upon that evening, and if she had not been, this would have made her so.

But, "Nonsense!" she said to herself. Her thoughts, her joys were so full as to be almost unseemly. They brought intimations of maturity. She longed to be a woman.

Her twin brothers were allowed to attend her party wearing their first evening coats. She looked, she seemed to them, like someone entirely new, a stranger, playing the part of their adored elder sister. Were the stages of life a series of escapes in which someone inevitably was left behind?

In her happiness something smote her with a pang. She took her brothers' faces in turn between her white-gloved palms and kissed each boy tenderly while her eyes filled with tears and she smiled and frowned in the uncertainty which created her hunger and also fed it. If this was an important moment, it was also brief, for she turned back to her duty, which was to receive her guests and make them easy.

The period which followed in her life seemed to others—though she never gave any sign to encourage the opinion—like an anticlimax.

She had many suitors but none quickened her heart. They came at prescribed hours to call, set their shiny silk hats—beaver hats had gone out—or army kepis or navy caps on the hall table which was covered with a Persian rug, and came into the drawing room to make a case for themselves. This was always done in the presence of Jessica and her chaperone—either her mother or one of her own young women friends, or occasionally a cousin who was a nun stationed in a Washington convent. Young men from the foreign embassies came, too, and Washington was sure at various times that Justice Dryden's daughter could have become a lady of title on a number of occasions. Such opportunities seemed to be lost on her. She kept her popularity, in an enjoyable life, but she seemed to reach a motionless state. She was certain that she must not marry for position or amenity alone. She must wait until she should fall in love. When she did not, she knew she must make herself busy. She wondered if she might not obtain a position as a teacher in some—perhaps her own—school for young ladies.

The issue was discussed at length in the Dryden household.

Justice Dryden was weightily against any daughter of his undertaking employment unless she needed to earn wages, which was manifestly not the case.

Mrs. Dryden had no such qualms. She had come from a family heavied by debt in her childhood, and she was entirely without snobbery in respect to money—its value, desirability or power. What she minded was the thought that her delightful Jessica might through the life of a teacher imperceptibly pass into the condition of old maid. She knew Jessica was too truly in need of a woman's creative life to be content, however strongly propriety might press, with the lot of the spinster.

The difficulty was politely and considerately held in abeyance by the family, but everyone knew that sooner or later Jessica must take a stand. She insisted that she must have something to do. She hated idle women. They seemed to her wasteful in the worst way. She loved and respected her father and mother, but their view of her life would not forever be hers.

What would bring her her own?

lxxii

Like so many other conditions and circumstances of a private sort, this one was changed if not immediately resolved by the trouble that came to the nation as a whole in 1861 when the Civil War began. Personal concerns seemed to subside, overcome by the great implications of the War in the life of every citizen. The Dryden twin brothers went into the Army. Washington was threatened by the Confederate forces. The justice aged visibly at the tragedy which overwhelmed the nation of which he was an idealistic and severe servant. When the wounded began to arrive from the South filling the hospitals, established or improvised, Jessica Dryden at last had "something to do."

She went to work as a volunteer visitor at the Armory Square Hospital. Her whole self was consumed with interest, compassion and inguenity on behalf of her assigned patients, whom she believed she regarded with enlightened impersonality.

This was true, but only until after several days of high fever and coma, during which he seemed to be living in dreams of desperate battle, Captain Hiram Hyde Prescott returned to consciousness and saw her, learned her name, and looked forward to her next visit.

When she returned to Armory Square the next afternoon she went in the usual order down the row of her assigned patients. She kept herself by will from glancing ahead to the captain's cot. Surely the other men were precisely as important to her as he was. It was over an hour before she came to him. Then she put her hands to her cheeks and laughed in astonishment.

"Well?" he said, weakly, but with a smile.

He had been shaved. His mustache was still rich and full, but it was trimmed, and his cheeks and chin were clear. He was pale, but for spots of color over his cheekbones. His eyes were brown, as she now saw for the first time.

"You are better!" she cried.

"I am almost well." But this was nonsense and they both knew it. He looked at her in such frank wonder and curiosity that she raised her head and dismissed the effect of interest in him. In a simply dutiful tone she said,

"Captain, is there any particular thing you would like for me to bring you, if I can find it?"

He was too weak to think. It had been a great exertion to be shaved by an orderly. He preferred now to look and enjoy the sight of her. She was rather tall, very slim, and held herself almost like a soldier. Her hair was a dark gold, and her eyes were clear gray. They were deeply set and her cheekbones rose against them when she smiled. There was something tawny in her looks; she was not beautiful in an ordinary way, but if she reminded him of anything unlikely, it was of the way a young lioness looked, though you had to add human charm and individuality to such a comparison before it could be right. Her voice had a cool sound to it. She was the most composed young woman he had ever seen. Her question remained unanswered. He scowled to recall it.

"If I think of anything, I will ask," he said. His voice was shallow and husky with weakness, but he tried to give it resonance, and she noticed this. It touched her.

She glanced down the long, high room where the ranks of beds contained so many poor histories, so much unspoken fear, so much flickering hope. It troubled her still to breathe the fetid exhalations of sick breath in the air. But she angrily told herself that she had to be here only six hours a day: what about those men who were trapped here day and night in their infirmity? She knew enough about the night-time hours when pale, wide rings of light from half a dozen oil lamps revealed themselves on the dingy white ceiling and threw long black shadows everywhere else, and the narrow windows let in glimpses of sky and perhaps now and then of a star. In the corner of the ward stood a rank of folding screens made of shirred muslin held by wooden frames. They waited to be unfolded around a cot where death might come. Jessica never caught them in her glance without feeling an impact at her breast. Captain Prescott followed her glance and said,

"I guess all of us in here think about those, and wonder if we'll get them."

"Hush, captain," she said with humorous asperity.

"They won't tell me what my chances are. I think they don't know."

"The surgeon tells me you are progressing, now."

"Did you ask him?"

"Of course."

He looked at her like a tired child, full of wonder at something he could not understand, but which gave him a sense of well-being and peace. He closed his eyes to keep the feeling; and thinking he was going to sleep, she was about to tiptoe away when he looked at her again and said,

"What is your name?"

"Miss Dryden. I told you."

"Who are you?"

She opened her hands in a gesture meant to say, "I am what you see." It did not suffice.

"No," he insisted, "where do you live?"

"Here in Washington."

"Are you a nurse?"

"Not actually, just a helper."

"You are not married. Who is your father?"

She went a trifle taller at his insistence, but then she shrugged and thought that if he wanted to know so much, and was so direct about it, she might as well humor him, which would tire him less than a snub.

"My father is Associate Supreme Court Justice Dryden."

"Lycurgus Tewkes Dryden?"

"He."

"I once thought of going into the law."

"But you didn't?"

"No. I went into the Army when this war came along."

She thought of him. He was like so many thousands—so many hundreds of thousands—of young men whose aims in life had been turned away by the shots fired on Fort Sumter two years ago. With a breath, she made herself come to duty, for if she stayed to talk, she would tire him.

"Have you not yet thought of what I could bring?" she asked.

"Yes."

"Why didn't you tell me?"

"I wanted you to ask me again."

"Now captain: why?"

"It would show you were interested."

"Interested? I am interested in helping everyone who—" But she was sorry at once, for his deep brown eyes were flooded with pain. In his condition, all feelings and reactions were exaggerated, and could not be hidden. She added, "But, since you have never before asked me for anything, I wondered, of course, more about you than I did about the others this morning."

"You did?" His eagerness was so transparent that it made her smile.

"Yes, I did. Now what is it you want?"

"Well, the thing I missed most of all during my army days"— he spoke as if they were over forever—"was the daily New York *Tribune*. So if you could find me a copy now and then, I would like very much to see it. I do not always agree with what Mr. Greeley says in the paper, but I like to read him, if only to disagree."

"But how can you read it, if you are not sitting up just yet?"

He smiled at her with some power of beguilement far beyond his strength to sustain, and said,

"If I cannot, perhaps you will read the paper to me."

Jessica lifted her chin. It was time to look superb and administer a snub. She said,

"Newspapers are frightfully scarce in wartime here in Washington, but I'll see what I can find," and left him.

At home that evening she said to Justice Dryden,

"Papá, what do you do with your New York *Tribune* every day when you have done with it?"

The justice slowly wagged his great head toward her and glared. If she reminded someone of a handsome lioness, her father would be the old king lion himself.

"Why?" he asked accusingly.

Isabel Dryden, his wife, sighed comically at her mending. How well she knew those two—the father always challenging and resentful of the daughter's separate life, the daughter always trying the farthest limit she dared in order to escape him, and yet keeping between them the family's strongest bond. Mrs. Dryden never worried about what might happen in the event of her own death; but if one of those two ever lost the other . . . she sighed again. But she also smiled, for she was warm in heart and lively in spirit, and refused at her age to start willing others to be what they were not.

"Answer your father," she said to Jessica.

"One of my wounded officers at Armory Square," said Jessica, "wants to see the paper. I am looking for copies to bring him."

The justice at once felt in himself a division between compassionate duty and jealous love. His wife saw this plainly in his face. She knew which impulse he would obey. The visible model of duty, he yet yielded to jealousy. When Jessica mentioned a man he always bridled.

"You must obtain copies elsewhere," he said. "Mine I find useful in official ways. The back numbers are filed in my office by Miss Cleary. They often contain matters of legal interest."

"Yes, Papá," said Jessica, and laughed at him for scowling at her with such painful inquisitiveness. She knew what worried him. She knew too how little reason there was for his present concern. It was a nuisance, but she would have to go back to Armory Square the next day with empty hands.

lxxiii

As soon as she arrived at the hospital in the following afternoon she found something else to give her more concern.

Captain Prescott was gone. Another man, bandaged across the eyes and emaciated to the bone, lay in his place, motionless and silent.

Or was this he? She felt something tumble deep in her breast. If it was he, what could have happened to him? She tiptoed to the foot of the cot to read the name on the card affixed there. The name was not Prescott. She turned. Where was he? He must not have died —this she could not think of. She went to the corridor where at his littered table the day orderly was leafing through his much-thumbed record sheets.

"Where is Captain Prescott?" she asked.

The orderly—he was a weary, unkempt and ill-spoken young man —replied,

"Who is Captain Prescott?"

She told him he should know, and described the location of Captain Prescott's cot. The orderly frowned at being bothered with so little a matter as some sick man's identity and scratched about at his papers.

"This one," he said, indicating a large black X on a diagram of the cots in the ward, "is Prescott." Her heart sank. The X looked like an erasure of a whole being. "I moved him. You'll find him in the far corner underneath the stovepipe."

She was so relieved that she neither reproved him for his bad manners nor thanked him for his news. She hurried to the stovepipe corner. There she found Captain Prescott. He was trying to lean up on his elbows and watching her come toward him. She had not yet changed into her working smock. Just above her eyes she wore a small round black hat with a feather. Her wide-hooped dress was of dark-green broadcloth with a long coat to match, both braided in black silk. She carried a sealskin muff to which violets were pinned. The captain all but called out to guide her as she came.

"What are you doing here!" she demanded, while at the same instance he exclaimed, "I was afraid you would never find me!"

They both laughed and she asked,

"Do you like this new location?"

"No—no. It is dark and has no air."

"Why were you moved?"

"I don't know."

"I shall see about this," she declared, and returned to the duty desk in the hall. There she asked that Captain Prescott be moved to a more agreeable location in the ward. The orderly stared at her in slack-mouthed amazement. What possible difference could it make where anybody was put? he seemed to ask. "Well?" asked Jessica with her eyes blazing, and power exuding from her whole attitude. She was her father's daughter. The orderly did not reply. Instead, he rose and walked into the ward. She followed him until they stood beside the captain.

"You making complaints?" asked the orderly, looking down at the captain. There was menace in his tone. It brought a surge of vitality to Prescott, who replied,

"I said I preferred the other place to this corner. If that is a complaint, I am complaining. You will address me as *sir.*"

"You think you're the only sick man around here?—*sir,*" added the orderly with heavy sarcasm. Jessica intervened. She saw the danger of further antagonizing the orderly. In her absence Captain Prescott, without defenders, might be really persecuted. She glanced about the ward. Below one of the tall windows she saw a clear space on the floor.

"Orderly," she said, with charm, for she was also her mother's daughter, "why couldn't you *give orders* for the captain to be moved over there by that window? I am sure he would be grateful, and so would I, for then I could find him more easily in my work."

The orderly enjoyed her idea that he might *give orders*. Out of self-respect he was obliged to raise an objection, but in the end, taken by the way of this young lady who made herself up to him, he agreed, though with a certain gloomy relish all his own.

"The man who *was* over there, by the window, he died last night. I was just fixing to set a new man there. But being 's you ask for it, Miss Jessica, the captain here might just 's well have it till *he* dies."

Jessica blazed out,

"He will not die!"

It was like a trumpet call, affirming for anyone to hear what the caller believed and wanted. The orderly shrugged. Jessica blushed deeply and dared not look at Captain Prescott, who lay grinning with pleasure over his champion. Jessica pointed to two soldiers who were mopping the aisle between cots. The orderly summoned them and under his orders they carried Captain Prescott, cot and all, to the open space near the central window on the far side of the ward.

"Now I'll have to change my diagram," said the orderly in a mixture of importance and resentment, and moved away. Jessica glanced after him.

"Poor wretched creature," she said. "You see what dealing with so much suffering does to some people."

"Nonsense," said the captain fondly, "you are too charitable. He's just a lout."

"I could not bring the *Tribune,*" she said, "but I'll keep looking for it."

"Yes."

She thought it best to leave him and change into her working dress and visit her other charges. When it was time for her to go home, he was sleeping. She tiptoed past his place, and she thought how touching it was, and—how odd, that when someone slept he seemed as far away as possible from everyone else, and yet in a strange, even a sweet way, in certain cases, he was most intimately present.

lxxiv

Going home that evening, she took with her an impression which had a strange energy in her mind.

Why, out of all the dozens or hundreds of wounded soldiers whom she had attended for over a year, should he take possession of her interest?

He was not remarkable to look at. She had met and excused herself from the company of dozens of better-looking, more impressive young men. It could not be that her sensitivity of the sad conditions of the hospital made her pity him until she thought about him more than she wanted to—after all, there were other young men suffering the same conditions and to them she gave hardly a thought once she had done her best for them and had passed on from their places in the rows of cots.

Why did it seem so significant that she had fought for him? To think of it: she had made herself up to that miserable orderly, she had flattered him with her expression, and she had prevailed. She had openly taken up the cause of Captain Prescott and now, in consequence, and uncomfortably, he had become a part of her.

At dinner that evening she felt cross and tired, rather as though she were coming down with something—a cold or Tyler's grippe. She was abstracted and silent, quite unlike herself. Her mother said,

"Your work at the hospital is plainly tiring to you, my pet. You must go to bed early."

She kissed her father and mother and went upstairs with a heavy heart. A family silence attended her until she had turned the last stair landing going up; then the voices of her parents, though not their words, followed her until she was in her room with the door closed.

"She does take it so conscientiously," said Mrs. Dryden.

"I don't like it and I never have, as you know," said the justice.

"She merely does what ever so many other girls are doing, Judge. I admire her spirit."

"I make no comment upon her spirit. It is quite something else, and I believe you know what I allude to."

Mrs. Dryden left her work and her chair and went and put her hands on his cheeks.

"I know," she said, "all those men. But my dear, don't fret yourself so. Men are everywhere. If Jessie were interested in anyone, we would be the first to know."

"No!" cried the justice. "She would not be afraid to tell you; but me? I would be the last."

"She loves you. She could not bear to hurt you, knowing how you feel."

"Ah. Ah." The justice's voice shuddered deep in his breast, and his wife stroked his great mane of shining gray hair, and saw, as only she was privileged to see, the vulnerable weak man inside the formidable person of the jurist.

Jessica sat in the dark, looking out of her window through the bare branches of trees. A few gas street lamps were burning. She could see across the square to the portico of the White House where a dim glow showed through the fanlight. She heard carriages and horses go breaking the frozen ruts of the muddy streets.

She could not put Captain Prescott out of her head. He had seized her imagination. She saw his bright color and his calm, deep dark eyes that looked at her from a world of experience which because it was his she wanted to know in every detail. He was still weak, but his voice had a curious burry richness to it. Something about the way he made the words he spoke—some cleanness of their formation by his teeth, tongue and breath—gave her an extra sense of what he said and what he meant. Nobody else spoke just that way. When had she ever before notice or remembered how someone spoke the common speech? Amidst all the squalid mercies of the hospital— "might just 's well have it till *he* dies"—he seemed curiously detached, as though immune to the foul odors, disheartening histories and poor futures that filled the long, whitewashed ward where an acrid scent of lime-and-water mingled with all else in the air. He had a spreading mustache, and if this made him look older, his eyes made him look younger—no, made him look ageless.

She was angry at her heaviness of heart, for she must believe that he saw her only as another volunteer female worker just like all the others, and no more meaningful for him than all the others who passed down the wards when nurses and orderlies were busy elsewhere. All her good sense told her to stop being a fool. He should mean no more to her than she meant to him.

But where could she find the New York *Tribune?*

If he was starved for the editorials of that tedious old Mr. Greeley,

she would go to any lengths to provide them. She thought of somehow intercepting Mr. Justice Dryden's copies and spiriting them
away to the Armory Square Hospital, all the while maintaining
innocence at home as to their whereabouts. When had all this started?
Shaking her head, she reviewed the helpless course of developments.
For a whole week while he had lain unconscious and near death she
had come day after day to watch by him. Would she ever know the
color of his eyes? The grain of his personality? She knew his voice,
but only in its anguish, for she heard him cry out wordlessly, and
then one day she saw him struggle to rise and she held him against
himself and heard him call in fevered urgency, "Captain! Captain!
Look out! Look out!" And then with the speed and force of a blow,
his delirium gave way to consciousness, however weak, and she saw
that look on his face of hungry peace when he realized that he was
awake and safe. That must have been the moment, she said to herself,
of the beginning.

She was in love. How would she ever manage matters? For nobody
must know it, not her mother, certainly not her father, least of all
Captain Prescott, whom she must go to see again tomorrow, and
again, however difficult this might be. She had no sleep that night.

What she did not know was that he did not sleep either, and for
the same reason.

But his feelings instead of bringing him sorrow brought him a
restorative kind of happiness.

He lay awake most of the night looking at the long shadows cast
by the low-turned coal-oil lamps in the ward, and he felt a promise
of strength flow lightly into him. It was a balm for his wounds and a
pledge for his future. His heart turned around for pity of the fellows
lying all about him. What did they have to cling to? He was lucky.
She was coming back tomorrow. She would come back every day or
two for a long time. His chest wound was the slow kind, they said.
He wouldn't be out of there for weeks.

With wisdom beyond speaking, and with memory rising out of the
uncounted generations from which he had come to be, he was absolutely certain that given enough opportunity to see her, and normal
progress in his recovery, he would make her come to him for life.

The next day just as Jessica was preparing to go to the hospital,
her father's Negro coachman returned to the house with a bundle
which he was to deliver to her.

"Mr. Justice Dryden's compliments, Miss Jessica," he said pulling off his rosetted top hat and handing her a roll of newspapers. She saw at once what they were—the most recent issues of the New York *Tribune.* She wanted to laugh and cry. The extremity of her feelings showed her again how her emotion had gone out of proportion to its prospects. How like her father this was, to proclaim openly only his harsh traits, and then, relenting, to reveal indirectly his kindness, which arose from his desire to please her. Her excitement was great at now being able to gratify Captain Prescott. In it, she all too soon forgot the little sacrifice of her father, and the grudging self-government it stood for.

For days, then, she read aloud from the New York *Tribune,* while Captain Prescott watched her rather more than heard her. The newspaper copies, she explained, were obtained only in "frightful difficulty" by the "most breathless exertions" (Jessica spoke the language of her sister debutantes). He nodded gladly. She thanked heaven that she had to read aloud. It permitted her to be impersonal. The opened pages of the newspaper were her refuge in his presence. But not forever.

lxxv

One day she found the captain feverish and flat on his back.

"It is nothing," he said, in a husky weak tone. The surgeon had been in and had found a little secondary infection flaring up at the edge of his healing breast wound. Said he'd been looking for it to happen, as so often seemed to happen from bayonet and saber cuts. Cautioned him to be quiet, and promised to be back in two days for another look.

"Two days!" she exlaimed angrily.

The news threw her into a panic which she could not entirely conceal.

"Don't you think you need a special nurse?" she asked. He laughed thinly and answered,

"Where in Washington is there such a thing?"

Desperation took her. She turned pink, and gave a likeness of distraught beauty which in his new weakness made his eyes fill, and she said,

"Well, then, if there is no other way, I would come and remain on duty, and nurse you. —We cannot tolerate the inefficiency around here!"

Her remark about inefficiency was meant to save her from sounding too personal; but her words were like a confession.

The captain gazed at her, smiling and calm, and hazy in the mind. He winked away the stinging in his eyes. He knew what he knew even if she might not. But he believed she knew too, now, and calling her for the first time by her first name, he reached out and took her hand and drew her down to sit beside him on the edge of his narrow cot.

She made to take away her hand, but he would not let it go, and rolling his head on his hot pillow, he grappled for her gaze with his, until she turned to look into his eyes, and then her own eyes filled with tears.

"Why will you cry?" he asked in a whisper.

"I do not want you to grow worse, with infection and fever, but to get well."

"Why do you want me to get well?"

"I want all of my patients to get well."

At that, he whispered a clouded laugh, and knew that she was evading the truth which was so dear and so troubling between them, and not meaning to be clever in pressing his advantage, but only acting with the genius of the moment, he said that he loved her, and that he had loved her from the very first day when he had awakened to see her there, and had begun to feel better.

To Jessica this was almost enough to make her faint, for through these weeks she had lost herself more deeply every day in what she was certain was an unseemly and hopeless infatuation.

Now Hiram lifted her hand slowly to his lips.

He asked her his question with his eyes, now himself unable to say anything, and, mute and trembling, she nodded her head.

In one moment she was delivered from her shaming anguish into the reward of her life.

She stayed with him till long after the usual visiting hours. She held his hand as he fell asleep. The tall window faced east beyond his cot, and as the night deepened in it from top to bottom, the evening star came out and hung faithful, pure and heartening, like a promise, in the immeasurable distance. The pulsations of its light were like the words of a prayer. Jessica said a prayer.

lxxvi

She found herself praying often in the next days that her will might be done without hurting anyone. By this she referred in her heart to her father. Her marriage? If anyone was to be in charge of that, and determine whom she must marry, and when, it was powerfully understood in the family that it must be her father. He would be prudent, for her sake, and weigh all factors, and require heavy promises of the future before he would consent to release her. She begged Hiram to give her his secret promise, and wait until the War was over, and then they would be able to make their own plans more sensibly.

"Wait!" he exclaimed. "I am going to marry you as soon as I am discharged from the sick list!"

He had no doubt that he would recover wholly from his wounds. He would return to duty with troops. He wanted her.

"I want you to come home to when the War is all done."

"Yes, oh, yes," she said; all he said was wonderful, but just the same, they must look at the world, the real world, through which they would have to realize their desires. It was not a promising view.

Captain Prescott had neither a fortune nor even a position of employment to which he might return after the War. He would like to live on his family farm at Batavia, New York, but this belonged to his two elder sisters who resided there as maiden ladies. Further, he could not see Jessica there for the rest of his life, unless he had a lot of money to bring it back from its rundown condition, and he had no money. He supposed he might return to Albany, where he had gone to school, and there establish a polite riding academy. Perhaps—an excellent amateur rider himself—he might breed race horses for private owners. He didn't know.

"All I know is, I will manage something when the time comes."

She embraced him and shut her eyes against the obstacles that faced them, and her heart against the judgments that she knew would be made against him, and said,

"You will, you will, I know you will."

If he was confident about his share of the future, she must be equally so, or pretend to be, about her share. The immediate form for her confidence to take was to bring Hiram together with her family under conditions which must not, at first, suggest anything more than kindliness to a convalescing soldier.

When he was well enough to venture forth on little expeditions, she walked with him. Their first promenade took them to the foot of Sixth Street to see the wharf where military supplies were docked. It was a busy place. Hiram was absorbed in watching this phase of the Army's work. He fell into a few words now and then with soldiers on the job, and Jessica saw him newly. He was no longer an invalid living a child's life under the care of women. He was a man of authority, full of powers that dealt with the hard materials of the working world.

Was it possible? He loved the Army. On another walk they saw a regiment in the streets, just arrived by troop train from the north. The soldiers were halted and they lounged in ranks. Hiram's eyes kindled when he saw them. The company formations stretched as far up the street as they could see. Hiram exclaimed,

"By jiminy! That's a fine bunch of troops. I could make something of these boys. I'd make them know before they got into it what they were going to face. They don't know now. Look at the little biddy fellow there—the yellow-haired one. I could keep him from scaring off. I could make a soldier out of him."

When they saw army wagons in other streets, he stopped and watched them if they moved or inspected them if they stood still. Army camps were everywhere—soldiers were quartered in the Capitol and drilled on the Capitol grounds, and soldiers slept in improvised bunks in the Patent Office Building. When he could, Hiram would ask men in uniform how the War went, and partake of their experience as they told it.

"Do you want to go back?" she asked.

"I do and I don't. You understand. The more of us that work at it, the sooner it'll all be done with."

She saw that it was the only work in his life of which he had had long and deep experience. He must have been a boy when he went to war. He was a man and an officer now and he was at home in the frame of the Army.

One Sunday they walked through the square in front of the White House. She pointed to a house on the corner across the way.

"That is Dolley Madison's house. I saw her just before she died when I was a tiny girl."

"How was that? Did you go to call with your mother?"

"No. Our house is next door. I was playing on that iron balcony there on the second story."

"You live there?" He stared.

"Yes. We are going to call there, as you put it, one day soon."

He was abashed at the grandeur of her place in Washington—living across the square from the White House. He flushed darkly.

"I suppose you've been in the White House?" he said.

"I have. As a matter of fact, Mr. Buchanan gave me my coming-out party there. He appointed my father to the Court, you see."

"Do you know the Lincolns?"

"I have met them. *Him,* I mean. He spoke to me. She did not."

"Well," he said, tightening her arm under his as they walked, "some day we'll go to the White House together, because of who *I* am, at that time."

Oh, she prayed silently, don't let anything happen to make him ever feel less confident and strong than he does now, no matter what happens! Even in her love, she knew that men could fail, and she pledged herself to him in her heart, whatever might come his way in life.

lxxvii

On the following Sunday afternoon after Jessica's carefully prepared occasion, he came to call at her father's house.

Lycurgus Dryden and his wife, Isabel, received him courteously. Dealing with an unknown man, their sense of caste was quieted by their patriotism, and here was a wounded officer to whom it was their duty to be kind. Mrs. Dryden felt no exaggerated qualms off-hand about the acquaintance between her daughter and Captain Prescott. It was the justice who, behind all his terrific front of judicial austerity, knew at once that from his point of view his daughter was in peril. His fatherly attunement to Jessica was acute, and he felt but concealed an immediate alarm.

They sat in the front parlor and consumed hot chocolate and *petits fours.* The conversation proceeded, then, without assistance from the justice, who sat massively silent in his great tufted armchair and gazed above their heads at the view through the looped lace curtains that hung before Lafayette Square. Mrs. Dryden did her best.

"My daughter has told us so much about you. How remarkable for you to make such a remarkable recovery!"

"I am lucky, ma'am."

"He's brave," said Jessica.

"I'm lucky to have had the kind of care I received."

"Yes, we are proud of our girls who work in the hospitals. It is such heartbreaking work, at times. . . . Do you expect to return to duty, captain?"

"Yes, the surgeon thinks he will discharge me as fit pretty soon."

"Ah. Well. I don't know what to wish for you. When my sons are out of the fighting—no, I would have to wish that they go back and fight if they wanted to. I suppose I would want them to want to. And yet. Captain? May I give you some more chocolate?"

He declined with thanks, and said he must be going. The justice rose and bowed gravely but said nothing. Mrs. Dryden shook hands and begged him to come back any time, until his orders should take him away from town. Jessica saw him to the door.

After he had gone, she watched him walking with his slight limp, and knew where in the family her trouble lay. It was more serious than she had even thought it would be, and it forced her to an imperative solution. She knew what she would do, if necessary, if the time should come.

The fact that she resolved upon her course without hesitating was proof of the strongest of all the bonds between her and Hiram. This was his complete absence of doubt about his power over her, and the gentleness of the way he used it. In fact, it was more true to say that he never used it at all, simply because its mere existence was known to them both. He never had to use it because Jessica acknowledged, in her every attitude, humor and response, that it was a welcome power.

A day or so later Mrs. Dryden said to Jessica,

"Would you like to invite your little captain for a meal?"

"Oh, Mamá. You know what Papá would be like. I cannot expose anybody to that. —I don't want to make Papá unhappy."

"Has he reason to be unhappy about this, my pet?"

"Yes, Mamá." Jessica went to her mother and put her face on her breast.

"Yes," said Mrs. Dryden, "I thought it might be so on the captain's part. But not really on yours. Has he asked you?"

"Yes."

"What did you say?"

"I want to marry him."

"Is he a Catholic?"

"No."

"I thought not."

"How could you tell, Mamá?"

"Isn't it odd? I don't know. But *who* is he, darling?"

"He is the dearest in the world, whom I love."

"Yes, yes, of course, of course," said Mrs. Dryden in almost a nursery singsong of fondness and memory, "but you know what your father will have to know."

"Oh, Mamá, how can we do this without hurting anybody?"

Isabel pressed her child to her heart.

"God knows. Isn't it dreadful? —You do know, my pet, nothing should even be thought about it until he talks with your father."

"I know."

"Waiting won't make it any better. Ask him to call on Sunday. Quite without thinking of you, I don't think I can stand uncertainty any longer than that."

If Jessica longed for her mother to embrace her with a rush of happiness mixed with compunction for the stages of life that must come to her when wed, she was disappointed. But presently she came to be thankful for her mother's grim determination to have the issue faced without delay.

On the next Sunday, while Jessica prayed for a miracle, Mr. Justice Dryden received Captain Prescott for the purpose now tacitly admitted in the family. In his library at the rear of his house, the justice said with impassive courtesy,

"Sit here, captain. Join me in a cigar. You have something about which you wish to speak to me."

Hiram could never remember afterward just what he had said, but somehow he managed to state his proposal. The justice left it unanswered while he asked a number of questions in a dispassionate tone.

"Your health, sir: is there promise of your complete recovery from your wound?"

"Yes, sir, so I am told by the surgeon."

"Your wound: has it in any way threatened your capacity to sire a family?"

"No, sir."

The justice was enacting the gestures of his professional style. His great head was immovable. His pale eyes were shadowed by his heavy brows. As on the bench, he looked neither stern nor indulgent, but only grave. His collars and cuffs, starched stiff, dazzled Hiram. His black satin neckcloth was rumpled in careless magnificence. His right hand, holding a lighted cigar, would have trembled but for the fact that his other hand held it steady. After a pause he asked his next question in his deep, growling, liquid voice.

"What are your personal financial resources?"

Hiram let go a long breath and confessed that only an inheritance, at an unpredictable time, of part of a New York State farm might be his.

"Then," said the justice, "no doubt you have employment in the civilian world, or a business, to which you will return on being mustered out?"

"No, sir. But I am confident that I will make my way in business."

"All young men are confident. But not all are successful. You have never received training for any of the more learned professions?"

"No, sir. But I am young, and I once thought of law, too—"

Justice Dryden dropped his gaze to his growing cigar ash. It was a restrained but skeptical gesture. Before raising his expressionless gaze again he asked,

"What do you know? In general: what?"

Hiram felt like a schoolboy whose mind empties when directly examined. It was therefore with nothing of the heroic in his tone as he replied,

"Well, I reckon, nothing but war, sir. Battle. Working to get men to do what they're told. I guess that's pretty much of life. And death. I know death, for I've seen enough of it. And then, duty. I know that too. And I suppose that's all I know, sir."

The modesty of this, and the size of the matters it spoke of, from the mouth of a man so young, who had known only these matters between boyhood and its end, endangered Justice Dryden's position. He was moved against his principles. What a son this captain would have made. Moving to recover himself, the justice said,

"In what business do you seriously think you might make your way, as you put it?"

"I had considered opening a riding stable and horse-training establishment in Albany. I am a cavalryman."

Now the justice looked at Hiram fully. By dropping his folded and draped eyelids the merest fraction he gave a greater impression of outraged sensibility than he could have given full voice.

"My daughter?" he said quietly. "You propose to make her a livery-stable keeper's wife? She who keeps her own carriage and pair, though now for wartime economy they are laid up? Sir."

Frightened and offended, Hiram showed spirit, though in another instant he feared it must cost him dearly.

"Whatever work I am going to do, I shall do honorably and without undue pride, Mr. Justice."

This brought a deep flare of light to the old man's eye for a second. Then he asked the question which he had held in the back of his mind since the beginning of the interview.

"Captain Prescott, do you read the New York *Tribune?*"

The captain brightened, for he was sure that in saying yes to this he was about to gain the justice's respect as a well-informed, alert citizen.

"Oh, yes, sir. Even in the hospital every day I can get it."

Mr. Justice Dryden felt a hot lick of fatality about his heart. So this was the man. Jessica had been taking him the New York *Tribune* for nearly two months now. His first instinct had been right. The affair was serious. It had lasted many weeks. The young people no doubt were certain of having their way.

"What is your religion, captain?"

"Why, I do not belong to a congregation, but I consider myself a Christian."

The father had his duty, no matter what else it might be called, and he would do it. He stood.

"Captain Prescott, I am obliged to say that I find unsatisfactory your replies to my inquiries. Your prospects are not those to which I may with justice commit my daughter."

Hiram also rose to his feet. Eagerly he detected a scrap of hope for the future. He must have Jessica, even if it should mean waiting.

"When I leave the Army, sir," he said, "and when I have shown what I can do, then, sir, may I speak to you again?"

"Thank you, sir, for your recognition of my stewardship in the matter. But I consider any further communication between you and Miss Dryden to be ill-advised, and I must ask you with all courtesy to desist from paying her further attentions, now or at any future time."

Nobody could look into the justice's heart and see there the fear that came to him with the idea of losing Jessica, his only daughter, his image, his other nature.

The father's position resulted in what he most hoped to prevent.

lxxviii

On the following day, Hiram Prescott received his discharge from the hospital. With it he received also orders to return to his regiment. He had five days' grace before he must leave Washington.

That evening Jessica said she would read aloud to her father and mother. The justice selected one of his favorite passages from *The History of the Decline and Fall of the Roman Empire,* by Edward Gibbon. He lay back in his grand chair and smoked and listened in deep contentment. His wife worked away with her needle and thread. Her thoughts flew faster than her fingers, but she must never speak them, even to herself, or she must say them aloud to her husband, and this, for her child's sake, she could not do. Moreover, what if she were wrong in what she was thinking? Nobody had ever given her exclusive right to the truth. But she sighed.

Jessica read slowly and clearly. Now and then her father would call for her to repeat a sentence—one which he particularly enjoyed for its balance, symmetry and for its merciless judgment upon the corruptions of the empire. When had man ever had a daughter so obedient and so gifted? Jessica gave her father great happiness that evening. When it was time to go to bed, she kissed him. If he had looked at her, he would have seen her eyes filled with unaccustomed feeling. He hugged her and let her go. She had never loved him more than then, saying good-by to him without his knowing it.

Jessica's greatest advantage in these hours was the certainty in her family that she would of course do nothing for which her father had not granted permission. They were not in the habit of thinking that she would do anything against their wishes. In the freedom of movement which she enjoyed under this blind assumption, she had her way.

On the next day, with a prayer at her heart that she would be forgiven by heaven and earth for what she must do, Jessica Dryden eloped with Captain Prescott. It was what she had always intended to do if denied a proper wedding under the loving protection of her parents, her friends and her Church.

They went before a justice of the peace who kept an office in a shack on the Port Tobacco Road and were married in a ceremony which lasted less than a minute, and which shamed her. She recited the Hail Mary all through it. Hiram felt her trembling and knew she was shaken by something in addition to the squalid formalities of the occasion. She must repose herself wholly in him. He would quiet her fears, whatever they might be.

The bride and groom took a room at Willard's Hotel, and left the world, and found it.

lxxix

Earlier in the day she had written a letter to her father and mother telling them of her inescapable decision, and promising to write again to ask their views. She was sorry to be disobedient, and had no wish to be forever cut off from her family. Would they not remember their own days of courtship, and understand hers, and by their consent let her return to be married in the church?

She could not hope for an early answer.

The newly married couple took the city into their love during Hiram's last days. They walked everywhere, only not daring to come too near to the Capitol, where Justice Dryden maintained his chambers, and where inadvertently they might encounter him. They strolled past an auction where a red flag stood outside on a staff, and where a Negro walked up and down ringing a big bell to call a crowd.

"Bless the captain and his lady," he cried, "come in, come in."

They did not enter the auction, but they rejoiced to hear the blessing. They bought hothouse strawberries for fifteen cents a quart, "with the hulls on," and ate them as they strolled. They hid when they thought someone approached whom she might know. They walked all the way out to Georgetown to the point opposite the island in the Potomac where a Negro regiment was encamped, and in the evening blue they saw the tents like great lanterns over the river, and heard the Negro soldiers singing together in voices that went deep into the tenderest feeling of those who listened.

At the Georgetown wharves sailing ships were moored and their masts rose on the sky like scratches on glass. One morning they saw coming along Pennsylvania Avenue a cavalry escort followed by a mud-spattered black barouche with its top laid open. In it rode President Lincoln, alone. He was making some marks with a pencil on a fold of paper held atop his high knee. He and his equipage looked seedy, common and poor. Hiram saluted his Commander in Chief and Jessica lifted her hand in its lavender silk mesh glove, and the President looked up just then, saw them, and gravely removed his scuffed top hat to bow to them. As his horses drew him by, something about the young pair arrested his gaze, and he turned to see them as long as he comfortably could. He smiled and nodded, smiled and nodded.

"I think he knows we are just married," said Jessica.

"How do you suppose he would know?" asked Hiram, drinking fondly of her shining look.

On the fifth day Hiram was to leave by railroad for the West, where his regiment had been shifted to the campaign in Tennessee. Jessica went with him to the station. They wandered for almost a mile along the tracks looking for his troop train. As they searched, he said,

"I have made up my mind, Jess."

"Yes, Hiram. To what?"

"To what I'm going to do after the War."

"Oh?"

"I'm going to apply for a regular commission and stay in the Army. We're going to make a career of it. I don't know why I didn't think of it when I was talking to your father."

She halted and faced toward him. She almost embraced him right there in front of all those hundreds of other soldiers looking for their railroad cars. But she knew he hated demonstrations or any conspicuous behavior, and she withheld the hug she wanted to give him. But her eyes shone, and her voice was wonderfully alive when she said,

"My darling, it will be exactly the life for us. I will be a perfect army wife and you are already a great officer."

"I don't know about great officer, but we'll be doing honorable work, and with luck I will become somebody, and our children will have position. We'll be poor; but I already know how to be, and you can learn."

She laughed in delight at the terms of his ambition not only for himself but for her. As for their children—she begged of her heart that she would have their first child as soon as possible. The War still carried dreadful risks. If she must lose him she would still have him in his child. She accused herself for what seemed thoughts disloyal to his life—that she should even consent to imagine him gone forever. But her good sense was equal to her love, and she was as she was.

Searching along the tracks of the busy railroad yard, they were happy beyond utterance, and ready to choke on grief. But in honor of the soldiers all about, they remained brisk and impassive. When the time came they said farewell to each other in a civil fashion, and each blessed the other for showing little emotion in a moment of extremity. His by nature, hers by breeding, this was their manner then and forever.

lxxx

Jessica went home, and she smiled to realize that by this she meant the room at Willard's Hotel. But she could not afford to remain there, for she must begin at once to use cleverly the money her husband had left with her. She would miss the convenience of the offices in Newspaper Row across from Willard's on Fourteenth Street, for the war news was posted several times a day in the windows there. But she could still walk by here every day to follow the campaign in Tennessee and share what she could of her husband's days.

Soon she found a room in a boardinghouse in Ninth Street for seven dollars a month. She wrote to her parents again, telling them where she was. She hoped her answer would come soon, but it did not, and she did not sit and wait for it.

It was her opinion that more than ever, now, as an officer's wife, she must proceed with her war work. Not quite able to understand why, she did not want to return to the Armory Square Hospital where she had found her love. Instead, she went to the Anacostia Hospital and again entered upon the duties of a volunteer visitor. Once again she read letters and wrote answers for the wounded. She brought an orange, or a page of engravings of the War from *Harper's Weekly* (the wounded men far from shunning the news or likeness of battle were eager for these), or even a penny toy bought from a street vendor. It always touched her to know that it was never the value of such little gifts that gave them meaning for her patients. The trifle

in each instance was treasured simply as novelty or change. That
so little could mean so much—she found eloquence and pathos in
this. And when some fellow whom she had brought to smile and
speak with her little mercies ended by dying in lonely agony or pure
resignation, she seemed less able than before to bear it. There were
perhaps forty military hospitals in Washington. She thought about the
inhabitants of them all. She overworked in her own, and one day a
doctor cautioned her.

"You must not continue too steady and too long in the air and
influences of the hospitals."

He looked more closely at her.

"Are you married?" he asked.

"Yes."

"Do you think you ought to see someone about your condition?"

"I suppose so. I have wondered."

"There is sometimes a sort of look, or more, even an air—if it is
true, then you should be even more careful about doing too much
here."

In answer to this advice, she reduced her hours at the hospital,
and instead, took long, slow walks during which she now and then
ventured near the Capitol. She hoped to encounter her father. Nobody's pride—meaning his—would be outraged if accident should
throw together a father estranged from his daughter. She longed to
see him. She felt sure he hungered for her, despite his silence, and
the silence he must have imposed on her mother. But she did not
meet him. Work on the unfinished Capitol seemed to progress very
slowly; indeed, in wartime it was practically at a standstill. She used
to tell herself that today she must wander over to see if any progress
had been made on the dome since her last inspection, and if in the
act she should chance to see a tall, heavy, beloved presence on the
steps of the Capitol, who knew what might happen?

In the course of those days she went to see the physician who
attended her family and had known her all her life. He confirmed the
intuitive diagnosis of the army doctor. He was astonished to hear
that she had been married, though to be sure he had not seen her
parents for many months.

"Would you tell my mother for me?" she asked.

"She does not know? Mothers always know."

"I have not seen her since my marriage."

The old doctor was willing to let it go at that. He patted Jessica's hand.

"If you don't want to tell her yourself, then indeed I shall," he said.

"I'd love to tell her, but they do not want to see me."

Since her family had not acknowledged her last letter, she could not bring herself to write to them again.

"Leave it to me," said the doctor.

lxxxi

Late that very afternoon her mother came to see her in the Ninth Street rooming house.

Isabel Dryden was grieved, but too she was stirred by the passionate independence of her child—and now she was touched to the heart by the news which the doctor had brought. She embraced Jessica, weeping very briefly, and then sat down and said,

"Oh, my poor, darling, grown-up little pet. Tell me all your feelings—physical feelings, I mean. The doctor hadn't time. All he said was he was sure."

They talked for half an hour about the sensations, duties, woes and joys of child-bearing. Mrs. Dryden was deeply interested, and she was also able to give her daughter much good advice. She was also realistic in worldly terms, and she would always feel responsible for her daughter's well-being. Opening her black velvet and jet reticule, she brought out a narrow leather case and handed it to Jessica. She looked about at the small, frayed but clean, rented room which so far promised to be the recurring atmosphere of her daughter's world, and she said,

"I must give you this, now, in private, my darling, while I have the chance."

Jessica knew what was in the case, for she had played with it as a child, and had seen it brought out into the light of evening gaieties at home long ago. It was her mother's chain of small diamonds in a long loop—an heirloom from her side of the family.

"I know," said Mrs. Dryden flatly, "that Hiram Prescott has not a dollar in the world, or a prospect, either, and I cannot bear to think that you might ever be in want. You must keep my grandmother's necklace against just such a moment, if it should ever come, my petty."

Jessica made a gesture which her mother repudiated. She wanted neither thanks nor protest.

"Fortunately," added Mrs. Dryden, "it is mine to give quite freely, as it did not come from your father. Even so, I think he would object if he knew this."

"He is angry, then, Mamá?"

A look of misery passed across Isabel's eyes. For a strange instant she looked like her husband, or so Jessica thought.

"Jessica, my dear, he has never in his life been so shaken by anything."

Jessica's lips were dry and pale. She asked,

"Will he ever see me again, do you think?"

Mrs. Dryden thought for a moment, and Jessica knew she was estimating just what degree of heartening deceit must now be invoked. This frightened her really. Presently Mrs. Dryden said,

"I think he may, eventually. But I think—yes, I do certainly think, even after today's news—I think you should not risk coming home just yet."

The two women understood each other. It increased both their heartaches.

"I must tell you, though," said Jessica, to change the subject and fling out a line of hope, "that Hiram does too have prospects. He will remain in the Army as an officer."

"Oh?" Mrs. Dryden swiftly evaluated this news and liked it. "Your great-grandfather Mercier was a colonel in the Revolution. One of General Washington's Frenchmen. How will you like the Army?"

"I am made for it."

Her mother laughed, like maturity laughing fondly at youth. She bit her lip thoughtfully then, and said,

"In time, this may make a difference to your father."

Jessica flushed. Her heart was sore and she wanted no concessions based on external advantages. But she was so happy to see her mother that she repressed scornful words that wanted saying, and for another quarter of an hour Mrs. Dryden dwelled delicately but with realism on the state of marriage, thankful, if Jessica must be lost to the family, that she was so sure in her happiness, and so proud of her choice.

Jessica, again alone, agreed that her mother's advice to let time heal her father's feeling was probably good advice. Yet if she could not be where Hiram was, she hungered to be home again in Lafayette

Square. There was where she wanted to bring her child to the world. There was where, if she could, she would wait out the War with her infant son—she was positive that Hiram would have a son—and it would be that infant son, she was sure, who would forge a living link between his father and his grandfather. It was a tender and powerful daydream, and she awoke from it many times to the realization that it broke apart each time on the rock of her father's hardness. At this her own pride would stiffen out of loyalty to Hiram, and she would say, "No, I will remain alone."

lxxxii

But in a few days, her own loneliness made her think more and more of her father's, and one afternoon when a thin snow was falling, and the sky over the Potomac showed pearly drifts of light that changed with the thickening of the air, she walked to Willard's Hotel and took a seat in one of the cars of the Washington and Georgetown Railroad, that ran to the Capitol. She felt a little tired and sickish, as her mother had warned her she would. The car would start soon. The horses were already harnessed. A stable scent of straw and ammonia rose from the red velvet cushions of the side seats along the car. Through the poplar blinds and damask draperies at the windows she could see the snow coming down harder. It was getting late. It was getting dark. She was done with waiting for accidents to throw her together with her father. She went expressly to find him when the day's sitting of the Supreme Court was ended. The driver took his place and jangled his bell and cracked his whip. The car moved out through the snow. Her heart was beating fast and hard.

At the Capitol, soldiers of the 8th Massachusetts Regiment, who were barracked in the Capitol rotunda, were now in spite of the snowstorm drilling on the north grounds. Jessica left the car and walked part way up the steps of the building which matched the drifting flakes, gray-white, in her vision. She stood outside and watched the gas lamps come on in the dusk through the falling snow.

She felt a pang for the sorrows to which men and women sometimes clung out of pride, and she prayed for anyone who fed on bitterness.

In the deep of twilight her father at last emerged from the building. She went to his side.

He lifted his hat and bowed to her as if she were a stranger whom he had once seen somewhere, and began to walk alone down the white steps toward his carriage.

But she came to walk along beside him.

Halfway down the long shallow sweep of steps he paused as though some shuddering power had stayed him from without. He began to shake. He reached for her hand and crushed it until she exclaimed, hurt. His massive head was trembling. She began to weep for the pain she had caused him and still brought to him.

In a moment he mastered himself, and continued to march down the steps. But he kept her hand, and when they came to the street, he took the handle of the carriage door from the coachman, and handed her in, saying nothing to her, but only a word to the coachman: "Home."

lxxxiii

Like many another robbed and troubled man, Mr. Justice Dryden, by submitting consciously to what life brought to him, mastered it, in a sense.

For the rest of the War Jessica Prescott lived at her family house, and there her first child was born in the absence of his father, who obtained no leave from his hardening duties for a year and a half.

It was then his son, rather than his wife, who most easily established his welcome when for the first time since his marriage he returned to Washington. The justice adored his grandson, and like most people of the nation during the War he had come imperceptibly to an acceptance of whatever life brought at the moment. The future, thus, was no longer a hard and bitter prospect to worry about.

It now had, in any case, a definite shape for Hiram and Jessica, for Hiram had already applied for a regular commission in the Army. He knew it would bring a reduction in rank, and many years of slow promotion, but he could imagine no other life to which he might want to give himself. He was a soldier. As an officer he would bring his wife and family a proper dignity. He was still young in years if old in experience. He was not looking for an easy life, but he hoped never again in his time even as an officer of the regular Army to meet, endure and survive the experiences which men—his men— gave and took in battle.

There would be plenty for the Army to do at peace. He would be ill-paid, but he would be paid more or less regularly, and he would be serving not only himself, and his family, but the United States, if the nation as such came out of the War. He felt sure it would, for he had absolute faith in President Lincoln, not only as a political leader but as Commander in Chief.

Hiram's plan for a career suited Jessica. It gave Mr. Justice Dryden, too, a sober satisfaction. To have a son-in-law in the regular Army as an officer was entirely compatible with his own view of the dignity of the judiciary. Mrs. Dryden had her own innocent business in the matter, and while her son-in-law was on leave in Washington she arranged for him to meet as many generals as possible at her spartan wartime dinner table.

One other great matter brought harmony and relief to the whole family during Captain Prescott's visit. He said to Jessica in private soon after his arrival,

"You wrote me that our child was baptized."

"Yes. Of course."

"What would you say if I said I was going to be baptized myself?"

"Hiram!"

"Yes. I became friends with a chaplain from New York in our division. He soon had it out of me, how we married, and the rest. I fought him off for quite a while, using all the excuses I could find— outraged privacy, individual dignity, no one else's business and so on. But you know? I was seeing more of men's souls than I would ever have a chance to see in peacetime, at my own business, whatever it would be, and I couldn't help feeling what no doctor or general or drill sergeant could explain away. A man is more, much more, than bone and blood and meat. Blood and meat we treat alike when we fight a battle, and we give our orders to them, and every man is as useful or not as his neighbor. But when he is hurt or dying or recovering, or longing for whatever it is he longs for, then— then there is something inside him that shows, in ways you cannot put your finger on, and it is the most true thing about him, and the most important. Father McManus listened to me talking this way one evening, and I think he made me understand what it was. When I knew that, then I knew what you pray for, and to Whom you pray, and why there was something very dear to you missing when we were married."

"Hiram."

"Captain McManus still had to struggle with me for a while. I had a thousand questions to ask, and I got few answers that satisfied my mind. But he was patient, and he was sometimes light-hearted, and the day came when I told him I wanted to take the regular instructions. He asked me why. Do you know what I told him?"

"No."

"I told him that the best commander I ever served under was General Sheridan. General Sheridan was a Catholic. I said that was good enough for me."

"And was it?"

"I was just putting him off, of course, by giving a rude enough excuse. But I think you know the real reason without my going on about it. Don't you?"

She found it impossible to speak. She nodded. She was flooded with gratitude. She bent her head under the mercy and grace of God. She felt that she did not deserve so much forgiveness and blessedness as were now hers. Captain Prescott was received into the Church in the presence of his parents-in-law and his infant son. Within the week he and Jessica were married under the rites of the Roman Catholic religion.

lxxxiv

In the following year Jessica's second son was born. When his father came home to see him the War was over, though not the agony of the nation, as other terrors than those of battle swept through the South.

Hiram was not only appalled at the assassination of President Lincoln on April 14, 1865—he felt a close, personal grief, and soon discovered that many of his fellow citizens felt the same. Who had bowed to him and his bride on his hidden honeymoon in Washington? The man had smiled at him. He would have known him again, if they'd ever met again. The sacrifice of the President's life brought a sort of purification to those who believed in his policies. Hiram took to his work as a regular officer (his appointment had come through, carrying the rank of second lieutenant of cavalry) a new, inner confirmation about which he said nothing, but which in his reflective moments he recognized clearly enough.

To his boyhood image of the country he loved, with its foxes in the sharp fields of autumn, and its hazy hillsides, its secrets of nature open to a boy; and to his youthful dedication to General Washington's endurances in behalf of the nation which he fathered; to these was now added a new sense of people—men and women, fathers, mothers, soldiers, prisoners, sons and foes—which the War had nourished in him. Was this the sense of charity, he wondered, about which his new friend Saint Paul wrote so much? Was there a glimmer for him here, a personal grasp of what Jesus meant when He spoke of human life? Hiram thought so. But he was after all no theologian, but a layman most recently come to the liberating humility of faith. What crystallized his view of human relationships was the death of Lincoln. It made him come to think of what the President had stood for in human ways.

Hiram said that Lincoln had the gift of seeing all men in one man, so that he could see the nation as an individual man, as it were, with all a man's familiar feelings, needs and hopes and failings and heroisms. What did that poet put down, who lived in Washington and worked at the Department of the Interior, and went visiting the hospitals during the War? "I contain multitudes," he wrote in a book of poems which Jessica owned. Hiram nodded his head over that, knowing what it meant without knowing why, exactly. He knew better than the next man that he was not brilliant, and his ambition, if ever he'd had any, was long since dissolved as trivial in the face of what he'd seen and lived with in the field. Jessica knew him better than anyone on earth, and she knew him for exactly what he was, and this was a comfort to him; for if, knowing his all, she approved of him, then he must be worth having around, anyhow. . . . So his thoughts would run.

lxxxv

If occasionally Hiram had a moment of low spirits over the unspectacular nature of the life he provided for her and their sons, she always had a remedy for him.

"Have I ever," she asked with love and comedy, "eloped with any *other* man? Or ever wanted to?"

In her crispness of mind and speech she could show him that he not only governed her, he also kept her amused.

His muscular exertions at his job, his stubby gestures, the quick temper that rose in him when faced with official frustrations or stupidities, and the slow, searching subsidence of it; the warmth of his loyalties and the sensitiveness of his sympathy for those of his command; his taciturn devotion to his children, and his wondering gratitude for Jessica's love—all these had enough variations and degrees to make him endlessly interesting to her.

When together they encountered real trouble, his impassive strength was like a garment which she could draw about herself as protection until she was able to face what must be faced.

It was so when their third child, another son, died in his fourth year. They were stationed at Jefferson Barracks, St. Louis. The little boy was taken with meningitis. There was no cure. He died after a week of torture which the parents had to witness helplessly. He was many years younger than his brothers. He was a late flowering of marriage.

His death drew Hiram and Jessica together more closely than ever, and in an oddly new way. It was the seal upon their ultimate maturity. They said nothing ever again could hurt them so greatly. Having conquered this, they were masters of life. Hiram said he did not think he could ever have come through it with a whole heart if he had not years ago brought himself under the will of God.

When the aching sorrow over the little boy was finally dissipated by time, duty and responsibility to each other and to the families of which they were in charge at their various posts about the country, Hiram and Jessica came to a second kind of youthfulness. It shed upon others about them vitality, humor and grace to a degree which they themselves never recognized.

Throughout many years they were stationed at various posts in the West—Fort Laramie, Jefferson Barracks, Fort Ringgold, Fort McIntosh, Fort Brown, Fort Leavenworth, Santa Fe, and finally they were posted to Fort Delivery, Arizona Territory. As expected, promotions had come slowly, and Hiram was still only a brevet major when he was sent to command the cavalry troop stationed at Delivery. About his new command he knew only that it was the farthest "one-troop" post on the Apache frontier. To another, assignment there might look like a bleak and disappointing job after all his years and variety of service; but he knew better. He believed it was precisely his experience which made him a good man for the duty. He thought that if he was able to help materially in the pacification of the last frontier, he might finally come to command his regiment, whose components were scattered all over the Southwest at different posts.

In any case, Jessica would be with him. The boys were both already in the Army; cadets a few classes apart at West Point.

"I shall soon be obliged to wear a lace cap and mitts and hobble about with a stick," Jessica said. Other army wives who heard her say it said she could afford to say it.

lxxxvi

My charming Laura darling [wrote Matthew], I write this late at night to be ready for tomorrow morning's ambulance to Driscoll, to connect with the mail eastward. I am well, busy and most of all, delighted. I shall say why.

The Prescotts have arrived. We have our new commanding officer and commanding lady. They came last week by the wagon from the tracks at Driscoll. We knew about when to expect them, and we had the troop in full dress, ready to turn out on parade. The timing was perfect. I was in charge. Just as the wagon and escort rumbled up to the main gate we had our trumpeter play flourishes and the troop in ranks at attention presented arms, quite smartly. We all held the salute until Major Prescott was able to descend and to help Mrs. Prescott out. Then they walked toward us, and he returned the salute to Teddy Mainwaring, and Teddy turned to me and asked for the order arms. It went off quite well. But for the surroundings, it was as smart a ceremony as any you ever saw up the Hudson.

Later we were all called to headquarters to meet them. Major Prescott is thickset, stocky, bald, frankly spoken, and quite evidently inclined to like people. He is not especially talkative, but you think he is always interested. His wife is as tall as he is, slender, and as far as I can judge most handsomely and fashionably dressed, in quiet style, but everything good. Her hair is graying. She has fine eyes— gray-blue, with dark lashes. She stands spendidly. Her voice struck me. She speaks in rather abrupt little rushes. She spoke to each of us about ourselves, and soon knew the best thing about me, which is you. She knows your parents. Your Uncle Alexander Quait was a great friend of her family's (they're all dead now, it seems). She understood me almost before I said a word, for she said to me, "We must arrange matters as soon as possible, so you can bring Laura here to join us." I am going to like her.

The Mainwarings are rather sorry to observe. They worked for days moving out of headquarters and taking their new and proper station in Quarters #3. (The Grays, he being a captain, rank them out of #2.) From commanding officer to Quarters 3! They knew it would come, all along, and you'd think they'd be used to it, and ready for it, but no. Mrs. Mainwaring has been red-eyed and too brave, and Ted has been downcast. I think he is relieved to be relieved of his responsibilities, but bitterly hurt that he was superseded before he could be promoted. He wants rank, but not responsibility. They have that greyhound, Garibaldi, by name, if I have not before mentioned him, and though the whole post is so small you can walk the side of the parade in a minute and a half, Mrs. Mainwaring has been fearful that their move to another house a few yards away will lead the dog to run off, so she had kept it roped, howling, to the front steps of #3, to get him used to his new home, *such as it is,* as she always adds. Being in 3, they are now my next door neighbors, as I repose in #4, along with my bachelor dreams.

Doctor and Mrs. Gray are delighted to have the Prescotts. The doctor is like a boy. He is sure our great day has dawned.

Certainly it got off officially to a right start, when Major Prescott made his first inspection. The officers all were directed to accompany him. I have never seen anything so thorough, or more deliberate. It took him all day to see the premises, and half the next day to inspect the garrison in formation, and the other half to examine the horses. I won't list—I wouldn't have space—the things he found wrong, or missing, or contrary to regulations, or neglected, in the properties. The men he found somewhat better in outward condition, but he felt at once their disaffection and lack of spirit.

To get to the causes for these, he interviewed the officers separately. My turn came last. When he saw that I was reluctant to make a full statement of my opinion of conditions prior to his arrival, he did me the grace of asking specific questions which I could not but answer truthfully. I had a chance to fit together in my answers a full account of the expedition of last month, and its results, and the state of affairs concerning the prisoners Cranshaw and Fry, who have been returned to us after facing court martial at Department Hq. They have been sentenced but nobody has been allowed to talk to them, and their sentence is known only to the Commanding Officer. Until this hour nobody has any idea of what Major Prescott is obliged to do in their case.

The feeling is very tense but for exactly opposite reasons to those which Lieutenant Mainwaring let loose upon us all. The troopers are full of rumors, all ranging from renewed certainties about death penalties to cheerful predictions that the new cndg. offr. will let the whole thing blow over, and the men go free. But uncertainty remains the key word, and I must say that it has chastened our garrison. Hardly knowing what to expect, the men work to make character for themselves no matter what is coming. They see Major Prescott all about every day at his duties (and he is into everything, all the time), and he looks so busy, so healthy and without fuss, that they cannot imagine what is going on in his head, and it has come to the point where they have to know, or burst. I think for myself that he is stretching the feeling as tight as he can, for the longer they wonder, and fret, and strive to deserve the approval of the cndg. offr., the more well-rooted will be his authority and his personal relation to everyone here. I may be wrong in this, for I admit I judge it in terms of what I would do in his position.

Night before last, about nine o'clock the suspense became too great for one of the prisoners. We heard a long, yelling cry come through the open but barred window of the guardhouse. It was Cranshaw. His nerve was gone for the moment. He sounded like an animal in a trap. Perhaps that is just what he is. Some of the men ran to the high little window to see, but the sentry quite properly dispersed them. Silence obtained, but Cranshaw's despair seemed to echo in it for a while.

I meant to note above that Teddy Mainwaring said to me that Major Prescott had commended him for ordering the revetments to be built at the corners of the parade. He had evidently forgotten who suggested to him the idea of throwing up earthworks instead of sweeping parade grounds.

I had two letters from you in the last bag. Mail service must be confused all over the West. I loved to have the two, but I grieved to think it must mean that another mail would lack any. I have a stunning solution to propose: for every two you used to write, please now write three. [He poured his love across another dozen lines, and then, after signing, he added something.]

Post Scriptum: On rereading this, I do not like that remark above about one of the prisoners as an animal in a trap. Please reconsider it with me. He is, of course, a fellow man, in grave difficulty, brought about by his own craven treachery, yet under military justice entitled to full consideration of his case. He must soon know what this will bring. We are all waiting to know. My dear love ever to you. M.C.H.

lxxxvii

At a quarter to eight the following morning the ambulance, waiting for the mail bag from headquarters, stood just outside the main gate. The escort soldiers were lounging by their mounts. Trumpeter Rainey was examining the stout mules harnessed to the wagon. He found a harness strap badly twisted through a brass half-circle, or D-shaped ring, and he called it to the attention of the driver.

"You'd better not let the major find you harnessing up like this," he said.

The wagoner swore at him and straightened the strap.

"What do you call this?" asked Rainey, fingering the brass link.

"What's it look like?" asked the driver sarcastically.

"Like a capital letter D."

"Well, it's called a harness D, then," said the other soldier, disgusted at the blithe ignorance of the trumpeter.

The adjustment was made barely in time, for from nowhere Major Prescott appeared. The men "came up" and saluted him. He put them at ease and began a careful inspection of the equipage and its men. When he was finished, he commended the corporal in charge and said,

"Stand by, corporal. There will be a slight delay in your departure for Driscoll."

"Yes, sir."

"Trumpeter, come with me."

He walked toward headquarters with Rainey at his left and slightly to the rear. As they went, the major instructed Rainey to go down the north line and ask Mrs. Gray and Mrs. Mainwaring to come immediately to headquarters and present themselves to Mrs. Prescott. The trumpeter was then to deliver the same message to the laundresses across the parade.

Rainey went smartly off. The major entered his headquarters and in the rear sitting room beyond his office found his wife. She was sewing. She glanced at him and her heart made a small secret jump and she looked down at her work again. Her fleeting sight of him was enough to show her a look of strain in his face, and the strong calm he had settled upon himself for some hard purpose. She knew the look.

"Jess," he said, "after studying my orders, I judge it is time to settle without further delay certain matters still outstanding from the previous command. I don't pretend to like it."

"Can I help?"

"No, thank you. It seems we are to *make an example* of a man for the sake of what may lie ahead. I have never believed in *making an example. Being one* is something else. Ah. Well. Let's get on with it."

"Yes."

"Close the blinds and keep the women here with you till I say."

She made no comment, but he knew her obedience, and he went to his office. When the trumpeter returned the major told him to sound officers' call.

While he waited for the officers he could hear the women coming up the steps and going past his closed office door to the sitting room where Jessica worked. The haste of their steps, and the silence they kept as to speech, revealed the excitement they felt at the unusual summons they had received, and at the sounding of officers' call on a day when there was no formation scheduled, no inspection, no ceremony.

lxxxviii

Jessica, awaiting her sudden callers, smoothed her needlework upon her knee, and in the same gesture smoothed her thoughts, especially those attached to Kitty Mainwaring.

When the Prescotts arrived at Fort Delivery, the Mainwarings, observing inevitable army practice, moved from headquarters to lesser quarters. Jessica took for granted that Kitty must have known for months that she would be dispossessed. She therefore did not expect what she saw—how noticeably Kitty concealed feelings of resentment with a bright smile. Kitty said to Mrs. Prescott on meeting her,

"I hope you will be most comfortable in 'my' house."

Jessica learned much from that nudge of the dispossessed, touched Kitty gently with her hand, and said in her clear, firm, fine voice,

"My dear, I hope you will always feel that it is your house."

Kitty's heart sank. The new commanding lady was another of *those* —an assured, well-bred, offhand woman who could do anything she liked because nobody questioned her inherent ladyship. Such a woman merely by existing seemed a living criticism of Kitty and all her troubled, hectic measures to proclaim her own indignant social position and to convince with brave allusions to a ruined but superior past.

lxxxix

Within two minutes after the dismissal of the officers from officers' call with orders, the whole garrison was stung with excitement. At one moment they had been a group of five dozen men, lounging their way into the day's routine. At the next, they were sprung together in a strict relation in a common design, rather like scattered iron filings drawn into an inevitable pattern when reached by the field of a magnet.

Lieutenant Hazard had ordered the troop into dress uniform with full equipment to await a special formation to be called in a quarter of an hour. The orders applied to the two prisoners in the guardhouse also. The lieutenant was already in full-dress blue uniform with saber. Across the parade, Lieutenant Mainwaring, having put on full dress, was leaving his quarters to return to headquarters. Captain Gray, in full dress, crossed the parade to enter the hospital bay at the end of the barracks.

At the blacksmithy, the troop saddler heard the commanding officer's orders from Lieutenant Hazard.

"Saddler, get up your forge in a hurry. Be prepared to fall out with a medium-sized brass harness D, and a small pair of iron tongs, and an iron bucket to carry live coals. Take one man to handle your hand bellows."

Doctor Gray soon came from the hospital where he had laid out various medications. He crossed to headquarters and disappeared within.

Lieutenant Hazard went to the guardhouse to see if their dress uniforms had been brought to the prisoners by their barrack neighbors, and if they were dressed. They were dressed. He returned to the forge to see if the coals had yet come to a glow. The saddler showed him the raw edges of fire deep in the bed of coals. All was ready. He crossed the parade to headquarters to notify the commanding officer that this was so.

It was a day of still heat and white sky. Thin high cloud filtered the sun's light until it made no shadows anywhere. Light poured wide and changeless from above upon all things. Color paled. Familiar objects—the line of a roof, the posts of the corral, the blocks of the buildings, the rod of the flagpole, the Mainwaring hound wandering at random over the empty parade—looked queer and new to the eye. No breeze moved. Sounds carried but were flat, echoless. The air was so hot and so dry that men inhaling it felt their tongues go rough under the roofs of their mouths. Many a younger soldier felt his heart beating hard and fast under his thick, hot, brass-buttoned tunic of dark-blue cloth, and wondered why it beat so.

To defeat weakening strangeness, a young soldier once again examined his dress cap and rubbed the brass shield on its front with his cuff. With one of his white cotton gloves turned inside out he buffed once more the brass sabers on his collar, and every one of the brass buttons that marched in double rank down his padded chest and belly. He breathed on his sleeve buttons and rubbed them against the blanket of his cot. He shined his belt buckle. Unable to reach the tail buttons of his tunic, he asked his neighbor to rub them once more. Critically he bent over to each side to examine the yellow stripe for cavalry which showed so bravely on each leg of his sky-blue kersey trousers. He swallowed over a hollow and yet lumplike feeling under his breastbone. Was something coming? What was coming? The day was so bright, and yet so washed-out looking. It was so hot and yet he felt like shivering.

All the officers were inside the headquarters. Its closed door seemed fateful to the troopers. Having been told to prepare to fall in for a special formation, for which the bugle call had yet to be sounded, they were apprehensive and restless. Those who were dressed and polished early did not wait for any bugle call, but drifted out to their own usual places for formation on the parade ground. Their skeleton ranks faced headquarters. The soldiers leaned on their rifles and wondered in silence or aloud. What were the officers doing behind the closed door under the deep porch? What was Major Prescott telling them? What would each officer do when the formation fell in? What was going on at Fort Delivery? Where, exactly, was Fort Delivery? If you wrote out the full address of the garrison, what would it be? It would be Troop F, Sixth United States Cavalry, Fort Delivery, Territory of Arizona, United States of America, North America, The World, The Solar System, The Universe, Creation . . . wouldn't it?

The door at headquarters was slapped open as no officer would ever open it. Trumpeter Rainey came smartly out and descended to the bottom step of the headquarters porch. There he blew first call.

xc

The troop was formed facing headquarters. Matthew Hazard was acting in command. To his left the two prisoners, under armed guard, stood at attention a few feet past the line. Fifteen feet to the rear of the rear rank waited the troop saddler with his equipment and a soldier who held a pair of leather hand bellows.

The commanding officer, accompanied by Lieutenant Mainwaring and Captain Gray, walking in step at march pace from headquarters came to a halt twelve feet from the troop commander and facing him. Having been designated as adjutant, Lieutenant Mainwaring came from the left rear of the commanding officer and stepped five paces forward between him and the troop commander. Drawing his saber, Matthew saluted him and said,

"Sir, all present or accounted for."

The adjutant returned the salute with his saber, made the about face, saluted the post commander and said,

"Sir, all present or accounted for."

Major Prescott returned the salute with his saber and replied,

"Publish your orders, sir."

Mainwaring saluted and sheathed his saber, turned about face, and drew two papers from his tunic. He lifted them until his arms were stretched straight before him. Every soldier could see that his arms trembled, and when he began to read the orders aloud in a barked tone, could hear that his voice might fail him at any moment.

"Attention to orders—" he said, and read the special order by which the commanding officer disposed of the case of Sergeant Fry. Sergeant Fry, for having aided and abetted a movement of mass insubordination which had come close to mutiny, was reduced in grade from sergeant to corporal, and following special duty to be given him in other written orders by the commanding officer, was to be transferred from Fort Delivery to the enlisted men's contingent component at Jefferson Barracks, Missouri, there to await reassignment. It was to be noticed that Sergeant Fry in consideration of his superior record previous to the present charges was receiving lenient treatment, under the circumstances. It was to be hoped that he recognized that in being the first to sign a petition questioning an action of the acting commanding officer he had committed grave infraction of discipline and had woefully failed in the duty incumbent upon all soldiers preferred by promotion to set a proper example for their subordinates. With the publication of these special orders, Corporal Fry was released from custody forthwith, and would assume the position of an extra file closer for the remainder of the present formation.

xci

For all the rest of his life Cranshaw was to be subject to two dreams recurrent at random intervals.

Both brought him to the scene of the parade ground at Fort Delivery on the morning of the special formation.

In the first of these dreams, the adjutant shifted his two papers containing written special orders, and prepared to read the second. The quiet was so breathless that Cranshaw heard Mainwaring's tongue sticking and pulling free from his lips which seemed to swell and dwindle.

"Special Orders Number Two," Cranshaw heard him say in the dream, and then heard him read how Private Cranshaw, for having abandoned his post while on sentry duty at night, and for deserting from the United States Army while in the field, and for stealing supplies, rations and other government property, was thereby ordered to be formally degraded in public formation by the stripping from his uniform of all marks and insignia of his unit and of the Army; and ordered to be branded on both hips with the capital letter D which was the officially employed and recognized mark of the deserter; and ordered to be dishonorably discharged from the United States Army and sent away under escort from his assigned post.

In dream, when the adjutant was done reading, Cranshaw heard a remote cry as though from under water where a man was drowning. He wondered who cried.

The sky was blinding white and made his head ache. Officers flourished their sabers in salutes and returned them to scabbards, and each blade made a wing of white light which was blinding to anyone who watched, and Cranshaw watching was both himself and everyone.

He would know Sergeant Fry all his life. He had been in the guardhouse with him and knew him well. It was most strange, then, when Sergeant Fry was ordered to go free and to take his place behind the troop as a file closer that the man who marched to that position from Cranshaw's side was a total stranger. Cranshaw wanted to cry out again in dream to say *No, no, you are setting free the wrong man!*

But it was difficult to remember everything while dreaming, or more properly, it was disobliging of the mind to remember, but not to realize, the meaning of everything, at the instant of action.

It was not until Lieutenant Hazard, whom he regarded as his best friend, turned around and gave more orders, that Cranshaw knew in a blow of meaning that struck him under the belly, and made him drown for breath, what the orders really intended.

How soon Cranshaw was lifted from one moment into the next! Lieutenant Hazard gazed at him, and Cranshaw saw himself smile, and he knew he shook his head as if to wheedle the lieutenant, and the longing in Cranshaw's mind said to the lieutenant,

"Oh, please, no, lieutenant, you know me, I'm your same old foolish and mistaken but dear trooper Cranshaw, please, lieutenant, with your deep black eyes and fine unafraid breast as you stand there so handsomely, you cannot do those terrible things to me, can you, even if they order you to? Will not we be somewhere else immediately, you and I, safe and forgetful?"

Cranshaw thought of himself in dream as so often he had been with his fellow soldiers.

"I used to sing to them, remember? They would sing with me. They would never let me stop. My voice was beautiful. It told them so much which they loved. And what stories I would tell. How they would laugh. And when they made me do my stunts for them, and act, and be somebody else for them, they clapped and yelled. Old Crannie was their hero. When I did my dirty show for them, about the castaway on the desert island with the mermaid, they made the barracks rock with their applause, and they got relief about love from Private Cranshaw's acting. They don't want me to be hurt, lieutenant, and you don't either, do you?"

"Hold the prisoner," said the lieutenant, and Cranshaw felt himself held, and in dream he fought not so much against force as against disappointment at betrayal.

Lieutenant Hazard stepped close to him holding a small pocket knife and with the pocket knife he cut away, and with his hands he ripped off, all he could from Cranshaw. From his cap he tore the brass shield that signified the United States Army and threw the shield to the ground. He ripped away the polished miniature crossed sabers from Cranshaw's collar. One by one he tore off every button on Cranshaw's breast, cuffs and coattails.

Every jerk and rip pulled Cranshaw's body awry in the grasp of his guards.

"I was silent and limp," Cranshaw told himself dreaming. "My eyes filled with tears that must not fall. I was a great big doll fixed up like a cavalry soldier. The fellows watching me didn't feel a thing because they knew I was a stuffed doll, too."

Cranshaw tried to swallow but his breath was thick and would not let him. He groaned in the dream.

"Done with buttons, the lieutenant took off my belt and threw it away. He leaned over and cutting with his little knife he tore off the yellow stripes from the whole side of my sky-blue kersey trousers, first on the right, then the left."

The lieutenant stepped back and faced about and called out,

"Saddler! Front and center."

And instantly the saddler was there, with his iron bucket half-filled with live coals, and his iron tongs, and a brass harness D in the bite of the tongs, and a fellow carrying the bellows.

The coals smelled hot and dusty, a sick smell.

Lieutenant Hazard's face became large and near and secret. He did not want anyone else to hear what he had to say. He said it to the guards and he sounded kind, so kind. Cranshaw took a deep breath of hope. The lieutenant, sounding so kind, was going to save him. The lieutenant said to the guards,

"Get his trousers down. Strip him below the waist."

"Oh, glory, God, no, I said with no breath left in my body," dreamed Cranshaw.

"Saddler," said Lieutenant Hazard, "get your harness D-ring red hot."

And the bellows pumped, and the smoke blew, and the coals went white. The ring went in, and the brass smelled hot, and the air turned black.

"On the right hip, first," said the lieutenant, and up came Cranshaw's tunic to bare his white hip.

"I'll bite my teeth not to yell," said Cranshaw then, but ever after his scream came anyway, as loud as it had to be. But it was loud inside his head. It was a strangled sound, exploding against his clenched, bared teeth, like an animal's.

"Did you see that soldier faint when he heard it?" asked Cranshaw, dreaming, for even in his own agony, he saw a young trooper fall to the ground. The trooper had to stay there. Nobody moved.

"Now the left," said Lieutenant Hazard, and the saddler shifted his place to burn his harness D into Cranshaw's other hip.

Lieutenant Hazard could not help turning his face away and putting his hand across it. The worst thing about it was the smell of burning, live flesh, and Cranshaw thought so too. The brand struck again.

"I made no sound then, for I went dark in my head. I can see it now, if I couldn't then, but they told me after that I fainted and fell to the ground. The guards were going to lift me up and carry me away, but they told me that Captain Gray, the doctor, came from out front and picked me up by himself and he carried me like a baby to the hospital and when I came to he was dressing my burns. I saw him. He didn't say a thing. They dismissed the formation outside. The doctor didn't say a thing. He worked at my hurt."

Dreaming, Cranshaw felt tears of self-sympathy sting and roll from his eyes. At that, peace came on him, and he smiled with relief, for he dreamed that nothing of what he dreamed was true, and that none of it had happened.

But waking, he would remember. It was all true, and it was exactly what happened that morning.

In his other dream, which did not visit him so often, but which was quite as powerful and clear as the other, the orders read that Private Cranshaw, for his dearness to everybody at Fort Delivery, was promoted to sergeant.

xcii

Half an hour after the dismissal of the special formation, the ambulance and escort left for Driscoll.

It carried the mail bag, with Matthew's letter to Laura unchanged. There had been no opportunity to add an account of the morning's events.

It carried also the commanding officer's brief report of the proceedings, with copies of the special orders read and executed that morning.

Finally, the ambulance also took Cranshaw, and, acting under the special duty given him after the formation by Major Prescott, Sergeant Fry, to serve as Cranshaw's guard until they should reach the railroad, where the Army's responsibility for the discharged prisoner would cease.

xciii

Matthew came to know a particular expression in Jessica Prescott's eyes whenever she heard of life's hardness—sin, crime, malice or sorrow. Her brows rose a trifle at the center of her forehead, and made little indentations of concern. Her eyelids were drawn and shadows seemed to gather about her eyes, and the light in her eyes seemed to come from a depth never to be measured. It was a direct look of the utmost compassion. It withheld judgment. It recognized human nature. Her eyes looked dark blue instead of blue-gray. She had no need to speak in words the feeling which then showed in her eyes.

It was so that Mrs. Prescott looked following the special formation. When it was all over, hardly any reference was made to it by the garrison. The shock was great, and it was over. The cases were closed. Finality was a relief. The new command was credited with creating instead of merely executing a resolution of the affair. Branding, said the troopers, was better than hanging or the firing squad. The Army, impersonally, prescribed the course followed and personified by Major Prescott. Through suffering, uncertainty, disgrace and firm action the garrison had become unified at last, under the impassive power of the new post commander.

Many days passed before Matthew could breathe altogether away from his head the odor of burned live flesh.

xciv

"I am favorably taken with young Hazard," said Hiram to Jessica a few weeks later.

"Yes. We must do all we can for him."

"How does he manage for his meals?"

She smiled at Hiram. So often they came to the same notions independently.

"I think he took most of them with the Mainwarings before we came. He still does, though the Grays have him now and then. And of course, sometimes, he throws together some probably appalling dish for himself, in his quarters."

"Yes. Well, Jess, I am not prepared to do anything official about it just yet, but I see that he will be the officer on whom I will lean most heavily."

"Ted Mainwaring ranks him."

"Yes, I know. But I can handle that tactfully."

"Will you keep Mainwaring here?"

"Oh, I think so. If I sent him off it might look to the troop as though I were after all siding with them against him. He showed poor judgment. He brought upon us much of the trouble we found when we got here. But after all, he was the commanding officer. No, I will keep him. He will make a better subordinate than commander. I can make something of him."

"I always said: give you a horse, a dog, or a junior officer, and you could make something of him every time."

"Would it look odd if we asked Hazard to take his meals regularly with us? The better I come to know him, the sooner I can really put him to work."

"It won't look odd, since he is single, and you can use him as a sort of aide, and that would justify having him here."

"Would you mind? A stranger, here, with us, more or less constantly?"

"No. I was thinking of it before you brought it up."

"You were? Why?"

"My reason is ever so different from yours. I don't know if you'll see it."

"Well?"

"Mrs. Mainwaring."

"What about her?"

"I thought you wouldn't."

"Jessie, I swear, sometimes you—"

"No, I suppose only a woman would've noticed. Well, I did."

"Notice what?"

"Kitty Mainwaring must be making matters quite difficult for Matthew."

"How, in thunderation?"

Jessica sighed.

"Oh, you'll say it is just female imaginings, and the rest, but when I've seen them together, that poor Kitty Mainwaring—she can't help herself, I suppose—she comes close to making a fool of herself over Matthew."

"Over Matthew!"

"Hiram, don't look so astounded. It isn't the first time a pretty and rather bored and quite unsure wife has thrown herself at a handsome younger man in some sort of desperate hope of something. It was equally plain to me that Matthew is troubled by the whole thing. So I thought if you ordered him to take his meals here, we would take him out of a situation he may not know how to escape by himself." She paused, then added, "Or even if he wants to escape."

"But Matthew is engaged. Everyone here knows it. She wouldn't— He wouldn't—"

"Oh, yes she would, feeling that way, and being what she is, poor child. And men get lonesome. Sad and hungry. So strong. So *weak*. Of course," she continued, "we may be too late."

They looked at each other. Neither wanted to speak further of what was in their mature thoughts. A brief silence fell during which Hiram reviewed the wholly new aspect of life in his present command which had just been revealed to him by his wife. Both felt obliged to withhold judgment. There was no real evidence, anyway. But beyond that, both knew the danger of openly admitting something which, once admitted, might suddenly have power to make trouble in the intimate garrison life they were in charge of. Jessica broke the silence by saying,

"You really ought to do two things. First, let him start messing here at once, and second, send him back East to be married as soon as it can be managed."

Hiram nodded thoughtfully. These things he would do. But,

"It will be hard to obtain leave for him much before a year's duty here has gone by."

"I suppose so. And he tells me that he was to wait a year, anyway, to satisfy the girl's family."

"Jess, you really do amaze me. How do you know so much about this place, so soon?"

"I'm a friendly creature."

"What will Kitty do if things are as you say, and we rather interrupt them?"

"We must all work hard to make Kitty happy. This is not only charity, but wisdom. An unhappy wife can have a terrible power over everyone around her, even those she may not know well. We must keep the peace within our little fort."

"While we work ahead to keep it outside."

"Can you tell me anything of plans?"

"Not in detail. But before we left I gathered a large-scale plan is being studied which will take a year, maybe two years, maybe more, to end the troubles once and for all. The War Department may or may not order it into effect. But if they do, we'll eventually feel the effect of it, in our small share here."

"Why on earth wouldn't they order it into effect?"

"Policy, policy. Mysterious as always. Thank God I don't have to make policy."

"You'd be heavenly at it. All it takes is common sense."

"Thank you, ma'am. —And I hear, besides, that the plan is the product of General Quait. That may be enough to kill it in Washington."

"I know, they do say he is unpopular. Too brilliant, I believe."

"Too odd, you mean."

"Yes. He is odd. But if he knows what to do, they ought to let him do it."

"You've been in the Army long enough to know it is never that simple, or sensible."

"Of course I know it. We'll simply do our tasks here, and who knows? It may turn out that we'll been using *policy* all along. —Shall I plan on Mr. Hazard for dinner tonight?"

"Well, yes, then, Jessica, and thank you."

Major Prescott fell comfortably silent, and his gaze, with his thoughts, drifted ahead.

It was many months of hard work which he saw ahead of him before Fort Delivery and its garrison would be at the beginning of real effectiveness in defense and in the field.

Crossing that thought was another: in his experience, it was wise to assume that the enemy—whatever form he took—was always ready.

BOOK TWO

Love and Duty

"Love and duty, my dear child.
Let them never be separated, but
equally kept."
—Alexander Upton Quait,
Major General, USA.

i

Early in the following month of June Lieutenant Hazard had a significant conversation with his commanding officer.

"Sir, it seems that plans for my wedding have been settled, if I can obtain leave to go to Buffalo."

"Thunder," said Major Prescott. "What is that going to mean?"

"Mean, sir?"

"Do you plan to return here afterward?"

Matthew was astonished at any other assumption.

"Why, certainly, sir. I never thought of—" He paused and his face flushed and he said, "Unless, sir, for some reason, you'd prefer to have me transfer."

"No, Matthew, I would not want you to transfer. It just seemed to me that perhaps—there might be a dozen reasons for not wanting to bring your bride out here."

He looked at Matthew with kindness and also with direct eloquence. They both knew what he was talking about. Neither intended to speak of it. What hovered between them was the image, the meaning of Kitty Mainwaring. She meant more than she had any right to mean in the life of a small garrison. Major Prescott was not at all certain how far matters had gone. Mrs. Prescott may have had clearer notions of all that, but he was reluctant even to probe for her opinion in so delicate a matter. If the young officer facing him in the headquarters office at Fort Delivery chose to take him into his confidence, he would accept that confidence with all good faith. But Matthew showed no more inclination now than ever of making plain a situation which everyone at the post had conspired to ignore.

"Sir," said Matthew, "Laura knows all I could write her about Fort Delivery. I don't think she will be surprised by any of the living conditions she will find here."

"It is always hard to visualize the real state of affairs when you're far away from it."

"Yes, sir."

"How long will you need?"

"I'd say six weeks, sir."

"Does anybody else know you plan to go?"

"I believe the Grays know I have been hoping to go. And the Mainwarings, too."

"Mrs. Mainwaring knows?"

Matthew frowned.

"Yes, sir."

Major Prescott put away his short wet cigar and took up a fresh one and lighted it.

"I'll trust you to know what you're doing, then, Matt. You may have leave, but I won't conceal from you that it would be awkward, and probably dangerous, if you should arrange for a transfer of station while you're away. We've just gotten ourselves into good shape here after months of working together. I can't spare you, or Gray, or Mainwaring, or a single one of our soldiers. You can imagine how long it would take to work somebody else in to take anybody's place. I don't know what exactly are the dates, but I have reason to know that Washington is starting things to roll. It'll take some time to feel it out here, but it's coming. I want this troop to be just as it is when the time comes. So if you think you can handle *all the private aspects* of this big change you're going to make in your life, you come on back here as ordered, you hear?

"Yes, sir."

"Put in your papers. I'll approve them."

"Thank you, sir."

"Buffalo, eh? The Greenleafs, isn't it? He's in command at Fort Porter, I believe."

"Yes, sir."

"Yes. Poor fellow. He might have gone far in the Army. Huntleigh Greenleaf has never had a day's real soldiering. I don't happen to have ever met him, but we've all heard of him. —You know his wife?"

"Of course, sir."

"I hear she takes a very strong position, at times. Rather high style, isn't it, at the Greenleafs?"

"Oh, yes, sir."

Hiram Hyde Prescott suddenly stood up and put out his hand to Matthew. His brown eyes went a little vague. For a moment he felt like the young officer, and he was moved by all the confusions of honor and nonsense, health and desire, hope and certainty which stood before him so handsomely bundled together in flesh. They shook hands. Matthew wanted more than anything in the world to make a father out of Major Prescott for five minutes, to tell him what he must of what troubled him; but instead, he saluted and left the office.

ii

In order to bear herself at all, Kitty Mainwaring had to pretend that "she was leaving him" instead of the other way round. When Matthew told her that his request for leave was granted, and that the commanding officer had emphasized that he was not to arrange for any transfer to another post while away on leave, she laughed in her highest and most breathless voice, putting her hands to her cheeks, and said,

"I am not to be spared even that!"

"What do you mean, even that?" asked Matthew grimly.

"I mean, having you bring your wife back here, where I'll have to see her day after day, and see you with her, and know that I must love her, and be nice to her, and keep up this miserable false effect of *nothing* in front of all the others."

"It won't be exactly easy for me, remember."

"You! It will mean nothing to you. None of it has. Well, if it is any comfort to you, I decided long ago that it has all been a mistake, and the sooner it is forgotten, the better."

But her eyes looked like coals in dark smudges of ash, and he lowered his face away from her in pity, not to see the suffering she could not conceal. For the thousandth time he bitterly rebuked his own nature, and longed for the peace of Laura's love, where again he could feel himself at one with his own honor.

"Kitty, I have told you I am sorry."

"Oh, sorry," she hissed in a whisper. "How cruel and conceited is a man! He takes another life and changes it forever, and then when he is through with it, he lets it go, and says he is sorry, and that is the end for him. But not for her!"

Her pretenses left her and she put her face into her tense, bony little hands and wept.

They both knew that she had never rested until she had known him as her lover. But the convention now required by her was that overpowering her he had cruelly shaped her weakness to his desire. He could only now leave her her pride, and agree, as Teddy Mainwaring had long ago in another event come to agree, that she had been "taken advantage of." How difficult, she seemed to say with her quivering life, how mean a task, to reconcile appetite and ladyship!

It all had much to do with how she must "see" herself. On first meeting Matthew, she was the beneficent, comradely, neighboring wife who must do kind things for him simply because her nature required this of her when she caught herself at random in any mirror. Then came her gasp of tenderness for him which she betrayed when he rescued Garibaldi from the poison of a scorpion. Matthew's dismay at her revelation brought her good health through her pride. She even sighed with relief that she was safely past a danger. But she reckoned without the astonishing result of another of her self-seen attitudes. This was the attitude of the worldly army wife who dared to tease young men with knowing assumptions about their habits.

"You're quite content to be alone here, I gather," she said to him once while he supped with her and Teddy. "I think you must have plenty of memories to live on, then?"

"Now, Kitty," said Teddy in his mealy and mellow voice of comic remonstrance.

"Now, Kitty," she mocked prettily, and put her head sidewise, and half-closed her eyes at Matthew. "I can imagine the broken hearts you have left behind. The empty nights for plenty of girls who had your promise to come back. You couldn't help yourself, of course. I suppose that is what bachelors are for."

To her astonishment Matthew began to blush heavily, like a schoolboy. This was not how a worldly man acted when chaffed about his philandering. He blushes! she thought, and then a thought struck her with the impact of truth. His hot face, his downcast look as he worked to recover his cool presence, the thumb of one hand pushing into the palm of the other, betrayed him to her feverish interest. He was—she would swear he was—without experience of women. It seemed almost incredible for an officer, a handsome young man, a man whose healthy powers and wants were manifest in every bulk and line of his person. With this intuition of his chaste strength, she was lost. She must have him.

From that moment her coquetting ceased to be harmless; it turned into an anguished, a sick and imperious desire which must end by tasting his very purities. She daydreamed how it would be.

Somewhere—in the country, under the wall of an arroyo, or on some hot afternoon in his quarters when her husband was occupied with duty—somewhere she would know him in that condition of man which though she had known it often had never yet brought her all that she asked of it. Now, she thought, now: to change and make awry a well-ordered man, a young man, a beautiful young man; to make his pleasant habit of speech turn into wordless gusts of voice against her mouth; to heighten his breathing—above all it was this detail of dreaming awake which made her wanton to think how it would beat against her cheek, and mouth, and cheek, as she turned her head to escape and yet invite it, so that the flavor of his life hotly arose from deepest within him and blew into her own breath; to create this sightless and mindless possession of a man by another self until it could die inside him of what she took from him in dearly wanted and yet finally unwelcome peace . . . These were imagined powers which crazed her until she must make them true. Lost in them, she could still see herself clearly and mourn for what she must do, and, in the end, for what she did do.

She knew shame for herself, for Matthew, and for Teddy Mainwaring.

Teddy had once made a storm over her making a set of curtains for Matthew's quarters. It was a storm he could afford to indulge, for he was certain there was no real occasion to be jealous over the curtains.

But when by her behavior, overcasual and lilting about the house like the very image of a suddenly satisfied and single-minded wife who never mentioned their neighbor, Teddy was brought soul-wrenching suspicions, he could not dare to utter them for fear they might be too true. He was too weak to risk the fact. If what he suspected were true, what must he do? Kill Lieutenant Hazard? Kill her? Kill himself? All sorts of witless splendors in folly occurred to him as he imagined what must follow disclosure. But he knew he would never be equal to them. He became the complaisant husband who must never risk doubts not because he trusted his wife but because he did not dare not to. The brief affair, precariously managed as it was, could proceed with no threat from Ted.

"What shall I do! Where can I go!" cried Kitty, when it was over. "After what I have given you—" she sobbed to Matthew, acting as though it was her virginity which had been the prize, though there had been no doubt of whose initiation had taken place. She could think even of this while creating her drama of sacrifice. "Have you no gratitude for someone who made love so lovely for you the first time?"

Matthew pushed the thumb of one hand into the palm of the other, and tasted every cost of man's power and weakness, and did not reply to her.

iii

Long thoughts of these conversations, and all that lay behind them, occupied Matthew in his journey eastward a week later. He finally had to pull himself up short, and say that henceforth nothing was to be gained by shaking his head over his guilt, however much his conscience told him to do so. He vowed himself to a long and honorable life with Laura, and the farther away he went from Arizona, and the nearer he came to her at Lake Erie, the lighter his spirits were. Her recent letters to him sounded before his eyes again, if he could put it that way, for he both saw them and heard her voice in them. Her happiness at the approaching wedding was like a song. Her mother had, amazingly, agreed to permit all preparations to proceed, but Laura had to warn him that Mrs. Greenleaf still intended to "Talk" with him, after he reached Fort Porter. She couldn't say just what the Talk was to cover, but she felt obliged to warn him to be ready for Drusilla Greenleaf's most important powers.

He laughed.

Mrs. Greenleaf held no terrors for him now. He was a soldier returning from life on the frontier. He was a man who knew women as he had never before known them. His own strength seemed to extend itself to every line and volume of his trim, hard, lean body, sunburned where it could be seen bare, and sprung with energy when it acted.

Laura's written concerns delighted him. They were innocent and intense—her kitten had consented for a whole week to wear a large blue satin bow about its neck, and then one day, quite contrarily, had torn it off and after pretending that it was a mouse to be tortured before the coal grate of the back parlor had torn it delicately to shreds; Bismarck was thrilled to hear about her approaching wedding, for the announcement only seemed like a further challenge to him to sweep her off her feet just before it was too late and cause a glorious scandal by carrying her off from the very church door; her brother Harvey was coming home on leave to be with his old classmate and to see him through "the dark days ahead," as he put it. Harvey was a wretch, he mocked everything sacred in the world, including marriage; they all quite despaired of his ever finding a nice girl and settling down, but she adored him, and perhaps Matthew's example would help guide him to every man's intended course.

And her father: what could she make of her father? Matthew would find him quite changed. He had not been well lately, odd, obscure pains in his limbs, and a strange light in his eye which they could make nothing of. He was cross at times, which was so unlike him, and even stubborn, which was even less like him. Mrs. Greenleaf was now and then concerned about him, but she said that they must all simply smile away dear Papá's moods, and realize that he was no longer exactly young, and that old men had these little storms of temperament, and that the wedding naturally was a strain—all these dressmakers around, and decorators taking measurements, and caterers drawing diagrams of the rooms for the reception arrangements. Laura was puzzled but pleased by something her father had done a few days before the present writing. He took her arm one afternoon and strolled her out to the long sloping lawn above the river in front of The Castle, as the commanding officer's quarters at Fort Porter was called, and when they were well beyond earshot of the house, he turned her to face him, and said, "Now, daughter, don't you let *anything* change you, do you hear me? You still love him, don't you?" and she scoffed and said of course she did, and then he shook her by the arms and said, "Well, then, don't you let *anything* get in between the two of you. That's all I want to say. But you remember it."

It had quite dismayed her at the time, but she kissed his cheek, and loved him for it, and it wasn't until later thinking of it again she had a little chill about her heart, wondering what he was warning her against. Was there some power working against her happiness? Did he know something she ought to know in order to be strong against it?

Matthew found his guilt once again in her report of this incident. He stirred against himself.

Did a man have to be as strong to deal with knowledge of himself as he did to put his power upon the world?

iv

Thanks to the telegraph, Laura and Harvey were there to meet him when his journey ended at last in the Exchange Street Station at Buffalo, New York. Suddenly he felt uncertain; perhaps even a little foolish. Everything here seemed strange to him, after the wastes of the frontier. From dealing with Apaches, had he become part Indian himself?

In the midst of the bawling confusion of hacks, porters, street vendors, the Greenleaf brother and sister received him almost formally. Laura came to him first, giving him her cheek. He bent awkwardly into the sweet-scented shade of her wide, ribboned hat. Harvey, who came from Fortress Monroe for the wedding, shook his hand and smiled enthusiastically at the changes that showed in him. Matthew thought the two of them stared a little, and he knew his uniform was gray with cinders and his face burned to leather by the sunlight he had left. It appeared that Colonel and Mrs. Greenleaf would receive him at the post where he was to stay with Harvey in a guest room of The Castle. They moved toward a carriage that waited on the cobblestones outside the station.

"Harvey will take your luggage in the second carriage," said Laura, glad of anything trivial to say. "Is the man bringing your things?"

Matthew showed his worn carpetbag.

"But this is all I brought," he said.

"Yes, well, excuse me," said Laura, motioning Harvey to his

duty. They entered the open victoria carriage and Harvey set the carpetbag on the dark-blue broadcloth seat facing them. Colonel Greenleaf's smart, paired bays took them over cobblestones through shaded streets.

Matthew looked at Laura and spoke to her silently.

Whatever else might be strange, she was not. Her parasol cast a waft of golden shadow over her but could not extinguish the radiance that she gave him, even though she could think of nothing to say to him. She was afraid to offer endearments to Matthew before Harvey, who would tease her with his sardonic eyes and his downward smile. She was suddenly shy to expose her love to Harvey's view of "all that." His illicit world, which she so well knew from his enthusiastic confidences, was like a dark reflection in which all that she loved in the daylight of her heart would be drawn downward to loveless regions and distorted.

"You are looking well. But you are thin," she said to Matthew.

"He is hard," said Harvey with expert appraisal. "It must be a razzy sort of duty."

"It is," replied Matthew. "But you get used to it. —I have lived for your letters," he added to Laura.

"That kitty, you know?" she answered with sudden animation, and Matthew's breath shortened for a second when he heard her speak what seemed like a proper name, "the one who tore her blue silk bow to shreds? I wrote you? Well: only yesterday morning she managed to get into the spring house, and was locked inside, and when we found her, she had tipped over and drunk a whole pint of cream!"

"A mistake, to keep cats," said Harvey. "They're too much like women."

"Oh!" Laura was exaggeratedly cross at this.

"Yes," persisted her brother in the comic insincerity which he was always allowed, "they get in where they want to be, no matter how much you don't want them to be, and then once there they always have the best of it. Cream and silk bows and little cushions and the rest of it."

"You may not keep cats," said his sister, "but nobody notices that you starve for women."

"Here, pussy, pussy, pussy," said Harvey.

Laura glanced up at the coachman's back with an air of warning propriety that recalled her mother.

When the sparkling, varnished victoria drew up before The Castle at Fort Porter, Matthew gave Laura his hand to help her down, and at the ardent weight of her gesture in his as she dismounted he felt all her longing and trust, and his heart sank with doubts about his fairness to her.

"My father is waiting to see you," said Harvey; "he has a particular reason, he says, and wants me to take you right in to him."

"Can you tell me what?" asked Matthew.

"Not really, Matt. Come along."

Matthew turned to Laura, asking with an opening of his arms when he could really see her alone. She smiled and made him a promise with silent lips and a close of her eyes.

"Go to him, darling. You can find me later."

The Castle was a wide, low house of finely quarried limestone with miniature towers flanking the main door and low crenelations along the lines of the flat roof. Vines clung to its corners and tall elms threw a play of shade over its pale elegance. The sun was warm and a lively breeze came off Lake Erie. The fort overlooked the point at which the lake narrowed into the Niagara River. The lawns were clipped and rolled, and, in front of The Castle, sloped sharply down to the water's edge. Fort Porter held only a token garrison on its high bank—The Front, as Buffalo called it—but all was splendidly maintained. The flower beds were on parade, the white trim of the rosy brick row of officers' quarters and soldiers' barracks gleamed, the fieldpieces mounted in grassy plots were polished.

Matthew and Harvey entered The Castle.

A long wide central hall was flanked by drawing rooms at the front of the house, and, deeper, by a grand dining room opposite to which was the commanding officer's study. A back parlor, pantries and the kitchen completed the main floor. Bedrooms, an upstairs parlor and a sewing room occupied the second floor.

Lieutenant Greenleaf knocked at the tall, walnut doors of the study. The white china knobs ringed with gold leaf turned almost at once, and the commanding officer of Fort Porter swung both doors open in a sweep of ceremonial welcome. He put out his hand to Matthew and said with warmth,

"Well, well, Mr. Hazard, we're glad to see somebody in the Army who's really doing something."

"Thank you, sir."

For the younger man was plainly a field soldier, and, without meaning to, by his mere presence brought shame to any man who was not.

The colonel turned to his son.

"Harvey, if you don't mind?" indicating the door.

"Yes, sir. —I'll wait for you outside, Matt," said Harvey, as the doors closed him outside the study.

v

In a great bay window under miniature battlements Colonel Greenleaf seated Matthew and himself in two deep velvet armchairs against double thicknesses of lace curtains, much looped and tasseled. In these Matthew saw Mrs. Greenleaf's style. Elsewhere in the room he recognized the colonel's. Over the marble fireplace hung the colonel's collection of engraved flintlock pistols, and in a narrow glass case on a marble-topped table was arrayed his collection of Georgian silver snuffboxes, and hung on the red rep-covered wall was his framed collection of royal autographs with the famous Louis XVI in the middle. A bronze bust of the great Duke of Wellington stood on a marble pedestal in a corner. This was a recent touch added to the self-portrait which Colonel Greenleaf assembled in his intimate possessions.

"Just a word or two with you, my boy," said the colonel. "Difficult to put it well, my dear fellow, but believe you will understand, later, if not now."

"Yes, sir."

"But let me ask you, first: you actually have taken to the field on a war footing, after Apache Indians?"

"Oh, yes, sir. Not long after I reported to Delivery I was ordered out on a detachment to pursue a party which ambushed and murdered two of our people."

"Yes. Yes." The colonel's eyes were diminished and his mouth was slightly open. His vision and his breath reached for the experience his prospective son-in-law had lived. He maintained his composure but could not conceal his interest.

"Pretty dangerous, at times, I imagine?" he asked hungrily.

"It could have been, yes, sir. The people we pursued were murderers and thieves."

"Yes. Overland marches, deserts, mountains and so forth? Danger of running out of rations and water? That sort of thing?"

"Yes, sir. One time on a march we had a deserter who ran away with half our food and water. Another time the sun melted our bacon. On long patrols men have suffered from the heat enough to lose their minds, temporarily. The things that Indians can endure seem at times beyond the strength of white men."

"Ah. And are the things true which we hear of Indian cruelty?"

"I have not myself met this cruelty, but I have seen remains of it, and yes, sir, it is all true."

"Torture, and so on? Mutilations?"

"All that. First they kill a soldier or a rancher as slowly as they know how. When he is dead they cut him apart and dishonor his manhood in every kind of mutilation. It is dreadful to find the evidences of this."

"You have done so?"

"Yes, sir. And it makes a serious problem for the command when soldiers see what might happen to them if they are captured."

Colonel Greenleaf straightened himself in his chair at the word "command." He was of a proper rank to command a regiment, though he had never done so. The young officer gave his blood a new race in his veins.

"What is the matter with these savages?" he demanded fiercely, like an inspector general determined to get at the root of a nuisance. "So far as I can see, there is only one way to treat them, and that is crush them out of existence, man, woman and child!"

Matthew was silent.

"You do not agree, Mr. Hazard?"

"If I may say so, sir, I do not."

"And why, may I ask?"

"There are many good people among them. They have ambitious and determined leaders. These have to be dealt with. But I have seen individual Apaches—like my own Indian scout—turn into loyal and devoted soldiers. Good example and fair treatment will in time help to put down the troubles. Before that, I fear, blood must be shed to bring the war chiefs down."

"You have thought about the problem."

"No, I don't think it's that so much, but I've lived with it."

"Who's your commander?"

"Major Hiram Hyde Prescott. Do you know him?"

"I do not. How many men have you?"

"Fifty-eight men, four officers, three wives, three laundresses."

The colonel made a knowing scowl.

"The laundresses—I take it this is only an honorary title for a position quite different?"

"So far as I know, sir, they are merely laundresses."

Colonel Greenleaf, rebuffed, cleared his throat and turned his leering scowl into an official frown. Hardly waiting for replies, he barked a series of questions intended to show his expert knowledge of how a post should be maintained—placement of batteries, sanitation, cubic feet per man allowance of air space in barracks, routine for stables, drill schedules, hospital discipline, mess-hall inspection (frequency of), fire-fighting equipment (replenishment and placement of): how were such matters managed at Fort Delivery? Without smiling even inwardly, Matthew sharply gave him exact information for each subject. However far from the scene of their exchange, and however different in their experience of it, they were two soldiers absorbed in professional affairs.

"Very good, very good," said Colonel Greenleaf at the end of his verbal inspection. He looked at Matthew with a deep inward look at himself, and he sighed. "Well, Matthew, I got you in here to say something to you." He stood up and made a breast for himself under his perfectly fitting dark-blue tunic, and a bantam rump under its tight, braid-bound rear. "Just you remember to do one thing, my boy. Just you do what you make up your mind to do, and stick to it, and don't pay any mind to anybody else. Hear?" He leaned toward Matthew and gave out a blaze of energy from his usually mild eyes. "I'm pulling for you, Matt, and you do what you ought to do, regardless. If you have to be a soldier, and I mean a real soldier, doing a soldier's work where it has to be done first, and that is where the enemy is, you just go and keep on doing it, spite of hell or high water, and you . . . " he waved his hand in the air vaguely.

Matthew stood up. The colonel's outburst troubled him. Why was it necessary that these things be said at all? And especially just after he had arrived to take his bride?

"Thank you, sir, I'll remember what you said. I don't just know, though, why you—"

The colonel halted his words with an uplifted hand.

"You remember the old army saying, Matt; it says, 'Never cross a railroad track or you'll get a change of orders.' Well, you've crossed a railroad track in getting up here to Buffalo from Arizona Territory. Things might begin to go against you, whether you want a change of orders or no. That's all. *Now that's all.* You'll be wanting to talk to Laura. Thank God you're here at last. She's been impossible. Where's Harvey. Harvey?" he called, opening the doors and turning his unnerved visitor over to his son again.

vi

Matthew looked for Laura, but was told that she was being fitted. Two dressmakers were behind insubstantial barricades in the upstairs sewing room where women, including several he could not account for, came and went with impenetrable importance. Lacquered cabs rolled up to the door with messages, parcels or visitors hour by hour. Decorators came to take measurements in the air with finger and eye. A personage with a German accent and a wheezing voice considered one place after another in which to install his orchestra. Pretty girls all exactly alike had charge of the back parlor downstairs where wedding presents were being arranged and critically rearranged for display. Harvey, who was to be best man, set a tone of affable distaste for all such concerns, and consumed time and beer with Matthew in their upstairs guest room while they overheard the hum of preparations and talked of what interested them more.

For Harvey, this meant "seeing through people." Any old thing meant something else, if you looked at it hard enough. He said now,

"Bismarck is coming," referring to their old classmate.

"To the wedding?"

"He's coming from Washington, where he commands a desk outside the door of somebody in the War Department."

The two young officers smiled with the superiority of field soldiers.

"I don't know who invited him," said Matthew.

"You don't? You could guess. He's rich, and social, and a general's son, and my hunch is that he's never given up, yet, on Laura."

"Did he really propose to her that time?"

"Yes, and again, even after you made it, and were too far away to do much about it."

"The devil he did."

"Yes, Laura told me so. She was flattered, like any scalp collector."

"Not Laura!"

"Good grief, Matt, like any female. Besides, he had encouragement, I think."

"Not from Laura!" Matthew rose a little from his chair.

"No, no, sit down, but you're warm. —Mother. He's exactly what Ma wanted for Laura. Money. Style. Talks French. Glorious in a drawing room and sublime in a conservatory. Can be managed in everything by the right woman. Something like Pa."

That the son should so coolly make game of the father confused Matthew. He looked at the rose-garlanded carpet and said nothing. Treading hard against the front of his silence was the thought of what he acutely wanted to speak about with Harvey.

"Yes, between us, Matt," said Harvey, "my dad is a disappointed old soldier. He let me know it once. Every time he had an assignment to a real command, out West, or in the Northwest, Ma made him take a transfer. They stayed in Washington, New York, Fort Sheridan, and once they were sent abroad with a legation, and all for what *she* wanted. He hasn't really been with troops since before he was married. Think of that."

"I see. Yes."

"He thinks you're great because of what you're doing."

"I know. I know."

"What did he talk to you about just now?"

"He told me to stick to what I wanted to do, no matter what anybody else—" Matthew broke off and stared into Harvey's smile. Harvey was "seeing through" everything so clearly that bright pleasure danced in his fine, indulged face. Matthew resumed, "What would possibly change what I want to do?" he asked.

"We'll wait and see," said Harvey. "We'll wait and see. You needn't look so worried. Nothing has happened yet."

"I don't look worried."

"Oh yes you do. I've been wondering if you'd like to get out of the whole thing."

"Harvey!"

"Oh, just because it's my beautiful sister, there's no use for me not to think of all possibilities. Am I right?"

Matthew took a swallow of beer.

"No. Not about that. But maybe there is something else you could give me your ideas about."

He raised his regard and looked straight out of his dark-shadowed black eyes into Harvey's friendly skeptical face. Harvey simply nodded. He knew that light indifference often produced greater confidences than earnest sympathy.

"Shoot," he said cheerfully. "If you want to rob a bank I'll help you. I'm broke."

"No," said Matthew, shaking his head, too serious to acknowledge the joke. "It's whether I ought to tell Laura about something before this whole thing goes much further."

"Something?"

"I think you know more about this sort of thing than I do, Harvey. You've taken me into your confidence often enough about your own affairs of this kind. You know a lot more about women than I do."

"A-ha. Women." Harvey stretched out his magnificently tailored legs and smiled with an expert's content. "You've gotten yourself in trouble and you are worried that Laura is going to find it out."

"Not exactly. I *was* in trouble, but it's all over. I swear it." Matthew was pale and his forehead shone with sweat. His miseries of conscience were coming clear at last to someone else. He needed to confess, and suffer, and define his honor provided it could be recovered. Harvey burst out laughing at his honest remorse. When he could catch his breath, he asked,

"Who is she—or was she, I'd better say, in view of your vows of renewed virtue?"

"The devil of it: she is the wife of another officer at Delivery."

"Oh, so. Are they still there?" Matthew nodded. "Will they remain after you return?" Another nod. "So there's a first-class situation awaiting your bride."

"Yes. But I think I can manage that. What bothers me is whether or not I ought to tell Laura everything, now, before—"

Harvey jumped to his feet exclaiming,

"Good God, no! Not in a thousand years! Never tell her. Never tell *any* woman. When she meets that other woman out there, Laura will suspect enough even so. Women have the most active nose for that sort of thing. But you'll do far better dealing with suspicions than with facts. For God's sake put it out of your mind forever." He smiled with relish. "Anyhow, it is nobody else's business, not even your wife's, what you do with yourself in all that."

Matthew grew a little formal.

"I don't quite agree with you. I feel it is a matter of honor to be completely honest with Laura in everything—especially everything that happens from now on. I have felt rotten about this whole thing for her sake. I don't know if anybody else would ever understand how it happened. I hardly do. But I was lonely, and Kitty—"

"Kitty!" said Harvey grinding his jaws in appreciation of the name and half-closing his eyes to see how someone named Kitty would make love.

"—I didn't mean to speak her name," said Matthew.

"Well, Matt, you're the limit. Quit being an old-fashioned man of honor and just be like everybody else. You're not the first fellow to get tangled up with a female, and you won't be the last who goes on his honeymoon with memories of other women. —I take it Kitty was more than ready for an affair, also?"

Matthew nodded. He knew shame for talking about her in this way, but he knew too a lifting of his burden, and though he did not cease to blame himself for his weakness, he was comforted to know that someone else regarded it as an amiable and familiar failing.

"Do you love her—this Kitty?" asked Harvey.

"No. It was just . . . " Matthew shrugged in puzzled regret.

Harvey exhaled with relief.

"Thank heaven for that, then. I hope nobody else out there knows anything about it?"

"I think not. We were discreet. It wasn't easy—it is a small post, and we're all much together, and besides, we—it only happened a couple of times. I came to my senses."

"I'll bet good old Kitty hated that."

"She's not like that, Harvey."

"Oh yes she is, whether you know it or not. Well. You asked my advice. I'll repeat it: never say a word of this to Laura, ever, and if anything like it ever happens again, and it probably will, never mention that either. In time she'll be wise enough to take you as you are. But it'll be a long time, and by then you won't *want* to do anything that she'd have to forgive. So speaks your friend, classmate and counselor." Harvey stretched and grinned, enlivened by the general topic. He yawned like a long muscular cat and unbuttoning his tunic scratched his belly enjoyably. "I'm tickled to death you told me, Matt, and I'm even gladder you had it to tell. I was getting worried about you. You've always been so damned good."

Matthew took a deep breath and looked out the window. The color had come back into his face. He seemed to have recovered his will.

He looked younger. He looked happier. His black and white gaze met Harvey's, and without any clear thought of why they did so, both young officers broke into a short, ringing laugh.

Deep in other rooms, the bridesmaids heard them and paused in their work for a second; and one of them had on odd feeling, as of some obscure shift of fluids within her, and she blushed so hotly at the sound of the young men's laughter that her vision swam.

"I'm going to find Laura," said Matthew.

vii

In the wide hall downstairs he encountered Drusilla Greenleaf. She put out both hands to him and gave him her charming smile, confident of her years and her position. Her silvery blond hair was swept back into long curls. Her face was thickly powdered. She wore an elaborate morning dress of heavy lilac silk, tight at the waist and falling in so many tubes and aprons of pleated silk below her back that she seemed to bring along behind her an extra presence.

She drew Matthew into the blue silk-brocaded drawing room to the left of the front door and brought him to sit with her in a ferny corner. The room was a bower of fresh green—tubbed ferns and potted palms sitting against the white marble fireplace, and before the two long gilt-framed mirrors which faced each other across the room. A gas chandelier with many round frosted globes hung from a molded plaster medallion in the center of the ceiling.

"Matthew," said Mrs. Greenleaf, "it is so good to have you. We must begin taking care of you. You look so thin and worn after all those impossible experiences out West. When can we expect the rest of your things to arrive?"

"My things?"

"Yes, I noticed your hand luggage: surely there must be more than that to ship from the Territory?"

"Why, yes, I do have a few other things at Fort Delivery, but I won't need them here."

"Perhaps not here, my dear boy, but surely at your next station?"

"Maybe I would, but we're going to be in Arizona for quite a while yet, Mrs. Greenleaf."

She put her hand into the lace of her bosom.

"But why?" she asked winningly, "but why? You're only just here. And surely you have had enough service out there! Isn't it time to go elsewhere, somewhere more suitable?"

She looked about her at the order and richness of her house: she had known order and richness all her life, and she wanted them for her daughter.

Matthew felt a threat in her words, and so spoke more roughly than he intended to.

"I don't dictate my service, ma'am, and wherever I have to go, shouldn't my wife go too?"

He did not intend this to sound like a veiled criticism of the life of Colonel and Mrs. Huntleigh Greenleaf, but this was what it sounded like to her. She said coldly,

"My dear lieutenant, you do not need to lecture me on the Army. I have been in the Army all my life. I therefore know perfectly well you could apply for a transfer. With your new connections, I know perfectly well it would be granted."

New connections. He tightened his jaws.

"May I see Laura?" he asked.

"And that's another thing," said Mrs. Greenleaf. "Have you no consideration for her? Can you imagine taking her back with you to a place like that? Why, I thought you loved her!"

"I do." He stood up. "Maybe you're right. I don't know who's right. Maybe she does. Where is she?"

His dark grimness was dismaying to Mrs. Greenleaf. Indulging the pleasures of management, she had not expected to go a little breathless at a turn of mood in this strong-willed young man. She knew a challenge. She hardened visibly. What rude force was this intruding into her established terms of life and threatening to take away something frail and precious? She was not entirely certain that she would permit this wedding to proceed in any case. Her eye lighted with sapphire lights. She was always in battle trim. Her strategy was to permit the enemy to destroy himself. She could then openly seem full of pity for his tragic errors of judgment. She now suffered in silent refinement for a moment before replying,

"Laura, as you might know if you thought about *her* problems for a moment, is an extremely busy young lady just now. I will tell her you asked, and you may see her later." She suddenly went fragile and winning all over again. She played with her lace and freed a warm sweet scent from it. She put her hand on his arm. "Matthew? I am sure, when you see her, you will do the considerate thing?"

She left him with a harsh whisper of silk, and now he understood the warnings which Laura had given with mystery in her recent letters, and the private stiffening of resolve which her father had offered him this morning.

His heart turned heavy. In spite of all the active preparations for the wedding, he felt he was just where he had been a year ago. This was precisely what Mrs. Greenleaf wanted him to feel.

viii

But at last he stood with Laura, when the post turned out for retreat, which under Colonel Greenleaf was a ceremony of some style. The officers were in blue dress with epaulets and swords. The ladies were dressed for tea. The field music wore white pantaloons, gloves and belts with their dress-blue tunics. An honor guard in dress uniform was drawn up beside a brass howitzer that commanded the river whose surface danced with lights along breeze-topped waves. Orderlies at the flagpole stood ready with the lanyards. Over the bright figures reached the long rays of the setting sun, gilding in bright fire the edges of all things facing it.

When the gun sounded and gave golden smoke over the dark green river, the flag came slowly down as if to join with its own colors a brilliant, quiet garden. And then in a moment, the picture moved, the guard marched briskly away to bugles and snare drums, and the grassy bluff above the river was animated with the released ladies and gentlemen. Long shadows were falling in Canada across the river and Matthew had her hand and took her with him to an old stone revetment grown with moss and violets.

He laughed, shaking his head.

"You ought to see how we do it out there."

"Retreat?"

"Nothing but bare hard clay, and one trumpeter—though he's the best in the Army, and a rascal—and not a stir of wind, but you breathe the heat that comes up from the ground. You step out of your hut to salute the colors and then step back in to wait till dark before lighting a fire to cook with."

"It doesn't matter. However it is—we'll manage."

She smiled sweetly up at him, but it was plain that she had no idea, even yet, after all his letters, of what life was like at Fort Delivery, Arizona.

"I want you to understand, Laura," he said. "My quarters on the desert are a one-room adobe house with a hut out in back for cooking. You go in a door and facing you across the room is a square window. Right now there's nothing but a big bed, a table made of a plank, and a lamp and some candles, and a few books. The next house has *two* rooms. The man who lives there is a *first* lieutenant. There's no grass, and the C.O.'s house is the only one with a roofed porch. The men live in a long row of one-story barracks. The horses live better, almost."

"Shall I be able to ride?" she asked with animation.

He looked at her gloomily. He was determined that she should know what she was bargaining for. In the climate of warnings, compromises, surrenders which surrounded him, he must test her to the utmost. If then she should still want him, he would be the more content.

"Yes, you can ride, under proper circumstances, unless most of the garrison is off on a chase. Then the women are alone with the maintenance people, and at such times the Apaches might raid. They know everything, such as what troop movements we're making. Do you know what we have to do when we leave? We have to leave guns and ammunition with the women. They must all learn to shoot. If there is any danger of their capture, they are ordered to use the bullets on themselves."

"Oh!"

"Yes, it is hard, but not as hard as what would happen otherwise."

"Oh, Matt."

"Yes. We know. We have seen the things."

"Tell me."

"I never could. Never. Laura," he said against her cheek, holding her. "I am asking a tremendous lot of you."

"Do you want to ask it?"

"Oh, yes. Oh, yes."

"Then ask it, my darling."

"You still—"

"Matt, darling, you don't know how clever I can be. The first thing I shall do when we get home to our quarters in Arizona—

the first thing, I'll make some pretty curtains for the window. Curtains make every difference. You'll see."

"Oh, yes, I already have some curtains, and they do cheer the place up."

"Where did you get them?"

Something—a warning—turned over in his breast, and he regretted that already he must unite Laura and Kitty in a common matter. He was poor at inventing. He said,

"A friend made them for me."

"A friend? Where? A woman?"

"On the post. The wife of the other lieutenant. My neighbors."

"You mean Mrs. Mainwaring?"

He had a stab of panic.

"How did you know?"

"You wrote me long ago about her," she said. "What's she like? Do you like her?"

"They've been very kind to me. Her name is Kitty."

"I hate her."

"Ah, Laura, dear."

"I've hated her ever since you first wrote about her."

"Ah, Laura."

"I do. What right has she to make curtains for you? What right have you to *accept* them?"

He sighed. He had asked himself the same questions many times, and because he had no answer for them but his own weakness, he was for a moment angry at Laura. Recovering, he said,

"I could not offend her by refusing them. She was just being kind to a lonely newcomer."

"You don't know a thing about women. Is she pretty? You said she was, in your letter."

Oh, Lord, said Matthew to himself and then aloud, he said,

"Yes, she's quite pretty. But she's not a raving beauty like someone else I know."

He embraced Laura and overcame her jealous dreads. He murmured into her cheek, her hair, her ear, her mouth. Her love beat in her throat and roved him through her longing hands. Together they lifted into sight their own vision of their life together. It brought them peace and certainty. Presently he said,

"There are other things just as true that I should speak of. Fort Delivery is not all hardship and blowing dust."

"For example."

"Mostly a feeling, it comes to you slowly, but it has much good in it. The commanding officer and his wife—they are wonders. And the post surgeon, the Grays, you'll find them lively and sensible. And then, it is hard to put it all into words, but there are moments. Sometimes the evening is glorious, everything so still, and the west falling away in fire and gold skies, and then in the twilight you can hear some of the soldiers singing together across the parade ground, and I don't know, something fine happens inside you. I've had the same feeling, too, riding on a patrol in the absolute wilderness, with good soldiers along, and all of us knowing where we are and what we're doing. And then sometimes in camp at night, quite late, with the stars so near above and the world quiet but for a night breeze, and the little embers under ashes waiting to be revived for the coffee pots at daylight, and you feel you've had enough sleep never to need any again, then your faraway thoughts become so clear, just like the starlight. I can't tell you. It's something."

She felt his deeply taken breath as his breast rose under her face where she lay against him. He was making a song without knowing how. It told her of the male sweetness of the calling he loved, and the empowering innocence of the moment when a man felt, even if he could not communicate, his gratitude for his life. She smiled into her fingers to realize that everything he described to encourage her about the life he was taking her to had little to do with her concerns, or any woman's. And yet she must love whatever made him happy. She lifted away from him and, returning to her own affairs, said,

"Yes, well, Matt darling, you don't know how clever I can be with all our things. You won't know our quarters when I am done with them."

"Things?"

"You haven't see our wedding gifts. They're heavenly. Come see."

He could not help laughing, even while he felt hopeless because she would not really believe what awaited her out West.

"But, my sweet child," he said, "we cannot take anything with us but what we can carry. How would we get them there? And once there where would we put them? Some day we will settle down with all your pretties, in some nice old stone army post, but not yet."

"Oh, but when I show you—"

"Yes, we'll look at them this evening. I am sure everybody in the

Army has showered us. Perhaps your father would store our things for us."

"But there must be *something* we could take—let me think."

Yes, he thought with a smile, some little thing; it is hard to ask her to leave every single thing behind . . . we'll see. Who could blame her for wanting to bring some small reminder of her life here, with its amenity, its possessions, its style?

"Very well," he declared handsomely, "you decide. But be sure you really want it, because one present is all we can manage to take along."

"Oh, but wait till you see. They are all so beautiful."

He blew out his breath. She was like a child, insisting upon her view of the life before her, no matter what he said to prepare her for reality. She read his troubled silence and said,

"Matt, my dearest, you don't have to convince me. I am convinced. Only, for everybody's happiness, could you do one more little thing? Could you just make Mamá see how everything will be all right, and how you will take care of me, and I will be safe? She worries, you know, Matt."

He took a deep breath.

"You would not come with me in spite of your parents?"

"There is no point in letting it come to that. You can *make* her believe. There is no point in making her unhappy. It is such a shock to her."

"Shock? She knew I would never give you up."

"Exactly. She felt so certain that when the time came, everything would work out, and you would be transferred. She cannot believe you really intend to go straight back West."

He could imagine Drusilla Greenleaf's complacent mind at work all that year, making its plans for everyone else according to what it believed desirable or proper for others.

Matthew stiffened in his own attitude.

"I'm afraid your mother already knows my decision."

"Yes, but you can flirt with her, and make her believe everything, the way you can make *me* do it!"

Oh, your mother's daughter! he sighed inwardly. He saw that there was great danger to his happiness quivering just below all the high social animations that held The Castle. He hardened himself against it. She saw his love grow distant, and she whispered passionately,

"Oh, Matt, without you, I could never—"

Never what? They had no words to say, but knew what they meant as they embraced. Never prefer safety; always abandon the self, stare down danger, pursue the unknown; all in honor of life and making life.

ix

In the blue drawing room later they found a tableau.

Sitting in a small silk chair facing a half-ring of ladies who had come to dine was a plump young man in uniform, with a yellow mustache cupping over his lively mouth. He was spellbinding his listeners with social reports from Washington, flipping a pair of lavender kid gloves as he talked. It was Lieutenant Adrian Brinker. The other gentlemen were in the dining room talking about something else by the punchbowl on the great silver-laden sideboard.

"Bismarck!" cried Laura, while Matthew darkened his stare, and all shook hands.

"Laura, I could not bear to come, and then I could not bear not to," said the visitor, pleased that she had called him by his nickname. Matthew noticed without satisfaction that she seemed genuinely glad to see his rival.

"Bismarck, you angel, it is too lovely, your gift."

"Oh, that," he said with a flip of his gloves, "a mere fraction of what I'd like to give you." He turned to Matthew and added, "Ah, well, Matt, I'll have to forgive you, old fellow."

"For what?"

"For beating me out, of course."

"Oh? I wasn't aware," said Matthew.

Laura tactfully drew him away. They went to the back parlor, leaving the latest wedding guest to resume his thrilling news from Washington.

"Matt, you are too dreadful."

"That pincushion."

"Yes, you *are* jealous," she declared, and laughed sandily. She was delighted. All things conspired to make her happy. "Now see," she said, and took him down the long tables where the bridal loot was arrayed. Silver in every form. Painted clocks. China. Lamps. Linens. Objects of obscure purpose but evident price. The raw materials of caste. She was innocently exalted by all of it.

"And look, these are wonderful," she cried, indicating a sparkling decanter and twelve goblets. "Real Waterford, from England." She lifted a glass and turned it until it made prismatic flashes.

"At least you can drink out of them," he said. "Who sent them?"

"Bismarck." She smiled. "They cost millions."

"Yes," he said, and spitefully used a familiar army expression, "he has money on the outside."

"Oh, Matt. Don't be mean." She pulled him along to other exhibits. "See, this epergne is from Uncle Alex."

"General Quait?"

"Yes, yes, isn't it lovely? Imagine it for our centerpiece when we give dinners."

It touched him to think that he might have some share in the intention of this gift from the great veteran of the plains and north Mexico who might this year or next—if he could dwell for a moment on information that was not for publication—take command in the long-planned move against the last Indian renegades. He saw Arizona again and his temper improved. They were both happy when Mrs. Greenleaf came to find them. She was resplendent for evening. Her curls were now piled on top of her head and retained with diamond crescents. Her gown, as Matthew thought, was made up of many departments, all of black satin. She carried a small fan of gold lace.

"Come, children," she called lightly, "it is time. We'll go ahead with dinner, anyway."

With a beautiful and somewhat unnerving smile she swept them back among the company rapidly spanking the air after them with her fan. Matthew disliked the effect of being shooed along like a barnyard fowl. Presently dinner was going along rather in the manner of a stately concert, with the hostess as soloist and the host accompanying in a climate of candlelight. The men were all in uniform. The women rustled in their voluminous silks. Suitable toasts were proposed—the President, the nation, the prospective bride and groom. In a chance moment of general silence, Drusilla Greenleaf said to Bismarck, her left-hand dinner partner, loudly enough to be heard by all, and with deadly playfulness,

"He is obstinate. A change of orders could be managed ever so easily, but no. He is talking of taking her right back to Arizona with him. As I say, there'd be nothing there but love among the savages. The poor impossible darlings. Well, we'll see."

She leaned nearer to Bismarck, and her eyelids drooped a trifle, and her bosom rolled visibly within its low bodice, and she seemed to be making unspoken encouragements of who knew what hopes.

Laura caught Matthew's eye and pleaded with him for silence. With heavy heart, for he saw calamity coming, he could not show restraint and remain himself. Taking up the other end of the little pause of general talk, he said to the young woman next to him in a voice for all to hear,

"And do you know what else? Not only do we kill rattlesnakes by the dozen every day, we are invaded in our quarters by even more forbidding creatures. Do you know what a scorpion is?" He made one in the air with a curled finger. "Those we slice apart with our sabers. And tarantulas?" He lifted a saucer. "Spiders this big. They crawl everywhere. Do you know what I do when I see one on my floor, or on my wall? I keep a bucket of fresh mud in my quarters at all times for the purpose, and when I see a tarantula, I take up a handful of this good, sticky mud, and I hurl it at the big black hairy thing, and if my aim is good, I imprison him in a dome of mud. When it dries a little, it can be shoveled outside with its victim nicely immobilized."

Little cries of proper horror came from young ladies. Matthew did not look at Mrs. Greenleaf, who heard him with a faint level smile. She knew a declaration of war when she heard one.

Oh, Matt, why must you, cried Laura in silent fear. He turned and smiled at her. Her heart calmed down under his strong look. Something valiant in his thought reached her. He was thinking that what had been meant in a mockery of sentiment—"love among the savages"—was good enough for a life, if he was man enough to make it so, unless all opportunity were already lost this night.

x

After the guests were gone in their carriages, Mrs. Greenleaf asked her husband, her daughter, her son and her expected son-in-law to accompany her to the blue drawing room. There she opened a family council, first addressing Matthew, and employing an official style.

"Mr. Hazard, have you possibly reconsidered our conversation of this morning?"

"I have recalled it, ma'am, but without a change of views."

Laura took her breath sharply. How reckless of him.

Mrs. Greenleaf lifted her bosom grandly and sadly, forced, as she was, to a melancholy decision.

"Colonel," she said to her husband with a tragic air but with undertones of satisfaction in her fine voice, "have you an orderly on duty tonight?"

"Yes, my dear, I have, as usual."

"Then I shall ask him to dispatch a number of messages at once."

"For what purpose, Drusilla, if I may ask?"

Harvey and Laura exchanged glances. Their father did not often dare to quiz his wife about her operations.

"By all means," said Mrs. Greenleaf with determined courtesy. "I feel obliged to notify the seamstresses, and the decorators, and the caterers, and all, not to come tomorrow, as I feel further obliged to cease preparations for the happy event that must now be canceled."

"Mamá!"

"My poor child, we had better be clear about this now than sorry about it later. You will hate your mamá for a week, but you will thank her for a lifetime. I have written my little notes. Huntleigh, if you will just have your orderly saddle up and call by for them?"

Colonel Greenleaf sat in his silken armchair like a model of deportment. His ankles were neatly crossed. His body was erect. His hands were folded with laced fingers in his lap. His pale gray hair and mustache were perfectly brushed. The only change in his appearance which anyone noticed was that his face had gone white. His voice was steady as he said to his wife,

"One moment, my dear, if you please." He turned to Matthew and asked quietly, "Matthew, do you grasp precisely what this is about?"

"I do, sir." Matthew smiled in an effort to show self-control, but the effect was only that of a sickly grimace in his sense of injustice and rage. "I gather that my failure to ask, or to permit it to be asked that I be given a transfer of station has led Mrs. Greenleaf to withdraw her consent to my marriage to your daughter. But in the first place, I have pledged my word to my commanding officer not to take new orders while on leave; and in the second, I do not consider it proper for me to marry upon a set of conditions established by anyone other than my promised wife."

"By God," said Harvey softly, in admiration.

"I see," said the colonel. "Laura, do you still want to marry Matthew Hazard and go West with him?"

"I do. I do," said Laura, in tears.

Colonel Greenleaf tugged hard at his mustache. His face was a sudden mottled red. His light eyes darkened with intensity. He stood, magnificently delineated in his uniform, gripping and ungripping his hands behind him.

"Yes, now that it is plainly understood," he declared, "*I* will make a few remarks. Lieutenant, you are to be commended for devotion to duty. Dangerous duty, and I hope you will remain all your life as sure of your soldier's vocation as you are now." The colonel faced toward his wife in irrepressible fury. "I wish with all my heart that I had been!" He turned back to Matthew. "If you are prepared to sacrifice everything to it, then be assured, by a paradox of God's mercy, everything will be yours!"

"Huntleigh!" Mrs. Greenleaf lay back against stuffed velvet, herself as inert as a cushion.

"And now, to my wife, I will say that under no circumstances will she be permitted to send out any notes by orderly this evening for the purpose stated. There will be no interruption of preparations, and all will proceed as planned. That is an order!"

"Huntleigh Greenleaf, I have never in my—"

"And you, my child, my Laura," said the colonel, taking his daughter in his arms, "you have now the chance to be a true soldier's wife, and I pray you will meet it fully, with courage and independence and faith. If there is hardship for your husband, it must be yours, if by sharing it you can lighten his burden. God bless you, my dear child, and keep you if dangers await you."

Colonel Greenleaf swept them all with a fierce and happy glare and stalked from the room, slamming the door righteously for the first time in thirty years.

xi

So it was that, after all, on the appointed day, Matthew Hazard stood with Laura his wife in the other, or yellow, drawing room of The Castle, ducking his head and murmuring his thanks for kind sentiments to the slowly moving file of guests who passed on into other rooms for champagne and tidbits and lively conversation about the ceremony which had just taken place.

Drusilla Greenleaf was under strain, but only her family knew it. Early in the morning she had fainted out of simple exasperation. Revived, she had let one after another of the family come to hold her hand outstretched from clouds of laces and sachets. But as the hour for public appearances drew near, she showed them all of what stuff heroism was made. She rose from her couch and strapped herself together with layers of satin and velvet, and when the wedding started, she was radiant, taking all eyes by her animation, her late-glowing beauty, and her personal notion of what queenly grace must be.

At the reception she gave a performance as hostess. Matthew saw her when he could and marveled at the range of her talent, from deathbed in the morning to grand conductress of the wedding and its aftermath in the afternoon. He wanted to laugh, but at the same time he could not withhold a certain grim tribute from his mother-in-law. She was tremendous, managing guests with the proper word, or two, or three, depending on their relative importance. She could give exactly the brilliant recollection, or the lifting allusion, or the dazzling gift of an epigram, according to whom she addressed. The drawing room was her stage, and she was the prima donna, and everyone was brought to recognize this. The selfhood and the insincerity of the display made Matthew vow to take and keep Laura away from all that forever.

But Laura, meanwhile, knowing her mother so well that she hardly saw her, was exquisitely happy, speaking to friends. Bismarck held her hand longer than anyone else as he claimed his kiss from the bride.

On the wide stair landing Mr. Schlumpfig and his orchestra, all in scarlet coats, played furious waltzes, while out of doors under the trees Colonel Greenleaf's band blew its way through a succession of concert *galops* and polkas. Guarding the wedding presents at parade rest stood two young soldiers with fixed bayonets—Colonel Greenleaf's single and eccentric contribution to the amenities.

But the side-paddle steamer *Inland Queen* sailed from the foot of Main Street at three o'clock for Toledo, on Lake Erie, and it was a long drive to the pier from Fort Porter. Harvey had a carriage at The Castle's back door, already loaded with luggage. If they hoped to get away unseen Matthew and Laura were disappointed, for as they met at the foot of the kitchen stairs, Bismarck brought a cheerful crowd through the pantry to hail them and see them into their hack.

They made the best of it, and waved, called, smiled. Mrs. Greenleaf came forward and embraced them. To Matthew she said,

"You will see. But I hope I am wrong."

But, in the conflicting emotions of the whole event, her effort to sustain her tradition was a poor one, and to the enchanted astonishment of her public she burst into tears and turned to her husband for comfort, as she had not done for many years.

Harvey shook hands in the air at the bride and groom as the carriage moved away. Catching his classmate's eye, he laid his forefinger across his lips in final admonition. Matthew scowled and smiled. Laura looked up at him in sweet puzzlement and perfect trust at this exchange. Nothing was simple, everything was complicated, but nobody thought of that now. The string waltzes and the brass polkas mingled in the air. Everyone watched the carriage down the drive but as it reached the gates all were astonished to see it come to a stop.

It did so on Matthew's orders while he spoke to Laura.

"What is this?" he asked, pointing to a large square box heavily corded that sat on the seat facing them.

"You said I might," she answered, "it is the present I picked to bring along."

"But, my sweet darling, look at the size of it. And all the rest of your things—we'll never manage. What is in it?"

"My Waterford glass."

"Your what?"

"The decanter and goblets that you saw."

"Glass? To take to Arizona?" He was dumfounded. And then he was further outraged at a recollection. "You don't mean the stuff that damned fool sent you?"

"I do, Matt, I certainly do, and I intend to have it. You said I could choose, and I did so. And if you think it is going to be easy to go ten thousand miles from here and live in a mud hut without one single decent thing in it, and if you—why, then, I simply—" She burst into tears.

She is merely nervous, he said to himself.

"If," she said into her muffling fingers, "you can have curtains made for you by your precious Kitty, I don't see why I can't have the one thing I—"

"Laura! Quit this!"

"Well, she *did* make your curtains, didn't she?"

"Yes." He struggled to remain patient. He tried to smile.

"And you *did* keep them, didn't you?"

"Yes."

"Well, there!"

He almost said, What do you see in Bismarck that you should take his particular present, of all things? But he said instead, "I think that we'd better leave your box off here. I assure you we'll never get it there."

"Oh! You promised!"

"That is true. I did. I expected, though, that you'd take out something more sensible. Easier to carry."

He gestured at all her other fine leather and brass portmanteaus, and his own single, worn carpetbag. But, with her heritage, she was a woman of spirit.

"Very well," she said, and her eyes blazed. "I will carry it myself."

"Very well," he said frostily, "if it means something very great to you, you may carry it all the way. God knows I will have enough to handle. Drive on," he called, and the carriage moved out through the gates, toward the *Inland Queen* and their cabin; the vast lake and their honeymoon, with its mysteries, its prides, and its fond, enduring compromises.

xii

She carried the box off the *Inland Queen* at Toledo. Without any direct discussion of the matter, she had established the fiction that if she would let him, he would gallantly carry the box for her, but that it was she alone who could be trusted to handle so fragile an affair as a dozen Waterford glasses with their decanter. He was grateful for her device, for he had sorrowed deeply over having spoken roughly to her in their carriage at Buffalo. She was serene in escaping the blot upon ladyship which would attend any submission on her part to an order that she carry a bundle against her will. Whenever they rode on cobblestones she held the box on her lap. In crowded railway coaches she held it again. Between vehicles she grasped it by a handle made of raffia tied to a cradle of heavy twine. In St. Louis her pride came upon an extra dimension of pleasure. With time to kill before taking the train for the West, they idled among shops, and at Lingenfelter's she was sure enough of Matthew by then to risk a dangerous topic and share a discovery.

"Look, there is my same Waterford."

He saw a sample of a decanter and one goblet, marked:

Imported from England
Very Special
Decanter and One Doz. Glasses
$85
Special Orders Only. Allow Six Months

"Yes," he said, "well, week after next, you'll see my Pennsylvania tin cups and plates."

"You'll be proud enough when we entertain and use my fine glasses!"

Before they boarded their last train for the long ride to Arizona he telegraphed to Driscoll, on the main line west in the Territory, to have a message relayed to the fort, asking for an army ambulance and an armed escort to meet them.

"How will they relay it?" she asked.

"You will see. It is something the Army has put in during the last year. It is wonderful."

He felt a curious eagerness to get back to Fort Delivery. It would be good to be at work with Major Prescott again. However primitive the materials, it would be a matter of deep joy to begin making a home with Laura. Her love had, without knowing it, blessed him with forgiveness of his brief, troubled infidelity. It was now almost impossible for him to believe that he had made love to Kitty Mainwaring. She was now a figure so impersonal to him that he could look forward to meeting her again with no qualms of any sort. No doubt, he reflected, she was in an equally sensible frame of mind. How sensible Harvey had been, giving him such capital advice on the matter! It was wonderful to think that never again in his life would he have to entertain thoughts of any other woman but Laura, or work to forget his own errors of love. He thanked God that he was not like Harvey, who had had to perfect a resilient technique for disposing of women by the hundred, he supposed. Laura was all womankind to him. He took her in his arms, possessed by the overwhelming desire to give, which could be assuaged only by taking.

"Keep you forever," he murmured. "Protect you."

She completed the thought in her own good moment by asking, "Will we see any Indians?"

"I hope not."

"Yes, they are all dreadful."

"No," he said, "no, not all. We use some Apache scouts in our troops. Mihe is called Joe Dummy. He is a good soldier and tremendous on the trail."

But she shuddered invitingly, and in satisfaction he had to comfort her.

At Driscoll, Arizona, they had to wait two days for the escort, and then left early in the morning overland. She saw sunup on the desert. By noon they were in a baking wilderness. The party crossed, one after another, flatlands outlined by far mountains.

The ambulance was covered with canvas over bows, and she sat under the cover, clutching her box on her knees. Every lurch of the wagon threatened her cargo. It was not lost on her that the escort rode in loose formation, on constant alert. They watched for anything that moved, even rocks that would seem to waver in the heat; and otherwise the hungry spiral of carrion birds, and the jump of small game, and, in camp, snakes.

On the second day out of Driscoll, she saw a thing that she watched for minutes before speaking of it, for she was not sure it might not be an illusion brought on by the heat. The sunlight was captured in repeated, tiny blazes on a high rocky point.

"That is General Quait's heliostat," explained Matthew. "One of the great preliminary arrangements he has had done throughout the past months. It's relaying messages by mirrors, catching the sunlight, and alternately showing and shutting it off. Soldiers operate the mirrors as far as fifty miles apart. That is how I could order the party to meet us. The winks spell out words, by Morse code. It would take us nearly two days to cross the ground between us and that mirror. It may be saying that we are on our way."

Finally late one afternoon Matthew called Laura to look, for they could see their goal: long low piles of desert ground, that were buildings; and something that faintly moved like a patch of sky, that was the flag.

It was empty yellow evening when they pulled up before the headquarters of Fort Delivery. Any arrival at the fort was an event for the garrison; but one which brought home a popular officer and his bride was tremendous. Matthew saw all his friends—the officers and their wives, most of the troop, including his entire platoon, and the laundresses—gathered between the main gate and the commanding officer's steps. He saw them in a hot blur, and he waved when they greeted him with cheers. He vaulted from the wagon and Laura stepped down into his arms. He brought her to the Prescotts.

"Welcome home, Matt," said Hiram Hyde, and to Laura, "we're proud of you, Mrs. Hazard, for coming all the way out here to join us. This is my wife."

"My dear!" said Jessica, holding Laura's hands, "I am so very glad to see you." She drew Laura to her and kissed her cheek. "We love Matthew, and I know we are going to love you." She turned to those standing next in line. "Here are Captain and Mrs. Gray, our surgeon and his wife."

Captain Gray shook hands with a bristling scowl, for fear of being thought tender-hearted over beautiful young women just wed. Mrs. Gray said,

"Cedric and I are so glad. —Do you play whist? Here are the Mainwarings, Ted and Kitty, your next-door neighbors."

Teddy made a shambling lunge of geniality and shook Laura's hand with a murmured word. His wife put her two thin hands together at breast level and with brightness in her eyes said,

"Oh, Teddy, she is! I told you she would be! She's so lovely!" and on the last word her voice went away into a dry, clicking whisper.

Laura smiled upon everyone, and Matthew said,

"It is very good of you all to turn out for us." He faced toward the troop, gathered loosely in a little crowd, and waved both arms to them. They responded with a disordered yell of good will. Jessica Prescott moved the tableau into dismissal.

"Matthew, take your Laura to your quarters. She will want to see her own place first of all, and catch her breath. I'm sending a little supper down to you both in your place, and we shall see each other, all of us"—she smiled and referred to the inescapable intimacies of Fort Delivery—"in the morning."

Matthew helped Laura back into the ambulance and they drove the last hundred yards to their new home in Quarters 4. As they drove down the officers' line, he was moved to see what had been done to make his return with Laura as happy as possible. The gravel of the walk had been raked and nicely straightened at the edges. It even seemed that the white woodwork of the windows and doors set in adobe had been newly painted. At his own quarters he saw with a sudden catch of pleasure that a garland of red, white and blue bunting, tied with desert flowers, was draped above the shadowless front door. A sign with fancy lettering read, "Congratulations from 2nd Platoon." The wagon stopped and he jumped out.

"Come, Laura darling!"

He held his arms up for her. She came down and they stood for a moment looking at their house with its door open upon dense shade within, broken only by a brilliant square of yellow sky in the window opposite the entrance.

"It isn't much," he said, as if to take her thought away from her and rob it of power to hurt.

"It's adorable!" she said, and turned quickly to take up her box from the wagon seat. Holding it, and moving as though to take a fateful step, she started to the house a few feet away. Matthew took after her. He fetched her up, box and all, to carry her over his threshold.

At that instant in the window opposite appeared a wild vision in the strong last daylight.

It was an Apache Indian with two feathers in his headband, a silent shriek on his face, who made violent gestures with his arms as he bobbed up and down in the window frame.

Laura cried out in terror.

She threw her arms around her husband's neck. Her box crashed to the hard mud floor with the sound of a thousand breaking pieces of prismatic, imported glass. With it much else lay finally shattered. She sobbed against Matthew's breast, and he caressed her dearly, but to save his life he could not help the laughter that roared out of him.

It was many minutes before he saw her subside into calm good sense. When at last she was able to grasp the fact that the Apache at the window was only Lieutenant Hazard's Indian scout, Joe Dummy, who had come to make her welcome in his way, she consented to shake his hand, which was extended to her sidewise around the open door of her house. Matthew clapped him on the back and thanked him for his kind attentions.

When Joe was gone, Matthew knelt down to take up the wreckage of the box. A moment later the commanding officer's orderly appeared with a tray laden with supper under one of Mrs. Prescott's best damask napkins, monogrammed.

"Thank you, Rainey," said Matthew. "Just set it on the table. This is Trumpeter Rainey, dear," he said to Laura.

"Thank you, lieutenant, sir. Hello, ma'am, we're mighty glad to see you here."

In the room's gloaming, the trumpeter, by peering frankly, could just see that Mrs. Hazard was pretty enough for any man to be glad of her, and that those must be tears that were lingering after what must have been sobs. The trumpeter, as he often said, knew life, and he now sighed inwardly at the things a man did that could make a woman cry; and without judging his lieutenant, he felt sorry for the lieutenant's wife and wished he could have the chance to make her smile, for he knew he could make her smile, as he had made other women smile, and he was Olin Rainey, who knew how to thrust back at trouble with thrusts that were a pleasure to give.

"That will do, thank you, trumpeter," said Matthew, interrupting the hungry and flattering stare with which Rainey held on to Laura.

Later that night, Matthew kept himself awake until he was certain that Laura had fallen into an exhausted sleep from which no ordinary sounds could awaken her. Moving then with care he left the bed and took his way around to the other side of the two suspended army blankets which divided the small room. At his table—a board laid across two empty ammunition boxes—he lighted a candle and sat down. He took up a steel pen, opened his dusty bottle of ink, and in a sense of loving secrecy, he began to write with firm clarity as became a superior student of engineering drawing in the class of 1880.

He addressed a letter to Messrs. Lingenfelter and Company, in St. Louis. Before he went on with his letter he listened a moment, but she was still asleep. His throat thickened with swallowed laughter. Then he drove his pen again, to order for shipment as early as possible a set of one dozen glasses and decanter of Waterford ware, to be imported from Ireland (as per samples recently displayed in St. Louis), and to be consigned to the writer at Fort Delivery, Territory of Arizona, if convenient terms might be extended to a second lieutenant serving on the Indian frontier with the United States Cavalry.

In the morning, it was his turn to see that someone else, too, had had work to do in the night. Beyond the blanket partition the light was unaccustomed in its brightness. Matthew turned to see Laura beside him. She was not there. Now he heard her at little tasks in the other half of the room. He bounded forth to find her. She was setting places for breakfast at the plank table.

"Where are you!" he cried, referring to her absence from bed.

"Right here. I'm doing what I can, but you will have to help me get breakfast, for I don't know where anything is. You said we would do our cooking out in back, but where is the wood, and how do we start fires?"

Glancing toward the rear window to show her the outdoor stove, he saw why the light was bright. The curtains of Kitty Mainwaring had been removed.

She saw where he looked and she smiled with virtue and success at the raised furrows of inquiry in his wide brow, which she loved so for its dear youthful candor. His brow fitted her loving hand exactly. Now she watched his thought travel across his brow and saw him resolve to say nothing about even so astonishing a change in his living quarters. The whole subject was too delicate. The curtains were gone, and when he faced her, it was clear between them both that she had intended all along to make their removal her first act of possession here as Mrs. Matthew Carlton Hazard. He never knew what she did with them. This was interesting, for it was actually difficult to conceal any discarded object at Fort Delivery, but after a while he did not give the matter too much mind.

xiii

On his way later to report to the commanding officer Matthew was joined in front of Quarters 3 by Lieutenant Mainwaring. The two officers walked on to headquarters together.

"Let's see," said Teddy, "you've been gone four weeks, is it?"

"Five," said Matthew.

"Well, time certainly goes. Well, we've all missed you, Matt." Teddy looked aside at Matthew with an almost pleading expression, though what he pleaded for must never come plain. Let's let everything be all right, he pleaded. Don't let's let anybody ever have any thought of what everyone knows to have been the truth a while back. When a thing is no longer true, the fact that it used to be true doesn't really mean so much anymore, now, does it? He put his hand on Matthew's shoulder, and his pale eyes watered with the fellowship of forgiveness and self-preservation, and he said, "I'm just as glad as the major is that we've got you on our team."

"Thanks, Teddy, thank you, sir. You know? I'm glad to be back."

"Oh, that's good, that's just grand."

They turned to enter the office and Teddy hesitated.

"I think I'll let you see the major by yourself."

They nodded and Teddy went across the parade to the stables. Matthew entered after a knock and found Major Prescott at his roll-top desk smoking a cigar. He came to his feet and extended his hand. He looked past Matthew toward the hallway.

"You are alone? I thought I heard Mainwaring with you."

"He was, sir, but he had to get over to the troop."

"How do you find him?"

"Why, well enough. He gave me a royal welcome, I must say."

"Good enough." Major Prescott growled with relief. "Sit down. Quite a lot has gone on around here since you went away."

"Oh? On the post?"

"Not so much on the post, no. All out there." The major gestured with his cigar at the vast dusty pink land outside the narrow window. "Things here at home have been all right. My wife has taken to sewing with Mrs. Mainwaring every day or two." He paused. Matthew felt a hot surge of blood come up about his ears. Jessica was doing her best to occupy Kitty's time and give her extra attention to make her feel cherished, before the return of the bride and groom. Major Prescott continued, "I had a letter from your father-in-law."

Matthew was astounded.

"Colonel Greenleaf? What in the world, sir!"

"He told me that every kind of pressure was put upon you to ask for a change of assignment, and that you refused, and that by refusing you actually risked having your wedding called off. So it was difficult?"

"For a while, yes, sir."

"Well," said the major almost harshly, to conceal his satisfaction, "it is just as well you decided to come back. Things are building up out here."

He picked up a transcribed heliostat message on blue paper with dark blue lines.

"We've been getting these reports every few weeks. It appears that the leader of the troubles of ten years ago, name is Rainbow Son, was then put on reservation after General Quait put an end to his cutting up. Two years ago he ran off, taking a number of his old followers with him. Ever since then he has been hiding in Mexico, gathering forces out of some of the Apaches in New Mexico, and others who live in the Sierra Madre down below the border. When his information seems to justify it, he makes an occasional raid up this way into the territory. So far as the War Department seems to be concerned, he is at liberty to keep jabbing where and how he pleases. The only thing that will fix him is not a local twitch every time he makes a sting, but an over-all, comprehensive, map-wide campaign which will handle him wherever he turns up."

"What got into him, sir?"

"Familiar problem. Trader trouble, as much as anything, I'd guess. There's a man named Seeley Jones who came to see me while you were gone. You'll have to get the feel of him some day. When we have time I'll tell you what I know. He has a commission as a sutler, visits the Indians, undoubtedly sells them arms and liquor, and runs his own little empire regardless of the good of the country. It wouldn't take much encouragement from such a one for Rainbow Son to go wrong again, and feel righteous about it. I feel something in the air."

"Have we any orders?"

"Not anything new, except to increase all precautions. While you were gone we got a requisition for a herd of remounts from New Mexico. They're on the way here now. They'd be tempting game for raiders. I'm having patrols extended in our immediate area. Mainwaring is taking one out today. If we had the over-all patrol idea— but what's the use. General Quait recommended it ten years ago. I've read his report. It's a crime they didn't listen to him."

"Where is he now?"

"Back in Washington again. He was in New Mexico again last year, before we got here. After the last raids there, which he seems to have pretty well ended, he returned to Washington to work for his famous plan for a comprehensive campaign which would be final. If Rainbow Son and Sebastian cut up again, they may give him the ammunition he needs to persuade the government to get moving. My wife says not to get too het up, though, for she figgers it'll take a year to move the Congress. I believe she's right."

"Sir, do you know General Quait?"

"No. My wife's people knew him years ago in Washington."

"Neither do I. He's my wife's uncle-in-law, if there is such a thing."

"We may never even see him, even if he does come out here eventually to take command." Major Prescott was suddenly animated by a gust of angry energy. "I wish they'd give the whole thing to me. I'd handle it. I'd know what to do." He subsided as quickly, conscious of his low rank. Blowing smoke, he added in comic resignation, "But they won't, never fear, they won't. —Things go well with you?" he asked, turning his gaze up at Matthew and rubbing his stubby hand across his bald head which gleamed pale above his sunburned neck and cheeks.

"Yes, sir, first-rate."

"Mrs. Hazard going to be happy here?"

Their glances locked and referred to any number of factors which could promise unhappiness for Laura. But the major saw in his junior officer so much contentment and ruddy health and strength of presence that he could not imagine any failure of happiness in Quarters 4. He began to smile at precisely the moment Matthew did too, and they exchanged reassurances no less strong for being unsaid.

"Go along, then," said the major. "You'd better take your platoon personally for drill this morning. They've needed you."

"Yes, sir."

"I believe the girls are getting up something for the newlyweds. You'll probably hear about it later today. If you hate occasions of sentiment, you have my sympathy, for so do I. I'll tell you how to get through such things. Don't remember how little pleasure *you* take from such things, but on the contrary, try to remember how much pleasure they give to *those* who are trying to please you."

The major nodded with emphasis and sagacity.

Matthew laughed out loud at his commander's air of social wisdom, saluted, and left for the platoon. In the hall he paused to drop his letter to Lingenfelter and Company in the mail bag which hung on a wooden peg inside the front door. It might be two weeks before the bag even left its peg for the wagon trip to the railroad at Driscoll; but a letter once deposited there was considered already in the care of the United States mails, and out of reach forever of the one who mailed it.

xiv

Matthew made an informal inspection of his platoon's barrack area. All twenty windows of the barrack room were shining clear. Each man's iron cot was properly opened up for the day, with mattress

doubled back and bedding folded edge by edge inside. At the head
of each bed each soldier had three wooden pegs driven into the
adobe wall where hung his saber, forage cap, and uniforms. All
sleeves were flattened to hang at the same curve and face the same
way. All boots were polished and aligned against the wall space between cots. The floor of earth was oiled and hardened until it shone.
Near the door was a rack nailed to the wall from which hung two
brass bugles with long yellow silk cords braided and tasseled. The
bugles carried a blinding polish. Matthew smiled over Trumpeter
Rainey and style. The whole barrack was fresh and spotless. The
vision of Major Prescott was everywhere evident, both in how he
saw requirements, and in how the troopers saw him and his exercise
of discipline.

Matthew was happy to be again amidst such details. They were the
little particles which made up the large shape of his content in work.
It would be good to resume the daily schedule he knew so well—
reveille sounded by trumpets and drums; first guard mount before
breakfast; inspection of the soldiers' mess at breakfast, dinner, and
supper, with appropriate samplings of dishes prepared; inspection of
the heliostat station; dismounted drill and mounted drill according to
the commanding officer's schedule; inspection and supervision of
stables every afternoon; inspection of pasturage beyond the fort at
suitable intervals; second guard mount in mid-afternoon; calls upon
men in hospital; sanitary inspections according to rotating assignment
by the commanding officer; schooling of horses following afternoon
stables; study of regulations, orders and military court records in the
headquarters office when not otherwise occupied; retreat ceremonies
in fatigue or full-dress uniform as ordered; third guard mount before
taps; taps, and Trumpeter Rainey's invariable success with the last
music of the day, whose final notes, prolonged in silvery sweetness,
as though the trumpeter could not bear to suspend the nightly glory
of his making, said, "All is we-l-l-l."

XV

Soon after breakfast Jessica Prescott sent for Kitty Mainwaring.
    "I have a little task for you," she said.
    "Oh, please!" Kitty was aquiver with eagerness.

"Trot down to Quarters 4 and pay a little call on our bride, and tell her that the Commanding Officer and Mrs. Prescott, with all the other senior officers and ladies, wish to entertain Mr. and Mrs. Hazard at dinner tomorrow evening at headquarters at half-past seven. Full dress. —And then, my dear, I'll have to lean heavily on you to help me with plans and details."

This was the Wives' Army coming into action.

"Now?" asked Kitty.

"Right now, if you please."

Kitty arose and put her fingers over her mouth and gazed big-eyed and speculative at Mrs. Prescott. Why had she been chosen by Mrs. Prescott to carry the invitation? Was Mrs. Prescott deliberately throwing her together with Laura Hazard, so soon, so firmly, for a purpose which it was dreadful to think of? Who was she, Kitty, to be handled like a doll? What if she did not really choose to see Mrs. Hazard just yet? Didn't it seem hard enough to have her right next door, without having to go to call on her, and pretend that—that there was nothing beyond a simple call to be remembered? Did everyone think she, Kitty, was made of wax, that they could push her into any shape they chose? Or of stone, that she would not feel what must never be spoken of? How was she to look into that exquisite, sparkling countenance of Laura Hazard where love and confidence spoke out so dearly without knowing it? Why did "life" come to some people and not others, and why was she, Kitty, one of the others?

Such thoughts, based on long practice, raced expertly through Kitty's mind, creating a pause which Jessica had to break.

"My dear? Don't you think so?" said Jessica as though continuing her own thought out loud. "It will be so pretty, for you, her next-door neighbor, to make our first gesture of welcome to her. I think Matthew would be grateful, too, and I am sure Teddy would be proud of you. I'll run down and see her later, but for now: yourself: just you."

With her tawny lion-like smile, and deep meaningful light in her eyes, Jessica exercised command as unmistakably as her husband. Imposing a discipline at this moment which, however it might hurt for the time being, must be met in order to insure the health of the small society over which she presided, Jessica was as strong as need be. Kitty submitted.

With a sharp intake of breath against the back of her hand, she turned and went as fast as she could walk to Quarters 4 and knocked on the door.

Laura came.

"Oh! Mrs. Mainwaring! How nice of you. Do come in."

Kitty entered. Facing her was the rear window, bare of her calico curtains. A gust of sick, hurt feeling seemed to cloud up inside her brow, but she knew she must not seem to notice anything, and with a glance around the little house she said,

"How much you have already done to make a home for Matthew."

"I'm wondering if my husband will even notice," said Laura with a laugh.

"Oh, my dear," said Kitty putting forth a hand to touch Laura's arm, "you will find that he really sees everything, though he may not always *seem* to see!"

"How kind that you should instruct me about him," said Laura, with a hazy, elevated look which recalled her mother's way with a snub.

"Oh, not *I*," cried Kitty, "not I alone; we all know Matthew so well, and do so very much like him, you must know how it is, living as closely as we do here, he's quite famous with us for his powers of vision, almost like an Indian, we have always said!"

It was too much of a recovery. Laura rejected it by changing the subject. She knew well enough when a woman spoke for herself and when for society.

"Aren't these pretty?" She touched a little bouquet of wild flowers in a tumbler of pink cranberry glass. "Mrs. Gray brought them a moment ago. She went gathering them after breakfast."

"Maud is a dear," said Kitty. "What a pity I am not after all the first to run in upon you, but there it is. What I came about is a message from Mrs. Prescott."

"We plan to call on them this evening," said Laura, "when my husband is free of duty."

"Yes, within twenty-four hours of arrival at a new post," said Kitty, to show that she too knew the Army etiquette of calling on the post commander. "But that is not what I came about," and Kitty gave the invitation.

"Oh! So soon!" said Laura. "What on earth shall I wear! I have hardly shaken anything out at all."

"Full dress, Mrs. Prescott said. It might as well be. No matter what you wear here, you'll always feel just as warm at Fort Deliver-

Me. And what else is there to do but dress up and pretend?" asked Kitty in a voice which suddenly went lightly away from her.

Laura looked at her with a sudden turn of kindness. Something made her visitor extremely nervous. Laura in her happiness felt almost ashamed to be happy in the presence of this troubled energy before her. How silly she had been to feel jealous of a pair of calico curtains put into this house a year ago by a kind neighbor. Impulsively she took Kitty's hand and said,

"Help me find a dress, then, for tomorrow evening. Everything I own is in this hamper; I'll have to work fast to get rid of wrinkles. This one, do you think—" lifting out of the raffia-bound hamper a satin evening dress which she said was of the fashionable new color called London Smoke.

But this turn of humor, so unexpected, touched Kitty in a desperate way, and to keep from bursting into tears at Laura's innocence and warmth, she said to herself, Who does she think she is, to come here with "fashionable new colors" and make the rest of us feel like the hired girl who hasn't a decent rag to her back!

"Of course," she said aloud, "none of us here have been able to shop for ages. I'm afraid you'll find us a dingy little crew! This *is* a lovely thing, how pretty you must look in it, with your eyes, let me see, what color are they, they're really almost violet, aren't they! London Smoke! What a clever thing to call it."

Laura sighed inwardly. She would have to try again to make friends with Kitty Mainwaring, but not just now. She tossed her ball dress back into the hamper and said,

"I'll find some old thing. If you're going to see Mrs. Prescott soon, do tell her we are overjoyed, and we look forward to the party tomorrow."

Kitty took this for dismissal, which it was. Holding her head high and smiling fixedly, she left Quarters 4 and went back to headquarters hardly able to wait until she could tell Mrs. Prescott that the first thing Mrs. Matthew Hazard had done was to rip down the curtains which a neighbor with no motive but the simplest kindness had once been fool enough to make for a lonely young lieutenant arriving in the most outlandish of all posts in the U.S. Army.

xvi

Laura could not help wondering if she might not have owned two selves. Lying awake in the dark while Matthew slept, now inertly peaceful, and again almost strenuously in search of healthy replenishment, she remembered what, before her marriage, she had thought of love. It was largely a view influenced by her mother's. The coupling of man and woman—in marriage of course, for Mrs. Greenleaf in her propriety never acknowledged any other circumstance of carnal union—was a preposterous arrangement whose purpose of propagation brought with it an elaborate system of advantages and sacrifices. The advantages were there to be had if the woman who would be wife knew how to establish her conditions and then how to see to their fulfillment. The sacrifices were involved with consents of purpose and yieldings of person which ill became any lady of strongly fastidious tastes. Laura knew from her mother—or anyone else— nothing in detail about what a husband would demand of a wife in his conjugal joy. Even from her brother Harvey, who took and gave so much pleasure in his tales of indulgence, she had no real notion of the ultimate intimacies around which all his scandalous experience revolved.

She expected of marriage all kinds of silken satisfactions which would have to do with being settled for life in a position of power and style. To be sure, she knew that she and her husband would sit together at table, and spend long evenings side by side; and of course, they were expected to share the same bed, and kissing was delicious, and made her love her lover till she could die of the sweetness of her feelings. What a joy it would be for two people to know each other so well that each would smoothly and gradually evolve an image of the other which would be endurable for life and durable in the public view! This was to come about without any change of any sort in herself.

But now: after astonishments imbedded in raptures, and bolt upon bolt of stricken discovery of another's life and flesh: she was unable to recognize herself in the wife who gave and sought love without reserve. Where was Drusilla Greenleaf's system of balance between fastidiousness and advantage? It was lost, forgotten, in a glory of selflessness which leaped alive like fire in Laura's heart. And yet,

even at the same moment, she found voracious happiness in being
acutely aware of herself as she made rapt celebration of her husband's dearness in flesh and mind and spirit. To fill with joy the
heart of his being even as he made her the same gift—this brought
the two Lauras together in one, and at their fusion, she felt like
someone wholly new. She had not sought change, but already it was
upon her. He had asked nothing of her; but by his very being, to
which she gave hers, he made her his. The simple confrontation of
his life to hers was the power through which all things must ever
after become known to her.

Upon the meaning of this thought, which presented itself to her
with lucidity not to be recovered in daytime, she slept.

xvii

Somewhat later, about half an hour after sunrise, Trumpeter Rainey
on duty as the major's orderly ran down the gravel walk in front
of the officers' line and banged on the door of Quarters 4.

"Lieutenant! Lieutenant!" he shouted. His young, excited voice
seemed to do as much violence as a bugle to the calm of the desert
that lay rosy and hot in the early light of August. Almost at once
the door was opened from within by Matthew, who stood in dark-
blue flannel shirt, sky-blue kersey breeches and black boots, holding a
silver-backed hairbrush in each hand.

"Yes, orderly?" he said gently.

The trumpeter glanced expertly into the room hoping for a glimpse
of connubial suggestions, saw none, and said,

"The commanding officer's compliments, sir, and will the lieutenant
report to him on the double?"

"Thank you, orderly, and my respects to Major Prescott, and I
will report immediately."

The youngster in tight flannel saluted and ran up the line. Matthew,
watching him, was already at work on possibilities. If it should happen
that he must leave her for field duty, there were things to tell his wife
before he was gone. He turned back into the minutely crumbling
adobe hut.

She came to him. She touched him and he felt her tremble faintly
as she questioned inwardly the meaning of the hasty summons so early

in the day with no previous warning. But she mocked the unknown, saying,

"Matt, don't be too long. I shall die of curiosity until you come back. Do you suppose our party tonight is to be postponed?"

Almost in one movement, he kissed her, took up his yellow neckerchief and his black, yellow-corded hat and left her, thinking, Perhaps it has come sooner than you might have expected.

At headquarters, the flag was up at the top of the tall pole out front. It hung inert, making pale shadow on the hot, sandy ground. Matthew ran up the two steps to the tin-roofed porch and into the wide hallway. He paused before the major's closed door to the left and straightened the knot of his neckcloth. The door to the Prescotts' living quarters, to the right of the hall, was also closed. Matthew knocked and entered.

Major Prescott was at his desk. His right arm was already raised forward in mid-air, and hanging from his right hand was a pale-blue paper. The single suspended gesture told Matt several things. He was to read the paper. It was about something urgent. A decision had already been made. The commanding officer disliked waste motion and liked to anticipate. Without speaking, Matt took the paper and read it standing. In Major Prescott's clear, heavy writing, it stated:

Received at Hq. Troop F, 6th U.S. Cavalry, Fort Delivery, Territory of Arizona, 23 August, 188–, 6:10 A.M., by heliostat.

1. Horse herd, escort waggons, mounted squad proceeding to Fort Delivery ambushed night of 21-22 August near Ransom Rock by undetermined number of Apache under Chief Rainbow Son.

2. Fire exchanged, with four seriously wounded in squad. All horses scattered and driven away to southwest. One Indian killed and abandoned.

3. Survivors commanded by Sgt. Burns reached Ransom Rock relay station last night with news.

4. Sgt. Burns of opinion that Rainbow Son and followers driving horses toward Half-Moon Canyon as nearest natural refuge.

5. Awaiting signalled instructions.

"Well, it's hit us, sir," said Lieutenant Hazard, putting the dispatch on Major Prescott's desk.

"It happened night before last," Major Prescott said. "If it took Burns till the next night to reach the relay station on foot, under scouting conditions, the column was about thirty miles away from there. They must have been trailed and watched for several days. There must have been a good many or the squad would've handled them. Rainbow Son has turned those men into foot soldiers, not only there, but, unless we recover the herd, even here, in time, since we needed those remounts badly, with our troop horses in the condition they're in. If the Apache *have* headed for Half-Moon, we will find one advantage and one disadvantage in that. First, we will find them gathered instead of spread around the map; but second, if they have enough to eat they can hold us off there indefinitely. Is this pretty much as you see it?"

If Major Prescott sometimes looked most comic when he was most serious, those who served with him soon forgot to notice his bald head, his stony little brown eyes, his great brown mustache and his stocky build. What impressed them instead were his directness of manner and his powers of dedication.

"Yes, sir," Matthew answered, but saying nothing of the question in his heart. His whole bearing asked what was now to be done, and whether there was a place for him in any plan of action. The troop's other line officer, First Lieutenant Mainwaring, would have preference, he was sure. Captain Gray, the surgeon, was not on duty as a line officer.

"We must do three things," said Major Prescott, screwing up his right eye to see more clearly in his head. "One, we have to get our people, especially the wounded, out of there; two, we have to get those horses back; three, we have to show the Apaches that we will strike back, and fast, even at heavy cost to us. And we have to do all these things at the same time. You remember what Half-Moon is like, don't you?"

"Yes, sir. I've been there twice." Matthew's heart began to feel solid and able. What was coming?

"Then you can see the problem."

"Yes, sir. Or I will, sir."

"Yes. After all, I haven't stated it in your terms."

"Mine?"

"Yes, I'm giving it to you. There is other work for Mainwaring." The major gazed at Matthew to stifle any betrayal of opinion. "You will take out two squads of the second platoon, find Rainbow Son, recapture the herd, and kill or bring in all the Indians you can. Mr. Mainwaring will head a relief party, with led horses and supplies, to pick up Burns and the first platoon near Ransom Rock. With two operations mounted out of this post in opposite directions at the same time, I'll have to stay here at the center. What will be the first thing you'll do?"

"Sir, I'll personally supervise getting my men and equipment ready."

"Then?"

"Then I'll move out in scouting order in the general direction of Half-Moon Canyon. It's the only lead we have."

"And then?"

"If I find them there, I'll work out something on the spot."

"The cave is a natural fortress, you know."

"Yes, sir, I know."

"Their line of fire above you will come from sources invisible to you."

"Yes, I've been thinking of that. But there's a way to beat them and I'll find it out."

The major stood up.

"It'll do. But I'll tell you what. I'll see to getting your outfit ready, if you want to have a little time with Laura. And I'll ask Jessica to take her on while you're gone. Those two have hit it off, you know."

"Yes, sir. I know. Thank you. I'll take a few minutes to give her some target practice. I'll feel better if she can shoot."

Hiram, looking at Matthew with an age-old compunction, was secretly moved by life as seen through the young and loving, and as met by the young and brave. It was early to take the Hazards away from each other, possibly forever.

"Yes," said the major, "now git."

xviii

They went arm in arm, rapidly, under urgency, toward the hot shadowed arroyo.

"I've told you, Laura," said Matthew in a voice dry and unlike his own, "what has sometimes been known to happen when the garrison of one of these posts is away."

"Have you? You did, but I've forgotten."

She looked at him prettily, as if they were strolling at a garden party. He wanted both to shake her and kiss her.

"If the Indians know most of the troops are gone, they might attack. If they get in, the women are then in awful peril. You must know how to shoot, Laura. I'm going to teach you what I can right now."

"So I can shoot Indians? How primitive."

"Listen to me. If they are in final danger of capture, our women are strongly advised to shoot the enemy if they can, or if this cannot be, then to take their own lives rather than allow themselves to be captured alive."

She was finally shaken by his gravity, and they stopped walking. She pressed his arm to tell him that he must not worry. He took her in his arms. They were lost until she remembered her duty, which was to protect him from any weakness that he might feel for her sake, and she made them walk again.

"What about where you're going with the troops?" she asked.

"A place called Half-Moon Canyon, two days' ride from here. They call it that because in its deepest part there is a huge, shallow cave, part way up the cliff, shaped like a half moon, straight side down. The thing arches like a big, perfect shell. The cave floor is flat, and has boulders along the front. You never saw a better natural fort. It can't be reached from the top of the cliff, and the trail up to it can be easily guarded. People must have lived in it centuries ago. I wish you and I could."

"Alone?"

"Alone."

"Why don't you build great enormous fires and have the smoke drive them out?" she suggested. He patted her hand kindly. "I know," she added, "you cannot bear it if I try to be clever about the Army."

They came to a miniature canyon in the dry, rosy arroyo. He helped her down the bank. Up the draw a little distance, he found a place. As targets he set up a row of three scrap pieces of tanned leather which he'd brought in his hip pocket. He stuck them in a sloping shelf of loose earth, and they were backed at a distance of a yard or so by the sunny arroyo wall with its overhanging rim of exposed hard gravel and sharp desert grass. He marked a place to stand facing the target across the draw.

"Here," he said. He saw her smiling at him, and he scowled. "This is no game. Now, here."

He drew and handed her his heavy Colt .44 Peacemaker cartridge revolver. Its weight dragged her light arm down, and she took it with both hands and wavered it up to breast height. He was hotly exasperated now by what he most loved in her, for in her playful frailty lay danger if she should have to meet the duty he was preparing her for.

"Laura, Laura!" he cried, and stood behind her, his arms around her, holding his hand over hers on the pistol grip, and beginning the lesson that was so hard for her to believe in and for him to be calm about. He raised her arm and brought the weapon's mouth down in a strong, steady arc until the gesture of aiming was made. He then stood away and let her do it alone. He talked about sights, and proper pressure on the trigger, and loading and unloading, and what to do with a firearm not in use. Then he stepped back and let her shoot.

Upon the explosion, there was an insect song from a ricocheting bullet, and a spray of dust, and one of the upright pieces of leather fell. Matthew laughed.

"You knocked it down, all right, but the wrong way. Try it again."

"What did I do?"

"You hit the bank above, and the bullet glanced off and struck the target from the rear."

"Oh, dear. Let me do it again."

"You couldn't do it again. What's more, it's dangerous, this close. The bullet might glance our way. You have to be pretty far from the point of impact to be surely out of the way of a ricochet."

"Oh, dear."

"Laura." He took her hands and spoke soberly, leaning down. She looked up. He was tall, and she made him feel taller. They were powerfully alive to each other. "You are supposed to hit the target from the front. Now aim lower, and do it right. There's a reason for all this. All right, now."

She fired. There was no result but the ringing of the shot.

"What did I do then?"

"You shot right over the bank at the sky. Lower."

He held her tightly again, and again rehearsed how to aim. "Exaggerate the low aim," he said sternly, while his blood pounded at her nearness. "Evidently you sight high."

He released her and when she fired the bullet sang sharply off the bank, again in ricochet, and struck the loose earth behind the bits of leather that remained. Dust came up.

"That's impossible, to do it twice," said Matthew. "Here."

He took the revolver and fired and hit his target in the center.

She called out with admiration and begged to try it again for herself. He remembered again why they were there, and thought wryly of the mixture of love, duty, comedy and danger in which he was caught. The emotions of the morning left him. What he wanted was a perfectly clear head and strong recollection of all the experience he had known or heard of that concerned desert warfare against a brilliant, horse-mounted enemy. He handed the revolver to Laura and said, "Unload," and then, "Load," and then, "Fire," and, for as long as he could allow, he made her familiar with the weapon. She was an excellent pupil. Presently he had to say to himself that if the fearful need arose, she would, in respect to handling a firearm, know how to do what was required. It was hard comfort. Taking her back to their quarters, he walked rapidly. She felt he was already gone.

"Here," he said at their door. "You stay here."

He went inside and put the revolver with a belt of cartridges on the box table, gathered up his readied field equipment, and returned to the bare ground before his threshold. There he embraced her.

"Inside, inside," she whispered, faithless to her duty.

"No. Here. That's why. It's hard enough this way. Good-by, my . . ."

Across the quadrangle there was a glisten of distant and continued activity at the picket line. The horses were saddled and packed. The troopers repeatedly inspected buckles, straps, canteens and arms. Joe Dummy, standing motionless by his mount, saw everything. Everything was in order. The soldiers prepared for their mission with speed, smoothness and care. In their action together, Joe Dummy read with satisfaction the signs of his friend's nature. Lieutenant Hazard, he would now admit, was a warrior. For nearly a year Joe Dummy had watched him perfect the second platoon in its habits of work. It might be that very soon he would be able to watch the young officer to see if he had learned the lessons of the country as demonstrated for him by Joe Dummy himself. It was strange that in any group of warriors going out in that land it should not be Joe Dummy—or rather White Horn—who was the chief. But if he was not the chief, he would give the man who was every wisdom and power in his knowledge; for that man was his friend, and a friend was he who above all things permitted dignity to even the least of his friends.

With all but one standing in place, the trumpeter, at a nod from Major Prescott, sounded assembly. The call was for Matthew, and he turned from Laura, shutting his eyes against her real image so as to

keep its last likeness in his mind. Out of other doorways in Officers'
Row, and across the parade from behind the laundry, other women
appeared. They stood silent and watched. They shaded their eyes
with their forearms against what blinded them, inside and out. They
heard a series of commands, small-voiced in the open quadrangle,
and they saw the guidon on its lance come up, and watched the
column move out at a nodding walk toward the silky waves of heat
in the distance, where, said Laura in silence, everything she hated lay
in wait for everything she loved.

xix

The commanding officer's wife seemed to be everywhere all morning.
She was in the laundry room, working the women hard, and earning
their gratitude because they saw how she intended to make them rule
their emotion. She called on Mrs. Gray, whose husband was preparing to accompany the relief expedition to Ransom Rock in order to
care for the wounded.

"I actually believe," said Mrs. Gray, "that my husband is delighted
to have all this to do. Not that he's glad for anybody's suffering, you
understand, but—"

"But he is just as willing to be at work, of course," interrupted
Jessica Prescott. "My husband is fretting because he feels he must
remain. Isn't it true: the hardest lesson for any commander is to
learn to send someone rather than go and do. Good morning. I'll be
looking in on the others."

She called next at Quarters 3 and found Kitty Mainwaring drying
her eyes in time to be caught at it.

"Now in heaven's name, Kitty," said Jessica, "Teddy is not going
to be in any particular danger on this relief march! Come, my child."

Kitty groaned. Once again her intentions had been misread, and
what she wanted sympathy for had been misread, and it would now
be tiresome to explain what had moved her. It was a tiny drama of
complaint and consolation which she had prepared.

"I am entirely aware of that," she said in a muted voice which
bespoke injury to pride. "But what have we come to if rank means
nothing any more? Teddy had a *right* to the dangerous assignment.
He is the first lieutenant."

Jessica took several deep breaths and regarded her.

"Can't you leave these judgments to the one who has to make them?" she asked, with difficult calm.

"Oh, I know, I know, I shouldn't imply this to the commanding officer's wife. But all our life, the same, it's been quartermaster, quartermaster, and the like, and every other woman's husband goes dashing off on a horse with a drawn saber!"

Jessica felt her distaste turn into a gentle regret that anyone must be so consumed by envy as this small woman before her. She deliberately did not let thoughts of withdrawn love enter into her mind, and the jealousy which these must feed. She took Kitty's shoulders and gave them a good-humored little shake and said,

"Well, my child, not that it will do you any good in your mood, but my husband, in eighteen seventy-six and -seven, was ordered to spend his days making an inventory of unused clothing intended for soldiers in the Civil War and never issued. I could give you some of the figures which he finally arrived at, but they'd bore you to death. For months and months we lived in a ridiculous nightmare of undervests and drawers, jackets and trousers and socks. But I don't really think we minded, though we were glad when it was over. We were still who we were, you know, no matter what."

Kitty turned white at this, and Jessica saw that somehow she had managed to add an affront to Kitty's grievances. What in the world, thought Jessica, was wrong with being who you were, no matter what? And then she thought that perhaps the trouble was that the Mainwarings hated themselves for who they were; and if this was true, then indeed, she must have given offense. But there was nothing to do about it without doing much more than she had patience for just now, and with a kind little nod which Kitty saw as condescension, she left the scene of this miniature disaster, and went with feelings of gaiety and relief to Quarters 4. There she entered and sat down with an air of planning to stay a while.

She wore a broad, flat straw hat, a white shirtwaist and a gray flannel skirt with a wide belt and a silver buckle. From the belt hung a leather purse. The army wives knew that in it she carried cigarettes and matches, and though she never smoked in public, she enjoyed her cigarette with friends whenever she felt like it. It was now a relief not to be careful in what she might say. Making an effect as abrupt as the rapid-fire syllables of her name, Jessica Prescott said,

"Well, Laura, I'm exhausted. You must take care of me for a little bit." She had come to take care of Laura, and they both knew it, but it was diverting to use this tone of comic heroism. "Won't you have a cigarette with me?" she asked, tapping her reticule.

"I've never tried it," said Laura. "My brother Harvey always tried to get me to—he is a wretch—and I always refused."

"I cannot think of a better time. Even if you dislike it, you'll feel that you've had a fling at something outrageous, and right now that'd do you as much good as anything."

They lighted cigarettes and Laura puffed hopefully.

"Don't do it rapidly," said Jessica. "Well, of course, my dinner party is ruined. Don't say postponed. That never means anything. We'll have other dinner parties, of course, but this particular one, which was no other dinner party, is in ruins. The reason we all respect."

It was like her that she would so soon release into words the purpose behind her call. She glanced about the little house. Laura in so little time had turned a bachelor's hut into a dwelling which, if it had no style or riches, was given character by certain placings of objects, and Jessica nodded, glad to recognize that army habits always showed, even in a one-room mud house. She brought her gaze back to Laura. Tears from the smoke had invited others out of a deeper cause. It was the first time this young wife had ever seen her husband depart for unknown dangers. Laura put her cigarette down and covered her face with her hands in a sudden, timeless gesture.

"Yes, well," said Jessica, "the first time may seem unbearable, but I will tell you something. It never gets one bit easier."

"What makes it worse," Laura said, "is that I deceived him at the very last. And now he's gone."

"You deceived him? How on earth could you. Do you want to talk about it?"

"When his orders came this morning, early, his first thought was for me. He wanted to teach me to shoot, in case—"

"Yes, I know. It sounded like the battle of Bull Run. That is all simply true, you know. Well?"

"So we went to the gully out back there, and he gave me a lesson with that." She pointed to the big Colt on the table. "I acted out a lie."

"How?"

"I was already a very good shot. My brother Harvey used to take me out with him and we'd practice for hours."

"You let your husband make a fool of himself over you today?"

"Yes, but I never thought it would matter, so long as he never found out. And he won't find out, but it matters horribly!"

"Indeed it does. Why'd you do it?"

"Mostly, I wanted him to make all that fuss over me," said Laura, with difficult honesty.

"It's a fright, how much of that we need, and the lengths we'll go to get it," said Jessica.

"I love him so."

"Yes. So much that you'll risk everything just to express it, like any of us. Well. Are you going to keep worrying over that?"

"I suppose so. I was really wicked. I shot several ricochets just to show off, and pretended they just happened. Something he told me made me think of trying it."

"What was that?"

"That cave where they've gone to—Half-Moon—was like a shell, he said, and he told me how hard it would be to get at men gathered together in the cave. I had a picture of it in my mind, and I thought the shots could just hit the back wall, and bounce forward and hit whatever was there from that angle. It was rather like that at the bank where we practiced this morning. It worked."

"Why didn't you tell him, even then? It might turn out to be useful on his mission."

"No. I'm learning not to talk about his work with him."

"I see." Jessica felt serious doubts and she showed them. "Why do young people always make everything so difficult? You should simply have *told* him. There's always a moment when it can be done, but it doesn't last, and when it's gone it'll always be too late. And if whatever it is ever comes to light by accident, then there's trouble. I think *trust* is the first thing to protect, no matter how hard it may be at times to admit deceits."

"When he comes back," said Laura, with some effort at confidence, "I'll have to see that he never finds me out in this one little thing. But I swear it will be the only one all my life that won't be open as day."

"I came to ask you, actually," said Jessica, sharply changing the subject to avoid open judgment of Laura's pathetic moral compromise, "if you want to come to stay with us at headquarters till the troops return. My husband told Matt we'd look out for you," she added, for fear of having a kind heart herself. "It'll be almost a week, at best, you know."

The challenge, as she made it, was supposed to hurt as much as possible. She watched Laura frankly and fondly. Laura looked about at the hovel where she dreaded to be alone, but she could not abandon what her few days with Matthew had laid upon the room and she replied,

"Do thank the major, but no, I think not. I'll stay here."

Mrs. Prescott merely nodded; but she was prouder of the young wife than she wanted to say.

xx

Condemned to inactivity at the center of things, Major Prescott for days was, as Jessica lightly said to anyone, impossible to live with. He told himself bitterly that he should have led the troops out south-westward to Half-Moon. Was he insane to have given the command to a youngster not two years out of the academy? He liked the boy, who was serious about his work, much in love, and strong. But with what was at stake!

And then the major convinced himself that, given the character of First Lieutenant Mainwaring, he had had no choice but to send Matthew. Next, he set about reproaching himself for not personally having gone northward to the rescue of his first-platoon troopers now abandoned to the desert near Ransom Rock. Men wounded, suffering, hungry, without horses, under the August sky—the picture tortured him. Yet—his mind came full circle—what if in the absence of most of the troops an attack should come to the fort? Should not the most experienced, the most responsible officer be on hand at the home station to defend that upon which all else rested?

His first relief came when Sergeant Burns, riding a mount bor-rowed from the few maintained by the Ransom Rock station, rode in to report that none of the wounded had died, that Mainwaring and the doctor and their wagons were well on their way toward reaching the dismounted platoon, and that they had picked up a stray Indian, wounded after the ambush and left to die after a few days of travel. This Indian, with the fatalistic candor that often came just before death, had confirmed that Rainbow Son and the stolen herd had in fact retired to Half-Moon. The sergeant also gave over a sack of mail that had come by train to Driscoll.

Major Prescott could now believe that his plans were sound. He must only hope that his men were equal to them. His thoughts kept drifting to Half-Moon, where there was action. How he longed for action. The best he could manage was to devote himself to the mail bag. There was a letter or two for half of the people on the post—there was one for Matthew—and he filled a little time by going personally, quite unlike a post commander, to deliver the mail at the various quarters.

Laura took from him the envelope addressed to Matthew.

"How nice," she exclaimed, turning it over. "It is from my brother Harvey, at Fortress Monroe. Thank you, major."

"Getting along all right here?"

"Yes. Yes, thank you."

"Well, I'm glad you say so. But you don't look as if you've had any more sleep than I have had."

"When will we know?" she asked, putting her head down, and then looking up at him again with startling seriousness. She looked like a haggard child.

"I give them another three days, maybe four," said the major.

"Yes. Four. Thank you. I wondered."

But her effort at resuming a social lightness was a failure, and they both admitted it by the look they exchanged. The major indicated the letter in her hand.

"Well, anyway, you can read news from home, and the like, from your brother."

"Oh, no! I would never dream of opening a letter addressed to my husband. Even from a member of my family."

Yes, he thought, nodding good-by to her, the bride and groom may live together in marriage, but they do not yet know each other very well.

xxi

But Major Prescott had deliberately given Laura a pessimistic guess as to how long it might be until there was news. In the afternoon two days later, a thin cry went up beyond the corral, making an instant effect in the almost empty fort. It was a sentry who called out, and when others came out of their black doorways he pointed, and they saw the little trail of smoky dust moving, yet barely moving, on the white horizon. As they watched there were flashes of sun off metal, and half an hour later a tiny flutter of yellow that was the guidon. It was Hazard's second platoon, moving at a walk, for that was the pace of a band of captive Indians who were marched by mounted guards. Once certain of the identity of the distant party, the commanding officer ordered up his horse and rode out to meet it. Lieutenant Hazard made his report to him as they rode homeward side by side.

"You did it, by thunder!" declared the major.

"Yes, sir," said Matthew.

"Which one is the chief—Rainbow Son?"

"We didn't get him, sir. He made it away with a couple of others. They had a few horses hidden just for the purpose. I should have thought of it."

"Yes, you should have. I've no doubt we'll have to deal with him in more difficult matters after this. Well. Go on. Where'd you find them?"

Matthew pointed to the band of recaptured horses in his train.

"The horses were half a mile down the canyon from the cave, under guard. We managed the horses first, and fairly easily. I put Joe Dummy in charge of that, and he did it well. We lost only a few of them, I figure. Then we got on to the cave."

"People actually in the cave?"

"In the cave. There they were, behind their rocky barrier in front, and thirty feet above us. We had cover on the canyon floor, bushes and rocks, but that was about all. I went myself the first night to see if we could do anything from the top of the canyon walls on either side, and we couldn't. And they had the trail—it reaches both ways from the cave down to the creek—well policed."

Major Prescott knew the place and he saw the picture. The Indians had gone to their great shallow cave as if to draw the pale sandstone cliff about their shoulders like a garment that would protect them now as it had protected their ancestors. He could not see how twenty men attacking it from below could have overwhelmed it. He said as much.

"I know. I wondered too, sir." Matthew was animated. His face, burned by the sun, was alight with vitality. "But I think I managed to do it in the only way possible."

"And what was that?"

"I shot them in the back."

The major reined in his horse in an astonished gesture.

"You *what?*"

"I shot them in the back, sir. I issued orders to every man—we had eighteen firearms—to watch for my signal when daylight came—this was the second morning—and when I gave it, to fire together at the curving shell of the cave, about twenty feet down from the dome, above the heads of the Indians. The bullets sprang off, and even on the first volley, some took effect. We used the Indians' own chief defense to destroy them. As I say, we shot them in the back."

Major Prescott stared at him.

"Weren't they surprised?" he asked thinly, in his amazement. A man with perhaps less than average imagination, he was moved by evidences of it in others. Shaking his head, he gathered his horse into a forward walk again.

"Sir, they were demoralized. They didn't know at first what was hitting them. They had no place to hide. We got better and better at calculating our ricochets. The damage was great."

"Wasn't it dangerous for you, if some of the shots angled back on your position?"

"No, though a few dropped around us, but they were spent. We had enough distance."

"Didn't the Indians fire? What did they have?"

"Rifles," said Matthew grimly. "How would they get rifles?"

"Their great white friend, Mr. Jones, trades rifles to them. I'll have to give you more about him when there's time. —Our people didn't take any wounds?"

"A few scratches. But we had superior cover. Joe saw to that. It wasn't long till the Apaches came down. You know, sir? I think the *idea* defeated them as much as anything else."

"How in thunderation did it ever occur to you?"

Matthew paused. He frowned. If an elusive recollection drifted across his thought, he shook it loose and dismissed it.

"I don't know, sir. It just did."

"I never heard anything like it." The major rode near and reached for Matthew's hand and shook it. "I'm not sure *I'd* ever have thought of it. But you did, and by God, I'm going to see you get recognition for it."

When they reached the post in late afternoon, Matthew called his troopers to attention and led them into the quadrangle. Herded horses were turned into the corral. Prisoners were locked into the black-smith shop and other sheds, there to remain until they could be marched to department headquarters for disposal. The skeleton platoon was then formed up for dismissal at the picket line. Facing them Matthew said, "I'll be glad to have every one of you with me any time I go out on a job." It was a simple statement, in easy words, but he invested it with so much gravity and significance that the troopers knew a sort of angry joy at belonging to him, and made their faces hard and empty in honor of their private feeling. He saluted and dismissed them.

Hiram Hyde Prescott took Matt by the arm and led him across to where Jessica and Laura were waiting. He announced that to celebrate the brilliant battle of Half-Moon, and the commendation of the officer who fought it, which he intended to include in his report to the Adjutant General, the Prescotts were going to have the Hazards to dinner that very evening.

"Nobody else," he said, "just us four, Jessica. You can have a big dinner when Gray and Mainwaring get back. Their wives won't expect to be asked this evening without them."

"We never really know about that," said Jessica. "But in any case I'll manage. Put on your grandest dress," she said to Laura. "We believe in all possible dog, if any."

xxii

Later, in the early twilight, after newly pledged endearments, Laura said she would dress for dinner behind the blanket partition while Matthew—oh, yes: she had nearly forgotten. There was a letter for him from her brother Harvey.

"Read it to me while I dress," she called.

He sat in the open doorway to take the failing yellow light of day over his shoulder, and read aloud.

Dear Matt [wrote Harvey] it is certainly good to think of you and Laura at your last ditch of wilderness out there. It makes this water-logged old dungeon seem like Paris by comparison. You'll have to

give me credit for one thing, anyway. I did my little bit to get Laura
ready for the wild and woolly. She made me—

Matthew's eye, traveling ahead of his voice, told him what was
hard to believe. He stopped speaking and read swiftly and in silence.
"What is it, dearest?" called Laura.
He did not reply. He put the letter on the doorsill and walked out
into the evening.
Laura, carrying rather than wearing all her laces and ribands and
silky pleatings, came to find him, and saw only the letter. She stooped
to take it up. Sudden fright destroyed her principles about reading
other people's mail. She read the letter kneeling against the door
jamb. She turned white as she saw what had driven Matthew away.
Harvey went on to write,

She made me swear secrecy till she could prove it to you herself, but
by now you must know what a good shot she is. We went out time
and again to practice. She got so good she could even trifle with
ricochets, though I discouraged this as somewhat dangerous sport. I
used to tell her that if there was one thing you couldn't safely predict,
it was the angle of a bullet. But you know the fair sex. (Or do you?
Not the way I do, old fellow.) Anyway, a little peril only adds spice
to—

and the letter went rambling idly on, having driven Matthew from his
house, and her heart into her mouth.
It was falling dark when he came back. They were in danger of
being late for dinner with the commanding officer. She spoke to him
and he answered shortly.
"Matt, my dearest, let me—"
"We'd better just get ready and go to the Prescotts'."
"But if you knew why I—"
"Why did you let me make a fool of myself? I imagine I'll never
really know. If you could do it once, it could happen again." He
gave a bitter laugh. He was so unlike himself that she was desolated
and alone. "It's taught me one thing, anyway."
She asked him with stricken face and silence what that was.
"To be more modest," he explained icily, "in the future, over any
small accomplishments that may at first glance have seemed my very
own."
She saw then how deeply she had hurt him. Could a great, huge

fellow, becoming used to the duties and responsibilities of life and death on behalf of other men, a man to whom others turned for natural protection in his competence, could such a man be as sensitive as a disappointed boy? With tears welling in her eyes she turned her shoulders to him and said,

"At least, hook me up."

He did so dully. Her shoulder, pearly and bare, was there, as so many times before, to be kissed. He only fastened the hooks in her silks of London Smoke and went to set a fresh stock in his blouse collar.

xxiii

In a few minutes they walked out in the hot night to dine, a handsome officer in dress and a lovely lady in yards of whispering shimmers, who had nothing to say to each other on the greatest day of their young marriage.

The party began as a failure. Laura confided to Jessica Prescott in the bedroom before dinner that the most unforeseen accident had befallen her to show her up as a liar and a busybody. She told of the letter, and ended,

"He's furious. It's frightful—I knew it would be if he ever found out. I'm miserable."

"He's furious because you deceived him. But he's more furious," said Jessica, "because he managed to deceive himself as to where his great idea came from, and is now exposed. He did a great thing in his battle. Hiram told me all of it, and I did not say I knew where Matt must have got the idea. But evidently he cannot do a greater thing, if it means admitting credit where it is due. Come, dear child, you look glorious. Flirt with Hiram. It'll be the easiest way to conceal how you feel."

They went in to the gentlemen, who were drinking whisky. The ladies were offered nothing to drink. Jessica produced her cigarettes. Laura took one. Matthew stared at that, but he could not comment without seeming to judge his commander's wife. Hiram was startled by the black looks of the young man for his beautiful bride, and was touched by the young lady's high-chinned efforts to be indifferent to them. If two people ever had reason to be happy, those two did. He growled gently at his puzzlement. Laura kept up a desperate running sprightliness in his ear, while he simply gazed at Matthew.

"I'm going to drink to our bride and groom," Hiram announced, rising. They all rose, and he drank alone, while nobody looked at anybody else. It was for such moments of social unawareness on his part that Jessica Prescott sometimes mildly said she could kill him. An honest professional, he had little of the trivial sensitivity which, applied to people, went far to make careers. As they sat down again she saw that she must close a gap, as hostess, and she resolved to make a point, as ranking lady.

"Families are wonderful," she said. "I'll never forget something my cousin-by-marriage—"

"General Van Landingham," interposed Hiram, to identify the reference within the Army.

"—something my cousin-by-marriage used to remind us of. When he was courting my cousin Lily Mercer—we were all in Washington at the time—he went as her escort to one of the Lincolns' receptions at the White House. They went down the line together, and when they got to the President, he shook hands with them and said he'd heard they were going to be married. They said yes, they were going to be married. And President Lincoln asked, 'And who is going to be the boss?' And my Cousin Lily looked right at him and said, 'Why, Mr. President, there isn't going to *be* any boss. There'll be just us, together, with *the better angels of our nature,* as you said in your speech.' And with that, the President leaned down and said to my Cousin Lily, 'Well, I know you're a Democrat, Miss Lily, and I'm a Republican, but I'm going to give you a kiss in the name of such a good heart.' And he did, right there in the receiving line. We always loved the story, at home."

Her listeners were quiet, and she added,

"Yes, because marriage above everything else is being without pride of self, but being grateful for, and holding pride, in the other. And isn't it odd? Sometimes the hardest thing for some of us to do is to accept what those we love can teach us!"

Matthew looked at his hands. Jessica saw that he was thinking over what she had said to them all. Another silence fell. It was too much for Hiram.

"Jess," he asked in his roughest voice, "what in thunderation is the matter with this dinner party, anyway?"

"I think," she said, rising, "we may all be starving. Come along, Matthew, will you take me in?"

They moved to the dining room and sat down in the candlelight. Jessica had prepared her meal alone, and simply.

"Supper party of the second degree," she said.

At the head of his table, Hiram breathed deeply, and resolved to begin the entire party over again. After all, they had met for a celebration, and he revived the splendid topic of the day.

"Yes, young fellow," he declared, leaning toward Matthew, "you'll go down in the history of the United States Army for your solution of Half-Moon Canyon."

Matthew gazed at his plate. He seemed to bow his head modestly under such praise, but he was fortifying himself in his heart. When had he ever shied away from what was hardest to do? Looking up, first at Major Prescott, then at Jessica, and then at Laura, he said,

"I think none of us realize that my wife gave me the key to the problem. I have only lately come to realize this myself."

"What in thunder are you talking about?"

Matthew, looking with a hard eye at nobody but his commanding officer, told the story of the pistol practice. When he was done, Jessica Prescott put down her napkin, rose from her place and, dragging a rustle of watered silk, walked around the table to him. She bent over Matthew and kissed him on the cheek. In the kiss was a great body of good sense, love and affirmation.

The major leaned back in his chair.

"Now what is that for?" he asked, as Jessica returned to her place.

"You'd never know, and neither would Matthew," she answered, "even if I told you. So I won't. What I do know is that now"—she turned to Matthew—"you are really married, Matthew Hazard."

Matthew looked at Laura. There was joy between them again. Sweet promises were alive in the candlelight. After that, it seemed that everyone had so much to say and said it with such brilliance that the party must never end. Matthew thought that Jessica, by her own efforts as much as her husband's, certainly would be a general's wife some day.

At the end, she said to Hiram,

"I think, don't you, just one song with your guitar, before we must say good night?"

"Which one, Jess?"

"Oh, I don't know. . . . 'Johnny, Did You Say Goodbye?' "

Glad of the suggestion, the major fetched his guitar and began to pick out the melody, to recall it.

"It's the first song I ever learned when I got in the Army in sixty-one. It was a new song, then. An old sergeant taught it to me. I was a private. It goes like this—"

> Johnny, did you say goodbye?
> Oh, yes, Father.
> I kissed them one and all goodbye,
> I said now don't you go and cry,
> For I'll be homing by-and-by,
> Oh, yes, Father.

His voice was deep, true and gentle, and the guitar throbbed and hummed in the hot, still August night. The stars trembled like shining drops of water above the desert. Whatever the residents of Fort Delivery had in the way of entertainment, they had to provide for themselves.

> Johnny, did you march away?
> Oh, yes, Father.
> The drum and bugle they did play,
> I marched through all the summer's day,
> I slept by night in new-mown hay,
> Oh, yes, Father.

Matthew and Laura glanced at each other as they listened, and for a brief instant they were each conscious only of the other. Their eyes shone. The mystery of their meeting and marriage—out of all possible combinations of people in the world—amazed them as always. Their feeling was as apparent as the comeliness and well-being of their flesh. They were blessed in their desire. The Prescotts observed and understood the exchange and smiled an old married couple's smile over it. Hiram gave an extra strum to the guitar strings and his voice increased.

> Johnny, did you fight the war?
> Oh, yes, Father.
> That is what a soldier's for,
> To listen to the cannon's roar,
> And fight till he can fight no more,
> Oh, yes, Father.

The singer's voice dropped again and he sang of what he knew as a war veteran.

> Johnny, did you see the worst?
> Oh, yes, Father.
> I saw what men will do athirst,
> I saw what rendered Cain accursed,
> I wish that I had perished first,
> Oh, yes, Father.

Laura smiled with formal pity at such allusions to human trouble about which she knew nothing. How much time old people seemed to spend thinking and talking about unfortunate things that happened. She knew life was not like that. But her manners sustained Laura and she kept her knowledge to herself.

> Johnny, did you see the best?
> Oh, yes, Father.
> The love that's in a soldier's breast,
> The love that never is confessed,
> To die if it will save the rest,
> Oh, yes, Father.

Why it came to her just now, Jessica could not say, but she had a thought for her little son who had died in childhood. Perhaps a child's death and a soldier's death were alike, for neither could have had enough of life when his moment came. She did not grieve. It was long too late for that. On the contrary, she had a thankful turn of heart for the abundance of life. The player slowed his fingers on the guitar strings and lengthened his words for the last stanza.

> Johnny, did you come on home?
> Oh, yes, Father.
> The government, they brought me home,
> And laid me underneath the loam,
> And here I lie, no more to roam.
> Oh, yes, Father.

Softly the song ended. The listeners were silent, clinging to the last notes hungrily. The major broke the spell.

"When I fit the Civil War as a youngster, I thought that song was about me."

"And so it was," said Jessica briskly. "And I've heard you sing it for years, and do you know? Only just now it occurs to me who 'Father' was in the song."

"Oh, it does," said her husband; "now who could that be?"

"Father Abraham."

"Who else?" said Major Prescott. "We always knew that. I thought everybody knew it."

"Yes," said Matthew, "I saw him when I was a boy. He put me where I am today."

"Put you where? In Arizona? What thundering rubbish is this?" asked the major, who disliked any figure of speech.

"President Lincoln, personally, himself, put me in the Army. That's all I mean."

"He did? How? How?" asked Hiram.

But Matthew, remembering how, remembered also the value of a life-giving secret. No one here—not even Laura—knew of the Lincoln cap. He only smiled, shook his head, and kept his private spell just as he had kept it on that day in 1864 running away in the meadow at Fox Creek from everyone who wanted to pick his brains. The famous cap was at the bottom of his private locker. There it would remain until he had a good reason to bring it forth.

"Come, Mrs. Hazard," he said. "It's time we went home."

"Lieutenant," said the host, detaining Matthew with a raised fore-finger, "report to me in the morning after inspection. There are certain matters I want to discuss further with you." He dropped his finger and released Matthew, "Good night."

"Yes, sir. Good night."

xxiv

In the morning the commanding officer and his junior lieutenant met in the headquarters office.

"Now I want your second thoughts about Half-Moon," said the major.

"Well, sir, I don't know as I have any, except to redouble our watchfulness."

"That should rank as an immediate reaction, not as a second thought. No. What do we conclude from the whole affair?"

Under fire, Matthew gave the effect of raising his breast to the attack.

"Oh. Well, I must not take credit for it, but I think Joe Dummy had an interesting thing to say on the way home. I thought there still might be Indians about and I was inclined to march with extreme care. But Joe shook his head."

"Why?"

"He said—"

"Said? He never talks."

"Not much, I admit. He prefers to use nods, shrugs, and dabs of his fingers here, there, and all about. But he does know quite a fair amount of English, and Mexican too, I gather, and he has taken to talking to me some, now and then. Anyway. He said he did not expect more Indian raids for some time. Perhaps months. I asked why. He said the Ransom Rock attempt was just to see what we would do about it. Were we strong enough? Were we willing enough? Were we smart enough to do right away what we ought to do? Joe says we proved that we were, and that is what they came to find out. They never meant to do more than this on this raid. Next time, he said, they will come in greater numbers, prepared to make a stand. I asked him, Why would they just wait for us to come and get them? And he said if they ran away they would never find out what they meant to find out. He said they did just what he would have done, and had done, in the old days, when he was a chief."

"They've tried us twice, haven't they. Once before I came—you know all about that; and now this time. Well, we'll try to know it before they hit us, next time."

"Joe Dummy said also that we must keep an eye on Mexico. They'll come with allies from Mexico next time, he said."

"Your man Rainbow Son will be the boss, I expect."

Matthew colored.

"Sir, I can't explain how he got off, except to think that he always intended to get off. I asked Joe this. I said, If we had captured Rainbow, would that have broken up all the enemy plans and actions in the future? He said no, Sebastian, the other chief, would just go right ahead. Joe considers Sebastian more clever than Rainbow. But Rainbow has the power."

"This is one of the hardest things to endure about our kind of duty," said Major Prescott. "Waiting for Washington to make up its mind to clear the whole thing up, while we fight local skirmishes.

What we need is a campaign. Where is General Quait? They don't *see us* in Washington. They see a good deal more how the politicians want it to look than how it really looks."

"What can politicians do if they don't know the fact?"

"They get information from out here, but they ought not to trust it. It often means someone is working things around his own way. I mentioned a Mr. Jones to you, the one who came to see me here at the fort while you were off getting married. He'll never come back here while I am commanding this post. He made me think of a scorpion to be stepped on."

"Who is he, sir?"

"Mr. Seeley Jones. You want to know where Indians get rifles? Mr. Seeley Jones. You want to know who knows what they plan to stir up before the Army knows it? Mr. Seeley Jones. You want to know who's got himself a private connection with various members of Congress? Mr. Seeley Jones. He says he used to work for a congressman, and once thought he might run for a seat himself, in Texas. But he says you can do a sight better at the very same thing outside of Congress than inside. What he means by the *thing* is to make private money out of public concerns. He is worse than the Indians. At least they are fighting for their own side. But Mr. Jones is on their side, too, or makes them think he is, which is just as bad. Of course, his only side is his own interest. But they don't see that, and if his friends in Washington know it, they're as bad as he is, and out after the same bag of loot. I tell you." The major shook his head. "I tell you."

"What was he doing here?"

"Oh yes. How do you like this? He came here to offer me—us— the Army—security from Indian troubles if I would make a deal to give him army horses which he would then trade to the Indians for his own gain. What they were supposed to trade him for the horses was their obedience. He says he is more or less the white chief of a certain lot of Apaches. You know what I think? I think he's crazy. But that don't help any, when he's making things work his way. Here's another thing. He files on land and gets himself a lot of claims over vast acreage, and then he says he can grant these lands to the Indians. Then when settlers come along and move in on some of these lands, not knowing who owns them, he files claims against the government on behalf of the Indians. It isn't legal in any slightest way, but with his friends in Washington to press his claims, he makes his way quite well. When he collects on his land claims, he is supposed to pay the Indians the big share of it. But you know as well as I do who is going to keep his own pockets full. I tell *you*."

"Did he tell you all this, sir?"

"Oh, some of it, and I found out the rest by writing to Department. They're on to him there. But Washington isn't. Oh, he made it all sound so pretty, and so nice, and such a favor to the robbed and downtrodden Apaches, and he himself sounded like a hell-fire revival preacher putting on his pleading voice. But he didn't fool me. When he said it was my duty to save American lives by coming to terms with him about the horse deal, I got up and picked him up by his galluses and I threw him bodily down the front steps here and ordered him off the post never to return. I was ashamed of it right away."

"Why, sir? A rascal like that."

"Yes, but he is sick. He didn't weigh more than a hundred and ten pounds when I picked him up. He went on smiling, too, sort of sickly, as if he couldn't believe it was himself to whom this was happening. He picked himself up and walked rickety over to his horse and rode off. Seeley Jones. A man hadn't ought to have to fight the likes of him in addition to Indians. But he is just as much of a killer. Only he goes about it roundabout. I wrote all about Mr. Seeley Jones to Washington. It may cost me my job, if his confederates get on to me. But somebody up there may see it who ought to see it. Even so, I feel certain I don't know all there is to know about Mr. Seeley Jones."

xxv

It was not only more charitable, it was also more precise to think of Mr. Seeley Jones not as a human creature with free will and a responsible intelligence, but as a growth from an anonymous seed which took its course blindly and often destructively through a compelled life.

Seeley Jones's father might have been any one of several men. His mother bore him in Tennessee, in a mountain cabin, in the vicinity of a work camp where lived surveyors and laborers who were driving a government road across the mountains toward the West in 1835. A number of these men were her visitors. She was certain that Seeley's father was among them, but it was not until the boy was ten or twelve years old that she began to detect a resemblance which would justify fastening his name upon him. Up to then she had called him just Seeley, a name which seemed to her elegant and unusual. But his last name was bestowed when she suddenly realized that her oldest son (she had eight more children after him, the last four by a husband with whom she stayed) was beginning to look like the handsomest man she ever saw in her born days—the young boss surveyor, Captain Mordecai Jones, back there on the mountain years ago when she was a girl, and crazy for anything and everything in britches, as she herself was known to say.

Even just remembering Mordecai Jones years later, she shifted at the heart, and went hot, and something fell heavy down inside her belly, and she blushed to remember *how he was* and *how he did*. She would fall to wondering if her son by his get, Seeley Jones, for this was now his name for sure and honest, would grow up to be as *you*-know as his father, with the same *you*-know to drive girls crazy-mad with wanting. Sighing about it ten-twelve years later, Seeley's mother, as she celebrated the past, accurately felt the future that awaited her boy.

Seeley Jones grew up to be a tall, amazingly handsome and prepossessing young man. His family could do little for him after he was about fifteen, for they were poor, and babies kept coming to make them poorer, and times were hard, and his step-father was jealous of the way his wife favored Seeley, just as if he reminded her of somebody else she would make love to. Soon the youth was sent out to make his way alone in the world, like many boys of his age. He had the clothes that he wore and that bulged with his comely hardnesses of flesh; and he had a jug of white corn whisky made by his step-father and presented as a grudging farewell present. Finally he had a word of wisdom from his mother.

"With your good looks and all, from your daddy, you hadn't ought to do but one *thang,* and that is, to find yourself some kind of work b'which you'll *meet the public,* for I will sw'ar by ev'thang I ever knew in my born days, if *ever* I saw *any*body who c'ld charm the chicken raght off the egg, it's my boy Seeley Jones.

"Look at him," she said, her heart aching to lose him so soon, and pretending lightness in her flattery, "with that shiny yeller hair s'sweet in the sunlight, and them ol' blue eyes lak cornflowers, and that curly, pink mouth, grinnin' s'nice, and them big ol' arms lak cottonwood branches, and them long ol' legs, fit fer dancin' and prancin'.

"Listen to him," she said with comic scorn which yet told him truly of his excellence, "listen to him taolk, and hear that voice of his, s'smooth and sort of dovey-like, why, I'll tell it to you sure and straight, honey, if you can find yourself any kind of work before the public, and dealin' with *wimmin* in pertikler, honey, you are a made man."

It was a passionate and powerful valedictory, and it gave Seeley Jones a picture of himself, and an opinion, which he never lost. He ever afterward considered himself irresistible, and thus excusable, in any circumstances.

His first employment came with a troupe of evangelists who were drifting across the South holding prayer meetings. Soon enough he was one of their major attractions. He became a heart-warming gospel singer. He learned to become a stirring preacher who was able to speak not only with the innocence of youth but also with the fascinating voice of sin.

"Oh, I know," he would say to his hearers in the guttering light of the snake-oil lamps, "I know what sin is, youthful though I may be, for measured by my iniquities, I am a ver'table Methuselah, for the good Lord saw fit to visit me with the curse of being attractive to wimmin"—and on he would go, washing white in public the titillating history of his obsession with women and his performance with them. For his mother was right—they could not leave him alone, once he had revealed behind his boyish comeliness his appetite and his astounding capacity for indulgence. He made an excellent living until he was twenty-six, traveling with the preachers, and making love, often in the name of the deity whom he professed to serve in his work, to many a girl or woman who, having come to pray, remained to have their aroused emotions assuaged by the young gospel singer. He received many favors in money, clothes, jewelry and the like, from the women who took from him love which he gave in almost abstract approval of his own prowess and splendor.

In 1861 he was mustered in as a foot soldier of a Georgia regiment. He fought all through the War as if it were a camp meeting. At first he avoided battles when he could, and if he could not, he lagged as much as possible for he wanted to live and live whole to be admired again.

But one day he could not escape facing direct combat, and to save himself, he killed a Union soldier with a bayonet. He felt a strange exhilaration after the act. His excellence seemed to him increased because he had taken a life. He was never again reluctant to fight in battle. He lost his fear of injury to himself—surely he was too good-looking, and he had too much of everything, to be spoiled by a wound, or anything?

After the War he migrated to Texas like other soldiers who had surrendered. Texas was big and everything was to be had for the taking there, so they heard. Seeley was now a man, and he wanted wealth, much of it, and quickly, and he knew he was now able to do anything that needed doing to get it, even to killing somebody if somebody got in his way.

He made a quick start in Texas when he met two Confederate gentlemen who, having refused to accept postwar conditions in their own defeated states, were emigrating to Mexico. Vast properties, limitless riches, even patents of nobility were possible in Mexico under the Emperor Maximilian for men of courage and conviction. The Confederate veterans could use just such a man as Seeley Jones, with his brawn, his charm, his war record. He joined them when they crossed the Rio Grande at Matamoros to ride over the deserts of northern Mexico to file their land claims with the Mexican government at Saltillo.

In the course of the journey it occurred to Seeley that he might just as well be in their boots as in his own—they had the sacks of money on their saddles, they were going to be the bosses, they were going to own the land—why not he?

He had several days in which to plan, for the journey was long and required many encampments at night in the wilderness. During one night he did what seemed necessary to him if he would acquire improved position.

Thereafter, riding on alone, it would be he, and no one else, who would file that claim, and spend that money in the buckskin bags, and get him a bunch of Mexican señorattoes, about whom he had heard enlivening reports.

He never reached Saltillo.

Within a day he was overtaken by a party of Mexican horsemen who had found the remains of his double murder. They captured him, took his money, and said he was now theirs.

"Are you police?" he asked.

"Police!" They roared with contempt. No, the police would give anything to catch up with them. No, they were a company who called themselves The Pacifiers, and at this they laughed again in innocent relish of the joke: they went about the country taking what they needed, and sometimes a little bit more, and if anyone objected, they *pacified* him, if the *point* was clear? It was the *point* of a pistol or a dirk, and Seeley Jones understood. Good. He had proved his knack for their kind of work, they had seen the evidence of this, had followed his tracks, and now he belonged to them, whether he like it or not.

For five years Seeley Jones was an accomplished member of The Pacifiers. There was hardly a crime of greed or lust, hardly a form of imaginative torture or murder, in which he was not directly implicated, if not actually the leader. The fact that these deeds were always the work of or witnessed by all The Pacifiers seemed consoling to the individuals in the company. Each man's guilt was subdivided and shared to the number of his comrades. If a man raped or killed, he did it not only for and by himself, he did it also for and as if by all his companions. Seeley Jones had a natural style, a muscular grace, in all he did, even of the darkest nature, which brought him the esteem of his friends, and also its dangerous corollary, jealousy.

It was this latter emotion in his Mexican band which led to his parting from them. He heard from one friend that three others, fearing he must one day seize command of the outlaw troop, were planning to have him murdered the next time they invaded and looted a town. They were operating near San Juan, Tamaulipas, opposite Camargo, Texas, at the time. Seeley decided it was time to go back to the United States and make his way there with the benefit of his recent experience.

One night he had sentry duty. While The Pacifiers slept, he deserted, swam his horse across the rain-swollen Rio Grande, and by morning was well on his way toward San Antonio. His money bag, almost as though it were an attribute of virility, comforted him by its weight. He had vague dreams of running for Congress from Texas, and getting to be somebody. He kept wondering how he'd look in a frock coat; but he knew—magnificent.

If he did not go to Washington as an elected congressman, he went as the next best thing. He was attached to a Texan member of Congress as personal representative. The title covered a number of duties —bodyguard, messenger, doorman, confidential operator, personal substitute on official occasions. The congressman had various interests with which it would be embarrassing to be openly identified.

Seeley Jones acted for him as go-between, and learned many secrets
and knacks of operation in the public trough, all of which he harbored
for his own future application. The congressman was at times too
drunk to make his appearance, and then Seeley Jones would put on
his new frock coat with satin lapels and appear instead, making a
charming little talk with overtones of the evangelical style in it. He
would excuse the congressman as "a man s'busy he just couldn't do
all the thangs he'd ought t'do, what with the fact that the good Lord
had only a-given him two hands and arms." In his glowing health, his
sparkling blue eyes, the yearning in his voice for the love of all who
heard him, and the kindling *you*-know that happened in him and as
a consequence happened in women when, staring at them, he thought
of them in just his way, Seeley Jones was always effective.

He had a daguerreotype taken of himself in that period. It showed
him in his frock coat, tall, nobly proportioned, open-faced with a
quizzical charm which seemed like character but was really the result
of holding an expression under the photographer's skylight for a long
moment. Ever afterward he carried a copy of the picture with him,
and was always ready to show it, happy himself to be seeing it again
through the eyes of a new beholder.

Oddly enough, the more prominent he became as a fringe figure in
the life of government Washington, and the more unofficial powers
he gained through associations with powerful men, the less easy he
became in his own mind. He had come across printed reports of
congressional investigations of outrages committed on or near the
Rio Grande border, and in some of them he found information uncomfortably precise about the operations of the bandit troop called
The Pacifiers. Settlers and travelers in Texas and Mexico had given
testimony. Though they did not identify him by name, they mentioned
a tall, blond American as one of the ringleaders, and it was possible
that one day a Texas witness in one of the hearings might just happen
to be in Washington, and might just recognize him. As a precaution
he grew a mustache and beard, and he resolved to make his way out
to the West as soon as he had a good plan for his future. One thing
was sure—he would not go back to Texas. Farther west—that was the
idea. A man could lose himself out there, or if necessary skedaddle
into Mexico.

His official post in the congressman's office brought him much
knowledge of how the Army on the Indian frontier was provisioned
and supplied. It seemed to him that if he could manage for credentials

as a sutler, he could come close to the source of a large and continuous stream of expenditure. He would need a sizable supply of cash to set himself up with stock in trade. In his enchanted fortune, he knew too much about his congressman to be refused a courteous but menacing request for money. The congressman gave him five thousand dollars to be quit of him. Seeley Jones outfitted himself and went to Arizona Territory.

But not before he had evolved a grandiose scheme which had to do with the Indians. There was a strong faction in Congress which had no intimate knowledge of frontier conditions. Its members discounted the sufferings endured by white settlers at the hands of Indian raiders. Indians—in the view of these congressmen—were more often victims than aggressors. Seeley Jones saw how a brisk trade might be built up by someone who took advantage of this sentiment. Such a man might become the champion of the Apaches, gain influence over them as their white brother, and develop a profitable traffic in handling Indian claims against the government, especially if he could contrive to fabricate those claims in the first place. If he wasn't smarter than all the Indians that ever scalped a white man, reflected Seeley Jones, then he had ought t'be scalped himself.

He intended to look into the possibilities and work out the details while serving the Army as a sutler. When the time came, he would make his switch to the side of the Indians—and *then,* he said to the unknown opposition which he imagined as waiting to catch him, *then* see who got rich, and got aholt of Indian lands, and got his hands on all the Indian wimmin a feller could want. "Shit, fire and corruption," he exclaimed in his favorite phrase, what color a wumman was, or where she came from, didn't signify—she was still a wumman, wasn't she? In every detail, his past was creating his future.

He went west in 1874. For the first year or two, in order to establish himself plausibly, he worked hard at legitimate trade with the Army. In the course of it he acquired a large private stock of firearms. When he judged the time was ripe, he traded these to the Indians for horses stolen from Mexico which in turn he sold to the Army. As a sideline, he sold whisky to the Indians, though this was equally risky. Rapidly he made a small fortune, meanwhile gaining the confidence of several powerful Apache chiefs. He married an Apache woman according to the Indian ritual. His work took him on long journeys across the territories of New Mexico and Arizona, and even into northwest Mexico, for which his desert travels with The Pacifiers had prepared him.

After some years of his double trafficking he began to feel poorly, as he said; said he had this sick-tasting cough that shook him like a ol' daog in a shiverin' fit. He lost weight rapidly. His eyes sank into their sockets, his cheeks went hollow and waxy, and he spat blood now and then. He wondered if it could be possible that just as he was gettin' t'whar he wanted to get—rich, powerful, and ready to work on his Indian claims plan—he was goin' t'come *daown* with something?

He shaved off his yellow beard and mustache to see how he looked. He would not believe what he saw. Instead, he pretended to be still the hardy, handsome man in the daguerreotype. He would pull out the picture and show it to anyone who would look, and say, there, that was him, that was how he looked, nothing could spoil that—and he never knew how much he had changed. Consequently, he still used all his old tricks of seductiveness and charm, all his equivocal and obscene suggestiveness. But now in his physical change people shrank from him, for he was grotesque and repulsive. To see him in his gallantries of manner was like seeing a spider try a swaggering bow or a centipede attempt a caress. He was dying of tuberculosis—"galloping consumption," as a trader called it to his face one day.

If his plans had once been grandiose and bold, they now became feverish with fantasy. He refused to concede that he was no longer equal to vast travels over desert and plain, under the drying burn of the sun, and through the freezing wakes of the nights. He sought shelter and comfort more often than before in army posts, and he began to notice that he was not so welcome as he once had been. More than one commander, having no proof, but believing what he had heard about Seeley Jones, sent him packing on his way.

How could any man treat him so, he would wonder, and his eyes would fill with tears to think of what he had once been.

Of all his memories, the one he most frequently evoked for his own comfort was one which reminded him of the time—the one time in his adult life—when he had done a good deed. It was, he remembered with a lump in his throat, sure 'nough a good deed, too, and if folks only knew about it, they'd b'nicer to him than they were.

It was this way. One time, years ago, during those adventures with The Pacifiers, they came down on a party traveling from Monclova to Eagle Pass. The Pacifiers took the draft animals, and the cargo, and the money and clothes and possessions of the men and women travelers, and violated the women, and tormented the men, finally killing everyone, as they thought. But there was one young man whose fate fell into the hands of Seeley Jones. The young man was silent, white with fear, degraded by his nakedness, but too spirited to beg for mercy. His dignity in his defiance struck Seeley Jones as novel. He decided to spare the young man's life, threw him to the ground, covered him with a serape, told him to play dead, and when The Pacifiers were gone, to ride off on a horse which Seeley Jones would hide for him behind a clump of greasewood. Why had he done it? He didn't mind killing. Was there something about the young man to affect him? Did the young man make him think of himself? He never could say. But something about the whole incident gave him a new feeling, and it now made him water at the eyes and cough just to think of it. Just out of the goodness of his heart, he guessed, he had spared that young man's life years ago.

He would look at the daguerreotype to see the man in his years of glory and power who had done such a fine thing.

Reassured, then, justified, excused, in his latest undertakings, he went feverishly ahead with his plans to defraud both the Indians and the government with false claims, when chance should present itself.

He had lately attached himself to the camp of the runaway chief Rainbow Son. There he kept his women. Refusing to admit that he was dying, Seeley Jones saw himself as the white chief of the large camp of Apaches who kept sanctuary in Mexico, from which they made raids into Arizona or New Mexico according to their opportunities. Hardly able to sit his horse when the camp moved, Seeley Jones went along, traveling the grand sweeps of earth which he vaguely saw as his own empire. His vision, awry with the disease which was touching from his lungs to his brain, had a last strange force. The Indians were reached by this, and if they knew that death was in him, they also knew that sometimes at the very hour of death the secrets, and thus the powers, of the world might come to a man.

xxvi

In mid-autumn the furnaces of the desert began to cool toward winter. The days were still hot at noon, but morning and evening were brushed with a breath off the mountains which brought the flavor of transpiring pine forests and cold rock. A sense of relief eased the garrison of Fort Delivery. The future had its appeal once again. The commanding officer was expecting the arrival of new recruits, and Laura Hazard—the whole post knew it though only the women spoke of it—was expecting a child.

After several days of containing his happiness, Matthew called on Captain Gray with a troubled question.

"Doctor," he said, "my wife has talked to you."

"Yes," said Cedric Gray, "and if you are not willing to say what she talked about, I am. She is pregnant. The common and desirable result of marriage. Please do not be dainty with me."

"Dainty!" Matthew was briefly outraged, but the doctor was both smiling and scowling at him in a furious kind of blessing, and he came back to good temper. "Yes, I want to ask whether you think she should stay here to have her baby or go back East to her parents."

"Your child will be born sometime in April. If your wife is to go East she should depart three months before that time, to assure her of safety while traveling. My view is that she would do well to go. You have no reason to trust my competence in delivering infants."

"Oh, no, sir. I did not mean that I did not trust—"

"Indeed you did, my boy, though you did not expect the issue to be baldly exposed. Well, I have exposed it, and I agree with you—for it is clear that she should not bear her child here in the wilderness, removed from every sort of amenity and convenience."

"Did you tell her so, sir?"

"I did not. She made no mention of the idea. I assumed from her demeanor that she regarded me as her doctor."

"I'm sorry, captain, I have been awkward and rude. But I am—"

"You are naturally concerned. Aagh. Don't be false with me. If I were you, I'd send her back, and I mean it without pique or pride."

"Sir, as an army doctor, have you attended at births?"

"I sh'd say roughly about seven dozen. I lost three; but Joseph Lister himself could not have saved two of them, I am certain."

"Sir, what if military action should have to come on us when the baby is still very young and small? Would it not be a great risk to move him if necessary?"

"I know of nothing, lieutenant, connected with very young and small babies which is not accompanied by great risk. It is a wonder of Divine Providence that any of them survive to grow up and beget more of their own helpless kind."

Captain Gray sat at his table with his large cranium supported by his spread hand. His china-blue eyes were squinted almost out of sight by the quizzical screw of his expression as he regarded the young man whose fatherhood brought him new emotion and eclipsed old politeness. Here was a young man suddenly filled to the brim with concerns that demanded new ways of viewing all life. The doctor brought his hand down and slapped the table.

"Send her off," he said and stood up. "I would do it in your place, and I would have no more interest than you have in what anybody else thinks about it."

Matthew also arose. Was the post surgeon reproving him? He looked and saw that he was not. Doctor Gray was simply stating exactly what he believed, without rancor, vanity or concession.

"Sir, thank you."

"You, Matthew," said the doctor, "you will always believe you can direct the events of your life and the lives of those you love. Some people can and some can't. You can. Go right on doing so. Good morning, sir."

Matthew would like to shake the doctor's hand, but the doctor had no interest in showing the deep run of feeling which flowed through his craggy heart. Not to see the fine young face which besought him, he turned his back and began to rearrange a small stack of foolscap pages at which he'd been working. Matthew left him and went to take his new information to Laura.

In reply to his decision to send her back to Fort Porter in good season, she said,

"We'll see."

"See? There is nothing to see," he stated. "I have made up my mind."

"And mine?" she asked with alarming sweetness. He saw a shadow move across her face, now newly rounded and softened by the stir of the ancient secret within her.

"Laura, certainly not, not that way. But we must simply do the sensible thing. Doctor Gray agrees with me."

"I am not at all sure that our child should not be part of our life in every particular, wherever we are, and if we are in danger, then so will he be, and you will protect us."

"Of course I will protect you. But here"—he waved his hand at all that he knew so well and all that she would not see—"here there are extra difficulties nobody need face unless absolutely necessary. I want you to have the best of care."

"Doctor Gray is highly regarded."

He flushed with exasperation at her weight of reasonableness. What weapon could he bring against such softness which yet had the power to rest like a rock on its position?

"I don't mean to say he is not. But all circumstances indicate that I am taking the proper precautions." He enfolded her in his arms. "Laura, nothing must happen to you. I could not bear it."

"You're willing to do without me, though," she murmured, "if you are planning to send me away."

Oh, this dodge and shift of the female mind. He let her go and then at once repossessed her, saying,

"I need not answer that. All I know is that all sensible people must feel the way I do about this."

"Mrs. Prescott does not."

"What? Have you asked her?"

"We talk about everything."

"And she thinks you should stay?"

"I did not say that. She just thinks there is no reason yet to make any decision. She had two of their children on army posts, one of them when there was no doctor at hand, but only a laundress who was also a midwife."

"I feel you might have discussed this first with me, before taking it to the commanding officer's wife."

"Oh, my darling, you are more put about by our baby than I am. Come to me."

She took his head to her bosom and its nearness and its weight upon her turned her heart over. She stroked his hair and made him know her love, saying in the faintest of whispers, "Hush, hush, hush," against the thoughts that still made turmoil in him, and that would come into words if she would let them. In a few minutes he was at peace. This was an achievement of some size, for she had brought it about without in the least changing the opinion which he required her to change. This, for the moment, he forgot.

But when he could, he summoned an old enemy to his aid.

He wrote to Mrs. Greenleaf, giving her and the colonel the happy news that they would be grandparents, and then ventured to hope that, in view of the primitive conditions and the possibility of active danger from enemy action at Fort Delivery, the Greenleafs would

ask their daughter to return to her parental roof in good time to see
her child into the world under expert care, fond affection and traditional well-being. Closing the letter, he sighed sharply at the turn of
life which could cause him to enlist the dangerous powers of his
mother-in-law to work against the calm stubbornness of her own
daughter.

He frowned. No matter. He was the head of a family and he would
do what he thought best for all. The letter went into the bag which
would leave in four days for Driscoll. All he said to Laura about it
was,

"I have written our happy news to your people."

"So have I," she said, and with clear eyes did not look into the
matter any further.

xxvii

One morning while Major Prescott was inspecting horses at the corral
after reveille, Trumpeter Rainey approached him with the air of a
man who had an irresistible bargain to offer.

"Sir," said the trumpeter, "may Private Rainey speak to the major
informally?"

"Go ahead, Rainey. I'll just keep on looking over these animals
while you talk to me. We could still do with another score or so to
work with."

"Yes, sir," said the trumpeter fidgeting slightly.

"Look at this one," said the major, deliberately postponing Rainey's
chance to speak, to determine whether he would persist—always, he
felt, a good thing to know about a soldier. The horse he indicated
was poorly fleshed, and if it moved at all seemed to be in a state of
somnambulism. Rainey held his breath to fill himself with resolve,
and then, to the major's pleasure, persisted.

"Sir, is it true that we're getting some recruits?"

"Why, yes, Rainey, we are. I put in for six. I expect they'll come
with the next mail wagon from Driscoll."

Rainey frowned like a man of affairs, and said,

"Sir, I have the first sard'n on my side in this, and if you approve,
he says I may go ahead."

"Approve what?"

"I thought maybe you would let me take charge of the recruits, sir. I can do it, sir, don't think I can't, just because all I get to do is blow the bugle, and—"

"And run yourself ragged as my orderly?"

"Sir—"

"I see, trumpeter. You want to be a soldier, is that it?"

"That's what I enlisted to be, sir."

The major saw that here was the old headquarters troop trouble. At first troopers in headquarters felt lucky; but when they saw how other men measured them at their soft jobs, some of them wanted to earn equality with the men who were in ranks and who handled troops and who—some day—might bear the brunt of battle.

"You're a first-class trumpeter, Rainey. Anybody who can play the bugle like you ought not to be ashamed of it."

"I'm not, sir. But I can do anything any other trooper can, too."

"How can you have a command? You're only a private."

The trumpeter answered his commanding officer with a sudden grin, putting his lower lip over the upper. What he meant was that there was nothing to prevent the major from promoting him. His proposals, spoken and unspoken, gathered force the longer the major considered them in silence. He watched the major closely. Finally Major Prescott took off his campaign hat and rubbed his bald head and Rainey eased a trifle, for he saw that he'd made his point.

"Very well, trumpeter. As of now you are Acting Corporal Rainey. We'll see how you manage. When the recruits report in, you report to me with them. You will give them their preliminary training in addition to continuing your other duties."

"Yes, sir."

Rainey saluted and was about to go elsewhere to expand with his news, but the major detained him to listen to opinions about the next horse, and the next. Rainey, though visibly impatient to be gone, listened sternly. To the major this was an encouraging sign. Command carried with it many sacrifices. Others would soon have to listen to Rainey. In honor of that, Rainey suffered Prescott. The major tried not to smile.

xxviii

Between two and three o'clock in the afternoon Laura went for a little walk to think about her life. Though she would never let her husband know it, she wondered if he might after all be right about her going to Fort Porter before the birth of her child. I wish, she thought, I wish this was my second child. I could be anywhere for that, knowing what I'll know after the first. She moved idly along the edge of the shallow arroyo behind Quarters 4. The day was hot but overcast and all was still. She noticed an extra pungency in the herblike scents of the dusty brush. Would it rain? Probably not. Was she right or wrong about anything? Who knew. All at once she heard odd sounds. If there was anything more strange than the silence of the desert it was a sudden sound there.

She heard someone shouting, a man's voice, a strangled voice, and at once she thought of Indians and a victim.

She was about to run for her house when she realized that what she heard was someone yelling out numbers—"one, two, three, four!" She began to laugh. It sounded like someone drilling troops down there, out of sight around a turn in the arroyo. The idea was absurd, but she went a little farther along and found herself gazing down upon Acting Corporal Rainey, entirely alone, giving out commands in a sustained rage of power. His face was contorted and his arm pointed with scorn at an imaginary mistake by an invisible trooper.

"All right, all right," he said before each of his bawled remarks, and then followed with what as a lady she assumed to be profanity of an original sort. "All right, once again, and let's get it right this time, you goddamned —, —, —," he shouted, as he turned to sweep his boxlike parade ground with a commanding eye.

Laura was about to retire to spare not herself but him. She was not quick enough. He saw her. He shut his mouth, pulled off his hat and feeling foolish slumped against the pink wall of the arroyo opposite to her. He threw his hat on the ground and looked at it. His thick sandy hair was plastered down by sweat. He mumbled something.

"What was that, trumpeter?" she called in her clear, pretty Eastern voice, with its confident authority.

"I said," he answered with miserable resignation, "that I was just practicing."

"How splendid!" she exclaimed. "And what for?"

He looked sharply to see if she was mocking him, but she was not. He straightened up. He picked up his hat and brushed it off. He put it on and smartened his chin strap under his lower lip.

"I've been promoted, and the major has ordered me to train the recruits who are coming."

"And you've been getting ready for them! I think it's perfectly splendid!"

"You do, ma'am?"

All of a sudden he was a hard, healthy young man who was being taken seriously by a lovely young woman.

"I certainly do. —Aren't you frightfully hot? Aren't you thirsty? When you're done here, come by my quarters and I'll give you a glass of lemonade."

"I was just about finished already," he called, and scrambled up the arroyo wall. When he reached her side he suddenly blushed violently. He remembered what everybody knew. She was going to be a mother. If ever he had looked upon her with desire he now felt a surge of what he was certain was a nobler emotion. Chivalry. He would serve her and protect her and when she had become a mother she would always remember the young soldier far away in the Arizona desert who had done so much to make her life more pleasant and easy. At all costs, however, she must never know that he knew that she was pregnant. In his propriety it must be insisted that any baby would arrive as if without cause or long preparation for birth.

At Quarters 4 he refused to go in out of the glare but lounged in the doorway while she drew some evaporation-cooled water from a Mexican clay jar and mixed his lemonade. She brought it to him with a little plate of sand tarts, and she let him stay where he pretended to be comfortable. He ate and drank rapidly for now he had nothing he could say. He only gave her his worshipful, blunted look over the rim of his glass before his lowered face, while she mentioned how clever it was of him to go off alone in that way to learn how to give commands—seemed very original, for though she had grown up in the Army, she'd never happened on it before, in all the posts where she'd been stationed with her father, Colonel Greenleaf. Shouldn't the Army, she wondered, be told about it so that everyone could—

At this point Matthew came home to find the young soldier returning Laura's act of kindness with a gaze of confused worship that faded swiftly in the presence of an officer. The acting corporal swallowed his last drop and crumb, coughed in a social way, saluted and wandered loosely across the parade ground toward the enlisted men's barracks. Laura watched him for an instant, and Matthew watched her. Both thought of, then spoke of, how much drift there was to a soldier's life, even within the Army's sharp outlines. Then in a flood of affection for her husband and their sharing of the trivial, she told him word for word of her encounter.

"Well," he said, "you've made a conquest."

"What silliness!" she exclaimed.

But Matthew saw that she lifted her chin a trifle in thoughtless satisfaction. Women! he thought, feeling like Harvey Greenleaf.

xxix

When the mail wagon pulled in from Driscoll bringing the recruit detachment, it brought with it an element of surprise. Acting Corporal Rainey, eager for his new responsibility, was the first man on the post to meet the wagon. What he discovered drove him full of wrath to see the commanding officer.

"Sir, you know? The recruits?"

"Yes, Rainey."

"Sir, you said six?"

"Yes, I said six."

"Sir, there's only one."

Major Prescott refused to show feeling before his most youthful subordinate, but his perpetual rage against the War Department was always ready and he now felt it start up behind his enforced calm.

"Very well, bring him to me and wait in the hall while I look through the mail bag."

"Yes, sir," said Rainey and departed.

In the mail the major found an official communication that acknowledged his request for six men, and stated that they were forthwith ordered to Fort Delivery. The next paragraph amended this information, explaining that five of the six would be detached and assigned to Fort Union, New Mexico, en route, leaving Private Brian Clanahan to proceed alone to Fort Delivery, Arizona.

Major Prescott felt almost a pleasure in the degree of disgust which filled him at this news. He rapidly wrote an endorsement on the War Department letter and made a copy for his files, and put the original in the outgoing bag. He then opened the door. Rainey was waiting in the hall with Private Clanahan.

"Corporal, please wait here while I speak to our new man. Come in, Clanahan," said the major, shaking hands with him.

He took Clanahan into the office, stood him at ease, shut the door and looked him over. Clanahan was tall and thin, a black, white and blue Irishman eighteen years old—black hair and heavy eyelashes, blue eyes, white skin. He gave an impression of points—the bones of chin, shoulders, hips. He contained a sort of wary excitement in his strange new surroundings.

"Where are you from, Clanahan?"

"New York City, sir."

"How did you come to the Army?"

"I enlisted in New York."

"How was your trip west?"

"They put me on a boat for Albany, and then I went by the cars to Buffalo, sir. Then I had a boat to Detroit, and the cars again to Chicago, and then a canal boat to La Salle, and then a river steamboat to St. Louis, and then the cars to Driscoll."

"What do you think of the Army by now?"

"Sir, it's all right," replied Clanahan, looking past the major, "all but one thing I saw."

"And what was that?"

"Something at St. Louis. They did it to a man." Clanahan's Irish came up. "They'd only do it to me once." He gripped his forage cap hard. The major nodded and he continued. "He was a soldier who had done something and they punished him. They stripped him naked, tied a rope around his ankle, and threw him in the river, and hauled him out, and threw him in again, and they did it many times. A lot of men came to watch. He was nearly drownded. There wasn't nobody to help him."

Many against one—power over a fellow man: the recruit was a little wild at the memory. The major asked,

"Do you know what he had done that was wrong?"

"No, sir."

"Before you judge the Army, remember that he may have deserved harsh treatment."

"Yes, sir." But Clanahan was not convinced. His spirit flared in his hot blue eye. Major Prescott stood up.

"Well, Clanahan, we don't have any rivers near here, and anyway, if you do your duty, and try to learn, you'll soon be one of us. Now, just step to the door and ask Acting Corporal Rainey to come in."

The major solemnly introduced the two young men. They shook hands as if they'd never seen each other before.

"Corporal Rainey will be in charge of your training for the present. Good luck. I'll be keeping an eye on you myself."

Rainey exaggerated his position of attention and said,

"Sir, may Acting Corporal Rainey speak to the major alone?" Prescott nodded, and after Clanahan stepped outside, Rainey went on. "Sir, I don't want it."

"Want what, Rainey?"

"Sir, how can you drill *one man?* It will look funny. I thought there'd be six of them, almost two sets of fours."

"So did I, Rainey. But in the Army we do with what we are given. That new man has got to become a soldier. You asked for the command. You've got it. You will keep it."

"Sir, it will make *him* feel funny, to be marching around and drilling all by himself."

"It is your duty to see that he does not feel funny. That is all, corporal."

Rainey glanced down at his chevrons. They were bright, new yellow. He would hate to cut them off.What a nuisance it was to discover that authority could have its disagreeable aspects. Feeling trapped, Rainey went out, picked up his one-man detail, and led him off the head-quarters porch, saying, "Private Clanahan, your first duty will be to clean and brighten brasses, with acid and ashes."

Hearing this, "Good enough," said Major Prescott to himself, and went across the hall to his quarters with something to tell his wife.

"Look here, Jess," he said, showing his copy of the endorsement he had written on the War Department letter. She was sewing. She said, "What is that?"

"You know about the recruits?" She nodded. "I asked for six?" She nodded. "They sent me one." He waved his paper. "This is what I told them."

"Read it to me."

He took up a position and read aloud in an inflection which combined angry vigor with exultant satisfaction at what he had written:

Endorsement.

1. Arrival of Private Brian Clanahan, recruit, for duty is reported.

2. Request immediate assignment of five additional recruits for duty at this station on basis of need clearly and responsibly outlined in letter of 6 July.

3. Pending adoption of balloon travel for by-passing dangerous areas, suggest travel of subject recruits be routed by ship to San Francisco, thence overland from west coast, to this post, to obviate temptation on the part of post commanders in New Mexico to intercept recruits westbound from the east coast, and with these to overpopulate army installations in an area already pacified and overgarrisoned.

Signed: Hiram Hyde Prescott,
Maj. Cav., Commanding.

Reading signature and all, he concluded his performance with the happiest expectation of applause.

Jessica only sighed.

"Well?" he said, brought down by her.

"Oh, my dear," she said, biting at her thread, "when will you ever learn that plain indignation, even, is better understood in the Army than sarcasm?"

"Well, I think it sounds indignant enough."

"Yes, of course it does. But it is flippant, too. Have you posted it?"

"I put it in the bag."

"You can always take it out."

"I think not. The bag is as good as a post office. It will go off today."

She sighed again, but she also smiled. He was who he was, said her loving habit of thought.

"How is your new man?" she asked.

"I don't know too much about him. But I have an idea he'll do. We'll see."

The incoming wagon brought also mail and express. Among the shipments was one from Messrs. Lingenfelter and Company, of St. Louis, marked *Fragile—With Care*. It contained a set of Waterford decanter and tumblers to replace Captain Adrian Brinker's broken wedding gift. Lieutenant Hazard, with much satisfaction, delivered the box to his wife Laura, who was able once again to say, "My Waterford."

XXX

The great spectacle of the day at Fort Delivery was the sight of Acting Corporal Rainey drilling Private Clanahan.

"It is as good as a play, for the rest of the troop," observed Captain Gray.

The men gathered to watch it at every chance. They were free with advice from the sidelines. Their critical comment often took the form of whistles of astonishment and disbelief. Rainey they called "General," and Clanahan his "Army." If Rainey gave his commands in a loud voice, the spectators pretended to be deafened. If he modified them to an ordinary tone, they strained to hear, saying, "How?" and shaking their heads in bewilderment. If Clanahan made a mistake as to which was right face and which left, they broke out in dispute as to which the acting corporal had called for. When he counted the cadence out loud, they joined him in chorus, altering the beat in unison until he had to call a halt and begin again. Starved for novelty, the troopers made the most of this one, and the two lonesome figures, one ordering and the other obeying, out in the middle of the bare parade ground, were objects of comic scorn and concealed good will. Watching the proceedings without seeming to, Major Prescott said that so long as the men preserved this balance of attitudes, no harm would come of the cutting-up.

It was not long before the acting corporal showed a certain ingenuity in the embarrassments of his command. As trumpeter he had represented the garrison's field music all by himself. But on the third day of his dismounted drill sessions he found another way to keep the recruit busy and for a little time relieve himself of the exhibition he had been forced to make of them both. He informed Clanahan that what was needed in support of the trumpet was music on fife and drum.

"Here," he said to Clanahan, handing him an issue fife and a dusty drum which he had found in the loft above the smithy, "I'm going to teach you how to play these, and then you will practice by yourself out in the arroyo when not at drill."

"I did not join the Army to make a racket with these things," said Clanahan.

"You will do it," shouted Rainey with an oath, taking offense at a reflection on his own military specialty.

In the following afternoons, during the hottest hours, when all was still but the spinning little winds of dust off the desert, everyone at the fort could hear the piping of the fife or the muttering of the drum, and knew, whether in headquarters, quarters, corral or smithy, that the new man, off by himself, was at work. The arrangement was convenient for Rainey, since wherever he might be he could tell simply by listening whether his charge was doing his duty.

If there was something disconsolate there was also much that was laughable in the vagrant sounds of the fife and drum in the dusty afternoon. Laura Hazard found Clanahan down in the arroyo one afternoon and asked him in his turn to come for refreshments at her front door. He accepted with somber alacrity. The ensuing silence presently took the notice of Corporal Rainey, who went to investigate it. He met Clanahan walking away from Quarters 4 and demanded an explanation. Hearing it, Rainey was furious. When he met Lieutenant Hazard later, this exchange followed:

"How is your man doing, corporal?"

"Fair, sir, fair. Only—"

"Well? Speak up!"

"If the lieutenant will excuse it, sir, he shouldn't be spoiled."

"Spoiled? Who's spoiling him?"

"Sir, he's been having lemonade at the lieutenant's quarters."

Matthew laughed, though he was not pleased by what sounded almost impertinent. Then he saw a sick look of pleading misery on the corporal's face, and he saw what was really the trouble. Corporal Rainey was inwardly shaking with jealousy because the beautiful lady, remote as the stars from any real concern for him in a personal sense, who used to give him lemonade and sand tarts, was now giving them to another. Matthew saw that the truth and depth of his feeling about the matter would not be credited by anyone who had never served month in and month out in the desert without ready female companionship or any other gentle influence. Matthew Hazard swallowed the rebuke that rose naturally to his lips and said instead,

"Perhaps it is time to get Clanahan up on a horse, corporal."

"He says he hates horses, sir."

"And what did you say to that?"

"I says, I ast him, I says, 'What the hell did you join the U.S. Cav'ry for, then?"

"A proper answer, I should say."

"Never fear, sir! He'll ride!"

xxxi

"I don't know," said Major Prescott to himself, in the course of keeping an eye on the training of Rainey's army. He often wondered how it was that the influence of women could enter through the smallest opening upon affairs that could not properly concern them; and once entered, there exert such power that before you knew it all things seemed to be happening not according to your plans but according to what some woman had made up her mind to. She might be right, he reflected. God knew they often were. But that was not his point. His point dealt with *how,* not *what.* The major knew what Laura Hazard thought because her husband told him.

She said she could hardly bear it, to listen on those hot days to the ridiculous and pathetic noise from the arroyo—*Bum. Bum. Tiddy-bum-bum-bum*—over and over, the recruit's drum practice. Making society out of her sympathy—as women do, mused the major —she asked Clanahan to come again for refreshment. She was astonished at the boy's reply.

"Lady, I thank you kindly," said Clanahan, making the elaborate manners of a street boy, "but I can't."

"You cannot? I see. Why not?"

"The corporal told me I couldn't."

"*What!*"

"That's right, lady. He says if I'm asked again I'm to say thank you very much, and no."

Laura smiled gently at him, and out of her life in the Army produced a wise reply.

"Then of course you must obey that order until it is reversed, as I have a notion it will be. You'd better trot along, now. We must not get you in trouble."

She told Matthew that the affair made her cross beyond all sensible measure. The idea that Acting Corporal Rainey should determine to whom she might or might not show an act of responsible kindness as befitted the wife of an officer—this she could not accept. She watched for a moment in which to encounter Rainey.

It came late in the afternoon when she strolled back to headquarters with Matthew. On the piazza was the trumpeter. She said good-by to Matthew, who joined the commanding officer inside. They could see and hear Laura through the open window whose shutters were turned up level. She was carrying a parasol. She was lovely in a blur of light. To Rainey she said with calm charm,

"Oh, corporal."

"Yes, ma'am?"

"Aren't you looking out for Private—who is it?—the new recruit?"

"Yes, ma'am," he said suspiciously.

"Yes. I'm sure you're doing splendidly with him. Well, then, please send him to my quarters after drill tomorrow afternoon. I have promised him some of my sand tarts."

She smiled and nodded as if there could not possibly be any resistance to her light command, and left him to stare after her bitterly. In the office Matthew looked at the major and sighed. Neither of them said anything.

The next day Major Prescott made a point of being near Quarters 4 when the sounds of one-man drill arose. There as close as possible to the little adobe house Rainey was drilling Clanahan. The spot was too near Officers' Row for the usual gallery of troopers to be present with their marveling remarks. Rainey gave his commands in full voice, quite as though conducting squadron drill. Clanahan, bright red, streaming with sweat, marched, countermarched, pivoted, faced and marked time. Rainey put him through the manual of arms. If he faltered, Rainey removed his forage cap, clapped himself in despair on his head, and rubbed his skull, bawling out uncomplimentary views, though without profanity. Every now and then he turned to glance at the doorway of Quarters 4, hoping to see Mrs. Hazard there lost in admiration of his zeal. But the door was closed. When it was time to end the drill, he marched the recruit to the door and in a loud voice commanded,

"Detail fall out and report to Mrs. Hazard!"

Clanahan looked at him to see if he meant it, and at an angry nod, turned to the door and knocked. Rainey lingered close. Surely, seeing him there, Laura would invite him too? But when the door opened, there she was, with a little tray for Clanahan, and only a cool smile for Rainey, and the words,

"Thank you, corporal. I am glad you remembered."

Then like a hostess who is serene in her choice of guests, no matter who remains outside her circle, she ignored him and turned to Clanahan to ask,

"Wouldn't you like to come in out of the sun for a minute?"

The two of them vanished within the house leaving the door open. Rainey stood fast. He could not believe such rudeness and for a moment he looked pugnacious. And then he realized that his feelings were hurt, and he seemed to crumple up inside. Slowly walking away, he saw Major Prescott and saluted. Afraid the major might talk to him, he smartened his pace and made off alone in his misery. For a moment or so Major Prescott wished that Laura Greenleaf Hazard were his daughter, so that he might have the authority to say what he wanted to say to her. As it was, he could but wonder what effect Laura's attitude might have upon the two young soldiers. If it should have any, he reflected, the chances were it would end up by spreading further in the garrison. If it should do so, he thought, he would have to intervene, though just how, he could not yet say.

As an immediate aftermath of her behavior, Laura received a gift on the following day. Acting Corporal Rainey stayed up most of the night making it. In the morning he asked Matthew to present it to Laura for him. It was a small oval picture frame tooled out of leather with a border of braided loops fashioned out of horsehair. Across the bottom of the frame worked in thin copper wire was the name, "Lady Hazard." Matthew delivered it, repeating a sober compliment from the artist. Laura put her hands behind her and said,

"Matt, what a hideous object."

"Maybe so. He made it for you."

"Take it back," she said with a shudder.

"I certainly won't do that."

"It looks like a new sort of tarantula."

He could not understand why she wouldn't accept it. How could she tell him that she felt guilty for her behavior of yesterday? Matthew teased her.

"I *said* you'd made a conquest!"

She turned white. She clasped her hands. Suddenly furious at him, she said unloving things. He was amazed—and then he recalled that in her "condition" such caprices were to be expected. He tossed the horsehair tarantula on the table and put his arms around her.

"How can you be serious about it?" he asked gently. *"I'm* not. All I mean is that sometimes a young fellow wants to find someone— a pretty woman—to idealize."

His generosity made her think of her own highhandedness. Her sweetness battled with her pride. Though her eyes filled with tears, she winked them away and replied coldly,

"I should think you'd protect me against such attentions from enlisted men."

He was about to make a remark about lemonade and sand tarts, but held his tongue.

xxxii

Innocently caused, the emotions generated throughout Fort Delivery by the arrival of the recruit presently troubled someone who must make the most of them. This was Kitty Mainwaring. Like everyone, for there were few secrets in that small society, she knew that the junior lieutenant's wife had been kind to the trumpeter, and then to the recruit. Kitty, unlike others, could put only one meaning into this fact. When alone, she swept herself through storms of daydreaming about it. The scenes she saw in her mind were as vivid as life, and the speeches exchanged were fluent and, on her own part, brilliant.

"Mrs. Hazard," she said, "everyone else may be fooled, but I am not. First you made up to the trumpeter, and then something happened; and to make the trumpeter jealous, and come back to you, you made up to the new recruit. I know men. Oh, and I know women," she said, gazing at all women through herself. She assumed a ladyship so exquisite, in her reverie, that it was a reproof to Laura whom she addressed in solitude, saying almost aloud,

"If no one else will do it, I will. You must be told that you are not worthy of your husband if you can trifle with this soldier, this trumpeter, for of course it is still he whom you want—I am not deceived by this Clanahan affair. Oh, to have Trumpeter Rainey in your house in the afternoons when Matthew—and I have a better right to call him Matthew than you know—when Matthew is away on duty . . . oh, it is warm, and private, and dusky, and close, and the trumpeter is a hardy young man, and any other woman might well—but not you, not with what you have, oh my God, if you knew how he loved me, your husband, some day you will find out, and it shall be myself who will tell you, I do not know yet just how, but the chance will come, and when it does, watch out for your pride *then,* my fine pretty high-toned lady! Have you no thought for the good of the troop? Turning the heads of young soldiers, and you an officer's wife! That's bad enough, but to make a fool of that dearest Matthew, I know him so well, I know what this would do to him!"

Remembering Matthew as a lover she grew warm and her eyes began to sting and she stormed on in her daydream, taking a new direction.

"And you, my dear lieutenant, you may think you have had me and thrown me away, but I am not finished with you yet, no, not by a long shot. I have my plans. No, you must wait, I will tell you nothing. But you do not know your darling Kitty if you think she will be satisfied just to let go. If I can't have you, I can certainly manage to make you suffer for that simple fact."

She saw herself as an avenging goddess, and the authority of her suffering seemed to justify whatever she might do. Then the images drifted and she assumed a different style.

"Mrs. Prescott," she said in her prettiest air of intimate modesty and charm, "I know there is a matter in which I can help you," and in the daydream Jessica kissed her on the cheek and said,

"Kitty, my dear, what would I ever do without you? What have you come to say?"

"Oh, my darling Mrs. Prescott, it is about poor Laura Hazard. I know, of course, that you must be half out of your mind trying to think of a way to bring Laura to her senses, in this thing about young Trumpeter Rainey. Well, I have come to relieve you of the burden. Let me go talk to her. I will tell her she cannot do this to *you.* She will be wild when she realizes that we all see—we all know. It will save everything. But you must promise not to tell anyone that I have done this for you—let us keep it our secret?"

"Oh, Kitty," murmured Mrs. Prescott with tears in her eyes, "what an angel you are. Yes, do, go, do it, and I'll not tell a soul." The commanding officer's wife now had a brimming smile. "Except one. I will tell my husband, and he will see, as I do, that with such a wife to help him, your husband should be promoted to captain at once!"

When her mind clouded and cleared again, Kitty was again addressing an absent Matthew.

"You will now feel what I have felt ever since you betrayed me," she said in tense but quiet tones. "Oh, no," she said, raising her hand to arrest his reach toward her. "It is too late for that. You should have valued what you had at the time, and now it is too late. But you shall not be spared. When you see me laughing with happiness in the love of another man, then you will have the torments of the damned. What is more, your vain and faithless wife will enjoy the same torments, for I can take young Rainey away from her, if I want to, and if she thinks, and if you think, that I cannot do it, just watch. That's all. I know myself. I am not so humble that I don't know what I can do to a man, any man, when I set out to do it. . . . No. I'm sorry, there is no use pleading. Olin Rainey! Where is he? He's really quite handsome, you know? Wouldn't it be wonderful if he should turn out to be the one I have been waiting for all my life? Olin. What a beautiful name. I wonder how he would say 'Kitty.' "

She lived so intensely in these scenes that when she came out of them into reality, her head ached a little to see where she was, and in what character. But her desires to punish and to love stayed with her, and among those who watched the acting corporal at his duties, she watched him with a hungry purpose.

xxxiii

Where before Rainey had resented his somewhat absurd duty, he now showed a personal hatred for Clanahan which aroused new comment. Rainey could only take out his jealousy and unhappiness on the recruit. Spreading the word that he was about to teach Clanahan the rudiments of horsemanship, and inviting all to witness the awful results when a man who "hates horses" should meet his mount, he made certain of a heavy attendance at the corral, which he would use as a riding hall. The corral was otherwise empty during the day, when all unused mounts were taken out under guard by a grazing party.

Rainey's decision came after a day's anxious waiting for Mrs. Hazard to thank him for his gift, with full reinstatement in her lofty favor. It did not come.

He led in a single horse, a ragged buckskin that stood sixteen hands high. There was no saddle or bridle—only a hackamore. Waiting in the center of the corral, as ordered, was Private Clanahan with a straight line to his mouth. Corporal Rainey led the horse up to him.

"Private Clanahan," he announced with a comical glance at the audience on the corral fence, "this is a horse." Clanahan simply gave him a blue-black gaze, and he grimly continued, "I will now demonstrate how to mount an unsaddled, unbridled horse."

With that, Rainey grasped the horse's mane with his left hand, faced widely out from the horse's left side and then from a quick crouch threw himself in a sailing arc up the horse's barrel and on to his back, where he ended sitting astride. There was a trick to it, as the watching soldiers knew, and it came only from long practice. The crowd cheered and whistled in an effort to give the occasion the feeling of a show. Rainey bowed cordially in acknowledgment and then folded his right leg and brought it neatly over the horse's neck and carelessly slid to the ground, his rump against the horse.

"Private Clanahan," he said in the thick voice of comic anticipation, "you will now repeat the demonstration."

All held their breath except Rainey, who stood back a foot or two and lounged confidently with his weight on one leg.

But not for long. Clanahan, longer and leaner than Rainey, executed the mount-up without a wasted movement, and sat looking coldly down at Rainey, while the gallery hooted and catcalled not at the recruit but at his trainer.

"All right," shouted Rainey in a choked voice, "all right, dismount!" and Clanahan did so, cocked knee and all, just as Rainey had done. "I thought you said you hate horses!" shouted Rainey.

"I did. I do. But I didn't say I couldn't ride 'em."

"Goddamn it, where'd you ever ride a horse?"

"Goddamn it, on my uncle's farm in New York State!"

"Well, by God, you're going to learn the U.S. Cav'ry's way, anyhow!"

The novelty was gone for the crowd. They drifted away.

But the next day, and the next, they came back to see the contest of endurance that was going on.

Rainey was out to break Clanahan and Clanahan was just as

determined to exhaust Rainey. The recruit rode the corral in a circle, at all gaits, bareback, all day long. He turned raw from the hairy, itchy, sweaty hardness of the horse, that he was obliged to grip without stirrups. Endlessly it seemed he was ordered to make his horse lie down—a drill which under attack made the horse a smaller target and in extreme necessity served the trooper as cover.

Clanahan was next issued his saddle and all equipment, including carbine, pistol and saber. Having been shown how to place these on the horse, he was told to place them over and over, with the order, "Faster, Private Clanahan, faster next time," and once when a few were watching with sympathy for the recruit, Rainey was heard to add in professional justification of his grinding hatred, "Your life may depend on it some day."

When drill had to end after all, he contrived extra tasks for Clanahan, such as painting the wooden frames of barracks windows in their adobe walls, or "cleaning and brightening brasses with acid and ashes," or sweeping down the mess-hall floor with wet shavings from the carpenter shop.

Strong feeling was contagious, and could be dangerous, in an isolated group. It was not long before Fort Delivery was broken into two factions in the situation. Major Prescott saw signs of this starting up everywhere. In Lieutenant Hazard he saw a certain gloom which reflected the views he had to face at home as Laura's championship of the abused recruit grew more indignant by the day. The major said to him,

"Females are at perfect liberty to be females, as far as I'm concerned, *until,* by *being so,* they upset the routine of my command, and then, by thunder—"

Matthew gave him a clear look that brought him down. Then? Matthew seemed to say, and then what would the major do? What single, small, effective act would correct matters, without at the same time bringing down about their ears the respected balance by which all must continue to live together in that desert? At the moment Major Prescott had no answer for the lieutenant.

Later he heard that Laura Hazard had gone to Jessica Prescott with her feelings.

Apparently, Laura talked as though she alone had any sense of justice. If a son of *hers* would ever have to go through what Private Clanahan was going through—her eyes blazed, and seeing life through the burden of unborn life which she carried, and forgetting that the

Prescotts had grown sons, she became the champion of all the down-trodden in the world. Jessica was patient, at first. She said,

"We have to leave these things to those who must be responsible for all, not just one. Are you ready to be responsible for your part in this conflict, Laura?"

"My part? What on earth are you talking about, Mrs. Prescott!"

"Oh, rubbish! Have you no idea that you helped to set these two high-tempered troopers against one another?"

Laura rose grandly from her chair beside the Prescotts' cold base burner and prepared to depart.

"I thought perhaps our commanding officer's wife might have some unofficial understanding of simple acts of kindness."

"Ah, well, perhaps I have, Laura my dear. And when you are a commanding officer's wife—as I am sure you will be some day—perhaps you will have too."

Laura tossed her head and went away. Jessica said she was never handsomer.

xxxiv

Early one evening the general feeling reached the point of explosion —not between the principals of the case, but between their opposing partisans. There was a fight between two of the other troopers out behind the blacksmith shop. The commotion was high. Matthew Hazard went to investigate, stopped the fight, sent everybody scattering and reported the affair to Major Prescott.

"Thank you, Matt," said the commanding officer. "Please send Clanahan to me."

While he waited, the major debated several courses, one of which he must follow. His wife always told him that after weighing the obvious solutions to a problem, he generally ended by discarding these in favor of another that he had thought of from the beginning, but had been unable to select with finality until by living with it in his mind he had become thoroughly used to it. "The military mind," she cited in such event, and "Hiram," she said to him, "don't be afraid to be Hiramish. You are always at your best when you are most yourself." Shrugging to excuse her compliment, the major went over his thoughts of the past several days:

"Rainey wants to be a soldier, to lead troops. He is going too far and must be controlled, but I don't want to discourage his ambition.

"Clanahan has to learn the Army, but in the process he must not be allowed to turn sour on it.

"I could take the trumpeter's command away from him.

"I could order the two young men to keep away from each other.

"I could order them to fight, and so spend their hatred on the one side, and sense of injustice on the other.

"But these would be short-term solutions, for in none of them would the two fellows settle the affair for themselves. And only if somehow they do this will the future be right for them here on a post where all have to live so close. Something has to happen that will sharply change their attitudes toward each other. Any change must be for the better, and must contain the seed of a solution at which they will arrive together."

So far so good, he thought. But better was on the way, he was sure, for what his wife would call a Hiramish notion had been edging into his mind for a couple of days. Whether he could put it through reasonably must depend upon two factors. The first of these had to do with the whereabouts of the nearest Apaches. To the best of his knowledge, based on scouting reports of his own patrols, and on information relayed from the other stations, there had been no Indians within a hundred miles of the fort since the engagement at Half-Moon. The renegade tribesmen had found sanctuary in the wastes of northern Sonora, though there was no promise that they would remain there. The second factor was Clanahan's state of mind, character and body, which the major was about to estimate, for he had sent for him.

The recruit reported to the office in a few minutes and stood at attention gazing past the commanding officer. He looked like a figure carved in black walnut. The days of sunlight had tanned him dark. If he was thin when he arrived, he was now thinner but harder, all sinew. Having come as a water-front idler, slack with purposeless freedom, he was now like a wild young animal in a cage, dumb with misery and alert for escape. As always happened with recruits, the same uniform that gaped and bagged on him at first now fitted him.

"Clanahan," said Major Prescott, "have you anything that you'd like to say to me about your life here?"

"No, sir."

But his hands flexed by his thighs and his lips looked white.

"Clanahan, I gather you have not yet had any target practice in your training. Can you shoot?"

"Yes, sir."

"Where'd you learn?"

"All Americans can shoot, sir. I just can."

"Yes. That is so."

A light fired in the young man's eyes. He was ready to shoot someone. The major could guess whom.

"How long is your term of enlistment, Clanahan?"

An expression like a racing shadow went over the recruit's face—an Irish flash of countenance that told of what despair thrust itself through his heart for an instant as he faced his future.

"Five years, sir."

He wet his dried lips. He darted his glance to the corners of the room behind the major as though trying to find freedom. He looked to his commander as close as could be to breaking into pieces. In another hour or so, a day or two, he might desert. And yet, thought the major, Clanahan, though the motive behind the treatment he had suffered was a bad one, was now as a result, physically at least, a hard soldier instead of a suspicious recruit. He seemed ready for the Hiramish plan. It had a risk in it; but almost any decision in the Army included a risk, and the major took it.

"Clanahan, I'm going to give you an important responsibility. It may be dangerous one, but I think you're ready for real duty."

For the first time the recruit looked at the officer. Responsibility? Duty? He? The lowest of the low? He swallowed and his eyes came alive with a gleam of hope.

"Yes, sir?"

"At exactly thirty minutes after taps—you have a watch?—you get yourself quietly out of barracks and meet me at the west sally port. Say nothing to anybody else about this. Don't be observed. If you think some of the men in your barrack room are still awake, then don't leave till they're all asleep. I'll wait for you. But make it as quickly as you can. I will have a horse and all equipment ready for you. We have some distance to ride tonight."

"*We* ride, distance, tonight—yes sir!"

He was alerted and taken by all that, which the major purposely kept as mysterious as possible. A sense of adventure was a large part of the major's plan.

"Are my instructions quite clear, Clanahan?"

"Yes, sir!"

The major dismissed him. He saluted with energy and strode out with new spirit.

"Now," said the major to himself as he enacted his thoughts. "I must go to find Matt and complete arrangements in which I will need his help. He will take over as officer of the guard, and relieve the sentries at the west sally port, sending them on an errand up the arroyo eastward just before half-past ten to investigate a suspicious —and imaginary—movement. They will be instructed to remain for an hour to make certain that there is nothing there before they return to report to him. And by then," concluded Hiram, rubbing his head with a certain pleasurable excitement, "Private Clanahan and I should be well on our way over the desert in the full moonlight of this night."

xxxv

At ten-forty Major Prescott led Clanahan out the sally port toward the grazing pasture where the troop horses fed by day on meager and bitter grasses. The two riders crossed it the long way and rode out to the open desert beyond toward the southwest. For what seemed a long time to Clanahan they rode at a walk and the major, feeling when Clanahan must burst into speech, hushed him with a raised hand; but at last they were safely beyond all possible notice from the fort, and matters could be explained a little further.

"We are riding out to a place called Arrel Spring, some thirteen or fourteen miles from the fort," said Major Prescott. "We have used it from time to time as a bivouac, and Apaches did so too, at one time. Now I want this spring and all the country that can be seen from there to be kept under observation for a period not to exceed three days. I have to know what the condition of the water is. Don't drink it until you inspect it. Use your canteens—I put two on your saddle. Dig to see if bones or carrion lie in the spring. Watch to see what animals, if any, come to visit it. So far as we know, the raiding Indians are all camped in Mexico, but if any should appear nearby, we have to know it. I'll show you where to hide if you have reason to think Indians are around. We must know all these things because we may want to set up an advance camp there if our garrison extends the patrol. I've picked you to do this duty."

"Yes, sir."

There was awe in the recruit's voice which he tried to veil. It was cool in the night, and under the moon the distant country was the color of turquoise against the sky. The riders rode toward the southern tip of a far mountain. Arrel Spring lay in a line between that tip and the fort to the rear. There was mystery over the desert —a mystery of calm and vastness. The major felt it, as always, and assumed that Clanahan did too, until a question showed the direction of Clanahan's thoughts.

"Sir, does Corporal Rainey know I am doing this?"

"No."

Clanahan could not suppress a sharp little laugh of gratification.

"A few more things, Clanahan," said the major.

He was to make no fires, day or night. He was to sleep in the early night, and make himself awaken well before dawn. The major quoted the axiom of the Indian fighter—"When you see Apache sign, be careful; and when you see *no* sign, be *more* careful." If by chance he ran out of water and had to subsist without it, he could quiet his thirst a little by putting a pebble or a twig in his mouth to suck. Before he slept on the ground he would be wise to scrape out a little trench in a half-circle around the place for his head, and continue it in a straight line away from each side of his body, so that if it should rain in the night, the running water would be channeled away from him.

Clanahan listened without comment; but the major felt the young man's alert excitement, and something hung heavy inside his ribs when he thought of a youth alone in the wilderness for the first time.

They came to Arrel Spring after midnight. They approached cautiously, but they found it abandoned. The spring seeped out of sand and rock at the base of a low desert terrace whose face was several yards wide and about twenty feet high at the highest. A single cottonwood grew by the spring. In the crown of the terrace was a narrow rocky gash like a miniature canyon, five feet deep below its rim. It could be approached and entered from the top. A man could hide in it and see the spring below. To conceal his horse from the spring side he would have to tether it out of sight where the rearward slope of the terrace faded into the flat desert.

The major and Clanahan went over the ground in the bright moonlight. As the soldier was about to leap down into the little cleft the major stopped him.

"Do it by daylight, when you can see what may be in the shadow. It is a perfect place for snakes."

"Say—" whispered Clanahan, shocked at his own carelessness.

The major inspected his rations once again, his arms, ammunition, canteens and leather, all of which he had put together himself. All was in order. The major bit down his doubts now that he was about to leave his man on duty here. He said,

"You stay here for three days, and then come back, unless I send someone after you."

"Yes, sir."

"Think you'll manage?"

"Yes, sir—and thanks, sir."

While the commanding officer was worrying about him, Clanahan was smiling in the white moonlight. The major gave him a small brass compass from his pocket and told him how to line up off the needle to bring him home, said, "Very well, then, Clanahan," and rode off northeast by the stars.

He reached the sally port between three and four o'clock. The sentry was ready for him. Matthew had told the guard that he had passed the commanding officer out, and to keep a strict watch for his return. After being challenged and passed back in, the major asked,

"Anything to report, guard?"

"No, sir."

"No activity earlier tonight at the arroyo?"

"No, sir. The first guard detail went to see, but found nothing."

"Very well. Carry on—" But he spoke with accents of doubt, as if this night were charged with mystery. In fact, before many hours, there would be a mystery, so far as the troopers were concerned, to end the feud of the past weeks. The major went to the corral, unsaddled, turned his horse in, and walked to headquarters. All was quiet but his thoughts. It remained to be seen what Acting Corporal Rainey would feel about the disappearance of his command. If the major was right, suddenly and without explanation to be deprived of his "army" should make the first sharp change in Rainey's attitude. "After that," said the major, "we shall see whether, given an opportunity to do so, the two young troopers can compose their troubles for themselves."

Not long after reveille the major in his parlor heard Rainey's heavy steps on the piazza of headquarters. The trumpeter entered the hall and turned into the office opposite the living quarters and paced about the office waiting for his commander with impatience. Once he went to the hall and listened for him at the parlor door, then returned to the office. In easy time the major walked in there. Rainey exclaimed excitedly,

"Sir, he's gone!"

"Who is gone, corporal?—At ease."

"Sir, my man is gone!"

The major was interested in the possessive pronoun.

"Clanahan?" he asked.

"Yes, sir! I've looked high and low, and he's not in the fort!"

"Ah, well, he can't be far."

"Oh, yes, he can, sir. A horse with full equipment is missing too!"

"That is impossible, Rainey. Stop talking nonsense. The guards were posted all night."

"I know, sir, but it's true. Nobody saw him go."

"I thought you were responsible for him, corporal?"

Rainey was wild with professional outrage. He was not comforted by the major's cold stare which rested first on his chevrons and then on his face. The major said,

"What have you done to recover him, trooper?"

"Sir, I have been out the gate, and I found hoof marks, but they led to the grazing pasture, and there are thousands of hoof marks there, and you can't follow among them"—as the major well knew and intended. He asked,

"And what do you propose to do next?"

"I could look for him if I knew where, sir."

"I think you'd better. Ride widening circles around the fort, but always keep us in sight. And while you're thinking of what might happen to *you* out there, you might also think of what might be happening to *him*."

Rainey caught a breath at that. For the first time he thought of Clanahan as a man—a man like himself, who could be lost, wounded, or killed, and who could feel what would hurt. The major decided that this was enough for the moment and dismissed him with orders to report back late in the day.

The day was a Sunday, and all day the fort was like a small community visited by the impossible and the ultimate—mystery or death. Speculation among troopers free from duty on the Sabbath ranged from the morosely suspicious to the happily fantastic. No one questioned that it was proper for Rainey to be out looking for Clanahan or some sign of his passage. A dozen times the whirling dust devils of the winds had been mistaken for a horseman's dust. But the desert on every side was empty all day long except when Rainey rode back an hour before retreat. On Sunday, Fort Delivery held dress parade and he must give the trumpet music. He reported to Major Prescott with nothing to report.

"Sir," he said, looking sickly under his freckles, "we'd better do something about it."

"Let me ask you something, Rainey. Have you considered why Clanahan might have gone?"

Plainly he had, but was obliged to reply,

"No, sir. What do you mean, sir?"

"Maybe somebody here has been pretty hard on him."

Silence. Then, in false innocence,

"Yes, sir?"

"Have you considered who may have been?"

Rainey threw his hand awkwardly and answered in a rush,

"Sir, I only meant it for his own good, and the good of the troop—"

"Bosh, Rainey. Maybe Clanahan has deserted. Do you know what the Army can do to deserters?"

"Yes, sir. Cranshaw, right here. I saw it."

"What can they do, Rainey, more than they did to Cranshaw?"

"They make them forfeit all pay and allowances they ought to get." Rainey paused to gather details which soldiers often talked of. The major nodded and he continued huskily. "If so ordered, they have their head shaved, and they have to get naked from the waist up and then they get fifty lashes on their back with a rawhide whip, and everybody stands there in formation to watch." He paused, sweating. He did not want to remember or tell more. The major made him.

"What else, Rainey?"

"They make them pull down their breeches and they brand them on their right and left hip with a letter D an inch and a half big."

"Yes. Then?"

"Then they cut off all their insignia and buttons and give them a dishonorable discharge. They march them off the post in front of fixed bayonets and the band plays."

His mouth dried. He saw all this happening to Clanahan, and he knew if it happened who would be partly to blame. In spite of himself he had come to know Clanahan well. At what point might a constant enemy turn into a friend? The major was now certain that he saw Rainey begin to feel the other half of command—not only to direct, but to protect.

"Sir," said Rainey, "will they do that to him?" For the first time in his life he was shaken by the thought that by his own acts he might wreak consequences in the life of another. "They just *can't* do that to him."

"I don't see why not," said the major, "if he deserted and is caught. It is a traditional punishment provided by the Army."

"Sir, maybe he will just come back, and everything will clear up," said the trumpeter energetically, pressing upon fate a wish so strong that it was like the incantation of a savage.

"Maybe he will and maybe he won't. We must wait and see."

Major Prescott then dismissed Acting Corporal Rainey to the hardest kind of punishment—waiting for an outcome which he terribly desired but was powerless to influence. The major wanted Rainey to have a full day of that.

In a few minutes the garrison formed for parade. When it was over, the major said to his wife, who knew all his thoughts and acts,

"Jess, I'll never forget the sound of 'To the Colors' and 'Retreat' as the trumpeter played them this afternoon."

"As music," she said, "they could not have been worse. Quite unlike him."

"Just so. But they tell me something I want to hear about Acting Corporal Rainey."

xxxvi

"He looks like a lost soul," said Kitty Mainwaring to herself when she saw Trumpeter Rainey during the next day as she came from a call at the laundry to return to her quarters. He looked at her but did not see her.

"Good morning, Rainey!" she called out in her most companionable voice. The light gilded her hair, and a beat at her heart gave her the feeling of being pretty. It was a feeling she both loved and dreaded, for once it was alive in her, it must grow, she knew, until it should find expression, for the pleasure of a man. The trumpeter came to himself and said,

"Good morning, ma'am."

His voice was hollow and rueful. The poor boy, she thought. She paused in her walk. Her head felt wonderfully clear with sweet powers that gave her strength and certainty. It was in her hands to bring consolation to this downcast trooper. Convinced of her own innocence, and yet yielding happily to obscure thrusts of desire, she said,

"Corporal, I do think it is a shocking shame that you have been treated this way by that little coward."

Rainey's eyes opened wide at this idea.

"Clanahan, you mean, ma'am? Coward?"

"Yes, coward. He has run away, hasn't he? He could not take the discipline you were trying to teach him, could he? I think he owed you more than this, and I am sure all of your other good friends here think so too."

Her sympathy spoke to him, and he had an impulse to forget his troubles in seeing just what she might be meaning otherwise by her presence here with him, for she was looking fresh and sweet, and her eyes were soft and heavy-lidded, and she held herself tenderly pulled together at shoulders and breast as though feeling a caress. But when she saw that she had made her effect, she was content for the time, and with a quick, sibilant breath she lifted her head, smiled and went on her way, leaving the acting corporal in a state of uncertainty and interest. She knew—she felt it almost physically —that he followed her with his eyes. A small pit of joy made itself felt somewhere within her. As always, she was grateful for proof of her charm.

Rainey, after her passing, lapsed into his gloom again. The usual work went on, and he took his part in it, but in such a disconsolate spirit that even those troopers who had been most bitter toward him now seemed to go out of their way to cheer him up. None succeeded for long. Major Prescott saw him frequently during the day and found errands for him to run. Between times, Rainey waited on orderly duty in the headquarters office or on the piazza. Every time he looked at the major he silently besought him to *do something,* find Clanahan, end the awful uncertainty which hung over the fort. Could not the officer in command manage fate by giving orders? But the major gave him back his look each time and left misery—and responsibility—with him. Rainey grew almost surly in speaking to the major. "Very good," thought Major Prescott.

Rainey was not the only one who held views.

Laura Hazard hoped the commanding officer was satisfied now that the thing had happened which anybody could have foretold must happen if a high-strung youth like Clanahan were persecuted beyond endurance. Under strict orders not to tell Laura the real state of affairs, Matthew had no means by which to soften her opinion. But she was a lady, and ladies did what they could for those of their friends who make foolish mistakes, and on several small pretexts she found occasion to run in at Quarters 1 to see the Prescotts. To Mrs. Prescott, Laura brought little bulletins of how she felt in her condition, and to the major, little snippets of army gossip gleaned from letters out of the recent mails, and in general, indications that if she could judge, she could also forgive.

"Laura," said Jessica to her husband, "is a lamb, and I adore her, but I do wish she didn't feel obliged to put us at our ease."

For everybody's sake Major Prescott was glad when he judged the moment had come to get on with his plans. One morning he called Rainey in and said,

"Corporal, I have a little job for you."

The acting corporal attended him in bruised silence.

"Do you know where Arrel Spring is?"

"Yes, sir."

"All right. Saddle up with full equipment and ride on over there."

"Alone, sir?"

"Yes. We have no reports of Indians around here recently. But keep a sharp eye out anyhow. When you get there, I want you to measure how far down the water is in the spring, even if you have to dig for it, and to see if it can flow enough to water say a detachment of eight men, and their horses. Get me this information, and don't loiter. You report straight back, hear?"

"Yes, sir. —Maybe I'll come across the trail of that no-account New Yorker."

"Well, if you do, bring him in. But you needn't give him hell, hear? I'll do that."

"Yes, sir."

"You ought to do it easy in two-three hours each way. Take a good, fast horse, and if you see any 'sign,' turn right around and get back to me as fast as you can. If there are any Indians around, we'll want to know it."

"Yes, sir."

"All right. That's all. Git."

Half an hour later the major saw Rainey move out through the sally port.

"It is now my turn to wait," mused Hiram, "and I'm no good at it." Night fell without Rainey's return.

After midnight Hiram had not yet found sleep. He lay still beside Jessica, who slept at peace. If Rainey had not returned, neither, then, had Clanahan. Hiram could not command his thoughts. His mind was lighted like a stage where he could see all that could have befallen his two young troopers, to whom he had wanted to give a chance, after first separating them by unexpected means, to come together and on their own terms to make up their differences, away from the people and conditions which had bred these. That this must follow, Hiram still believed, after watching Rainey for the past two days—but only if nothing unforeseen had happened to the two of them. Had Rainey reached the spring? Had Clanahan been there when he arrived? Had their hatred started up anew? Had they fought? Both were armed. Plenty of men had shot their differences out on the frontier. Had they? Or if they had started back, were they now lost?

His impulse was to go to find them; but if all that he had hoped for had happened, might not at least some of its good be undone by any sign of oversolicitousness on his part? There was just as much chance that the return of the troopers had been delayed by something harmless as by something dangerous. A mistake, thought the major, a mistake often made by commanders was to try to do everything themselves, even to the point of carrying out orders given to others to execute. Patience.

But all his thoughts as they swung back and forth through the still hours could not conceal what they worked so hard to conceal from the major in alternate anxiety and optimism. If all his scouting information had been faulty, and if Indians. . . .

He sat up. What did he hear? From the sentry post at the sally port a challenge sang out and in a moment the sound of horses entering the quadrangle reached the commanding officer. Quietly he left his bed and crossed to the office to look out the window, pulling on breeches and shirt. Were these visitors who came so late, or the two soldiers he awaited? If they were visitors, their horses would be put in the corral and they themselves would be taken to beds in the barracks, and he would not see them until morning. If the others, they would, seeing his light, report to him without delay.

He did not have long to wait.

Hearing the thumping walk of horses coming toward headquarters, he felt something big and cool strike about his vitals, where for hours there had been something hot and tight. In a hurry he turned to his desk, pulled out a sheaf of War Department orders and busied himself with these, while picking up one of several dead cigars from his ash bowl. When discovered, he would be a perfect picture of an overworked man busy late into the night with a stubborn problem on paper.

Outside headquarters the riders dismounted, came thundering up the steps and into the hall, and knocked on the office door.

"Come in!" growled the commanding officer, "and be quiet about it!"

They came. They were rubbed with dirt off the ground. Clanahan had a black three-day beard and on his left hand a bloody bandage. They were unbuttoned and gaunt with fatigue and their eyes were haunted by excitement and they scowled over smiles of exultation. Lining up facing the major, they both saluted, and as the senior soldier, Rainey said loudly, staring at nothing,

"Sir, Acting Corporal Rainey and Private Clanahan reporting back from duty, sir!"

"Rest." The major glanced impassively at the clock on his wall. "Aren't you somewhat late?"

"Yes, sir!" they said in unison, and standing closely side by side they nudged each other for what they knew. It was all they could do not to laugh out loud over the surprise they had for their commanding officer.

"Well, what do you have to report?"

They nudged again, each to start the other talking. The result was that both started and the major held up his hand. They stopped, and he pointed at Clanahan's dirty bandage.

"Are you hurt? What is that?"

"It's nothing, sir. Just a cut from a chip of rock that flew off when a bullet hit near me."

"What bullet?"

They looked sideways at each other with pleasure now that they had got to the point.

"One of the bullets fired from out in front of the spring by the Indian, sir," said Rainey.

"You met an Indian?"

"Two of them, sir," said Clanahan.

"We didn't exactly *meet* them, sir," said Rainey, "they had us under attack for hours—"

"—An hour, anyway, sir," amended Clanahan.

"Yes, more like an hour," agreed Rainey, "one out front, and one up in back, on top of that slope above the spring."

The major stood up and sat down again.

"By all thunder! You mean you had a skirmish?"

"A battle, sir," stated Rainey.

The major nodded at chairs behind the two soldiers.

"Pull up and sit down, and let me get the whole thing. Clanahan, you start. You were there first."

Clanahan said nothing much happened all day Sunday. The first thing he did was to clear out the little rock rift above the spring so he could establish himself there. It was wise to have waited for daylight, for actually there was a rattlesnake among the cool rocks of the wedge-shaped cleft. He shot it and threw it up to the bare top of the terrace. Hours later a shadow came suddenly brushing across him out of nowhere, and he looked up, and saw it was the shadow of a buzzard, circling earthward to feast on the dead snake. He smiled at being so startled by such a natural thing. No other creature visited the spring that day, or the next. Late on Monday he went down to the water and using his saber dredged for carrion or refuse, and found an animal skull, a coyote's, perhaps.

"Possibly thrown in there by an Apache Indian," said the major. "It is the sort of thing they might do, either for sacrifice, propitiation, or to cast a spell. —Go on."

Monday night was peaceful, except that it seemed to Clanahan he never saw so many shooting stars. Before dawn on Tuesday the wind blew and woke him. He stayed awake. He ate the last of his issue canned peaches, and was glad they were gone. It was odd how sleepy it made him to sit there in the rocks and look at the spring, and then the whole desert scape in front of him, and watch for anything living. It was funny how much he thought about things, and how different some things began to look to him.

"What sort of things?" the major asked.

Oh, he didn't know, exactly. Oh, things like the Army, and how they had to do things. Things certainly seemed to look different when you were off by yourself for a long time. You got so you wanted to see *anybody,* you wouldn't mind seeing your worst enemy after a long time in a place like that. Noontime was hot and made him drowsy. The sun was directly overhead. He was half-asleep when he saw a shadow go over him again from above, fast, like a blink of an eyelid, and he thought, Yes, another big bird, and he looked up, saying out loud, "You can't fool me again," but there was no bird. He leaped to his feet and peered over the edge of the cleft and ducked down like lightning. A few feet away, crouching to cock and aim a rifle was a young Indian, who, after looking in upon him, had swiftly dodged back for concealment. Beyond him were two horses, standing near Clanahan's own which was tethered halfway down the slope behind.

Clanahan saw this much in his one empowered look. His heart began to thunder away and somehow he felt wildly pleased at his circumstances. On his saber he lifted his forage cap just over the edge of the upper rocks and at once the Indian rifle fired. Clanahan came up to fire back. In his haste he missed the Indian, who rose and ran back to the horses, twice falling prone at exactly the instant before Clanahan fired again. "Two horses, two horses," Clanahan kept thinking, without then just knowing why.

In another moment his thoughts cleared, for from below him, about fifty yards out on the plain before the spring, another rifle cracked like a bullwhip, and he turned and saw where the smoke drifted over clumps of mustard-yellow rabbit bush, and he did not know which bush concealed the Indian who belonged with the second horse. Clanahan fired generally at the clump, without effect. He turned to look down the slope behind and saw that the first Indian was working to untether the cavalry mount. Horse thieves! thought Clanahan, and fired to make him take cover.

Just afterward, the rifle beyond the spring fired again, and Clanahan turned hoping to see exactly its position, but again he was too late. He was in almost a direct line between the two Indians. Dealing with one whom he could see, he could not turn fast enough to detect the other one. It seemed to him that his neck was on a swivel, as he kept turning so often and so rapidly from one to the other. "Holy gee!" he said when, facing for an instant to the plain, he saw dust coming after a horseman who approached in the distance. "Another one!"

"That was me, sir!" exploded Rainey. He had contained himself with much strain, and the major now nodded to him to tell what he knew.

Rainey was riding along at a slow trot in the hot noontime and everything seemed so still until he began to notice an odd little sound now and then. Something, at irregular intervals, would go *crack!* somewhere over the desert, and he would look about for what it could be. Soldiers had often noticed how in absolute emptiness under the bearing sun such a sound would go off, dry, sharp, hard to locate. It made them think now of a breaking stick, again of a hard-shelled insect. Or was it a rock cracking? But rocks cracked at night, from cold. He gave it up and rode on, until above the mound of the terrace of Arrel Spring he saw a feather of smoke that vanished swiftly, and he leaned forward with his horse reined in, and heard the crack again, and he knew what he was coming toward. It was rifle fire.

He didn't know what to do. He nearly turned to run away as fast as his horse could carry him.

"You better not of!" exclaimed Clanahan, looking first at the major, and then at Rainey, with a grin.

Rainey showed him the back of his hand in a comic swipe, arrested before it became a blow, and went on talking.

He had dismounted and led his horse cautiously forward. What made him do it instead of running was this: he reasoned that if there was shooting, it wasn't Indians shooting at each other, it was more likely to be Indians against white men. If that was so, he had a soldier's job to do. He carefully came closer. He could not say just the moment when he could see sharp detail of what he peered at. It was always strange how as distance contracted in the desert you could suddenly see rocks and earth wrinkles and bushes where before you had seen only pale shimmers and depthless foregrounds. The firing continued, now near, now far. Soon Rainey could see that some of the shots came from among bushes on the ground in front of the spring, where whoever fired was absorbed by thin shadow under the brush. Other shots came in reply from the cleft in the terrace. He began to discern movement now in the narrow rock opening. Always coming slowly closer in the strong noon light that shafted down to the rocks he next saw color. He saw blue. He saw a uniform. He couldn't tell anything about how he made up his mind to what he did after that, he just knew he did it, as if something had knocked him on the back of the head and told him to do it.

He moved toward the clump of yellow brush until he came within what he was sure was dead-shot range. Dismounted, he made his horse lie down, and he fired toward the clump from a position left oblique to it. An Indian rolled himself half around toward him, showing himself for the first time. Just as he got his rifle up, he threw it in the air and fell back, and then Rainey heard the delayed sound of a shot from the rocks, and saw the man in uniform wave at him. He waved back, mounted, and rode to the Indian to see if he was dead. He was dead.

"The most beautiful shot you ever saw," said Rainey. "It got him between the ribs and must have hit his heart. That trooper can handle a carbine."

Clanahan cleared his throat and stated,

"Rainey gave me the target, sir."

Major Prescott bit down hard on his dead cigar to keep from showing anything at this exchange of compliments.

Rainey resumed his account impatiently. He mounted and rushed the terrace. Then he tied his horse to the cottonwood tree, scrambled up into the cleft, and found the recruit there. He stood amazed and started to speak but Clanahan pulled him roughly down beside him, and Rainey knew why when a bullet went stinging against the rock just behind where his head had been visible above the cleft. A splinter of rock flew loose and hit Clanahan's left hand, making a deep cut. "You got another Indian out there?" asked Rainey and Clanahan nodded. They held a consultation, and when Rainey understood the problem, he took command and made a plan. After waiting a minute or two to catch his breath, he would go down to his horse at the spring. He would ride around the flank of the terrace in a wide arc to surprise the remaining enemy from the rear and draw his fire. When Clanahan heard a shot or a yell, he was to come up with his sights over the edge of the rocks and fire. It seemed like a good plan, and Rainey remembered that just before he left to carry out his part, they shook hands on it.

"He forgot to mention how long it might take to get around behind the other Indian, sir," said Clanahan. "I thought he'd never get there."

"I took it on a real wide circle," said Rainey. "I didn't want the Apache to catch me out of the corner of his eye, did I?"

"Finally I heard a shot," said Clanahan.

"That was me," said Rainey again.

"The corporal was way out behind the Indian," said Clanahan, "and the Indian turned toward him, and then the corporal fired again."

"So did you," said Rainey. "We fired at the same time, exactly the same time. —You got him."

"I did not. You did."

"It was yours," insisted Rainey. "I could tell when we looked at the body."

"Sir, he's a liar," declared Clanahan. "He did it all. I'd have been a dead duck if—"

"Who's a liar!" demanded Rainey with his jaw out.

For a moment they glared in their desire to yield credit to each other.

"Men!" said Major Prescott, "hold on!"

Out of respect, they eased up, and then accepted their triumph together. They looked at each other, and Major Prescott knew their trouble was over. He rose and went to his wall cabinet from which he brought out a bottle of whisky and three glasses. He poured three drinks. Lifting his and nodding to them to do the same, he said,

"I'm proud of you both."

They exchanged a glance as if to say, He better be.

"Now," said the major, "why did you take so long getting home?"

"When we fired last time, so close to the horses, one of the Indian horses broke and ran," said Rainey. "It took us a long time to catch him up. We wanted to bring them both in."

"And did you?"

"Yes, sir."

"And then," said Clanahan in his turn, for it was their joint story and they wanted to tell it together, "we talked a long time about how to bury the two Apaches."

"—But we had no way to do it, so we had to leave them to the big birds. We straightened them out right where they dropped, and folded their arms"—Rainey was proud of the proprieties—"and I got Clanahan to say a prayer, very elegant, as he is Irish Catholic. Everything had to be done twice, in different places."

"Then we had something to eat and talked some more, and before we knew it it was getting dark. We started out, and got lost after dark."

"You had a compass."

"Yes, sir, but I didn't want to make a light to see it by.

"Finally, after midnight," said Rainey, "we began to make out your light, here, in the office, sir. It got us home."

"We was very glad," said Clanahan.

"So am I," replied Major Prescott.

The two soldiers were so tired they didn't want to move, even to find sleep. Before sending them off, Major Prescott had one more instructive endurance for Acting Corporal Rainey.

"All right, Rainey, now how about your report?"

He was startled.

"Sir, I have told you all about it."

"Why did I send you to the spring?"

"Oh." The trumpeter rubbed his head in the manner of his commanding officer. "To measure how far down the water is."

"Yes. Well?"

"Sir, I forgot to do it."

Clanahan gave the major a pleading look, and said,

"Sir, we can tell you that. It's down from the surface about that much—" and he measured his left forearm with his right forefinger.

"I didn't send you to find out, I sent Rainey. I'm glad to have the information, though. —Corporal, why did you forget?"

"All the excitement, I guess, sir."

"I can understand that. Do you understand why I brought it up now, even after the great things you have both told me about?"

Rainey turned his whisky glass slowly from one hand to the other, and said,

"I guess to have me remember to obey orders, sir."

"I think you will, too. Well"—they all stood up—"you'd better get your horses taken care of and get some sleep. I'll look over the Indian ponies in the morning. They may tell us something. And corporal?"

"Yes, sir?"

"You may keep those stripes permanently. Tell Private Clanahan" —Clanahan listened with a burning interest in his dark-shadowed eyes—"tell Private Clanahan that we can't promote him till he's had more time in the service. But you tell him he's promoted himself the first step, from recruit to soldier."

In the morning Major Prescott sent for Lieutenant Hazard.

"I want you to look over those Indian ponies that were brought in last night. I'll go with you."

"That was a story, wasn't it, sir? It's all over the post already."

The major gave a low laugh made of wet wheezes.

"I suppose," he said, "when they catch their breaths, those two will wonder how they happened to meet at Arrel Spring, and they will ask each other if it was all my doing. They will say yes, and have some second thoughts. But in light of the results, I don't care if my little plot is exposed, or if the rest of the troop will try to figure me out all over again, the way men always do with their officers." The major lifted his stubby hand, screwed up his face and adopted a voice. " 'How did he know?' " he asked in the character of an enlisted man, " 'how did he know that there would be an Indian fight where them two troopers would have to face a common danger, and that they would come out alive, and come out friends?' " Resuming himself, the major said, "I did not know, of course. But that was a risk I had to accept. I did so then, and I do so now. What I know clearly, Matthew, and what the rest will feel, is that by the new league of Corporal Rainey and Private Clanahan the total security of Fort Delivery, and of this United States Territory, is improved, if only by a fraction. I must say I find this gratifying, in a professional way."

Matthew smiled and mused over the major's part in the story. Then he said,

"Sir, after what we've been talking about, what I have to ask may sound a little foolish. But I think in view of how all this began, I'd better not make any decision on it by myself. There might be much in it that could go wrong."

"Speak up."

"Laura wants me to have Rainey and Clanahan to come to the quarters, and tell her the whole story, and have some lemonade and sand tarts, in their first free moment. Do you think I'd better, sir?"

"Did she ask for them both together?"

"Yes, sir."

"Then that's all right," replied the major. "Now let's get on over to the corral and have a look at those ponies. I would not be astonished to find the U.S. Cavalry brand on them."

But when they found the two horses in question, no brand showed —only wide and deep scars where not long ago someone had burned away with searing swipes of red iron all traces of whatever brands may have been there.

"They took some trouble about it, didn't they?" said the major. "You could not tell for the life of you whether it was the Army's brand or a rancher's that they burned away." He leaned down and took up the left hind hoof of one of the horses. The horse flinched and the fabric of muscle under his coat did not shift smoothly. The major led the horse forward in a few steps. The horse limped slightly. "Yes," he said, "it is clumsy, they burned so deep that they have permamently injured this animal, and probably the other, too. Well, Matthew, who *did* own these horses, then?"

"Certainly an owner who had them branded."

"Yes, yes, who was it?"

"Sir, I cannot read any trace of a brand."

"No, but there is another condition which speaks plainly of the real owners of these stolen animals."

Matthew gazed at the horses, and then his recognition cleared, and he said sharply,

"Of course, major. These were army mounts."

"Tell me how you know."

"Their coats. These have been clipped not very long ago. The hair is long, but not as long as the hair on an Indian pony or a cowboy's, which are never clipped. I should have seen it right off."

"Better late than not at all. I believe these were some of the horses stolen at Ransom Rock. Their presence hereabouts means that our elusive friends still have us on their minds. I trust they will know we return the compliment if they ever find the bodies left yesterday at Arrel Spring by our young men. I'll go and prepare a report." The major glared at Matthew impersonally. "I wish I had a star on this shirt collar and a brigade of even two squadrons for just thirty days! What I would show them!"

Space, distance, uncertain information, the dead weight of inertia in the government back home—all these were present among Major Prescott's occasion for honest rage.

xxxvii

Winter came not with snow and ice but with cutting winds bearing whole skies full of dust out of Mexico. In the bitter dust storms people had to lean forward if they would walk through them, and turn their heads aside, and shut their eyes. The winds were sometimes so strong that a weaker person was grateful for the guiding hand of a stronger. Corporal Rainey came upon Kitty Mainwaring in the afternoon of such a storm as she was struggling to cross the parade on her way to Soapsuds Row.

"It's a bad one, ma'am. Better let me give you a hand."

He put his hand under her arm. She stopped walking. The wind tore her words out of her mouth.

"Take your hands off me, you insolent brute!" she cried, but he heard only her furious tone. He stepped away and in the cold stinging blow of sand his face turned hot and dark.

"Excuse *me,* ma'am," he said, and walked rapidly on ahead of Kitty. Now having lost him, out of what false self, she bent into the wind and ran as well as she could after him. As they came to the buildings on the far side of the quadrangle, she overtook him, and in the lee of the smithy, she caught her breath and detained him with a gesture.

"Oh, corporal, you must forgive me, I did not recognize you, I was so startled; you know I would not speak so to you!"

He was grave and honorable in the name of his hurt. He gazed across her shoulder and said colorlessly,

"Never mind, ma'am. It won't happen again."

She twisted her hands together in pretty anguish.

"Oh, *please* don't be offended with me, we are so few people so far away out here, if any of us can take an interest in any of us, we ought to be grateful and take advantage of—" She paused. She saw Matthew coming out of the smithy. Her heart tingled at her opportunity. She put her hands to her cheeks and gazed up at Rainey with whimsical charm, like a lovely young woman considering an appeal to her heart. How often she had gazed up at Matthew in the same way! What a pang it would visit upon him to see her look so upon another! She felt her powers rise and she put her hand forward as if to touch the corporal and then withdrew it as though she had approached it too close to flames. Her little laugh rang out and she buried her face in her hands as though sweet confusion forced her to hide from it. Matthew walked by and against the wind which swept past the corner where they took refuge he called out cheerfully to them,

"Hi, Kitty! Hi, corporal! Isn't this a regular blizzard!"

Leaning into the wind, Matthew began to dogtrot away to his quarters. Kitty dropped her hands. Matthew had seen nothing, or if he had seen anything, it had meant nothing to him, which was worse. Kitty's eyes began to shine with determination whose purpose was not yet clear even to her. It showed itself in another instant, when she seized the corporal's wrist in a twiglike grasp whose great strength made him open his eyes.

"This is not the time for it," she said in rapid breathless exhausts, "but it will come. It will come."

Pulling him awkwardly off balance in a final communication of her feeling, which held as much exasperation as desire, she dashed past him to resume her errand. Rainey wondered what it was whose time would come. He knew what he wished it was, but when Mrs. Mainwaring, for reasons unknown to him, acted like three different women within five minutes, he thought he had better not get his hopes up for nothing.

xxxviii

It was like Mrs. Huntleigh Greenleaf that her answer to Matthew's letter should be addressed not to him but to her daughter.

> The Castle,
> Fort Porter, New York,
> Wednesday.

Laura my darling,

You must listen to me, now, my darling, and pay attention to what is for your own welfare. Your husband wrote to me soon after certainty of your condition was known to all of us. It is of course an occasion for great joy and your father and I and your brother in his dutiful letters home to us are all full of happiness and all send you their congratulations. It is the most happy occasion which can visit a family, and I am proud and grateful that in all our life as a family, we have all known what such happiness is. But of course everyone must be sensible and responsible in taking part in the happy event, and it is this which your husband wrote to me about, and I am grateful, as well as astonished, that he should feel just as I do about what must be done for your safety and the proper care for your baby.

You realise what this is. You cannot doubt that my experience and judgement in these matters are superior to your own. Your father agrees with me. I know Harvey would if I consulted him. After all, I have had two children, and I may say that they have had every advantage and condition to make them strong, healthy, and worthy of their position. But would this be so if I had consented to have them brought into the world under primitive conditions in the midst of danger and squalor? No, not at all. You must agree. What you must do, and what your husband feels you must do, and what I insist that you do, is come to your loving mother, and let her make all arrangements for the birth of your baby here at The Castle with splendid doctors at hand and expert nurses and every comfort. Indeed I have already sent for the decorator Mr. Kleinschmidt in Buffalo to come and redecorate the upstairs north bedroom for you. The room next door will be made into your sitting room and the nursery will be right next to that. So you see. I understand it is to be in April. Well April is lovely here as you know; the winter will be breaking and there will be less risk of pneumonia. Your father has always been subject to pneumonia and I would never allow you to take a risk of pneumonia with your baby so you see this will be the right time of year. I think you should plan to arrive in February or early March at the latest. Then you can get into a nice comfortable regimen before the happy event is consummated.

Now Laura my darling you know I would never do anything but for reasons of what is best for you. So plan to come and let us know when to meet you at Exchange Street, or if you come by boat, the foot of Main. If I were you I'd bring everything you have for of course after the baby comes you'll remain here for at least six months or a year as travelling to the far west with a baby would be difficult if not ruinous and your husband by that time surely will be ready to serve in somewhat more acceptable surroundings.

Now Laura don't forget what your own mother did for the sake of her babies when they were born. Do you remember how I told Harvey and how I told you when you were old enough to understand? I went to our place in South Carolina just so my babies would be born in their ancestral mansion in the dear wonderful old South where all proper care was possible with all our servants and friends, It was great effort for me but I made it for your sake and Harvey's. So think of your little dear one who is coming and come home to your darling mother who has never a breath or a thought for anything but the health and happiness of others especially those of her dear family.

Write at once and tell me when you will come.

With my love,

Drusilla Greenleaf

Your father is not too well. Nothing serious. But the Congress adjourned again without acting on any new promotions and this was naturally a blow to all of us. I cannot see why this should be denied me. So much for all the help your precious old Uncle Alex has been to us!

D. G.

"Here," said Laura, extending the letter to Matthew. "This seems to be an answer to a letter you wrote to my mother. It really concerns you more than me."

He read it.

"Yes," he said, "it answers my inquiry."

Laura smiled faintly. Her dark blue eyes had far lights in them. She seemed as elusive and impersonal as the stars.

"Well?" he said, "don't you agree, now that your mother thinks it is the thing to do?"

She smiled again upon him, like every woman who says she can see the child in every man, and deal with him accordingly.

"No, Matthew, I do not agree, and if you thought to make me go by stirring up my mother, you were wrong."

"Then you will not?"

"No."

"Laura!"

"No, I am going to stay right here and have my baby come right here. I am not the only woman who ever had her child in difficult surroundings. I consider it my duty to stay here, and I shall."

"Laura, you don't know what risks you may be taking! If you don't care for yourself, or the baby, think of what it would mean to me if anything were to—think of *me,* Laura!"

Now her eyes fired with feeling and her smile retreated before anger.

"What else do you think I am thinking of, Matthew! Why do you suppose I intend to stay! Who is it I don't want to leave!" She began to cry. Her voice went thin and high and soft. "Why can't you see that I want us all together always, no matter what or where! Why don't you know I love you!"

She turned and sobbed in anguished privacy. He was astounded. He was humbled. Her courage and sweetness and doubtfulness smote him with heavy blows.

"Laura!" he whispered, "oh my wonderful darling one, here," he stroked her head as she came into his embrace, and "here," he said, "here, darling, here, you and I, ah, forgive me, Laura, forgive me, my only one, my darling only, my only, only."

Soon enough Laura had a call from Doctor Gray.

"What's this?" he said roughly. She knew what he referred to, for Matthew must have told him.

"No, I'm not going," she said. "You will have to give me the most lavish care."

"Lavish, then, hey? Well, I will say you are a spirited one, and do you know?" He put his head on one side and a shock of his frosty thick hair fell over his brow like a boy's, and he loved the marvel of what he would tell. "Do you know what Maud Gray told me? She said, 'Cedric, I'll have you know something. When her times comes, that pretty little Laura Hazard will no more go way back East to have her baby than she'll fly,' she said. How did she know? Great God almighty, don't ask me, for I cannot tell you. But she was right, wasn't she? And I'll tell you one more thing, my fine young lady, I'm glad she was right."

"But you thought I should go."

"Aagh, all I was thinking was that there are better doctors than Cedric Gray in the world, and that if you could get one, you should. But since here we are, and here we're going to stay, we're going to do more than make the best of it. We're going to be proud of the work we're going to do together. Now answer me some questions, and then, if you will permit, I will make a brief physical examination, my child."

For the next months, time at the Fort seemed to pass in the measure of Laura's advancing motherhood.

xxxix

One day in March the troopers found a paper posted on the portal of their barracks. It was a printed excerpt from a speech made on the floor of the House of Representatives at Washington by the Honorable Granville Joe Squillers, Member of Congress. At the request of the author, the document was distributed by the War Department to all army posts and installations in the United States. Major Prescott had required all his officers to read it, and now he placed it for his soldiers to read. Those who could read spelled it out to those who couldn't:

My honourable colleagues, let us dwell briefly on the so-called crimes of the aboriginal American Indian concerning which you and I and all of us receive a constant stream of allegations from partisans of various special interests in the glorious empire lands of the Far West, where the eagle soars free and the breezes of the Gulf of Mexico and the far Pacific meet and mingle above those rocky crowns which are the glory of the North American continent and the sons of nature roam an earthly paradise unparalleled since our first parents knew their domain in innocence and contentment.

What are these crimes? Some transgressions there may indeed be, though I have documentary evidence in my desk to prove that they are almost to a jot grossly exaggerated. But assuming, my honourable colleagues, for a moment, that in some instances there may have been acts of unlawful violence committed by certain individual Indians against white settlers and their nascent communities, what, I ask with all the passion for justice which I or any right-minded citizen of these broad and glorious States can command, occasioned such acts? What indeed but the natural impulse of the human soul to defend that which bred it and that which in consequence, under a natural law, it must love to the death?

Now I have evidence to show that in doing its duty in guarding the westward advance of the rolling tide of American civilisation, the United States Army has consistently, as a matter of policy, habit and conviction, committed wanton depredations upon the persons, property, domain and freedom of the Indians of the Far West. In vain have I and my like-minded associates in these great halls made vigorous protest to the authorities. The President of the United States and his Secretary of War have but turned us aside with open contempt and have on the other hand encouraged both settlers and soldiers to massacre at will, to pillage, steal and convert to often very dubious uses the territories owned for lo, these thousand years by the natural noblemen of the plains and the mountains.

Even now, my fellow guardians of the national welfare, even now we hear of discussions taking place in various military committees and bureaux which will lead to plans for further armed aggression against the wards of our sympathy. I call upon you, as I call upon my own conscience, to lift your strength against all such evil and wanton depredation to be visited in cold blood upon a people who desire naught but the arts of peace, the fair fellowship of unmolested existence, and the pursuit of their ancestral ways.

Great heaven, gentlemen, is not the Far West also called the Great West? Is there not sufficient space in its lordly sweeps for all manner of men to subsist each according to his way in comradely peace and justice? To see those great steppes and savannahs stained with the blood of their aboriginal owners is to make us cry 'Faugh!', and turn away from a spectacle unworthy, in its ignoble outlines, of the grand nation whose destiny has led it into lordship over the most glorious territories ever granted by a just God to a God-fearing people!

Honourable colleagues, in the struggles soon to be felt on the floor of this honourable house, I enjoin you to throw the weight of your wisdom on the side of the despoiled and calumniated Indian. Might rarely needs a champion. Let us champion the victims of might, until once again, riding his gilded chariot fro' out the auroran east, and proceeding o'er the zenith unto the raven deeps of the west with fall of night, the sun himself may shine out upon a nation of brothers, who in peaceful contentment, will be relieved at last of burdensome taxes for the maintenance of an enlarged military arm. I thank you.

xl

Answering a summons delivered by Corporal Rainey, Captain Gray reported to the commanding officer.

"Sit down, Gray," said Hiram. "I need a professional estimate from you."

"Yes, sir?"

"How soon do you expect to deliver Mrs. Hazard?"

The surgeon calculated briefly, putting his lips forward and grinding his jaw gently, and then replied,

"Five to six days from now."

"Thunder."

"Have you objections, sir?"

"Yes, I have."

The way he said it caused both officers to laugh, and then the major continued,

"We have a job of duty to do, and I need Hazard for it. You know, Gray, that I cannot repose the same confidence in Mainwaring that I can in Hazard." He turned to his desk and fingered a blue dispatch paper. "Heliostat gives us orders from Department to send out a scout southwest as near to Mexico as we can go unobserved. There are reports of a massing of Chiricahuas across the border, and we're the nearest post to it, and Department has to know as soon as possible what it looks like. It will take the scouting party two to three days to find the Indians and as much time to return with their information. This is the difficulty about Hazard. He would want to be here when his child is born. Laura would want him. —How is she?"

"Sound as oak, sir."

"No nerves, the like?"

"Plenty of nerves. I see her frightened now and then. But I also see her ride it out."

"If she has to go through it without him nearby, what then?"

"I'd say she'll do it."

"Thank you. You are fully prepared?"

"I am, sir," said Captain Gray stiffly.

"No, no, I don't mean to question your arrangements. Naturally, we all feel concern, in our keen interest."

"Naturally." The surgeon rose. "If that is all, sir?"

"Yes. Thank you, captain. I will just go down to Quarters 4 and explain the matter to her myself."

The post surgeon softened with the effect of melting ice.

"Aagh, major," he said, allowing his Gloucestershire accent full color, "when'll we ever see another like you?"

xli

Three days later at sundown, Matthew, approaching Mexico, came to the execution of his orders: to find the massed Chiricahuas, to estimate their number, their temper, and the direction of their travel, to avoid a fight, and to return to Fort Delivery within six days in any case. With him was the soldier he had chosen to accompany his mission. This was Joe Dummy.

They saw a towering cloud of dust in the golden distance. Joe indicated the height of the dust cloud, and sprinkled with his fingers to indicate that the number of the distant band was great. Heading north, they could have no business but outrage. Coming cautiously in their horses' walk, Matthew and Joe discussed a plan to circle southward and under the cover of dusk to take up a trailing position far enough to the rear to avoid detection and yet close enough to watch until absolute dark the movement of the traveling throng out of Mexico. Earth's shadow began to show on the eastern sky as the sun dropped under the west. The ground was veiled in its own colors of gold, pink and gray. A premonitory chill came into the air.

"Ay!" said Joe, a sharp exclamation. He pointed and then turned his mount and slapped Matthew's to make it lunge into a gallop. Matthew saw a little spurt of dust detach itself from the main mass of the Indians. It stirred itself forward toward the two soldiers. Here was a clue as to the temper of the Indians, for having sighted the two cavalrymen at an incredible distance, a dozen Chiricahuas were coming in pursuit.

With Joe Dummy slightly in the lead, Matthew bent over his horse's laboring neck. They rode eastward into the rapidly deeping twilight. Ahead of them the full moon began to rise, whitest silver in the ashy blue of twilight. In the last fade of daylight behind them, they saw that their pursuers still came, and they knew they must run for cover wherever they could find it.

Joe kept the lead, for he knew where to go. They seemed, actually, to be racing the moon, for as it rose above a low mesa, it cast a long shadow to the west, and the two horsemen were riding to gain it.

"If we gain that shadow," thought Matthew, "they may never find us." He spurred his horse. Ahead, the moonlight lay like a shining sea. The young officer and his scout could hear nothing of their pursuers over the sound of their own galloping blood. So it was that the first they knew of how closely they were being overtaken was the sound of bullets and of arrows coming over them. If shots could come one way they must go the other. Matthew remembered his orders— "to avoid a fight"—but his first duty seemed to be to survive in order to make his report.

"All right, fire!" he called to Joe, turning in his own saddle and firing his carbine at the pursuit. The aim was general, for the light was gone, and as the sunset died into darkness, all chances for marksmanship disappeared. He heard Joe's carbine, and mixed with the shaking thunder of the earth beneath hoofs he heard the faint crack of answering shots, and again the airy exhaust of arrows stinging the air beside him. "How is it going to be?" Matthew asked in silence, and soon had the beginning of an answer, for the army mounts were the sounder, and under spurs they drew slowly ahead of the pursuit. The two cavalrymen bent forward into the dark, running for the mesa.

Soon the ground lifted under them in a long slope covered with tall, dry grass. They were suddenly at the edge of the shadow; they plunged into it. Behind them the moon shone in the dry golden grass.

By contrast the shadow was dense and engulfing. Joe led the gallop in a long oblique change of direction for a quarter hour. Then Matthew heard Joe dismount and dismounted also. Leading their horses they walked far along the base of the mesa.

"What is he looking for?" asked Matthew, but with no doubts of his scout. Joe knew the whole land, not only its sweep, but also its detail. Their eyes were now able to use the shadow and Matthew saw Joe dimly crouch, then rise and beckon, and then disappear. An instant later Matthew himself came to the edge of a wide earth bunker at the foot of the mesa and went down over its edge. It was like being in a revetment. Whatever man built, nature had somewhere built it first. Behind them rose the sheer bluff; ahead of them as they turned to see where they had come from lay, moon-silvered, a stand of tall grass and then the desert. Their pursuers must be some time deciding which way to turn if they should in their turn enter the shadow.

"You knew just where to come," said Matthew. "This looks like a camping site."

Joe replied with a whistle of breath to indicate agreement. He held up some charred mesquite roots left by earlier visitors. He shut off his whistle and then let it go again, but now in a blast of breath through clenched teeth with lips skinned back like an animal in fury or pain.

"Joe, what's that?" asked Matthew.

Joe Dummy bent forward in a kind of convulsion. Matthew went to him and turned him around. He saw, in silhouette, how Joe held up an arrow.

"Where did you get that, Joe?"

For answer Joe sniffed the arrow point, then threw the arrow as far from him as he could. He then sank down to his knees into darkness and refused to speak.

"Joe, what is the matter? Where did you get that arrow? Did it strike you?" Matthew was shocked by his own words. "Did it hit you, back there, where we fought them? Are you hurt? Answer me!"

In the starlight, Joe finally answered. He took Matthew's hand and showed, on Matthew's own shoulder, where the arrow had struck, how it had quivered and stayed, how deeply it had bitten, how he had ridden miles with it in his flesh, and how only now, in safety, with duty done, had he pulled it out. He had smelled of the arrow's head. Did the lieutenant know what this meant? It meant death.

Yes, Matthew knew. The arrow was poisoned. The Chiricahuas made baskets of spring willow canes. Into these they put captive rattlesnakes which they teased with arrows thrust through the woven willows, until the snakes struck again and again at the iron points, leaving on them the crystalline venom that when dry gave no odor but, when wet, as with man's blood, smelled to make the tongue come up in the throat. Such an arrow smelled of death. Joe Dummy, as Matthew knew him, and more properly White Horn, as he knew himself in all his knowledge and dignity, was now preparing to die.

"Like hell!" said Matthew. "We'll do something."

He pushed Joe about to face him and tore down his shirt at the right shoulder. Lighting and shielding a phosphorus match, Matthew looked at the wound. It was raw and already puffy. He leaned and sniffed it; there was a faint stench. Suddenly the match went out. Joe had put his fist about it. He indicated the open desert. A little light would show for miles and call for anyone to come near, enemies first of all. Joe took Matthew's hand and waved it as if to dissuade him from foolish hopes confronting death.

You go and leave me, said White Horn in Joe Dummy, with gestures and few syllables. *Live or die: who can know? But do not wait for me.*

"No, if it's true and that is snake poison, you'll die unless we do something. I will think what to do."

Yes, I will die. But I will die anyway with time. You go. Now. Before they come. You must find the fort from here.

Matthew thought over what he knew of army field medicine. Haste was all he could think of for conditions like the present—haste and something red-hot. Feeling about the bunker he gathered up mesquite roots and branches and twigs and laid a fire. White Horn breathed out protest. A fire at night would summon all desert life.

"Sure," said Matthew. "If I have to, I can hold them off with our firearms. I need the fire for you."

He lighted it. White Horn stared at the wild light. He stared at his commander. He could not believe that he was not to be abandoned. He saw Matthew remove a spur and thrust one long blunt rowel into the heart of coals. Matthew blew and fanned; he nursed every scrap that would burn. Presently he was astonished to see the scout slide forward toward the fire. From a pouch at his waist White Horn took with the finger tips of one hand a fine yellow dust. Uttering sacred words deep in his throat he released a pinch in all six sacred directions: north, south, east, west, up and down. He then made a puff of the powder over Matthew's head and then another over his own. Then in signs he explained.

In his own time and among his own people, years before he had come to the Army, he had been a chief and a doctor, with powers. The yellow dust was pollen of tule, or cattail. It was called *hoddentin* and was used thus in an act of prayer.

"Ek!" concluded White Horn, in a sudden, constricted, explosive sound, like a sharp breaking of a dried branch. It was a sound meant to startle supernatural powers into paying attention and hearing a prayer.

"Very good," said his lieutenant. "Let us use every means, including this one," and he took the spur, red-hot, out of the knotty fire. He slapped his man on the belly. "Lie down and hold on to me." He plunged the spur deep into the poisoned-arrow wound and, sweating with sympathy, made it grind out a burned crater deeper than he guessed the poisoned area to be. White Horn lay inert and silent as a sleeper who felt nothing, with his eyes open, staring at Matthew in amazed subjection. He believed that his young commander was giving him life. Fire and smoke ascended against the dark face of the mesa. Matthew sat back on his heels.

"Well, I hope that'll do it," he said. He went to the fire and kicked it apart, leaving a few veiled coals. He then took his canteen and gave the scout a drink of water. In response, White Horn took from his waistband another sacred accessory. It was a twig from a tree that had been split by lightning. With this he made a wide looping gesture over Matthew, in thanks and blessing. Matthew said,

"Yes, fine. Now rest a little, and I'll watch, and then we'll try to move out for home."

The two soldiers said of each other in their thoughts that this was how a man should be: on the one hand quiet about pain and death, on the other loyal to life.

Matthew faced out, on guard, over the immense night.

xlii

He shivered. He wanted to build up the fire again. In the moonlight there was no enemy to be seen, but he could take no risks. He began

to invite his thoughts, which warmed him like desire. He had much
to think about.

But the quiet night was now broken by a plaintive, smothered
cry that came from the tall grass out in the moonlight.

Matthew tightened everywhere in him. He leaned to peer. The cry
came again—a rolled, sorrowful inquiry of the wilderness that ended
with a little throaty yelp. At that, Matthew sat back on his haunches
and laughed. The fire had attracted attention after all, but it was only
the attention of a coyote. It spoke again, nearer, with a wheedling
cajolery that was almost human.

And then Matthew jumped in astonishment, for immediately behind him in the earthwork spoke another coyote, exactly mimicking
the heart-hungry voice of the animal out on the desert. Matthew
turned.

There was White Horn, with his nose raised like a snout, his mouth
closed around a little "o," his cheeks drawn in, delicately managing
the tone; and in his throat the soft, trilled phrases of treachery replying to those of the desert. In another instant he was at the fire. He
took up a last glowing coal with tongs made of sticks, blew on it and,
before Matthew could speak, threw it out into the tall, dry grass. He
then threw Matthew and himself to the ground out of sight of the
light. The grass took fire and, the wind being right, began to roar
down the slope in a wide front away from the bunker. In its savage
glow Matthew saw the naked figures of his Apache enemies leap to
their feet and run away. One or two turned and fired rifles as they ran.
They had crept forward so slowly that any movement of the grass
must have seemed to be caused by a breeze or a wandering animal,
and in case any movement had been noticed, they had taken the voice
of the coyote to account for it.

Matthew raised his carbine and fired as long as he could see running shapes. Through the flicker of flame and smoke he thought he
saw some fall. The grass stretched for several miles. It would burn
the Indians back to their train. Meanwhile the spectacle was remarkable—a grass fire running through darkness over flat land.

Rid of the attackers, Matthew felt excitement really rising in him
now that the threat was over, thanks to his companion's understanding of the wilderness and all its creatures. With a stern obligation to
be matter-of-fact, he went to his saddle bag. Of the usual rations only
one item seemed appetizing. He came back with a can of peaches,
opened it and offered it first to the scout. They ate together in silence.

The sticky fruit tasted good. There was a future for both men now, and time to consider it.

Matthew thought of Laura, and of what this cold, bright night might have brought to her and to him. Tomorrow would be the fourth day since he'd left her. Major Prescott and Captain Gray, not to mention their wives and the women of Soapsuds Row, would all do their best for her. But Matthew still hoped he would be back at the fort in time to know it the instant he became a father. She needed him near her. She had wept, only once and briefly, at the prospect of bearing her first child while he must be absent on duty. He had held her close to remind her that he would soon return, and then they would be a family. It seemed like a lame reassurance, and his breast filled with tender pain at the thought of how nearly this night he might have left them, his wife and coming child, forever. Far away by now a fiery ruffle showed its glistening retreat against the dark. Would Laura give him a son? If she gave him a son, Matthew would one day give him to the Army, that had given him miserable pay, danger, impersonal treatment—and everything he loved.

xliii

They stayed in the bunker until daybreak. Dawn brought its news. Joe's right arm was helpless, but otherwise he was no worse. One of their horses—Joe's—was dead, shot during the firelight exchange. The desert was black as far as they could see it, and no grass smoldered. It could be ridden over.

Matthew gave orders that they would both mount his horse. He took up Joe's rifle. To carry its extra weight, now that Joe could not use it, was not justified. Matthew swung the rifle and bent its barrel over a rock and threw it away, useless to soldier or enemy alike.

They mounted and at a rapid walk crossed into the burned-out grass. They came upon two dead and blackened bodies, at which they hardly paused, but rode on for the place where they had last seen the Chiricahua train; for Joe was certain that, having been observed and defeated, the migrant Indians would return to Mexico rather than pursue their rampage, to which the Army would now be alerted.

They rode without hurry and when they were across the black grass and into the bare, pink desert, they saw from afar what seemed to be a camp.

They halted to look long and earnestly. Bright scraps of cloth, there, against dark clumps of mesquite—yes, those were people, many people. But why did they not move? No one walked about in that camp under the sun.

Suddenly Joe struck his breast with his left fist to signify his understanding, and then motioned southward to indicate many Chiricahua people already out of sight on their return to Mexico.

"Then who are those, over there?" asked Matthew.

Joe replied with gestures, *Indians,* and then motioned, *forward.*

"Forward? Why? It looks like a lot of Indians, and we're in no shape for another fight!"

Yes, insisted Joe, *yes, it was safe, he would see. Forward!*

They rode on. Presently they heard dogs barking, and they saw to whom the dogs belonged. They were all old men and women, motionless on the ground. They were motionless because they were tied to mesquite bushes and left to die along with their dogs, which also were tied.

Aghast at the spectacle, Matthew stared, frowning, while Joe explained that when the Apache had to retreat in a hurry, he sometimes abandoned his old people this way; for otherwise, traveling on foot, they would have slowed down the march of the mounted warriors, with their women behind.

Matthew looked at the sun and the distance and the motley collection of old men and women, who gazed back at him out of their wrinkles. He dismounted and cut their bonds. He pointed south and urged them to travel after their sons and daughters. He released their dogs, which ran to their owners.

The old creatures lost no time. In their various racking gaits they set out for Mexico and the only life known to them. Matthew said,

"All I can do for them is turn them free."

Joe Dummy gazed around. There was plenty of signs that the warrior band was retreating toward Mexico. It was time, and it was safe, to turn toward Fort Delivery with this news.

xliv

Two nights afterward at about ten o'clock they saw what surely was a light at Fort Delivery. An hour later they were close enough to see more lights. Matthew, with a pounding in his breast, wondered what they could mean, so many showing so late, and said "Laura" to her silently in his mind, if she were suffering or in danger.

Behind, on the horse's rump, Joe made a tense small motion, pointing. Off in the moon-washed night was a figure on a horse riding cautiously toward them. Matthew halted and took his revolver in hand and waited. The approaching horse ambled forward at a peaceful jog and its rider presently asked in a mild voice, "Matt?"

"Yes, sir!" replied Matthew.

"Well, come on then," said the other, wheeling and walking his horse rapidly toward the main gate where a young sentry watched for the commanding officer to return from his midnight ride. Matthew wondered anxiously why Major Prescott was abroad. As he often did, the major answered the unspoken question.

"I just rode out for a little air."

But they both knew that a disguised concern for his command had brought him out to meet the young lieutenant and the Apache scout. Matthew knew also that the major never took up personal issues with any ease, and so he asked,

"How is Laura? Is there any news yet?"

"Any minute now. The Grays are with her, and so is Jessica."

"You mean it began tonight?"

"Just before supper."

"Is she all right?"

"Last I heard. Brave as a Mohawk."

"Is it—difficult?"

"My female informants assure me that it is never easy. What's wrong with that Joe, there, behind you?"

Thereupon, as they neared the fort, Matthew gave his report to Major Prescott, who remarked at the end of it,

"Too bad your orders read not to get in a fight. I'll have to report that you did. It may be looked into, even though by doing so you diverted the enemy and finally caused him to retreat. Yes, and I shouldn't be surprised if someone should file a claim against the government for getting his pasture burned out." The major's voice grew comically bitter, aping the Washington construction that could so easily be placed upon perilous acts of frontier duty. " 'Committing wanton depredations upon the persons, property, domain and freedom of the Indians of the Far West,' " he mocked, quoting Congressman Squillers, and went on to improvise. "Picking fights with innocent Indians, and running around setting fire to valuable grazing lands, and consigning destitute old men and women to cross the desert without providing for their subsistence and care. Well, Matt, I'll testify for you. Both of you did a job."

They answered the sentry's challenge and rode into the fort. Lights burned in all the officers' quarters but the last one.

"Laura is in headquarters," said the major. "We've put her in our bedroom. Jess and I are doubling up in the parlor. Come along."

He led the way to headquarters.

"You come along, too," said Matthew to Joe Dummy, unaware that henceforth it would take a direct order to keep Joe from his side. "I want the doctor to see you when he can."

"All this with Laura came along just in time," said the major. "Gray got orders after you left. He is to leave us for Fort Union."

They ran up the steps to the piazza at headquarters. Matthew was taken by a hollowing fear. They went down the headquarters hall to the bedroom door. The major tapped there. Jessica Prescott came to the door from within and opened it a little way, hushing them in her greeting.

Beyond her Matthew saw a pool of lamplight and a spread of high wings of shadow on the whitewashed wall, and Captain Gray bending close to the bed, and the delicate face and white hair of Maud Gray opposite to him. Between them was a lost face, older, younger, than the beautiful face he knew, turning from side to side on the pillow, saying silently and repeatedly what nobody could understand, in some fierce preoccupation with the tremendous task of giving life. Laura looked so frail and her commitment was so shaking that Matthew said to himself, "She will die," and with a look of shocked fear he implored Jessica Prescott to save Laura.

"Don't come in; she wouldn't know you," said Jessica in the abrupt kindliness he knew in her, "it can't be long. Just wait. We're so glad you are safely home."

She then retired and closed the door, leaving her husband and Matthew in the dark hall which showed at both ends the open air.

Joe Dummy sat on the front stoop waiting for the surgeon. His black shape against the paler night made Matthew think of responsibility, and this in turn made him recognize his own helplessness now.

He felt a disagreeable turn of temper. It was the other side of his hope for the future, which now depended upon whether life remained or departed in the closed bedroom of headquarters. What could he do to make up to her for this? She must hate the desert, where her child was now struggling toward open life. How could he carpet it with green lawns and visit it with cooling rains and sweeten it with kindly creatures? It was hard and gritty and gave off hot winds that blinded the eye and the soul, and in most of its creatures lived peril. Why did young people getting married pretend that life was beautiful and safe and always would be? Someone should tell them that it was not so.

His troubled waverings of mind were suddenly interrupted. A thin gasping cry came from beyond the door, then stopped, then tried again, gained in its tiny power, and established a hasty, regulated rate.

"Well," said Hiram Prescott, "it's all over. That's your baby, in there."

Gratitude swept through Matthew. It was like some unimaginable sweetness for the senses. The door opened. Jessica beckoned. He went in. Laura was heavily drowsy. She saw him, smiled as she shaped his name with her white lips, and fell asleep. Captain Gray nodded, indicating the baby whom Mrs. Gray was holding.

"A little boy," he pronounced silently, and looking wise behind his iron-rimmed glasses under his heavy fall of white hair, gestured with his head that Matthew should now leave.

"Yes," whispered Matthew, "but as soon as you can, please examine my scout. He's waiting outside. And thank you, sir."

Jessica took him to the door.

"Go into the office with Hiram," she said. "I'll be along when everything is quiet here. Who is that, back there?" she asked in the hallway, looking toward the back door. There was an irregular silhouette of heads. She went to them. They were the women from Soapsuds Row, with Kitty Mainwaring. They came for news of new life in the desert, that was like water in the wilderness. The commander's lady gave them word in vivid and brisk detail.

xlv

"The Army," said Major Prescott, pouring still another drink of whisky for himself and Matthew in the headquarters office later in the night, "has a peculiar nervous system. It always reacts to stimulus, but you never know how long it's going to take to do it, and you *never* can predict which *way* it's going to react. Just one thing you remember, young man. However, it reacts, it always *means something.*"

The major had expected this to sound somehow more profound and lucid. He set his head toward Matthew to see if Matthew were drunk enough to be impressed by a remark that had fallen short of its aim. It was his determination to see that Matthew got drunk tonight, under his rules. No officer of Troop F, Sixth United States Cavalry, Hiram Hyde Prescott, Brevet Major, USA, Commanding, was ever going to turn down a drink—or ever show any outward effect of it.

"Take this Gray affair, for example," he went on, wondering why Matthew was moving his mouth in silent speech. "Transfer to Fort Union, New Mexico, via Santa Fe. H'm? Mean anything to you?"

"They need a post surgeon, I suppose, sir."

"Too easy. The nerve system of the Army again. Touch the center, and a long time later a twitch reaches the farthest nerve. That's us. —What?" he broke off, scowling, for Matthew's lips were moving silently and his gaze was inward.

"Nothing, sir. I was just trying over something."

"Would be very grateful 'f you'd listen to me, sir."

"Yes, sir."

"All right. What's behind it, pulling medical officers back from the frontier? One of two things. The Indian campaigns are about to be abandoned, or," said the major with a rub of his bald head to indicate wisdom and its temple, "or there's going to be a big build-up for a new all-out campaign."

"When does Gray go?"

"Will proceed earliest practicable date," quoted the major. He took a brooding pull at his heavy mustaches. "Then what? I'll tell you. The Army just abandons F Troop without medical care, here at the most advanced regular post in the West. Why did you ever do it?" he asked earnestly. "You get out while you're still young, and pick any other p'fession but the Army. It's too late for me. I'm *in*. But *you*—" He waved at unseen worlds of opportunity elsewhere, for Matthew,

"No. I'm in, too," answered Matthew.

Major Prescott asked himself cloudily whether Lieutenant Hazard were drunker than he thought, repeating things that were said to him that way.

The young officer again moved his lips speculatively, and then said abruptly,

"I'll tell you something else, too, sir."

"Yes, *sir?*" in a parody of respectfulness.

"With your permission, I'm going to call him Prescott Hazard."

The major stood up and found at once that he had better sit down again, which he did. He regarded Matthew with a shiny blur in his eyes. After a long, breathy silence, he said, inarticulate with happiness, "Oh, thunder," and held out his empty glass.

Matthew was in the act of filling it when the office door opened and Jessica Prescott entered. She saw at once the state of affairs, and ignoring the major, said to Matthew with deadly pleasantness,

"I see my husband, who has never had too much to drink in his life, has set out to see that you do have."

"Jess," declared the major, "how's that new baby boy of mine?"

"Yours?" she asked.

"Ours, damn it! His name is Prescott Hazard."

Mrs. Prescott turned to Matthew.

"Oh, Matt, how sweet of you. How entirely dear. They are fine. Both asleep. I think we all need sleep, actually."

"Oh, no, you don't," cried the major. "You mean that for *me*. You let *him* alone"—waving at Matthew. "All right, I'll go. Good night, my boy. Think you can make it alone to your quarters?"

"Don't know, sir," replied Matthew loyally, and Jessica nodded at him for his sober tact. As he left she gave him a deep, searching look, thinking of the life that had come of his own, and all that it must hold of love, pride and duty. The last thing he heard as he went out into the waning moonlight was the voice of his commander, raised in glad song:

Put my little shoes away,
I'm going nowhere, dear.
The time has come when I must stay,
You'll always have me near.

xlvi

As Matthew went home along the gravel walk in front of Officers' Row, someone heard him as she lay awake. It was Kitty, lying beside her husband, who slept inertly.

Ah, she said in her scurrying thoughts, there he goes, no doubt proud of himself. And to think that at one time I was more to him than anything in the world. And now? How is it now? She gently lifted her thin arms above her head in a gesture of conscious grace. She smiled in the darkness. She quaffed deep draughts of breath through her smiling lips. I am free. This has freed me, tonight, the birth of his child. Anyone must respect that. All my darling goodness comes to the fore at the moment like this. He is a father. He is out of my life. He means nothing to me, less than nothing. I wish him well. I do not care what he thinks now. Why should I try to make him remember and be jealous? How wonderful to have this open feeling of lightness around my heart!

She turned to lie with her cheek to the pillow. The night was faintly lighter. Dawn must come soon. She closed her eyes. Whether she yawned or not she could not remember, but tears for something went slowly and blessingly forth from her eyes and dropped to her pillow with a tiny sound which she heard. How strange, the way happiness ended, and how it began again. She settled herself like the kitten she was named after, and as she fell asleep, she silently made the shape of a name with her lips. "Olin."

xlvii

Ten days later the spring was at its worst. Everyone at Fort Delivery longed for summer, hot as it would be. Now the wind blew and carried harsh dust. It was still cold. Animals stood together for comfort, and so did men and women. Laura fought her way against the wind from her quarters to headquarters. The journey left her trembling weakly by Jessica's Franklin stove.

"Yes, what a day," said Jessica, to dispose of the obvious. "The poor Grays, setting off this morning. Did you see them go?"

"No, but Mrs. Gray brought me a present and said good-by."

"Maud Gray is a little tower of strength. What'd she give you?"

"Some calico. She said she'd carried it around for years, from Fort Slocum to Jefferson Barracks to Leavenworth and here, and she refuses to take it another inch. It's pretty."

"Show it to me."

"I'll bring it next time." Laura glanced in the direction of her quarters. "I've never left the baby before. He's sleeping. I was lonesome. I can only stay a minute."

"He'll manage all right," remarked Jessica, somehow suggesting that even infants must learn to dominate experience. "How is your life these days?" she asked, as though they did not meet daily. She was a great believer in giving to an army post, with its forced associations, an air of a wide and complicated society which must enclose a variety of choice in activities. So she protected and educated her officers' wives.

"It is heaven, with the baby and Matthew—all of us together," replied Laura, and then scowled like a flower in shadow. "But oh, that Joe Dummy!"

"Yes," Jessica said, "if you're downwind from him, it is trying."

Jessica could not help smiling as she thought of him. Of middle height and in middle years, he looked to her twice as old as he really was. She always marveled when she saw him move on his moccasin pads like a wary bobcat. She thought the resemblance was helped by the tufts of whisker-fur now growing out from the corners of his mouth. The distinctive red headband worn by the cavalry's Apache scouts was rich with human grease. His hands and face were cured with dirt into another substance than flesh, surely. He wore a cotton shirt, a vest and striped trousers, stolen long ago from a Tucson gents' emporium, and these garments, mused Jessica, were so heavy and soft with dirt that they seemed to glide over his moving joints and muscles like accommodating membranes.

"Yet you know, Laura?" added Jessica Prescott, "Joe Dummy, all the same, is *somebody*."

"Then I wish," stated Laura a trifle shrilly, "that he'd go somewhere else and be somebody. He is always underfoot. He dogs Matthew. I hardly ever see Matthew alone any more. Joe is so dirty I cannot bear him near the house on account of the baby. When I scold about it, Matthew just says no woman could understand, men don't mind the things that bother women, especially if the men have fought through danger together. Matt said he saved Joe's life, and Joe thinks he belongs to Matt for it. I can't stand it. I would love to scream. I don't see why *my* life has to be ruined by it. Living here is hard enough without that dreadful creature squatting on our doorstep."

"Well, my dear, perhaps you are forgetting why we are *all* here. Your husband will do his work all the better for having Joe Dummy so close to him. It has taken *me* thirty years, but I do know at last that when you marry into the Army, you marry all of it. We also serve, child. And"—Jessica smiled delightfully—"that is why some generals' wives are so horrific. They're real veterans."

Laura was not ready for comedy. She rose.

"I really must run along and see if the baby is all right."

"Run right back and bring your calico. I'll have some tea ready. Wrap the baby up warmly and bring him, too. I haven't seen him since yesterday. We'll have a party."

"Oh, in this wind? He'll catch his death."

Jessica, who had made life for two sons, sighed at being educated by the young mother, let her go, and set about preparing tea. Hearing the boots of her husband and someone else come up the porch and go into the office across the hall, she added enough tea for everyone. She sat down to have her cigarette and wait for the water to come to a boil on her silver spirit lamp. The wind shrieked past. It imitated the oddest sounds, a woman calling and sobbing—or did someone just now run up on the piazza in distress? Jessica started forward as the door blew open before Laura, who was in hysterics, carrying in her arms her child, who was crying.

"Laura, my dear, what is it? Is it the baby?"

Laura could not speak. She went to kneel on the floor before the stove, hugged the baby and sobbed in anguish.

Jessica decided the baby was red and yelling with fright only. She left the room, crossed to the office and looked for Matthew. There he was, with Major Prescott. She brought him up with a commanding word, "Please, Matt?" and set him to manage his family. She believed that only husbands should manage their wives' hysterics. Both could learn in the process, if they were sensible. If they were not, then at least others were spared a task that had no claim on them.

"Laura!" cried Matthew, embracing her and the baby, "What is it?"

But it was minutes before she could tell, and when she did, Matthew pressed his lips together, shook his head and swallowed his regret and impatience.

". . . And when I started home," gasped Laura, "that filthy Joe was outside, holding the baby in nothing but his little gown, and lifting him high, then down low, and then pointing him four different ways"—Matthew recognized the sacred directions of life to which Joe thus offered the baby—"and then he took some stuff out of his belt and spread it over the baby, and then he took a dirty little stick and made signs with it, and then he took up some dust off the ground and rubbed it on Prescott's little cheeks, and all this time I was running and watching. It was a nightmare. I never seemed to get there to take my darling baby out of that horrible smelly creature's arms. God knows how long he held him out like that in the cold! And when I came, he shouted '*Ek!*' *Why did he have to say a crazy thing like that?* I can't stand it! And I took the baby, and he began to cry, and I sent Joe Dummy packing. Oh, why, oh, why—"

She broke down beyond speech, sobbing in her exile, her hunger for safety in the wilderness.

Major Prescott came in from the office.

"Ho-ho, where's my baby?" he roared, to bring cheer.

Laura hugged little Prescott closer and cried,

"Either that Joe Dummy goes, or I go!"

The issue was now administrative as well as material, and the commanding officer raised his eyebrows at Matthew.

"Sir," said Matthew, "Joe Dummy was only trying to bless the baby and dedicate him the way they do and pray over him. Laura caught him at it, and it upset her. He was probably doing it for my sake."

"Upset her!" echoed Laura, aghast at his reasonable tone.

Jessica brought the tea tray.

"This cures everything," she said, and poured four cups. But the gentlemen did not want any and returned to the office to think over their new problem. Major Prescott finally said,

"Of course it's all nonsense, but you know how touchy these Indians are, especially the indispensable ones. I leave it to you to manage it, Matt, but one thing is sure: nothing, underscore nothing, is to cause us to lose Joe Dummy. Is that clear?"

"Yes, sir," replied Matthew confidently, unable to imagine that there would be any consequences of the episode.

xlviii

He was wrong.

At midnight Laura awakened him. She held the baby. He was ill. She was frightened into silence. They heard his breathing that went fast and sounded like a tiny, wet, wooden whistle. His eyes were open and seemed without sight of the real world. He was in a high fever. The father and mother looked at each other. This was possibly pneumonia (my family have always been susceptible to it, thought Laura), and it was probably a result of today's exposure in the bitter wind. All conspired against them. The post surgeon and his wife with all their effects were a day's journey out on the desert, under escort commanded by First Lieutenant Mainwaring, on their way to Driscoll, Arizona, and the railroad to Santa Fe. This little boy, eleven days old, the substance of their joy and pain, might be about to leave the life they had happily promised him.

Matthew climbed from bed, put on some clothes, and with Laura, did what he could for his child throughout the night—cool cloths, steam to inhale, the comfort of being dearly held. The wind fell toward dawn, but after sunrise it rose again.

"I cannot do anything," said Laura wanly, in exhaustion.

"Let me see if Mrs. Prescott will relieve you for a while," said Matthew. He put his lips to her brow for a moment and left the quarters.

Outside his door he found Joe Dummy squatting with his back to the stinging wind. Matthew felt a stab of anger at the combination of devotion and ignorance which had made the misery inside his house, but when he spoke to Joe, it was with patience.

"Joe. My baby, you know? He is very sick. Here." Matthew pressed his own chest. "It was bad outside for him yesterday, without any blankets, and so cold. It has made him very sick. You must not take him again, any more. Do you understand?"

Joe showed no feeling. It was possible that he did not understand cause and effect in relation to the child's illness. He did understand blame, however, and making an impolite, if serious, Indian sign for woman, he gestured toward the interior where Laura was, and wanted to know if she was still angry at him. He rehearsed how she had flown at him yesterday. He rolled his eyes and flapped his tongue and his hands, to show that he had been stunned—killed, really— by her attack.

Matthew nodded. Yes, she was still very angry.

Joe all but said *Ah!* with his forefinger and screwed up his face in delight at being able to please the lieutenant by what he would now propose, that would take care of everything.

"Yes, Joe? What is it?"

Now White Horn spoke through Joe Dummy. He produced his sacred lightning-struck twig, and made it clear that, as a doctor with ancient knowledge, he had but to see the child in order to cure.

Let me in at once, White Horn demanded in silent fashion with his foot on the rock sill of the door. *I will bring down huge powers, and you may cease your worry.*

"No, Joe. Thank you. You're a good friend. Thank you, but no. My woman will never let you do that."

Woman won't? inquired White Horn in dismay, unable to understand why any woman should be consulted about such a matter. Before Matthew could stop him he pushed open the door and, holding his magic aloft, came upon Laura who was walking the baby. Seeing him she turned white and weak with fury.

"Oh, get out of here, you horrid, dreadful—" and her words dried up. But she made such sounds and shook with such loathing that Joe Dummy scrambled backward out of the door. His face, too, was now wrenched with anger. He spat and spat on the ground and stamped on his spittle. Then with a most abused look he turned to the young commander whom he worshiped and solemnly shook his head in reproof.

Matthew smiled warmly on him to claim him still as his friend and said,

"Come along with me. I'm going to headquarters."

They walked in the cold wind up Officers' Row. Captain Gray's house was being made ready for new occupants by a detachment of enlisted men under the command of Corporal Rainey. Mr. and Mrs. Mainwaring were to advance their position by one notch for they had now succeeded to the next higher ranking quarters. Their own quarters

in turn would be available to Mr. and Mrs. Hazard. As Matthew
and Joe passed the surgeon's vacated quarters, Matthew said,

"If only the doctor were still here."

He was sorry at once if Joe heard what he said for it seemed hardly
polite in the presence of one doctor to sigh for another. At the piazza
of headquarters, Matthew said,

"I'll see you over at the corral later on," and went indoors with his
poor news.

It was a measure of how remote, and commonly absorbing, was
life at Fort Delivery that the baby's illness became an event shared
by all. The laundresses from Soapsuds Row clustered about the door
of Quarters 4 in their shawls, proving sympathy by suffering the bitter,
dry cold. Jessica Prescott and Kitty Mainwaring spent much time
indoors with Laura. The work of the garrison went on through the
day, but only because Corporal Rainey or Private Clanahan ran
every half hour to fetch the latest bulletins. These were progressively
disturbing. As the day advanced the child seemed to be more ill. He
went into a deathly calm toward sundown, scarcely breathing, barely
responding to any stimulus. None of the women knew what more to
do for him. They could only make about him, and about his mother,
a cordon of fierce wills to live.

Jessica watched Laura with increasing pride in her. The young
mother seemed to grow stronger the more drawn with fear she
became. Late in the day she asked Mrs. Prescott,

"Do you think he may die?"

"Yes," said Jessica, "I do. I also think he may live, my dear."

Laura pressed her hands on her mouth, and her eyes filled with
tears, and then she said,

"If there is a chance for the other, I keep remembering that he
has never been christened."

"Yes, I have been thinking of that, too."

"My family are in the Episcopal Church."

"We are Catholics."

"Yes. I know. Isn't there something about what to do in an emergency?"

Jessica put her arm around Laura and said gently,

"Yes. Anyone may baptize a person in the face of death."

Laura covered her face with her hands and spoke into them softly.

"I don't want to seem to invite anything, but if it is near, then I want him to go to God. Will you do it for me if you think it may be near? I wanted you for his godmother, anyway."

"I do think it is, Laura, and I will."

The wife of the commanding officer took a little dish of water and while Laura held her child said over him, making the sign of the cross on his brow,

"I baptize thee in the name of the Father and of the Son and of the Holy Ghost. Amen."

xlix

As night fell on doubt and anguish Matthew had an official task to do which he would rather not have done. At headquarters he said to the commanding officer,

"I am sorry, sir, but Joe Dummy seems to be gone. I've looked for him all day, but when nighttime came, and he was not around, I felt I'd better tell you. There is a horse missing, too."

"Didn't I order you directly—" began the major in fury; and then, remembering what everyone felt in common throughout the fort, he took a deep breath and resumed quietly, "Have you an explanation of why he may have disappeared?"

"I'm afraid so, sir." Matthew described the morning's encounter between Joe and Laura.

"What did you do to mollify Joe?"

"Sir, I said I'd work with him at the corral later. He loves to work the horses with me on the different gaits."

"That all?"

"Yes, sir."

Matthew refused to claim, and the major would not do it for him, that worry over Prescott Hazard had taken all his attention during the day. The best Major Prescott could do was to admit,

"Well, I suppose nobody could have done anything. Once they get their feelings hurt! —He's made it off to his own people, I suppose. He will have a lot of information they will be glad to have and which we are mighty sorry to release." He screwed up his face in a wryly comic expression. "You tell *me* which is worse to handle—wimmin or Injuns!" He sighed and came back to seriousness. "Well, Matt, we've lost a great scout."

"Yes, sir," replied Matthew stiffly, feeling responsible both for his own and for Laura's part in what might become a military calamity.

"Oh, thunderation!" growled Hiram at the complexity of human affairs. "Let's go see how my baby is."

They went out against the wind through which the desert spring was trying to come, and at Quarters 4 entered with the women upon the vigil of that doubtful night. The commanding officer kept his own counsel, but he knew that early the next day someone would have to go out after Joe Dummy, recover a stolen horse, and bring back as a prisoner an old comrade in arms. He decided upon a stern mercy, contingent on what all dreaded. If Prescott Hazard died during the night, it would be his father who would be assigned the duty of capturing the renegade tomorrow.

In the lamplight turned low they all sat still, against the brushed adobe walls. They strained to hear, and the infant's breath that now and then came in small, fluttering flights was all they heard other than the wind pressing northeastward with its long, high cry.

Yet about four o'clock Major Prescott lifted his head suddenly, thinking that he heard something, a call along the wind. It was a sentry's challenge borne to him, made even louder by the wind. He glanced at Matthew and went to the door. The moon was gone, but there were stars overhead, and he could now see, as well as hear, a commotion at the main gate, where one horseman dismounted and another, passed in by the sentry, spurred across the parade ground and rode up to Major Prescott.

"Is that you, major?" asked the rider, sliding to the ground and unbuckling a small saddle bag.

"Gray!" exclaimed the major. "How in thunderation did you come here!"

"That Indian scout of yours. He overtook our train about sundown, gave me your orders to return at all speed. He is a devil mounted. I'm ready to put in for line duty again, now that I've proved I can still ride like that. How is the child?"

Major Prescott answered him by pushing him through the door with his bag of bottles, phials and powders. The surgeon called for more light, threw off his blouse, rolled up his sleeves and bent over the child who lay in the center of the big bed. Laura fell to her knees and put her forehead against the mattress and poured out her grateful heart in silence.

1

Shortly after reveille everyone knew the wonderful story of Joe Dummy's ride, and all day they told it to one another in various ways.

"Joe found the train just like that, and talked to Gray. Told him the major sent for him. Said he had orders to bring the captain back regardless."

"And he came?"

"He came, and that Mrs. Gray—"

"What did she do?"

"Well, Captain Gray asked her if she thought she'd be safe if he took up and left her."

"Yes, and what did she say?"

"She never batted an eye, but she said right off that, why, of course he ought to leave her. She told him, she said, the baby's new life was more important than her old one!"

"She never."

"She certainly did! And so she said she'd just go on to Driscoll with Lieutenant Mainwaring and the escort, and wait there."

"So then Joe and Captain Gray turned around and rode back here?"

"Yes, and the captain says he was entirely lost until he saw the lights of the fort. Joe made his own trail back."

"Now think of that."

"And the baby is already better. Doctor Gray is the best single surgeon in the whole damned United States Army. You watch. He'll have that baby waving his little fists and cooing in a day or two."

As this prophecy was borne out two days later, a feeling of heroism went through all the garrison, men and women alike. They told the desert, the enemy, to do all it could against them. What could ever hope to succeed against the United States Cavalry? Not even the weather could do that, for during the afternoon the wind rose to wild gusts, and then gave way to rain. Soldiers ran out into the rain baring their bellies to it. It rained into the night, and nobody but the sentries knew when it stopped, but in the morning, when the trumpeter called them all with his rooster music, and they went out, it was to see a day so pure, a sky so fresh, a land so fragrant and tenderly touched with green from which all dust had been washed away, that they had a feeling of being blessed in their lives, and they gave thanks that it had fallen to their lot to know spring in the desert.

Captain Gray was to leave to overtake the train. Matthew asked Laura,

"I wonder if I shouldn't go along with him. Joe will be the guide, but I could be an extra guard."

"I certainly do think so, Matthew, after what he has done for us."

She was sewing, and she bit her thread in a busy contentment which made him smile with love. He loved her to be so pretty, so free of anguish, so certain that, with her small affairs in order, all was right in the wide world elsewhere.

"What're you doing?" he asked, indicating her work—hummocks of calico, and pins, and a pattern cut from one of Major Prescott's old copies of the New York *Tribune,* to which he had subscribed ever since the Civil War.

"You will see," she said, "by the time you return."

li

Matthew forgot all about it, but eight days later when he returned near evening, she continued the conversation in perfect logic and instructed him to bring Joe Dummy to her.

"Joe Dummy? You want to see Joe?"

"Immediately. Don't let him refuse."

"I'm inclined to think, on the whole, Laura darling, that the less you do about Joe the—"

"Nonsense. Immediately."

It took Matthew half an hour to persuade Joe that he must go to Mrs. Hazard. Matthew could not endure to witness the meeting. He remained at the corral while Joe advanced sidelong across the parade to Quarters 3—the Hazards had moved—alerted to flee at any moment.

At the door Laura was waiting.

"Hello, Joe," she said, overloudly, as though Joe were deaf as well as alien.

The Indian did not answer, as he believed his presence was acknowledgment enough. He was fearful, for he had no recourse against the fury of a woman like this one. With one of his own, if she dared to abuse him, it would be proper to hold her by the hair and beat

her till she could shriek no more. But looking fixedly at Laura he
saw something odd. He saw that her cheek, her lips, quivered in spite
of the unimportant smile she kept on her face. Her hands trembled
so that she had to clasp them together. Her voice was dry. He thought:
she is afraid.

It was true. The impassive, grotesque creature before her seemed
to her the essence of all that simply could not exist among human
beings. Yet she was determined to recognize him as a man, to deal
with him at close quarters in the terms she might employ with any
stranger to whom she was indebted. If she could manage this, she
would gain a milestone of maturity, and she knew it. As steadily as she
could, she said,

"Joe, please wait just there for a minute. I'll be right back. Don't
you go, now!"

She disappeared into the house and then emerged bringing a large
basin of warm water with soap and a towel.

"Now use this, Joe. Take off your shirt, and wash, *hard*. Go on,
Joe. Right now. I'll be right back again."

She retired once more. He plucked at his dirt-velveted shirt as if
considering what to do. She appeared again holding something else.

"Go on, take it off and scrub"—she pantomimed how with one
hand and with the other held up a new shirt made of Mrs. Gray's
calico—"because I made this for you, and I want you to put it on!"

It was a beautiful shirt, with long tails which could hang outside
Indian trousers and be gathered by a belt laced with quills. The calico
was of turkey red and all over it grew lemon-yellow flowers with
bright green leaves.

"You'll *see*, Joe," said Laura in accents that promised even more
if he did as she asked. She nodded and withdrew; but out of sight she
watched him from the door.

He slowly undressed to the waist and then wildly attacked the soap
and water. He blew and whistled and tore at his face, his breast and
belly, and fought each hand with the other. Her fear began to dis-
solve in amusement. He was like a dust devil, stirred up from the
desert by the wind and dancing over one spot in brief fury.

"Good!" cried Laura, coming forward as he dried himself with
large, inaccurate swipes of the towel. "Now see how you will look!"

She handed him the new shirt. As he buttoned it with a look of restrained pride, she saw that his hands, while cleaner, were not what she
called clean. But it was as much as she could hope for the first time.

"Now. Don't we look fine?" she said, and added, "Now, what all this is *for,* Joe. You wait."

Turning to the house again she saw Matthew approaching cautiously to determine at close range the meaning of the curious performance which he had watched across the parade. Joe also saw him coming and, averse to being an object of curiosity, he started to make his way sidewise toward the corner of the house where he could disappear. Laura was too quick for him.

"Joe Dummy!" she called, "you come back here this instant!"

Her voice was clear and sweet. He turned. She came from her doorway with her baby in her arms. Joe walked back to her. This much Matthew saw clearly as he approached, but he could scarcely believe what he saw next. Laura, leaning forward with the grace of all springtime, laid her child in Joe's arms, as though to say that at last she knew who her real friends were.

Joe gazed with incredulous pleasure at the child he was given to hold. He looked up as Matthew's shadow fell across him. Laura watched an unspoken exchange between the two comrades. They were glad, both of them, that their recent trouble in connection with a woman was over, for that was the worst kind and always had to be met with special powers.

Joe Dummy was also White Horn. He now did a reverent thing. After a long, earnest look into the baby's face, he ceremonially handed him to Matthew to hold, and then motioned to give the baby back to Laura. It seemed a gesture larger than it was, giving life back to its source, from man to woman.

Laura held her child. Prescott Hazard, not quite three weeks old, lay with his face to the sky, where the light was changing. He could see light, vast and pure. It was reflected slate-blue in his clear, unfocused eyes.

Life at Fort Delivery was composed for endurances which were called forth in the coming summer.

lii

In June, the commanding officer received a communication which resulted in his immediate order to the trumpeter to sound Officers' Call. As soon as his lieutenants were seated with him in headquarters, he held up a piece of War Department paper and waved it slowly before him while a sardonic smile mocked the news he had to tell.

"Gentlemen, this little billet-doux from the adjutant general tells us that this command is to be the subject of an official inquiry, which will be conducted here, on the spot."

The lieutenants responded in their characteristic ways. Ted Mainwaring at once assumed that he, with his associates, was guilty of some unknown military misdemeanor. He said,

"What have they got against us, sir? I did the best I could last year, with that Cranshaw case, while I was acting in command."

Matthew had no reason to think the worst. He said,

"Well, maybe they have decided to inactivate this post again, and are coming to see about it."

Major Prescott studied the two young men for a moment, and then replied,

"No, Ted, I doubt if they're interested any longer in going back to the time when you were acting. As for closing us up here—I doubt very much, Matthew, whether they would send a two-star general all the way from Washington to go over a one-troop garrison just to close it up. No, they don't tell us what it is all about, but whatever it is, we'd better be prepared to the hilt. I want this post, from this day forward, to be in condition to be inspected at short notice, and I mean formal inspection."

"Sir, who is the general they're sending?"

"Alexander Upton Quait."

"Well, anyhow, they're letting him get out of Washington, at last."

"Do you know him, either of you?"

"No, sir."

"No, sir. But he is Laura's uncle."

"I don't know him either, but Jessica knew him years ago. He is the unknown quantity of the United States Army, I've always heard. Either ought to be the lieutenant general of the Army or locked up as a lunatic. Anyway. We have to face him, whichever. Now let's go over every detail here, and be quite clear on what each of us is to be responsible for."

Every day thereafter, Major Prescott expected the arrival—with trumpet flourishes and drum ruffles, artillery salute, guard of honor, dress review and white pipe clay and shined brass . . . the arrival —in a train of blue army wagons with white canvas tops pulled by six mules each and each escorted by six mounted cavalrymen . . .

the arrival of the president of the board of inquiry, Major General Alexander Upton Quait.

But days passed, and weeks, with no further sign of the War Department's ominous interest in Fort Delivery—indeed, with no unusual event of any sort to break the monotony of the crushing heat of the day—until one morning before reveille Major Prescott was visited by a rude shock.

The thing as a whole was such a thundering outrage that he was unable at once to estimate his anger at its parts. In his daily habit he was up and out before the summer dawn, to ride his favorite mount in a wide circle across the desert about the fort. He knew that if Apaches launched an attack it was usually just before daylight. He had a fateful belief that if ever he should miss his morning survey under the fading stars, it would be just that morning on which the enemy would strike. There had been an unsettling period of quiet for many months. The commanding officer during inaction was an unhappy man, prey to morbid worries and dire conclusions, but he had not projected in his most conscientious self-troublings the sight that met his gaze this morning in the smoke-colored world before dawn.

As he came around the unwalled fort area from the south and east, and rode at a walk along the north side, he saw with unbelieving stare that, no more than a quarter of a mile from the main sentry post of Fort Delivery, a camp had been set up sometime during the night and now was asleep under the breaking day.

He reined his mount and squinted at the incredible sight. There stood a single tent large enough to accommodate three or four bedrolls. Its flaps were open front and rear to take through any breeze. The prevailing wind was from the southwest and—someone in the tent knew the desert—the tent was oriented on the same axis. Six horses—three for riding and three for packing—were tethered at a little distance from the tent. There was an air of almost priggish neatness about the small establishment. Hiram Hyde Prescott felt as though it met his reddened stare with a smile of smug virtue.

A commander of troops in the wilderness could know nothing more humiliating than to have his boundaries breached without his knowledge. Major Prescott's first impulse was to ride forward to the strange camp and demand its identity. Yet in the habit of command he overcame this, in order to ask his own people first what they might know that he should know, before taking any action himself. He pulled at his bridle. His horse reared and swung its massive forequarters in midair toward the fort. The major galloped to the sentry post, raging with questions.

Who had challenged the new arrivals in the desert? At what time? Who were they? What was their business? And why had the post commander not been awakened immediately to deal with a matter so unexpected and strange?

Worse yet: if nobody had challenged the camping party, why not? There must have been something to see under the starlight as they had dismounted, unpacked and made their establishment. The distance between camp and fort was not great. Thunderation, if a man saw somebody putting up a tent in the desert in the dead of night, would not mere curiosity, let alone military duty, move him to go see what went on? Oh, thunder, what was the matter with even the most stupid recruit that he did not see danger in anything at all out of the ordinary at any time?

The major reined in at the west gate where the sentry recognized him at the present arms.

"Order arms. At ease. Look out there to the west and tell me what you see," said Major Prescott, clearly, and in spite of his anger, almost gently. He was patient with creatures like horses and dogs, and half-consciously included with them children and soldiers.

The sentry peered into the still dusky west, then saw. He was a young private from Ohio, innocent as wheat.

"Why, sir, it's a camp!"

"So it is. When did it come there?"

"Sir, I don't know. Not during my guard."

"Did the previous guard report it to you, so you might be especially watchful?"

"No, sir."

The commanding officer felt a qualm in his middle. If the sentries on their shifts had not reported from old guard to relief guard the presence and location of the strange camp, then the worst had happened: nobody had seen it. The sentry saw on his commander's face something of the professional misery this conclusion brought with it, and he hugged his rifle and smiled with a duck of his shaggy head and sought to absolve them both in the guilt of general humanity which in his youth he was content to live by, since it must always justify him in his clumsy pleasures.

"That'll do," said the major. "Resume your post."

The sun was announced by light and color on little high clouds over the east. It was nearly time for reveille. The flag orderly was already crossing the parade to his pole. The trumpeter, still pulling his shirt about him, ran sleepily to meet him. The major resolved to make one more inquiry before setting out to take stern measures with the occupants of the camp, whoever they might be. He sat his horse to watch the procedure of the next few minutes. The day was already hot. A gold light now lay upon everything. Trumpeter Rainey lifted his bugle and blew. The flag started up the pole. It was all smartly done.

It was, oddly, not done by itself. Major Prescott asked himself if he heard another bugle somewhere else playing the same call. He turned sharply in the saddle. It was true. Across the ground now revealed in a rose light he saw a little figure in the posture of a bugler before the strange tent, and he heard on the dawn breeze the notes he played, while another figure emerged from the tent with a staff which he planted, and from which then fell open a flag which at this distance the major could not readily see, but which accompanied by the bugle call could only be a flag of the United States.

Even before the end of the bugle call, the major was joined by Matthew Hazard.

"Good morning, sir."

"Matt. —Look there."

Matthew gazed to the west. He asked for information. Not replying, the major ground his jaws and gave an order.

"At reveille have all the sentinels of last night's details fall out and report to me here."

"Yes, sir."

The formation fell in slowly until the last second, and then it was suddenly complete and at attention. In a minute or so the guard detail fell out and marched to the main gate where, still mounted, their commander awaited them. He saw by the astonishment on every one of their faces that the camp he pointed out to them was as great a surprise to them as to him. He formally interrogated them. They confirmed his worst dread.

"Do you men not see," he asked with formality over his rage, "that if a friend can come so close to this post of the United States Army at night undetected, so could an enemy? Until now this has been the best one-troop post in the West. If I had more information I would take steps to discipline those responsible for negligence on guard duty."

He turned to Matthew, ordered him to dismiss the detail, then proceed to the corral and at once return mounted. He then rode over to the reveille formation and gave orders in the hearing of all that for the present all personnel were to consider the outlying camp off limits. He nodded to the first sergeant, who dismissed the formation. To a man, the troop broke ranks and ran toward the western line of the fort and gazed at the camp accouterments now lighted like toys in the risen sun.

Matthew joined his commander without delay. They rode off at a walk.

"Sir, they're Army all right," said Matthew as he picked up one, then another aspect of the camp, where smoke was now rising from a breakfast fire. "Why didn't they ride right in and spend the night with us?"

"That is among the things I intend to discover. The thundering fools. We'd have been justified in opening fire on—" He reined his horse. "Matt, what is that they're doing now?"

But the major knew, as he watched a man come out of the tent and plant in the ground with a hardy strike a lance from which a red pennon momentarily stood out.

"I think, sir," said Matthew, "that is the standard of a major general."

He was right. The pennon carried two large white stars in its red field.

"Now, then," said Major Prescott with an instant, bitter grasp of the significance of this, "there'll be the devil and all to pay. That must be General Quait."

"Yes, sir," murmured Matthew sympathetically.

They gathered their mounts and went forward the rest of the way at a slow trot. They could soon see in detail that three men were seated on the ground eating from mess kits. One leaped forward to take their horses as they dismounted. He was a middle-aged sergeant with a heavy, weathered face.

"Thank you, sergeant," said Major Prescott, and with Matthew advanced upon the other two. One of these slowly came to his feet. He was a captain, with pale eyes set forward in his wide pale face. His figure and stance struck Matthew with familar displeasure. Saluting correctly, but with an obscure effect of disdain, the captain spoke through thin pallid lips in a cultivated voice.

"Good morning, major. I am Captain Adrian Brinker, adjutant to Major General Alexander Upton Quait. Good morning, Matthew. Think of my arrival here! How is our charming Laura?"

For this was Bismarck, Matthew's old classmate, who could not seem to shed the airs of a potential rival in romance.

"Hello, Brinker. We are well."

"General Quait," said Bismarck, "this is Major—?"

"Prescott," said the major, looking at the still-seated figure. "Sir, this is Lieutenant Hazard, of my command."

On the ground, cross-legged before the campfire, shaded by a wide, East India sun helmet, clothed in a rumpled linen duster, and peering upward with a fixed stare of sharp black eyes, General Quait looked older than his sixty-odd years. He was bone thin. His skin was tanned to walnut color. Below his beaklike nose his mouth was wholly concealed by his flaring white mustache and long forked beard. Taking his last morsel of breakfast, his spoon found its way through his whiskers with some skill. Without blinking or removing his gaze from Major Prescott he laid aside his mess kit and with angular lunges uncrossed his leg bones and came to stand in his full six feet of height. Prescott and Hazard both saluted him. He returned the salute with a gaunt gangle of his right arm. They could see now that he wore black alpaca trousers stuffed into cavalry boots at the knee. In a thin, wiry voice, he spoke rapidly.

"*Anxius et intentus agere,*" he declared, "as you will remember from your Tacitus, which I translate to mean, '*Always active, never impulsive.*' How do you do, gentlemen. Tell me, major. When was Fort Delivery last attacked by an unchallenged enemy at night?"

"Sir, we have never been attacked at night."

"How curious. The opportunities would seem to be great, from the hostile point of view. It is my observation that the Indian enemy knows all details of how a post is operated. He knows every troop movement. Every security measure. Every weakness of a post commander. I should think a cavalry post a hundred miles from anywhere, unguarded by sentries, would be as inviting to him as it is astonishing to me." He turned to his adjutant. "Captain Brinker, please to present Major Prescott with copies of my orders. Read the pertinent portion."

From a wallet strapped to his belt the adjutant produced two sheets, in duplicate, of white paper with blue lines on which, written in a clerkly hand, were two paragraphs from which he read aloud.

". . . will proceed to Fort Delivery, Territory of Arizona, there to inspect conditions obtaining at that post, and to inquire into circumstances leading to certain recent combat actions, in the month of April past, including destruction of property and abuse of Indian persons, executed or authorized by Brevet-Major H. Prescott, United States Cavalry, or by individuals within his command. By order of the Secretary of War."

Under the reading of this the major and Matthew stood smarting like schoolboys while General Quait, taking sharp little breaths, watched them fixedly. Captain Brinker, looking at Matthew with a fastidious smile which implied damaging knowledge, at the same time handed to Major Prescott a copy of the orders. The major said,

"General, I have of course been expecting you, though I would have been happier to receive you on the post and provide more suitable quarters than—"

"Yes. Saluting cannonry, corrupting comforts, and the rest. Please to be at ease concerning my accommodation, major. You have nothing further to do about it. I shall remain here in my camp for such period as may be needed to carry out my orders."

"We are adequately established," said Captain Brinker with an air of virtue under powerful protection, "having come adequately prepared."

"Sir," continued the major with some desperation, "I cannot explain how you succeeded in making camp here undetected, but our guard details were all in order, as usual, all night. I'd be grateful to know about what time you arrived."

"Yes, that you may discipline those who have exposed you to an inconvenient opinion," said the General. "I shall with your permission, withhold the information you request. It is not for me to tell, since it was for you to know. I shall, however, reveal to you that my small detachment on my instructions moved in as quietly as possible, with a view to discovering what might be discovered about the defenses of Fort Delivery." He flicked his gaze, a dot of light in a black pupil, with the impersonal sharpness of a bird, to Matthew. "Mr. Hazard, you command, I believe, the second platoon of F troop?"

"Yes, sir."

"You have an Apache scout assigned to you who accompanied you in April of this year on a mission?"

"Yes, sir."

"Is he on the post at present?"

"Yes, sir."

"Please hold him in readiness for the hearings I shall conduct."

"Yes, sir."

"Thank you, gentlemen," said the general. "I shall ask for you as proceedings require."

They were dismissed. Major Prescott was appalled. Was the general not even coming to inspect the post, to meet everyone, to have a look around, to bring news and connection to a garrison so long isolated?

"Sir," he said with a suffering effort at good-fellowship in the wilderness, "my wife and I would be delighted to have the company of yourself and Captain Brinker to dine this evening, at any hour convenient to you."

General Quait's reply to this was a whiplike glance at his adjutant, who spoke for him.

"I believe the general has made himself clear, gentlemen, and until he requires your attendance, he does not expect your company in the meantime."

The officers of F troop, both of them, turned dark with anger under such treatment. In silence they saluted and turned to go. General Quait detained them with a long bony finger.

"*Omnia scire, non omnia exsequi,*" he said. "Again Tacitus. I shall render it. '*He knew all, though he did not always act upon all he knew.*' I commend these words to you as a motto for the next several days, gentlemen."

He gave them his flung salute, and—was it possible?—something more. As they turned to mount and ride back to the post, the major and Matthew believed, and then did not believe, and then again believed that Major General Alexander Upton Quait had ended his words with a sudden smile of unexpected warmth; though with all his whiskers, they were far from sure about it.

liii

The officers of the fort knew that the morale of any military unit could only take its character from the command. Accordingly, they did their best to conceal the uncertainty, the professional fear, that they felt now. But as the troopers of Fort Delivery were highly sensitive to their leadership in times of physical peril, so were they now in a time of undefined administrative menace. Fort Delivery was in a state of unrest. Jobs were done, but intermittently. Speculation was lively. Major Prescott's temper was recognized as awful. He had the two lieutenants with him all morning at headquarters. The troopers expected at any moment orders to prepare for inspection, but these did not come. In a powerful way, this gave the soldiers more concern than if they'd been told to do the usual things that were done when a major general appeared. The only order they had received was the one placing "Camp Two-Star," as they had immediately named it, off limits, and thus making it irresistibly fascinating. But if nobody knew any answers to the question that seemed to be poised above the desert a quarter of a mile away, all at the fort felt united by their common uncertainty.

The post commander seemed inclined both to invite and reject the advice of his lieutenants.

"I ought to go to the general," said Matthew, "and explain that I alone am responsible for what happened in April when Joe Dummy and I were out scouting to the southwest. If he is a reasonable man, he will understand, and that will be the end of the inquiry."

"Who says he is a reasonable man?" rasped Major Prescott. "Spouting Latin quotations at breakfast in the field. And who is always responsible, no matter what? The commanding officer."

Teddy Mainwaring must be useful if he could. He dislocated his soft, friendly face with an expression meant to be shrewd, and said,

"We ought to prepare a case, then, sir. Let's review the circumstances."

Major Prescott flared at him.

"We'll tell the flat truth. We don't need any other case. A case sounds like something fixed up. We have nothing to fix up."

"I'm sorry, sir."

"Oh thunder, don't be sorry, Ted, damn it."

In his trouble, the commanding officer had no mind for anything but the real source of it, as he saw it. "Nobody'll convince Washington—and Quait was sent by Washington—that Indians are dangerous. Sometimes you have to shoot at them." In his bitterness the major made a massive attempt at effeminate horror. "What? *Shoot* at them? —And sometimes you have to take desperate measures to defeat them otherwise. This is a war in which the rules have to be made up on the spot. We did just that, and we'll do it again, unless we're all in Fort de Russy prison or Leavenworth jail. I sent Lieutenant Hazard out last April to do a certain job, with orders not to fight. Well, he got in a fix where he had to, and he fought. I reported it, with my full approval of his course of action. Three thousand miles away someone in Washington—probably the Honorable Granville Joe Squillers—fainted when they read that an American soldier actually raised his muzzle in anger at a band of attacking savages, and drove them off by burning away a whole prairie of grass, and incidentally in all likelihood nipped a sizable invasion in the act. A case? Thundering multitudes of major generals can't change the *reasons* for what we did!"

"For what *we* did . . ." Matthew was grateful for the unconscious and enfolding responsibility which his commander revealed. Yet with all the sounds of confidence in justice that they made in the office that morning, they failed to encourage each other. Careers were at stake, and families, and self-respect. Remembering General Quait's attitude, and the chilled, the elegant, self-righteousness of Captain Brinker, Major Prescott was, for all his show of nerve, apprehensive.

His wife came across the hall to the office about noontime.

"Since I am denied a dinner party tonight," she said in her clear, rather loud voice, "I am having a lunch party right now. My army wives and I have worked all morning. Come now. All of you. No starving in the face of doom."

They could not help laughing. She was, in her quarter of their little world, quite as much of a commander as her husband in his. A lifetime in the Army had put a hard shine on her natural grace. They rose and went across the hall where Laura Hazard and Kitty Mainwaring awaited them.

Laura went to Matthew and embraced him with an ardor that made them both blush when they saw the others smile. In her caress she told him that however much he was officially at fault, nothing could ever convince her, after something over a year of marriage, that he was in any particular less than a perfect man and soldier. Watching them, the Mainwarings remembered each other ten years ago.

Kitty felt a stir of prettiness, which was deeply reassuring. How amazing, she thought, not to feel anything anymore when I see the Hazards together like that. Did it really happen. How can you ever tell by looking at them what strange secrets about strange combinations people carry around inside them! Now it is just as if we were all in the same boat. . . . Which was the truth. Something like a powder train of common loyalty fired through all of them as they sat down to lunch.

"Jess," said Hiram, brushing his heavy winglike mustaches up with his forefingers, "this is manna in the desert."

"Are you calling me an old crow—or raven, then? Yes, it's a good lunch," she replied. "I love, most spitefully, to think of that ridiculous old man out there with his adjutant and his sergeant eating government bacon and warm canned peaches out of a tin plate. Why *do* you suppose he acts as if we were quarantined?"

"Oh, no," said Laura necessarily, though with qualms at shattering the flow of total agreement they all must feel if they were to face danger together, "he is not ridiculous at all. He is my uncle, and he is a darling, and I love him very much. But I know him, too, and if there is a matter of duty, that will always come first, with him. I tried to swindle him one time and he wouldn't be."

"How?" asked Matthew.

"About you. When we were engaged I asked him to do things for you, and he refused. But he made me love the way he did it. Don't you think I should go to see him after lunch?"

"I forbid it," said Major Prescott gently but with finality. "He has made the rules for his visit."

"Very well, sir," said Laura meekly.

"I had a relative who knew General Quait in 'sixty-four," said Teddy Mainwaring. "Quait commanded a brigade in the Army of the Cumberland. Said General Quait never left his tent except to fight a battle. Said he invariably did that well."

"*I* know what he had in the tent," said Jessica.

"What was it?" demand Kitty, alert for something dreadful.

"A little book."

"What little book?"

"Any little book, so long as it was elevating and classical."

"All that Tacitus," grumbled Major Prescott.

"Exactly," said Jessica. Her face became hilariously open with what she remembered and they all laughed even before she resumed. "When Alexander Upton Quait was a young lieutenant he used to call on my family in Washington. They all used to die at him. If he had to wait, even for a minute or two, he always pulled a little book out of his blouse and fell to reading. Usually the Roman historians, they said, and *in Latin*. He would sometimes even forget where he was. One time when he was calling on Mamá she came in and he didn't hear her but went on reading. She sat down on the other end of the sofa from him, and then he saw her, snapped his book shut, and they began to converse. Five minutes later he suddenly stood up and then sat right down again. Mamá asked him what that was for and he replied that he had forgotten to rise when she came in. Imagine. She said he never knew where to put his feet. I always feel that a major general really ought to know where to put his feet. I wonder if he knows now. When you're a major general, you'll know, Hiram."

"I'll never have the chance, as a major general, after all this, but thank you just the same, Jess."

The lieutenants glanced at each other with the same thought. If Major Prescott was marked for sacrifice, they must discover some way to save him. They were discouraged in the same instant. What could subalterns do with major generals?

"Well," said Laura, "my father has been a colonel for twenty-seven years. He says being made a general depends on who is running things in Washington, the intellectuals or the practicals, as he says."

"Trouble with the stranger without our gates," said the major, "is that he may be both. He used to know these Indians like a book—and I am not referring to Caesar's *Commentaries*. Don't forget that he was out here in the seventies, after the War, and made history himself, and again in New Mexico three years ago. To be sure, that only makes it worse. Queer as he may be, he is a great professional."

Jessica was waiting to tell something else she recalled.

"General Quait always has had his own way of pronouncing some things. I remember when he wanted to say 'great deal,' he would say 'grade eel.' It always made me think of an especially *elegant* eel."

The room was sweltering. Their hearts beat with troubled hope. They ate their lunch with false appetite. When would come the first summons from Camp Two-Star, and for whom? Most of them were strong enough to spare each other any revelation of unease. But when the dessert—of army canned peaches chilled for hours under evaporation cloths—was served, Kitty Mainwaring, crowded by emotions so strongly shared and so valiantly concealed, suddenly put her napkin to her eyes and sobbed. Her little shoulders were racked. Laura went to her and put an arm around her, like a woman much older. Kitty shook her head and gasped in a pinched little voice,

"I hate wondering!"

liv

Soon after lunch the sergeant from Camp Two-Star appeared at headquarters with a note for the commanding officer. Major Prescott read it and tossed it to Matthew. It read,

Sir, with your permission, I should be glad of opportunity to pay an informal, unofficial call upon Lieutenant and Mrs. Hazard at three this afternoon. They are old friends of mine and Mrs. Hazard in particular, as she has no official connection with the mission of my party, it will be a distinguished pleasure to see. Please ask her to go to no trouble, as I should like to see them just as they live. With respect,

Yours etc.,
Adrian Brinker, Capt. USA, ADC.

"Who is he?" asked the major.

"General Brinker's son. We were classmates."

"And he's a captain and you're a second lieutenant. The harvest of Washington. What's he like?"

"I'm not a fair witness, major. He tried to marry my wife. He proposed to her several times. Once even after she became engaged to me."

"A fine friend."

"Everybody calls him Bismarck," said Matthew. "As a cadet he was always quoting Bismarck as his ideal of a soldier."

"Blood and iron, eh? Is that how he is?"

"Well, last time I saw him he came to my wedding at Fort Porter in lavender gloves and spent his time gossiping with the ladies."

"Does Laura like him?"

Matthew reflected. Laura was his, she had his child, she bore his hard life with grace. What reason remained for him to hate Bismarck? Yet anger tried to work his heartbeat, and he replied severely,

"I am sure, sir, I do not know."

For the first time in hours Major Prescott laughed. He hit Matthew a stout blow on the shoulder.

"Well, I hope he turns out to be your problem, not mine."

Matthew went to Quarters 3 with his news.

"I think you're going to have a visitor."

"Uncle Alex?" asked Laura with light in her face.

"No. Bismarck. He is the General's aide and adjutant. He sent a note to the major."

"Bismarck! Heavens! I must polish his glasses before he arrives!"

It was an unfortunate note.

"*Bismarck's* glasses?" said Matthew. "It seems to me *I* have just finished paying for the ones we have."

"Yes, of course, but as they were really a replacement, I somehow always think of them as his gift. He will be so pleased to see us using them way out here. You must be pleasant to him, dearest."

"I shall be Lord Chesterfield."

"Matt, darling, I can't help laughing at you. You need not hate him so. You need have no fears."

"I am not aware of harboring fears. Isn't it possible simply to dislike someone? Especially with good cause?"

"Possibly, yes, but such a waste of time."

Some imp kept jabbing Matthew to persist.

"What I have never been able to grasp is why if you see anything in me, you could possibly see anything at all in him. Oh, yes, his father is a general, and mine was killed as a private in the War; and his family are rich, so that he has money on the outside, while I live on a lieutenant's pay; and his battlefield is the drawing room, where you earn captaincies, while mine is a thousand square miles of sand, where you don't. I see all that."

"Matt, you're being absurd." It did not make him feel any better to know that she was right. "As for Bismarck," she added, "after all, I married *you*. Can you remember that?"

Matthew smiled and sighed. In marriage he had discovered how a lady could employ a sensible air to clinch matters. There was no defense against it, especially when the love beneath it was taken for granted. A year ago it was all rapture and nonsense. Now—more livable, surely—it was all good sense and fond habit. He thought of something he must not forget.

"Bismarck sent word not to take any trouble. He wants to see us *just as we are.*"

"Oh!" her eyes snapped. "He does! How touching!" She was suddenly more indignant than Matthew. No one lived who could condescend to Laura Greenleaf Hazard. She looked about at her earthen house with angry pride. "Well, he shall have a good look!"

Matthew laughed and she frowned. He kissed her for it.

"I'll go wait for Bismarck at headquarters and bring him here," he said.

Captain Brinker was prompt. He shook hands with Major Prescott, met Lieutenant Mainwaring to whom he said, "Mainwaring? I know that name in the Navy, we shall have to make it more prominent in the Army," and then addressed Matthew.

"Well, my boy, you look very fit. I can barely wait to see Laura, who must be as lovely as ever. And the baby. Tell him his Uncle Bismarck is here at last. As for you, old fellow," said Captain Brinker resting his easy paw on Matthew's shoulder, "we can leave official points of view to one side for the moment, though I must warn you, the inquiry will be quite impartial. In any case, I find I am still glad to see you, even though I owe you the grudge of my life."

They were now walking down Officers' Row toward Quarters 3. Matthew said,

"Grudge? Your life?"

"Oh, come, you know well enough. How often I think how much more it could all mean to me—position, worldly goods, future career —if only I'd been able to persuade her."

"Who?"

Bismarck, moved by his own generosity toward Matthew, let his pale small eyes flood with moisture. He laughed in that voice which when it sang had always been described as a "manly tenor."

"Does she know I'm coming?" he asked, walking ahead of Matthew in the habit of privilege. At the door of Quarters 3, Matthew knocked and Laura called, "Come in." Matthew thrust the door open upon a tableau.

There was Laura kneeling on the earthen floor with a damp rag in her hand. Beside her was a bucket of muddy water. Her hair—the first time Matthew had ever seen it so—was hanging in hanks from from under a wrapped towel. Her face was smudged. Her hands were black. Her outer skirts were pinned back revealing her petticoat. To Matthew she looked like an immigrant girl ready to cringe at a glance from above. At the sudden light of the hot sky in the doorway she blinked and wafted the back of her hand across her eyes. She made a wet sniff, like a slavey.

"Laura!" cried Captain Brinker at the spectacle. "Is this you!"

She rose to her feet with an effect of aching joints and hopeless soul.

"Why, Bismarck," she said quietly, "how do you do?"

"What are you doing down on your knees, looking that way, my poor girl," said Bismarck in a high, thickened voice; "what would they think at home!"

"Who?" she asked wearily.

"Your father the colonel, your mother Drusilla Greenleaf, one of my best older women friends, the ablest hostess I know! Is there no one to be hired to get down in the dirt to spare you?"

As he turned in dismay to see the spotless little room with its few accents of grace, Laura gave Matthew a brimming look of fun and then resumed her show. If Bismarck came to find a story of how low poor Laura Greenleaf had fallen by not marrying him, she was ready to supply it. Rubbing her hips with a humble gesture of servitude, she declared just short of a defensive whine,

"I'm sure I do the best I can. It isn't easy, the dust rises so; all there's to do is dampen it once a day, but it's an endless fight; and then the scorpions and centipedes we have to watch out for—" Bismarck started and glanced about his feet. She was not yet ready to let him go. "Of course, the cooking," she said, "look, outside, there, in back, where I cook. I have a range made of adobe brick and cast iron. I have to get him his three meals every day; and the baby, he takes my time, too. Here, you haven't seen him."

She went to the crib in the corner beyond a standing screen and took up Prescott Hazard and brought him to Bismarck, who was now slack-jawed with horror at her life. Automatically he held out his hands to take the child, but the child, after one look at that heavy white countenance with its yellow mustache, burst into yells and had to be handed to Matthew. As the cries subsided, Prescott Hazard, braced against his father's chest, kept looking reproachfully over his little shoulder at the cause of his outburst.

"I'd no idea, not the remotest idea," murmured Bismarck. "Something must be done. We must do something. This cannot go on. Why, in a year or two, she will be—" He gasped, shocked into silence by what he had almost said.

"—I will be an old woman, isn't that what you were going to say?" said Laura. She plucked at her lip and even managed to tremble a little. If Matthew was astounded at her talent, he was even more angered by it, and controlled himself with difficulty in the presence of condescension on the one hand and false humility on the other.

"But your things," said Bismarck to Laura, "all those magnificent wedding presents that I saw at Fort Porter!" His eye lit upon the Waterford decanter and glasses, newly polished, and set up in a row on the sideboard, which was made of a size B quartermaster box with a Turkish cloth over it. "But at least," he exclaimed, "you have one good thing to live with!"

Matthew made a movement that promised a statement about broken glassware and its replacement. Laura caught it and before he could speak, she cried,

"How could I forget to offer you a cup of tea, and I think we have some of those wafers left that came last time from Mamá. Let me—"

But Bismarck raised his hand and rubbed the bad dream in his brow and said,

"No, no, I just came to say how d'you do, and I'll have to be running along to join the General. He could give me only half an hour all told, as we have important work to do this afternoon."

With a heavy glance full of opinion about Matthew's brutality, he took his leave. When the door was closed on him Laura pulled off her towel, tossed her hair back and threw her arms around her husband's neck, enclosing the baby between them.

"I thought you'd never come," she said through her laughter. "I kept watching so I could strike my pose. Wasn't it wonderful? His worst suspicions were confirmed!"

"I don't think they had to be confirmed at my expense," said Matthew crustily, "though the show you put on was a good one."

"Your expense? What are you saying, dearest?"

"He will say everywhere that I treat you like a slavey. I have ruined your youth. I am too stingy to hire anybody. Your marriage is a dreadful mistake, just as he said it would be. It all made *me* look very fine indeed."

She fell away from him. Her fun was gone.

"Oh, Matt, is that how it looked to you? I only did it to show you

I did not care *what* he would think or say. I thought to make you laugh. You are suffering, instead. You think I made a fool of you. Well, it isn't true. All I did was make a fool of myself."

Young Prescott could not say what was wrong, but he knew something was wrong between his father and mother. There was a break in the protective relation that he knew as his daily weather. Staring away from his parents he began to cry. Rising from his troubled heart, his small mortal wail said that he was suddenly alone in the world, and that he could do nothing about it, and that he did not like it. Holding him, Matthew felt the energy of his cry and by its loneliness it made him aware of the desert all about, whose grit he seemed to taste now. Laura took the baby and hushed him.

"Another thing," she said, "you were going to tell him about the glasses, weren't you?"

"I was, and if I have another chance—"

"Matt, you couldn't!"

"Could I not."

With this, through a sudden shift managed by female skill, the sense of injury passed from Matthew to Laura; and he found himself presently suing for a smile, and making little promises, and exaggerating his natural clumsiness. Behind it all he marveled at the power to enter their feelings that could be held by someone outside their little family—by Bismarck, in fact.

lv

Watching Captain Brinker leave the post to return to Camp Two-Star, Major Prescott became aware of something to see far beyond. Drifts of dust were coming up off the desert to the southwest, such as would be made by a body of travelers. He at once alerted the fort. A field piece was run out to cover Camp Two-Star if enemy Indians might be converging here. The major rode forward to make his own observation, and soon saw that a great band of Apaches and dogs was approaching, on foot, with women pulling willow tent poles and general bundles. It was a party ready to make its encampment, and it was headed directly for Camp Two-Star.

Before Major Prescott could make inquiries about the purposes of the Indians he was intercepted by Captain Brinker, who overtook him on horseback.

"General Quait's compliments, sir," said the adjutant with his lips held fine, "and these Indians are not to be interfered with, as they have come here on his express invitation, and will encamp under his protection."

The commanding officer of Fort Delivery was forced back to his own official limits in a rage. This was puzzling and fearsome in a new way, this move to make an Indian colony right at the edge of the garrison's enclave, yet to deny the garrison any authority over it.

"They look like part of the north Mexican Apache crowd," said Matthew.

"Well, if they are," said the major grimly, "then they have been brought in as witnesses."

"Whose side is the government on," asked Matthew bitterly, in the style of his commander, "its own, or the enemy's?"

"I think you're beginning to see," intoned Major Prescott, feeling absently of his bald head.

All afternoon they watched from the post how more Indians arrived and put up their tepees until a little forest of topmost twigs made a grovelike enclosure behind the General's tent. In the end, there were enough Indians to overwhelm not only Camp Two-Star, but even Fort Delivery, if they felt like it.

"Presumably he knows what he's doing," they said at the fort, looking out westward.

In late afternoon arrived a final member of the General's colony. He was a white man, long and stooped, with insect-like legs and arms which he used in slow, careful gestures. As he moved, spoke, and coughed, he favored his caved-in chest. He rode a small horse that he could almost straddle while walking. Only he, of all the newcomers, approached the fort. Halted by a sentry, he asked to see the commanding officer and under escort was brought to headquarters. Whirling about from his roll-top desk Major Prescott saw who came and lunged to his feet in a fury.

"Seeley Jones!" he roared, "I threw you off this post before and I'll do it again! You know my orders to keep away from my soldiers and quit your dealings with any Indians hereabouts!"

"I knaow, majee," said Seeley Jones in a sick but satisfied whine. "I just thaought I'd take the pleasure of one last look at yew."

"Last look! What in thunder!" Major Prescott was choked with anger. "Go on, git, now! I won't have you tricking and stealing soldier's pay with your fifth-rate merchandise, and selling likker to Indians, and firearms stolen from army stores! Do you want me to have the guard handle you physically? I wonder you had the nerve to come here at all."

"Yew'd come too," said Jones in a hoarse, liquid whisper full of glee, "if yew was to be the guest of Majee Ginral Alexander Upton Quait." He broke into coughs, rapid and soft, which shook his flat body unmercifully.

The major gazed at the face of moral and physical corruption before him and now knew that if the most dishonest Indian trader in Arizona was summoned for witness, then indeed justice seemed to be fainting in the desert. He was disheartened, and tried to conceal it, but he was unable to do so. Seeley Jones saw with a smile that he could be proud of himself. Moving with the sticky reluctance of a heat-dazed grasshopper he withdrew from the office and the post, leaving the night to fall on a soldier's worst ordeal. This was the uncertainty of who, indeed, was his enemy.

lvi

The next morning brought the general's orderly, shortly after reveille, with another note for Major Prescott, directing that he and his officers present themselves together to General Quait at nine o'clock precisely for the hearing required by cited War Department orders. They were further asked to bring with them three canvas chairs for their own use.

They gathered to confer in the office.

"With three chairs," said the major. "It is a thundering wonder he didn't ask us to bring our own nooses."

"I don't know why he wants me," said Mainwaring. "I had nothing at all to do with that affair when Matt went out scouting."

"That may make you our best witness," said the major harshly. "I have no suggestions for you gentlemen except to remember that General Quait is a great student of rhetoric. Try to be as clear and yet elegant in your replies to his questions as you can. He will ask you very sharp questions. If he conducts a hearing as he fights a battle, it will be all point and no length. And keep your eyes on those

Indians. I do not trust them whatsoever. I want orders given here to the first sergeant to cover the camp, and at the first sign of anything wrong over there, to ride out and fight."

"Sir," said Matthew, "those people are definitely part of Rainbow Son's old crowd. I asked Joe Dummy to get around there during the night to learn what he could. He says Rainbow Son is still hiding in Mexico but that he talks to them and tells them what to do. They say his spirit never left him, but speaks to them through the second chief, Sebastian, who is with them here. They are waiting for Rainbow Son to come back to them in the flesh."

"If he ever does," said Major Prescott, "we—or somebody—will have a bloody job, and a big one this time, to do. *Can't he see that?*" he asked in sudden passion, jerking his head in the direction of Camp Two-Star. "He *must* know what Apaches will do at any sign of weakness, once they are sure of it!" He sighed with the regret of a rational man in the midst of the irrational. "We will meet, mounted, at the gate at eight forty-five. Don't forget the canvas chairs, which are sure to look splendid when carried by mounted officers. Full dress is in order. Yes. I know. In this heat. But I think we'd better."

So in their respective quarters along Officers' Row the gentlemen were helped by their wives into their padded dark-blue blouses, starched stocks, pale-blue breeches with yellow stripes, sabers, belt sashes, and brightly shined boots.

"Watch what he does with his feet," said Jessica Prescott. "It may make him self-conscious, and I hope it does." She knew her husband felt her more real concern, and so she did not bother to speak to him of it.

Kitty Mainwaring said to her husband,

"You look so handsome, Teddy, they can't do anything to you." He kissed her and in a sudden vagary she asked, "You *haven't* done anything, have you, Teddy?"—with her eyes wide and flaring, sending him off with a little chill about his lips and sorry that even her most witless drift of thought had power to affect him.

In Quarters 3 there were a few minutes to spare when Matthew was ready, and he sat holding his son. He felt the sweet delicacy of the baby's warm life, the pulse of its head, and the softness of its touch, with something like guilt. Was disgrace dwelling over this life that he had made? What, today, tomorrow, on trial, would he do to his little son's future? Laura knew his thoughts. She knelt beside him and kissed his big hand where it held the baby, and took into her

arms all she could of her husband and her son. Her beauty glowed
with her strength of heart. It was time to go. Matthew left, sure of
something, anyhow. It would be enough, her love, no matter what
might happen under the precise questionings, the thin, carrying voice
of General Quait.

lvii

But when the three officers came to Camp Two-Star and gave themselves to the proceedings, nothing was as they had expected it to be.

General Quait sat in a canvas chair before his tent, wearing his
Anglo-Indian sun helmet and his linen duster. He was reading a small
red-bound book. He rose to return the salute of the three garrison
officers and at once sat down again to resume his reading.

At right angles to him, and facing east, sat Captain Brinker. Before him to serve as a desk—symbol of his operations—was upended
a quartermaster's "chest, wooden, small." On it, weighted by a lump
of gypsum, was a sheaf of papers.

To the side of the adjutant sat the sergeant of Camp Two-Star,
who in addition to serving as orderly, cook and bugler, was now prepared to keep a record of the day's proceedings in the system of short-
hand devised by Isaac Pitman. On his lap he held a large bound notebook with marbled covers and in his hand he held a dozen sharp
pencils.

Major Prescott had not expected so much formality. If a word-by-
word record was to be kept, then the War Department would eventually read it. He meant to be sure that his own statements would do
justice to his cause and that of his subordinates.

With a gesture Captain Brinker directed the major and the two
lieutenants to place their chairs in a row facing him, at right angles
to the general's left. Thus they faced the adjutant at a distance of
about fifteen feet, with the general on the sidelines between.

Opposite to General Quait, in a great arc, and enclosing all the
military, sat the throng of Apache men and women, among whom
stirred dogs and children. In the center of their front row, and resem-
bling a poorly filled bag of bones, sat Seeley Jones. The sun, up five
hours, bore brassily upon them, and made vision quail and breath
scorch the tongue.

"The hearing will come to order," declared Captain Brinker.

At this, the general promptly shut his book and gazed in turn with a bird's eye at the three gentlemen on his left, while the adjutant read aloud the orders creating the occasion. They returned his regard, and then looked at each other with a last encouragement, wondering which of them the general would interrogate first.

But he spoke to none of them, then, or thereafter, throughout the whole interrogation. He listened, he watched, he made records in his mind. To their astonishment it was Captain Adrian Brinker who conducted all the proceedings.

"Captain Hiram Hyde Prescott, brevet major, United States Cavalry," said the adjutant, "did you, on the eighteenth day of April of this year, order one of your officers to take an Indian scout and leave Fort Delivery, with specific orders for an operation in the field?"

"I did, sir," said the major, leaning forward in his chair. Captain Brinker regarded him in silence for a moment, and then remarked in a flat tone,

"It is customary on such occasions as this for officers under examination to stand. However, I am authorized by General Quait to waive formalities in the interest of comfort under trying conditions." In honor of what he intended as a pun, he smiled aridly. His pleasantry was allowed to wither, and with it vanished the last vestige, for the while, of Bismarck, the drawing-room charmer. In his place appeared Captain Brinker, the very incarnation of power and right. In severe official bearing, he asked,

"Who was that officer, Major Prescott?"

"Second Lieutenant Matthew Carlton Hazard."

General Quait looked at Matthew as though to be certain of identity. As each man spoke, the general turned his gaze upon him. They were most conscious of his forked white beard, now pointing east, again west, as he followed, in alert silence, the development of information and the revelation of personality.

"What circumstances motivated your order on that occasion, major?"

"We had reports that a large band of Chiricahua Apaches was gathering in Mexico and moving north into the Territory. Department ordered me to ascertain whether this was true."

At the name "Apaches" the Indian crowd stirred. General Quait swept them with his vision and his beard from left to right across their whole arc, as though to tell them to hear well how he would consider their interest.

"What precisely were the terms of your orders to Lieutenant Hazard?"

"I gave him orders to estimate the numbers of the Indians, if he could establish observation contact, and to ascertain which way they seemed to be moving, and what their purpose might be, that is, were they peaceable or warlike, and to do this without getting involved in any fighting, and to return and report to me within five days."

"Yes. Thank you." The adjutant glanced at papers in his hands. "Your replies are so far in agreement with your copies of departmental orders and with your report as submitted to the War Department. Now: were these orders obeyed in every particular?"

Major Prescott scowled and gripped his hands. He did not like to answer the question until he could describe what the lieutenant had encountered in his mission.

"I should say they were obeyed as fully as possible under the conditions which the lieutenant—"

"Kindly answer the question, major."

"No. They were not obeyed in every particular."

"In what way were they violated?"

"Lieutenant Hazard was forced to open fire on an advance party of the Indian movement. It was undoubtedly necessary, as indicated by—"

"Did an exchange of fire follow?"

"Yes, sir."

"In other words, there was fighting, though the lieutenant had been ordered to engage in none?"

"Yes, sir, but—"

"Were there any personnel killed or wounded in the engagement?"

"Yes, sir."

"How many killed?"

"Two, that we were sure of."

"Yes. Who were these?"

"Two Apache Indians."

The Indian listeners made a coughing sound of confirmation.

"How many wounded?"

"One that we know of—our Apache scout, Joe Dummy, who was with Lieutenant Hazard."

"Who fired first?"

"The Indians."

"Is it possible that your detachment drew the Indian fire?"

"Oh, thunder, of course it is possible, if you want to put it that way. They chased our men and our men defended themselves."

Captain Brinker smiled and dropped his eyelids a trifle on his small eyes. It was rewarding to see a witness reveal the cumulative effect of skilled questioning.

"How did your men escape?"

"They outran the Indians, took refuge in a hollow at the foot of a mesa, and were later surprised by their pursuers."

"You mean, major, that the engagement did not end when your men outran the Indians?"

"I do."

"How did they escape the Indians the second time?"

"They set fire to a prairie of tall, dry grass through which the Indians were creeping toward them. As it burns rapidly and sweeps away for miles, the fire drove them off."

"And your men then made their escape?"

"Yes, sir."

"And returned to report to you?"

"That is so, sir."

"What did they report?"

"They reported what I have told you, and also, that they saw clear traces the next morning that the Indian band had beat a fast retreat to Mexico, without going on the warpath in the Territory."

"What signs?"

"Well, marks on the ground, trails the Apaches left at certain places. Also they had abandoned all their old men and women, in order to travel fast."

"Abandoned their—?" echoed Captain Brinker with a fastidious little gesture of dismay. "Kindly explain that further, Major Prescott."

"The lieutenant and his scout found a large group of very old men and women, Apaches, tied to mesquite bushes and left to die in the desert."

"What did the lieutenant do?"

"He untied them and indicated the way to Mexico, and left them free to return to their people."

"And he then returned to the post?"

"He did."

"What course of action did you then take with respect to his mission, major?"

Major Prescott flushed and said,

"I forwarded through channels a complete report of his mission, with copies of my original orders to him and covered all of it with my endorsement commending the lieutenant for his actions."

"Even though he did not obey your orders in every particular?"

"That is correct. But when you consider—"

"Thank you, Major Prescott, that will be all."

"On the contrary, captain, that is not all," said Major Prescott heatedly. "What the lieutenant accomplished has not been brought out here today. Without his—"

"I repeat, Major Prescott, that will be all."

The major stood and passionately addressed General Quait.

"Sir, I appeal to you!"

The general swiftly, neatly, turned his look upon him, then to Captain Brinker, and then pointed his finger like one designating a winner. Captain Brinker was the winner.

Across the patch of clear ground the Indians stood and waved their arms. They were elated to see Major Prescott discomfited—whatever over they were not sure. But they could see his temper and know his defeat. Captain Brinker permitted a small interlude of indulgence to the emotions that showed themselves. Feeding upon displeasure, he smiled. General Quait took out his little book and read for one minute, and then put it away again as the adjutant rapped for order.

lviii

"Very good," said Captain Brinker. "And now: Mr. Seeley Jones, if you please."

The exhausted bundle of cloth and bones that sat among the Indians next to a tall, sinewy man who led his people in their opinions, moved a few inches forward on the ground and answered huskily.

"Jaones, here."

"Mr. Seeley Jones, state your occupation and citizenship."

"I am a merchant, and I run a rainch, and I am a citizen of the Yew-nited States."

He ran a ranch? The post officers looked at each other. How could that dying cheat run a ranch; and where was it if he ran it?

"Yes. Did you, Mr. Seeley Jones, recently file claims against the government of the United States?"

"I did. I filed them through the office of my frind, the Honorable Granville Joe Squillers, Mimber of Congriss."

"Kindly detail their particulars."

Seeley Jones, trembling with excitement, lunged in a rickety way forward and supported himself leaning on his arms.

"I filed for myself, and I filed for my frinds the Apache Indians. I mean to press my—" he burst out coughing. His narrow body was whipped about on the ground by the vehemence of his spasm. Between coughs he hauled deeply for breath and pulled at one, then another, of the white men with his eyes, in mortal panic. Would they save him? Who would put off death? Animal fire burned deep in his eyes.

"Perhaps if I were to read copies of your claims, as forwarded by the office of Congressman Squillers," said Captain Brinker, "you could indicate whether they are correct." Seeley Jones nodded gratefully. The captain read aloud from his papers.

The first claim, in the amount of $14,750, alleged that the pasture on Jones's ranch by Moon Mesa had been wantonly, maliciously and without cause burned off to an extent of twenty-one square miles by United States troops from Fort Delivery on the night of April 20-21. The second claim, in the amount of $75,000, was made by Seeley Jones, agent on behalf of Chief Sebastian and other parties named as belonging to the Chiricahua nation, and alleged that humiliation, hardship, sickness and death did visit certain old men and women of the said nation, by reason of their being made to march on foot, unprotected and without food or water, across the desert into Mexico, upon orders of United States troops from Fort Delivery.

As the pattern emerged and became clear, Major Prescott felt grow in him a sickening wrath. He leaped up and roared at General Quait.

"Sir, I protest the construction that is placed upon these idiotic claims, following my testimony. Sir, I mean to insure fair treatment for my subordinates in these matters. What is more, sir"—his thought was desperate and he wished he could bombard it into the general's head without the Indians present to hear, for he was dreadfully certain that only great peril must come from so openly appeasing them— "think of the *real* consequences of all this, for the whole Territory;

sir, are we ready for—for . . ." He wanted to say a campaign of massacres and depredations, with only a handful of troops scattered at the various forts in Arizona and New Mexico. But General Quait merely seemed to taste his hidden lips in quick nibbles, which rippled his beard, as he turned to the adjutant with a nod to continue.

The major sat down swollen with ire and dazed with injustice. If every question was framed to prejudice the case against him and his subordinates, in the presence of a major general who refused to interfere in the interests of fairness, then nothing could be done. He meant to speak to himself, but his anger broke out in half-whimpered words that others heard.

"—To sit here and watch the whole shebang go to thundering hell and not be able—"

Captain Brinker gave him a lidded glance and then resumed his enjoyable work.

"Mr. Seeley Jones, you have, I presume, witnesses to support these claims?"

Seeley Jones indicated the arc of seated Indians, and tapped his neighbor, Chief Sebastian. Captain Brinker nodded.

"We shall secure depositions from various of these individuals and attach them to your papers here. Would you care to make any further statement?"

"I just waont to say that I'm going to see that my frinds here git justice, and I mean to collect every pinny asked for in the claims."

"You are legally their agent?"

"I am," said Seeley Jones, and at the prospect of a fortune in hand, fell to coughing again.

Major Prescott stood and asked in a shout, pointing at Jones,

"Does that mean he is going to do the actual collecting and handling of the money if the government pays it? If it does, not an Indian will ever see a penny of it! I warn you!"

In the hot shade of his helmet General Quait's eyes glistened as he looked at the major. Captain Brinker spoke sharply.

"Major Prescott, you will confine your part in these proceedings to supplying remarks that are requested of you."

With a majestic bow the adjutant then excused Seeley Jones as a witness. The major sat down in righteous gloom. The next witness was named.

lix

"Second Lieutenant Matthew Carlton Hazard, United States Cavalry."

"Yes, sir."

"Did Major Prescott correctly state here today the terms of orders given to you on April eighteenth?"

"Yes, sir."

"Did you understand them thoroughly at the time?"

"Yes, sir."

"Do you understand that in order to obey orders under certain circumstances a soldier might be expected to risk his life, and even to sacrifice it?"

Matthew bit his jaws to master his irritation.

"Yes, sir."

"Granted you were under attack. If you had orders not to fight, should you not have obeyed them even under pain of death?"

The question made self-defense sound like an act of cowardice. Matthew saw that the question was a pitfall. If he answered it one way, he convicted himself of wanton disobedience; if another, of saving his own skin first. But there was still another way, and he found it.

"Sir," he replied with formality, "if, through lack of self-defense, I had been killed, it would have been impossible for me to carry out the rest of my orders as I did, namely, to return to report."

His companions could not help bursting out with delighted laughter. General Quait's beard pointed in a swift transit toward them, and then swept ninety degrees to the adjutant. Captain Brinker gave the general a respectful and reassuring smile, to indicate that if he had lost that trick he would still take the rubber.

"Mr. Hazard, you have heard Mr. Seeley Jones claim that pasture grass on his property was burned by United States Army personnel on the night of April 20-21 near Moon Mesa to the value of $14,750. Where were you on that night?"

"At Moon Mesa, sir."

"Did you see any such fire as Mr. Seeley Jones mentions?"

"Yes, sir. As Major Prescott has already told you, my Indian scout and I set that fire, for the reason you know."

"Assuming—which this inquiry does not necessarily do—that such a measure was necessary for your self-defense, will you tell us what measures you took to *put out the fire* and save property after threat of attack was lifted?"

Matthew turned to the major in dismay. It was an astounding question. Put out a raging prairie fire . . . two men? Further, even if they could do it, why would they, since it was the fire alone which drove off the attackers?

"Answer, if you please, Mr. Hazard."

"I made no effort to put out the fire."

"Why not, sir?"

"Sir, it was impossible. Two men could not stop such a fire."

"Before starting it, did you pause to consider that?"

"No, sir."

The captain permitted a silence to underline this answer, and then asked,

"Mr. Hazard, when you came upon the band of elderly Apaches that were said to be tied to bushes and left by their tribesmen, what did you do?"

"As you have already been informed, I turned them loose."

"Why?"

"Why? For the love of God, I did not like to think of them there, waiting to die in the desert, without any sort of a chance."

"Yes. And then what did you do with them?"

"I didn't do anything with them. I simply indicated the way to Mexico, and saw them start off. It was their only chance."

"Thank you. How far is it to Mexico from that point?"

"I suppose about thirty or forty miles."

"What was the weather like?"

"Oh, very hot in the day, and cold at night. We had many dust storms last spring."

"Indeed. How was the road: was there a road?"

"It is easy to see that you have not served in these parts, captain. All there was, was sort of a trail."

"Your perceptions do you credit, Mr. Hazard. Now. How would those old people nourish themselves on that overland march back to Mexico?"

"Sir—sir—I do not know, unless they could somehow manage to live off bits of root and berries they found."

"But food was not easy to find, I take it, in that region?"

"No, sir." Matthew was heavy in the belly for the question that must come next. It came.

"Now tell us this, Mr. Hazard. What arrangements did you make to provide these people with food and supplies for their journey?"

"Why, none, sir. I had nothing to give them."

"Thank you, Mr. Hazard. That will do," said Captain Brinker with a sandy-lidded gaze of achievement. "And now, First Lieutenant Theodore Mainwaring, United States Cavalry."

lx

"Yes, sir," said Teddy, leaning forward with sweat rolling off his round, tanned cheeks. He was more plainly ill at ease than his fellow officers had been. He feared for the answers he must make. First Kitty had been afraid, and now he must be. He licked his white lips. Captain Brinker saw this with calm joy. The day's mighty heat, the discomfort upon all, the ordeal by innuendo, all had a sort of inverted propriety much to the adjutant's liking.

Just now, though, a break in the dignity of the hearing occurred when a stray dog wandered out of the ranks of seated Apaches and took its place in the center of the cleared space, curved itself on one haunch, and violently scratched itself for fleas. Captain Brinker rapped sharply on his box and wagged his hand to have the dog removed.

Chief Sebastian trundled forward and kicked the dog, lofting it through the air while it screamed. The sound caused Sebastian to smile. Visibly displeased at his various interruptions, Captain Brinker addressed himself to his witness.

"Mr. Mainwaring, in your capacity as an officer of the United States Army, do you consider that you have a duty toward property owners?"

"Why, yes, sir."

"What is it?"

"Why, to protect their property, if it is involved in any military connection."

"Do you consider burning grazing land grass to be protection of property?"

"No, sir." Teddy shone with miserable earnestness and sweat. What

ororrrrrr rrrrrr rrr

were his answers doing to Matthew? "But in similar circumstances, sir, I—"

The adjutant broke in.

"What are your views on treating Indians, Mr. Mainwaring?"

"Why, sir, if they are not enemies, they should be treated like anybody else."

"By that you mean they should not be *mis*treated, Mr. Mainwaring?"

"Yes, sir, of course."

"Yes. Thank you. Now, Mr. Mainwaring, where were you at the time Mr. Hazard destroyed private property by fire, and set loose a party of aged Indians without food or water in the desert?"

"Sir, I was on duty at Fort Delivery, as usual."

"Have you any idea why you were not given Mr. Hazard's mission?"

Teddy could say with bitterness that the commanding officer usually favored Mr. Hazard over Mr. Mainwaring, and he hesitated long enough to consider and reject this thought. The captain was about to speak when Teddy said, hurriedly,

"Why, no, sir. The post commander always makes the assignments and we do not question them."

"Are you not the senior lieutenant?"

"Yes, sir."

"It does not seem to you odd that the junior lieutenant should be given the assignment while you were available?"

"No, sir," said Teddy, but he swallowed uncertainly.

"I see. It just might occur to a disinterested party," said Captain Brinker, "that with your respect for property, and your feeling for the rights of Indians, you might have been regarded as a restraining influence, by higher authority."

"Oh."

"Unless, to be sure," added Captain Brinker, "you possibly made known your *preference* to be excused from the duty under examination?"

It was a thunderclap, an accusation of weakness, or complicity, or worse. Teddy rolled with shock in his chair. Was that how things looked to them! Was he, after all, guilty of something in the official mind? He felt of his shaking, plump jaws, and by the tyranny of fear he was forced to scramble wildly back to firm ground and official approval.

"Oh, no, sir, I had no preference; how could I, when I had no idea of what was going on, I knew nothing of what was planned, or what happened, till it was all over! Major Prescott did not inform me."

He pleaded with Captain Brinker through an air-eating smile. And then he felt a gaze upon him, and he turned to see the black eyes of Major Prescott. It was a gaze of compassion and sadness, and at its source it burned with brightness. It told Teddy Mainwaring what he had done, or seemed to do: how by repudiating he had, in spirit, anyway, betrayed his commanding officer. Teddy's mouth shook and he turned back to Captain Brinker and in a mushy kind of shout, cried,

"Sir, don't misunderstand me! I consider that Hazard did the only thing he could do, and I know the major has always ordered us to protect our citizens, and take care of Indians when possible!"

In its weak vehemence the statement was like a hasty bit of patchwork, and as such it seemed to suit Captain Brinker.

"That will be all, Mr. Mainwaring, and thank you," he said, looking first at the general, and then at the ranks of the Indians, that all should notice the near-collapse of one of the white officers whose systematic humiliation they had witnessed.

Major Prescott took a deep breath.

Now, he was certain, would come a chance for him and his people to state their view of the events under discussion. He had held his temper meanwhile for the sake of the record that was so busily inscribed by the sergeant of Camp Two-Star. But now on that same record he intended to establish the hard military necessities that had called forth the skill, heroism and sound judgment of his second lieutenant. When they would read it in Washington later, fairness might have a chance. The major was marshaling his opening statement when he heard Captain Brinker say, while standing at the salute and facing the general,

"Sir, the interrogation is complete, and the proceedings are closed. The stenograph will be transcribed and ready for your signature by this evening, sir."

"By thunder, I protest all the way down to the ground," cried Major Prescott, jumping to his feet and advancing a few steps toward General Quait. "In any fair trial, there is provision for an adequate defense, and an opportunity to cross-examine, to bring out an opposing view of circumstances. Sir, this is an outrage, to close this affair at this juncture!"

The general flicked the issue to Captain Brinker in silence. The adjutant said,

"Trial? Defense? Cross-examination, major? I believe you have misconstrued our efforts. This is no trial. Merely an inquiry. If the Army in its wisdom should proceed with trial by court-martial, there would be ample opportunity for the provision you demand now."

The Indians followed the dispute with open mouths. Led by Sebastian, they made murmurs throughout their throng, and released foreboding sounds that told of what they had suffered, and would not long suffer. Captain Brinker was not quite done. He added,

"As for characterizing an official inquiry, conducted under the presidency of a general officer of the United States Army, an outrage, I must plead incompetency to comment, for I have had no previous experience of such manners."

He glanced at the sergeant to note that these exchanges were recorded. Major Prescott saw that his own mouth only got him in trouble when he opened it. A hot, powerful impulse surged along his stout arms. He had a barely controllable desire, a passion to deal physically with Captain Brinker. But he suddenly looked forlorn in his storming fury, and he faced General Quait with a hopeless gesture.

With a small dry sound General Quait stood up and cleared his throat. He was going to speak at last. All looked toward him. Major Prescott and his young men felt a lift of hope. Their very careers now depended on the general officer presiding at the inquiry. They leaned forward to hear him.

lxi

But when he spoke it was with detachment.

"Captain Brinker, you may release to me, now, the record of these proceedings. I shall examine it with ease, as I am proficient in the system of Mr. Isaac Pitman." Ignoring the captain's open amazement and regret that even a single formality of the occasion was to be waived, he turned to the sergeant. "Sergeant: the book. I'll thank you."

The sergeant took him the stenographer's book. General Quait tore out the pages of the record, handed the book to the astonished soldier, folded the pages with a sweeping gesture, and set them inside his duster in an inner pocket. Then clasping his hands behind him, and with his duster lifted by the searing breeze, he walked across to the Indian ranks and faced them, raking the points of his beard across them from side to side. He then spoke.

He spoke to the Indians in their own language. They hung forward to hear him. His voice was changed, buried deep in his throat, baffled against his tongue in the explosive, hard sound of Apache words. A curious power gave gaunt grandeur to his sticklike anatomy in its curtain-like costume. He addressed his discourse to Chief Sebastian, who rose to face him.

In his discourse the general also used signs. Though none of the officers could speak the Apache tongue, they could recognize the subject of pursuit when the general alluded to it, and fight, and burning prairie, and death, and old people dying on the march, and sunset upon all Indian nations in their own lands.

But the officers did not know what else he said, and at one point the Indians gasped and touched each other out of amazement, and with their excited chatter obliged the general to halt his remarks for a moment.

What did he tell them? asked the officers of one another silently.

The general soon resumed. Speaking slowly and with great emphasis he told them something else that turned their faces to stone. He seemed to say it again and again. Then he put his long, bony hand over his heart and shut his eyes and lifted his face to the sky, and in a kind of blind, artless Apache song, ended his address with the effect of a blessing. He looked like a figure of the Old Testament, crying out of the desert for the redemption of humanity. He made an astonishing spectacle. For an instant Major Prescott and the others forgot their miseries and their angry doubts about him, and paid him the same awed attention as the Indians. And then in his rickety gangle of a walk, General Quait broke his spell, marched alone into his open tent, sat down, took out his red volume, and secluded himself amongst its ideas. The official meeting was almost over.

But not quite.

Just as Captain Brinker, rubbing his hands together in calm satisfaction, instructed the stenographic sergeant to dismantle the desk and chairs, first one, then another, Apache dog bolted out of the Indian crowd, and at the adjutant's very feet, and before the general's tent, began to fight. They made hacking sounds in their throats. They blew their spittle. Their mongrel fur flew, and the dust and gravel were spurned into the air by their frantic claws.

"Stop them!" shrieked Captain Brinker above the animal din. "I won't have it! Not here! Not now!"

But the Indians only made a ring around the fight, to enjoy the show. A dozen other dogs broke through the legs of their masters to dance with loud barks around the fighters, and one or two leaped into the fight and bit and were bitten.

"Do you hear me?"

Captain Brinker was beside himself. Did commands mean nothing? The Indians ignored him. He turned to the lieutenants, who with their commander were seeing the dogfight. "This is a disgrace, gentlemen! Separate them!" commanded Captain Brinker.

But the junior officers, squatting down, seemed not to hear him, and with a despairing glance at the tent where General Quait sat in stillness never once lifting his eyes from his Roman historian, Captain Brinker, a martyr to propriety, came into the shrieking tangle of dogs and began to kick.

At this new element in the fight, each dog redoubled its rage, bit more wildly, raked more viciously with its claws. Some included the adjutant in their aim. He cried out in pain and outrage but what he said was lost in the scramble. Blue sleeves, furry paws, white hands, blue trousers, shining fangs, a white shaking face, all merged in an animated blur. The captain sank into the whirl of dust. At this point Major Prescott, putting on a face of solemn innocence, caught the eyes of his officers and gave a command with a gesture. They folded their chairs, went to their horses, mounted and rode back to the post, laughing until they hurt over the inglorious finish to the morning's work.

lxii

But there was no laughter all the rest of the day, and all night, at Fort Delivery. The issue, even the purpose, of the morning's ordeal were unknown to the victims of it. In his own way, each dealt with his sense of injury privately, and in his thought went around and around with the single aspect of the case that fitted his nature.

The major kept thinking, The record, the record, when they read it in Washington! If all I knew was what appeared there, I would court-martial all of us. . . . The service seemed to him now the most beloved thing in his life, other than Jessica, whom he honored in his nature by not even considering her as apart from him. He was grieved for the depths to which the Army could fall in error and injustice. Knowing when it would be an affront to console him, Jessica refrained from doing so. This was all the harder for her to do since, inarticulate, he was like a trusted horse or dog who in pain could only tell that he hurt, but not where, or why, or how to ease him. She smiled over this notion, that made a pet animal out of her husband; and was true to her love that could bear fond comedy.

Matters were somewhat otherwise in the Mainwaring quarters.

"I know what it sounded like to them," said Teddy, shuddering upon Kitty's breast. "I never meant it, I never did. I was just trying to give everything a very good appearance, by cooperating with the inquiry, so the general would feel better about them too, and all of us. But the way Captain Brinker asked those questions! And then the way it sounded when I said I never knew anything about what Matthew's orders were till it was all over! The major turned and looked at me, he looked at me, and I knew what he thought, and I tried my best to say the right thing right away, for the record! Does it sound right to you, Kitty? I meant it all right, you know I did, and now what will happen to us all! What will happen!"

Kitty did not know, any more than the others. But in her need for emotion no matter where it came from, or where it led to, she shook Teddy by his shoulders and cried,

"You'll have to do something! Anything! I couldn't face it if they made you resign, or dismissed you from the service, or reduced your rank! Oh, why did you ever get mixed up in a thing like this! Did I deserve it? Is this why we have spent our years in this Godforsaken place?"

He angered. She replied tragically. Their voices rose. They quarreled bitterly, as so many times before. If enough were made wrong with their private world, perhaps they might endure the general wrongs which they felt amidst the other people of their daily lives. Each thinking of himself first, the Mainwarings exhausted each other with accusations, until they could sleep.

In Quarters 3 the thoughts were all for the future, also, but the future far distant, as it dwelt in the person of Prescott Hazard, six months old. At ten o'clock he woke for feeding, and by candlelight in the stifling earthen house he went for the food of life with blinking glee that always made his father and mother laugh together with pride in his healthy grasp of his duty and its fount. It was hard to think, as they now thought, of what a boy would have to look forward to if his father were cashiered from the Army. For themselves, they could manage. But it gave them a pang to consider that the presence of a fantastic old man with a small red book and eyes as brightly fixed and secret as those of a bird could have consequences for their child that no child could possibly bring upon himself.

"I know," said Laura, "that if only I could see Uncle Alex, I could make him be good to us. I'm the only one who really loves him. I used to think this didn't mean very much—but since I've been married, I know it means more than anything in the world."

"No, you yourself said he was not to be swayed in any matter of duty."

"Yes, that's true, I did. —Oh, Matt, all I know is, he is a good and wonderful man, and he can't do anything to hurt someone who is in the right, and you are in the right."

"That may depend on how things look to others." He stretched and yawned and said with humor that she loved him for, "Well, the next thing after a soldier that I wanted to be as a little boy back home in Fox Creek, Indiana, was a station agent on the Pittsburgh, Fort Wayne and Chicago Railroad. I think the baby might like that, with steam cars and engines and all."

The baby was done. She handed him to Matthew to replace in the basket cradle by the open south window. She refused to reply to his joke. Too much prophecy lay under it for her to contribute either to the joke or to the prophecy. When he returned to her she took him in her arms until she was in his. In shock upon shock of piercing sweetness they forgot all else.

Though so many of its people were wakeful, the fort was quiet. After midnight the commanding officer walked out by himself and inspected the sentry posts. The stars were out and made the sort of withheld light which revealed shapes or movements to the corner of the eye. For a long time he watched Camp Two-Star, trying to see what was happening there. Late, a wounded moon came up and after its first dwelling above the horizon in a golden cloud of heavy dust, it began to show the land, near and far. Major Prescott then knew what he saw, and all night long he watched the Indian encampment as its tepees came down, its dogs and women were loaded with their burdens for the trail, and all its people and things went away toward Mexico southward. By dawn they were all gone.

Only Camp Two-Star remained, like an ominous cloud calm on the horizon, from which sooner or later storm must break. Bored with waiting, the major said to himself, "Let it come, let it come," so long as he might learn its direction, its speed and its power.

He turned back when reveille sounded and watched the formation. Before dismissal he spoke to the troopers.

"As you have heard, Major General Quait, from Washington, is encamped over there. We do not know what his plans are, but it is likely that he will inspect the post at some time during his visit with us. Until further orders, I want every man, every animal, every piece of equipment and all quarters to be prepared for formal inspection at any moment. I'll give you all the time I can the minute I know what to expect. Preparations will start the second you are dismissed from this formation. —First sergeant, dismiss the troop."

The men broke ranks on command and amazed Major Prescott by sounding off with a spontaneous cheer in which there was much anger. He marveled again at the soldier's ability to know without being told what might prosper or what threaten his army unit. The cheer was clearly meant for him; the anger for what threatened him and his command. He was abashed by the spirit that supported him from the ranks. He didn't think he deserved it, for he knew he was not brilliant, though he often wished he were, so that at least he might know why he did what he did, instead of just doing what always seemed to him the thing a soldier, a horse, a wife, a friend, a child, or an enemy deserved to have done to them.

He was grinding away at a late breakfast as if to punish it when the trumpeter came up on the porch and knocked. In the knock sounded contemptuous lightness. Trumpeter Corporal Rainey, like the other soldiers on the post, had rallied behind the commanding officer with a disrespectful opinion of General Quait for causing all the troubled atmosphere throughout the fort. Major Prescott came to the door.

"Yes, orderly?"

"That sergeant over there," said Rainey, "just rode up to the west gate and said that the *general*"—the title was almost a sneer—"would be on the post in fifteen minutes to inspect everything."

Major Prescott scowling yet managed to smile at the trumpeter and said,

"Sound Officers' Call."

The trumpeter did so at once from the steps of headquarters.

lxiii

Within minutes Mainwaring and Hazard were at headquarters, the first sergeant was notified, and the troop was formed on the parade ground with all arms and equipment, each man standing by the head of his mount. All metal shone like knives in the unwavering sunlight. At the west gate the garrison officers, mounted, awaited the inspectors, who were prompt. They came at a canter from Camp Two-Star. Salutes were exchanged. General Quait at once dismounted, saying,

"Though, like Agricola, *intravitque animum militaris gloriae cupido,* or, *his heart was pierced by a craving for a soldier's glory,* I shall nevertheless inspect your post on foot, major. Please to dismount your staff and accompany me."

The old man then set off at a fast, long-legged walk that flew his duster out behind him and had his companions sweating and puffing in no time. It was a pace he kept up during the whole inspection and it gave him an aspect of angry gaiety.

He went first to the troop formation and paused at the small headquarters detachment before Corporal Rainey, who stood, a model of correctness, at almost swollen attention. The general eyed him, peered into the bell of his bugle for dust, and then, in a Gatling-gun rapidity, asked an inspector's question which was intended to test the alertness of troops.

"Trumpeter, if you saw a steam frigate manned for battle come sailing through the west gate, there, what would you do?"

"Sir," replied the trumpeter as rapidly, and scowling fixedly ahead, "I would ram it with an ironclad."

The troop officers glanced about in horror at this light treatment of a major general.

"Where would you get your ironclad?" asked the general sharply.

"The same place you got your frigate, sir."

General Quait paused for an instant on a divide of opinion. But even if this were insolence, it was of a gifted nature, and he suddenly put his head back and laughed, almost silently, but with all of him.

Tears rolled out of his small black eyes. Major Prescott was astonished and delighted. The old gentleman seemed someone wholly new, and almost likable. And then, as sharply, the entertaining moment was past, the general resumed his work, and the officers were again conscious of their yawning apprehensions, while Captain Brinker, following the general down the ranks, showed a reserved face that was unnerving to see.

They came to the second platoon, and among the file closers reached Joe Dummy, who stood motionless and casual. He wore his red headband. The tails of his new red calico shirt hung over his soft trousers heavy with dirt. With the general peering closely into his face, he leaned a trifle backward and obliquely, and his nostrils hardened, and his eyes grew remote.

"Who is this man?" asked the general.

"Our Apache scout, Joe Dummy, sir."

"Ah, yes." The general looked again. "I know him. I know you. That is not your name. Your name is White Horn. You were with me at Fort Bayard. This is the man I asked to see." White Horn showed recognition by a drowsy sort of letting down of his eyelids. "You see, you remember me, too. Major, please to require him to accompany me to my camp at the conclusion of inspection this morning."

"Yes, sir."

They passed on to the corrals. There the general strolled among the few extra mounts, examined one or two closely, asked how many at a maximum could be fed there, nodded at hearing the figure, and then, regarding the garrison officers in turn with a certain intensity which seemed both puzzling and oddly significant,

"No proper officer ever takes a horse for granted, gentlemen, or for that matter, a man, be he high or low, advantaged or humble. I should now like to see the barracks."

Again traveling rapidly he led the party. The three women of the post laundry watched nearby in curiosity. The General passed them without acknowledging them and entered the barracks. He strode down the rows of bunks. With the bone crook of his riding crop he raked the folded mattresses apart, scattered bedding and disemboweled wooden lockers open for inspection. He unhooked extra uniforms hanging on wooden pegs. With a white-gloved finger he tested for dust along the topmost moldings of the windows. Turning over ranked shoes with his own boot, he examined their soles. He squinted for cobwebs in the beams. Returning to the door to leave the room which he had reduced to disorder, he gave no opinion of what he had found.

Outdoors again, the general proceeded at his loping pace toward the smithy. As he went he said to the major,

"Those women, back there; laundresses, I assume?"

"Yes, sir."

The general gave him a roguish glance, like a man of mind who, without knowing quite how, yet must try to be a good fellow among lustier men.

"How many of the unhappy wantons," he asked, "can expect, after living at large with soldiers, to achieve a married state one day?"

"Sir, as far as we know, and we all know everything on this post, the women of Soapsuds Row conduct themselves pretty decently."

"Oh? Most extraordinary. I have misjudged them. I shall make amends."

At the smithy the armorer was ready to demonstrate his forge. Coals glowed. A new horseshoe was in the fire. The general took it up with tongs and put it back again. It was dark in the shop and the forge coals were brilliant. Half-closing his eyes, and tilting his head to see a remembered vision, the general asked Matthew Hazard,

"Have you ever seen a live volcano? After the battle of Lookout Mountain, above Chattanooga, the opposing armies were deployed from the crest to the base. In the dark of that night, their campfires looked like two streams of lava running down the slopes. It struck me." He reached his hand to the rim of the forge where lay cold bits of charcoal, picked one up, and ate it with crunching nibbles. "A practice I commend to you all. Charcoal. A capital eupeptic," he stated, and led the party almost at a run out of the smithy and across to the mess hall, kitchen and storerooms. Running his eye along the shelves of the stores, he selected a can of tomatoes.

"Please to have this opened. I will taste it. Thank you." He tasted and puckered his countenance thoughtfully over a mouthful, and then announced, "I find the contents to contain malic acid, with a trace of citric. The amount of the free malic acid I sh'd judge to be equivalent to perhaps three hundred parts in a hundred thousand, or a trifle over three-tenths of one per cent. As any officer knows, lemon juice contains about twenty-five times as much free acid. The amount of the present vegetable acid in proportion to the total solid matter is of itself sufficient to make tomatoes valuable as antiscorbutics. I shall let this be known as Quait's Law. Thank you. Proceed."

He was conducted to the root cellars. In the sudden cool gloom he was struck by another notion.

"Gentlemen, your animals here yield, of course, a grade eel of manure. With this resource, I offer you the suggestion—suggestion merely, mind you, in no sense an order—to establish in such a cellar as this a systematic culture of the edible mushroom. The spawn is readily obtained and crops can be had throughout the autumn, winter and spring. No doubt you know Robinson on *Mushroom Culture,* major? Ah, no? I commend the volume to you: W. Robinson, *Mushroom Culture, Its Extension and Improvement,* London, Warne and Company Limited, 1870. A suitable *vade mecum.* I have learned a grade eel from it. Thank you. I shall take a glance at the headquarters of the post. Proceed."

Coming to the headquarters he took the piazza steps in a single bound and entered the building. The office door was open.

"Here is your office, major. I would suggest that you turn the desk another way, to receive the window light over your left shoulder. And these boxes? Yes. Files of correspondence and orders. I can wish you nothing more satisfying than a fire of unknown origin to consume and destroy utterly these papers which cast a pall over man's thought and rob him of better uses of mind. —And your quarters? Along this wide hallway? Yes. And this is surely Mrs. Prescott?"—for Jessica came from her parlor—"Madam, good morning."

The general took up her hand and kissed it with a bony swagger. She raised her eyebrows and greeted him with official charm. He went on,

"Our work is rounding out to a finish, and if it should be convenient, Madam Prescott, I should be d'lighted to come to dine with you this evening at half after seven. My adjutant," he made an introduction, "Captain Brinker—Madam Prescott—will accompany me."

"How very nice, general. We shall expect you."

"Yes, how d'lightful. I shall not caution you to go to no trouble. In the first place, you would do so anyhow. And in the second, I have always found that going to some trouble for a social occasion in a remote place is salutary for all concerned. Thank you. And might I propose dancing after dinner? I am devoted to the dance.

Let the whole garrison take part," he added to Major Prescott. "I shall dance with the prettiest laundress."

He was animated in every feature—his little eyes, the whisk of his beard, his angular turns of body. With a wide look around that missed no detail, he said,

"I dare say you dance in this hall. Very good. Until this evening, madam," and he was off to the piazza, down the steps, and across the parade to the west gate, where his sergeant held his charger, and where White Horn was waiting on his pony. The general turned, saluted and then mounted his horse.

"Until this evening, gentlemen. Good day."

He rode off, followed by the Indian scout, the adjutant and the sergeant, leaving behind him an effect of exhaustion and low spirits.

Was the inspection satisfactory? He had not said. Was there hope in his decision to spend an evening socially with the officers he had come to judge? They could not guess. What had he told the Indians before sending them off in the night? Seeley Jones had gone. Where, and with what assurances? Joe Dummy was taken off for private quizzing. Beset by questions, the officers wondered if Major General Alexander Upton Quait was a mere crank, with his Latin saws, his bites of charcoal, his demonstrations of vitality meant to astonish in one so old with so white a beard. Going back to headquarters, they knew of nothing to say to encourage each other. Major Prescott dismissed his officers at the steps. Lieutenant Mainwaring lingered and asked if he might see the commanding officer alone for a moment.

"Sir," he said when the office door was closed, "I hope you did not misunderstand my testimony yesterday."

"No, Ted, I don't think I did."

'How was this statement intended? Teddy hastily broke into his defense.

"I only meant to help things out, but I was afraid afterward it may have sounded as though I didn't intend to carry my full share of responsibility for whatever goes on here. I thought you thought perhaps I let you down."

The major looked drawn and troubled; but for other people's troubles he still had a store of feeling. He looked earnestly at Teddy and replied,

"I thought perhaps you did, a little, but I don't now, Ted, since you bring it up yourself, and set me clear on it. I thank you for doing so. I do."

"Glory be, sir, I'm glad you say that." Teddy was shaken with relief. If his commander did not *think* himself betrayed by one of his officers, then he was *not* betrayed, and the officer was not a coward. Teddy, light-headed with restored innocence, said, "If I made a fool of myself it was because I was rattled by all that went on. They seemed determined to prove us all *guilty* of something in advance, didn't they, sir?"

"That's how it struck me, Ted. And I guess they have. I don't blame you for being rattled. Those questions. That Brinker."

Mainwaring's hopeful, infirm face went a shade pale under his sunburn.

"They have? They have proved us? What can they do to us? Have you any idea, sir?"

"Don't get rattled all over again, Ted. We may—*I* may—have a still worse time ahead on this whole thing. I won't make a good showing if I get rattled. Nobody will."

"No, they won't, of course they won't. That's just common sense, sir. I'm no good at being shrewd. I never could manage anybody like that Brinker, sir."

"Well, Ted, people can only do what they can do. Don't worry about it."

Power without the fort, weakness within—Major Prescott saw it all plainly.

lxiv

In the evening just before "half after seven" Jessica Prescott showed her husband her arrangements for the dinner party.

The table was laid for eight. The combined grandeurs of the officer families had yielded crystal (including certain Waterford tumblers), silver, linen and lace for the occasion, and the table looked heavy and rich. Jessica unrolled some damp napkins and took out candles she had so kept all afternoon against the heat. She put them now into silver candlesticks. As she made her last critical survey before the guest should arrive, she was abstracted with a glittering hardness of eye.

Her husband looked at her with a secret amusement. When she

worked at a job in her part of the army world, she was, as he thought, "hell-bent." She—and the other ladies—had made up their minds that Major General Alexander Upton Quait was going to be punished with excellence in all the details of the party tonight. It was a matter of their particular severe joy that, so distant in the desert, so lost to fashion, they should contrive an entertainment that would do credit to any army wife stationed in the civilized East. He —that elderly wretch with the beard that was always going in little whisks—he would have his eyes put out by the shining silver, the gold edged china, the champagne glasses from which they were actually going to drink champagne chilled all day by evaporation.

He could compliment them on the cold soup and the curry of lamb, and if asked how on earth they found curry out here in the wilderness he would be told that it had been ordered from an importing house in Boston, and had taken a year and a half to arrive. He would taste the salad of fresh cucumbers and long French lettuces, and learn that these were grown right behind the headquarters, and so was the melon he would have for dessert, with his champagne, and if he remarked how capitally such fresh foods served as antiscorbutics, he would, assuredly, be instantly killed by whoever first thought of doing it. And if he cared to, he might help himself to drops of German bitter chocolate in gold foil, that came from a cousin in the Army who had spent a year in Germany studying the German military system for the War Department. The sort of thing he would never notice, General Quait, as it had to do with beauty and its touch, was the cluster of wild desert flowers and dried stalks in a silver epergne that centered the table. But it was there out of the hostess' pride.

Major Prescott walked around the table to her. Her shoulders were bare, she had on her Paris dress and her mother's chain of little diamonds. He was moved by all her work, of which not a scrap of evidence would remain in a few hours. He bent over and rubbed his chin on her shoulder and murmured her name. Her eyes shone like a girl's, but she went on touching things aright on the table, and said with a laugh in her words,

"It's all a trifle ghoulish, isn't it?"

"Ghoulish?"

"I feel as if we were entertaining our own executioner at dinner."

"Ah. Yes, and his assistant, who carries the basket."

"Basket?"

"Yes. For the heads."

"Hiram! How dreadful, you wicked— Here they come."

It was the other post families, all in high full dress, like the Prescotts. The gentlemen greeted each other with a symbolic finger in the collar, to dispose at once of the topic of the heat. Kitty and Laura toured the table, as Jessica had done, marveling. And then they heard hoofbeats, and then steps on the piazza, and they went to receive the general at the front door.

He entered wearing full-dress blues with long frock coat, two rows of gold buttons, five medals sewed to the breast and heavy dress epaulettes with thick fringes. His dress boots had long spurs nailed to the heels. He wore a general officer's gold bullion belt to which was slung a huge saber which he held off the ground with his left hand. Captain Brinker was outfitted in similar dress appropriate to his rank.

"A dream of fair women," declaimed the general, swinging bonily from one to another of them, kissing their hands in a determined gallantry. When he came to Laura, he held her away for a second to look at her, and then his swagger fell off him and he enfolded her in his arms like a father finding a daughter. She blushed with joy and kissed his cheek.

"My very dear little one," he said, so softly that the others almost could not hear him, "you can have no idea of how happy I am to see you, and how I have missed the thought of your being near me somewhere!"

"Uncle Alex!" she said, and it was enough.

Bismarck came forward in his turn and said,

"But Laura!"

His face told plainly that he could not believe the vision before him, after what he had seen the day before in her wretched hovel. Matthew watched him with a smile. Laura had done all possible to show Bismarck what the smutted slavey could turn into. She looked like someone who had stepped out of a magic bandbox. She wore her wedding dress which was white and shining, with a tail to it, and covered all over with rose vines made of little pearls. In her hair she wore half a dozen crescent moons made of diamonds, and more pearls and diamonds hung from her ears, and around her neck was a string of pearls. Long white kid gloves reached above her elbows and she carried a small lace fan. Her eyes outshone all else.

When General Quait gave himself to social gaiety, he was as constantly in motion as in acts of duty. He removed his belt and saber, handed them to Captain Brinker, and went to sit down in a little horsehair-cushioned chair. He sat like a child's drawing of a man seated, all up and down, with lap and feet making right angles. His feet he placed exactly side by side and together.

Jessica, making an innocent smile, gazed at his feet. If he had to place them together that way, like boots left outside a bedroom door to be cleaned, he still did not know what to do with them, even as a major general.

He saw the direction of her gaze and abruptly rose to overwhelm his sudden self-consciousness, and began to tour the Prescott parlor. He peered at what rested on wall or table, speaking aloud the name of each article he saw, while Jessica, honestly pleased with the success of her malicious joke, withdrew for a moment to the cooking shed. There Corporal Rainey and Private Clanahan, in white jackets, were marshaling the dinner which they would serve.

The company began to understand that they would not be called upon for much conversation. General Quait was in brilliant spirits. His cheeks were hot and dark above his white whiskers, his eyes danced, his loose gestures were genial.

"Sea shell," he said for all to hear as he moved down the wall, "specimen of amethyst quartz, an Italian dish, possibly majolica? A French filigree scent box of silver-gilt. And here is a spray of cattails which the Mexicans call *tules*. And two horses after Sir Frederick Leighton. To be sure. The cavalry. And how do you do, a banjo clock, with gold leaf and color within the glass, I should think quite old, actually. And what is this?—a silver medallion of the Emperor Napoleon III, a good likeness, if somewhat less heavy than as I saw him during the retreat from Metz—United States military observer, you know." He reached the doorway and found Jessica in it. "And my Lady Prescott," he declared, "you have come to announce dinner, and will you do me the honor to go in on my arm?"

So they went to table.

"Ah," remarked the general, "as I expected, you have gone the whole hog, or, as I say, *totus porcus*." Seated, he leaned forward in his chair at Jessica's right and touched one after another of the desert stalks and flowers in the centerpiece. "Yes," he said, naming them one by one, *"verbena bipinatifida,* yes, *senecio canescens,* yes, *cassia bauhinoides,* yes"—and thereafter made no comment on the dinner or its details. His beard glistened in the candlelight. In their deep caverns his eyes gleamed out impartially at one after another guest down the board. His dry crackling affability had a terrible force in it. It was the same power which Major Prescott and his officers had felt in their official dealings with him, and it gave them now the same cold blood of apprehension. Did the General rattle his incessant words in front of them to distract them from the fate which already he must have prepared for them? The garrison officers ate their dinner obediently, like large boys, and left it to their wives to respond with animation to the egocentric merriment of their principal guest.

Like many extremely thin men he seemed unable to have enough food. Eating as rapidly as he talked, the General seemed never to need to draw breath. He saw everything—the faces about the table, the two young soldiers in their mess boys' jackets, the dishes awaiting him on the sideboard. He took his first topic from the matter in hand.

"I am a food crank," he declared, and launched into a smiling dissertation on a favorite aspect of hygiene. "All green matter has a degree of pernicious toxicity. I consume greens in moderation only, and 'twould be better if not at all. But in my edacity—a cherished word, from *edere,* to eat, of which *edacious* is the adjectival form, meaning greed and greedy—I sample all. Consider, though. Animals domesticated for food purposes do not eat other meat—that is for man. What do animals consume? Vegetable matter originally green at some stage. Thus, man acquires from meat all the values green foods give to beef cattle and sheep. However: let me hasten to assure you that I restrain myself from governing, or attempting to govern, the pleasures and habits of others at table. I speak out only because conscience requires me at least to share my theory. Meantime, perhaps, Madam Prescott, a bit more of that capital curry of lamb?"

He broke off to catch Laura's eye. Making a signal with a bony finger, he seemed to send her a message beyond the words he spoke.

"You are furious with me, Laura, my dear! I did not make my manners to you earlier! But with my work—!"

"But no, Uncle Alex!"

"Ah, but yes. How heavenly you look tonight, child. —Thank you, yes, delicious, just a bite more, if you will. —Yes, clothes, what a study for the reflective mind. If I may adduce another theory which may be called Quait's Law. Clothing, of course, is designed to go the farthest remove from man natural, *id est,* man naked. Garments I am convinced have less to do with warmth and protection—aboriginal habit around the world proves that epidermis will suffice if the mind agrees—than with occasion and identification. To be properly accoutered—this is assuredly more valued than to be comfortable. Clothing has symbolic purpose. It announces who we are. Seeing me, dressed as I am in the full agony of a major general of regulars, you make no mistake about who I am or indeed what." He peered about at them, and the garrison officers quailed invisibly. "One wonders, if one were to dress up a dog or a monkey in robes or uniform, whether the total result would not be believed in terms of the costume? Yes. And possibly the beholder would believe more readily than the wearer."

Kitty Mainwaring sneezed out of nervousness at such clever and trying talk. Lifting a small phial from an inner pocket of his heavy tunic, the general handed it to her and said,

"Syrup of violets. My constant specific against colds. Three drops in your water glass, please. Yes. Infallible. Yes. I believe Mr. Ruskin uses the same."

Having cured her cold, he returned the phial to his pocket and rattled on. His eyes danced across the laden table and sparkled with appetite, and if someone offered him what he saw, he would take, without comment, and go on talking. He talked of army life, politics, travel abroad, phrenology, burial customs of the Dakotas, Mr. Disraeli (whom he had met), Queen Victoria (whom he had not), and a dozen other things. Only when the dessert came and the champagne was poured and official toasts were drunk was there a pause, and then Jessica broke in saying,

"You know, general, my family used to receive you in Washington."

"Indeed? Indeed? And who were your family?"

"My mother was Isabel Mercer."

"Ah, yes. Secretary Mercer's daughter. I do recall. I do indeed."

His spirit flagged for a moment. A vagrant shame for all the absurdities of his awkward youth, with its violent longing for distinction that had led him to affectations, came back to him now. Jessica swiftly concluded that it had needed only her reminder to discomfit him with his young self in the Mercer household. With one half of her heart she was sorry she had summoned back the time of mockery for him, for she meant this evening to be hospitable, no matter what her guest might end by doing officially to Hiram, her life; but with the other half she could not help enjoying, in Hiram's name, what she had done.

Kitty Mainwaring was like a child at a party who has missed every prize. She kept looking at the general, and then at the complicated display of the table, of which he had noticed nothing but the spiny centerpiece. For her the party was a ruin because he had not exclaimed over every salted nut. She could not see how Mrs. Prescott could be so serene, so grand, in her low gown and her diamonds, or how Laura Hazard could keep her eyes on the general until he looked at her, and then lower them with pretty confusion, which made him brush his mustaches with the backs of his fingers, and ride his chair gallantly.

A small cry sounded from the bedroom. Laura rose.

"Oh, Mrs. Prescott, please excuse me. It is Prescott," and went to her baby.

"Prescott?" said the general, lifting his fierce white eyebrows inquiringly.

"My namesake and godson," said Major Prescott. "Matthew and Laura's baby."

"Baby? To be sure. I had intended to have him produced for me to greet. Will he come here?"

Matthew asked Mrs. Prescott with a glance and she nodded. In a moment he brought Laura, holding Prescott, to the candlelit dining room. General Quait immediately held out his arms to take the baby. With misgivings, Laura yielded up the child. But if her son was alarmed by so much white whisker and bright cheek and sparkle of eye, he kept it to himself. He lay looking up with a faint smile of drowsy curiosity while General Quait smiled upon him and addressed a speculative monologue in a soft voice to the transfixed company.

"Ah yes," he said, "every infant as it grows passes through all the stages of human history. Quait's Law, if you will. If the idea is not wholly new, still, it has its striking analogies, and it has long amused me to speculate upon it. Yes, you see, the time of ooze—I recall your Darwin to you—and the sea and the water and the fish and the gills and the fishlike sounds—did you know that fish are not silent?—of prenatality, yes, how fascinating. And then birth and babyhood—the dawn of time on earth is what the infant itself encounters. What matters it that others see him as coming into an advanced environment? To him the environment as he perceives it must seem like that which revealed itself after Noah's flood, when the first dry earth appeared.

"Comes then a happy short span of creature perceptions, and

motor training. And then—perhaps in the years of seven to ten—
a Golden Age, a time Hellenic in its classic charm and peace. The
child then exhibits an odd selflessness, in his citizenship among the
guileless young, when spontaneous gifts are made without reason and
accepted without greed. To be sure, gifts at times smudged and
sticky, but gifts from the heart all the same. And so, on to manhood,
which we will let correspond to the present age—this age of gallantry,
science and enlightenment, in which mankind has made such giant
strides toward a civilized millennium. Yes, we may read all this ahead
for this golden mite of life!"

He held the baby up to face him and the baby took it as a game
and showed his rosy mouth open in a soft chesty laugh. "How beautiful," said General Quait, "is the responsibility of educating the inherent faculties of this unformed spirit. If I were privileged to
oversee it, I would teach all the usual gifts of knowledge, deportment
and honor. But I would teach one thing more." His voice fell gentle
and he looked at the floor while he said, "I would educate this
wonderful small being not only for power and triumph, but also for
a day of sorrow, such as must come to him no less than to all others.
I would then, if my lesson were successful, know that there he would
go, a strong man. —Thank you, Laura, my dear, here is your darling
dandy."

"Yes, Laura, thank you," said Jessica, and gathering Kitty, she
withdrew the ladies and the infant, leaving the table to the gentlemen.

lxv

Major Prescott moved to his wife's place next to General Quait,
offering the general a cigar. The two lieutenants produced their own
and were about to light them, when they noticed that General Quait
was sitting bolt upright, staring at nothing with still eyes. His whole
bearing expressed shocked disapproval. Captain Brinker spoke for
him.

"Permit me, gentlemen. General Quait does not use tobacco in
any form; and it is his custom to leave any room where it may be
used by others."

"Very well, sir," said the major, putting away his cigar case and
motioning to the others. The general at once went easy and was

about to speak, but Major Prescott, filled to the limit with injuries and bafflements, firmly put his fist on the table and declared,

"General, forgive me if I take the floor for a moment. I know you are willing to forget official cares for this evening, and we hope you are enjoying our little function. But sir, I have had no opportunity to speak with you, and neither have my officers. I do not presume to judge your actions, sir, but I feel absolutely obliged by my duty to ask if you have considered how the Indians will interpret the hearings which they attended yesterday?"

"*I beg your pardon,* major?" asked Captain Brinker thickly. But for the first time, the general put the adjutant down with a finger and nodded to the major to continue.

"Sir, the Indians—for your own no doubt excellent reasons—came to witness what amounted to a display of bitter disharmony in the Army on this frontier. Sir, I believe most earnestly that they will only interpret this as weakness on our part. I fear very much for the effect of this on them, and on the whole Territory. If, for official reasons, my officers and myself had to be skinned alive, so be it— not that any of us enjoyed it." (Captain Brinker smiled modestly.) "But sir, let me urgently recommend that immediate steps be taken to strengthen defenses wherever possible, until we see the results of the Indian visit to Fort Delivery in these past few days!"

The general's head began to drift in little rotary motions toward the end of Major Prescott's remarks, giving an effect of amused thought going around in circles. He now looked at Major Prescott in silence for a long, probing moment, and then abruptly he stood up, saying,

"Thank you, major," in a deliberately colorless voice. "Let us join the ladies."

Major Prescott flushed and said harshly,

"You are wholly welcome, sir. I will say no more on the subject, but only hold on here, and watch, and fight. For it will come to fighting again if Washington goes on coddling the aggressors. What will happen in this particular corner when I'm relieved at Fort Delivery, I would not care to say."

The general led the way to the parlor. Major Prescott left the dining room last. He could only shrug in utmost discouragement at his officers.

lxvi

Out in the long wide hall that ran from front to back of the headquarters there were tentative blurts of music from a violin and a horn, a dimmed ruffle on a drum. Subdued but excited talk hummed over the waiting soldiers and the three women from Soapsuds Row. On the piazza at the front, the stoop at the rear, clustered those who could not find places in the long hall without filling it up in the center. They peered in from outside. At one end of the hall sat the orchestra—the trumpeter with his valve cornet, the armorer with his fiddle, and Private Clanahan with his drum. Three lamps hung in a row down the ceiling. As all remarked, the place was an oven.

But the excitement of the garrison at the high state of a major general's visit overcame all disadvantages, and when the parlor doors flew open and the music began on that signal, there could have been no greater satisfaction than to see the commanding officer's wife, to whom all were devoted, taken down the whole length of the hall in the arms of Major General Alexander Upton Quait in an evolution of remarkable energy and invention. He held her with his elbows lifted at right angles to his sides. His face was fixed in a scowling smile of fierce concentration while he counted rhythm in a whistly whisper. Launching his joy, he roved three times rapidly to the left and then violently whirled with a high backward kick that made his spur glitter in the air. He reversed the figure to the right. He then advanced down the center in long swooping steps, repeating his whirls and kicks and glides. He required, with his amazed partner, a radius of three feet about him at all times in order to accomplish his pleasure without offering serious danger to others from the kick of his spurs.

The valve cornet and the drum faltered now and then as their players watched the general taking Jessica Prescott up and down the rocking floor. But he nodded and waved to all others to show that they too must come on the floor and dance, only see how well he enjoyed it, let all join in—and soon the laundresses with partners and all the other lone troopers who could find space on the floor were dancing in pairs under the general's furious and yet systematic example. The first dance ended. General Quait returned Jessica to her husband.

"That," he said in the thinned voice of elderly excitement, "is what I call the Glide Waltz."

"Most remarkable, most extraordinary!" said Jessica.

The general bowed with a wrenching twist from the waist.

"Not at all, my lady," he said, happy in what he construed as a compliment. "And now, where is Mrs. Mainwaring? I believe her husband is next in seniority?"

Jessica wanted to laugh right out. The general, frank as a boy, was ticking off his social duty first thing. Again she had a curious pang of sympathy for one who after a lifetime of determined effort could not yet move with ease in his natural element of human company.

The dance was resumed and its gaiety went like a prairie fire. Captain Brinker, dancing with Mrs. Prescott, made eyes at her, and stumbled for doing so. She smiled over his shoulder at Hiram Prescott, sending him a silent message with face and finger to say that the adjutant, without anyone's noticing, had managed to get himself drunk on champagne at dinner. The major, with a heavy heart, gave her a smile to indicate that he had received her intelligence, and walked out to the open night for a moment with a cigar.

He was troubled for what he thought of as the shame of Fort Delivery, which had come so suddenly, and left so little hope, either for himself as man and officer, or, as he saw it, for that part of the nation which he defended and loved. He walked around headquarters to the west side, leaned on the wall under his office window, and lighted his cigar.

Through the walnut blinds of the window fell pale gold bars of lamplight on the dark ground. They lighted little for him to see. They seemed to him like his own quality of mind. Seeing things only in little slats of revelation, he wished he had the power to see grand prospects and big visions. He kicked the ground gently, musing. He supposed, finally, that he was at his best with soldiers in combat, horses, dogs, and his good wife. Why did not the Army let him alone to do what he could do? But for all his feeling of baffled modesty, he mourned now to think that he would never be known as colonel, much less general. It was hard in the prime of life to admit that a career was in all probability stopped in its tracks.

lxvii

It was there, in such a mood, that they presently found him. He heard steps coming off the piazza and around the weathered adobe corner of the building. When he saw who came first, he threw away his cigar and heaved his shoulder off from the wall. It was General Quait, followed by Matthew Hazard and Ted Mainwaring.

"Thank you, major," said the general coming toward him in a skeletal walk that expressed clattering jubilation, "the smoke of the ignited tobacco leaf causes some obscure agony to my breathing apparatus. My objections are, then, rather than moral or social, wholly physical."

"Yes, sir."

"Yes. I have personally brought myself together with you gentlemen now, alone, while my adjutant is dancing with the fair lady of the Mainwarings, for I have business with you."

He faced the window. The slats of light went across him. His medals, his gold fringes, glimmered as he unbuttoned his thick frock coat and from an inner pocket brought out a little sheaf of folded pages.

"Do you know what these are?" he asked.

"Sir, is it the stenograph of the—the inquiry?" asked Matthew.

"It is that precisely," said the general, "and it has never been copied. Permit me, major."

With that, General Quait tore the record in two, and then tore it again. He handed the shreds to Hiram.

"Sir!"

"Yes, major, burn them, dispose of them as you will. They have served their purposes. Among others, they have helped me to know the caliber of men whom I am going to need—how soon, none can say."

"Sir?"

"My official inquiry here ended only an hour ago, major, at your dinner table. When I said 'Thank you' as we rose from the table, I meant it. What I thanked you for was your devotion to duty, your concern for the whole outcome here in the desert, over and above your natural bitterness about your personal difficulties."

The major and his young officers peered at each other. Did they dare to hope that matters were improving? The general put his hands together with satisfaction and sent his thumbs spinning about each other. He resumed speaking, and they listened intently.

"I believe we have ended, at Washington, the period of do-nothing-ism. The President is finally determined that the frontier menaces must be crushed. But he has felt pressures, and while his purpose is firm, he has had to make certain trades to accomplish various purposes which have nothing to do with the West. I believe a certain clique in the House, led by a most curious specimen of congressman, the Honorable Granville Joe Squillers, was able to receive the latest favor. But I am assured it will be the last one. I do trust so, for we shall not be able to endure many more favors like it. In short, the so-called 'Indian party' in the Congress has managed to obtain amnesty for Rainbow Son and his followers."

"Amnesty, sir!"

"Yes. Charges against him have been dropped. He need not fear punishment now for past crimes."

"But sir," declared the major, "he will see this as sanction of any future crimes he may commit! They've turned him loose!"

"Ah, yes," said the general, and a smile all but whistled through his beard, "but at the same time, they have turned *me* loose. I have fought him before, you know. As of tomorrow I assume command of the Territorial Department. It may be that I will fight him again. Now. Pay attention. This is significant.

"I sent word to those Indians to meet with me here. They were a group out of Mexico from Rainbow Son's following. I wanted to say certain things to them in terms of honorable warnings. But I also wanted them to witness our proceedings. I believe you will recall? Yes. When I spoke to them at the end, I told them to remember well that injustice, wickedness, evildoing were not tolerated among our own people"—he pointed genially—"meaning yourselves, gentlemen, and that no more would they be in future tolerated among Indian people. They witnessed our crude efforts at a military inquiry and were impressed, as I could well see. And then I told them—you heard them gasp—how their head man, Rainbow Son, was being granted forgiveness by the good heart of the great father at Washington. Of course I said everything a dozen times, and made florid solemnities serve instead of logic, but the point was made. I told them they must go home to Rainbow Son and tell him that he must keep the peace and stay in Mexico, and I told them another dozen times that

I could promise him punishment, and war to the end, if he crossed the border and broke the peace. All his people would suffer with him. Well, as you know, they have gone, witnesses to our sense of justice. Indians know justice and injustice like anyone else. They heard me."

"This is immense, sir," said the major, "but it still occurs to me that they may take fairness as a sign of weakness."

"*Veritas, veritas,* and it is for just this reason that as I came west I laid down a mobilization that is already moving. This Department will presently receive new forces from Fort Union, Fort Bliss, and Fort Wingate. There will be a period of quiet, but it will be the quiet of creatures opposed to each other, listening as it were, for sounds of aggressive intention. And one day, if Rainbow Son, wild with license as a result of a quixotic application of the precepts of charity, if Rainbow Son should break over from Mexico in any force, this time the equation is to be factored out to its ultimate."

"General, I cannot tell you—" began Major Prescott, and found actually that he could not. There was a momentary silence while a new thought went through the minds of the garrison officers. They glanced at each other and hesitated to speak, and General Quait picked up their thought for them.

"Yes, gentlemen, you may well ask how it was that I permitted you to suffer the inquiry if it was meant chiefly as dramatics. Let me tell you. *Primo,* the Indians would know it at once if you were only pretending indignation and distress. Their talent for spiritual penetration is greater than any soldier's for acting. *Secundo,* there is the matter of Captain Brinker. He too believed that you gentlemen were to be found delinquent in your duties and he behaved accordingly."

"But why, sir?"

"He was appointed in Washington for this mission by those who feel the Army is always wrong, the Indian always right. Well, of course, nobody is ever always right or wrong. But this infantile observation is still beyond some members of Congress. Even certain statesmen of the *senaculum,* as I believe the Romans called their senate chamber, tremble professionally between greed and sentimentality. I was privy to certain conferences presided over by the grotesque Squillers, and I never listened to so many rose-water imbecilities, as Carlyle would have said, or to such unashamed plans for private gain at public expense. Communications from our friend

Seeley Jones were, cynically enough, part of the record. Well, to achieve justification for their unholy alliance with Jones and his kind, these guardians of the republic required evidence for their case. Captain Brinker was at hand to gather it. This being so, it suited my purposes to use his talent for the disagreeable. It is, may I add, considerable." He turned to Matthew. "In you, lieutenant, he had, I understand, a personal target."

"But sir," replied Matthew, "he was just as personally disagreeable to everyone else. I don't see why he had to be."

"Ah, my good young man, Tacitus said it for us: *proprium humani ingenii est odisse quem laesaris*, that is, *it is a human trait to hate whom you harm*. Poor Captain Brinker. He has worked most dutifully. But now instead of his stenographic report, there will go to the War Department certain recommendations I am making." The general turned to Mainwaring. "Lieutenant, you, having made clear that you took no part in the events under discussion, will understand that I do not include you in my dispatches."

Teddy smiled uncertainly and swallowed. Here was the just return for his earlier denials. He felt a sick qualm now when he thought of how he must tell Kitty that he had been passed over, and why.

"For you, major," continued the general, "I am recommending permanent promotion to major and a brevet of lieutenant colonel. And for you, Mr. Hazard, my nephew-in-law-by-marriage, if such a fantasy of genealogy exists, I propose a brevet of first lieutenant, with my complete endorsement of your action of last April. Now, when renewed warfare comes to us here, as well it may, I now know I can lean heavily on you both, with more responsible commands." He put his forefinger to the tip of his nose in order to announce that he meant to look wise. "It takes great fiber, in my opinion, for men to meet and transcend the sort of ordeal you have met and transcended in our few days here."

They thanked him shortly. He knew their feelings. He thought of something else.

"I am also making official commendation of your scout, White Horn—whom you call Joe Dummy, in the usual habit of our people to reshape the dignity of subordinate or alien peoples to suit ourselves, alas. He was one of my first crop of Apache scouts. He resisted me for longer than any other I recruited. I respected him for it. Here at my camp I asked him five several times to give me his version of the Moon Mesa affair. Five several times he gave it to me with no detail of variation at any time. He is a truthful man. A brave soldier. The best of the Apache nature, which is good to see when we must punish the worst. As we also punish *our* worst," he added with spirit. "Mr. Seeley Jones, for example. The marshal of the Territory has a warrant to arrest him, and may have done so by now. Mr. Seeley Jones holds no title to any property such as he based his claim upon. He will meet justice, gentlemen, if he lives one day longer—which very possibly he may not do. I know his disease. I once had it."

lxviii

The hot, starry night suddenly went quiet. Those under the office window heard that the orchestra had stopped playing. The dance number was over. General Quait twined his fingers together in finical merriment. The other officers had been so lost in respect for his unquestioned power in their profession of arms that they were now startled to see again his rattle-boned assumption of social postures.

"The dance is ended," he cried, "long live the dance. I must have the next one. Come, gentlemen. 'There was a sound of revelry by night.' "

He led them with his rickety stride back to the hall. At the door he paused to say softly, "Nothing of all this to poor Brinker, pray," and then entered to rove the ladies with his eye until he came upon the youngest laundress—it was Dutchy, with her fresh face and placid German eyes. To her he made his way, bowed with his arm bone across his gaunt middle, and took her off to glide strenuously away as the orchestra struck up, and the other two laundresses bridled at her luck, even as behind their hands they mocked the old gentleman who was so dizzily above them in station.

The garrison officers returned to the floor. Near the door they saw Captain Brinker breaking away from Kitty Mainwaring with desperate pleasantries of escape. Teddy went to claim her. The captain stood for a moment alone, wiping his face with his silk handkerchief. Kitty, like many small women dancing, had been heavy, inert, in his grasp. He was glassy from champagne, heat and effort.

Hiram Prescott and Matthew were in high spirits at the end of their ordeal. With suddenly inspired smiles they exchanged a look and, understanding each other perfectly, went together to the adjutant.

"Come on, Bismarck," said Hiram, hooking an arm through his, "you need a little restorative."

Bismarck was suspicious of such sudden familiarity, but allowed himself to be dragged to the dining room where under their example he agreed to swallow a half tumbler of whisky.

"We know what you've been through here in the last few days," said the major, "and I just suppose it wasn't a pleasant job you had to do."

For a moment, as the whisky made its strike at him, Captain Brinker became more himself than ever. His eyes went pinpointed and he said,

"The record is closed, gentlemen, and nothing you can do at this stage will be of the smallest help to you. I suppose you put him up to this, Matt. Well, it will do you no good."

"Help. To us?" said Matthew with an air of outsized virtue. "We know that, we know you could only do your duty, and we just wanted to let you know that we sympathize with you. It isn't easy to come in and be somebody's guest and cut their throat—we know that."

"You do see that it was my duty, then?" said Bismarck. His eyes filled in sudden emotion. The whisky softened his ordinary disdain and he had a pang for these splendid comrades in arms on whom he had sat in judgment.

"Yes, yes," they said, pouring another round.

"I don't know," said Bismarck weakly, "perhaps I was too hard on you."

"Oh, no," moaned Hiram, "what else could you do, with the general there, and the rest?"

"No personalities could be allowed to enter in," said Matthew mournfully, "we know that."

"Oh, yes," cried the adjutant, holding himself steady by their shoulders, "I may have been overzealous. Nothing is too much trouble for me when I am on a mission. I have been told that."

"Never!" bawled Hiram in a calflike voice, "never say that Adrian Brinker did not perform his assigned task with less than utter impartiality and devotion to truth! Never! D'you hear?"

"Sir, I hear," said Matthew, in a sort of howling piety, "I hear and I horrificate!"

"Yes, the record is closed," said Bismarck, searching their faces with his badly bent vision, "and there is nothing to be done about

it now, but I'll tell you what, I'll tell you that I will make a point
to report when I get back to Washington, report that, make a report
that I heard Jerl Quait say after inspection today, that he said, that
without any s'adow of a doubt, that he never saw cavalry horses better cared for anywhere *than right here at For' Delivery!"*

"*Did he say that!*" roared Hiram Prescott in enlarged awe, "and
will you really tell them that he did?"

"He did, I heard him. I certainly will. —It is just a shame, I can't
help being vexed," said the captain, weakened by the first good
fellowship since childhood, "that things are the way they are, especially after you've been so white to me, you fellows."

Without warning he bolted from them to the dining-room wall,
leaned his back against it and slid slowly to the floor where they
left him.

lxix

Matthew danced with Laura. Their pleasure was great. Their relief
was extravagant. It tried to speak through love.

"I tell you," said Matthew, "he is a great man! A very great man!
I wouldn't be surprised if he were the next lieutenant general of the
Army! I am going to name our next son Alexander U. Q. Hazard!"

Laura knew that time was a woman's great modifier and simply
smiled at his sparkling, black-browed face.

Across the hall General Quait came to the commanding officer at
eleven o'clock precisely.

"It has been a positively rattling party, major—I hope I shall be
saying *colonel* soon—but as we are to break camp in the early hours,
I shall now withdraw. To my Lady Prescott"—he turned to her—"the
thanks of an old scarecrow who has perhaps one more job in him to
do for his country. You will both be coming to Washington sooner or
later. Our hospitality cannot match yours, of course, but when you
come, I shall discover you, and I shall ask for an opportunity to fling
back the cutlet. Madam—" With a leg before him, he made an old-
fashioned bow that went back to cadet days before the Mexican
War, shook hands with Major Prescott, waved to the company, who
all waved back, and finding his saber carried it out to his horse by
the piazza.

There waited Captain Brinker in the spilling lamplight, barely able
to stand by holding to his horse's stirrup. Major Prescott went to help
him up. General Quait watched. When the adjutant was mounted, the
general remarked.

"What is not in the heart cannot be poured into it from a bottle.
Ah. Well."

He then brisked up in his own saddle, and in his old, official,
reduced but penetrating voice, said,

"Major? A final word for your ear—once more from the great
Roman whom I am rereading, and who is a great source of lessons
for any soldier: *inter somnum ac trepidationem vigilibus irrupere,*
which, for your lesson, please translate as follows: *overwhelming the
sentries, they struck terror into the sleeping camp.* Good-by, sir,
for the present. You shall hear from me."

Leaving the commander of Fort Delivery smarting in the dark,
Major General Alexander Upton Quait turned and rode off to Camp
Two-Star, followed in depressed silence by Captain Adrian Brinker.
Major Prescott watched them into the darkness, and then went to give
certain orders to his guard details. He did not tell them what to watch
for, for as he said to himself he would play it fair; but if during the
night they saw anything at all in the range of vision of the post, to
wake him first, and then Second Lieutenant Hazard in Quarters 3.

So it was that long before reveille, Major Prescott and Lieutenant
Hazard were before the west gate, watching in the starlight as Camp
Two-Star came down. They listened in the stillness to the tiny sounds
of hoof stamp, and a chime of buckle, a creak of rope as packs were
made and loaded.

"I suppose he would expect a sentinel to ride out and challenge him
at this point," said Matthew.

"Maybe so. I'd just rather let him know we saw, this time, Tacitus
or no Tacitus."

The major put a cigar to his mouth and struck a phosphorus match
and lingeringly lighted and puffed at his smoke. The little fire, its
long, easy breaths, visible far across the flat night landscape, told of
someone awake and confident, watchful yet willing to keep his distance.

"If I know my man," said the major softly, letting his match die,
"he saw that."

The camp moved away to the northwest.

The two officers watching lost it by ear and then by eye very soon.

But they stayed out in the night for a while, sharing conjectures of the future as hard as the challenging world of the desert and the horizon north of Mexico, which had seemed lost to them, and which now were restored to them in purpose and duty because they were the men to master it, when their time should come, as it must.

lxx

Some weeks later, behind the barracks, Corporal Rainey and Private Clanahan were working leather with saddle soap and a bucket of water. As they finished, Clanahan was about to spill away the bucket when Rainey stopped him.

"Wait. Keep that water. I promised to wash the dog for Mrs. Mainwaring. I'll be right back. You wait here. You can help me. He's a big dog."

Clanahan waited. Thoughts which had troubled him for some time now arose again and he knew that he would somehow have to let them come into words when Rainey returned. If what he thought was true, then he must warn Rainey, though Rainey might not like it.

"Here he is," said Rainey, bringing Garibaldi the greyhound around the barracks to the patch of shade where Clanahan waited. There was nobody else nearby. Clanahan's pulse began to throb. "Now we'll scrub him," said Rainey. "He got into something a day or two ago and he smells to heaven. She wants him prettied up."

He took a sponge and rinsed it in the saddle-soapy water and began to rub down the dog's smooth coat. Clanahan was silent and inactive.

"Here," said Rainey, "what's the matter with you? Come on. Give us a hand. This hound has two sides to him."

Clanahan moodily began to scrub at the dog. Rainey scowled. What had got into Clanahan while waiting for him to return with the hound?

"What're you so glum about, all of a sudden?" he asked.

"Nothing." Clanahan pushed hard along the dog's hair with his sponge. "Only I don't see why, just because she tells you to, you have to go giving her dog a bath."

"She didn't tell me to. She just said she wanted it and I said I'd do it. That's all."

"Well, I don't think that's all," said Clanahan, and now because he had begun to say what he had to say, he was dry-mouthed and a little breathless.

"Oh, you don't. Well, what else, then?"

"If I tell you you'll get sore."

"Maybe I will and maybe I won't."

"Well, I'm your friend, ain't I?"

"Oh, shit. What the hell makes you ask a question like that? Sure you're my friend. Hell."

"Well, a friend has to say something sometimes that is supposed to be good for a friend but the friend may not want to hear it."

Rainey sat back. His face hardened.

"Go on," he said.

"Well," said Clanahan, with almost a pleading voice, "it's about her."

"Her?"

"Yes, her."

"Who's her?"

"You know who. Mrs. Mainwaring."

For a moment Rainey was stretched between resentment and relief. He had been wanting to talk to Clanahan about this very thing for weeks, yet he disliked having it pulled out of him. But the excitement he had held in secret pressed him to share it with his best friend, and he now could do so. It was a pleasure he had looked forward to with hunger, but until now he had never found the way to break it upon Clanahan. He grinned and looked around him to all sides to be sure of privacy, and then leaned close to Clanahan and said huskily,

"Well, I want to tell you, but nobody else, you hear? Nobody knows and you got to swear not to tell anybody."

"I swear. But I know already."

"You do? How the hell do you know?"

"Just by the way you act."

"Act? I don't act any special way."

"I mean running over there all the time, and keeping yourself all shined up, extra, all the time. And then when you're off somewhere on a detail by yourself, I notice she's off somewhere, too, riding her horse along the arroyo, or walking off a little ways with her dog. I ain't blind. But I'm scared others may not be blind, too. I been trying to get around to warning you."

"Warning me? You think somebody else might be noticing?"

"Maybe not yet, but they will, soon. *I* seen it just because you was around all the time where I was until you began being around where she was. So that's all I mean. I just mean you got to be careful and you really ought to cut it out. If they ever catch you—an enlisted man monkeying around with an officer's wife—holy gee, Rainey, you'll sure catch it."

Rainey grew serious.

"Yes, I know. I have thought a lot about all that. I sure don't want to get in trouble. I told her once I better quit. She raised hell, she cried, and hollered, and said I don't love her, and all that."

"Do you?"

"Do I what?"

"Love her?"

"Hell, no."

"Did you—did she let you—?"

"What do you take me for? Sure I did. Sure she did. Every time."

Clanahan wished he knew everything that Rainey, and every man, knew about the subject, from experience.

"How was it?" he asked, swallowing.

"How was it? Like it always is."

"Did she like it?"

"What do *you* think?"

"Do you want to keep on doing it?"

"What do *you* think?"

"Are you going to?"

"I don't know. I know I hadn't ought to. It ain't easy to fix it up so we can meet where there's nobody around. And she always wants to *talk*. My God, she wants to talk."

"What about?"

"Oh, about everything. Her husband, he don't love her any more, and why ain't he a captain, and all the money her family almost did make, and how she could have married a French count and gone to live in high society, and what she wants to do for me, and we will run away to San Francisco, and I'll have my own brass band, playing the cornet, and oh, you know, all that muck. I said to her, I told her, once, I said, 'Honey, if you just shut up, we could have a nice time doing this.' She slapped me in the face and said I was a clod. I slapped her back and said good-by. She came after me and began to holler so I had to go back and stay to keep her quiet." Rainey shook his head. "Maybe it ain't worth it."

He looked up and saw Clanahan's black eyes fixed on him in confused intensity. Rainey smiled. "Old Briney Clanahan. I sure ain't seen so much of you, lately, have I? I guess I better call it off. She'll get over it. I guess it's too much risk to keep on taking. How about it, Briney?"

Clanahan took a deep breath, and went back to scrubbing the dog. "That's what I been trying to warn you about, Rainey."

"Well, you won't have to, again."

"That's great."

The two young soldiers fell silent, and then presently, without signal, but at the same moment, they began to whistle idly. Each had a different tune, neither heard the other, and both were content.

lxxi

Going through the mail in the fortnightly bag, Major Prescott attended first to War Department matter. What he read made him sit back and look out the window. He took a deep breath and said, "Well," and then again, "Well, sir." He then called his orderly in from the hall and said,

"Corporal, hike over to the corral and send Lieutenant Hazard to me."

"Yes, sir."

Until Matthew arrived, the commanding officer sorted out the rest of the mail into neat little stacks. In a few minutes Matthew stood before him.

"Here you are, Matthew. You're a brevet first lieutenant now. Congratulations, my boy."

Matthew took his papers. He turned pink under his tan. Reflecting upon his own first promotion the commanding officer could feel the young man's emotion with him. No promotion would ever mean as much as that one, even a general's star—but Hiram Prescott believed he would himself never know anything about that.

"Thank you, sir," said Matthew, going calm again. "Do I call you colonel, now?"

"Well, yes."

They shook hands. Matthew asked,

"Is there anything for Mainwaring?"

"No. You heard what General Quait said."

"Yes, but I thought perhaps at the last minute—"

"No, Matt, it was not justified. Tell me. Do you happen to know whether he's ever said anything to Kitty about the general's remarks that evening?"

"No, sir. But I don't think so. I doubt if he could. I think if he had, she would have said something to someone. Several times, probably."

"Poor girl. Well, I'd better talk to Ted myself, first. Send him over, will you? Then you go and tell Laura, but have her keep it to herself till we can lift Kitty over the thing, if we have to."

In a few minutes Mainwaring reported to the office. The commanding officer asked him to sit down, gave him a cigar and lighted it for him. Teddy was apprehensive at being called alone to headquarters at an odd hour of the day. It made Hiram Prescott a little impatient to see such a big man trying to look small, and such an uneasy man trying to smile.

"Ted," he said, "have you ever thought to mention to Kitty what General Quait said to us about promotions the night of our dance?"

"No, sir. She worries so, you know, and then, I thought—" He paused. Hiram was sorry for him, but irritably reflected that Teddy should have known there was not a chance of what he hoped for. Teddy continued, "I thought perhaps by some hook or crook something might come through for me after all, and if it did, why, then she'd have been upset for no reason." He squeezed his cigar till it flaked and asked, "Why, sir? Did something come through?"

"Yes, Ted. This morning, by the bag. I'm sorry to tell you you didn't make anything. I'm trying to figure the next step."

"I see. Did Matt? Did you?"

"Yes. Both of us, as the general indicated."

"I'm very glad, sir. Congratulations, colonel."

"Thanks, Ted."

Mainwaring began to sweat. He stared past the walls of the office, and what he saw of his life was nothing for Colonel Prescott to see. He raised his cigar and when he looked back at the colonel, he had tears in his eyes, perhaps from the cigar smoke, as the colonel preferred to think.

"I don't care, for myself," said Teddy. "But Kitty—she'll never—" Never what? Forgive him? Forget it? Understand it? Colonel Prescott sighed, and said,

"Ted, you just sit here and wait a minute. I've thought of something. Sometimes wives can handle these things better than we can. Excuse me, will you?"

The colonel crossed the hall to his quarters and said to Jessica,

"Do you know whether Kitty Mainwaring knows that Ted could not possibly expect to be promoted this time?"

Jessica viewed him with speculative exasperation.

"This time?" she repeated. "Do you mean that the papers have come?"

"Yes. Matt and I. Not Ted."

"And you did not inform me first thing that I am now a colonel's lady? Hiram, you're impossible. I wish you'd put your mind on me now and then. Come here." She embraced him. Then she said, "No, I'm sure Kitty doesn't know. Oh: the poor child."

"Question is, should you perhaps tell her, the way you can, you know—nice and direct, but count-your-blessings sort of thing? Or should we leave it to Ted, and God knows what?"

"I could try," said Jessica, "but you know women. She might think I was being grand with my new rank. —No, on the whole, I'm afraid this is one of those things in a family nobody outside can handle. Let's stay out of it, Hiram, now and afterward."

"As if we could," said Hiram. "All right." He started for the office.

"Good-by, colonel," Jessica called after him.

"Good-by, Mrs. O'Grady," he replied and returned to Mainwaring, who had a look of polite hope on his face which faded when the colonel said, "On the whole, we think you'd better manage this with Kitty by yourself, Ted."

In his fresh disappointment, Teddy cloaked himself in dignity. He rose and said,

"I never expected anyone else to do it for me, colonel."

"Good!" said the colonel heartily, confirming Teddy's poor dodge. When Teddy was gone, Colonel Prescott said to himself, half-aloud, "I'm a fool to hope so, but what if this should bring her closer to Ted, and break up the other thing?" He could prove nothing, and he deeply hoped he would never have to know proof of what he was thinking about. But as some people knew how to make things grow, others, equally true to their natures, knew how to destroy, and must do so. Poor Kitty, he said, poor, ruinous Kitty.

lxxii

"I have seen Kitty," said Mrs. Prescott. "You will never guess. She has taken charge of the celebration about the promotions."

"Thunder," said the colonel.

"Yes, she came over to see me this afternoon, trembling, all pale green, and smiling, and I wanted to hush her in my arms, she looked so *breakable*. She said that as the Mainwarings are the only family that did not get promoted, she was the only wife who could be hostess at a party to celebrate. None of the new rank could do it, she said, without seeming to congratulate themselves. So you see? she said, there's always *some* good in every situation, because now she was left free to do the proper thing. It was trying."

"Oh, thunderation. What's she going to do?"

"Yes, as she is so really torn apart by this, she has to make a really grand gesture to prove that she isn't. You'll never believe it, but here it is—she's going to give a hunt breakfast."

"Now, Jess, talk sense."

"I told you. —I said to her, a hunt breakfast? But without a hunt, of course, I said. We shouldn't ride out here as if we were all at Fort Belvoir, Virginia. But she said how could there be a hunt breakfast without a hunt before it? This was just my point, so I agreed, and then she said, yes, we were all to put on our best riding habits, and ride out tomorrow morning just after reveille, all of us—the Prescotts, the Hazards, and the Mainwarings, and of course Garibaldi, and hunt rabbits in the desert. Then we're to return to Quarters 2 for a delicious breakfast, with every possible trimming."

"In this heat? She wants to go to all that work?"

"I know, but she said I was not to say another word, her mind was made up, and if she wished to do this for her commanding officer, on such a wonderful occasion, and so on. She had tears in her eyes. So there you are. We hunt, then we feast."

"Have you accepted?"

"Tentatively, but of course I said I must ask you."

"I'm afraid we cannot. There are very real objections, you know. Military ones."

"Oh, Lord, isn't it frightful how the Army keeps getting in our way."

"We're in the Army, after all."

"As I say," murmured Jessica with radiant illogic.

"You've done enough on this, Jess, and thank you. I'll go see Kitty myself."

"You're going to regret it."

Since she knew the answer, he did not reply.

At Quarters 2, next door, Kitty received Colonel Prescott. She was hard at work, with Laura to help her, preparing for the hunt breakfast. She threw her arms around the colonel's neck and kissed him on the cheek, straining against him like an unwanted child. She was drawn with exertion. In a high, dry voice she exclaimed,

"Congratulations, Colonel Hiram, we are all so proud of you!"

"Thanks, thanks, Kitty, my dear."

"You aren't supposed to see what we're doing, yet, so please don't come in, there is so much to do, and we do so want to do it!"

Laura Hazard, behind her, gave the colonel a powerful glance of helpless understanding. With the indulgent look of a husband doing a job under a wife's orders, Teddy Mainwaring appeared in the background, lugging a packing box which he was to set up as a sideboard. The colonel said,

"Maybe before we get too far along with this activity, I'd better bring up my objections to it, Kitty."

"Objections?" she said lightly, while the others, in the presence of a contest, grew still.

"Yes," said the colonel, "sorry as I am to say so, I have to say that it would be wiser not to give this entertainment which you have so thoughtfully planned."

"Really, major—colonel," said Kitty, "I am sure my husband is prepared to obey you in all official matters, and I am mindful of my duty to you, also, but after all, I am only giving a party." Her voice went a little weak and wild. Her eye changed oddly. "I do not quite see how this can bring down your disapproval. Many ladies give parties."

The colonel did not like what he saw in her face. He took her hand and patted it.

"Yes, so long as your party is within the limits of the post, I have nothing to say. But you want to take us out hunting beforehand, and there's the trouble."

"I must say I do not understand!"

But the others did, at once, and knew she was lying.

"Kitty," said the colonel, "if we do go, it can't be much fun. We'd all have to remain so close together, including the ladies, in case we flush an Apache instead of a rabbit. The country all around us is still potentially a very dangerous area. Our wagons never move without escort. A single man or a pair with good mounts can maneuver safely alone. But not a hunt party. And I cannot see myself ordering out an escort to ride guard on us while we strain our eyes for rabbits."

"Why, it's like a table top," declared Kitty, "you can see everything for miles."

"Everything except a smart Apache who grew up knowing the country. I'd hate to be responsible if one of the women in my care met up with one."

"Isn't it strange," said Kitty with a mesmeric look in her child's-blue eyes, "I cannot bring myself to be afraid of a single living thing."

"Oh, Kitty, be sensible," said Teddy, looking at the colonel for approval.

She sank down on her doorstep and broke into tears.

"My poor, miserable party," she sobbed, "when all I was trying to do was—"

Teddy gave the colonel a look of anguished appeal which said, You have done this, can't you undo it?

Colonel Prescott reviewed the consequences of his implied command to cancel the hunt. Days of hurt feelings. Unnecessary politenesses in that intimate community. Unspoken reproaches that would eat at the heart of mutual confidence. Time spent at restorative, sentimental labors that more profitably must go to acts of duty. He could not separate the personal from the official on a post like Fort Delivery. He was trapped, both as friend and commander. Once again military effectiveness seemed to depend on happy relations within the small community. With a cursing thought, he went and took Kitty by the shoulders, feeling the almost laughable strength in her little bones, and hauled her up to standing. He lifted her chin against her will, and said,

"All right, we hunt. But under these orders, which I mean strictly. We will remain closed up; the ladies will carry pistols; if game is sighted no one will dismount to fire even though this means luck instead of marksmanship; and we will be gone no longer than one hour. Is that understood?"

Everyone broke with relief. The family was one again. Promises, thanks, exaggerated delight. Kitty smiled through her abating breaths, and said,

"I'm so ashamed, but I would have been simply killed—" and she turned to set her work going again. No longer an ogre, the colonel was allowed to go back up the line with his own thoughts, of which the uppermost was a question. Was he right or was he wrong to give in? The answer was not here, he thought, but out there, in the desert, and he would not know it until the hunt tomorrow.

lxxiii

He could not know how powerful in their effect on the events of that day were the hidden but painfully clear thoughts of Kitty Mainwaring. The more her thoughts raced across the backs of her eyes, the harder she must work at her preparations for the party. If she could die of exhaustion just before sundown, what a joy this would be to her! They would all shake their heads over her and her tireless efforts on their behalf. Look, she has killed herself for us, heart failure, that poor, gallant little heart simply tired itself out doing things for others, they would murmur. But a piercing memory would burn forward through the clutter of her mind like a red-hot poker through kindling, and she would actually gasp and bite her lips and drive herself onward.

She had gone to wait for him, as planned, they were quite clear about the plan as they parted the last time, and when he didn't come, and didn't come, she felt cold at heart. What was wrong? Had he forsaken her, as she had been forsaken before? If it should happen again, how could she endure it? And then she had made herself be calm, to remember that any number of interruptions, assignments, duties must have kept him from finding her in the arroyo, around that shadowed bend, where the bank overhung a little, and made a shelter from the too-explicit light of the sky, and where with him she had found again and again the proof of how lovable she was, how much she had to give, how dearly it was desired by one who must receive it or know misery.

He would come—but she waited as long as she dared, and returning to the post, she saw him sitting contentedly in the doorway of the barracks, plaiting horsehair in a long lariat, and whistling a little tune. Foolhardy with love, she went to him and asked why he had let her wait. He looked up with a vacant face and told her softly to get away before someone heard them talking, and she had better know right now that she could wait all she liked, he was never again going to risk everything to go and meet her alone.

Private Clanahan came out of the barracks to show Corporal Rainey a letter he was writing to a Swedish girl in Binghamton, New York, and when he saw the first lieutenant's wife, he ducked back in again *in such a hurry* that she knew he knew something he should not know. In this, betrayal was implied, and when she knew this, it unbearably demeaned the love she had given and already had lost. She turned and made her way unsteadily to her house. When her husband told her there that he had been passed over for promotion, she laughed before she wept. He had no idea of what she really wept for, or what actually drove her to efforts and words more intemperate than ever. Teddy Mainwaring could not know that if Kitty were not to destroy herself, which, for reasons obscure to her, all forces drove her to do, she must in various ways seek to destroy the life around her, wherever she could reach it.

Laura worked with her, trying with light talk to keep an agreeable atmosphere. Kitty said, remembering her words with the commanding officer,

"I think he might have shown more confidence in my judgment."

"Oh," said Laura, "confidence. Nobody ever means exactly the same thing by it."

"I never expected you to be cynical," said Kitty.

"I am not cynical. Perhaps I am realistic, though. It's amazing how realistic being married makes you."

"Were you a romantic little thing once upon a time?" asked Kitty with a ravaged face.

Laura laughed.

"I suppose so. Though I actually think my husband was—and is— the romantic of the family. He was so serious when he courted me!" She smiled reflectively. "I had all sorts of questions I was dying to ask him, but he was so *seriously* in love with me that I couldn't even begin to ask them. And now I know I was right not to ask them. Confidence, I said just now—well, it meant that I had confidence in him."

"What were the questions about?"

"You can guess. What his love affairs were before we were engaged."

The innocent statement struck Kitty like a blow. She knew that before knowing her he had had no love affairs. His image came back alive in her mind. Was it possible? She had thought herself free of him, for the sake of another. But that other one had cast her away, too, as Matthew had cast her away before him, and she was alone, alone, not in the world, but in her love for herself. She felt hysterical and struggled not to cry out. Laura noticed nothing and added,

"And then, the only girl he knew after we became engaged was you, Kitty, way out here at Fort Delivery. He wrote me about you. I was so jealous! I wondered how pretty you were, and why you made curtains for his room. Oh! I was a wretch!"

She smiled with the comfortable reliance of a wife and mother on the solid foundations of her world. It came close to destroying Kitty, already of desperate mind.

"Stop it!" cried Kitty. "What are you insinuating under all that! There was nothing, nothing at all, between Matthew and me! I tried not to let it go that far! He was so lonely, and nobody else seemed to understand him, here, and who could blame him if—who could blame me if—oh my God! What am I saying! Oh, please, never, never speak of it to him! He meant nothing disloyal to you—oh, it is so hard sometimes to know what is right and what is not! Laura! Oh my God! Why did you lead me into telling you!"

She covered her face and ran out the back door.

Laura watched her in bewilderment, and then the meaning of Kitty's vagrant and tortured words came home to her. First denying, Kitty seemed to end by confessing, without precisely saying so, that Matthew had been her lover. Oh, no, said Laura to herself; no, not at all. It was not so. But she had a dry sick taste in her mouth, and putting away what she was doing for the hunt breakfast she left Kitty's house. First she turned to go home, but if Matthew were there, what would she say to him of what she had just learned? She said she must have a little time to come to her senses and to know how to meet her husband. She turned to headquarters and sought Mrs. Prescott.

"Laura, my lamb, what on earth is the matter?" asked Jessica on seeing her.

"I can't have it," gasped Laura and fell into a chair. It was a few minutes before Jessica extracted admission of the heartbreaking doubts which Kitty had given to her. Jessica listened with a gaze of sorrow. Her brows were lifted at the center and her eyes were shadowed with compassion and through this shone a light which came from deep in her eyes and reflected her thoughts. She faced human misery and human evil and she was moved not to judge offhand but to save first what could be saved of life's dedication. When Laura fell silent, Jessica said,

"Well, Laura, my darling, I am glad you came to me first. A little time is good to have at a time like this. And, my dear, remember that Kitty Mainwaring is in a frightful state. How can we take seriously anything she may say? She feels a terrible snub, from forces too great to contend with, in this promotion thing. It may have driven her out of her wits in a way. And then, from what you tell me, she did not actually say what you think she meant, did she?" Jessica paused to see hope in Laura's face, but in her own memory she saw again the betrayals of feeling which Matthew and Kitty had made so long ago. But what, actually, had happened between them? She had no proof of anything. Laura had more, now, than anyone had ever had before. It was true to Jessica's nature that all possibilities must be faced, sifted and put in their places. Without now confirming Laura's dread, she moved to open out for the young wife a passage to safety for the rest of her life, if she should ever need to follow it.

"Laura, my darling, you must never lose confidence in Matthew, if you are to live with him and love for all your days. I do not for an instant concede that what that pitiful hysterical little creature said to you may be true. But listen to me: even if it *were* true—not that it *is* true, remember—even if it were true, do you think you would do well to let it destroy everything you love?"

"Oh, Mrs. Prescott! How can you!"

"Are you weak or strong?"

"I don't know why you ask that!"

"If you are strong, you will know how to suffer and yet still make a future for others which will do them good, not harm."

"But I could not stand it, if it were true, to think of him bringing me here, right back where that woman is, and going on, pretending that nothing—oh, no, I can't!"

Jessica put her arms around her.

"Oh, yes you can, or rather, you could, if you had to. Laura, look at me. Whom do you love?"

Laura looked at her with tear-blurred eyes.

"I did love him."

"You still do. You always will. Now, ask yourself this. Do you love him as he is? If you do, that means you love everything he has ever known, because that is what has made him as he is. Or do you love some other Matthew that you want to make him into? Is it really your husband you love, or only what you think your husband ought to be? If it is the latter, how do you know you are so right as all that, to take the power of making someone into someone else?"

Laura was ruefully interested in these arguments. Her breaths went easier, and she began to think instead of feel. She wished she might have time to think over what Mrs. Prescott had said to her. Her heart hurt when she thought of Matthew going handsomely and healthily about his day, all unaware of the crazy danger that hung over him and his family. She said sorely,

"What shall I do, though?"

"Do you really want to know, or are you just asking?"

Challenged, Laura said,

"I really want to know."

"Well, then, my dear child, do nothing."

"Nothing? You mean not even ask him to deny it?"

"Not even ask him to deny it. If it never happened, you must behave as if you never heard of it. Not that this will be entirely easy. I know that. But oh, Lord, Laura, which of us can't be an actress when she has to be?"

This forced a smile from Laura. She thought of her mother. Then she frowned and said,

"But how could I ever see or speak to that little creature again, after what she has said?"

"Oh, that'll come easy. You'll see. You know her pretty well, now. You can afford to be kind."

Laura stood up.

"I will not do anything for a day or two, I promise. But Matthew and I have to be honest with each other, and we shall have to talk about this eventually. But by then we can both be calm about it. Wouldn't it be terrible, Mrs. Prescott, *not to know* if it were true or not, all my life?"

Jessica wanted to say, Perhaps *to know* would be worse, but she held her tongue, and kissed Laura, and sent her home. Alone, she allowed her sorrow for Kitty to come forth. Lighting a cigarette, she said half-aloud, Oh, you poor, unhappy, driven, little wrecker!

lxxiv

Under the sunrise at twenty minutes before six the company rode out to the hunt. To find the best hunting country, they rode northwest. There lay a big lowered basin which was fed, when rains came, by several little gullies and miniature canyons which looked like spaces between spread fingers.

After the storms and doubts of the day before, everybody worked to maintain high spirits. The ladies were in formal riding dress, and among them, Kitty, in her sweeping side-saddle riding habit of sky-blue kersey uniform cloth with rows of brass buttons, and her military cap, and Garibaldi bounding along at her side, fulfilled the picture of herself which she had foreseen. Jessica glanced at her now and then. Kitty's face was haggard, and she tossed her head as though to dismiss troubling thoughts, or even tears. Her uneasiness made Jessica uneasy in her turn. Jessica took greater pleasure from regarding Laura, who wore black velvet, and a smile of marble calm. Beside her, Matthew rode all innocently. It was a white day, which meant that blowing dust might be expected later. The company moved at a slow trot, with Colonel Prescott leading.

He kept a sharp eye for the land all about. But even so, he was pleased by the spectacle they made—three ladies and three gentlemen, well-mounted, accompanied by a pure-bred hound, crossing wild land under a strong sun at an easy pace, in search of sport. It was an ancient pleasure, and without thinking about it explicitly, the colonel felt allied to one of the oldest impulses in mankind. He was glad that there were traditional garments of an appropriate nature to be worn on such an occasion, and he was proud that everyone with him had a good seat, and that some few were expert in the saddle. Now, if they would only see a rabbit or two, and take their bag, and go back satisfied—

He heard galloping to the rear and turned. He saw Kitty riding fast off to the right in pursuit of Garibaldi, who had strayed.

"Mainwaring," called the colonel, "go after her and bring her back and make her stay close up with the rest of us!"

In a few minutes, Kitty was returned to the cavalcade and the colonel rode back to speak to her.

"We'll ride back to the fort immediately," he said sharply, "if you do not stay close. You heard my orders yesterday. I mean them."

Her blue eyes flashed. In her state of bruised feeling she was look-ing for a challenge. She started to reply, hesitated and then made a bow of amused compliance, as if to say what a pack of timid souls they were; and rode on in exaggerated restraint. Her face was clouded by dark resentments. Must every move she made be wrong and bring disapproval of her? If anything should ever happen to her, how keenly they would all remember how unkind they had been to her, and how sorry they would feel! Sometimes she thought only her dog Garibaldi loved her for what she was!

As they rode, they sang little songs, and told stories, and watched for their prey. High drifting dust had come to diffuse the light of the sun without veiling its heat. There were few shadows. A band of dust now blurred the horizons and the riders could not even see the fort if they turned to look.

"Amazing," said Jessica, "one hardly knows which point of the compass one is riding toward."

Colonel Prescott watched for the faint change of color in the desert sweep which would tell him that he was nearing the basin. The de-pression had no rim but simply eased down below the level. They rode down the slow incline and across the bottoms until they were facing the far rise with its shallow gashes in which scrubby bushes grew. An occasional twisted desert juniper or cypress clung to dust-filled crevices in outcropping rock slabs. The colonel indicated a central cut with widely separated walls.

"We'll ride into that one. It is the widest and easiest." He led the way.

The gully made slow open bends. Vision went far. Once rising to the general level of the desert at the far end of the gully, they could circle the whole depression and make their way home, rabbit or no rabbit.

After they had come a quarter of a mile up the gully the colonel heard an eager panting and sniffing along the ground beside his horse. It was Garibaldi the hound, who seemed to express in every move-ment his joy at having again escaped the restraints of his mistress. How could she have let him come? Colonel Prescott turned to see her at the end of the column. She was gone.

"Mainwaring," shouted the colonel, "where's your wife?"

Everybody turned to stare in all directions. How had she vanished? They told each other that they must have been watching so intently ahead up the gully that they did not notice it as she fell away behind them.

"Oh, thunder and damnation!" called Colonel Prescott. "We've got to find her," and he turned the column about toward the entrance of the gully. Surely they would see her as they came around each of the slow winding curves of the dry course. But she was nowhere. They soon realized that if she had gone off alone on a private hunt, she might have taken any one of the many other gullies. Unless she found her way back to them, the search might take quite some time. When they reached the open shallow of the basin, the colonel halted the party, and fired a paced series of signal shots. They strained to listen. They heard no reply. Teddy was sweating with concern.

"You don't suppose she returned to the fort by herself?" he asked.

"How in damnation should I know?" snappel the colonel. "Why in thunder didn't you keep an eye on her? She belongs to you!"

"Hiram," said Jessica, seeing how alarmed Teddy was and how little her husband's rage would help anything.

"Yes," said the colonel, "I'm sorry. Matt, you take Jessica and Laura back to the post, and return as fast as you can with Joe Dummy and four enlisted men. We'll have to start a real search, unless you find Kitty there when you get there. Bring some rations and extra canteens. Arrange for a signal after dark. We may be out here all day."

lxxv

They were.

They searched the finger gullies, one by one, dividing the assignments, and found no trace. Some of the gullies had rocky steps beyond which a horse could not go, and in those, brought up short by the rock barriers, they turned back. In others the sandy bottom ran clear and free all the way to the far rim, and in those they saw nothing, not even a snake or a lizard. They rode the whole circumference. They fired signal shots. They watched the approach from the fort, hoping for a messenger coming to say that Kitty was home safely. In the white overhead the sun's light seemed universal, and as the noon passed, and the afternoon, it became more difficult than ever for an inexperienced person to tell directions. If Kitty was somewhere in the desert—as she must be—she was just as likely to ride toward Mexico as back toward Fort Delivery.

"What will we do if night comes and we haven't found her?" asked Teddy.

"We will ride in for the night. But perhaps we'll have a signal by then . . ." For Matthew had arranged to have the garrison send up a rocket from the fort half an hour after sundown that would tell the searchers if, late but after all, Kitty had returned.

"I must stay out all night," said Teddy. "What if she should call me? Poor girl, out here, alone." He shivered.

"You will return to the fort with the rest," said the colonel. "In the darkness nobody can search. We will resume in the morning, and you will help us then."

The great dome over them filled with twilight as the veiled sun went under. They all turned toward the fort to watch for a rocket. With sundown the air was clearing as usual. The colonel wished his thoughts could clear into certainties.

If Kitty were really lost in the desert, now, after so long a day, only chance could bring her safely home. If she had suffered an accident and was somewhere helpless, only chance could bring rescue to her. If Chiricahuas were near, and had found her, there were too many possible consequences to imagine, none of them without pain, some with horror.

The lights of the fort began to show tiny and clear far away. Hoping for the rise of a rocket, they held their mounts still, and straining all senses to know, they became aware of the little sounds of the desert in its general nocturnal calm. They heard now and then a singing and fading whir of some insect at work or travel. They heard the hollow call of the little desert owl, given at long intervals, as if asking the same question on a timeless line of thought, and expecting no reply. There was no wind, but they heard an occasional rattle of a dusty bush, and knew some creature of the dry and hot was stirring about a night's business. The colonel held the formation waiting for much longer than the prearranged half hour after sundown. There was no rocket.

"Come on, Ted," he said at last. "We'll have to go in. It's pitch dark."

They moved off toward their home lights. The stars were out. They rode at a trot in close order. When they reached the west gate they were told that Kitty's mount had come in riderless just about at sundown, but as there was no signal arranged to tell this piece of information, they simply had to wait to tell it themselves when they could.

The fort was alive with hushed concern. To those who knew her best, Kitty was vividly alive in thought. They remembered her at her best—the little darts of her wit, the impulsively kind things she often did for others and dismissed with brisk lightness, her way of starting an argument for its own sake, and how she would collapse with self-mocking laughter before the point was made, her frail prettiness that expressed her troubled nature as often as her grim small determinations. Corporal Rainey needed comfort from his best friend Private Clanahan.

"I could find her, if they'd let me," he kept saying in an angry whisper.

"No, not any better than anybody else, Rainey," said Clanahan. "Don't go thinking you're responsible for her."

"In a way, I am."

"Well, maybe you are."

Though they could not know it, nor could anyone else, they were right, to a degree.

lxxvi

Before daylight the search party assembled at the corral and saddled up. Matthew spoke to the colonel.

"Sir, Joe wants to try something."

"Well?"

"He thinks we ought to search the upper ends of the gullies where the rock steps kept us from riding further yesterday."

"If we couldn't get up, how could she?"

"I know, sir. But he thinks she might have come into one of the gullies from the other end."

"We'll do it, of course. But why would she still be there?"

It was an appalling inquiry, and the colonel abruptly turned away, gave the signal to mount, and led the party out northwestward.

Daylight was over them when they came riding around the northern curve of the basin. They were approaching the first of the gullies by the flank, and soon they entered it from its upper trough, where long ago it took its beginnings from rain runoff. They saw Joe Dummy dismount and walk ahead of them and they yielded to his natural authority in that wilderness. In a long slow walk during which he examined every rock and shadow, every sweep of sand, every ragged bush or overhanging cypress, he brought them to the top step of the rocky flight which broke the gully, as it broke the next three to the west, where the same shelf outcropped from the earth which buried it between the draws. He had found nothing.

"We'll try the next one," said the colonel.

"What can we do, what can we do?" asked Teddy Mainwaring, more of himself than of any of the others.

They knew how his belly must be stretched hollow with concern, and how through his scattered thoughts must drift views of the future which twisted his pale, full face with pain.

Once again Joe Dummy, at the next gully, began his examination of the earth. They penetrated the draw to a distance of a few hundred yards when he arrested his slow tread and looked intently upon an object which lay against a rock twenty paces ahead.

As they looked, it moved.

Joe Dummy spread them all to a halt behind him with his hand. They were facing a large lion-colored animal with a scowling cat's face and bared cutlass-like teeth. It was a puma. The animal raised his heavy head and flared a great paw to show his claws, and tried to rise in defense and preparation for attack. But he was wounded. Blood showed in a drying seep at his left shoulder, and his huge wound glistened with moving insects.

"Great God," said the colonel, "someone shot him."

Joe turned to nod yes, yes, and then he pointed past the cat along the gully, and they saw a trail of dried blood on the exposed rocks and wind-cleaned sand. The wounded cat had come from deeper in the draw. They must go past him. The colonel drew his revolver and advanced a few paces cocking his weapon and raising it for the aim. The puma made a warning cry and threw himself up against the rock behind and took up a tense position as if ready to spar. His whitish breast and belly were exposed. Pain made him snarl with a riplike sound. Colonel Prescott shot him in the heart. He fell magnificently inert, with his eyes open and still, and his mouth relaxed in what looked like a witty smile.

"All right," said the colonel. "Get along."

They moved around and beyond the great lion and came toward a bend in the draw. Before they came around it, the colonel halted the party, and said,

"You people stay here. I will go forward with Joe." He looked severely at Teddy, and they all knew what the colonel thought to find. If there was a chance of finding it, he must spare someone the first sight of it unprepared. While they waited, he walked on around the bend with Joe Dummy.

Kitty, like all the women, had been armed with a pistol. If she had come here and had met the puma she had shot at him. If she had done so, why had they not heard the shot? But they knew that if they had been miles away at the other end of the basin they could not have heard. And of course, someone else might have come upon the puma and wounded him. The puma had dragged himself, leaving a trail of blood, from a spot around the bend which, from where they waited, they could not see.

"Why do they take so long to come back?" asked Teddy.

Nobody answered him.

The fact was, Colonel Prescott and Joe Dummy, having found what all expected they might, spent a little time in making it less hideous to look upon, the better to spare Teddy Mainwaring what he would have to see.

lxxvii

Jessica Prescott, like everyone else, must speak of it. She said to Hiram, almost as though musing, in the cool, quiet voice he loved to hear when they were alone and perhaps drowsy and reassured simply by their nearness to each other,

"Poor, poor child. At least the essential part of her at last knows peace. I've been wondering for weeks. She has not been herself. Or perhaps she was more—too much more—herself then ever. She was so ready to have her feelings hurt, and she couldn't keep out of the way of feeling sorry for herself. Who knows why? I have ideas, but I shan't say them. But she seemed to beg everyone to pay attention to her. I've seen that in children. They will need something so much they will go to any lengths to get attention. They will make everyone sorry for them. They will show us: they will run away. Maybe they will get lost. Maybe they will get killed, and then—oh, and then—

how sorry everyone will be for the way they acted! Poor Kitty. Maybe she had to go off and make her little sensation and get us all worried and make us go to every kind of trouble to find her and save her and bring her back and prove that we love her—and then, suddenly, everything went too far, and turned real, and—and the end!"

"Yes, the end. I am glad you did not see it," said Hiram.

"So am I, though I could have if I'd had to."

"Ah, Jess."

"Poor Ted."

"We must have him in for meals until he feels like being by himself," she said.

"There's a risk," said the colonel.

"Yes, I know. But that can be managed, too. I can have the Hazards take him on now and then, and in time he'll be weaned."

If only a commander could always pick everyone to serve with him, mused Colonel Prescott.

"Hiram. Yes. Do you know? Why wasn't I more kind to her? Kitty. Not kind. More *with* her, in feeling? I wish. Oh, I don't know. Perhaps I could have helped."

"I don't know how."

"Neither do I. But there was probably a way. How little we ever give ourselves, really."

"Jess."

In another house, peace came to someone else. It was Laura. In her first intimate contact with death, she felt that the life that was taken was purified of all things. Laura knew pity and mercy for the woman who had come close to destroying all that she cherished. She resolved never to speak to Matthew of Kitty's revelation. She vowed to put it from her mind whenever it should find its way there. From the horror of Kitty's death she took refuge in her husband and her son in renewed love.

Kitty was buried in the cemetery southeast of the post. Hers was the fifteenth grave in the little fenced enclosure. Corporal Rainey sounded taps over her small mound after the commanding officer read aloud the prayers for the dead. The corporal said later to Private Clanahan that he had thought, for a moment, there, that he wasn't going to make it, remembering how she was, and how she had been, and the rest of it, but when he got his mind on blowing the bugle, he stopped thinking of anything else, and he played taps just like he always did. Now that everything was really over that he had talked about with Clanahan, he had to swear Clanahan to secrecy once again, on the grounds that what somebody don't know is the better for them, and everybody owed respect to the dead. For his part, he found, after a while, that he had no regrets, because, he said, "It ain't my fault if I am a man, and have to have a woman when I can get one." He said he was still a soldier, and he still had a friend he could talk to about anything.

When the wind would come up at night, Teddy would lie awake, and think of how it blew across the earth vault of Kitty's grave, and he would see the sand taken off the small mound and blown away, and how in time there would be no sign of it left; and the image of this gave him his most forlorn sense of loneliness. Often he would lie awake until daylight, he who had always slept like an old dog, shapeless and content. So much was different now, perhaps he would be someone else, himself. Perhaps he would have a chance, if General Quait ever came back, a chance to *show him*.

The opportunity, complicated and extended as it was, came sooner than anyone expected.

BOOK THREE

Trial at Arms

Honour and arms scorn such a foe,
Though I could end thee at a blow,
Poor victory to conquer thee
Or glory in thy overthrow!
Vanquish a slave that is half slain!
So mean a triumph I disdain!
                    —From *Samson,* by
                    George Friedrich Handel

i

Corporal Rainey and Private Clanahan were out with a grazing party east of the fort under the command of Lieutenant Mainwaring. Their duty, like that of the other five mounted troopers who rode guard over the grazing horses, was to keep a sharp eye out on the distance.

"Rainey," said Clanahan, "what's that, there?"

"Where?"

"There—see, due east, just this side of that bunch of brush. It's moving. It looks like someone."

Rainey squinted and stared.

"Yes, it is someone. Look there. He fell down."

"Yes—but now he got up again. We better tell the lieutenant."

They rode to Lieutenant Mainwaring and reported what they had seen. He focused his binoculars and exclaimed,

"It's a white man! He's alone. Ride on over there and bring him to me. Watch out there's nobody hiding anywhere around. —It's an old man; he can hardly walk. Say, he just fell down. How could he ever get here?"

The two troopers spurred their mounts and rode fast toward a thick bush of mesquite a half mile away. A few feet from it they reined up and looked down to see an old man with thick white hair lying face downward with his arms outflung. His left eye, which they could see, was open, and his mouth worked in the dust, though he

493

said nothing. They dismounted and turned him over. He looked at them with a smile of great weariness and sweetness, and nodded his head weakly, as though to say that he always knew, if he came far enough, that someone would find him and take him up and save his life.

"Say, there, dad," said Rainey gently, "who are you? How did you get here?"

The old man put his tongue through his lips. He was parched with thirst. Clanahan went to his saddle and brought his canteen. They gave him a few drops, which he smacked up faintly, like a small bird drinking. His eyes filmed over and closed. He seemed to fall asleep.

"Say," said Rainey, "he must be pretty far gone. Help me up with him. I'll hold him on my saddle."

The old man awoke and showed by his effort that he would help them if he could. But he had no strength and they had to lift him and place him in the saddle. Rainey vaulted up behind and held him. Clanahan mounted up, and they rode at a careful walk back to the grazing party. The old man was like a child in Rainey's arms—thin, clear-boned, and compliant. His strength seemed to return somewhat, for he made efforts to hold on to the pommel and otherwise maintain himself. He was sun-burned a raw pink. His cheeks were ragged with a short white beard. His eyes were a filmy blue. He had no hat. Over a torn red shirt he wore a loose vest of checkered homespun. His trousers were of bottle-green broadcloth, thick with dust and torn. They were stuffed into heavy buckled boots. When he saw Lieutenant Mainwaring, and rode up to him with Rainey, he made a feeble gesture of saluting, and said a few syllables which nobody understood as words.

"Who is he?" asked the lieutenant.

"Sir, we don't know. He was lying there almost dead of thirst. He can't seem to help himself."

"What's your name, sir?" asked Teddy. The old man bobbed his head and tongued his lips as if making a reply. He gazed smiling all about, waving his dried hands in a little dance of courtesy before his caved-in breast. He was a shell of life at its simplest, with no more mind than an infant. "He's crazy," said the lieutenant, and the old man, animated by the sound of another's voice, bobbed and smiled again in general good will.

They gave him a few more sips of water, and then the lieutenant said,

"Get him back to the post and report to the colonel. We've got to try to find out how he got here and what he was doing out there."

With their charge bobbing shakily in the saddle, the young troopers rode to the fort. Because a sentry saw them coming, the colonel was waiting for them at the steps of headquarters.

"What's this?" he asked.

They told him what little they knew. He saw immediately that the old man needed care. They took him down from the saddle and carried him to the settee in the headquarters parlor where he could lie down. Jessica brought tea which he drank avidly; and then a soft-boiled egg which he ate in one swallow. The colonel made no attempt to question him until he had napped for a few minutes after his meal. Then, awakening, the visitor tried to rise and make his thanks with little bobbing bows. His strength was not equal to the gesture and he sank back again and looked up at Colonel Prescott with a puzzled expression. He gave the effect of begging the colonel to tell him where he was, and how he had come here, and what had happened which lay clouded in the back of his mind. The colonel ventured a question.

"Were you traveling alone?"

Oh-yes-yes-yes, the old man seemed to say, smiling a baby-gum smile, and working to do what was asked of him.

"How did you get lost?"

The old man spoke the first clear words they heard from him.

"I was lost."

"Where were you coming from?"

"Coming from—"

"Yes. Can you tell us where?"

"Where?" The old man looked around at those listening—the colonel, Jessica, Matthew, and the two young soldiers who had brought him in. His eyes clouded and his face broke like a baby's into a silent grimace of grief. "Where are all the others?" he begged to know.

"Others? What others?"

He waved his arm and seemed to see a company of people in his thought. His voice caught on his breath and he began to sob against his small, knotted fists. The colonel approached and put his arm on him. When the old man's grief abated somewhat, the colonel asked,

"You said you were alone. But you were not alone?"

"Oh, no, no, no. All the others!"

He stared wildly up at Colonel Prescott.

The colonel said,

"We think you should have some sleep now. Just rest awhile. We will take care of you. We will be right here."

Confident as a child, the old man nodded and with a few shudders of relaxation, shrank into himself and was soon asleep. The colonel took Matthew to the office.

"He is out of his wits," he said.

"Yes, sir, he will agree with anything we say to him."

"Yes, but something happened to him. We have to hope that his mind will clear with rest, and that he will be able to tell us. He must have wandered two days, at least, to be in such condition. We'll let him sleep. But be on hand to help me when he wakes up."

The old man slept until twilight and awoke to call out, rising against his blanket,

"Let me go!"

They were with him, and they turned up the coal-oil lamp and showed him that he was free. He sighed and sat up, rubbing his brow. He eyed them one by one. His eye was clear. His cheeks were flushed with sleep. The colonel knew that he was somewhat restored. He gave him a glass of water.

"Drink this. We will bring you a little food. Are you hungry?"

"Yes." He drank noisily and gave back the glass, and said, "I got away and I walked on for three days."

"Did you know how to find us?"

"No. I just walked."

"Were you alone?" asked the colonel softly.

"Yes, while I walked. But not before, not before."

So the old man's earlier answers, though confusing, could both be true.

"Were there others with you before?"

He bent over into his shallow little lap and began to weep almost soundlessly, shaking his head. Through his wet, slaking sobs, he said,

"All the others, my son, my daughter, my grandchildren, and all the rest of us, all the others, yes, all of them."

"All of them," said Hiram. "Where are they? Can we help them?"

"Gone. All of them. Dead. Nobody can help them. Oh, my poor honey little ones."

He bent his head and put his hands upon the back of his neck and pulled himself down into a feeling of darkness and privacy. Gone was the obliging old baby with toothless smiles. Those watching him had never seen such an image of sorrow. They waited in silence for him to come back to the world. Presently he came. He could say no more until Jessica fed him. A little while after that he was able to tell what he had witnessed. It was recorded in Colonel Prescott's official report, along with the actions which immediately followed.

ii

Headquarters,
Fort Delivery,
Territory of Arizona,
Oct. 11, 188-.

Report for: The Commanding General, Dept. of Arizona.
Subject: Massacre of Edwards Party, Oct. 5, 188-, near this post.

1. On Oct. 8, members of a grazing party of this command while guarding horses at the grazing grounds east of this post sighted and brought to the post an American citizen named Amos Edwards, aged 76, of Black Rock, Erie County, New York. He was nearly dead of thirst and starvation, and was in a dazed condition for several hours after rescue. He had walked for the better part of three days, moving westerly, though without fixed plan or guidance. He was the sole survivor of a massacre mounted against his party by a large raiding party of Chiricahua Apache Indians.

2. Mr. Edwards, with his two sons, their wives, his daughter and her husband, nine children extending in age from three years to fourteen, three married men and their wives, with five children ranging in age from one year to nine, and two single men, comprised the immigrant party. Their names, ages, and home addresses are appended to the end of this report. They were travelling with three waggons, fifteen horses, nine oxen and six head of beef cattle, on their way to take up a homestead on which they had filed in Tucson. The site of their new farm was a tract east and south of Ransom Rock, roughly midway between this post and the railroad station of Driscoll. They chose to travel with waggons rather than by the steam cars as the former mode of conveyance permitted hauling of more household goods and possessions than the latter. Likewise livestock could thus be brought from the home farms of the party. All members of the party were in good health but Mr. Edwards,

who rode in one of the waggons, as he was a sufferer from rheumatism.

3. As all adult males of the party were armed, to the number of nine, and were able marksmen, they felt secure in travelling by compass in the open country, without military escort. In their seven months on the trail they had encountered no dangers of attack until the early morning of Oct. 5, when occurred the incident which is the subject of this report.

4. Sentries were posted at the open side of a compound made by the three parked waggons. Shortly before dawn they heard a disturbance among the tethered animals a short distance from the waggons. Going to investigate, they discovered four Indians cutting tethers and preparing to make away with the horses. One sentry immediately fired. The other ran back to alarm the camp. Adult males of the party seized their weapons and came out to fight off the marauders. They found the first sentry dead and they fired at the Indians who were taking cover behind the horse herd. The Indians were armed with army rifles. Hot fire was exchanged for a minute or so and then the immigrants saw a large party of Indians riding fast toward them. Mr. Edwards estimated that there were over a hundred Indians in the party. He was in one of the waggons, unable to descend because of stiffness in his limbs. He witnessed all that followed.

5. The Indians swept over the camp on horseback in such great numbers that resistance, while gallant, was useless. Within a few minutes not a man of the camping party was left effective. Three were dead, the others disarmed and tied. An Indian reached into the waggon for Mr. Edwards who shot him. But just behind, another Indian seized Mr. Edward's rifle away from him and pulled him out of the waggon. He was about to be killed when another Indian, apparently in authority, caused the first Indian to desist. Mr. Edwards was taken a little distance away and tied to a bush facing the camp. The children were pulled away from their mothers and held under guard in one group while the women were herded together a little distance away from the waggons. Indians removed everything portable from the waggons. They then set fire to the waggons. Mr. Edwards remembered that the sun rose at the same moment and he said that the fire was wild and hot as the waggons burned. The bodies of the dead settlers were thrown into the fire to the accompaniment of jubilations.

6. Movable property was then examined by the raiders who made bundles of such objects as could readily be transported. These were loaded on the stolen horses.

7. The oxen were slaughtered and butchered into parts for transportation by the Indians.

8. The five male captives other than Mr. Edwards were then led

into an open space and denuded. Before the eyes of their families they were subjected to tortures and mutilations, details of which, being shocking in the extreme, are submitted in the attached sealed cover for the eyes of those only who will be authorised to read them. Only one of these victims, staked to the ground, failed to succumb immediately in the course of the torment.

9. The children were then led forward and with two exceptions were all killed outright by blows on the head from clubbed rifles. Their mothers had to see this. The exceptions were the oldest, a fourteen year old boy, who was tied and mounted on a horse, to be taken away by the raiders; and the youngest, a one year old boy, who was deposited at the feet of Mr. Edwards. The infant was crying.

10. The women were then taken, denuded, and subjected to violations described in detail in the sealed attachment. All were shot to death at last. It was then about nine o'clock, Mr. Edwards estimated.

11. Mr. Edwards was untied but not otherwise touched. He picked up the baby at his feet. The marauders left him thus, laughing and pointing at him. It was his belief that this was their final torture, to leave the oldest and the youngest of the party, alive in the desert, without food or water, or strength to survive for long, and in the presence of the carnage wreaked upon their companions.

12. The raiders then resumed their mounts and rode away rapidly toward the south, taking with them the captive youth and their stolen horses and supplies.

13. Mr. Edwards went to the staked man who was still alive, who died as he watched. Mr. Edwards laid the baby down and looked about for anything to cover the dead men, women and children with, but could find nothing. He felt he could not remain there helpless in the presence of so much indignity and horror, and accordingly, took up the infant and began to walk in a westerly direction. He was in pain from rheumatism and proceeded slowly. The child was hungry and fretful, seeming feverish. He walked all day and part of the night. It was cold at night and the child took a chill. By noon the following day, the child was dead, of congestion of the lung. He buried it with small rocks as best he could and continued his wandering course which brought him, exhausted and out of mind, to the immediate vicinity of this post.

14. The foregoing account was gleaned from what Mr. Edwards was able to tell after resting and taking nourishment. His ordeal was too much for him in the end. He died at Post Headquarters early in the morning of Oct. 9. He was buried in the Post Cemetery with honours.

15. With the coming of sunrise on Oct. 9 news of the massacre and

subsequent movements of the Indian party was sent by heliostat relay to Department Headquarters.

16. The Second Platoon of this component was ordered to prepare for expeditionary march, pending orders from Department, under the command of the undersigned, with Bvt. 1st Lt. M. C. Hazard as second in command.

17. The post was placed on full defensive basis under command of 1st Lt. Theodore Mainwaring with the first platoon remaining in garrison.

18. All women were removed to post headquarters to remain until further orders. Arms were issued to all women.

19. Late in the afternoon of Oct. 9 using the last sunlight, messages were received from the Commanding General, Department, for the 2nd platoon of this component, under command as noted above, to move out with maximum speed to rendezvous with other troops making rendezvous at Bear Mesa.

20. Movement accordingly was initiated and rendezvous reached in mid-afternoon of Oct. 11, when the undersigned reported, with his second in command, to the General Commanding.

Respectfully submitted:
Hiram Hyde Prescott,
Bvt.Lt.Col., Cav.

iii

"Please to be seated, gentlemen," said General Quait to the officers who had come to their feet upon his entrance among them.

They were gathered, seven officers and the Commanding General, in a great cleft of shadow in the southern face of Bear Mesa. Skin-colored walls of sheared rock rose above them on both sides like mighty wings reaching toward the pale blue sky. The gentlemen sat on the ground in a half circle facing the general, who reclined against a low rock. If they had been photographed they would have come out looking like members of an outing on an occasion of sentiment. As it was, they were intensely earnest. General Quait swept them with his lighthouse gaze and they kindled to his power of mind and purpose. He held their attention entirely as he spoke.

"Gentlemen, we are now complete in our components. The units ordered to this Department from New Mexico and California are distributed. Some parts have been assigned to double the guard at the Apache Reservation of San Carlos. Others are deployed at significant stations along the border of Mexico. The remainder are here with me. That you may understand in common the details we represent in particular, I shall inform you that we are a brigade—understrength, to be sure, but still in size the greatest yet gathered in these deserts. We in this bivouac represent one portion of a concerted effort. I shall attempt to sketch for you the whole grand scene in all its rich design."

Colonel Prescott and Lieutenant Hazard felt a settling of heart at hearing him again. They knew him well by now. His style was no longer eccentric to them. He was a master of his craft and theirs. They took his every word and glance with stern eagerness.

"This rendezvous, Bear Mesa," he said, "is now a great castle and fortress. Our troopers are encamped at its base. Sentinels guard them from its crown. Its small catch-pools will afford them a little water to drink, and if rain should come, a little more in which to disport and bathe. You will observe tonight how watch fires will blaze from the rims above us. You are astonished? Does this not proclaim us to the desert enemy and invite attack? It so does, precisely, by my command. I want the Apache to know that we are here, in greater numbers than ever before. If he will offer us battle, we shall accept. He will think that by defeating us here, he will have defeated us everywhere. Our thought is to the converse. If we defeat him here we know that we shall not have defeated him everywhere. We know that we must do him down in many places. But he does not know how we plan for this. It is our largest weapon—our plan of enfoldment and extermination. I believe, of course, that our soldier can manage himself in physical opposition to the Apache, but without undue advantage. The Apache is lord of his own country; our soldier is not. If we are to conquer, we must conquer with more than the body's force. We must invoke our priceless heritage, the civilized mind. In the end we shall, I daresay, have to invoke that which contains this mind—human character in all its high possibilities of honor and steadfastness."

If some of the listening officers, not yet used to the general's ways, were ready to fidget, those from Fort Delivery were not only patient but reassured, for they knew how General Quait always meant something by what he said, however oblique it might seem.

"Let us reflect for a moment on the reason why we are here. We are here because massacres, touched off by the Edwards tragedy last week, have sprung up in separate areas of the Territory. Reports came to us within the span of a day and a night of outrages committed against settlers, travelers and soldiers over a widely scattered area. It is obvious that we observe a concerted scheme. It is one which calls forth our fullest effort. We shall not pause until all such events are made impossible for all future time.

"But if we are to act in fullest understanding we must understand more than hideous crimes—but must see beyond them to causation. Given his mode of response to injury, the Indian is not wholly without justification for his return to the uses of outrage."

Colonel Prescott saw that some of the listeners were shocked by such a statement. So did General Quait.

"Yes," he insisted, "wicked white men, certain citizens of the United States, have robbed and swindled the Indian in his own land. Outlaws have committed horrors against Indians which any Apache virtuoso of fiend's work might well envy. Moreover, even in the reservations, where their care was pledged, Indians have been starved and left to suffer sickness unalleviated. Cattlemen have come here to obtain leases and have fenced vast areas, dotting them with great herds. Such leases have been investigated in Washington, and the President has caused many to be revoked. But too late. Too late. The Edwards massacre in all its pitiable savagery was induced, I have no doubt, because the attackers, having watched the Edwards train for days, determined that it was yet another expedition on its way to settle on lands which the Indians believed their own in perpetuity. Once so determined, the event invited its own fearsome issue. I do not condone or excuse, gentlemen—I merely elucidate the nature to which we oppose our own nature. A corollary is that if we must defeat a limb of our common tree of mankind, we must do so in mercy equal to our power."

The general paused for a sip of water from a tin dipper in a bucket beside him.

"Now: I have a map in my head. It embraces this whole Territory and a corresponding contiguous area of Mexico. Think of a great tablecloth, gentlemen. Take it and fold it across the center. Make a crease there. Open it up. The crease is the border of Mexico. Crumple the cloth below the border. The crumples are mountains—the grand Sierra Madre, in its northernmost upsweeps. There is the fortress of the enemy. From it he issues in forays, as presently. To it he retreats to gather new power of soul and body. After he troubles us on our half of the tablecloth, he invariably retires across the crease to his own crumpled fastnesses. There his commander the chief Rainbow Son, maintains his power. To him they will always return. If he dare, he will come forth himself. I believe he may now be with his warriors in one of the parties, perhaps the Edwards raiding party—in any case a large one—on its way back to the mountain crumples.

"Now: there are certain established routes by which to travel to the Mexican lands across the borderline crease. Trails existing since prehistoric times. I have ordered these crossings to be patrolled. In addition, the border can be crossed almost anywhere that an escaping marauder will choose. It is obvious that the nation itself does not have in standing order sufficient troops to police the entire line of the border. To meet this difficulty, I have set in play two measures."

The general held up his bony right forefinger and tipped it with its mate of the left hand.

"First: I have set to roving three detachments of strength of which we are the largest. We shall, starting with dawn tomorrow, be on a constant move, sweeping the desert as the frigates of Decatur swept the ocean wastes, in search of Indian war parties as they rove." The general switched to a new signal with his middle finger and said, "Second: I have detailed eleven small parties to keep watch on the trails to Mexico and certain other conspicuously plausible areas for crossing the border. These parties are not to give combat. They are to give reports to me, which I shall receive almost instantaneously upon their dispatch."

He paused to brush his beard and to take several audible indrawn breaths of satisfaction. An officer who had accompanied the 4th Cavalry from Fort Union, New Mexico, said,

"But sir? We are more than a day's ride from the nearest crossing as it is! How can dispatches be ridden so fast?"

The general eyed him closely.

"Do I not know you from the Cumberland and Dakota, captain?"

"Yes, sir. I am the former Major A. Cedric Gray."

"Ha-ha yes. The surgeon to whom I once gave a line command?"

"The same, sir."

"Capital! Delighted to see you back with me, though regrettably at a lesser rank. And still asking questions. Well, Captain Gray, there is a key to it, a curious key with which you are surely familiar in a previously established use. It is composed of a refined combination of silica, mercury and uncounted billions of candlepower of light. In short, a little mirror reflecting the light of the sun. In short-shorter, the heliostat."

"But, sir, no heliostat stations have been set up that far south."

"True, true. —By the way, have I ever shared with you gentlemen the process of thought which led to the adoption of the heliostat in the United States Army? Possibly not. Yet it is worth telling. Soldiers in the field tend to take for granted the equipment devised for them by command and staff. Let me take you back with me to the inception of this *weapon of thought*. I do so not in vanity but to offer a lesson in the processes of reason.

"I shall state and dismiss at once the fact that the whole procedure was the work of the present speaker. I encountered a grade eel of opposition from my colleagues but in the end prevailed. I shall trace my course.

"What, I demanded of my all too reluctant brain, what were the elements of our greatest disadvantage in the Indian deserts? Answer: first, on this thumb, the forbidding mountain towers thrown across so much of the region. Second, on this finger, the pitiless glare of sunlight over the desert: third, on this, the clear desert atmosphere devoid of moisture; and lastly, on this, the vast distances over which the fastest dispatch rider often seemed to make so more headway in emergencies than a man walking down Broadway.

"If, then, these were the grand, fixed obstacles, to oppose them in themselves must be useless.

"But there was another thing to do with them. It was this: it was *to use these very obstacles to our own advantage.*

"This conclusion was inspired by a line of reasoning I had pursued for some time but without discovering the key. The key I found in my reading of reports of military services from all about the world— in this case, the reports of the British Army in India. There, as here, the greatest strategic problem was to obtain information as soon as possible from stations scattered in a landscape almost identical, in the major aspects, to these deserts. The British Army in India had solved the problem through the invention by a British officer of the device variously known as the heliostat, or heliograph, from the Greek *helio,* sun, wedded to *stat,* render stationary, or *graph,* write. A small mirror placed at a suitable angle to the sun could reflect its light in a blinding flash which could be seen—and read, once a code was established—across a distance of fifty miles. The angle of the mirror, steadily changing in an accommodating inclination toward the sun as it traveled the arc of the heavens, was controlled by a small clockwork mechanism. By alternately shuttering and exposing the mirror the message could be sent. Stations were set up on high mountain eminences.

"Delectable. I sent a small detail of signal officers and men to India to study the heliostat to determine whether it could be employed in our vast geographical responsibilities here. My elation on receiving a diagram of the device and later the full report of our observers can be imagined. I had the answer to the line of reasoning which I had pursued, for this small complex of glass, mercury, clockwork and shutter was the very instrument which would employ to our distinct *advantage* those cosmic *disadvantages* I cited—mountain, sunlight, clarity of air, distance. All these were conquered for us by the device. And as you know, we erected many months ago a chain of fixed heliostat stations, to communicate between our fixed army posts here.

"But if we were to have the advantage of the device in the field, captain," he addressed Cedric Gray, "one further refinement must be created. This is the *portable* heliostat, which I asked the signal officers to design for me. It was finally produced, though not without a grade eel of opposition. But now our patrols on the borderline can carry with them the small tripod with its small platform at the apex where rests the precious mirror. All our roving detachments contain soldiers whose duty it is to sweep all vision as far as the earth's curve permits, and watch for flashes. With the speed of sight we shall be informed when there is something to know, from all quarters. It is my aim, gentlemen, to enclose the Indians in a constantly moving network of little mirrors. Thus the tale behind a military novelty."

He ended on a note of such guileless triumph that the listeners stirred, giving the effect of applause. The general bowed in acknowledgment, and added with an air of comic deprecation,

"Thank you. To be sure, in short order this military novelty will have become a moldy military chestnut. But let us hope by then that its work will have been done. —A drink, gentlemen?"

He passed the dipper, full, to the next officer, and it went around the half circle. The process reminded him of something.

"Almost the gesture of the Dakota peace pipe," he said smiling, as the dipper returned to him and he drank. "I feel we should found the Order of the Dipper, to commemorate the work we are about, and those who work it. I smoked a cigarette of peace years ago with Rainbow Son. Wretched stuff, tobacco. When you see Rainbow Son, as I earnestly trust we shall all do, he will puzzle you by his appearance for a moment. He looks like someone we all would recognize. It held me for a few moments and then I caught it: he is, especially in profile, the double of the Duke of Wellington, whose portrait every soldier must know by heart. From this likeness, at first I conceived that he possessed a spurious nobility. Later I was unsure of both attributions of quality. I do not think him in any way spurious. It is safer not to. As for nobility, this must always include magnanimity, and I misdoubt whether our man possesses a shred. It will fall to one, some, or all of us to encounter this man before we are done. He is the central problem of our mission.

"For the rest, take back to your troopers, who will move out with you at the end of starlight tomorrow morning, a reminder of how the Apache enemy is wedded to his land in war. Let them be suspicious of every clump of brush. You will more readily discern a speckled bird or a banded serpent against mottled rock than you will see the Indian enemy right out in the open when he does not wish to be seen."

Towering shadow was crossing slowly over them as the afternoon leaned westward above the great rocky wings of Bear Mesa. General Quait rose and all stood with him. He hooked their attention with a bent finger.

"A last word, gentlemen. Your components include Apache scouts. Let me say to you that I have never found an Apache scout or soldier to be faithless to my trust in him. I venture to add that without him we would now be in poor case. Thank you. I shall dismiss you with words to harbor before battle. The noble Virgil said it for us. *Possunt quia posse videntur,* said he, and Dryden made it into English for us, saying, *They can conquer who believe they can.* Posts, gentlemen."

Taking them toward battle, he was master of the distance and the circumstance in which they must use their lives in the near future. Feeling calmly classic—Virgil and Caeser and Tacitus breathing in his soul—he made his officers feel dimly but powerfully classic, too. Colonel Prescott, leaving the general's meeting with Matthew, was a member of a great line of commanders reaching as far back as his emotion and his ignorance of literature could take him. His feeling gave him a formidable aspect, in spite of which one of his own troopers came up to address him. It was Private Clanahan.

"Sir"—with a salute.

"Well, Clanahan? What're you looking so mad about?"

"Sir, I'm not mad, I just want to ask the commanding officer something which I've been thinking about. Rainey said just to ask you."

"Well, if Rainey advised you to ask me, you'd better do it, since he ranks you."

"Yes, sir, that's just it."

"Just what?"

"Sir, we're going to get into something on this march, and we're going to need all the good noncommissioned officers we can get, in case any of us get separated, and if there's no corporal, or sergeant. Sir, I—"

The colonel scowled not to smile.

"Your remarks are somewhat confused, Private Clanahan, but I believe you are trying to make a case to get yourself promoted."

"I am, sir!" said Clanahan with Irish truculence to cover his flooding embarrassment.

The colonel turned to Matthew.

"Lieutenant," he said with severity, "do you have any recommendations to make in this astonishing request?"

"Yes, sir."

"Then come along and make them to me in private. —Private Clanahan, your request will be considered." The colonel and Matthew strode on to their camp at the base of the mesa.

Clanahan watched after them wondering what the devil the colonel meant by his last remark. He shrugged. Rainey would know. But he supposed it meant that he would have to wait a while longer, anyhow. What the hell did Rainey mean by getting him stirred up to go and ask, anyhow? He felt like a fool the minute he began to ask for the honor of chevrons. Something told him he should never have asked—he should have just waited, and one day when he least expected them, they would have been given to him. Damn Rainey, anyhow. He may have spoiled all chances with his advice.

"What did he say?" asked Rainey when they met at their bivouac area near the eastern tip of Bear Mesa.

Clanahan looked resentfully at him and said,

"He said it would be considered. I suppose that means I was

supposed to go home and mind my own business and not put my nose in where I would only spoil my chances."

"Who says it will spoil your chances?" snorted Rainey, taking offense at Clanahan's tone. "A trooper is supposed to be able to talk to his C.O. about anything he wants to, if he has permission."

"They made a sort of a joke out of it," said Clanahan.

"Who did?"

"The colonel and the lieutenant. They called it an astonishing request. They told me off, all right. I wisht I hadn't listened to somebody who told me what to do."

"Oh, you do, hey? Well, you needn't listen again, get that? Because I'll never try to help you again, see?"

"That's good enough for me."

Side by side, they went in silence about their affairs, taking mess kits to the stew pots, sitting after dark by the fire to listen to songs, watching the firelight waver tall on the rosy rocks above them. They were sore at heart. There was nobody to tell them that small matters could grow huge in the lonely, monotonous life of men soldiering together for months on end in the wilderness. They did not reflect that if an officer made a joke about an enlisted man in front of him to another officer, the joke might as easily be a token of good-hearted interest as a sneer. It did not occur to them that each was hungry for the other's success in the Army. When the songs were done and the stars wheeled the vast night over the brigade, the two troopers rolled their blankets out side by side in their usual habit and, still not speaking, went to sleep.

Late at night, in the cold, Rainey sought warmth. He awoke to find his arm around Clanahan's chest which rose and fell in shallow draughts of sleep.

"You poor kid," thought Rainey. He was suddenly full of angry responsibility. "I'm going to get you those stripes. I'm going to look out for you. But before I let you know I'm looking out for you, I'll spit in your mess kit."

Comforted by these sentiments he went back to sleep.

iv

For a week the mirrors winked reports along their networks, and several times a day General Quait gathered his immediate staff to evaluate the intelligence received. He kept a diagram tucked into his saber belt. On this he marked the area reports and daily he traced with his finger the invisible track which the massed Indian marauding army must be following, since no crossings of the border had been observed to the south, and no further attacks were reported to the north.

"I perceive," he told his commanders one day, "a curious structure in all this. It is a trough, long, wide and invisible, as though made of great plates of glass, or vast sheets of light. Through this trough, marching with skill and caution, the Indian army must be going toward the west. If I am right, they will advance until almost they reach the Californian line, and then they will turn sharply south, awaiting their opportunity to cross the boundary in small units, and then again assemble and run for their mountains. The country where we must arrest their progress is country where seven years ago I had occasion to be active. Odd indeed to be returning, and on the same mission. I will confess frankly that I failed then. But perhaps I know rather more than I did then, and we shall not fail again."

He put his finger on his diagrammatic map. "I promise you wonderful country as we advance. It is a wild park of fantastic rocks. Is it fate which takes me there again? I choose to think not. I choose to think that in history there rests a certain propriety. Its benefits are now extended to me once again. I shall hope to achieve now what was denied me before. The areas north and south of the park I refer to are covered by two of our squadrons—one marching parallel to us, far to the north, and one to the south, to seal the border. If we are right, and the enemy is feeling his way through the sides of the trough which we have created, in the end he will have nowhere to go but where we send him. One thing is certain, however. He will not await us at our convenience, but at his. I will coolly admit to you, gentlemen, that he has the advantage. But a great soldier is one who can succeed against disadvantage, and you are great soldiers. Thank you.

"And now from here forward, the marching order of this brigade will be as follows: an advance guard composed of one platoon, under its regular commander, with whom I shall march daily. For this duty I designate the second platoon, Troop F, Sixth Cavalry, Lieutenant Hazard commanding. The main body will be commanded by Lieutenant Colonel Prescott, and will follow my advance by two thousand yards, holding the interval strictly. I allow so wide an interval in order to permit movements to be detached on either flank from the main body as required by local observation. The rear guard will consist of eight troopers from the Fourth Cavalry under a noncommissioned officer and will maintain an interval of five hundred yards. Nightly bivouac will draw all our elements together in a single camp. Watch fires will be kept up all night. Troops will bivouac in a great circle enclosing horses and supplies as in a corral or paddock. Questions, gentlemen."

"Sir, how do we know that the Indian party has not crossed into Mexico already, under darkness?"

"Sir, our patrols, though widely separated, are yet sufficient to ride the border in daylight to look for massed hoofprints or other evidence of the movement of a crossing by day or night such as would be discerned by the Army's Apache scouts. They have reported none."

"Thank you, sir."

"Sir. —Posts, gentlemen."

v

"Yes," said General Quait to Matthew Hazard riding beside him, "precisely seven years ago I crossed this same waste of desert land, and for much the same reason."

The time of day was about noon, when even in the month of October the heat of the desert rose sharply, lifting strange winds, such as had done strange work on the features of the earth throughout thousands of centuries. In the distance on all sides rose separated towers of rock, each different from the other, all fantastic, all eloquent of the unseen struggle between that which moved and that which rested in the desert nature. General Quait himself seemed to echo that same struggle. An old man, to whom nature might already have given the word to rest, he contained in his tall, bony, expressive figure a leaping spirit. It shone in his lively black eyes, it agitated his forked white beard about his stream of conversation, and it even qualified what clothes he put on his back.

As a general officer was privileged to do, he had long ago modified his own uniform, and now wore his favorite desert dress, which included his Anglo-Indian sun helmet, the familiar linen duster which now flowed over his horse's rump giving an Arabian air, black alpaca trousers stuffed into cavalry boots, and gauntlets with fringed cuffs that reached the elbow. Lieutenant Hazard rode in the Army's regulation dark-blue flannel shirt, light-blue kersey breeches and black boots, with campaign hat creased down the center. The troopers in the platoon following looked much the same. Two miles or more to the rear the main body was stretched out in a mighty column which raised a high-curling wave of dust which drifted away to the south.

"How timeless is man's self-conceit," the General continued, sweeping the horizon, the foreground, every bush, with his sharp sight, both to gratify his theory and to watch against individual enemies. "I have looked today for visible changes in the rocks, forgetting what made them as they are, and how long it took to make them. So much has passed in my life in those years since I have been here that unless I govern my sense I seem to expect all nature to show corresponding change."

He waved his hand toward the rocky fantasies in the distance.

"Those are created by what we call erosion, action of the winds carrying small particles which grind against solid stone, and in time make the jagged pinnacles we see about us. Think of how long! And think what a rock is made of, to let wind change its shape!" The general glanced sidelong at Matthew and smiled in a wag of his head. "You must think me a teacher, lieutenant, making a pupil of you. Well, I am a teacher. Anyone who must lead is a teacher. He knows the lessons aforehand and he must hand them on to those who follow. With me it has become a habit, as you note. I shall continue. Thank you.

"This whole land has layers of hard, then soft, then hard, materials, and great heaps of loose soil. These winds come and shift a whole desert, and expose soft rock and wear it down until hard rock is revealed, and then the winds look again for softer places to change, and drill away and drill, like the railroad tarriers, and accomplish wonders and mysteries our eyes can scarce believe. Yes. Yet we must pierce them if we would be true to our own currents of thought.

I refer less to myself as an individual than to mankind altogether in man's eternal quest to know all he can."

"Yes, sir," said Matthew, aware that this was an inadequate reply, yet feeling that he must say something out of wonder and politeness. Now used to General Quait's studious cast of mind, he had come to regard it as a source of power, even of physical strength in the old gentleman, who campaigned in the wilderness with the endurance of youth, while interesting himself with the reflections of a sage. Matthew felt rather a swindler, to be giving an attentive ear to a dissertation which though perfectly clear was still allied to habits of mind entirely foreign to his own. It seemed to him that if the general was a genius, he should have another genius to hear him. Matthew sighed. Himself, all he was, was a strong, healthy, ordained young soldier who could see well enough what his eyes beheld, but who would never, of his own interest, peer beyond to derive from winds and rocks and aeons of time the story of creation.

"Possibly you see all this quite differently?" asked the general, as though he read Matthew's thought. He swept the landscape with a gesture. "The Indian sees it differently, we may be sure, and yet he has found a system of truth in his life on the wasteland which we could never use, much as we might want to. I cannot tell my people often enough how I have seen Apache Indians appear in the desert and vanish. Individually and in groups. It is not magic. It is skill. Lieutenant, please to halt the column."

Matthew gave the hand-signal command and reined in his horse. The troopers halted and watched the general, who leaned forward in his saddle and peered all about in a slow arc.

"This looks very much like the place," he said, "as I saw it years ago. Then as now we were chasing after Rainbow Son; the problem is similar, and the lie of the land, I believe, identical. It was in just such a place as this—I remember fixing it in my vission by making a straight line which anchored on that tower of spools there far ahead, and on myself at the center, and behind me"—he turned in the saddle and pointed—"on that vast mushroom of rock in the bright distance. It was very close to here that we lost Sergeant Reimmers, and had to retreat that day."

"You had a skirmish here, sir?"

"We had a skirmish," said the general, suddenly dismounting with odd anglings of his long thin arms and legs. He fell to the ground, and Matthew thought something was amiss with him; but the general was only assuming the prone position of a rifleman the better to sight the country as he remembered from fighting on it long ago. "Yes," he said, lying there in some inert content with the mindless earth, "we are very near to the same place, if not precisely upon it." He stood. "I relish a mystery if I can solve it —that is to say, if I can meet its conditions with sufficient intelligence. But how vexed I am when there is no hope of a solution, and the mystery continues!"

He mounted again, and asked Matthew to signal "At a walk, forward." When the column in good order was again under progress, with nodding horses, sandy whisper from the walking hoofs, creaking leather, the low clanking of bit and saber, canteen and spur chain, the dim hum of troopers talking idly—all the music of a commander's ear—he said to Matthew,

"I am bitter and confused when I remember it. Sergeant Franz Reimmers was the only soldier I ever lost to the unknown. I shall never understand how it could have happened, or how I failed to recover him, alive or dead. There was never a better soldier. I never knew a truer friend among enlisted men. I see again how it was, in this same wind-freaked wilderness. Let me tell you as we go."

vi

While Matthew listened he kept his eyes piercing ahead and on all sides, to open the secrets of the open day and the open land. There was nothing to see, yet how could he know, under the tutelage of General Quait, what might not betray the presence of Rainbow Son and the warriors after whom the Army was now riding to kill or capture? It was an abiding desire with Matthew to recover the kidnapped grandson, fourteen years old, of Amos Edwards. Where was the boy? Where were his captors? All was hidden in light and space. The distant land, pale yellow, was broken here and there by idle lifts of dust on the warm wind. Nothing else moved.

And all seemed just as still, said General Quait, on that day seven years ago when another army detachment waited for Sergeant Reimmers to return from a scouting foray. General Quait had every confidence in him. The sergeant was a young man of excellent education. He was a German, an ex-student of the University of

Bonn, who had left the Germany he loved because it was being turned into a Germany he detested. He came to the United States to live in the freedom that was being destroyed at home by Count Bismarck and the German imperialist politicians and army officers. In the United States he found employment as a dispatch runner on the docks of New York, where he could meet the German vessels that docked, and carry manifests, news and instructions between the ship captains and the agents of the owners in the offices in Water Street. He would stand on the street waterfront under the ropes and chains of the great bowsprits which the ocean-going ships thrust out over him when they docked, and cry his credentials up to the deck officer above him. They would take him on board, and though there he spoke German, he always represented himself as an American.

The surge of life borne into New York Harbor by the sail-masted steamships from Europe week after week made him wonder. Where did so much cargo and so many people go from New York? He listened to talk of the West. He had read at home in Bonn all the novels of Fenimore Cooper which he could obtain, and these had told him about Indians and savannahs and prairies. Immigrants spoke of going west—even those who had never heard of Fenimore Cooper. Dimly he felt that Cooper's world must have vanished. Another world was coming alive in the great inland. He was poor and he was ambitious. He knew that he would become a complete American. To do so he must know the whole country. One day he enlisted in the Army and was sent as a recruit to Fort Union, in the Territory of New Mexico. He found a land he loved, the whole Southwest.

By the time he was assigned to the Arizona campaign of the '70's under Major General Alexander Upton Quait, he was proficient in English. He became the general's orderly. Of all the soldiers in the command he was the only one—officers included—with whom the general could converse on matters of history, philosophy, natural science, art and literature.

"He became a student of the desert wilderness," said the general, "and he soon became an expert Indian fighter. I promoted him to sergeant."

Sergeant Reimmers was not a big young man, but he was hardy and agile, with a capacity for work that burned in him—his German heritage—like a passion. He was yellow-haired, his eyes were blue, his face was round and smooth-shaven and serious, and he had a reluctant, kind smile which served him when other men laughed out loud.

"Every night he wrote a half page," said the general, "in a little pocket journal. This is also my habit. I asked him about it and he replied that he was keeping it to show his parents one day, whether they ever came to America from Bonn, where his father taught philosophy in the university, or, timid in their maturity, stayed home, where as a successful American he would go to visit them before they died."

On that day seven years ago this particular passage of country was new to the commander and his troops.

They had ridden in the pale wastes for so long without seeing a sign of the enemy that this very circumstance seemed more and more significant and dangerous—for they knew the enemy was there.

"But we had not the present advantage of our wide-flung snare of mirrors, and I did not know," said General Quait, "whether the enemy had opened a passage for me, or whether he had closed behind me and was trailing me with deliberately prolonged pleasure in the feast of blood and shame which he would finally make. It was also a simple possibility that the enemy was ahead of me on my march. Yet with my skyglass I saw no evidence of this."

On the noontime of that day so long ago the general gave the order to halt in a faded pink stretch of sand. He told his subordinates that if they were all entirely visible and exposed in such a position, then any enemy coming upon them must also be.

"I took refuge in sheer conspicuousness; and if the enemy responded, he too must be equally ostentatious, and the battle could be joined in frank array."

But he was not so inexperienced as to imagine that even in the most bland country the Apache could not at times find cover, and accordingly he rode forward a few yards with Sergeant Reimmers and asked him to make a scouting foray on a long, shallow arc, from south to north, never to lose sight of the halted column, and to return instanter if he came upon any sign, any trail, new ashes, recent horse droppings, or human offal by which (as desert craft required) the late presence and the direction of the enemy might be determined. Meanwhile, the column would be deployed in positions which would guard against all approaches.

Before he left on his mission Sergeant Reimmers said an interesting and curious thing to General Quait.

"Sir," he said, "I have formed the opinion that every field commander and scout should be trained in the art of landscape painting."

"Have you, indeed, sergeant? Yes, of course. In order that military personnel in the field may enhance their reports with scenes taken on the spot, no doubt."

"No, sir, though that would be useful. No. I was thinking how different this very landscape must look at different times of day. A trained eye would know at noon what differences must show at four o'clock. The differences might be strategically vital."

General Quait put his head on one side and squinted at the land to change its aspect.

"Imagine," continued the sergeant, "a table top lighted from above. All is flat. But throw light from the side, and little rumples in the tablecloth might show."

The general saw the implications at once. He exclaimed,

"Capital, sergeant! Please to detect all rumples as you ride! I shall sight you frequently from here. Proceed with speed, care and the universal vision of a bird."

In hilarious imitation of a bird, the general cocked his head, and made Matthew smile now as he had made Sergeant Reimmers smile at the same gesture then.

Sergeant Reimmers saluted and rode toward the south till he was a rock, a bush, a clump of grass, in size and pallor, in the distance, save that he moved and those did not. He turned northward to ride his long arc.

The troopers watching him were dismounted. Their horses were held at picket. The men, with carbines ready, were ranged in a thin line facing west, but sentries were set out a hundred yards from the main body, facing the cardinal points, and ready to fire or call an alarm. General Quait remembered how he himself had paced in a circle around the troopers as a sort of universal sentinel. He swept the horizons with a beam of vision like the ray of a lighthouse. Each time he completed his circle, he found Sergeant Reimmers, moving north half a mile away, and he measured the sergeant's progress by how much nearer he was to crossing in front of the far distant tower of rock which was eroded into what looked like a pillar of great spools. When the sergeant would have passed before the tower of spools his mission would be half finished, on the arc of his ride. The general calculated, at a certain moment, that the next time he saw the tower of spools in his own conning of the land, he would see Sergeant Reimmers riding right across its base.

He came about with his vision, saw the tower, looked for the sergeant, and could not find him.

He peered again. Some illusion of light, some jump of the eye against the tower's rocky rose color must have obliterated the sergeant, at this distance, until he was lost to observation. Once past the tower, the sergeant would show again, against the simpler horizon of bleached earth and white sky. General Quait watched for this materialization to take place.

It did not come.

The general took his spyglass. At first he saw nothing but a pale world rimmed in the blue and yellow unreality of the lens. And then he picked up a horse, the sergeant's mount. The horse was running riderless, tossing its head, turning in random lunges, as if in pain or terror. Sergeant Reimmers was nowhere visible. The land on which he should show was a long flat line with hardly any growth, and only the crazed horse to give it scale. It was a strange picture to see in the glass. It broke from sight to sound for the general when on both his right and his left the outposts gave yells and fired their carbines.

"I lowered my glass, and swiftly looking to right and left, saw the unbelievable, which was that from two directions, the south and the north, Indian warriors in great numbers were riding down upon my deployed detachment. They had appeared from absolutely nowhere. If they had come straight up out of the ground they could not have been more startling. It was impossible to explain what concealment they had used, or how they had managed to attack me not on one but on both flanks. They ran at full gallop, and their cries came clearly. You will hear them, lieutenant, before we're done. Let me see. What did they sound like? Yes. They were small, plaintive, half-strangled animal sounds that could almost stir pity for the blind animal appetites they proclaimed."

General Quait shouted commands to bring his outposted sentries to the main body. He redeployed the troopers, with the picketed horses in the center, and two lines of riflemen facing out north and south to meet the impact that was coming. It was coming heavy on the ground, and the soldiers felt the Indian hoofbeats tremble into their own bones through the common earth. They saw the naked bodies riding air just above their horses' backs, and speed became the same thing as dust and noise as light, and the explosions began on both sides, and a few iron-tipped arrows went with the sound of a gut guitar string. A horse gave out a scream, and the first pass went by.

"I could estimate their numbers, by then," said the general, "and I saw that they exceeded my own force by four to one. It was a matter for thought."

The Indians rode out to reorganize and sweep back again from opposite directions. The general found an instant to scan the distance again for Sergeant Reimmers, and again saw only his horse. The horse now came in a runaway to the troop position with an arrow sticking out of its left side.

"When I saw that, I saw that Sergeant Reimmers had met the Indians in their invisibility, and somehow had not been able to escape when his horse escaped."

In a thrust of painful thought, the general knew what he must do. He must mount his men, get them in motion, and, with a whole platoon of men and horses to animate and save, he must abandon to his fate, whatever it might be, Sergeant Franz Reimmers, lost in distance.

"I knew I had only one advantage over the enemy in that moment. Apache horses suffered the same steady abuse as Apache dogs, women and old people. The Army's mounts would show superiority any day. I braced my unit to meet the next attack. I told them that the Indians, riding at full gallop, would not be accurate in their aim, while on the ground, we would be. I ordered my men to stand ready, after the next enemy pass, for a command to mount."

The assault came, a soldier was wounded, a handful of Indians felt the carbines and one fell. As the waves passed by each other from opposite directions, General Quait called out, the deployed line broke for the picketed horses, and with the Indians widening out on the desert to make their next turn, the Army moved eastward at an extended gallop. Heading for that thick mushroom of eroded stone which loomed at the entrance of the rock-rimmed desert, the cavalry ran for refuge across the country over which they had just come.

"It was a retreat," stated the general, "but it was not a rout. In direct combat, with anything of a defensive position, we could have handled them, numbers or no numbers. What we did not know as well as they, was how to use the land."

By nightfall the general and his men found their refuge in a natural fortress of rock, waiting for an attack to come at dawn. It came. The Apaches were driven off by superior fire from an en-trenched position. By mid-morning the Indian survivors, including their leader, ran away under the protection of a rear-guard action. As soon as possible, General Quait hurried to retrace his course of the day before. He tried to bear upon the very spot where he had lost Sergeant Reimmers, but he must have missed it widely, for he found nothing—no trace of a struggle, no body, no break in the open land. Pressing on, he abandoned Sergeant Reimmers for the second time, and tried to pick up the trail of Rainbow Son. After days of footless search he returned to his headquarters.

"I reported the whole episode in detail to Washington. You will know what resulted. I was sharply censured by the War Department for my failure to win a single day what decades of frontier effort had been unable to win. There was talk in the *senaculum* that the con-duct of the Indian war in the Far West should be investigated. *Iniquissima haec bellorum condicio est,"* said the general while Matthew strained at the Latin saw with respect and ignorance, *"prospera omnes sibi vindicant, adversa uni imputantor.* An observa-tion from the *Agricola* of Tacitus which I always bring over as: *Of all the conditions of war, this is the most unfair—that all take credit for victory, while in defeat giving blame to one."*

vii

Both musing, they rode in silence for a moment, and then Matthew asked,

"Was there never anything more about Sergeant Reimmers, sir?"

"Nothing. After his horse came back to us that day, we led it until it fell down of its wound. At our rapid pace, the animal could not survive. We shot it forthwith, and I took the sergeant's saddle and pack. Later I found a few personal effects to send to his father and mother in Bonn. Among them was his diary. I read it, the better, and finally, to know my friend." The general smiled with a scholar's pleasure. "It was written in English, with an occasional Teutonism in construction. Verbs uneasily located, and the like. There were a few loose leaves with notes made on the trail, to be elaborated later when he wrote with care in his diary by the campfire. He always carried a pencil and some folded sheets of paper. I used to see him scribbling observations even on horseback, at the walk or halt. A lively, a most lively student of his environment. Who knows? If he were still with us, he might have become a later Humboldt."

"Did you ever hear from his people, sir?"

"Yes, I did. Professor Reimmers wrote to me, just one letter. I still have it. In it, he said that his son had written home many times about the United States, and had always used the expression, 'We Americans,' and spoke often of how the whole country was the creation of all the people, voluntarily, and how a man was willing to do his duty because it was not required of him by force. Coming after the sergeant was gone, his feeling carried a quite extraordinary weight. Most moving, you see. Yes. Extraordinary. Yes. He was a romantic, like the German poet Schiller."

Matthew felt a little chill. What if, in some still hidden day, his beautiful young wife and his infant son should have to be told that he was lost to them forever? Many another soldier's family had heard such news from his commander. He put down his emotion by staring ahead at distant little whirlwinds which took the loose face of the desert into the air, spinning awhile, and fading into nothing against the sky. He gestured at these. General Quait nodded.

"The dry winds at their work. Imagine the millions of years needed for them to change the earth as it was changed here." The general glanced with rueful humor at Matthew. The lieutenant was an excellent officer, a good companion, but he did not have a darting mind, and the general must answer his own speculations for himself. Following a new train of thought, the general closed one door and opened another. "Our tasks, like the winds, are never finished. A soldier's work, to be done, sometimes has to be done over and over— today, and seven years ago."

"Yes, sir." Matthew rose a little in his saddle and pointed. If he could not be scientific, he could at least indicate the stuff of science. "There's a beauty, sir."

A particularly high, thin and powerful column of whirling pale sand was moving in the distance straight ahead of them. It seemed to approach them, dancing mightily as its tip touched, and leaped, and touched the earth.

Suddenly, as it touched, it violently changed color.

"How incredible!" cried General Quait. "I have never seen that happen before!"

Before their eyes the whirlwind sucked up and in an instant made into a flying column some earth dust of a heavy, dull yellow which took the light brilliantly. And then in another instant the yellow fell like scattered powder against the sky, and the color of plain sand once again whirled across the ground.

"But we must see what caused that!" said the general. "It lies right in our path." His eyes burned with scientific interest. "It was precisely like changing the color of smoke from a fire by adding certain minerals. When will one ever know enough about the desert? —Lieutenant, please to signal *trot*."

Matthew gave the hand signal and the column broke into a trot. The privileges of rank! Matthew smiled uncritically at the whim that permitted a major general in the field to hasten forward with thirty mounted men who would probably retain their composure in the presence of one man's interest in natural science.

"Lieutenant," called the general in his voice which he could thin to make it carry in command, "take over the lookout. It was very close to here where they came the other time. I shall watch for the yellow earth."

They trotted for perhaps ten minutes. If Rainbow Son and his marauders were in the land, there was no sign of them. But by now Matthew was schooled to take particular care in the most innocent of situations.

"Ah, yes!" abruptly cried General Quait. He saw something. He called, "Signal *walk*."

The column came down to a walk.

"Signal *halt*."

They halted.

"How perfectly and superbly extraordinary," said the General softly, gazing at what he saw. It was the mouth of an open pit in the earth, roughly triangular, about a yard wide. Its edges were worn by weather and dusted with the yellow earth the color of which they had seen staggering rapidly into the air. Otherwise, the ground nearby was of ordinary sand. "You see, lieutenant? You see? Here is a weak place in the earth's crust. The wind has drilled this pit and touched soft yellow—ocherous—soil. The dancing updraft whirled across the surface and lifted ordinary soil. Then it crossed this mouth and instanter it sucked up the yellow soil which lay below its path. We saw it taken high in the air by the spinning wind. Then it passed beyond this mouth and took up again only the plain sand. How beautiful. I must see more."

He dismounted, handed his reins to Matthew, and walked to the edge of the pit. He peered into its dark depths, murmuring with delight, and ended by slapping his leg and saying to Matthew,

"You do see, don't you? This is a wind creation, an *inverted* tower, as it were, created by just what made the rock forms we see yonder. How classically beautiful."

He stood up and threw off his linen duster.

"I must descend," he cried.

Ah, that's too much, said Matthew to himself, while retaining a respectful bearing. The old gentleman was all but dancing with pleasure. His Anglo-Indian sun helmet, his white beard, his long-boned gestures suddenly seemed to Matthew like laughable if not irritating extensions of his unpredictable personality. Aloud, Matthew only replied, "Very well, sir. Give us instructions."

"A rope about my upper middle," said the general, "with the other end tied through your pommel"—the Army's McClellan saddle had an opening there—"and at my signal, you will walk your horse slowly forward until I am on the bottom, or have, quite literally"—he laughed drily—"reached the end of my rope. I shall take a quarter-master's camphine lantern by which to see down there. When I tug on the rope once, please to pull me up by backing your animal. If I tug twice, do you arrange, in the same way, to join me. Is this clear? —And see that the lookout is sharply maintained in all directions while we are halted. If we take too much time, please to send a rider to instruct Colonel Prescott to hold his interval with the main body."

viii

To the incredulous interest of the troopers, the exercise was carried out just as the general had ordered. As he went over the edge he peered at them all, and something in his face made them laugh out with admiration at his juvenile zest for investigation.

Matthew rode slowly forward. His rope was sixty feet long. When about sixteen feet were payed over the rim of the pit, the rope slackened suddenly. All observers knew that Major General Alexander Upton Quait had reached bottom. A little haze of yellow dust drifted up from the pit.

There was a long pause while the men on top tried to read in each other's faces what could have happened below.

Then there came two violent tugs at the rope. Matthew with a sigh dismounted and prepared to join his commander down in the ground. He turned the command over to the first sergeant with strict instructions, and in his turn was lowered into the blinding darkness of the pit.

For moments he could not see, and could hardly breathe. The confined air of the pit was dense with disturbed dust. He could hear the general's voice close to him.

"Lieutenant, lieutenant, what a tremendous moment. Move gently, or you will free more dust and we shall choke. But look, my boy, look!"

The general's voice trembled with exaltation and awe. He put his hand on Matthew's shoulder and held high his camphine lantern. Now the darkness cleared for Matthew, the dust fell slowly about him, and his faculties returned. Under the vibrant hand of General Quait he looked at the wall of the pit opposite. In shock at what he saw, he opened his mouth and choked on a draft of yellow dusty air.

At a sharp incline, a slope of earth reached out from the pit wall toward the center of the deep dusty floor. Leaning on it was a figure of a man, face downward, with his head resting on his raised left forearm. His right arm was curved under his belly. In the dim lantern light he was dusted thickly with the golden earth of his open grave. His cheeks were parched and gaunt, showing skin, not bone. So too with his hands. His hair was long over his collar and a silky beard grew along his jawbones. He was clothed in garments that were bulky on his shrunken figure and smoothed by heavy dust into soft contours of sculpture. He was a mummy, preserved by the dryness of the desert air and the driftings of the yellow earth about him.

The general and the lieutenant in the sifting silence listened to their hearts beating and heard eternity.

Gradually they came to detect in the air a dry herbal scent which was laden with sweetness. It was this which unlocked the jaws of the living. General Quait spoke first.

"One thinks of balsam," he said, and his voice was hushed against the cushion of the golden dust, "the balm which the Shades leave behind them as they journey far." He raised his hand toward the still figure. "The chevrons will show under the dust. There will be crossed sabers on his collar, his belt buckle. His shirt is dark blue and his trousers sky-blue kersey. Somewhere under the soft floor may lie his carbine. Sergeant Franz Reimmers, leaning here for seven years."

Matthew stared at the general.

"Is this he?" he asked in awe.

"I know him. At last I am answered."

They fell silent again, until Matthew asked,

"How—"

"Yes, you see," interrupted the general. "He was attacked, for his horse showed it. He was dismounted and ran for safety and fell into this." The general glanced up at the patch of sky in the opening sixteen feet above. "There was no way out. We searched for him but this could only be found by accident. —What is that in his hand?" he asked, peering sharply.

Matthew leaned forward while the general held close the lantern.

Showing under the left side of Sergeant Reimmers was his right hand, holding three things. One was a small crucifix, one was a big silver watch that he clutched by its heavy chain, and the third was a scrap of paper.

"Let me have them," said the general.

With strange feelings Matthew took the watch and then the cross from the withered fingers and handed them to the general, who said,

"Yes, he dwelled on time, measurable time"—the watch—"and eternity"—the cross. "Yes, the ultimate objects for a philosopher. —And the paper?"

Matthew blew dust from the paper and saw lines written on it. He began to scan it in the lantern light.

"Read it to me," said General Quait.

Matthew read aloud.

"For General Quait, or whom otherwise it may concern: in the last possibility that this may be found in time to be of service, if ever, it is a matter of duty for me to report—"

[The general interrupted. "Duty," he said softly, "even to this. Go on."]

"—to report that, west of this pit into which I fell while after my wounded horse running, there is another break in the earth. It cannot be seen any more than this ground opening until immediately you are upon it. It is a long trough of ochreous earth reaching from north to south about fifty yards wide and eight to twenty feet deep. If from the west approached it might from a little distance be seen. If from the east, as we approached, it is invisible, for the near lip is higher than the far one, and in a full overhead light no difference between them shows. I came upon it in astonishment, dismounted and crawled near. There were the Indians, hidden from view, yet mounted and ready to go forth. Riding to right and left to the ends of the trough they could suddenly appear on the desert with terrible surprise. I started back to report. However, they saw me and gave their attack order and rode out two ways. One came to deal with me. I ran and made a long race thinking to win it. He fired at me. He saw me fall, but not from his bullet I fell. In here I fell. I pray they brought us no harm. I feel shame for failure of my duty to return with warning. May God keep me if I am to remain here. *Für mein—*"

Matthew paused in difficulty with the writing which changed into German. The general took the sheet and finished it.

"*Für meinen Vater und meine Mutter, Liebe und Trost—for my father and mother, love and consolation. Für Amerika, Glaube und Dank—for America, faith and thanks,*" read General Quait.

The paper was not signed. The hand in which it was found was its endorsement. The general frowned at the paper for a moment as though to force from it a living vision of the man who had written it.

Then he whirled to the lieutenant and struck him sharply on the arm, and for one of very few times addressed him by his first name.

"Matthew!" he cried, and the dust came up about them, and the air throbbed with his excited voice, and the agitated lantern shifted the shadows of the figure leaning on its arm until it too seemed to move, "we must go up! Instantly!"

The general tugged at his rope once, mightily, the signal to be hoisted away.

"The instant I am clear, you will follow," he said with a crackle in his voice. "I shall order the platoon mounted immediately, and the main body to come up at full gallop. I shall take command. I shall order the charge!"

The rope went taut and General Quait began slowly to rise, gently turning in midair. If under the circumstances the spectacle had not been ghostly, it would have been comic. "We must risk being fools," he said in wry excitement, "if there is one chance to be heroes." He reached the opening, and with an angular scramble, was gone.

Matthew, bearing the lantern, was taken aloft immediately afterward.

The action of the next hours was "rapid and multiplex," as General Quait wrote of it in his published account *—the most authoritative source for knowledge of what happened that day.

ix

Upon my emergence from the pit I saw that the main body was nearer to us by a half mile or so. I dispatched a courier to order Colonel Prescott to join me with all his men at uttermost speed. I then ordered the advance guard into line, with drawn sabres. It gave me satisfaction to set the silver watch of Sergeant Reimmers and to wind it up. Acting upon dutiful warning, we would move in his frame of time.

Prescott came up to us in speed. I deployed his squadrons in line, and after quickly giving him my view of what might lie ahead, I told him to give the command for charge. In turn, the bugler gave that call as if to crack the very air with it, and prick the blood alive in men's veins.

In a great ragged leap the brigade broke forward in the gallop, going directly to the west where the land seemed to be but was not, as we now knew, unbroken. I led this charge. My horse gave me a kind of animal trust which was most exhilarating, and which made me feel that I rode him lightly as a child.

In the charge our numbers were grand, and the distance to cover was not great—perhaps three quarters of a mile—and the objective was not really certain. But my officers and men caught together with me some sense of the marvellous, for all rode with exulting spirit. We made the thunder of heroes on the ground. It travelled ahead of us. It gave our news.

For just before we sighted the hidden break north and south in the ground, we saw perhaps half a hundred mounted Indians swarm up from the trough and break away over the far side on to the open land. Our pace was so heavy that I could not at once detach a party to

* *Honour and Arms.* The Autobiography of Alexander Upton Quait, Major General USA. Philadelphia, Adam & Blaine, 1892.

give chase. But my thought of Sergeant Reimmers was proud, for he had told us where the enemy waited, and once again the enemy was there. In the full splendour of our power, we swept on in the charge and came to the near edge of the depression. It was a steepish bank. No matter. We flew down it like a tidal wave, and there in the hollow, waiting for us with a positive sheet of bullets and arrows was a great war party. It was a hot discharge which they threw at us, but they could not stand and make another. They divided and rode up the draw. Our momentum, in three waves of squadron fronts, was too great to let us halt and immediately give battle. But out on the far side of the depression we turned and divided, and drove the escaping enemy back into the trough. There the god of battles shook us all like peas in a split pod.

What is the genius which seizes men at such a time? My troopers, and no less the Indians, coming face to face and, in a hundred incidents, hand to hand in combat, declared themselves in valour and power. The enemy fought fiercely even though all knew, including himself, that he was doomed. I saw, from my command position on the eastern lip of the depression, many a valiant act in our ranks. One young soldier saw another about to be killed by a blow from the side, and threw himself in the way of it to save the other, and was himself cut down. I saw another trooper, fighting with his sabre, knock down an Indian with it. In an automatic gesture whose origin in memory nobody could define, the trooper reached down, pulled the Indian to his feet again, and continued the duel. I did not observe the issue of this, as my attention was required elsewhere.

I sent for Lieutenant Hazard, 2nd pltn., F Troop, 6th Cav., and commanded him to take his own platoon and one other, constituting together a troop in strength, and give pursuit upon the Indian party which had fled on our approach. It seemed highly possible that they had gone to do one of two things: a., either they had Rainbow Son with them and were his escort to safety, or b., they were in flight to give warning of our tremendous arrival. Mr. Hazard had his pursuit in train in all possible haste modified by order.

The waggons were slowly overtaking us from the east, and I was not sorry. Our toll in wounded was high. I could not yet know how many we lost killed. Captain Gray, surgeon, reported to me at this point, and asked for permission to detach a squad of men to assist as bearers. Granted. He soon had his patients moving to the rear to meet the ambulances. Colonel Prescott accompanied one small party of his own men for a little distance and then returned to report to me for orders.

The fight was suddenly more fierce in the center, and then, in a trice, it was over. Our heavy numbers had pressed in so closely, after the first shock and recovery, that the enemy was enclosed. The effect was as if in the end he could not lift his arm to wield his weapon, so closely was he pressed. On my instructions, Colonel Prescott rode down to the floor and gave the order to disarm all the enemy and herd every Apache to the south end of the trough there to remain under guard as prisoners. The count was taken, including dead and living Indians. It came to one hundred and twenty-one. Our men were given to rest. Their elation was great. I went among them and heard their exploits; for a soldier's greatest need after giving of his valour is to tell of it. In all, as in myself, the day's deed was a marvel because it had come before us in surprise. How did we know? I heard them ask, when we charged, that the enemy would be there? In time they would know. But meanwhile all must have seemed to them the favoured outcome of rashness, and they felt irreducibly aggrandised by fortune, men whom none could now defeat, men who chained the very unknown to their service. For myself, I took comfort in reflection, drawing strength after the deed, as it were, from Macaulay's remarks on Chatham, which long years ago I memorised to my profit: 'The Minister, before he had been long in office, had imparted to the commanders whom he employed his own impetuous, adventurous, and defying character. They, like him, were disposed to risk everything, to play double or quits to the last, to think nothing done while anything remained undone, to fail rather than not attempt. *For errors of rashness there might be indulgence. For over caution . . . there was no mercy.*' In this I found both precept and consolation.

There was a lull now during which I canvassed the captives for their chief. He was not among them. I asked who led them and who had escaped with the first party? After much reluctance it was admitted that Sebastian was their man. I awaited the results of Mr. Hazard's chase.

In about an hour I had these. He returned with forty-six prisoners including Sebastian the chief. In dune-like formations to the southwest he had overtaken the escaping party. Resistance was brief, though fire was exchanged, and two troopers were wounded, and five Indians were left dead. These new prisoners were added to the others, and Colonel Prescott ordered plans for an escort to march the whole bag back to San Carlos Reservation. From thence they were to be transported to Florida, there to be resettled under guard, far from the scenes of their offenses. Meanwhile I dealt with Sebastian. The dialogue ran quite closely as follows, with the benefit of my own Apache and Spanish words.

"Do you remember me?" I asked.

Affirmative, was the reply in sign and mutter.

"Did I not warn you at Fort Delivery in council?"

Yes.

"Why have you and your people disobeyed me and ignored my warnings?"

We have grievances.

Even so, I went on, these would have been dealt with honourably if they had been presented properly. Meantime, where was Rainbow Son? I wanted to know. He delayed his reply until I asked again, and then he told me, with a gesture, that Rainbow Son was in the north. I permitted silence to answer this, and then I told him that he and all his people here were prisoners and would be marched away under guard, never to be free again, until peace was made with Rainbow Son. I asked him again, where was Rainbow Son? He gave the same answer—*in the north.* I then told him he lied, for I knew better. My mirrors with flashes of sunlight told me better. At this Sebastian held his breath and scowled for a long minute then exhaled and said that Rainbow Son was not in the north. He did not know where he was. I said that we would know soon enough, just as we knew all things that we wanted to know. I said,

"I suppose you observed us?"

Yes.

"Why did you not attack? Did you know our numbers were too great for you?"

Yes.

"Then if you did not attack, your only chance was to lie hidden here thinking we would pass by all unknowing."

Yes.

"Then you could have fallen on us from the rear."

Sebastian remained silent, but this was confirmation enough. I asked,

"Why did you not open fire when you heard us coming?"

He looked at me deciding whether to answer. I did not threaten him in any ordinary way. I leaned forward a trifle in my saddle, and I pierced his resistance with a terrible look which did as I intended it to. It was like a fatal blow from an infinite superiority of power—the multifarious power of an educated mind. Sebastian felt that power. He gave up. He replied,

We still did not think you knew we were here. We did not dare to let you know. And then you did not pass by but came here. And then it was too late.

"Thank you, that is all," I said.

But now Sebastian made an inquiring gesture.

"Yes," I said, "you wish to ask me something?"

How did you know, he said, and with a swing of his head indicated the long hiding place and the presence of all his Indians there.

"I will tell you," I answered. "I went deep down in the earth and met the spirit of all that is good in mankind. He told me."

For the first time Sebastian put down his head. He was really defeated and now knew it.

The second plase of the day's action was ended. The third and last developed a little later when the scout White Horn reported to Lieutenant Hazard who had sent him to reconnoitre the vicinity. White Horn reported that he had observed significant activity in the reddish rocks that loomed to our right at a distance of a thousand yards. He indicated that still another band of enemy warriors lay there embastioned. I ordered Colonel Prescott to go in strength to reduce any resistance there, while I accompanied him to observe. It was an extraordinary and final spectacle. Kneeling up in my saddle I regarded all. It was as if I witnessed the polarities of human nature all exposed. In skirmish or battle all occurs too swiftly to create philosophy by the moment. But if one brings one's philosophy along, all is to show in its light, and struggle, goodness, evil, and sacrifice stand forth plain. Any man is then all men, proclaiming the worst and the best that dwells within him and his kind.

We moved against the reddish sandstone escarpments to our right in mid-afternoon uncertain of what awaited us. But not for long.

The enemy made little attempt at concealment. Indeed, he seemed in a rage to give battle. As we came near, we could see gestures of defiance scarce worthy to be told. On the rocks, enemy warriors leaped up in nakedness, showed us their posteriors in obscene mockery, and made vile gestures to accompany shouts of contempt. At the same time a shower of arrows and even small rocks came at us, and then rifle fire was exchanged. Sixty to eighty feet above us, the enemy held a physical advantage. Colonel Prescott advised me that he would send a detachment to the side and above, to divert the enemy, while a heavy effort would be pressed from the front.

This operation was carried out, led by a volunteer of his own troop, the trumpeter, who accompanied him in the field. With what seemed almost foolhardy valour, this young soldier took his squad up the escarpment with its irregular fallen stones at times in sight of the enemy. But our distraction from below guarded the scaling party against the enemy's full attention, and with cries of fury and triumph, the trumpeter and his small band reached a shelf above the Apache nest in the cliff and directed a hot fire down upon it. At the same time Colonel Prescott ordered a full broadside from the front, and then, dismounting to join his already dismounted troopers, led a charge against the rocks which took the form of a swarming climb toward the ledges where the enemy was lodged between two fires.

I was witness to many deeds of valour on that day, but none seemed to me more inspired, as with some aethereal superiority to man's natural condition of earthbound weight, than an exploit of the trumpeter's. As he saw the troops moving up from below, he threw himself forward in a rage of selflessness, and bounded down from pinnacle to platform to ridge, until he was able to leap into the enemy camp with sabre and pistol, and there, like a titan in Homer, to deal fury and death about him. He must certainly have been destroyed if the upcoming troops had been delayed by an instant. As it was, they swelled in numbers over the last edge of the hanging entrenchment, and with him, and the men who now followed him down the cliff, joined forces to carry the day.

It was at this juncture that a grievous blow befell the army. Coming with his men up to the ledge, Colonel Prescott was severely wounded by the last bullet discharged that day by the enemy. He fell back and was only just caught by arms below him. Taken carefully down the escarpment, he was unconscious and bleeding sorely. I assumed active command in his place, and after seeing him borne to the rear with all considerate haste, I superintended those duties and functions which attend the return of the normal pulse after an engagement. Then the breath of battle slows itself down. Transcendent vision clears into ordinary sight. The body has time to feel its aches. The mind resumes its balance between what is fear and what caution. The heart is able to measure the loss which the eye observed during the conflict. The world all about once again becomes real, and once again expands to include more than a pinpoint of light on the tip of a sabre at the throat of an adversary. Our men acknowledged their hurts and assuaged each other's. The senses again served consciousness, and soldiers smelled the wool of their own uniforms in sweat and dust. The afternoon was falling toward evening. Taking our prisoners, and carrying our wounded and dead, we retired from the rocks and returned to our main body at the long earth trough.

There I found a message awaiting me. My staff had received in the last daylight a heliostat signal from the southern system which told us what we had all come so long and far to discover. A patrol had reported evidence which indicated that a strong mounted party had crossed into Mexico during the previous night. Our total for Indians captured and killed now stood at one hundred sixty seven. Any large remaining band must logically be that of Rainbow Son. We had rather have taken him here, in the open wilderness. Now he was running for the *sierra* where our task would be immeasurably greater. I was not at once resolved on how to manage it, but only knew that it was a task which must be done.

x

When the troops first swept down into the trough, the confusion was great, and many troopers saw that they must dismount to fight if they would reach their enemies. Rainey and Clanahan both did so, and fought side by side with sabres. At one moment Rainey turned in the direction of a shout which he heard, and just then an Apache closed toward him from the other side, with a long knife raised to come down on him. Clanahan saw this too late to parry it. Instead, he threw himself against Rainey thinking to butt him out of the way. The knife came on its way and instead of Rainey it was Clanahan who received it. He fell against Rainey, who turned to resist. But he saw Clanahan, and what had happened to him, and who had done it, and he killed the man who had put down his friend.

Temporarily, the battle was over for Rainey. He took Clanahan up and helped him to walk away. They climbed the eastern wall of the trough with serious care.

"Shut up, Briney, now don't say a word, not a word; save your breath," Rainey said repeatedly. Clanahan, who had said nothing, was bleeding internally and choking. "I'll get you out of this, and set you down. I'll get you some help, before I get back to it down there. Easy, now, Briney. That's right. Now we're coming along fine. Just hold on. Now tell me when you have to rest. We've got all the time in the world."

But Rainey knew they hadn't, and his throat thickened with feeling. At the top of the slope leading out of the battle, Clanahan must go down to the ground. He lay on his side holding himself up on an elbow, and he looked at Rainey with huge childlike eyes in his whitened and sunken face. His lips were open in the shape to drink, or sing a song. Instead of a tune his breath came fast with a few whispered words—"Hail Mary, full of grace, the Lord is with thee." Clanahan pulled at a chain inside his flannel shirt and brought out a medal he must see. His mouth drank air now, as if he needed air to sing, through lips reaching forth like the mouth of a fish. Rainey felt a hot pain go through his head at the thought of what was happening to Clanahan. Another thought came to thrust it aside. He said, "Briney, will you just wait here a second? Just a second. I'll be right back. Don't you leave now, Briney. Hear?"

Clanahan did not change in any feature. His immense blue eyes were dark with mystery and inquiry, and his mouth went on singing its fixed and soundless song. Rainey ran away to find the colonel.

He found him, mounted, at the north end of the trough, looking through his field glasses.

"Colonel, colonel, come on, come on!" he cried.

"What's the matter, trumpeter?"

"He's dying. They killed Clanahan. Please, sir, please come, just for a second. I can't stand it, sir. Please, sir!"

Words so wild and simple carried something more than they could say. Rainey pointed. Clanahan was not far away. Rainey was full of power. Colonel Prescott did not know how to refuse him. He nodded and while Rainey ran alongside, he trotted his horse a few hundred feet to Clanahan's side. Dismounting, he knelt down by the young trooper. Clanahan saw him but in no way changed his attitude.

"Well, Clanahan, this is too bad," said Colonel Prescott. "We'll get you taken up and looked after."

"Y'y'y'y," said Clanahan in a rapid whisper. He lifted his medal and pressed it toward the colonel. The effect was that of saying, "Please, please!" Colonel Prescott said,

"You want me to say your prayer for you?"

"Y'y'y'y," which urgently said yes.

"Yes, my boy," said the colonel. He took Clanahan's hand holding the medal and shut his eyes, and said close to the young soldier's face, in his deepest, burry voice, softened to extreme intimacy, "May Almighty God have mercy on me and forgive me my sins and bring me to everlasting life through Christ our Lord. Amen." Clanahan's eyes clung in fixity to the colonel's face. As he prayed, the colonel heard behind him an odd ripping noise. In a moment Rainey thrust his hand about the colonel's side to hand him something. The colonel looked up at Rainey's desperate face, and then saw what Rainey had handed him. It was a pair of corporal's chevrons newly ripped off his own sleeve by the trumpeter. Rainey nodded forcefully at the colonel and jerked his head sideways toward Clanahan, and silently but clearly shaped the words,

"Promote him, sir, please, promote him."

Colonel Prescott was reached by the intensity and the purpose of Corporal Rainey. He looked down at Clanahan. There was very little time left. The colonel leaned over and said gently but clearly,

"Clanahan, can you understand me? I want to tell you something important."

Clanahan saw him.

"Private Clanahan," said Colonel Prescott, "for gallantry in action against the enemy, you are now promoted to the grade of corporal. Here are your chevrons."

The colonel held them up.

Clanahan saw them and his face cleared. His eyes went calm and his mouth closed and then opened again. He nodded slightly and gave a faint smile. A little color came to his face. Rainey clapped his hands and hugged himself.

"That's the old Briney," he cried, "by God, it's Corporal Clanahan, that's who it is! Hi, corporal, by God!"

"Hi, corporal," repeated Clanahan, but the words he uttered called up the blood on his breath, and reaching for his chevrons, and grasping them in his white hand, he fell back off his elbow, and choked on a crimson pour from his throat, and died.

After another moment, Colonel Prescott remounted and returned to his post. Later in the day Corporal Rainey, in a splendor of rage and grief, volunteered for the duty and the joy of destroying the enemy in the rocks from above, in the name of Brian Clanahan, who was buried at nightfall with the others lost that day by the Army, and one other who had been lost years before.

"Sergeant Reimmers," said General Quait, "has stood for seven years as if at a post of duty. It is time we relieved him and gave him rest."

A special detail under Lieutenant Hazard rode to the pit and raised its occupant into the desert twilight. They brought him back to join the others who awaited him in the common grave prepared by their comrades. The grave was lined with pack mantas. The dead—five in all, including Sergeant Reimmers—were wrapped in bedding rolls. While the edges of the grave were manned by troopers watching with bent heads, General Quait read aloud prayers for the dead. The grave was filled in and over it was pitched an officer's tent. At the proper moment the bugle sounded taps. It was not Trumpeter Rainey who played it that evening. A bugler from the 4th Cavalry took the duty. A salute of rifle shots rang out. Rainey stood beside Lieutenant

Hazard. Tears went down his cheeks. He did not care if they showed. He wept for Brian Clanahan. When the formation broke, he said to his lieutenant,

"He did it for me, you know."

"Yes. I heard about it. I don't blame you for feeling sad."

Rainey dried his face against the crook of his sleeve and leaning confidentially to the lieutenant, said with a last anger on behalf of so poor and short a life,

"And another thing, sir, you know? He was a virgin!"

Matthew had no idea of what to say to this, but he felt for the general turmoil of sentiment in his trooper, and he was glad that he was there for the trooper to spill his feelings to, if it would help. Rainey seemed delivered for the moment, and turned to go off alone to his platoon bivouac.

Matthew went to the ambulances where Colonel Prescott lay. The colonel's wound was grave. He was still unconscious. Matthew saw him for a moment by lantern light. It was odd. The colonel looked smaller than he had remembered. He seemed to be at peace in his coma. Later, Captain Gray told Matthew in reply to a question,

"Yes. It is entirely possible that we may lose him before morning. But if I keep him until tomorrow, we may save him. He is not strong enough now for me to go after the bullet. When I can take that out of him, he will very possibly recover rapidly."

"We've got to keep him, sir."

"You needn't tell me, lieutenant."

xi

The Army camped in the open that night. Extra guards were posted over the prisoners. Fires were kept up at the edges of camp. Some of the troopers, too tired to be wise, threw themselves down in their clothes to sleep in the mild evening without taking their blankets from their packs. They forgot that the desert night could grow bitter cold.

Late, late in the darkness, with only the low light of the watch fires showing, General Quait lay thinking, though he seemed not be be awake. He had much to speculate about.

Bonn. What must he write to Bonn? How many days did it take to die in a dusty open grave? For how long every day did sunlight shaft

into the pit? Was it the ever-increasing cover of dust which had preserved the pencil-written lines against fading on the clutched paper?
Would there ever be a stranger document to add to the archives of
the War Department?

Prescott. How gravely was he hurt? And what did his wound
mean to the mission at large for which the Army was here?

But the general knew well enough what it meant. It meant a
major change in assignment of command, for General Quait had
intended to go himself to take Rainbow Son, however far into the
Mexican *sierra* the job might take him, and in his absence, he had
planned to leave Colonel Prescott in command of the Army in the
field. The Army would have much to do until Rainbow Son was
taken. The whole outlying territory must be patrolled. The central
deserts must be roved in constant lookout for other last war parties.
The prisoners must be transported to the reservation, their families
gathered, their effects examined, and their whole beings shipped by
train to internment camps in Florida, there to "await the pleasure of
the President." Colonel Prescott could not now undertake these
responsibilities, which called for an officer of maturity and experience.
Who could assume them? The general knew at once that evasions of
the truth would not profit him or the Army. It was clear who must
take the place of Colonel Prescott. It was the Commanding General
himself. General Quait actually squirmed with regret at this conclusion, which seemed to him inescapable.

Very well, then. No self-indulgent regrets, if you please. But who,
then, if you please, was to be advanced to perform the intended duties
of General Quait in Sonora? The objective there was nothing less
than the surrender of Rainbow Son, once and for all. And how was
this to be attained? By a penetration in massive forces? By lightning
movements in scouting strength? By prestidigitation? The general's
unsolved problems led him briefly into a vein of farcical irony. Or
must not another way be found—some wholly original way—a way
dazzling in its simplicity, its daring and its entirely novel view of the
Indian nature?

As a young officer, Alexander Upton Quait had formed the habit
of analyzing whatever problem lay before his mind by writing down
on paper its various aspects and its alternative solutions. With experience and age, he had come to a purely mental exercise of the
same practice. He could now see a sheet of paper in his head, and
make writing come on to it in plain inner sight. He could erase the

lines one by one until there remained only that one which was his choice of a solution. He now wrote such a page in the area of intense thought behind his eyes, which were shut. He listed the salient events of the Indian campaign, culminating in today's action. He outlined the geographical conditions of the north Mexican deserts and mountains. He sketched the logistics of travel in such areas. He calculated distance against time and supply against mobility. He catalogued the salient traits of the Indian nature and made common case with them of certain traits in the white man's nature, and out of such a comparison he hoped to discover what all men, Indian or white, had in common as human beings. Perhaps just there might lie some key to a solution—some penetration not physical but spiritual —some entry along a channel of electric fluid, as it were, between man and man, which might. . . .

The general was suddenly distracted from his lively thoughts by a sense of some small but perhaps significant change in the condition of the camp about him. Even behind his closed eyelids he perceived it. Opening his eyes, and leaning up under his blanket, he saw that someone was moving quietly through the camp among the sleeping troopers, bending over them one by one. The General was about to go forward to investigate, and then he recognized what was happening.

Someone was looking to see if all the sleeping soldiers were covered by blankets. For those who were not—one was Trumpeter Rainey—he quietly opened their packs, unrolled their blankets, and covered them against the sharply fallen temperature of the night. His task done, he rose and stood for a moment in the still bivouac. Something of his stature against the starry sky, the spring of his character in the lines of his body, told General Quait who it was. It was Lieutenant Hazard, not yet gone to his own rest after the hard day.

"Yes, duty," said the general to himself, with a pang of pride for the young officer, "there is this about it. It never ends."

In another moment, the general felt a wonderful, wide easing of concern in his mind. The page in his thought, with nothing yet erased there toward a solution, disappeared. He now saw all his speculation resolved in terms of human character, an individual, a junior officer of his command. With the very man for the problem came the terms of its solution. The general lay back and in hungrily comforting motions took his blanket more snugly about his long, thin, aching, old person.

"There is my man for Mexico," he said, and lay awake till dawn, refreshed not by sleep but by intense activity of mind, as he made his plans for the last mission of his campaign.

xii

"I had thought," he said to Matthew and Joe Dummy in his tent early the next morning, with the flaps laced back to admit the last cool air of night and the pale violet and blue sweeps of the distance, "to take Rainbow Son on our own territory. Now impossible, this must give way to another plan. How now: the main force of our brigade? No, for a mountain campaign with regulars in strength might never end. Then? Scouts in platoon strength? A possible solution— yet certain to bring battle. The sight of any sizable force would re- quire Rainbow Son to stand and fight. I dismissed this. H'h'h'h—" The general inhaled several shallow, rapid draughts of breath which gave the effect of representing his swift succession of thoughts. "No, what we want is some new design for an approach to Rainbow Son."

Matthew, as he listened, leaned forward and held his hands clasped between his knees. He wondered why he rather than some officer of field rank was here in the tent of the commanding general, attending a monologue on the problems of the command. Beside him sat Joe Dummy with a fixed countenance. The general said to him,

"Do you understand everything I say?"

Joe Dummy nodded.

"Listen to what I say next, and then tell the lieutenant what I said. Yes? Are you ready?" The general spoke a long sentence in Apache, while Matthew restrained a laugh at the curious clicking and softly strangled sounds which the old gentleman made with every sign of earnest proficiency. "Now," said the general, in English, "tell the lieutenant what I said."

Joe Dummy gathered his thought for a moment and then said slowly, but without uncertainty, in a thin, husky voice,

"When big chief captured, is big trouble to know what is make and do him long time he live."

"Capital!" cried the general gaily. "Lieutenant, you have made a habit of understanding this man. Do you grasp the concept in his statement? Please to restate it for me in acceptable English."

Matthew frowned over a smile. This was like going to school. When would the surprises inherent in relations with General Quait ever end?

"When a big, or important chief, or enemy commander, is captured, it is a great problem to know what to do with him for the rest of his life," recited Matthew.

"The equation is complete!" exclaimed General Quait. "We have the perfect channel of communication for what lies ahead. This man's understanding is equal to ideas in his own tongue, and he can quite evidently reveal these to you in primitive form. You, in your turn, are equal to framing them for the information of the Army. Remarkable." He turned to the scout. "Your name is White Horn. Why do you answer to the name of Joe Dummy?"

"I am White Horn," said Joe in Apache.

"Sir," said Matthew, "the soldiers gave him the name because he is usually so silent. Everybody calls him Joe Dummy."

"You will henceforth call him White Horn, lieutenant. Let us restore his dignity as we dispatch him upon a grave task."

"Yes, sir."

"White Horn," said the General, "do you know Rainbow Son?"

"*Sí!*"

"Tell me what you know about him."

Well, and this, and so. And a long time of knowing Rainbow Son. And thus he is. And so. Rainbow Son was one of the bravest and most clever commanders in the world. He was full of power, he could not stand to be laughed at, and if anyone ever broke a promise to him, he would try to kill such a one, and he would kill somebody just as quick as he would eat a piece of meat. One thing he never did was take risks. He was practical. He saw no reason to do something unless it would succeed. That was why he was such a great war leader. He always knew what would succeed. Other men took chances and acted like boys with sudden ideas. Not he. He was always willing to wait. And then, some day, it would be time for what he would do, and he would do it. He was still strong though now an old man. He had had four wives and his children and grandchildren were everywhere. One trouble with him now was that he had long ago promised them that they would never have to give in to the white people. He was trying to keep his promise.

"Why does he break promises to white people?" asked the general.

Promises to white people were not the same.

"Did any white man ever make a promise to him?"

White Horn did not know.

The general stood up and slapped his boot with his riding whip. His eyes burned black with pleasure in a notion.

"Yes, lieutenant, I do truly think we have it. I think our case is developing. I keep insisting that the key to all is Rainbow Son, and we shall never make progress unless we know him and understand him. I have made enough case for good Indian people in my time to be in a position to speak honestly of the bad. Rainbow Son is one of the bad—very possibly the worst. He is clever. He is vain. He is neither a fool nor a saint. They will die for an idea, but not he. Abstractions will mean nothing to him. He is an intensely practical man. I find this most satisfactory, as I believe an intensely practical man can be overthrown in only one way. This is to attack him with something which is, from his point of view, *entirely impractical.* H'h'h'h. I believe I know what this is, in respect of Rainbow Son, and it is to you, lieutenant, that I owe my certainty."

"Me, sir?"

"Yourself, sir. There is one instrument of human affairs which has never yet been tried with our present enemy. It is trust. I have seen this work with our Apache scouts—it was the basis on which I enlisted them to fight the devil with fire, as it were. They have kept honor. Honor is thus not inherently alien to the Apache nature. To convince the enemy of this, we need a vehicle of character and trust on our own part. All we seek to bring to peace and order is one man, for if he will come the rest will follow. I propose to take him not with a brigade or a troop or even a party of scouts, but with one man. It is you, Lieutenant Hazard."

Matthew sat back in his camp chair and then leaned forward again. His mouth fell open. He lost his breath for a moment and could not speak. His brow was dark with a scowl of interest and his eyes were intensely black in shadow. He looked furious, though he was only trying to embrace the news he had just been given. The general continued,

"I propose that you and White Horn, and no one else, proceed into the pursuit of Rainbow Son, and bring him back to me. White Horn will be your guide and your interpreter. You will wield the honor and the faith of the Army in its invincibility. Rainbow Son will come in only if he is convinced that it will be to his advantage to do so. You will so convince him."

Matthew found enough breath to laugh shortly.

"Yes, I know," said General Quait, "it is made to sound easy, while of course we know that it is not. And yet—and yet, what greater demonstration could we have of our confidence in the certainty of the outcome than to send not a thousand soldiers, but one, to win a campaign? He knows me. I have dealt with him before. You will be my official representative. You will bear terms of surrender for him to accept. He knows already that he must lose. He knows that Sebastian and the rest have lost here. Why else has he run away? You will come to bring him not war but peace, and he will know this when he sees that you are the only soldier now dispatched against him. Do you know Helmholtz's theory on 'The Principle of Least Action'? In sending you alone, rather than a brigade, we shall apply this theory by analogy. Through White Horn you and Rainbow Son will know each other's mind. You will take notes of all he says and keep these for me. I can foresee how your encounter will be.

"Somewhere, somehow, you will find him in his mountains, and there will be a conference. Once it has been established that there will be no immediate bloodshed—and only a zany would discount the possibility of bloodshed—there will follow elaborate exchanges. There will be speeches and dialogues. Obstacles will be thrown up in argument, all for a purpose. You will have to counter these with the wits—the, the, the, *character*—of the moment." The general gave Matthew a serious look. It was character on which he was risking all. It was the character of Lieutenant Hazard which had caused General Quait, on the inspiration of the night, to conceive of his whole new strategy. "You will have to make him know that your word is honorable, and that he must meet it with honor on his own part. Your pursuit of him, in itself, will fascinate him—for he will of course be informed of your movements if you should come close. The essence of my scheme is to reduce the war to an exchange between two men. Will you be one of them, sir?"

Matthew showed a quizzical face which looked like the cheeky impudence of a boy taking a dare and asked,

"Do you think there is a reasonable chance to succeed in this affair, general?"

"You, too, are a practical man, I see. Well, I do think there is a reasonable chance for success in this affair. I do not minimize in any way its difficulty. You will have to survive hardship almost unimaginable—I know that country where you will go. You might be absent for more than a month, depending upon how far our quarry has drawn ahead of you. Mishap from other sources than the enemy may befall you. Risks are everywhere in the matter. Might not a man's very willingness to meet these give us a dramatic advantage over the enemy we seek? But though all be difficult and dangerous, it may well enclose the result we hope for."

"Yes, sir. I will go."

"Ah," said the general softly, regarding Matthew with almost an awesome sweetness of countenance, "ah, *deligebat idoneos homines huic rei,* by which Caesar said in his *Commentaries,* lieutenant, *He selected suitable men for this affair!"*

"Well, let's hope so, general."

"You, Mr. Apache Scout," said the general to White Horn, "I promote you to sergeant. You will need a sense of our power as well as your own. Take your chevrons from the quartermaster, and wear them at once. Your papers will be arranged."

White Horn put his chest upward the smallest lift and said nothing.

"How soon will we go?" asked Matthew.

"I should think perhaps within five hours. You will have arrangements to make."

"Yes, sir. I would like to send a note to my wife, if there is a way to get it to her. And I would like to see Colonel Prescott, if possible."

"By all means, your letter. And the colonel is conscious this morning, for I have already seen the surgeon, and he is hopeful. Pray attend to these personal matters, and then prepare your packs, and report to me at noon. I shall give you luncheon here. I shall henceforth on occasion address you as Matthew. Good morning, sir."

xiii

Matthew returned to General Quait at noon.

"And the colonel?" asked the general.

"Sir, I am not happy. He could barely speak. The surgeon had taken the bullet, and I was permitted only a few minutes with him. He is weak and he is distant. He keeps slipping away, and then he comes back, and looks at you again. I hope, sir, he can have all possible care."

"You may rest assured, Matthew. —And the rest? You are ready?"

Matthew produced a folded and sealed letter addressed to Laura Hazard.

"May I leave it with you, General?"

"Leave it with me. I believe you have no possible idea of how devoted I am to your wife."

"She has told me, sir, how close she feels to you."

"I do trust she has a notion of what duty must do without regard to persons—?"

Matthew smiled.

"She will storm at you, sir, for sending me out, but she will know that you had your reasons."

The general fingered his beard and gazed at the dirt floor of his tent. Both officers in silence considered, and then dismissed, the soldier's opposing selves—that which would live with love, and that which would leave it for duty. The general broke the little spell, and said with animation,

"Take that chair. My striker is bringing us a bite of lunch. Now that my wagon has caught up with us, he has found a tin of deviled goose livers from Strasbourg, and somehow he has mastered the knack of making a sauce for jerked meat out of flour and sherry, and I believe we may expect biscuits and London jam. To top it, there is to be some Dutch chocolate and coffee. I regret the absence of salad. You shall have it with me another time. To return to the subject: Rainbow Son will remind you of the Duke of Wellington in the Pistrucci bust. The same fixed crease above the high-arched nose, the thin lips set almost as if pursed in fastidious skepticism, the smooth-balled chin. But here instead of high-bred intelligence you detect cunning, and rather than an effect of immovable conviction you suspect a capacity to scamper when expediency suggests. I should say he stands five feet seven inches and weighs perhaps one hundred sixty pounds. Every inch and every ounce will be fixed against you. But all will collapse together if the right nerve is jabbed. I have faith that you will find it, if you can find him. —A bit more of the pâté?"

"Thank you, sir. —What am I to tell him?"

"That you have come to save his life."

"Save his life?"

"And the lives of his family, friends, people."

"That's a tall one, sir."

"Not at all. For you may tell him what he must already know—that the Army took him once before, and it will take him again, but this time if it must come after him, it will take him dead, and it will kill all who help him to fight. Let me assure you, Matthew, that an Indian has quite as high a regard for his own life as we have for ours. You shall use an invariably persuasive argument."

"Why would he believe me, sir?"

"He will believe you because you have come alone, with nothing but your own life, to tell him."

"All right, sir. What am I to tell him to do?"

"You will tell him to give you his unconditional surrender. He is to come with you and give himself into my hands."

"He will ask what will become of him."

"You will tell him that he and his followers and family will be taken safely to Fort Marion, in Florida, there to live until the President makes disposition of all."

"What if he says he might be executed?"

"It is probable that he will not be killed. I promise him safe conduct. Nothing further. But if he refuses, I promise him certain destruction."

"I see."

There was a thoughtful pause, and the general then said,

"Why would he accept? Would anyone? Has anyone ever? In the face of the alternatives, he would accept. A king once did accept analagous terms—one thinks of Ferdinand VII, who was offered nothing but exile and captivity by Napoleon at Bayonne. We must require our man to do as much. By his course Napoleon precipitated a disaster. By ours we shall pacify a continent. At Austerlitz, by the way, I should have given orders quite the contrary to Napoleon's, in the episode of the famous 'left wheel,' and by it, I should have saved half the casualties."

Matthew allowed himself a doubtful smile.

"I'm not Napoleon, sir. I'm not very good at arguments."

"To be sure. Yet knowing your cause, you can, and you will, invent agreement upon matters of detail on the spot—ways and means of doing the will of the Army. But the main points are grand and simple: absolute surrender, and trust in my promise."

"I see. —How will I find him, sir?"

"We know where he crossed into Mexico. You and your scout will go to that point and pick up his trail. Thenceforth, the very country itself must be your informant."

"What is it like, sir?"

"For a very great space southward, it is very like this country here. If you must persist deep into Mexico, you may come to semitropical lands. I trust you will find your target before then. You will encounter few people. Many of these may be hostile. Some of them will help you, for Mexicans as well as Americans have suffered outrage at the hands of Rainbow Son and his kind. Your chiefest enemy, though, will be the hardness of rock, the power of light, the vastness of space between you and where you would go. It will not be a rapid progress, Matthew. Let me see. Upton's *Cavalry Tactics,* page 477, if memory serves, tells us that twenty-five miles a day is the maximum the cavalry can stand. You will perhaps exceed this rate—but not at an average, for you will at times be climbing instead of advancing on the level. The Apache, says Upton, can travel, week in and week out, at the rate of seventy miles a day. A brave and wonderful fact. Our man has by this reckoning already a lead of perhaps a hundred and fifty miles on us. But there must come a point where he will halt to consider his future, and slowly you will close the gap between you and him, and the day must come—God willing—when you will confront him.

"You may have to travel a thousand miles. Suppose you manage twenty miles a day. This would amount to fifty days. I shall await you during two months. The mirrors will find me when you need me at the border. If at the end of two months I have not received your return, I shall then mount an expedition in pursuit and enter Mexico myself with force. I shall come to find you and Rainbow Son and reopen the war. God knows how long matters will march thereafter."

"Well," said Matthew, "I am packed and ready, and so is White Horn."

"Bravo, lieutenant. I have two things for you to take to Rainbow Son from me. One is this packet of tobacco—ten pounds of it. The other is this talisman which he gave to me as a gesture of undying friendship many long years ago." The general handed Matthew a canvas-wrapped package of tobacco—and a fetish carved of polished porphyry representing a lizard. It was about three inches long, very old, with eyes and tail of inlaid turquoise. "The tobacco will be a politeness; the talisman will prove that you come from me."

"Yes, sir. Well? I suppose there is no use delaying anything any further, then, general?"

General Quait stood up and so did Matthew.

"None whatsoever, sir. We do try to give form to our experience.

Like the young hero in the epic, you will probably have a number of gates to open and pass through. How many? Who knows? Yes. Seven. Probably seven. Why seven? Who knows. But it is a mystical number, and mythology has always settled upon seven. Thank you. And the gates—what are they? You will know them as you come to them."

Matthew looked at the old man and saw that he was prattling in order to diffuse the emotion he felt at this moment of commitment and farewell. Nothing gave Matthew greater proof of the seriousness of his undertaking than the general's employment of literature just now.

For his part, General Quait, in choosing Matthew to go forth on this mission, knew nothing in detail about his qualifications. He knew nothing of the high sense of vocation given into a little boy by Abraham Lincoln; nothing of the power of intention by which a boy had overcome Mr. Clarny and a youth the congressman; nothing of the strength in love and self-respect which had prevailed against the Greenleafs. But the general could see the result of all these moments of power in his lieutenant, and what had been ordained in the young man's early life was accessible enough for the old man to put to use now.

"Yes, good-by, Matthew," said General Quait. "But yes. One more thing. Honesty compels. If we succeed in this great enterprise, I will receive the credit. If we fail, you the blame." He smiled frostily, to make a signal of humor, but it was a thin effort at professional cynicism with which he sought to veil his true feeling, and he disposed of everything by nodding rapidly several times, hustling Matthew out of the tent without even a handshake. He did not stand to watch as Matthew went. He returned to his field chair, sat down, pulled out a small book in marble boards, and began to read with vacant eyes the splendor of words he knew by heart:

> *Arma virumque cano, Troiae qui primus ob oris*
> *Italiam fato profugus Laviniaque venit*
> *litora. . . .*

xiv

"Out of impulse, purpose, daring and sacrifice, an orderly chronicle can be arranged with benefit of evidence gathered from many sources after the event," wrote General Quait in his autobiography.* He continued:

Late in the day of his setting out, Lieutenant Hazard, with the scout White Horn, came to the border where all reports pointed to a crossing by Rainbow Son and his remaining army. There he was met by Lieutenant Fleetwood, 4th Cavalry, and a detachment of signallers, who gave them encampment for the night and sped them across the border at dawn. Before them lay that country of vegetable spike and rocky crown; torrent and drouth; furnace and ice; glory and shame—in short, Mexico. The early fathers of the church used to know times of trial, endurance or temptation. To undergo one of these was, in their parlance, to go through *a passion*. Lieutenant Hazard now entered upon the country of his *passion*. It was a country known to me since my own campaign there many years before.

The great earth feature which dominated that portion of Mexico into which our small expedition had entered was, and remains, the *Sierra Madre del Occidente*. To apprehend its character, fantasy is required. Imagine, then, the *sierra* as a vast armoured lizard, fixed and petrified a hundred thousand aeons ago. Its scales were single mountains; the chinks in its armour great canyons unmeasured by man; its dorsal crest a jarring succession of spires and fins upthrust in alien majesty. No wonder this continental ridge was called *la espinosa del diablo* by the native—*the devil's spine*. Extending from north to south for virtually the entire length of Mexico, this terrible fixed evidence of an ancient earth convulsion was paralleled on the west by many lesser ranges which shared its character if not its scale. Suffice to say that a man crawling upon such mountains was as insignificant in scale as a sifted grain of sand in a whole desert, or a single lappet in a sea of waters. Pursued or pursuer, man seemed to disappear there into the gigantic secrecy of the land.

From a general altitude of three to five thousand feet, the mountains swept up to heights of ten to twelve thousand feet above the plain. Mountains by their nature invite the formation of clouds and

* *Op. cit.*

the condensation of vapour into rainfall. Yet here the aridity of the climate is almost constant, except for seasons of rain in spring and autumn which when they arrive bring too much moisture where otherwise there is too little. Rivers abound—but many of them are like features in some hellscape—rivers without water, whose wide shallow beds show accretions of white boulders tumbled from the slopes in times of cloudburst and torrent. Locked between towering canyons, whose walls often reach a mile in height, hidden rivers almost invisible from above go their secret way cutting away rock for their passage, while denying passage to man. On the great dragged upsweeps of the foothills which share the character of both plain and mountain, occasional relief from forbidding earth circumstance is found in unexpected catchpools and springs. These take away the breath with their jewel-like serenity and their accompanying shade in the surrounding harshness of rock and thorn and unremitting glare. Here, after primordial trials, man finds easement for flesh and spirit, and himself feels primordial satisfaction in his compact with nature—until once again he must take up the march, for whatever purpose brings him thither.

Temperatures vary in extremes upon the peaks—oven by day and ice cave by night. In the plain below I have measured temperatures at midday registering as high as 130° F. A man so incautious as to breathe through the mouth in such heat will find that for days thereafter he will be unable to taste food, for having scorched the interior of his oral cavity.

Here subsist creatures of claw and scale, beak and sting. The wild peccary or *jabalin,* the reptile creation in all its dread variety, great ravens and vultures, the prowling wildcat, and his relations, the scorpion and other huge venomous arachnids, all are formidably common. Relief comes now and then from observing a platoon of blue quail pursuing comic evolutions of dismounted drill, or from suddenly hearing the wild sweet fancies of the mocking bird, or— in silent canyon or upon rock platform in the sky—from seeing deer or mountain sheep. Most wisely noticed from a distance, the great brown bear sometimes shows the way to combs of wild honey which a starving expeditioner could well use. Clinging in airy architecture to some pinnacle, the huge nest, fashioned not of small twigs and scraps but of large sticks and branches, of the mountain eagle, proclaims a fiercely independent life.

So, too, must be the life of what few human inhabitants are to be found outside the scattered towns and villages of north Mexico. The larger communities lie far from the mountains. An occasional village, in a cluster of *jacales,* holds to life where some mountain stream wanders forth upon the plain. Now and then in a lost, interior basin, remnant of volcanic action long ago, grazing pastures and a release of underground water will permit of settled habitation. But in the country of primitive trails and hiding places and great natural dens within mountain walls open to the sky, wanders a restless population of predators whose quarry are the scattered *rancherias* of the plain and the foothills, or whatever traveller happens, for whatever astonishing reason, to be faring precariously so far from more reasonable places of travel. Some of these creatures of prey are Indians, some are of Mexican stock, which in itself contains so much admixture of Indian blood. The authorities of the Mexican states —Chihuahua and Sonora—assigned regular troops to the task of controlling these wild bands of self-promoted soldiery. Their problem in its essential nature was familiar to me and my associates. Their failure to solve it out of hand touched all our understanding and fellow-feeling.

There, then, went Lieutenant Hazard and his Apache scout. Aside from my necessarily general instructions, his only accessory of information was a woefully inaccurate map of the region, engraved in 1861, under the imperial license of the Emperor Maximilian, which I had purchased in a Paris bookshop in 1870. If I knew the map well, I knew the country even better, and after I sent Mr. Hazard into Mexico, I could fancy in those moments of mental activity before sleep that I could see tiny dots of motion on the rubbed and creased page of the map, whose interior boundary lines were washed with faint stains of water colour, where he went southward, with his scout, along the immense eastern flank of the Sierra Madre.

Rumour and report in the villages of the wasteland told him that Rainbow Son with a large war party had indeed gone that way and was heading south. Sergeant White Horn found many evidences of trail, from which it seemed clear that the chief and his band were gradually drawing ahead of their pursuers. This was a remarkable, and discouraging fact. It would seem that two men could make more rapid progress than a hundred. Yet as ten days passed Mr. Hazard and his aide were unable to close the gap. It must seem that Rainbow Son knew that he was being followed, and was anxious not to be found. Why did he not wait in ambush for his pursuers and destroy them? It is a mystery in a land of mysteries. Both pursuers were in the uniform of the army—Sergeant White Horn wearing a soldier's blouse in order to bear and display his chevrons.

Hardships were visited upon them almost at the outset. They had a week's supply of dried meat, but when that would be gone, they must subsist on the meagre fare of the land. Game was scarce, and it was a rare day when one or the other of the expeditioners brought down a rabbit or a quail to cook over a small fire of dry wood which would show little or no smoke. It was not to avoid notice by Rainbow Son that the lieutenant must show no smoke—on the contrary, he would have been glad to be noticed and sent for by him. But the "irregulars" of Chihuahua were abroad and must be avoided at all costs. (The vast depredations visited upon Mexican ranchers of beef cattle must explain the failure of Mexico to grow a cattle industry comparable to that which Texans developed so rapidly and efficiently.) Mr. Hazard on his first thrust southward narrowly escaped two encounters with the "irregulars," and his escape was owed to his scout's extraordinary percipience in examining the conditions of the surrounding country. In one of these two instances, Sergeant White Horn actually *smelled* a hostile encampment before he could see it. Warned by his olfactory sense, he brought his officer and himself safely past the encampment without detection.

At last after a ten-day mounted march along the roughest of foot-hill country, they reached the west-flowing Pamphigochil River, which cut through the *sierra* a little way south of the settlement called Mulatos. The river was flowing shallow when they first found it. By the intaglio of many hooves, which would re-create the dancing movement of horses waiting to cross, they saw that their quarry had forded the river. They must follow. They crossed late in the day and remained to camp for the night, hidden from the water, but within sound of its grateful purling amongst boulders and other obstructions. Late at night the sound was magnified. They awoke to hear the river's roar as it charged along swollen by cloudburst up-stream. If anything could have made the small party feel to the utmost their isolation now, it was to realise that the rising of the waters had cut them off by one more barrier from the home country they had left.

On the following morning they resumed their travel westward across—or rather, through—the *sierra*. The river was still high and their way along its southern edge was precarious. Presently they noticed that the character of the canyon was changing. No longer a gorge with narrow trail beside the cutting waters (which had sub-sided somewhat), the river's passage became a canyon within a canyon. The walls widened above, and an irregular ledge hung about halfway up the sides, at a general tilt toward the river. The travellers took to the ledge to make their way. Now the army boots they had started out with proved to be encumbrances, for often they must dismount and lead their animals at a walk, and then upon the stones

of the way they slipped and fell in miserable frequency. They ended
by discarding their boots and donning moccasins which they had
brought, at Sergeant White Horn's insistence, in their packs.

The crossing of the *sierra* was to consume seven days, though Mr.
Hazard was certain that he must be able to manage in less time.
And so he might have, but for a pair of circumstances which dashed
his expectations. The first was a calamity from without—the second
from within.

On the second night in the canyon of the Pamphigochil, while
encamped in a natural redoubt of boulders and wind-torn scrub pines,
the expeditioners were awakened by a soft, mysterious touch upon
their exposed faces, and with a sinking of the heart, realised that
they were in the midst of a mountain snowstorm. Winds flew past
them from the peaks, and swept the substance of cloud in extreme
condensation relentlessly down upon them. It was the first stroke of
winter in the hanging canyons of the inhuman *sierra*. The cold was
terrible. They made a fire and huddled up to it. With dawn of the
second day the storm was over but now all things were encased in
ice. Movement was virtually denied to the travellers until warming
air should heat the ice away.

But before it should become possible again to take up their march,
they were delayed by the second calamity, when Lieutenant Hazard
was stricken with an onset of fever which rendered him at one
moment inert and palsied with weakness until he felt he must die,
and at the next, infused with wild strength in delirium, when he
strove to fling himself against the rocks and even across them into
the dreadful gorge a thousand feet below. Awakening from one
such seizure, he found that he was bound with rope and unable to
move. In his depleted reason he believed that his scout had turned
traitor and had made him captive, and must soon dispatch him.
But it was only as a measure of safeguard that the faithful Sergeant
White Horn had tied his commander to prevent him from destroying
himself in his ravings.

For three more days they were unable to proceed. The fever persisted for the first two. At the end of the second day, the lieutenant
ordered his scout to leave him, to retrace his steps, to save himself,
and report to me the failure of the mission. The Apache sergeant
heard him but gave no sign that he understood. For three days he
nursed his leader. He made poultices of boiled pine greenery which
he placed at the base of the lieutenant's spine. Heating rocks, he
surrounded him with purging heat which fended off the shaking
exhaustion of chills. His cures were also metaphysical. Reverently
rolling himself on the ground in the four cardinal directions, the scout

invoked the powers which governed mountains. He blessed his patient with puffs of *hoddentin* and he made the signs of power and safety over him with a sacred accessory described as a twig from a lightning-struck tree. Placing the dried head of a blue quail over the lieutenant's heart, the faithful thaumaturge worked to impart the quail's quickness in life to the labouring heart of the sick man. With night-long fires whose blowing light made the towering rocks all about resemble vast curtains in a ruined castle, he re-created as best he could, though alone, the fire-dances which his people performed for curative purposes.

At last, on the third day, the lieutenant was free of fever, but he was still too weak to rise and make his way. Now it was Sergeant White Horn who said that they should return to the border, and this time it was Lieutenant Hazard who did not listen. After resting for that day, and lying all night in heavy mountain fog which their firelight turned into a great frosted lantern about them, Mr. Hazard on the morning of the fourth day gave the command to continue the march westward in pursuit of his assignment.

They had yet to pass the crest of the *sierra*. It was impossible in the wandering canyon to recognise their progress by any distant landmarks. They would not see the highest peaks when at last they would pass these, for their vision was confined by the lesser, but still formidable, heights between which they crawled. Sergeant White Horn announced that when the river at last found its open way on the western slopes of the *sierra,* they would see from a great height and distance a sight to give them relief. This was a *ranchería* or small village lying far down the western approaches to the mountain. It was a place he had known years ago. There they would find shelter, and a renewal of their food supplies, and news of the people they were seeking. It was a tempting thought to Lieutenant Hazard that there, too, he might rest for a while, to recover his strength, which was slow in returning. As they advanced in the last reaches of the Pamphigochil through the mountain barrier, he was forced to stop many times a day to rest. As such times Sergeant White Horn would sit a little distance apart and keep watch, possibly wondering, as soldiers will, over the thoughts which his comrade must harbour, when chance is compounded by peril, and both may be stronger than the human will.

What it is in man which, though he falls fainting and can no more, tells him to rise and do? What told Ulysses? And what Xenophon? Classic antiquity breathes upon ancient eposide an aura of splendour and an illusion of size which events in our own lifetimes rarely seem to share. Yet whether it be an army which is moved to thrust grand impulse against all obstacle, or only a man alone who so strives, the essence of spirit is the same, and equally calls forth our praise.

Exhausted by illness, hunger and what we might call mountain *malaise* (that is, an enfeebling sense of being endlessly trapped in canyons whose turns reveal not space and freedom ahead but only another great rocky barrier), Mr. Hazard received the first relief in his persistence in late afternoon of the seventh mountain day. Then, coming with Sergeant White Horn over a last ridge, he saw to the west, lying far down the apron of the mountain flank, the little cluster of hovels which he had been promised. It was the first *rancheria* beyond the mountains.

Weakness gave him the emotion, now, of a home-coming child. It was too late to go on as nightfall was near; but he slept that night sustained by the happy prospect of coming before noon the next day to the *ranchería,* which, from descriptions, I identify as the settlement of San Vicente de las Palmas. It was so called because of a great concentration of yucca palms which covered the plain all about. When I saw it in '74 the palms were in bloom, and their myriad waxy cups actually perfumed the air at night. A dozen or so buildings were centered about a small *placita* one side of which was formed by the main house of the rancher. All was crudely made —stakes plastered with mud and vegetable fibre roofs and stockades of the long, stiff blades of yucca spears—but somehow appealing to the sympathy for the spirit of independence which alone must have brought life to settle so far in the wilderness. A small earthen chapel at one corner of the *placita* proclaimed the main source of strength of the *ranchero* and his family.

Thither, with the earliest light, went the lieutenant and the sergeant. They had come several miles when Sergeant White Horn arrested their progress and pointed. Lieutenant Hazard strained his eyes to see what was indicated, but declared that because of his weakness he could see nothing but black specks drifting against the hot white sky above San Vicente. But this was precisely what the sergeant saw too, and in a word he explained that the black specks were vultures, circling in their deathly spirals above the little community. Their presence in such numbers could mean but one thing, and the troopers rode on in caution and anxiety until they reached the village.

It was silent and empty. But if there was no one present to speak to them, there was plenty left to tell them that Rainbow Son and his band had come this way. Every classic outrage was represented by its poor remnants, now many days dried by the sun and picked by the birds. The buildings had been put to the torch. The stockade corrals were empty. No human beings were left alive and among those left dead were several who had been thrown upon the hideous daggers of the yucca spikes. The chapel was despoiled and profaned, with excrement deposited upon its altar. In the center of the *placita,* the single water well gave forth the stench of decaying bodies in its shaft. Trails showed that in riding away the marauding party took along the beef cattle from the corrals. The familiar thoroughness of the acts represented here must have conveyed not only horror but also a curious sense of ceremony, performed under some almost righteous obligation.

But such reflections were surely not then the concern of Mr. Hazard. His disappointment at not finding succor was submerged in feelings of enraged pity. Summoning what strength he could, after a tour of the ghastly exhibit, he gave, with the aid of his sergeant, what little dignity and final order he could to these corpses which had been most mistreated; and then gave the command to go forward on his mission.

The finding of San Vicente was the last event of particular interest for many days. It was perhaps the most disconcerting feature of such desert and mountain travel that after a while, persistence loses its relation to common modes of reckoning, and experience, extended over days, in monotony, can only be apprehended by the mind through a process of simplification in which the particular becomes universal, and the factual symbolic. Time is confused with distance, and new experience with old. This is not to say that all mountains were alike, and all rivers, as the lieutenant and his scout passed across successions of these, but rather that the human organisation, when subjected to continuously alien condition, must, in order to persist at all, focus its powers upon its end of action, and devote little attention or energy to the terms of passage which must lead to it.

Let it suffice to say that for twelve more days, Mr. Hazard and Sergeant White Horn followed their quarry westward, across two mountain ranges. Beyond them they saw another range, and before it lay the Yaqui River which they must cross. The river was low, and they crossed, and then bathed, refilling their canteens and canvas bags. The trail led them around the southern tip of the range before them, and then northward in a great open basin flanked by mountains. Though well into the month of November, they were also well removed from the temperate zone, and the heat of the day was extreme, while the nights were formidably cold. It was a constant matter of concern that they might run afoul of wandering members of the Yaqui Indian tribes, whose distaste for strangers is exceeded only by their spontaneous ferocity. Owing chiefly to the uses of caution, in the degree of genius, by the sergeant, they passed up the vast basin for six days without encountering danger from other persons, though on a certain night, while encamped in the desert, they were subject to manifestations difficult if not impossible to explain.

Shortly after midnight, a sudden wind arose and threw coarse dust and sand levelly through the air in such density that suffocation seemed inescapable. It must have come but for the equally sudden cessation of the dust-squall within half an hour. There followed a brief fall of rain, which in turn was succeeded by a stillness more acute than could be imagined. All nature appeared to have its head cocked, listening with bated breath, though for what, who could say? And then the silence was broken—even shattered—by a series of sudden loud cracking sounds which seemed to occur at varying distances from the camp. What was the origin of these? Science might perhaps declare that desert fibres, long dry, were now, in the absorption of the sudden drench, demonstrating the law of the co-efficient of expansion. Or perhaps they might be of origin in the insect world, if a single, sharp stridulation could be produced by enough insects to cause the spattering series of noises. Or were rocks cracking asunder after a million years of integral form? There was no answer. But this was not all to bewilder and awe the travellers, for slowly, in the northern heavens, coming like the materialisation of interstellar ghosts, vast wavering curtains and scrolls of light became visible. They loomed and faded and loomed again, in some grand freak of the atmosphere. The desert voyagers were seeing the *aurora borealis*—but to see it so far to the south was extraordinary, and to see it at all, after the strains and visitations of their passage, was portentous in the extreme. They watched for well over an hour, while the lights went from white to rose to electric blue. When at last they disappeared, the night was of Stygian darkness. And then, in the effect of a final episode of what must have seemed a night of cosmic lunacy, a long, quavering scream sounded from a great distance away, and though they said to each other, "Coyote!" when the silence fell back upon them, Mr. Hazard and his scout (who for all his impassivity admitted his fearsome awe at these events) remained awake until daylight.

Mr. Hazard had by now traced upon his map a great U-shaped image of his travels, southward down the eastern side of the Mexican *cordillera,* westward across the *sierra* and two more ranges, and then northward in the basin lying between the Sierra de Sahuaripa and the Sierra de Antuñez. Having traversed perhaps seven hundred miles, he was now, curiously enough, travelling toward the border of the

United States. Soon he would find the outpost town of Avanzada, Sonora.

Worn and exasperated as he was from the failure to find Rainbow Son before now, he yet felt some quickening of spirit at the belief, based upon topographical calculations, that if he was coming again to the United States in pursuit of Rainbow Son, then Rainbow Son must soon make a stand in Mexico rather than cross again himself into territory which he had fled out of prudence.

Sergeant White Horn was now in country which he knew intimately as the southern range of his homeland. The Sonoran deserts reached deeply across both sides of the international boundary. He was able to state when they were but two days' ride from Avanzada, where they would hope to hear news of the object of their search. Avanzada was a garrison town whose relations with the Chiricahuas swung like a pendulum from hostile to friendly, and from the boycott to the market place. The trail leading toward the town was marked, though more faintly with the passing days, with the signs of a large party proceeding northward. It was possible that Rainbow Son was on his way to stage one of his peaceable interludes with the citizens of Avanzada. If so, his encampment would be seen on the outskirts of the town, and the inhabitants would experience a period of nervous compliance with the indicated wants of their unpredictable visitor. Commerce would be conducted, and bargains would often be disastrous for the Mexicans in their market place.

On the other hand, Rainbow Son might be withdrawing to the mountains, either to the east or west of the settlement, there to gather his intentions in a natural fortress, while the Avanzada garrison was left to wonder what to expect.

In either case, the trail should show where he had gone—ahead, or aside. And so it would have, under dry weather. But the land was swept by cloudburst one midday, and all records of passage were washed away. The rivers rose; the arroyos ran; the flat desert floor was scoured by rain driven like bullets by the explosive power of the wind. The expeditioners took shelter in a great grove of greasewood, and when they emerged, there was no evidence upon the ground to tell them where to follow Rainbow Son. They could but resolve to find Avanzada, and learn there what was known.

As they set out on the last day before Avanzada, they were finding their way precariously across an arroyo still muddy from the previous day's tempest, when from the earthen rim above them they heard shots, and an instant later, from impacts about them, knew they were the targets. They took cover under the cheek of a wet earthen buttress carved by erosion in one of the banks. Shots came again, and they saw their faithful animals—two horses and a pack mule—destroyed before their eyes. The figures on the edge above vanished, only to reappear in the arroyo from a slope around a bend. They were five mounted men, dressed in the serapes, great conical hats, Philippine shirts and silver studded trousers of the Mexican horseman. They rode up near to the refuge of Mr. Hazard and the sergeant, and dismounting, called out to come forth without resistance.

"Who are you?" called the lieutenant in turn.

"Friends of the poor," cried one of them, and all of them laughed. They were a band of "Irregulars," out for booty.

"I am an officer of the United States Army," shouted Lieutenant Hazard, and brought his carbine carefully about the earthen bank to train on the leader of the party.

Silence fell. The announcement seemed to bring the bandits to take thought. They held a whispered colloquy. So near to the border, they were evidently saying, perhaps it would be folly to engage the enmity of the United States Army. Homeless travellers, Mexican pedlars—well and good. But people who spoke English and had someone along to translate for them? —The whole condition seemed awkward. The bandits were sporting losers at their game. They called out to put away arms and come forth, for they guaranteed safety.

The lieutenant ordered the sergeant to remain out of sight and on the alert, while he would go forward alone to confront the bandits. He appeared before them in his uniform which by now had lost almost all semblance to military dress, for it was torn and stained beyond recognition. At sight of him, the bandits seemed to reconsider their policy for a moment, and made light-hearted gestures of resumed hostility, raising their guns; but the lieutenant showed with one hand the brass belt buckle of the army and with the other the army weapon he carried, and *took a step toward them.* They shrugged, laughed, and lowered their weapons. The leader made a speech. Its refinements were lost on the lieutenant and the scout, who was listening in his burrow, but its general notions came clear, as these will always do despite all obstacles of language, when there is genuine desire to communicate.

The speech, in effect, said that the Friends of the Poor regretted having been so intemperate as to shoot the horses and mule of the United States Army officer, for now he and his companion would be deprived of their means of rapid locomotion. Still, it could be assumed they were on their way to Avanzada, where the Mexican army kept soldiers, and the Friends could not but be content that the travellers must now proceed slowly, on foot, to their destination, where, even if they alerted the garrison to the presence of the Friends, so close by, the Friends, by the time this intelligence reached its goal, would have a chance to be far away—though from that garrison, they declared sardonically, they really had little to fear. Meanwhile, they were pleased to offer the lieutenant his selection from his own packs of anything he desired to carry with him on foot to Avanzada. What was left, they would, out of self-respect, attach as their own booty.

It was a poor bargain, but Mr. Hazard resolved to make the best of it. Calling Sergeant White Horn, he went to the dead animals, and there, with his help, he extracted ammunition, food, canteens, his compass, his map, the notes already made of the expedition, and paper and pencil with which to make more, and—lastly—the packet of tobacco which I had consigned to Rainbow Son, and the lizard fetich of porphyry, for these were the strategic resources to be used at the outset of any encounter with the chief. The bandits watched with curiosity as he made his choice of belongings, but true to their promise, did not interfere. When the lieutenant and the sergeant were done, the bandit leader made them a low bow, indicating that they were free to depart. They did not delay, but found their way up the arroyo wall and set out on foot for Avanzada, which now, as they were dismounted, was not one but three days away. Their last view of the Friends of the Poor showed them stripping the dead animals of their United States Army equipment.

Almost it would seem that the journey on foot to Avanzada was longer than all the weeks spent previously on horseback, crossing a great loop of Mexico. Every mile ahead was ten times as long as every one behind. The young officer and his scout—assuming they would survive—were drawing to the final test of their efforts. Within a few days they must report either failure or success. Meanwhile, their moccasins wore thin, and the moment came when actually they must proceed barefoot. The ground was rough. It reached away on all sides in the inescapable images of the northern Sonoran desert. Giant *saguaro* cactus stood all about, lifting their fluted arms and headless necks in eternal vigilance, like fantastic soldiers stationed on sentry duty. Dusty, olive-green desert growth, pale dusty land, far mountains showing their blue trace against white horizons— the travellers had seen almost no other sort of country for a thousand miles.

It was thus somewhat in the nature of a blessing when, at last, they saw in the hot late light of falling afternoon a low dome of green trees, somewhere in the midst of which rose two church towers of pale plaster, and knew they were within sight of Avanzada. When darkness fell there were lights of the town to see, and they came at night to the dusty street which took form out of the desert and led them to the town plaza, where a drowsy sentry on guard duty before the local command post aroused his guard officer, who took them in for the night. They had seen no sign of a large Indian encampment near Avanzada, which would have proclaimed Rainbow Son.

In the morning they were the marvel of the town. Children clustered about the headquarters, peering in past the iron grilles set over against the windows in the pale pink plaster walls. The local priest came to gaze and estimate, and ended by offering his services as interpreter—which the lieutenant politely declined, already having tested the talents of Sergeant White Horn in that direction. After their breakfast, appeared the commandant, who had reserved the privilege of interrogating them. The discussion opened on a note of suspicion, and proceeded to an exchange of information, substantially as follows.

COMMANDANT: How do you explain your presence in my district, without previous permission to travel here?

HAZARD: I am on orders of the United States Army to find and treat with the Chiricahua chief Rainbow Son. My government has permission from yours to enter your territory.

C.: True. There is a treaty. But surely you do not intend to go alone to find him?

H.: Those are my orders.

C.: Why do you think he is anywhere near here?

H.: My scout and I have trailed him for almost a thousand miles [indicating on a wall map the course of the travel]. I lost his trail south of here.

C.: It is a veritable Odyssey. What do you mean to accomplish with him?

H.: I will take his surrender.

C.: [showing melancholy mirth] May God preserve you.

H.: Do you know, sir, where he may be?

C.: It is possible.

H.: [making a tactical move] Before you tell me, sir, I must hasten to inform you that four days ago, roughly here on the map, my scout and I were attacked by bandits who killed our animals and robbed us of all except what we carry. They seemed discomfited to think of our telling you of this. It is my duty to do so.

C.: I shall order an immediate pursuit. How many were there?

H.: Five. They called themselves the Friends of the Poor.

C.: There is no such band. It was a joke. Nevertheless, we shall look for them. Permit me.

The commandant gave orders to his subordinates and presently a mounted detachment rode out of the courtyard of the headquarters and down the dusty street to the south, making a fine clash and clatter, to the cheers of children. The colloquy continued.

H.: And now Rainbow Son?

C.: Ah yes. Have you had service in the Indian troubles?

H.: I have, sir. For over two years—ever since my graduation from the military academy.

C.: What! You are only a youngster! Forgive me, but your appearance misled me.

H.: I have had a hard journey.

C.: For the love of God, it must have been a hard journey. Well, if you have had service against Indians, you know, then, the problem. Now we fight, now we are at peace. Peace is better than war, but with those people, peace is just as full of risks as war. You will understand if I do not wish to do anything to disturb the present balance of peace in this district of mine.

H.: You are in a state of armed truce with Rainbow Son?

C.: If you like. Expedient cordialities are preferable to massacres and reprisals.

H.: Our countries face the identical problem, sir. It would seem that we should aid each other in solving it.

C.: Give me a division, and bring one to match it, lieutenant, and I will help you solve it soon enough.

H.: Well, I have come alone, and I will go on alone. But first I must know where to find my man.

C.: [after taking long thought] You have proposed an inconvenient affair, lieutenant. Perhaps you will drop it.

H.: I shall find Rainbow Son with or without your help.

C.: It is a large country.

H.: It is small enough in which to notice him and his works.

C.: My garrison is to be reinforced during the coming months. I shall prefer to wait for my increment before making any moves.

H.: I ask for no moves, sir. Only tell me where to look.

C.: [confounded by persistence] You are very sure of yourself, sir.

H.: I have no one else to be sure of, sir.

C.: [giving in with a weary smile] It is the will of God. Very well, lieutenant, I will tell you this much. Two days ago, three women from Rainbow Son's band came into town to buy some things. They remained for a day and then returned to him. They came from Torres Mountains at the upper end of the Sierra de Sahuaripa. There they returned.

H.: [to Sergeant White Horn] Do you know where that is?

W. H.: Yes.

C.: Southeast of here, you will find the Bavispe River. The mountains are beyond. But do not think that it will be like walking into a house and finding the right room.

H.: I do not think so, sir, after what I have passed through in these months.

C.: I question your fitness to proceed further in your condition.

H.: Perhaps you will permit us to remain a day or two to gather our forces?

C.: Gladly. My house is yours. We shall have to arrange for some clothing, too, and boots. Possibly you would sign a receipt for these things, and for new horses, which your government will later honour as an obligation to repay?

H.: By all means, sir.

With further conventional courtesies, the interview was concluded, and Lieutenant Hazard arranged to sleep for two days, awakening only long enough to take food, and one or two little strolls in the cool of the evening about the plaza. He was treated with curiosity and kindliness by the inhabitants. Their little city produced upon him an effect of charm and quaintness, with its few streets all of which lacked cobblestones, and its houses of pale pink, yellow, or blue plaster, whose corners were painted with imitations of Doric columns or other decoration, and its great overhanging cottonwood trees which rose from hidden patios where played children, parrots, cats and dogs. At the end of every street was a vista of mountains far away. So soon as he felt confident of his strength for the final trial which awaited him, Mr. Hazard set out again with Sergeant White Horn for the Bavispe River and the mountains which lay beyond it.

It can be imagined with what anxiety and impatience (and yet what resolute trust) I awaited, during all this time, news of what was transpiring in Mexico.

Vacillating between sanguine certainty, and self-reproach at having demanded more of Fate than she could give, I found reflection of my conflicting thoughts in the 129th *Rambler* paper of Dr. Johnson, whose works I carried with me in the small edition of 1811.

"Among the favourite topicks of moral declamation," wrote the Rambler, "may be numbered the miscarriages of imprudent boldness, and the folly of attempts beyond our power. Every page of every philosopher is crowded with examples of temerity that sunk under burdens which she laid upon herself, and called out enemies to battle by whom she was destroyed.

"Their remarks are too just to be disputed, and too salutary to be rejected; but there is likewise some danger lest timorous prudence should be inculcated, till courage and enterprise are wholly repressed, and the mind congealed in perpetual inactivity by the fatal influence of frigorifick wisdom.

"Every man should, indeed, carefully compare his force with his undertaking. . . ."

Had I promised for Mr. Hazard that which he must better have promised for himself? I could not believe so, and yet it was but feeling which told me so, not reason. But if I was cast down at moments by doubt, I was raised again by the great flourish in Ovid, which Dr. Johnson set at the head of his essay, and which was enough to set me right again:

> *Restat iter caelo: caelo tentabimus ire.*
> *Da venium caepto, Jupiter alte, meo.*

That is:

> *The skies are open—let us try the skies:*
> *Forgive, great Jove, the daring enterprise.*

Even so, as I waited, there were duties to occupy me throughout the Territory—in particular, at Fort Delivery.

xv

General Quait, acting immediately upon information which reached him by heliostat in the field, left the vicinity of the border in mid-November and hurried, with the 2nd platoon of F Troop, back to Fort Delivery. In his absence, extended patrolling action was to continue under the command of the lieutenant colonel of the 4th Cavalry.

At three in the afternoon two days later he came to the scene of the battle in the trough, where the graves of the fallen had been left. He ordered a halt. The graves had been opened and desecrated. Scraps of uniform were lying about, and alongside the edge of the soldiers' common grave was a tumble of bones, already whitened by picking and the light. The tarpaulins were missing. Nearby there was a single grave which had been similarly treated. It was that of Brevet Lieutenant Colonel Hiram Hyde Prescott, 6th Cavalry, dead before the main column moved on to the border.

"They always find us," said the general, and gave orders for the remains to be separated as well as could be determined into the constitutions of individual men, and gathered up in blankets to be carried home to the Fort. In the work detail performing this service for lost comrades was Corporal Rainey. He worked calmly. Rage was burned out of him; but not sorrow. It was sorrow, now, not so much for a lost man, but for all men in their time, himself included. When it was time to remount and go on again, he knew an unformed joy in having done one further service for Corporal Brian Clanahan.

At sundown the next day the general and his trotting column came in sight of Fort Delivery. The eastern sky was a dark sullen twilight. Against it, illumined over the shoulders of the returning troops by the last rays of the sun, leaped into brilliant vision the flag at the pole-top in all its color. The troopers could see it wave gently in a sundown breeze. Not one of them failed to be moved by the sight. They thought of the dead companions whose bones they were returning to the flag. They thought of the word home, and saw its utmost sign in the sky. They thought of who they were, and in what country, and some felt greater than they were, and some humbler.

The sun was down when the column reached the main gate. The general sent the trumpeter ahead to speak to the sentry on duty. His orders were to bring the person in command of the post to report to General Quait.

Until this order was executed, the general detained his detachment a hundred yards from the gate. Within a few minutes the trumpeter returned, accompanied by the acting sergeant of the first platoon of F Troop. They halted facing the general. The sergeant saluted.

"Acting Sergeant Drew, first platoon, reporting to the Commanding General, as ordered, sir," he said. He was a thickset man of middle age with few teeth left, and a flinching air of self-distrust.

The general returned his salute and said,

"Sergeant Drew, state your position of duty at this post!"

"I am acting in command, sir."

"How many men have you in the garrison at present?"

"Fifteen, sir."

"Where are the remainder?"

"Absent with the acting commanding officer, sir—Lieutenant Mainwaring."

"How many of them went with him?"

"Fourteen, sir."

"When did they leave?"

"Nine days ago, sir."

"Where did they go?"

"I am not sure, sir. All I know is that the lieutenant said that things were quiet enough around here, so he would take the platoon and go out to find some action."

"Find some action? What did he mean by that? Were there reports of fresh enemy activity which caused him to leave the post in pursuit?"

"Not that I know of, sir."

"Since his departure, have you had any signs here of enemy activity?"

"Yes, sir."

"What sort of sign?"

"Five nights ago the sentry heard something in the corral, and turned out the guard, and we chased away a small party of Indians. We fired on them but didn't get any. We figured they must have known we were under strength here, or they wouldn't have dared come in so close."

"A reasonable assumption, Sergeant Drew. What else have you to report to me about the condition of the post?"

"Nothing else, sir. The ladies are all safe, and they have all done their best for everybody. I made sure they had their firearms by them at all times."

"Most proper. Thank you. Have they received any news of the events in the field which followed the departure of the second platoon three weeks ago?"

"No, sir. But they sure have been perishing eager to know anything."

"Thank you, sergeant. —What is that sound?" asked General Quait suddenly, raising his head to listen. From far across the quadrangle rose a doleful, sustained, moaning call.

"It's the hound, sir. Mr. Mainwaring's dog. A greyhound."

"Does he always make that extraordinary noise?"

"No, sir. I never heard it before. He usually bays like a hunting dog when anybody comes."

"Where is Mrs. Prescott, Sergeant Drew?"

"Sir, she's in the headquarters, with Mrs. Lieutenant Hazard and the laundry ladies. We've kept them all there during the time. We thought it best to have them keep together, until the garrison comes home."

"Again most proper. That will do, sergeant. I now relieve you of command, and commend you for doing as well as you could. I will proceed to headquarters, and will inspect your men in the morning."

"Yes, sir. Shall I turn them out to take the horses, and the pack horses? I see you have some extra packs, there, sir."

"Thank you, Sergeant Drew, my men will attend to all. They have instructions about the extra packs already."

"Sir."

"Sergeant."

The acting sergeant saluted and moved aside for the general, who led his column through the main gate. Once inside, he dismounted and gave his reins to the trumpeter, who led his charger away to the corral, where the rest of the platoon went. Then taking a deep, staggering breath, the General braced up to his full lean height, clasped his hands behind him, and strode rapidly to headquarters, up the steps, and into the hall. The hanging oil lamp was lighted. He stood under it. It gave a heavy golden light over him and made shadows as black as char. Bolt upright, he was like a carving of some pilgrim out of the desert with his white beard and bony hand. The burden of his news brought up so much feeling in him that he could only stiffen over it. Now, now, of all times, he needed the ease of amenity in which for all his life he had been wanting. In the silent moment of taking heart for the task that lay just ahead, all his sense of awkwardness showed plain in the somber lamplight, and could be taken for grief. He faced the closed door of the parlor.

"Yes," he said to himself, "I must knock upon the door," and was about to raise his gnarled fist when the door opened, first in a thin crack of light, while whoever held the knob turned to say a word to someone else inside before opening the door all the way. The general's heart began to beat slowly and heavily. The door opened all the way and he saw Laura. She was astounded to see him. She stepped forward with her hands to her cheeks. His rigid figure spoke out to her of calamity and sorrow.

"Uncle Alex!" she cried, but without sound. "What is it! Is it Matthew!" she cried, finding her voice.

He embraced her.

"No, my dear Laura, no, no," he said. "I have no recent news of him. We shall talk of his duty later. Here is a letter I brought you from him." The general took it from his tunic and gave it over. "Later. But tell me, Laura, is Mrs. Prescott here? How can I see her? Is she—is she well?"

Within the parlor, beside the open door, Jessica stood. She heard.

She pressed her heart until she made it hurt from without. Who asked for her? Who wondered if she were well? Why must she be well?

But something in the troubled, whistly voice of General Quait told her what she must hear, and how discomfited he was in his task. A beat of her thought gave her a little respite—she could take refuge for a moment longer in a lesser emotion. It was a feeling of pity for the poor old creature, who had not the grace of a broomstick in matters of this sort, and surely she must put him at his ease? Winking back any telltale light along her lashes, she came into the hall extending her hand, and saying,

"But General Quait! How good it is to see you! You have so much to tell us all, and it is so good to have an officer on the post again."

He took her hand and bent over it, murmuring her name.

"Laura, my dear," said Mrs. Prescott, "take the general into the parlor. I will make him a cup of tea, and then we can discuss dinner, for surely you will be with us, general?" Taking his reply for granted, she strode off down the hall.

He looked mutely at Laura and shook his head over a lady who helped him to find his ease before permitting him to say what he had come to say. Following Laura to the parlor, he murmured,

"Most incredible. It was like a mystical signal."

"Was like what?" asked Laura.

"As I rode in, some hound, somewhere, raised a mournful cry. I must say it made me shiver. It was quite as though he knew what I brought with me."

"Yes, Uncle Alex. I was about to go see what disturbed him when I found you here. Since the attack the other night, we have been nervous. —What is it, Uncle Alex? What have you brought?"

"I brought home to bury again the men we lost in our first day of battle. There are four of these. There is another whom I lost many years ago and found again. And there is another, who died of wounds. This is your colonel, Laura. This is what I must tell Mrs. Prescott. I am glad you are here with her now. And with me."

"Oh, the colonel!" said Laura softly. The tears which had been ready to spring forth for Matthew now rose for Hiram. Laura put her hands over her mouth and gazed at her uncle, shaking her head. Strong feeling always disarrayed the personality which he had created and sustained through long practice. To retain himself, he strode up and down the floor with his hands clasped behind him, saying,

"Yes, most wonderfully appropriate, the hound baying out his certain awareness of death as I arrived with the remains. What a study. The classification of portents traditionally associated with dumb beasts—a veritable footnote to mythology."

"Oh, my dear Colonel Prescott," said Laura. "Whatever will she do, when she hears? How can she ever bear it. I could not. Is Matthew really safe? You have not told me."

"He was when I saw him last. It was many weeks ago. I expect to hear from him at any moment."

"Where is he?"

"In Mexico."

"Mexico! What is he—"

"Hist! My dear, we shall talk of it all later. I hear her coming."

Jessica came bringing a tea tray. She kept a veiled smile on her face, as though lost in a far world of unbreakable contentment. Nothing could be true until she knew it, and for as long as possible, she would refuse to know it. She set the tray down and seated herself before it on a small horsehair sofa. Then she looked up at Laura.

Laura, unlike her mother, Drusilla Greenleaf, had no gift for concealing what she knew. In Laura's face Jessica read the certainty of what there was to know.

"Laura," she said, "you have been crying, and you tried to stop when I came in." She turned to see the general. She stood up. Holding her hands tightly together, she said,

"Yes, General Quait?"

He knew what she meant by asking this, and he replied,

"Yes, Mrs. Prescott. We lost the colonel of wounds following our day of battle. I have brought all our dead to bury here tomorrow."

Laura was watching Jessica, waiting for the sign of permission that she might go to embrace and comfort her. She saw light come into Jessica's face. Jessica raised her head a trifle. The certainty of what she now knew filled her to the utmost. Light trembled in her eyes but her tears did not fall. Her mature face suddenly looked young. The girl who had married and lived with Hiram Prescott was there to be seen for an instant, and Laura saw her. It was a revelation of love and realization which moved Laura almost more than the news which caused it. Perhaps it was too much for anyone else to see. Jessica put her face into her hands and Laura then went and put an arm around her. General Quait left them.

xvi

They worked at sunrise with their spades, and six graves were ready when at eight o'clock the small procession reached toward them from the post. By command of General Quait the reduced garrison of Fort Delivery observed as strictly as local conditions permitted the order of honors for the fallen.

With slow tread first walked Trumpeter Rainey playing on a fife "When Johnny Comes Marching Home," in half-time, which made it sad to hear. Beside him walked a soldier beating the march cadence in half-time on a drum with loosened laces and muffled with a square of blanket. Followed then in order, the firing squad of twelve troopers; remains of the six dead in coffins made during the night, and covered with flags, borne by troopers with crepe on their arms; the commanding officer's charger equipped with a black pall, saddle, bridle, saber, and boots reversed in stirrups; the private soldiers of F Troop; General Quait; and Mrs. Prescott, accompanied by the other women of the post.

When all was ready and the coffins were in the opened ground the general came to the head of the row of graves and, holding the colonel's prayerbook in which Jessica had marked the page, read aloud the prayers for burial, first in Latin, then in English.

"The Latin," he said to himself in thought behind his spoken words, "will do for the Catholics, and the English for the others, and the mercy of God between the words for all of them."

When he was done, he stepped back. Trumpeter Rainey raised his bugle. He closed his eyes and took a slow breath. If he ever did it beautifully he was going to do it best of all now. Under great control, he released his tone. The notes were as pure as a long silver cloud in the still sky of early winter in the desert. Each note lasted forever, it seemed, and yet none broke the lengthened design of the rhythm of taps. The trumpeter was moved by the beautiful sounds he made. Two tears came from his closed eyes. His throat thickened and to control himself he threw more control into his bugling, and with his song of glory, sorrow and peace, he pierced all who listened. His last note held them in a spell even after it died away.

A nod from General Quait to the corporal in command of the firing squad broke it. The twelve rifles came up and pointed over the graves at the sky. The volley crashed out. The day changed. Earth fell on the pine boxes below. Gravel rattled against planking. Finality was harsh, as befitted the facts. But by then Mrs. Prescott was walking slowly back to the post.

Laura walked with her. She was full of pity—for whom it was hard for her to know. She was young—she felt young and invulnerable, yet some day what might befall her? This trial which Jessica now endured—if it should ever happen to her, thought Laura, she would simply be unable to bear it—she would *die*. But this was only a way of thinking or talking, and she knew it. If she had to do so, she could go on. Life was planned that way. She had always heard that this was so, but now she knew it. Walking back to the fort with Hiram's widow, Laura believed at last, as she had never really believed before, that she herself and those she loved were not exempt from sorrow and loss.

Later in the day, Jessica said to her,

"I always knew he would go first."

"Oh?"

"I have some sort of tiresome strength. I simply know how to live on, I suppose. It's a bore to be competent. My mother warned me about it in a general way when I was a girl. May I give the baby his supper? How Hiram adored him. Well, he's the future. Let me do for it."

xvii

"Now what can you tell me, Mrs. Prescott," said General Quait in the evening, "about Mr. Mainwaring's present"—pronouncing the next word in French—*"escapade?"*

"The poor creature," said Jessica. "Ever since he lost his wife—no, even before, I'd say—ever since he was passed over for promotion, he has been odd."

"Quite how?"

"It is difficult to say. But there was a sort of simmering discontent in him. What. How to say it. Perhaps an upside-down sort of humbleness which didn't seem real at all. I used to wonder what would come of it. It was the kind of thing that a man must eventually break out of. I believe that is what he did this time, when he suddenly took half the garrison and went off."

"Did he say anything to you of his plans and intentions?"

"Yes—Laura, you remember. You were there."

"Yes," said Laura. "It was not pretty. He is madly jealous of my husband."

She suddenly blushed and exchanged a glance with Jessica. It was the first possible reference in months, and it was accidental, to Kitty's desperate revelations. They had always wondered how much Teddy knew of the affair. Jessica moved calmly to return their thoughts to professional matters.

"Yes, I think Lieutenant Mainwaring felt that Matthew was always preferred to him in official ways."

"Without doubt," said the general. "And with reason."

"Ah, he knew that, of course. That is what ate him up. Anyhow, he did say to me one evening that a man could take only so much, until he had to get up and prove himself. I believe he declared that you, General, had an unfortunate impression of him. He intended to erase this. He intended to earn promotion to captain. He owed it to Kitty—his wife, now dead. He grew almost passionate about that point. I asked him how he would set about all this, and he said he was going to take just under half the remaining men of the garrison and go into the field in search of action. He was bitter. He declared that nobody ever won his spurs sitting around a practically abandoned post. If there was a fight to be found, he was going to find it, and win it."

"What did you say to that, Mrs. Prescott?"

Jessica smiled ashily.

"I suppose I am hopelessly full of rank, but I asked him whether his orders gave him authority to leave the post open to almost certain capture by a raiding party of any size. He was very superior with me, reminded me that *he* was acting in command, and it was for him to decide what was and what was not safe to do."

"He was even more unpleasant than that," said Laura. "Tell the General."

"I think I should not."

"I will," said Laura. "Teddy also said that it was clear that Mrs. Prescott was afraid, and that was why she tried to keep him from going off."

"Poor wretched fellow," said the general. "How dreadful to be doomed to do always the hopelessly wrong thing."

"It really was wrong, don't you think?" asked Laura.

"Wrong! My darling child, it will cost him everything, if we ever see him again. Ambition of the weakest sort led him into endangering all that he was given to defend. It was the greatest luck that the party which raided the corral here was so small. It was also, if I may say so, fortunate that I received signals—delayed, to be sure—from heliostat relays saying that he had been sighted roving north of the Phantom Mountains with his garrison party. I sent orders for his instant return to his assigned duty here, but either he did not receive them or he ignores them. And of course I came at once, to reinforce the garrison. I shall remain until an officer arrives to relieve me. I have sent for him. It is Captain A. Cedric Gray, who is as good a line officer as he is surgeon."

"How nice to see him again," said Jessica.

"He may be the last commanding officer of Fort Delivery. If all goes well we shall deactivate here after—after I know what comes out of Mexico."

"Mexico," said Laura. She now knew all that there was yet to know of where Matthew went, and for what.

xviii

It was close to noon the next day when a column of fourteen troopers and an officer rode into the main gate of the post. First Lieutenant Mainwaring dismounted and gave his reins to a trooper. The sentry said to him,

"Report to headquarters, sir, by command of General Quait."

Teddy's mouth fell open and he looked around at headquarters in dismay.

"General Quait! Is he here?" he asked in a mealy voice.

"Yes, sir. He has taken command of the post. We were all alerted to watch for you."

Teddy wavered for a moment and then turned and ran after his troopers, who were on their way to the corral. Overtaking them, he said between long breaths,

"Listen, you men. Now you let me handle this. General Quait is here, and he is going to want a report on our march. If he asks any of you anything, you just tell him I was suspicious of Indian movements across the mountains up there, and let it go at that. You hear?"

The troopers stared coldly at him. No one replied.

"Now don't you say anything about how we decided to come back, you hear? I can make it mighty unpleasant for any man that doesn't do as I say, now. Now go on, that's all. But you just remember, all of you!"

They resumed their walk to the corral. He watched them with a cold weight above his stomach. His legs felt chilled and feeble. He had an impulse to run away out the gate, and was suddenly aware that he was walking to the headquarters. On the steps was Trumpeter Rainey, who saluted him.

"Hello, Rainey," said Teddy. "I hear we have a high-ranking visitor."

The trumpeter did not reply but only threw open the office door. Rolling his dry white tongue over his dry lips, Teddy said, entering the office,

"Corporal, you will answer me when I speak to you."

"That is all, trumpeter," said General Quait, facing about in the colonel's old high-backed swivel chair. Rainey left and closed the door.

"Why, General, this is a fine surprise," said Teddy.

"Mr. Mainwaring, our discussion will be neither social nor informal. You will stand, though not at attention. Repeat now to me the gist of the orders under which you were left here at Fort Delivery when the commanding officer took the field."

"Why, General, I—"

"*General* is a possibly social address. Please to address me as *sir.*"

"Sir, I was placed as acting commanding officer of Fort Delivery, until relieved."

"Mr. Mainwaring, who relieved you on the eleventh of November?"

"Nobody, sir."

"Yet you left the post?"

"Yes, sir. But I left a competent man in charge."

"How was leaving the post an execution in any fashion of your orders?"

"Sir, I thought the defense of the post extended out beyond the actual limits of the post. I went to do what I thought best for the safety of the post."

"Leaving a garrison of fifteen men and five women?"

"Sir, I took less than half the platoon. I left more than I took."

"In the amount of one man, I believe."

"Sir, there was no activity going on near here."

"Your post was raided seven nights ago, in your absence, by a horse-stealing party of Indians. Sergeant Drew and his men managed to drive them off, as they were a small party. I leave it to you to consider what might have occurred here had they attacked in numbers."

Teddy turned gray. Sweat glistened on his full cheeks.

"Sir, I never imagined—"

"Did you find enemy action in your scouting expedition, Mr. Mainwaring?"

"No, sir."

"Why did you decide to return?"

"In—in my judgment, we had fulfilled our mission. Our rations were running low. I made the decision to come back "

"You did not receive my orders to return?"

"No, sir—I did not know you knew I was out."

"It is among your unluckiest assumptions, Mr. Mainwaring. Who was your second in command on the march?"

"Corporal Simmons, sir."

"Please to step to the door and have Trumpeter Rainey bring him here. You will remain while I interrogate him."

"Sir, I assure you, I have all information which you may need."

"Mr. Mainwaring."

"Yes, sir."

Teddy went to the door and gave the general's order to Rainey. Returning, he found the general facing the desk, reading with composure a small brown leather volume. The old man's long thin brown hand veiled his face from anyone in the room. Teddy was left to stand alone, in silence, in the middle of the office until seven minutes later when Corporal Simmons appeared. This was a lean, soft-spoken Kentuckian about thirty years old. Even at attention he gave the impression of lounging, and his calm was unbreakable.

"Corporal Simmons, were you the second in command of Lieutenant Mainwaring's recent expedition?"

"Was, sir," replied the corporal slowly, with little liquid sounds of saliva edging his words.

"Did your troopers ever express an opinion of the undertaking?"

" 'S, sir. They thaought it was just all wraong."

"Why?"

"To leave Fowart Delivery undefinded thataway."

"Did you have reason to believe you were on a fighting mission?"

"Nao, sir. We nivver heerd of any Indians to go out and fand."

"Why did the lieutenant order the detachment to return to the post?"

Teddy hupped a sharp breath and turned toward Corporal Simmons forcefully. The corporal ignored him and said with deadly precision,

"We taold him to."

"We? The troopers?"

" 'S, sir. We knew we was off on some wald-goose chase, it nivver made inny sense, start with, and fanally, the other troopers and I, we taold the *lieu*tenant we was coming bayack, and he could come with us or no, just as he lakked."

General Quait swung slowly from side to side in the swivel chair. Its creaking springs made the only sound in the office for a while. Then he clapped his hands once and stood up.

"Thank you, corporal," he said, "that will do."

They exchanged salutes. When the corporal was gone, the general said,

"Mr. Mainwaring, my impulse is to shout at you to vent the rage I feel at your various betrayals of trust. I restrain myself because the luxury of exhibited contempt is in this moment superseded by what I can only call emotions of bewildered pity for you. If your judgment has been disastrous, it is as nothing compared to the disgraceful loss of respect you have achieved among your troopers. I must ask you to consider yourself in arrest, to await orders which will take you, in due course, before a court of inquiry at an appropriate army post. There will be determined the degree of your future usefulness to the United States Army. That is all, sir."

There could be no torture greater for Teddy Mainwaring than to see himself facing an ordeal by inquiry. They would try to find out all about him. He would try to be clever and keep them from doing so. But maybe they would find out anyway; and if they found out, then he would find out too, and this was a thing he had never found out before—who Teddy Mainwaring really was. He did not want to know, he did not want to know. In his darkened quarters in Officers' Row, he put his face on his fists and shut his eyes against himself. "Kitty!" he whispered. "Oh, Kitty!"

Two days later Captain Gray arrived to relieve General Quait of the command of the post. The general departed at once, with the same small escort which had come with Gray. By rapid stages he returned to the border, at a point opposite the Sonoran town of Avanzada, which lay forty miles below the international boundary line. There he took up his position again, waiting for word out of Mexico. It was a task, as he wrote in his autobiography,* which gave him "new notions of patience and discipline."

xix

For it had now been forty-four days since I had seen Mr. Hazard into the interior, and no word had come from him. Later it was possible to know that, just as I resumed my vigil on the border, he and Sergeant White Horn were approaching the Bavispe River after a two-day mounted march from Avanzada. And now, after those weeks during which time itself seemed hardly to crawl on its course, all seemed suddenly to quicken, so that events all but anticipated the intentions which called them forth.

At the Bavispe River, Mr. Hazard and his scout made an encampment in a ravine which gave to the eye all the delights of a romantic scene such as would put a lettered observer in mind of the dramas of Schiller. Rippling water played against rocky walls dappled with silvery lichen and emerald moss. A narrow white sandy beach looked as clean as bone. Above this sloped a bank of wild grasses from which rose a grove of mixed trees whose shade, teased by the playful wind, danced upon river and bank alike. There stood the smooth, white-trunked, long, slender sycamore, the varnished-leaf cottonwood, the plumy willow, the spurred buckthorn. A trail in the rock walls led down one side and up the other, reaching beyond into the Torres Mountains whose blue crowns could be seen on the horizon from the top of the ravine.

At the top of the miniature gorge Sergeant White Horn kept watch while his lieutenant refreshed himself in the stream below. Mr. Hazard was in the water, bathing, when a cry from above brought him to the alert. The sergeant indicated with a gesture that someone was approaching on the trail coming from the mountains. Not stopping for his clothes, Mr. Hazard sprang for his carbine and watched for whatever visitor might come. In a moment Sergeant White Horn began to back down the trail into the ravine, beckoning someone to follow, and Mr. Hazard was astonished and embarrassed to see an

* *Op. cit.*

Indian woman in slashed buckskins appear. She came calmly down the trail, unruffled at surprising a white man in a state of nature. Mr. Hazard worked hastily to correct his exposed condition, and by the time she and the scout were at the shallow ford, ready to cross to join him, he was properly attired in the somewhat fantastic costume which represented the best which Avanzada had to offer.

The squaw was a messenger from the camp of Rainbow Son. She spoke to Sergeant White Horn of her lord. He was established in the Torres Mountains on a crest roughly eleven miles distant. With him were his warriors, and their wives, children and livestock. He was strong and powerful, and he was sick and tired of being followed. He was not yet ready to be angry, but he was close to it. He wanted to know why he was being followed, and to find out, he now sent for the Apache scout to come and tell him what the white army officer with him was after. The officer would remain at the Bavispe River while the scout went alone to the mountains to talk to Rainbow Son. If the scout could give acceptable answers to his questions, Rainbow Son would consider next what to do. He wanted to spend no more time on nonsense and delays. It was time to end this annoying condition of being followed for over forty days without knowing why. It might be that he would send for the officer. How soon, would depend on how promptly the scout came to see him and how well he spoke. The woman messenger would conduct the scout to the mountains. Meanwhile, the officer was to remain where he was.

"Alone?" asked Mr. Hazard in English, in a colloquy slightly withdrawn from the woman.

"Yes," replied Sergeant White Horn.

"They intend to separate us."

"Yes, but I do not think that means any additional danger. If they wanted to destroy us they could do so immediately. He wants to see me alone. He wants to see if we are bringing danger to him. If I go alone, he will see that we are willing to be separated."

"You should go," said Mr. Hazard.

"Yes, I should go," agreed Sergeant White Horn.

"I will wait here. Come back as soon as you can."

"Or I will send a message."

"No," declared the lieutenant, "he sends for you and takes you away. He must send you back before I will agree to go to him. I will not be sent for by him. If he will see me, I will go. But only in my own way, and with you along."

"Yes, you are right."

"Then go. Be back by tonight if possible."

"Nobody knows what is possible."

"I am here to make everything possible."

The Indian woman made a remark in the clicking strangled Apache speech, and the sergeant nodded to her. She was bidding him hurry and he agreed. In a few moments, after assembling his usual small possessions, he gave the lieutenant a rudimentary salute and without again looking at him, crossed the river and mounted the rock trail, with the woman following him. (An Apache male would never follow a female even though she were sent to guide him.)

What we have just seen was an exercise not only in the Apache nature, but also in the style of manners common to occupants of high places. It was like the Apache to impose a test of bravery and determination upon the officer sent to confront him; and it was like a reigning monarch to deny access to himself until after certain conditions had been met. If we are to believe Tallyrand, his master Napoleon snubbed, scolded or rejected the emissaries of lesser monarchs in much the same fashion. Rainbow Son in his time and place conceived himself to be a great man, having never known evidence to the contrary. If he gave himself airs, he had reason to do so, if power is all.

In imposing his test upon Mr. Hazard, the Chiricahua chieftain also imposed danger. The outcome could be mortal for either Sergeant White Horn or for his commander. To face this possibility promptly and with no quibbling was the only way to impress Rainbow Son. My representative, simply by enacting his character, did so.

During the day at the ravine then, Mr. Hazard took full advantage of his enforced idleness. He lay several times in the shallow, cool, trifling waters of the Bavispe River, as though he had never seen water before. He slept in the grove, he wrote pages of thoughts for his wife, and he brought up-to-date in some detail the notes he was keeping for me. Having lived for so many weeks with no thought but of advancing through rock and desert, with no expression but a scowling stare into the distance which he must conquer, he now found that he could lie inert and awake, and take power from his rest. Looking into a still backwater of the river he was still astonished at the change in his appearance which he had first noticed in a mirror at Avanzada. There, shaving with a borrowed razor, he had discovered how haggard and exhausted he was. He laughed to see the changes wrought in him by his experience.

One entry in his notes reveals a certain aspect of his nature.

"It is a flaw in my character," he wrote, "that I am poor at the task of waiting. If something is to be done, however difficult, disagreeable or dangerous, I want to do it immediately, and have it behind me, rather than before me."

For a man who had so little of the philosopher in him, this was a respectable effort at self-regard. It also, for the task which lay ahead, betrayed a manly impatience which must serve him well when the time should come for him to act.

It was not until the following afternoon that Sergeant White Horn returned. He came alone, having learned the way to the fortress of Rainbow Son. He was unharmed. His commander immediately interrogated him.

"Well? What does he say?"

"He wants to know what you want," said the Apache sergeant.

"What did you tell him?"

"That you want to see him."

"What did he say?"

"He says you will come to the mountain tonight, and that he will see you tomorrow morning."

"How will we go?"

"On foot, the way I did."

"If we both go, who will take care of our horses?"

"He says we will have to take a chance that nobody will steal our horses."

"I do not like that."

"It is all we can do."

"Was he bad to you?"

"He was bad to me at first."

"Why?"

"Because I am in the army."

"And then?"

"Then he was good to me because I am a Chiricahua."

"How will he treat me?"

"He does not yet know, therefore I do not know."

"He will wait and see?"

"Yes."

"Then so must I."

"He does not know who you are."

"But you told him?"

"Yes. But he says how will he know that you really come from the army, and from the general."

"I can prove it to him."

"He says you will have to."

"If I can, then what?"

"Then he will have to think about it."

"Has he many men?"

"Over a hundred."

"What is his place like?"

"The high part of the first mountain in the *sierra*. There is an open space, with high rocks around, and no trees, but some grass, and water. The women have built shelters out among the high rocks. We sat by the creek on the grass and talked."

"Did it rain?"

"No."

"Did it snow?"

"No. It was cold but the sun shone."

"Where were you at night?"

"They put me there by the creek for the night. They all slept in the rocks. But they watched me."

"Did they let you keep your gun?"

"Yes. But they did not give me anything to eat."

"Have you eaten?"

"No."

"We will eat and then we will go."

They made a meal and packed food to take along.

"How long does it take to get there?" asked Mr. Hazard.

"Three hours."

"There must be a good trail?"

"Yes—they took their animals up with them."

"We should ride."

"No. He says no."

They tethered their animals, hid their supplies and proceeded up the trail at midnight. It was a clear, starry night, and they had eyes for darkness. Now that he was approaching the very climax of his ordeal, with its unknown quantities before him, Mr. Hazard felt a grand calm settle within him. Going upward, always upward, in his night march into the Torres Mountains, he reviewed my instructions, and found comfort in the resolve to do his best, after which success or failure, life or death, while holding preferred alternatives, yet could not exact of a man more than he could offer.

Before dawn, in the drift of air off the peaks which chilled the climbers to the marrow, Sergeant White Horn suddenly arrested their progress with a touch upon the lieutenant's arm. They must go no farther. They were already near. They were not to show themselves before morning. They would remain where they were until daylight.

"How do you know we are near?" asked Mr. Hazard.

Sergeant White Horn made plain that he knew with his nose. Still two miles away from the castle of Rainbow Son, he could smell the presence of the Chiricahua band and their animals.

In the first white sky of dawn, they resumed their march, and when the sun was up and sending long shadows westward, the lieu-

tenant and the sergeant came from the last reaches of the trail between a gateway of rocks into the open place on the mountain top
which was the natural palace of the chieftain. A small creek bisected
it, running westward and falling off with the slopes. The great open
room was empty. The early sunlight stood like shining swords against
the encircling pinnacles of high rocks. A perfect silence reigned. It
was so complete that Mr. Hazard must break it.

"Here I am. Where is he?" he asked the sergeant in a loud, clear
voice. The sound of it was doubled by the rocks. Startled, an eagle
made a slow, slapping rise from a rocky spire and took the sky.

Though he saw no one, Lieutenant Hazard had a strong sensation
of being observed, as he stood to his tallest measure, holding his
carbine across his belt, and searching the circumjacent partitions of
stone for signs of life.

What impression must this arrival have made on Rainbow Son? I
can but think that Mr. Hazard's very approach to the last mountain
fortress of the Chiricahua nation, alone but for a single companion,
must have brought to that imaginative people an effect almost of
mythic power. Knowing what he had endured, they saw him unruffled
in the face of such endurance as might still await him. In him they
saw a veteran of the deserts, the canyons, the cliffs, the rocks, the
heights, the depths; the pumas, the eagles, the serpents; the pitiless
light and the spacious dark; the pressing solitude and the undiminish-
ing distance; the freezing fogs of the crests and the sun at midday.
His arrival in itself must have been a weapon of astonishment.

So gradually that he could not determine just the moment of its
beginning, a movement showed amongst the rocks. Slowly the Indians
came forth, a great crowd of them, as momentous as conifers would
be if moving from their roots across the ground. They came until well
over a hundred men were standing in a wide circle about the lieutenant and the sergeant. The last to come was the man they had
come to find.

Rainbow Son at this period of his history was a living contradiction
of his lyrical appellation. As such he would induce hilarity if he did
not create chill apprehension. He was now fat where years before
he had been lean and muscular. His face in profile still suggested the
grand crag of Wellington, but fully seen it was an asymmetrical melon
whose rind had split, then dried, then contracted, so that more wrinkles at greater cross purposes could not have covered a human
countenance. Scars added to the display. His eyes were almost pale.
In that dark face they were like a cat's eyes. The left was paler than
the right—a condition later discovered to be caused by advanced
cataract. He saw well enough with the right. All lines and eminences

of that visage were fixed in an expression of unremitting bad temper, which varied in one direction toward the furious, and in the other—almost more unnerving—toward a grimace intended to demonstrate the cordial. If—to change the metaphor—you imagine a double handful of thickly whorled lava, and imagine further the possibility of kneading it into changes of expression, as it were, without losing the character of the lump, you will have the physiognomy of Rainbow Son. His hands were blackened by sun and dirt. He moved with lightness amazing in so gross a person and his voice was thin, high, husky and penetrating. That there was intelligence within such an unpromising envelope there could be no doubt on the part of anyone who ever encountered him.

Not glancing at Mr. Hazard, he came now through the ranks of his courtiers with a majestic tread. He seated himself on the bank of the little stream with his back to it and as if at a signal his followers sat down in a grand demilune about him. He spent several minutes in thought, patting his scarred heavy lips with his crusty fingers. Mr. Hazard waited aside at a distance of fifty feet. Then suddenly, with a lunging heave of his thick person, the chieftain commanded with a gesture that he be brought forward. Two Indians went to take him by the arms. The lieutenant stood fast, putting them off from him with a severe stare and only when they had stepped back did he come forward, taking Sergeant White Horn along as his interpreter.

The lieutenant walked slowly ahead until he was face to face with Rainbow Son. At distance of three feet he seated himself before him, and greeted him with an inclination of his body. The chief bowed back and there was silence for a moment. The lieutenant spoke first. The conference was opened. Its laborious and repetitious progress is reduced here by my paraphrase, which modifies the original notes in the direction of coherence and lucidity, and seeks always to reveal the intention of the speakers, substantially as follows.

HAZARD: I have come from your old friend General Quait. [Sergeant White Horn proceeds to translate—though then and throughout it is clear that the chieftain understands more English than he likes to admit.]

RAINBOW SON: I do not know that this is true. [Mr. Hazard jots down this exchange in his notebook. Rainbow Son makes a waving motion of distaste for having recorded what is said. The lieutenant ignores this and produces the porphyry fetich of the lizard to establish his identity as my emissary.]

H.: This will tell you that I come from General Quait.

R. S.: [Taking the fetich and turning it over.] Yes. You come from him. He is the old White-Bearded Lizard. I remember him. Yes.

Here my vanity requires me to assure the reader that in so referring to me the chief was not necessarily resorting to insult. Use of animal names for human beings did not, in Apache habit, any more than among other primitive peoples, carry with it anything of the pejorative. Nonetheless, it is possible to smile at this hint of the grotesque or the eccentric, and since others will smile, perhaps with some vague recognition of myself, I hasten to smile first.

Rainbow Son composedly put the fetich, with its turquoise eyes, into his shirt. Mr. Hazard did not object, since it had accomplished its purpose as a passport. He produced the bundle of tobacco I had given him.

H.: Here is tobacco from the general for you.

R. S.: Please give me a bottle of mescal.

H.: I have not brought any liquor.

R. S.: The Lizard knows I like to drink mescal.

H.: There is none.

R. S.: I drank much mescal in Avanzada. I have fire in my mouth for it. Give me some.

H.: I have none.

R. S.: Where is the Lizard?

H.: He is in Arizona, as you know.

R. S.: I do not know.

H.: He is waiting to know that I have seen you.

R. S.: I do not see you. [Looking past Mr. Hazard with a runnelled expression of injury.]

At this there was a fierce murmur through the camp. The tribesmen were of independent temper, which they expressed through attitudes of ferocity under restraint. Wearing blankets which they threw open as the sun went higher, they revealed shirts of German cotton in all colours and patterns, such as are sold in Mexico. Each man carried his traditional medicine charms—buckskin bags of *hoddentin,* red-bird feathers, feathers of the woodpecker, the head of a quail, the claws of a prairie dog, a small silver crescent, or a split twig. Most significant of all, they sat holding Winchester or Springfield breechloading carbines and they wore bandoleers which held metallic ammunition.

H.: If you do not see me, why am I here?

R. S.: Yes. That is a good question. Why are you here?

H.: [Instantly saying what he had come so far to say] I am here for your surrender. Surrender to General Quait, with all your people, and you will live a long time. You will all be sent with your women and children to Florida. The President of the United States will decide what will be done for your future. Everyone else of your nation is already being taken there. Agree to go, or fight until you are killed. That is what General Quait tells you.

As his last words died away, a bolt of silence struck the party. Inducing a nightmarish air of naturalness in the preposterous proceedings, Mr. Hazard occupied himself by writing his notes. Not looking about at any of his hearers, he felt rather than saw evidences of the tension which held all. So, also, he felt the faintest of changes in the presence of Rainbow Son and knew that a response of some sort might be coming. He snapped his notebook shut and looked up.

If the countenance upon which he gazed was made of lava, the good eye in it further supported the volcanic analogy. There was a smouldering light inside which meant no good if it should leap into fire. Mr. Hazard gave back look for look and waited for his answer. After an interval sufficiently protracted to convert astonishment into dignity, the chieftain replied.

R. S.: I heard what you spoke. I must hear it in my head. I must think about it. I have nothing to say until I think about it.

H.: When will you talk to me about what you think?

R. S.: Tomorrow. Go back to the river now. Come here tomorrow.

H.: I would rather have you speak to me now. It is a long walk to the river, to go now and to come back tomorrow.

R. S.: Come back tomorrow.

H.: I will come back tomorrow. But I will ride my horse.

R. S.: Walk.

H.: Ride. [Standing up with an order to the sergeant to follow.] I can see that what I ask is a big thing to ask. I see that you must think about it. I want you to think about it. The more you think about it the better you will see it is. I will go to the river now, and tomorrow I will come back, with my scout, on our horses. Thank you and goodbye.

He turned and walked down the creekside and then turned to take the entrance to the trail. Behind him he heard a chorus of metallic parts moving and accommodating—the cocking of half a hundred carbines. He said in a subdued tone to Sergeant White Horn,

"Do not look around or take cover."

The few steps to the trail and invisibility seemed endless; but they passed, and Mr. Hazard and his scout were soon making their way down the mountain. They watched to see if they were followed but could neither see nor hear anyone behind.

At the Bavispe River they found their possessions intact. Mr. Hazard fell down exhausted. He found he had little nervous reserve. He slept hours before nightfall and all night. In the morning, preparing to return to the height, he knew serious apprehension for the first time; for now Rainbow Son knew what he had come for, and it was wholly possible that for bearing such disagreeable tidings, he might pay the supreme penalty. Before they arrived at the crest, Mr. Hazard arranged a signal with Sergeant White Horn which would tell him whether, in the sergeant's judgment, Rainbow Son would be telling a lie at any given moment. This was the signal: the sergeant was to put his lower lip up toward his nose. Thus, at a glance, the lieutenant could know when to doubt.

This time, when he arrived, he found the conference already assembled. The sergeant tethered their horses just inside the rocky gateway to the pass where they could be watched. Advancing then to resume their places at the council circle, the young officer and his scout sat down in silence and waited. Finally,

R. S.: You brought your horses.

H.: Yes. I told you I would. If there is a trail a man is a fool to walk when he can ride.

R. S.: I told you to walk.

H.: I remember. But by riding I came to you faster than I could if I had walked.

R. S.: You will go away faster, too, that way.

H.: Did you not ride when you came here?

R. S.: I did. But it is my mountain.

H.: I do not ride because I want to make you angry. I ride because it is the way I go. [Silence again while Mr. Hazard's air of respectful independence has its chance to make effect. Evidently it does so, for the chieftain now changes the subject, venting on a new cause the irritation denied to an old one.]

R. S.: [As Mr. Hazard jots down his notes.] That writing. That paper. I do not like it. Stop it.

H.: Excuse me. The general ordered me to do this writing.

R. S.: The Lizard is not here. He is not in charge. I am here and I am in charge.

H.: Excuse me, but wherever I go, he is in charge of me. I must do as he says. When you send your young men far away to do something, they do what you tell them. This is how it is with great commanders. I must make my marks on this paper.

R. S.: When something is written down about a man it takes part of the man away from him. Why do you want to take part of me away from me?

H.: I do not want to do that.

R. S.: Then stop.

H.: No. But I will tell you that if I take part of you away from you, when I do this, then I take part of myself away, too, because I put down here what we both say. So it is the same for both of us. [It seems clear that even in such trivial matters, there is a struggle of powers going on. So far, it is the will of the young officer which is prevailing. As he finishes his next notations—] Well, here I am again, waiting to listen to what you think about the gift I bring you from General Quait.

R. S.: Gift? [Bitterly.] A pinch of tobacco. Gift? Not even a bottle of mescal.

H.: I do not mean such gifts. I mean the gift of life which he offers you.

It was a striking way to regard the proposal I had sent. Rainbow Son was tipped off balance by it. He threw himself into the lead by making a speech as a distraction.

R. S.: The Lizard does not know what I have suffered. No man should be asked to accept insults and betrayals. Your people have told lies about me and have told the whole world that I am a wicked man. They have started rumours about me. My people came and told me what everyone was saying about me. It was disgusting. How would you like to have people going around saying terrible things about you? You would not be as patient as I was. All a man has is his pride and his manliness. Do you think I should have sat by like an old woman without any teeth or hair and let those things be said about me? I was told that you were all looking for me. You were going to arrest me and put me in jail. I will die if I am ever put in jail. Do you want me to die? They said you were going to hang me. Do you think I want to be hanged? I tell you these are disgusting things to hear about yourself. This was long before I went on the warpath. Do you think I would have gone on the warpath without perfectly good reason? I am not such a fool, or such a small boy, that I would do things without any more reason than the thing that makes a grasshopper jump, when he does not know how far he can jump every time. A time comes when a man has been abused all he can stand, and then he gets on his feet and goes out to stop all such wickedness. [His self-righteous expression changes and he becomes sad and tender, with all the warted delicacy of a peccary, and yet with some eloquence.] I was living at peace with my power. The shade of the trees was over me. My grandsons were at my knee learning the lessons of a man. I was praying four times a day to the six directions and to my power and to the sun and the moon. Nobody was ever so full of peace and goodness. All I wanted was the blessing of the mountain all around me and hours to think about all that I had learned since I was a boy. How fine it is to be a boy and train your body with hardship. My father told me to take my hands and have a fight with a great rock and make it give up to me. I did so. He told me to run barefooted in the snow. I did so. I sat in the sun for three days without eating because it would give me power. I kept my eyes off girls until I took my first wife. When I became a doctor and then a chief I fasted longer than anybody and I wrapped my loins in rags with thorns in them, to keep me from having women when I was busy with sacred matters, working for the good of my people. The shadows of vultures never went across my heart. My sons and their sons were learning to have my life and my knowledge in them. Don't you know what it is to be in the shade of the trees without wanting to do anything? [If this is a farrago, it yet has some psalmistic spell about it. Mr. Hazard writes intently as Sergeant White Horn transmits in a halting flow the remarks of Rainbow Son. Rainbow Son continues.] Now what happened? I will tell you. Whenever I left the reservation it was because I heard the bad talk about me. [His temper changes. His voice rises.] Don't blame me. Blame those people who spoke badly of me. Blame the man who lived with me and made fine words and faces for me and then caused me more trouble than anybody else, though I did not know it then. He showed me newspapers and read me what they said there. Your people all read the newspapers and see what is said there, and you saw that they said I was this and I was that—terrible things. It was Seeley Jones who told me all this. He said he was disgusted with the disgusting things white people did to me. But he did not mean it. But I did not know it then and I had to go out and do the things I did. [He is indignant.] No man can stand all that forever. I am a man and I act like a man. What is the worst is this, that it was Seeley Jones I should have killed, not so many other people. I would have killed him but it was too late.

H.: Too late? What do you mean?

R. S.: He was already dead when I thought of doing it.

H.: Who killed him?

R. S.: All I know is that he was dead. Too soon. [Now, whether the pathetic self-portrait of a man slandered beyond endurance loses its conviction even for the speaker, or whether his tactics of distraction call for a new tone, Rainbow Son suddenly shifts his interest.] Of course, I knew every move which you made, and White Horn, when you came along after me. I could not understand who was such a fool as to follow me.

H.: Why didn't you stop and wait for me?

R. S.: I did not want to. I wanted to come here. I wanted to see how far you would come, too. I wanted to know who you were. [He becomes fatherly. His smile is like a crack in a lava flow. He points to

Sergeant White Horn.] He left us and became a soldier. Look at his coat. Look at his marks of power on his arms. [Chevrons.] I wondered and wondered if I would ever see him again. I am glad to see him. We are the same man. Now he is your man. If we are the same man, that should make me your man, too. But how can I ever be your man when such terrible things have been said about me? Now if I made war, one reason was that I wanted to get White Horn back again, to be with our own people, and be on our side. I knew I would find him. He was worth fighting for. [Sergeant White Horn puts his lower lip upward, and Mr. Hazard is confirmed in his recognition of a florid lie. He says nothing, but writes. The chieftain half rises from his haunches and then settles back again.] Why are you so silent? You do not even look at me. You should speak to me. I want to see you smile. It is good for men talking to smile and show a pleasant face. We are men together. I am like you. [He leans forward and roughly touches Mr. Hazard at each part of the anatomy he cites.] I have hands, like you, and feet, and belly, and loins, like you. Be pleasant to me. All men have the same powers. All men feel the same.

Mr. Hazard now recognised that he had, by preserving an air of stony disbelief in the face of Rainbow Son's elaborate evasions, gained a certain advantage in the spirit of debate. Rainbow Son was now asking something of *him,* even if it were no greater thing than a smile.

H.: I will speak to you. First, as for threats to arrest and hang you at the time you speak of, that is all nonsense. Nobody wanted to arrest and hang you until after you had done many bad things.

R. S.: I was told they were going to hang me.

H.: Not before you did all those things.

R. S.: Why do you want to punish me because I make war? The Lizard makes war. You make war. Why don't I punish you?

H.: Why don't you keep your promises? Sebastian promised General Quait this year, and you promised him many years ago, not to make war again. Why did you break your promise?

R. S.: We don't want white people here. They burn our grass and take our water. They do not care what becomes of us.

H.: We do care. We are trying to show you how to live in peace. And then what do you do? You murder and torture and steal. Why did you do all that to the Edwards party two months ago near Fort Delivery?

R. S.: I know nothing of this.

[Sergeant White Horn lifts his lower lip.]

H.: That is not true. We know all that you did.

R. S.: How did you know?

H.: The old man lived long enough to tell us. Why else do you suppose the army came after you in such great numbers?

R. S.: Yes. You must have many men to get me.

H.: We have many.

R. S.: How many?

H.: We have nearly a thousand here, and if we need more, the President will send us more.

R. S.: How many?

H.: Nineteen thousand more.

R. S.: How many is that?

H.: If you put all our men in a long chain holding hands, they would make a chain reaching from here on this mountain top all the way down to the Bavispe River without a single break. That is one hundred times more than you can show in men. For every man you have I can send for one hundred. General Quait will bring them.

R. S.: What if you do not send? [This is not a simple question. It is, in the context of sudden expression of savagery in Rainbow Son's face, a mortal threat.]

H.: If I do not come back or send any word, General Quait will come to find you. [This, too, is a threat. It produces silence. Presently, in a thoughtful tone, the chieftain resumes.]

R. S.: It is Coyote who sometimes makes people do unfortunate things. Some of my men have done bad things. I always wanted to put bad things away. We all want to be quiet, with our people, on this land. What do we need? We need water, wood for fire, grass for our animals, food for our bellies. All men need these. That is all we look for when we go out.

H.: Very well. Come with me and you will have water, and fire, and food.

R. S.: I will speak to you again tomorrow.

H.: You said you would answer me today.

R. S.: I said I would speak to you today. Come tomorrow and I will speak to you again.

H.: Will you give me your answer then?

R. S.: You keep asking me questions. I will ask you some questions.

H.: I do not want to go on talking for days. I want to settle everything.

R. S.: You can settle it now.

H.: How?

R. S.: Go back to the Lizard and do not return.

H.: Come with me.

R. S.: Where is he?

H.: He is waiting where we cross the border.

R. S.: Why did he not come to see me himself?

H.: He had other things to do.

R. S.: No, it is because he does not like me.

H.: No, that is not the reason.

R. S.: Go and ask him to come to me.

H.: No. I will go to the river and come back here tomorrow. I will expect to hear your answer.

R. S.: I do not want all my sayings put down on paper. [Matthew Hazard has a sudden idea. He takes his binoculars and unscrews one of its lenses. He tears out the last page of his notebook jottings and crumples it into a loose ball. Focussing the sunlight on it through his lens, he speaks.]

H.: To please you I will destroy some of your words. In a moment this paper will turn to fire and then ash. You will see. I can do this because I have the power to do it. In just this same way, once we have promised to do something, General Quait, and all his soldiers, and I, have the power to do it. Watch.

[The paper begins to scorch, then smoke, and then with a little snap it bursts into flame. There is an intaken hiss of dismay in the crowd of silent Indians, and the chieftain stands up and takes a step back. He scoffs, but his voice is unsteady.]

R. S.: That is not real fire.

[Mr. Hazard picks up the burning paper in his bare hand and swiftly transfers it to the hand of Rainbow Son.]

H.: It burns my hand, and it will burn yours.

[The chief drops the paper quickly enough. It falls to the ground and dies away into crinkling ash. He stands watching it. He seems heavy and dispirited. His head aches with arguments, and now he is depressed by a marvel. He comes back and sits down facing Mr. Hazard.]

R. S.: Very well. I will give you my answer now.

H.: Good.

R. S.: I will give up and go back to the reservation and bring everyone here, if you promise that there will be no punishments.

H.: No. [Standing.] You heard what I said yesterday. You will be sent to Florida and what will happen after that is in the hands of the President. [He turns to go toward his horses, followed by Sergeant White Horn.]

R. S.: Wait. Then I will agree to go to Florida but only for one year and then I will come back to wherever I want to be.

H.: No. [Mr. Hazard unties his horse.] I cannot promise how long you must be in Florida. [He mounts.]

[Rainbow Son rises to his feet, bellowing.]

R. S.: Then I will go on making war just as I like!

H.: I will take your answer to General Quait. [Mr. Hazard turns his horse's head toward the rocky exit from the council place. The chief waits until he was almost gone, and then calls out.]

R. S.: Then come back tomorrow. I have already told you to come back tomorrow. You must do what I tell you. I am the chief here. This is my mountain. We will talk again.

[Mr. Hazard, though he is shaken and drawn by his ordeal of playing a lone hand against extraordinary odds, preserves his severe demeanor.]

H.: I will consider overnight whether to return. If I do, I shall expect the answer I want to hear. We have already talked too much. If you see me after the sun comes up, you will know what must be done.

R. S.: Leave White Horn with us overnight. I will talk to him.

[The lieutenant turns to the sergeant.]

H.: Are you willing to stay? Will you be all right?

[Sergeant White Horn nods. He tells his officer that Rainbow Son evidently does not believe what had been said to him. He believes he can convince him that the lieutenant tells the truth.]

H.: Then stay. I will come for you in the morning.

So it was left.

When he returned for the third day of conference, Lieutenant Hazard found the mountain top empty. He went to his accustomed place by the stream and waited. It was three hours before he saw any sign of life in the rocks, and then Sergeant White Horn came from the rim and sat down beside him.

H. Where are they?

W. H.: They are coming.

H.: Why have I had to wait?

W. H.: They have been talking. Some of them wanted to kill you. Others said no, that would do no good, for the army would come anyway. They talked to me all night. I told them what I knew.

H.: Are you all right?

W. H.: I am all right. Some of them wanted to kill me too.

[At this juncture the council returns. Rainbow Son sits down.]

R. S.: What were we talking about when you left yesterday?

H.: [Unable to help laughing at this question—] We were talking about what you would agree to do.

R. S.: What did I say?

H.: I would rather have you tell me.

[The chieftain deliberates, and then repeats his three suggestions.]

H.: I reject them all.

R. S.: What did you tell me to do, then?

H.: I repeat. Surrender to me without conditions. Come with me to General Quait. You will live. Your children will be better off. I am ready to go. Come with me.

R. S.: Are you crazy? How do I know this? You will take me down the mountain and we will all be killed from behind the rocks.

H.: Trust me. Trust General Quait.

R. S.: Why?

H.: I have trusted you.

As though no one had thought of this for the past three days, the statement caused a minor rustle of sensation throughout the council, which moved Rainbow Son to say, "Yes, that is so."

Lieutenant Hazard noted on his page at this point, "tug of wills." It was now that both adversaries felt bereft of further arguments. There was only force left—force of two kinds. One was physical, and in this the chieftain and his Chiricahuas were superior by a preposterous margin. The other was force of spirit, and in this Mr. Hazard was obliged to put his faith. His arguments had been powerful, and he embodied them in his abiding presence. Facing the chief, he waited. He never took his eyes off the face of his adversary. There is no record of how long he waited. Rainbow Son finally spoke.

R. S.: If I agree to surrender with all my people, and to go to the Lizard at the border, will you agree to do these things—one, that you will send White Horn to the Lizard to have him send us food, some clothes, and tobacco. Two, that you will stay here with us and sleep in our camp until White Horn returns. Three, that we will keep our arms until we see the Lizard. Four, that if we have to defend ourselves on the way, you will fight on our side.

H.: [Instantly.] Yes.

His immediate agreement brought dismay, for each point would have been a pretext for luxurious wrangling in the true style of Apache statesmanship. The young officer agreed because the conditions made no reference to the terms of the captivity which he had promised to the Indians. He leaned forward and grasped the hand of Rainbow Son. They shook hands energetically. Seeing this, the other Indians insisted on shaking hands also. The ceremony consumed some fifteen minutes before all had been accommodated. The occasion seemed to call for further observances, and accordingly, Rainbow Son spoke.

R. S.: If I have surrendered, do not think it is because I was afraid or because of all your soldiers reaching from this mountain top down the river. Not at all. I had a dream last night which told me what to do. It told me about sending for tobacco and food, and having you remain here, and how we would fight beside each other if we met the Mexicans. So you see, these things are important, these ways of knowing what to do.

H.: Surely, surely.

R. S.: Now your old White-Bearded Lizard will have charge of us. He must be our father. We must have all things at his hands. He is the highest chief. The greatest man. Tell him this is how he is. Tell him he must from now on be our God. He must make clouds and rain, and put berries on the bushes, and send us rabbits and antelope. He must bless our children and send grass for our cows and horses. Your God will be our God. Tell him to stand with us on the seventh day [—here Rainbow Son's sense of the deity shifts from his ancestral concepts and merges with a notion of the bleak missionary Creator whom he had encountered during his reservation days—] and wear black clothes and sing together with little books in our hands and not drink mescal. You see? We know all about your God. Tell him we do.

H.: I will tell him.

R. S.: Tell the Lizard he must not let anything bad happen to us. We have surrendered to him and we will keep our promise and he will keep his. [He tugs at Mr. Hazard, shaking hands, pulling at his belt, invading his person to seal an exchange of promises. As the lieutenant steps back, the chieftain thrusts his neck forward and bobs his head in the lieutenant's face, all but breathing into his mouth.]

H.: Yes, yes. We will all keep our promises. You may trust us.

R. S.: Now that I have surrendered I am happy. No more hiding in rocks. No more war and killing. No more running away. Now we will have a green valley to live in. Now all around us will be trees with nuts and bushes with berries. We will see antelope at midday standing off there like little trees. The water will run all day and all night in the ditches. We will eat and dance and sleep. You will see how it will be.

Mr. Hazard knew misgivings about the precise fulfillment of this vision of Rainbow Son's future life, but did not feel it dishonourable not to say so at this juncture. He contented himself with a bow, and a question.

H.: One more thing. Where is the Edwards boy?

R. S.: I know nothing of this.

[Sergeant White Horn makes the liar's signal.]

H.: You took a fourteen-year-old boy with you when you ran off after the Edwards massacre. I want him back. Where is he?

R. S.: I thought we were now friends. Why do you start asking questions again?

H.: This is the last one I shall ask. I want this boy to send back to General Quait with White Horn.

R. S.: Well, I will tell you. He is dead. He tried to run away five days after we got him. I sent after him and when he fought, one of my men killed him.

[Mr. Hazard looks at the sergeant. There is no signal that the statement is false. He has to accept it.]

H.: We shall now send White Horn to General Quait. I shall wait here with you.

R. S.: When I was a free chief, I was the one who gave the orders. Now I bow down to hear your orders.

The conference was adjourned. The sergeant came to me at the border within three days, bringing his own account of what I had been waiting to hear, along with Lieutenant Hazard's notebooks. I instantly complied with Rainbow Son's requests, and sent Sergeant White Horn and a squad of men into Mexico with tobacco, coffee, dried beans, and a few articles of extra clothing—enough to meet the promise given by the lieutenant.

I followed within a few hours, taking along a platoon of the 4th Cavalry. At Avanzada I halted and made my camp. There I encountered the local commandant, who after he brought himself to believe that I had come to receive the surrender of Rainbow Son, gave me all accommodations. One of the most difficult for him to grant was to yield up his claim to the right of receiving this capitulation on behalf of his own government. He gave in only because he was convinced, to the last, that it was impossible for Mr. Hazard, virtually single-handedly, to bring Rainbow Son, his warriors, their women, children and animals, down from the mountain.

I could have no precise knowledge of when I might expect the lieutenant with his procession, but I calculated that he would appear during the day of 12 December. Night fell upon Avanzada with no sign of the arrival which I so earnestly desired. In the morning of 13 December, the commandant paid me a visit to offer his condolences, for, he declared, he knew Rainbow Son, and he could not, on the basis of experience, put faith in any of his promises. I thanked him and resumed the study I was engaged in.

The confidence which I exhibited but, in all honesty, did not wholly feel, was revived at a little past noon, when Sergeant White Horn arrived at my temporary headquarters with a message from Mr. Hazard. It said that Rainbow Son was reluctant to meet me at Avanzada, for fear of treacherous action on the part of the garrison there. He proposed that instead I march to the Bavispe River, where he would give his surrender.

The delay was exacerbating, the new condition a nuisance; but since it was possible that Rainbow Son had grounds for his fears, I determined to do as he asked. On 15 December, at twenty-one minutes past eleven o'clock in the morning, on the west bank of the Bavispe River, I exchanged salutes, and then a hearty handshake, with Lieutenant Matthew Hazard, whom I could scarcely recognise as the same young man who had left me fifty-eight days before.

Behind him stood Rainbow Son. In another moment he came forward to extend his Winchester carbine to me, remarking with an air of complacency and historical consequence, "This is the third time I have surrendered" (i.e., the first time to me in 1875, the second time to Lieutenant Hazard, and the third time to me on this occasion). At the same moment, his followers laid their weapons on the ground. My troopers passed among them and took up all the carbines and rifles, and there, in that most lovely of ravines, where the Bavispe River mildly went its sparkling way, and the shade trees afforded cool and comfort in the universal light, was brought to its end "an Indian war that has raged since the days of Cortez," as I characterized it in my general order no. 14, series 87.

BOOK FOUR

Recessional

"That's my dandy boy," said the
photographer, fixing eternity in
the instant.

i

General Quait, and the other soldiers who knew Matthew Hazard, saw in him, as he returned from Mexico, a man tried and transformed. His youth was gone. Still tall, he carried himself with a slight twist at the shoulders. He had lost thirty pounds. As soon as possible he shaved his face, thus revealing gaunt cheeks and a jaw whose square bones showed clear. His eyes were deeper in their sockets, and his gaze was blacker and brighter than ever, under a frown which had been fixed for life by the empty light of the Mexican desert. Like any survivor of marvels and ordeals, he saw the commonplaces of home with a stare of hungry discovery. In General Quait's camp he found a fresh uniform, hot food, and all the organized reassurances of the society which he knew best. His first want was for news of those to whom he had said good-by so long ago.

"Yes, she is splendid," said the general in reply to Matthew's question. They were taking supper in the general's tent. "I was at Fort Delivery a few weeks ago. I saw her. I saw your child. It was beautiful and touching—how Laura considered everything in relation to you. Poor child. Yes. I came to bring a certain word to Mrs. Prescott. Laura saw me first. She was convinced that it was she to whom I brought the message which it is always so hard to give."

"Then Mrs. Prescott?" asked Matthew, with concern. "Did you see her? How is the colonel?"

"Yes. Ah, lieutenant, it is never any easier to tell it, even now. I carried her word that her husband died of his wounds. We buried him first at the battle site; then later we reburied him at his post. You may see his grave when you return."

"The colonel."

The death of his commander was one more blow which maturity aimed at Matthew. He leaned over in his chair with his hands clasped between his knees, and looked at the earthen floor of the general's tent. His eyes felt dry and hot as he contemplated the inner vision of Jessica Prescott's life henceforth. He felt again the power of his old commander who had sustained him in charity and fondness which he had taken for granted, until now. Now he knew what it was to have someone who suffered you day by day, permitting you to be as you were, only helping you, with scarcely noticed guidings, to be as you were at your best. He would not have been ashamed to show grief, as he might have shown it two months ago; but now all feeling was contained within him and would not reveal itself. Having borne much, he could bear more, and show nothing.

"The colonel," he repeated.

"Yes," said General Quait. "Your good commander. Yes." But life continued. The general extended a flat opened tin to Matthew. "Will you have another trifle of these mushrooms in claret which my man in Philadelphia imports from Paris?"

"No, thank you, sir."

"Then permit me." The general helped himself. "Yes. I do think, that, in this context, sad as it is, we might as well project the next moves which await us."

The old gentleman was the world. Matthew straightened up. The abounding and disciplined energy in the commanding general had its instructive aspects. For the next hour Matthew learned what his future duties would be, and where, and what must be done with the surrendered Indians.

Fort Delivery would be deactivated as rapidly as proper regard for government property and disposition of the garrison would permit. Mr. Hazard would return there forthwith. He would find Captain Gray in command, instead of Mr. Mainwaring, who by now had left for Fort Leavenworth, there to await official inquiry into his serious dereliction of duty.

Mrs. Prescott would also have gone by now—she had relations in Washington, it was her old home; there she would without doubt feel well enwrapped in the comforts of the familiar and the concern of her friends. If Matthew was disappointed at not being able to see her immediately, he would be gratified to know that he would see her very shortly in Washington, for it was General Quait's desire that, so soon as Mr. Hazard's final duties with the garrison permitted, he enjoy a period of leave, and then take his family and report to Washington, where for perhaps a year General Quait would require his services in concluding the preparation of official reports and assigning to proper bureaus the records of the campaign just ended. At the end of that time, they would consider what would next prove to be the suitable assignment of the lieutenant. There was one further occasion for his early return to Washington which General Quait had in mind but need not now elucidate.

To continue. Fort Delivery would remain under the command of Captain Gray until its deactivation was complete. This was a task for an experienced officer, and Gray had proved himself equal to any task which required common sense, and any situation which deserved severe analysis. Meanwhile, the garrison must be transferred, with all its animals, wagons and movable equipment. This meant a march overland to Fort Union, New Mexico, where Troop F would be stationed until reassigned by the adjutant general. Lieutenant Hazard would command the march. It should entail little hardship and hardly any inconvenience. The Indian difficulties were at last all done for. It was the season of the year when the desert was most clement. A march to the Rio Grande, and up its grand meandering valley, then to Fort Union in the fine meadows of northeastern New Mexico, would be an idyllic journey—granted there would come no sudden sweeps of blizzard off the buffalo plains or across Texas from the Gulf of Mexico such as sometimes, it must be admitted, broke upon the land in that season. It was entirely within the discretion of Lieutenant Hazard whether he would carry his family with him in an ambulance comfortably fitted out, or whether he would dispatch them by rail to the East.

For the rest, tomorrow morning, the surrendered Indians, under an escort from the 4th, would proceed to their old reservation, there to be sorted, as it were, ticketed, and divided into small bands which would be conveniently managed, each by an overseer, and put upon railroad cars for their removal to Florida. The Apache scouts of the Army, having proved their trustworthiness, were to serve as overseers, translators and comforters of the Indian people on their long journey.

"Then Joe Dummy—White Horn, sir?" asked Matthew. "He will go with them?"

"Indubitably. One of the best. Perhaps our very best man in this category. I am citing him for extraordinary valor, in his long duty with you."

"I am glad, sir. He deserves all recognition. When do they start? I must see him before. He is a friend. I have often wondered what was to become of him."

"It is a difficulty. I trust the Army will always have a place for his sort. I am asking that he be ordered to Fort Wingate or some other post in the Southwest when he returns from his brief trip to Florida. He will never be content anywhere but in these spaces."

"Thank you, general."

"The march will start early tomorrow. Do you get to your sleep now, if you would be up to see them off."

ii

Long before the bugle, Matthew was awakened by the gathering of the marchers. In the slowly fading darkness they milled in loose circles. Their voices rose in complaint. Soldiers gave orders which nobody understood. When Indians did not leap at once into formations upon command, the soldiers were angry, and began to push the Indians into ranks. Day broke upon a scene of indignity and misery. General Quait came from his tent to observe the event. By the time he reached the throng, some sort of order had been established, and he was called upon to do nothing but stand and watch. Matthew stood with him.

"Ah. It is sadly prophetic, I fear," said the general.

"Sir?"

"This sort of treatment—it is so immediately the reflection of the attitude of our people toward these others that I fear the Indians will meet similar behavior wherever they may be taken."

"Our men should be told—"

"They have been told, lieutenant. First they must feel. What's this? I do believe we have a visitor. Yes, sergeant?"

It was Sergeant White Horn who came to salute the General and speak to him. He spoke Apache. At the end of his message, General Quait turned to Matthew and said,

"He brings me a request. Rainbow Son wants to see me. Come with me."

They all strode over to the long, straggling line of the Indian families in the middle of which stood the chief, hugging his blanket about him, and showing a face of numb concern which gave him almost a youthful look. When he saw the two officers approaching he hugged himself upright into a stance of sprightly charm, lifting his face like a boy, and making every effort to present himself appealingly.

"You want to see me, my man?" said the general, and repeated his words in Spanish.

"I do. Yes. I forgot something. It is strange. How could I have forgotten? But now I remember. There is something I must do. I thought I must ask you about it."

"And what is that?"

"You see, everything happened so fast, I did not think of all the things I should have thought of." He turned to Matthew. "The other commander, my friend here, gave me no time to make all my arrangements. I completely forgot a most important matter."

"Well? Well?"

"You see, I have a herd of cows, quite a large herd of cattle, that belongs to me and my people, and I forgot about it. The herd is down near Mulatos."

"Do you know where that is, lieutenant?" asked the general.

"Yes, sir. It is on the eastern side of the Sierra Madre. Three hundred miles or more from here. We passed by that way."

"Yes," said the general to Rainbow Son. "And what do you propose to do?"

"Ah, yes," replied the chief, coming close and showing his jumbled teeth in the general's face, "I thought the great Lizard would tell me to go and get my cattle, and take care of them, and bring them back, so my people will have meat, and so nobody else will steal the cows. Cows are valuable. Everybody wants cows. Mine are fine cows. I will just take some of my men and go to get the cows and we will come back as soon as all this is managed. This is what I forgot and what I say must be done now."

General Quait stepped back a pace and clasped his hands behind him. He tilted his head and a filmy expression of compassion went over his face as he looked at the Indian. Matthew glanced at Sergeant White Horn, who slowly and firmly put his lower lip over his upper lip as if to touch his nose with it. Matthew nodded and was about to warn the general of falsehood when the general said,

"Rainbow Son, you desire to run away. You have no cattle. If you had cattle they would have been with you on the mountain, and you would have driven them here with you. I understand how you must want to run away. But if you were to run away, you would soon make war again, and we would have our work to do all over again. Every man wants liberty. But every man wants life and safety, too. When you have liberty you destroy another man's life and safety. It cannot be so. For a time you must now be without your liberty until it is safe to give it back to you. You will be kindly treated. You will live and your people will live, and so will my people whom you would otherwise endanger. Go with your people now, and remain peaceful, and show them how to be good people, and the time will come when you may all have your own lives again. Now go. Go."

Rainbow Son stood irresolute. Black rage began to change his dark seamy face. He looked around. Soldiers were everywhere. The wagons for the march were drawing into line ahead. Mounted guards were patrolling the whole long formed procession of his followers. Women gazed at him in heavy spirits. All was lost. He had lost it. Indian children watched to see what was happening. Their lives were about to be forever and entirely changed, though they could not know it. Full realization seemed at last to come to Rainbow Son. He turned to the general and said,

"We are alone."

"No—some of your own men—some of your best men will go with you and help you. Here is Sergeant White Horn. He will talk for you, and help you. He will help the Army, too, so everybody will understand each other. You will not be alone if you have him and others like him."

"It is a strange thing. I used to know what to say to everybody. Now it is you who know what to say to everybody."

"That is what I am here to do."

"How did you know where we were? For a long time we could not go anywhere without having you know where we were!"

"Did you see sunlight flashing from the mountains and the hills?"

"Yes. I saw the flashes and I said they were spirits, and I refused to look at them again. I was afraid they were telling you things."

"They were. That is how I knew. I knew as fast as the eye could see the sunlight. My soldiers told me with little pieces of glass."

"That is what defeated me. I could not move. When I went to the mountains I went at night and nobody was there to see. And yet you knew what trail I took."

"I knew from my little flashes the next day."

"Signals. Like smoke."

"Yes, like smoke, but quicker and farther. You could see my lights ten times—twenty times, as far as you could see smoke."

"Everything now is ten times more. Twenty times more."

Saying nothing further, Rainbow Son turned back and stepped into the waiting column. The sun was rising. It washed everything showing toward the east with a pour of glorious light, like molten gold that clung to every sweep or wrinkle of surface. Far ahead, a command sang out and was relayed down the line through the mounted guard. Almost imperceptibly the column began to move out. In a disordered shudder the movement begun at the head of the column traveled down its whole length until here, where stood the general, the lieutenant and the scout, it was taken up in shuffle and push by the Chiricahua followers of Rainbow Son. Their long walk had started. General Quait turned away. The sight moved him and he did not want to be moved.

White Horn looked at the column and knew he must assume his duty alongside it. He came near to Matthew and peered closely into his eyes. He said nothing, but his eloquence was enough to reach the lieutenant. Matthew put out his hand. White Horn shook hands with him.

"I will look out for you, White Horn," said Matthew. "I will see that the Army takes care of you. I will see you again somewhere."

White Horn nodded and nodded. He stepped away backward. He turned and walked a few paces. He stopped and turned around and saw his officer again for a moment. He turned and went again. Again he paused and faced Matthew. When he wanted to speak from his deepest feeling, White Horn spoke from the past which had created him, with the land which was his mother, and out of dreams and visions which even he might not remember but only carry within him all his life. From long ago, something made him think of ghosts who had coarse dust running out of their eyes in dry streams. He bent to the ground and took up in each hand a palmful of dust. Rising, he looked at Matthew, and then he lifted his hands to his eyes, and through the funneling of his fingers he let fall to the earth two streams

of dust from beside his eyes, like dry, unnatural tears. More sad than
tears, the dust of the earth falling from living eyes spoke for him to
Matthew, mourning the end of a time, and a people, and a friend.
When the dust had all fallen, he turned and fell in beside the moving
column and with them trudged away.

iii

Prescott Hazard, on seeing his father at Fort Delivery a few days later,
did not know him.

"Let me take him," said Laura, reaching for the child who wailed
with fright in the arms of this tall, gaunt stranger. Matthew yielded
him up and saw as Laura turned her face to the child's to comfort
him that she too was struggling to restore her image of her husband,
which had been broken by the long ordeal from which he now returned. "He will be all right as soon as he is used to you," she said.
"He is just at the age when he learns so many new things, and you
have been gone so long, he remembers how you looked, and now—"

"Am I so changed?"

"You have been through so much. Everything you have told me is
still so strange and I see the marks of it all over you. You have
changed *inside.*"

"Ah. Laura, my dearest, not here." He pressed his heart. He
hungrily touched her. She hushed the child and put him down. She
turned to Matthew and took him in her arms, looking up into his
face. Her expression mirrored his. In her lovely face he saw the reflection of his suffering, his gratitude and love. She was timid with
him, as though with a stranger.

"No," she said, "not there—or here, either"—her own heart. "You
are here, and safe, and so am I, now."

They made finish with words.

iv

A week later they were ready to go. The troop stood in mounted
order. The garrison wagons were filled and waiting. Every movable

object had been either packed or destroyed. All rooms except the bed-room at headquarters and the office were empty. There was a cot in each of these. One was to be used by the last post commander, Captain A. Cedric Gray, the other by Trumpeter Corporal Rainey. These two soldiers would be the last to leave. They awaited only an inspector from Department who would give final approval for the abandonment of Fort Delivery.

"Until then," said the captain to Matthew, "I'll be sitting here, thinking about where to go when I retire. Not that I will be idle. It isn't in me to be idle. I am making an album of water-color drawings of this forlorn place. I can always look at them and see what went on here."

"I don't like to leave you here, sir."

"Rubbidge. It's all very well to be sentimental about places. Now don't be getting sentimental about persons."

"Laura can't make up her mind whether she is glad or sorry to go."

"She is sorry now, but she will be glad in ten days."

"Is the trumpeter ready, sir?"

"He is waiting by the flagpole."

With the departure of the garrison, Fort Delivery would officially cease to be an active post of the United States Army. The two men left behind would remain merely as caretakers until relieved.

"I am ready, sir, if you are."

"We shall go."

The old post commander and the young commander of the garrison, which was drawn up ready to march out through the main gate, walked to the flagpole together. Laura and Prescott got down from the seats of their ambulance, which was parked at the head of the column. Trumpeter Rainey was standing at the base of the flagpole holding his bugle. At a nod from Captain Gray, Matthew turned to the formation and gave the command,

"Tro-o-o-o-p—attention!"

After a brief pause, he commanded,

"Pre-e-e-e-sent—arms!"

The sabers flashed up before the faces of the troopers.

The trumpeter, with no further command, but after a moment like a drawn breath, in which all the silence possible in the world seemed to enfold the buildings, the open dusty ground, the scrubby desert reaching away everywhere, the wind-softened graves in the cemetery lying off to the east, the men and women waiting on horseback or in the wagons, brought up his bugle and sounded To the Colors. When he paused, a young trooper came forward and took the lanyards of the flagpole in hand. The bugle sounded Retreat, and the youngster with the ropes slowly fed one upward and the other downward, and the garrison flag, at ten o'clock in the morning, came slowly traveling down to the ground for the last time. The trumpeter played the call slowly, extending the last four notes as though they must never cease to sound. But they ceased as they must.

"Or-der-r-r-r—arms!"

Since everybody knew what to do, the next moments were active, the farewells short.

"At a walk, forwa-a-a-r-d—march!"

The command rang forth in Matthew's voice. The column moved. In the leading ambulance sat Laura. She pressed her lips together. Prescott watched her with concern. Her effort at control was useless. Her feeling welled up and broke. Matthew was riding at the head of the column. She was glad he could not see her. He would ask her why she wept, as though he would not know that she wept with love for all of life itself which she had known there with him.

One day soon the last two men would leave the post, and the quadrangle would be empty to the workings of the desert. Matthew had seen ruins of adobe walls. He remembered General Quait's lectures on erosion. The Mexican winds, the rain when it finally came in season, would take off the shoulders of the buildings. Settlers far away might think it worth while to come for timber and whatever metal might be had. Topless doors would lead nowhere. Floors open to the sky would rise up gradually in the corners of rooms, and grasses would spring up. The walls would fall unevenly and at long intervals. Little mounds would remain where houses stood and then melt away into the flat desert. Made of dust, they would surrender to dust. Old wagons ruts would hold longest, coming nowhere. No one would hear what would sound—the sun-rising cry of a cicada, the sharp click of some shelled insect, the question of the prairie owl. The column drew away, taking its memories along.

V

Four weeks later, Lieutenant and Mrs. Matthew Hazard and their
infant son Prescott, on their way to Washington, D. C., paused for a
visit at Fort Porter, New York, with the Commanding Officer and
Mrs. Huntleigh Greenleaf, at The Castle. They were received in
Buffalo at the steamer landing at the foot of Main Street by Lieutenant
Harvey Greenleaf.

The greetings were scarcely done when Laura exclaimed,

"Harvey! Something is wrong! Is it Papá?"

The lieutenant blew a breath and shook his head.

"No," he said, "it's Mother."

"What do you—you don't mean—"

"No, not yet, but they tell us she hasn't much time."

"Oh, no! What is it? When did it happen?"

As they went in a closed carriage to the Front, he told them what
they must hear. Four days ago, while the Hazards were still traveling
homeward for a happy reunion, Drusilla Greenleaf lost consciousness
at the dinner table in the evening. She was just saying how many things
she must do to prepare for their visit when she fell back in her velvet
chair. The post surgeon was called and she was taken to bed. At first
they feared a stroke, but by the following day it was evident that she
had suffered a spasm of the heart. She was in bed, very weak,
wretched with worry over the arrangements for the visit which now
were in disarray, and above all astonished.

"Astonished?" said Laura.

Harvey remained himself.

"She cannot get used to the idea that it isn't Father who is ill.
This seems all wrong to her. She has always been the strong one. It
makes her furious."

"Harvey. How can you talk so now?"

"We never fooled ourselves over anything before. I don't see why
we should begin now."

Mockery which had once given Laura a tingling delight of cleverness and guilt now offended her. She now knew more about everything of any real importance in life than her famous brother, with all
his experience. She looked at him. He was still handsome, clean and
ruddy, beautifully put together out of flesh and cloth and leather,

with a sweet, teasing light in his eye, and on his fine lips a smile which suggested the joys of tasting. Everything was his, but nothing touched him. She turned to Matthew, who held his little son on his lap. She saw a seamed face and a fixed gather of brow, and under this a strong, black and white regard which saw whatever it looked at. Her heart turned over.

"Father is holding up remarkably well," said Harvey. "He seems to know what to do. Perhaps he has known all along, but has never before had a chance to show anyone."

"When did you come home?" asked Laura coolly.

"They sent for me by telegraph. I reached here yesterday."

"Shall I be able to see Mamá?"

"She is waiting for you. Father is waiting to see his grandson."

Harvey leaned across her to nip Prescott by the cheek. The child knew at once that this was a friend. He gave a broad, delighted smile.

"That is your Uncle Harvey," said Matthew. "Give him a nice big kiss."

Harvey took the baby, rode him on his knee, and said,

"Matt, by God. I used to think I was the smart one and you the slow one. But damned if I don't think you have put it all over me. This fine boy. That fine record you made out there. A married man."

"I wish you meant that, Harvey," said Laura.

"Maybe I will, some day."

They rode in silence through the snowy streets over cobblestones. The movement of the carriage pleased the baby. He played with the gray silk-braided window strap. The trees were black and bare against the pale gray sky over Lake Erie. In the air a pungent wintry dampness, sweet and piercing, brought Matthew sharply back to the feeling of life in the eastern United States. Unless he shut his eyes he could scarcely remember waverings of crystal heat above bare rocky outlines of distant mountains.

If he expected another image to persist—his memory of Mrs. Greenleaf—it was gone when he saw her.

She received the Hazards in her blue silk bedroom on the second floor of The Castle. Surrounded by all the gleaming surfaces, the gauzy comforts, of her taste, and attended by two nurses and her anxious husband, she was no longer the luxurious and commanding woman who had lived so firmly by the mirror and the banknote for sixty-one years. Matthew, through his fixed consoling smile, had to work to recognize his mother-in-law. For one thing, she seemed greatly diminished in size. The removal of all accessories of style brought her outline in. Her hair was drawn flat and plain across her skull. Her face was without rouge or pencil. Its whiteness was shadowed by hollows under her cheeks and jaws. Her nose seemed prominent. Her eyes searched and searched for life, which she knew was leaving her. She touched Prescott Hazard with her pallid fingers when he was held above her by his father. The child rounded his own eyes big and wide, looking at his grandmother's, which were as big and round. He was quickly taken away by his father and grandfather, and Laura was left alone with her mother.

Mrs. Greenleaf shut her eyes and held Laura's hand in a grasp of thin, dry, hot fingers. Through them Laura could feel her mother's strong desire to live, and in her mother's closed face she read the uselessness of that desire. Mrs. Greenleaf's lips moved and Laura leaned down to hear her.

"It hurts all the time," she murmured, faintly gesturing toward her breast, her heart. "I should think they could make it stop."

Laura could not help smiling a little at this, even as she felt a sting of sympathy rise to her eyes. It was so truly like her mother to repose confidence in giving an order and expecting it to be obeyed. She sat with her in silence for an hour. Only twice again did Drusilla Greenleaf speak to her daughter. She said,

"Where will you go from here?"

"To Washington. We'll be stationed there for a while."

"You see. How foolish not to go years ago when I said you should. You're going after all."

"But we're going now only because we were out West—"

Mrs. Greenleaf rolled her head from side to side. She lapsed into silence in which a bitter line came to her mouth. Presently she opened her eyes and asked,

"Will you do something for me?"

"Oh, my darling, everything."

"Have the chaplain come to see me."

"Of course. When?"

"Now."

The nurses returned and Laura went on her errand. She was moved by this most unexpected evidence of her mother's acknowledgment that she must die. Aside from weddings, christenings and other people's funerals her mother had never given interest or confidence to religion or its deputies. Now it seemed that Drusilla, with the courage of finality, would order her soul before God. There could hardly be more ultimate, more severe, realism than this, and Laura hurried to do her mother's wish with a sense of the largest moments in her own life, of which this was one, along with her wedding to Matthew, the birth of her son, and Matthew's return safe, but older, from Mexico.

In a quarter of an hour she brought the post chaplain, a Major Lowell, to her mother. Drusilla motioned to her to stay. The chaplain, an Episcopal clergyman, produced a narrow purple stole which he put around his neck. He went to the bedside and knelt down. Drusilla, with great effort, gave him her hand in one of her old gestures of social grace.

"You are kind to come," she said.

"I am grateful, and God is glad, that you wanted me, my child."

Drusilla's eye regarded him with a remote flash of opinion. Laura translated it later to Matthew. It said that no one had ever before said "my child" to the wife of the commanding officer. She seemed to doubt that anybody with such manners could speak accurately for the gladness of God. She shut her eyes and indicated with a finger that the chaplain should proceed with whatever it was he was accustomed to do at moments like this.

Major Lowell, a tall, thin man with piercing dark eyes in a hawk's face, put his face into his hands and began to pray in a cavernous rumble. His prayer was devoted to the stark matter of petitioning Almighty God to receive in mercy an erring soul about to take leave of the human condition. He was moved by his own agency in this august and grave duty, and by the words he uttered, as they treated of contrition, judgment, mercy and eternity. Drusilla Greenleaf was unable to see herself in any of it. She opened her eyes and spoke sharply to her comforter.

"Stop that muttering," she said, "I don't like all that. I want you to tell me all the loveliest things you know!"

The chaplain glanced at Laura in dismay. She could hardly suppress a smile over an intuitive glimpse of her mother's vision of heaven—it must be a boudoir swathed in lace and shining with satin, and scented with hothouse flowers in silver trumpet-like vases, where celestial voices repeated soothing mottoes chosen from albums covered in watered silk. Raising his shaggy black eyebrows at Laura, Major Lowell asked silently if her mother were out of her wits. Laura shook her head. Mrs. Greenleaf had never been more herself than just then. If he disapproved of her mortal desires, he must simply do his duty as he saw it. Shaking his head, he turned back to the bed-side and said, earnestly,

"This is no time for soft sentiments, my child. I am making your last petition to Our Heavenly Father. Pray with me in your heart for His mercy upon your repentance."

He resumed his prayer. Drusilla lay with her eyes shut and her brows arched in repudiation of the chaplain's view of her future. Repentance? What on earth had she to repent of? She let him pray, if that was what he came for, but she made no further acknowledg-ment of his presence. In a little while he finished and went away. Mrs. Greenleaf was sleeping. Laura left her and went downstairs to her father.

It was comforting to see how much of life there was where she found her father making friends with his grandson. Prescott and his grandfather were on the floor of the commanding officer's study, sur-rounded with toys. These were some of Colonel Greenleaf's most treasured books, now used as building blocks; specimens from the colonel's collection of old pistols which made satisfactory clicking noises; and a few of his stouter silver snuffboxes, whose lids could be endlessly opened and shut. With the snuffboxes the two had in-vented a game—hiding a box behind him, the colonel would put into it a coin or a twist of paper which the baby could discover and move into another box. She had never seen her father more content, or her son, either.

In the yellow drawing room Harvey and Matthew were having a cigar. With all they had to talk about, it was odd that they both found it difficult to say much to each other. The reason, though neither thought of it clearly, was that while Harvey was the same man as ever, Matthew was not.

"Yes," said Harvey, "it must have been quite an experience."

"It was," said Matthew, and could think of no way to bring Mexico with any particular true effect to his classmate.

"Fifty-eight days of it? By God, no wonder it wore you down. But it was worth it, eh? You brought in the old villain, after all, and that's what counts. It must have tickled my uncle Alex, that queer old bird. I never could understand how he got where he did in the Army."

"General Quait," said Matthew, unable to help the sounds of priggishness he made, "is one of the greatest soldiers and most re-markable men this country has had."

"You really think so, eh?"

"We won't see his like again."

"Well, that's a fact, anyhow," said Harvey with a laugh. Moving on to more congenial matters, he said, "Tell me, Matt, how did you manage things with that girl, that lieutenant's wife, you told me about when you were here before—Kitty?" His eyes kindled and his lips shone. "Yes, it was Kitty."

"She is dead."

"Ah. Too bad. Did Laura ever find out?"

"No. Shall we go to her?"

They went toward the study where they heard sounds of merriment arising together from age and infancy. It was a funny thing, reflected Harvey, how a friend could go off on another track, and get away from you, perhaps forever. He would miss old Matt, whenever he should happen to think about it.

Late at night all the household was awakened. The doctors had returned to The Castle. Before dawn they came from the sickroom with final news. Mrs. Greenleaf was gone.

The funeral was held three days later. Colonel Greenleaf expected now to retire, and after being relieved in due course from his command at Fort Porter, he thought he would go down to Washington and take a house—a rather fine house, as he was now rich. He would be glad to be near Laura and her family. She was happy at the prospect, and asked him to have her wedding presents, which were boxed and stored at Fort Porter, sent to her as soon as she had her own address.

The Hazards soon left for Washington. They were eager to see Mrs. Prescott and General Quait, whom they would find there.

vi

In her bag of black silk cording she carried Laura's note, and now that she was about to mount the stairs leading upward from the lobby, she made a considerable matter of opening the bag, finding the folded note and bringing it out to read in it again the room number she must look for. Even as she did so, she smiled and shook her head with impatience over her own dishonesty. She knew the room number by heart. She knew every step that led to it up the stairs and down the corridor. If she had pretended to have forgotten the room number it was probably—she told herself without mercy—to put off for as long as possible a recognition which must move her more than she would like to reveal.

She must find the third floor. The stairway rose in a golden gloom, with spherical lanterns on each newel post. At the end of the second flight she paused to catch her breath, and she felt her heart beating once again at that final landing. How it had made her laugh, to feel so breathless with love, so long ago. And now she was breathless for another reason—she was old and climbing was not easy for her any more. In a moment she stepped along down the wide corridor which smelled of dampened dust and furniture polish. At the far end she saw again a window misted over with heavy lace curtains. In front of it was a tall taboret supporting a potted fern which looked black against the sweet gray daylight of winter over the Potomac. At the end of the corridor she turned to the right where another hall at right angles took her along within the front of the hotel. The carpeting was worn, but the colors and the design were the same—large pink roses amidst green leafery against dark brown, with borders of Prussian blue.

The floor creaked once, slightly, under her step, and she smiled to think that she might be heavy enough to cause the flooring in Willard's Hotel to creak beneath her. But the fact was she had grown thinner in the past weeks, and surely all she heard was the voice of an old building making complaint at being used. The door was the second from the end on her left. Before she knocked on its panels, just below the white porcelain plaque with the room number on it in black enamel, she stood and shut her eyes. It was most ridiculous at her age that so much feeling should rise within her at returning here, and she must control it before she saw the Hazards. They were dear, good, kind young friends, but—she was certain—nothing in their lives had yet fitted them to know how susceptible under sorrow a person could become, despite every consideration for others and good sense for one's own sake.

Within her closed vision she saw the room in every detail. She held her black-gloved hands across her heart and breathed against them as slowly as possible.

It was a large, high, square room, with a ceiling of white plaster molded in a design of vine leaves and grapes along the edges. From its center depended a gas chandelier with shades of etched ruby-red glass. There were two tall windows overlooking Pennsylvania Avenue. These were faced inside with dark walnut shutters divided halfway up. Many combinations of light and shade, shutter and pane, were possible with them. Long ago she had tried them all. Lace curtains hung straight to the floor from the tops of the windows, which, like the top of the doorway, were arched and outlined in white plaster molding. The door was thick and wide, with six panels of black walnut. The doorknob was breast-high, and made of cast brass which used to require two small hands to turn it, while someone stood by laughing and holding gloves and reticule and whatever else had to be set aside for the handling of the doorknob. The walls were covered with paper generally pale green on which wide vertical stripes of yellow roses and green leaves reached from floor to ceiling. Between the windows was a white marble fireplace with a Franklin stove in it which gave forth a glimpsing firelight and a warm inviting breath on a winter day like this, or any other winter day when it was happier to be indoors. The floor was solidly covered with a carpet like that of the corridor outside—pink, green and brown. In the center of the room stood a marble-topped table with beveled edges, supported by a carved walnut standard which divided itself into four feet with little brass claws. By the table rested two low-armed walnut chairs covered in forest-green velvet, and two more like them stood against the wall.

At one side of the room was a towering wardrobe of walnut with two doors and carved wooden handles. On the inner face of the right hand door of the wardrobe the wood was unfinished. She knew that near the center of the panel was a little cluster of three dark wooden knots. They were placed in such a position to each other as to make a face, with two eyes and a mouth. By the lines of the grain about the knots, the face seemed to have a hazy smile. Facing the wardrobe beyond the center table was a wide bed with a walnut headboard as high as the uplifted hand of a man standing. From the bed the eye looked out through the upper panes of the windows above the wooden shutters closed below, and saw the sky over Washington, which always held so much watery color, and told so much about the flavor of the day outside, from which it was possible to judge whether it would be wise to arise and go out, or wiser to remain here, for as long as could be, with someone never to part from willingly.

Jessica Prescott opened her eyes and smoothed her black gloves and knocked on the door.

vii

How difficult, for almost half an hour, to find each other easily again! News of Matthew's exploit, the effects of it upon him, the sad events at Fort Porter, all diverted them from the difficulty of speaking of Colonel Prescott, hearing of him, acknowledging his widow. It was fortunate that Prescott Hazard was there, for in his assumption of being delightfully the center of this, like any, occasion, his father and mother and godmother found a common refuge from the feeling which both united and divided.

"Even in these weeks," said Jessica, "how he has grown! How adorably fresh he looks!" She held him on her lap. "And will you stand up, and will you sit down?" she said to him, "and will you stand up, and will you sit down, and down, and down?" while the baby, smiling aloud, executed the evolutions proper to her chant.

"Don't let him tire you," said Laura, reaching for him.

Jessica yielded him up with a droll sigh.

"Ah, when will I ever learn to be an old woman? I don't feel like it at all."

"Oh, no, my darling Mrs. Prescott, I did not mean at all to—"

"It is time you came to call me Jessica. Both of you. I am not your commander's wife any longer. I command nothing, so you can be quite free with me."

Matthew on an impulse, blushing deeply, went to her and kissed her cheek.

"You will always be the wife of our commanding officer," he said.

"Matthew, do try to find something to blush over whenever possible. It is most becoming."

"What a becoming dress," said Laura. Jessica wore black ribbed silk, made into a small jacket with velvet frogs. Her skirt was full, draped up at the sides, and edged with a deep ruffle at the bottom. At her throat was a white lace collar and bow, fixed with a large amethyst surrounded by small pearls. On her head was a small oval hat of black sealskin with a cluster of small black ostrich plumes at the front. Her black dotted veil was drawn up above the tip of her nose. Her deep gray-blue eyes were vivid and shining behind the veil. She wore a little cape of black sealskin that came to her elbows and carried a black sealskin muff to which a bunch of violets was pinned. Her face was white.

"Do you know it is over ten years since I have been in Washington?" said Jessica. For the first time since they had come together again, they all felt an easing intimacy in the air. It was Jessica who brought it. "I was here then when my father died. All the changes in our family since then have been dealt with by mail. It is so strange—and do you know? I feel quite detached about all of it. I walked past our old house on Lafayette Square, and I saw myself on the iron balcony with my mother when I was a tiny child, when Mr. Polk used to drive by and tip his hat, and I thought he was tipping it to me, but of course it was to Mamá. And though the house looks exactly the same—Washington doesn't try to change itself much—I hadn't a qualm about not being in it while I am in town. My brother, who owns it, has rented it to somebody in the cabinet. He offered to recover it and let me have it, but I said no, I could not possibly keep it up. He wanted me to come to live with his family, then, but I said no, I was perfectly comfortable for the moment at my cousin Lily's. My other brother's widow asked me, also, but I do think—two widows under one roof? I think not. And do you know? My boys both wanted me near—they are at the military academy. But I said no, the thing for me to do was to take the advice I gave to Papá when Mamá died. I told him not to make up his mind to anything for a year. I said he was in no state to decide anything wisely. So I have decided not to decide anything just yet."

Matthew and Laura exchanged a meaningful look. Laura's face showed forth a deep disappointment.

"What are you looking back and forth about?" asked Jessica. "You make me feel like someone prattling nonsense."

Laura nodded to Matthew, who said,

"Mrs. Prescott—Jessica—we hate to hear you say you won't decide anything. We have something we want you to decide to do."

"And what, my dear?"

"We are looking for a house, and when we find one, we want you to come and be with us, for good. We have had this all planned for several weeks."

It was not easy for Jessica to believe that she was so well loved. She came up straighter in her green velvet chair and blinked several times. Her lashes, wet with tears, caught in her veil and she had to draw the veil a trifle away. Her voice when she could speak was reduced and edgy under her control.

"You will have to let me off from saying anything except no, just now," she said. "I can tell you more another time. I cannot do as you ask, for everybody's sake, but that you asked me, is—is wonderfully dear to me."

Laura was about to urge the claim of their love upon her, but Matthew restrained her with a little shake of his head.

"We will say no more about it, now," he said, "but we will always be ready for you, if you will ever come."

"My darlings, that assurance is better than having a house to live in. I'm sorry if I am all too full of feeling. I am really quite all right. It is really such a good thing to be able to be with you and talk. You know I have been to Batavia?"

"Batavia?"

"In New York State, where Hiram came from. I went to see his two sisters who are still living there in the great, square farmhouse on their family place. Such old, *old* ladies, all full of memories of his boyhood, and the gossip of the Mexican War, and not much since. Two tiny gray wrenlike creatures. All the rooms but two are kept closed and dark. They let me see everything, and I saw so much of Hiram as a boy. You know he always kept something boylike about him? You must have felt it, even if you could not put your finger on it. I found so much peace in the place where he grew up. It was like knowing more about him, and that is a very dear thing to have happen now. It was good to see what made him. I took many walks in the fields, the woods, the little hills and creeks about the farm. What lovely places for a boy to discover things! I felt renewed. It was most curious. But most true. And when the Army brings him home to me, it will be there that he will be buried. He will lie there forever. Do you see?"

She suddenly stood up and took a step toward the wardrobe. She touched the right-hand panel.

"May I open this door?" she asked.

"Of course," said Laura, wondering.

"There is a face inside it," said Jessica, "a little smiling, rather sleepy face, I am sure there is."

She opened the door and there it was—the little cluster of walnut knots, making the face of some secret guardian of the room and its passing lives.

"How in the world did you know!" exclaimed Laura.

Jessica shut the door and faced them.

"I suppose I never told you. I know every stick in this room, though it is all faded and worn, now. Hiram was wounded and in the hospital here during the War. I worked in the hospital. We fell in love and we eloped. This is the room where we spent our honeymoon. We had four days here before he returned to the War."

They had been hearing about Colonel Prescott, but now, for a moment of power which seized them all in the tightest feeling, he was in their midst. The Hazards had never seen anyone else in the light of their own love and its discoveries. Now they saw Jessica and her lost husband so, and the room took on an energy to move them, and memory was not only a reference, but a force. The young man and wife saw themselves in all others now. The moment passed, but not its meaning. Their love became large enough to hold the world.

"We had nothing," said Jessica, "everything was against us, we did not care. How amazed you are, my dear children. But yes— we were *young*, once, and what anybody ever feels has always been felt before by someone. I must go. Lily is expecting me for tea. You are coming to us for tea soon. I hear the general is in town. You must bring him. Matthew, what will you be doing?"

"I'll be in the War Department with General Quait for a while."

"How proud of you Hiram would be! And so am I." She came to him and embraced him. "What a boy you were when we took command. And now look at you."

This very room, thought Laura.

viii

A week later when his leave was up, Matthew reported to the office of General Quait in the War Department. He was ushered through a bare spacious outer office by a civilian clerk into a long narrow room which was the general's private office. Wearing uniform, Matthew was surprised to find his chief in civilian clothes. The general wore a tall starched collar, a green silk cravat, a long, tight, black frock coat faced with satin lapels, and old-fashioned trousers in a large black and white checked pattern strapped under his black boots.

His tall thinness was exaggerated by the costume, which hung upon him as though on a clothes tree. He had worn a uniform for such a long lifetime that he looked ill-fitted and awkward in any other clothes. Even so, it was clear that he felt like a beau and a dandy, for he stroked his shining lapels and he frisked the pleated tails of his frock coat.

"Ha, Matthew," he called, tipping up and down on his polished boots, "welcome, most welcome. I trust you can find your way through my fine philosophical clutter." He advanced the length of the narrow room through a path scarcely clear amidst a profusion of objects on all sides. Shaking hands he drew Matthew to the far end of the room, indicating, as they went, something of the character of his collections.

Bookshelves reached to the ceiling and books were piled in every possible space. Having run out of shelving, the general had set books on the floor, in columns and pyramids, and on table and desk tops. Matthew was dazed by the jumble—stuffed specimens of small animals and large birds perched anywhere a precarious foothold was available; a terrestrial globe, a celestial globe, an astrolabe; a microscope; a scales; boxes of papers on the floor; an alabaster model of the Temple of Vesta; plaster casts of the busts, or life or death masks, of Julius Caesar, Wellington, Napoleon, Goethe, Shakespeare, Händel, Voltaire, Franklin, Helmholtz and Alexander von Humboldt; a scatter of curious weapons from India, Africa and the American West; and a model of a steam frigate in a huge glass case. The room was heated by a base burner in the center of the narrow passageway leading to the far end. The air smelled of dried leather bindings, dried fur, dried feathers, the coal oil of several green-shaded student lamps, and an acid essence which rose from inkpots kept open for immediate use before an idea to be noted could dwindle and vanish.

"Here we are," said the general, finding a small open space where two arm chairs of black biscuit-tufted leather stood facing a long narrow desk by a window whose light must fall over the left shoulder of the occupant. "Sit down and bring me up to date."

Matthew glanced about the room.

"Yes," said the general, "you are wondering how all this will ever be moved when the time comes. It is coming next year, when I am to retire. It has taken full fourteen years to come in. I am not sufficiently gifted to project a method of taking it out. H'h'h'h. Perhaps some kindly pyromaniac will save us all the trouble. On the other hand, I should dislike to deprive the Smithsonian Institution of the eventual ownership I plan for my lifetime's collections. Do you know how I am referred to here in the Department? They do not know I know, but I know. I am called the 'Antiquary.' I believe the joke began with a reference to my possessions, and has been modified into a linguistically misapprehended reference to my age. Are you ready to go on duty?"

"I am, sir. We are temporarily settled at Willard's. To tell you the truth, I am eager to get back to work."

"Excellent. I have no plans for you today except for a visit, at precisely eleven o'clock, to the office of the Secretary of War. You will have the occupancy of the outer office here. The clerk will acquaint you with our routines and systems. I count on you mostly to help me in the preparation of an orderly study of our recent campaign, and I shall lean heavily on you for ideas formed of experiences when we shall reach the portions of our study which will propose recommendations to the Army for the formation of future policy. You are well again?"

"I believe so, sir, though I expect I must give up on regaining the weight I lost."

"Yes. I assure you that it is the thin individual whose mind can dash along best, and the unimpeded muscle which can manage most action with least fatigue. Have you any questions which will help you to find your duties here?"

"Not specifically, sir, but I do want to ask what arrangements are made to recover and bring away the bodies of those we buried out West? I have seen Mrs. Prescott and she would be heartened to know, I am sure."

"Yes. It is all in train. The survey is now being conducted. Those of the fallen who lie in continuously maintained army posts will abide where they are, for their premises continue to receive every care, and the government has ruled that the expense of removal is not justified out of public monies. Individuals may request removal at their own expense. In the other cases, where sites are deactivated, the government will bring home those who are buried in such locations. There are several, including Fort Delivery. All will be transferred from there, and I believe applications are already on file for the ultimate disposal. Mrs. Prescott may be easy."

"Good. I suppose the Indian transfer to Florida is completed by now?"

General Quait settled his mustaches with both forefingers before replying. His hesitation made Matthew lean forward with a frown. At last the general replied,

"Yes, it is done these three weeks past. We had reports a fortnight ago, giving us the final details."

"No escapes?"

"None."

"Was there any difficulty with Rainbow Son?"

"None."

"Then that is good. It is really all done with, sir."

"I'm afraid it is."

"Afraid, General? I do not think I—"

General Quait stood and began to pace a few steps up and back in the pathway. His voice became dry and breathy. He was attempting to govern his temper.

"Yes, afraid, since there is one aspect of the government's final arrangements which I have tried to overturn, but without the smallest success. It will distress you, Matthew, to learn what this is, and yet it is something you must know."

"Yes, General?"

"Matthew, the government has broken trust with some of the very soldiers whose faithfulness and intelligence helped us to win the campaign. I refer to such men as Sergeant White Horn, and the other Apache scouts whom we trusted and who never betrayed us. We assigned eight of them to accompany the transfer of the Apaches to Florida. When they arrived there, the commander of the internment camp had orders to detain all Indians, regardless of their relation to the Army. White Horn and the others are prisoners like the very ones they had charge of."

At this, Matthew jumped up. Nowadays his responses to feeling were hair-triggered. He went white.

"Now, by God, General, that isn't going to be allowed!"

"Of course it is, for it is done, and there is nothing we can further do, for I have tried everything. I feel that nothing is too great an effort to free those particular men and return them to honorable duty. But the Adjutant General has confirmed the orders in Florida, and they have been initialed by the Secretary himself. I personally have protested. It is a stain of the darkest shame on our arms; but nobody in Washington is rational where Indians are concerned, and I can only hope that I am still about when the Indians are returned

home, in order to be of help to those scouts. It is all I can say. I
dislike to tell you. Your man White Horn was invaluable to you, and
to us. It is a bitter repayment we make for his labors."

"Why, General, I could not have succeeded at all without him!
They might as well put me behind a wire fence if this is the regular
repayment for our service in Mexico!"

"Indeed they might."

Matthew was not used to feeling anger. It weakened him. He sat
down and he licked his lips and stared up at the general out of
eyes that showed red coals of light in the dark caverns beneath his
brows. He was turned sick by the disgrace of honor committed by
the Army he loved. It seemed impossible that he, who was a limb
of that great body, could fail to share in the dishonor it had brought
upon itself. He was helpless to think of how he could redeem the
Army and restore his sergeant scout to a decent place in the world.
He felt his mouth dry up and his throat tighten at the notion of what
White Horn must now be enduring in his heart at the betrayal with
which he would associate his lieutenant. Matthew saw again in his
thought the last gesture of White Horn in the dawn of the marching
day, when he took dust from the earth and held it to his eyes and let
it weep back to the earth in some fateful finality. The general was
troubled by what he saw in Matthew's face. He leaned over him.

"Don't be wild, don't be," he said. "It will do you no good. It
will do good for no one. It is a dreadful affair, but it is behind us,
and we must only hope to find in the years ahead some chance to
make amends. Meantime, Matthew, it would appear that duty is
with us always, and we have seven minutes to arrive at the Secretary's
office for our appointment. Do come up, now. I am proud to have
you with me and I desire that you make an excellent impression."

"Sir, I should be grateful to be excused for this morning. I do not
feel I am in a proper state to go with you."

"No, no, no, lieutenant, I must require you to come. There is a
reason, and you will know it soon enough, and I trust, with some
pleasure."

"General Quait, I promised Sergeant White Horn to look out for
him."

"So did I, Mr. Hazard. I promised all the scouts. We have been
overruled. We will go now."

Getting to his feet felt to Matthew like climbing a steep hill. It
was necessary to obey. He did so with difficulty. His sorrow was heavy.

ix

It was strange to find Laura and Jessica in the office of the Secretary of War. When he looked at Laura, she thought he must be ill, from the drawn, burning look in his face. He gazed about with wonder at the gathering in the Secretary's room. The Secretary stood behind his great desk. Beside him was the Adjutant General of the Army. Matthew had never seen them before. He bowed to Jessica. She smiled and bowed in return. He had a thought. It brought a small gleam of light into his angered gloom—this occasion must have been arranged to do honor to the memory of Colonel Prescott, else why was his widow present? General Quait brought Matthew forward to the side of the official desk and introduced him.

"Mr. Secretary, I have pleasure in bringing before you my most able subordinate officer, Mr. Matthew Hazard, who is here by your request."

The Secretary came from behind the desk to shake Matthew's hand.

"Yes," he murmured, "yes, indeed. We are indeed pleased to have you with us, lieutenant, and the ladies whose right it is to be present. I believe we may now proceed," he added, turning to the Adjutant General with a nod.

The Adjutant General lifted a large square of heavy paper from the desk and read aloud from it.

Second (Brevet First) Lieutenant Matthew Carlton Hazard, United States Cavalry, having proved his selfless devotion to duty in the discharge of an extraordinarily arduous mission, calling for every example of ingenuity, courageous endurance, diplomatic skill, utter disregard of his personal safety, and a proper grasp of the historical interests of the United States, which directly created the circumstances leading to the capitulation of the last enemy among the aboriginal Indians of the west, thus bringing to an end a war which has persisted for many generations costing grievously in lives and property, is hereby, under the direction of the President, and with the consent and approval of the Congress, granted the highest military award within the gift of his nation, the Medal of Honour, with all the rights and privileges thereunto appertaining.

Matthew was like a frozen figure. He saw nothing and felt nothing as the cabinet officer stepped forward and placed the blue ribbon collar of the medal about his neck, and seized his hand again, and shook it. The Adjutant General shook his hand, and then General Quait, and after that, Laura came to kiss him, and Jessica came to kiss him. He was cold and pallid. His eyes were lost in their shadows. Silence fell in the room, broken only by the slow, marching cadence of a tall hanging clock on the wall. It was General Quait who broke the pause which created increasing uneasiness as it persisted.

"Lieutenant, possibly a word in response to the Secretary before he dismisses us?"

Matthew nodded sharply and wetted his lips. His cheeks were fallen in under the strain of his emotion. He wore an expression of grief, and he knew for what he grieved. He knew what he might now lose, and it was all he loved, beyond his wife and child. It could not be helped. He must say,

"Mr. Secretary, thank you for the mark of favor you have presented to me. I was not alone in my expedition in Mexico. The man who accompanied me, and who made possible any effect I may have had with the enemy, was an Apache sergeant and scout in the United States Army. He is now interned and denied his freedom along with the very enemies he helped us to subdue. I should like to appeal for his release, Mr. Secretary, and the release of all the other Apache scouts who served with us. They never broke their trust to us. They are now being dishonorably treated. We have broken our trust to them, sir. That is all."

The clock was louder than ever for a moment. Then the Secretary of War turned to the Adjutant General of the Army, and asked,

"Are you familiar with this situation, General?"

"I am, sir. It is being carried out in accordance with War Department orders, and your own approval, and that of the President, as General Quait well knows."

"There is no occasion to reopen the matter?"

"In the opinion of the Army, there is not, Mr. Secretary."

"In that case," said the Secretary of War, turning back to Matthew, "I feel there is nothing I can do about the matter. Justice is at times hard, yet it must be visited upon the transgressors."

"All Indians are not alike, sir."

"It is not for me to say, but it would appear that if we are to start differentiating among these people, we shall never stop."

"On the contrary, sir, it is exactly what we must start doing if we are ever to solve their problem! We should start by keeping promises made to individuals among them."

"Your concern does you credit, Mr. Hazard. And now, before we adjourn this little gathering on this splendid occasion, let me congratulate you once again on attaining the recognition which has come to you here today. I feel a pleasure which I am sure your ladies, here, share in all pride."

Matthew looked at Laura in appeal, and then at General Quait, and then in a rapid awkward motion lifted from around his neck the blue ribbon with its pendant star-shaped medal and laid it upon the desk of the Secretary of War. He stepped back a pace, saluted, turned, and left the room.

x

"And now?" asked Jessica Prescott. She was conversing with Laura and General Quait in the Hazards' room at Willard's. Snowflakes were just disappearing on her sealskin furs, her fresh bunch of violets, for she had come indoors from a heavy snowfall.

"And now," said Laura, "he has taken Prescott with him to be photographed down the street at Sarony and Major's. It was the strangest thing. He asked me early this morning for his small locker-trunk. Something which he had not opened for years, and which I have never opened. It was down in the basement here with our other things. The porters brought it up, and Matthew found the key and opened the trunk, and sat on the floor a long time looking at the things in the top tray. He made me think of the time when I met him. Except that now he is so full of care."

"Has he slept any since the other day?"

"I think not much, though he tries to remain quiet all night for my sake. He remains too quiet, so I know he is awake."

"Do you think he is sorry, now, Laura?" asked the general.

"Oh, no, Uncle Alex. He has told me many times that he could not keep the medal, and if he could not keep the medal, then, for the same reason, he could not remain in the Army, and that is why he sent his resignation in the next day. What is to become of us? What is to become of us?"

"He will know what to do," said Jessica. "Do finish about the trunk."

"In the trunk, way down inside, he found a cap—an officer's cap, like the kind they used to wear in the War—you see them in all the pictures, crushed in at the front, and with a square visor."

The general and Jessica exchanged a smile, and Jessica said,

"We saw them on the soldiers themselves."

Laura nodded, and continued,

"Do you know where he got it? He said it was given to him when he was seven years old by President Lincoln, and I never knew it before, but all his life he has felt that his career, his commission, everything, came from Lincoln. He said he always meant to keep it a secret, as long as he was a soldier. But now that he is no longer a soldier, there is no point to keeping it a secret, and he told me the story. Now the cap has to go to Prescott, and he wants Prescott to know about it when he grows up. So they have gone to Sarony's to have a picture taken with the cap. Oh, how could everything go to ruin so fast? What are we going to do? We have nothing. When I wonder out loud, he tells me to remember the Prescotts." She turned to Jessica. "He tells me to remember how you told us the other day here in this room that you and the colonel had nothing, either, when you lived here."

"Nor did we. Except that we had each other, and that is everything."

"Oh, yes, oh yes," cried Laura, "we are the same, I know that, we have each other, there is no question of our not facing everything together. But sometimes I think and think so about it, and I cannot help myself, I think how frightful, to throw away a career, and a great honor, and a position for his wife and child, all because of an odd, unsanitary creature who has had a stroke of misfortune! What did Matthew see in him? Oh! it used to make me so cross! I suppose I must not let it do so now."

"No, Laura," said Jessica, touching her arm urgently, "oh no, it is not the man alone that concerns Matthew now—it is something even larger—an individual man, yes, but even more, a principle is the matter here, and oh, Laura, my darling, suffer as you do, don't, I beg of you, ever let it carry you to the point of saying to Matthew what you have just said to us! It is dreadfully important, I promise you!"

Jessica knew better than anyone what Matthew's decision had cost him—it had cost him the Army. She saw ahead for him what she had seen in other soldiers, old and young, who had for whatever reason left the service. They were clothed in the past, brave and yet lost in the present. Some of them worked mightily to make their old ways serve them in the new, and more than one of them lived out his life with a look of disguised wonder and longing seamed into the very lines of his face. Jessica knew nothing of Fox Creek, Indiana, and the mansion called The Fortress, and an unwanted benefactor named Major Pennypacker, and a small boy's fixed desire for inner independence, but it gave her no difficulty to conclude that Matthew had only done what he must do.

General Quait tried, too, to help Laura.

"*Having nothing* is either temporary or relative, my dearest child. I am sure Matthew already has plans."

"Plans—of course. He talks of our going out West."

"He is right. There is an immense future. He helped to claim it for all of us."

"Railroads, he has said. They are building railroads. There will be towns. If we care about having a fortune, he has no doubt we can make one."

"All that," said the general. "I mourn losing him, but I haven't a qualm about the future for you all."

"If only he could have given back the medal, but stayed in the service!" said Laura.

"Ah, my dear," exclaimed her uncle, "I do not think it could have succeeded. He would have been regarded during all his service as a crank. I am afraid I know something about that. It is a lively destiny, perhaps, but not a comfortable one. Cranks make their way with a grade eel of difficulty. It was only my inherent superiority of mind which forced the occasional recognition of my labors. Matthew's great quality is a different one. I should call it goodness unaware of itself. It is the greatest weapon of all, but it takes more than a lifetime for it to be effective. Now"—he raised his finger like a lecturer— "the question whether Matthew's repudiation of the Army is an act occasioned by a moral position, or on the other hand, merely by an act of personal loyalty, is, finally, irrelevant to this discussion. What figures is that the issue was determined long ago. The very nature which won for us in Mexico must, given the givens, as I say, have done what it did in the office of the Secretary of War. I, for one, would not have him do otherwise. Did I do likewise? No. Why?

Perhaps my lifetime in obedience held me fast. Perhaps my retirement next year beckons in the name of peace and order. Perhaps futility wedded to heroism does not seem to me an intelligent union. H'h'h'h'h. All these are evasions. He knew himself well enough to be true to his nature. I did not. —Look. The snow is falling thicker. I hope they will be home soon. We must have a happy welcome awaiting them. What must snow look like for the first time to an infant boy? I can imagine no finer wonder for such great, longing eyes."

General Quait failed himself in his effort to change the subject. After a pause, looking inward, he said in a remote voice,

"I wonder whether Matthew ever had a chance to educate himself for a day of sorrow. I hope so. I do hope so."

xi

"Would you like to look?" asked the photographer, holding up his black cloth above the opened accordion pleats of his box. Matthew bent over and looked, twisting his head to reconcile the image upside down with how it must be seen right side up. The light from the skylight was silver gray, and the heavy flakes turning through it made a quiet fall of a myriad little shadows over the lens, and seemed to put outside of time the instant which was about to be recorded. In the private dark tunnel of the camera, Matthew saw his son Prescott, over a year old, sitting gravely upon a hassock with a Turkey carpet thrown over it. He wore a gray broadcloth suit with a tight jacket and a knee-length kilt trimmed in black braid. His stockings were black and his small boots were buttoned up to the ankle. His head was lifted to watch the lens. Light dwelled sweetly on his brushed hair, which had a long wave over his wide clear brow. In his fisted hands he held the Lincoln cap against his breast as he had been fixed to do. His father looked for an isolated, long moment, and saw both a memorial and a pledge. Then, as if to break a spell, Matthew stepped out from under the cloth and nodded with a scowl. The photographer took his place, made one more adjustment of the focus, and then, inserting his boxed plate, lifted his hand beside his smile to enliven his subject and hold it still.

"That's my dandy boy," said the photographer, fixing eternity in the instant. He pressed the bulb. The picture was a success.

Now and then, in later years, when Matthew Hazard looked at it, he knew again something of the feeling that had brought it to be, and this in turn made images and sounds, all brought together for the son whom he hoped to give to the Army, with such a blessing as had been his own, in the possession of the Lincoln cap, and in such a heart for the soldier's life as sounded again in the memory of his commander's voice singing,

> Johnny, did you say goodbye?
>   Oh, yes, father.
> I kissed them one and all goodbye,
> I said now don't you go and cry,
> For I'll be homing by and by,
>   Oh, yes, father.

POSTSCRIPT

AS A WORK OF FICTION THIS BOOK invokes appropriate indulgences in respect of historical fact; for while I have taken much profit from reading the literature of my period, I have not been strictly bound by it in my pursuit of design and form, in the course of which, where suitable, I have fitted events to my characters—all of whom are of course fictitious except those presented under historical names—rather than the other way round.

Yet too this is a historical novel, which means that a period and a scene have been enriched—indeed, largely created—by general reference to known circumstances. I am therefore constrained to list here with gratitude and respect a little catalogue of those materials which gave me the most of pleasure and instruction in preparation for the task of many years which this story represents.

Louisa May Alcott, *Hospital Sketches;* John Russell Bartlett, *Personal Narrative of Explorations and Incidents in Texas, New Mexico, California, Sonora and Chihuahua;* James A. Bennett, *A Dragoon in New Mexico;* John G. Bourke, *On the Border with Crook;* Mrs. Orsemus Bronson Boyd, *Cavalry Life in Tent and Field;* John C. Cremony, *Life Among the Apaches;* Thomas Cruse, *Apache Days and After;* Britton Davis, *The Truth About Geronimo;* John Van Deusen DuBois, *Campaigns in the West, 1856-1861;* William H. Emory, *Report of William H. Emory, Major First Cavalry and U. S. Commissioner, United States and Mexican Boundary Survey;* John K. Herr and Edward S. Wallace, *Story of the U. S. Cavalry;* William H. Keleher, *Turmoil in New Mexico, 1846-1868;* Anton Mazzanovich, *Trailing Geronimo;* Nelson A. Miles, *Personal Recollections and Observations;* Morris Edward Opler, *Myths and Tales of the Chiricahua Apache Indians;* Frances M. Roe, *Army Letters From an Officer's Wife, 1871-1888;* August Santleben, *A Texas Pioneer;* Martha Summerhayes, *Vanished Arizona: Recollections of My Army Life;* Matthew W. Thomlinson, *The Garrison at Fort Bliss;* Walt Whitman, *Specimen Days in America,* and *The Wound Dresser.*

Also, files of *The Cavalry Journal;* various United States Government publications of documents—Congressional hearings and reports on Indian affairs and frontier troubles, indemnity claims, military policy and experience, Surgeon General's records, etc.; and Signal Corps photographs of early Army posts.

—P.H.